McGee #4

PALE GREY FOR GUILT

Tush Bannon was in the way. It wasn't anything he had done. He was just there, in the wrong spot at the wrong time, and the fact that he was a nice guy with a nice wife and three nice kids didn't mean one scream in hell to the jackals who ganged together to pull him down. But one thing they never could have figured . . . Tush Bannon was Travis McGee's friend.

"Travis McGee is back and that's good news for anyone who likes a taut, well-written, properly-worked-out thriller." *Evening Standard*

ONE FEARFUL YELLOW EYE

Glory Boyle had been one of the broken birds. McGee had taken her aboard *The Busted Flush,* patched her up, and turned her loose to make another try at life. Now she was calling for help again. Someone had very quietly very skilfully, extracted six hundred thousand dollars from her husband during the last painful years of his life. Blackmail? Obviously.

"An intensely readable and absorbing as one automatically expects from MacDonald." *New York Times*

A TAN AND SANDY SILENCE

Until Harry Broll turned up out of the blue, waving a gun and accusing McGee of spiriting away his wife, Travis was blissfully contemplating the well-rounded bikini-clad joys of life aboard *The Busted Flush*. Now all those sun-warmed lazy days of love and leisure would have to be scrapped. Because he had to find Mary Broll.

"On no account miss it." *Sunday Times*

Pale Grey for Guilt
One Fearful Yellow Eye
A Tan and Sandy Silence

McGee #4

by

JOHN D. MacDONALD

ROBERT HALE · LONDON

© *This omnibus edition Robert Hale Limited 1986*
First published in Great Britain 1986

ISBN 0 7090 2723 0

Pale Grey for Guilt
Copyright © 1968 by John D. MacDonald

One Fearful Yellow Eye
Copyright © 1966 by John D. MacDonald

A Tan and Sandy Silence
Copyright © 1971 by John D. MacDonald

Robert Hale Limited
Clerkenwell House
Clerkenwell Green
London EC1R 0HT

Printed in Great Britain by
St Edmundsbury Press, Bury St Edmunds, Suffolk
and bound by WBC Limited.

Pale Grey for Guilt

Tush Bannon was in the way. It wasn't anything he knew or
anything he had done. He was just there, in the wrong spot
at the wrong time, and the fact that he was a nice guy with a
nice wife and three nice kids didn't mean one scream in hell
to the jackals who had ganged together to pull him down.
And they got him, crushed him to hamburger, and
walked away counting their change. But one thing they
never could have figured . . .
Tush Bannon was Travis McGee's friend.

CHAPTER ONE

THE next to the last time I saw Tush Bannon alive was the very same day I had that new little boat running the way I wanted it to run, after about six weeks of futzing around with it.

So on the test run I demonstrated one of our contemporary maladies: You can't just go out and ride around in car, boat, or aeroplane—you have to have a destination.

Then you feel purposeful.

So in the early morn on a flat, calm, overcast day I stocked the ice chest on the little *Muñequita* from my ship's stores on *The Busted Flush*, locked up the *Flush*, dropped down into my new playtoy, and, as what faint breeze there was seemed to be coming out of the south-west, I stuck my nose out of the pass to see if I could run north outside. The long, slow grey-green lift and fall of the ground swell was all of a towering five inches high, so I took it a mile off the beaches and fooled with the rpm and the fuel flowmeter, until she was riding right and sounded right and just a hair under 3,000 on each of the OMC 120-horse stern-drive units. I then turned the steering over to the little Calmec autopilot, took a bearing on the Lauderdale Municipal Casino and noted the time.

That, of course, is one of the fussy little enchantments of a new boat—new being either brand-new or second-hand new. What you are hunting for is the optimum relationship between fuel consumption and distance. You tell yourself that maybe someday you are going to get caught very short, and you are going to have to squeak back into port with no more than half a cup of fuel left, with luck, and it would be very nice to know what rpm leaves you the least chance of running dry.

But like the exercise of caution in almost every human activity, the fusspots who make it their business to know are the ones least likely to ever have that ticklish problem. It's the ones who never check it out who keep the Coast Guard choppers busy.

The little boat was aimed back up the Florida east coast toward Broward Beach, where I had picked her up on an estate sale from a law firm. She'd belonged to a Texan named Kayd whose luck had run out somewhere in the Bahamas.

It's a funny thing about boat names. She had that *Muñequita* across the stern in four-inch white letters against that nice shade of Gulf Stream blue when I brought her on back to Bahia Mar. Spanish for "little doll." One night Meyer and Irv Deibert and Johnny Dow and I sat around trying to dream up a name that would match *The Busted Flush*. Little Flush? Inside Straight? Hole Card? The Ante? And I forget which one we decided was best because when I got around to changing it, I looked at the name it had and I decided that trying to match it to the name on the mother ship was a case of the quaints and the cutes, and I liked the name just fine. It was a little doll and had begun to acquire in my mind a personality that could very well resent being called anything else, and would sulk and wallow.

I switched the FM-UHF marine radio to the commercial frequencies and tried to find something that didn't sound like somebody trying to break up a dogfight in a sorority house by banging drums and cymbals. Not that I want to say it isn't music. Of course it is music, styled to accompany teenage fertility rites, and thus is as far out of my range as "Rockabye Baby." FM radio was a great product when it was servicing a fringe area of the great American market. But it has turned into a commercial success, so they have denigrated the sound, and they have mickey-moused the stereo, and you have to really search that dial to find something that isn't either folk hoke, rickyticky rock, or the saccharine they pump into elevators, bus stations and Howard Johnsons.

As I was about to give up I found some pleasant eccentric, or somebody who'd grabbed the wrong record, playing Brubeck doing Cole Porter, and I caught it just as he opened up "Love for Sale" in a fine gentle manner, and then handed it delicately over to Desmond, who set up a witty dialogue with Joe Morello.

After telling myself that ten of eight in the morning is beer time only for the lowest types, I cracked a bottle of Carta Balanca and stood in the forward well, leaning through the centre opening where I'd laid the hinged wind-shield over to port, out of the way, forearms on the smoke-blue foredeck shell.

Well, I was on my way to see old Tush after too long, and I had wind in my face like a happy dog leaning out a car window. The wake was straight. The engines ran sweetly in sync. I could feel the slow rise and fall in the imperceptible ground swell. The overcast was starting to burn off, the sea starting to glint. I could see pygmy figures over on the beach by Sea Ranch. Even with the investment in the playtoy, I still had a comforting wad of currency back in the cache aboard *The Busted Flush* at slip F-18, Bahia Mar.

It had been a fine long hot lazy summer, a drifting time of good fish, old friends, new girls, of talk and laughter.

Cold beer, good music and a place to go.

That's the way They do you. That's the way They set you up for it. There ought to be a warning bell on the happymeter, so that every time it creeps high enough, you get that dang-dang alert. Duck, boy. That glow makes you too visible. One of Them is out there in the boonies, adjusting the windage, getting you lined up in the cross hairs of the scope. When it happens so often, wouldn't you think I'd be more ready for it?

I took my right-angle sight on a water tower just beyond Ocean Ridge, one that measures almost exactly thirty miles north of the Municipal Casino, and my elapsed time was sixty-two minutes. I wrote that down, along with fuel consumption, so I could do the maths later, breaking it down in the way that to me is easiest to remember, statute miles per gallon at x rpm.

The wind was freshening and quartering into the south, and though I was still comfortable, I decided it wasn't going to last very long, so I went through Boynton Inlet into Lake Worth. The OMC's were still green enough so that too much constant speed wasn't the best thing in the world, so as soon as I had a nice open straightaway up the Waterway without traffic, I pushed it up to 4,200 rpm, estimating it at about 45 miles an hour. I estimated I had fifty if I ever needed it, and hoped I'd never get in a bind where I needed it. I held her there for five or six minutes, then dropped it way back, getting it to that minimum rpm that, depending on gross weight at the time, would just hold it on the plane. It wasn't a rig I was about to take out and see if I could get to Nassau ahead of Wynne and Bertram and those people, taking those thirty-foot leaps and turning your spine into a concertina every time you smash back into the sea, pulping your kidneys and chomping your jaw into the foam rubber tooth guard. The little *Muñequita* would have had to be turned into a racing machine, with a hundred more horses in each mill, special wheels, a lot more bracing and reinforcement to keep the engines in her, and then she would not be much good for anything else.

Besides, I had been talked into trying it once. I think you could maybe argue the point that it is a little more fun than a hungover, carbuncled cowboy might have while trying to stay aboard a longhorn in a dusty rodeo, but it would be a close decision.

When I reached the bay north of Broward Beach, I had to look at the chart to see at which marker I should leave the Waterway to hit the mouth of the Shawana River. So it was ten thirty of that Tuesday morning, or a little later, when I eased up to one of the finger piers at Bannon's Boatel, put a line on a piling and cut the engines off.

I stepped high onto the pier decking and looked around. He had a dozen outboards tied up, and maybe half as many inboard-outboard rigs, two smallish cruisers, and, neatly aligned in their slips, the dozen rental houseboats, outboard rigged, fibreglass, white with orange trim. I saw that he'd put up the in-and-out storage he had told me about the last time I'd seen him, over a year and a half ago. Fifteen racks wide and three high. The forklift could tuck forty-five boats in there on monthly storage, but only the bottom row was full, and the middle layer half full.

Up the river from his place and on the other side, where it had all been marshland the last time I was there, I could see, maybe a mile away and more, some squat, pale, technical-looking buildings and a glinting of cars in the industrial parking lot next to them.

There didn't seem to be anyone around the little marina building, or around the white cement-block motel with the red tile roof that sat parallel to the river and parallel to State Road 80D, and about a hundred feet from each of them. I remember Tush talking about how he was going to expand the motel from ten units to twenty.

"Now that there's the three kids, me and Janine are taking up two units, and having just eight rentals, I couldn't tell you the times we've had to turn folks away, Trav."

The slab had been poured for the extra ten units, and the block had been laid up to shoulder-high on about three of them, but some kind of a coarse green vine had taken hold and had crawled along fifteen feet of the wall, spilling tendrils down.

Some of the dock pilings sagged. The pennons on the marina building were bleached grey, wind-ripped and tattered.

"Hey!" yelled Tush. "Hey, now! Hey, McGee!" He had come around the corner of the motel and came toward me in a kind of Percheron canter. A big man. Almost as high as I am, and half again as big around.

Long ago and far away we'd been on the same ball team. Brantley Breckenridge Bannon, second string offensive fullback. First string if he could have got into his stride quicker, because he was hard to stop when he was in gear. The nickname had started as BeeBee and had been shortened to Beeb, and it was that season it suddenly turned into Tush. He was a man totally incapable of profanity. The most we ever heard from him, even in the most hideous, unlucky and painful circumstances, was a mumbled "Durn!"

Then in one game we tried running a play that was designed to make up for his slow start. They set him out to the right, and on the snap he had to run to his left, go behind the quarterback who had taken some quick steps back and who had faked a handoff to a wingback slanting right, and who would then spin and stuff the ball into Bannon's belly on a half cut and an off-tackle slant left.

The first time we ran it, and I was offensive left end at the time, a linebacker thought he smelled a pass, blitzed through, saw what was happening, and rolled his shoulders right into Bannon's ankles. The second time we ran it, he had a good head of steam but there was absolutely no hole at all, and as he tried to spin along the line and find one they tore him down. The third time we tried it, we were fourth and two at their eleven, so late in the game that we had to go for six points, being four points behind. He got a fine start. We got a good jump and cleared him a big hole. But as he went through the hole he was juggling that ball, hand to chin to chest to forearm to hand, too busy to keep from getting hit, and was hit from the side and the ball floated into the hands of their squatty defensive centre, who after a considerable pause to realize he actually had a football right there in his hands, took off in a lumpy little grinning gallop out to their forty before he got pulled down from behind. Bannon, on his knees, ripped off his helmet, whammed it against the sod, stared skyward and yelled, "Oh . . . TUSH!"

When things went badly for him on one play in the next game, about four of us yelled, "Tush!" And Tush it became, then and forever.

After he was converted to a tackle, he stayed with an AFL team four years, during two of which, being married to Janine, he saved his money. A pinched nerve in his neck turned him into an insurance salesman and he did well but got sick of it, and then he sold houseboats, and then he bought the ten acres on the Shawana River on which to act out and work out the American Dream.

So after the obligatory thumping upon each other, our words of greeting were drowned out by an oncoming roar, deep and grinding, and three big orange Euclids went by on their six-foot tyres of solid rubber, loaded high with yards of wet marl, kicking up a powdery dust that drifted north, across the palmetto and scrub pine flats on the other side of the state road. I saw then that the blacktop was gone, and the right of way widened.

"We're being improved around here," he said in sour explanation. "Everything is going to be first-class. By and by." He stared west, after the fading roar of the big earth movers. "Worries me the way they bucket through here. Janine should be on her way back from town by now, and there's some bad places where she could meet up with them. She does more than her share of driving now that the school bus can't come down here."

"Why can't it?"

"They can't use roads that are officially closed, that's why." He looked toward his waterfront. "What'd you come in. You can't get the *Flush* upriver in this tide."

"Wasn't there a good deep channel?"

"Until they did a lot of dredge and fill upriver. Now the first half mile from the bay up toward me is pretty bad. They say they're going to scour it out, but they won't say when."

We walked out and I showed him the *Muñequita*. He knew that good honest T-Craft hull, the semi-V that Rodney Thompson makes in Titusville. When people from the Kansas flats get the marine fever, it is a dreadful addiction, and Tush had a bad case. He looked over the custom installation of the two dual-carb OMC's and listened to my explanation of why I'd pulled the Chrysler-Volvos the original owner installed. He was intrigued by the special engineering of the Teleflex panel and control system.

I heard myself talking too much. Things were going well for me. And the world was a little sour for my friend Tush Bannon. In repose his broad, heavy, freckly face sagged. So when it happens like that, you talk too much. The small breeze stopped, and the October forenoon heat leaned hard, in that 95°-95 humidity that makes the sweat pop out.

So we went up to the motel and sat in the kitchen alcove under the rackety-clatter of an overworked little window air-conditioner, drank beer while he said Janine was fine, the boys were fine, and we talked about who we'd heard from and who we hadn't, and who was doing what. I stood by the window with the cold can in my hand and said, "What's all the big industry over there, up river?"

"TTA," he said with a tangible bitterness. "Tech-Tex Applications. A nice clean industry, except every now and then any fool fish that comes up the Shawana turns belly-up and floats back down. And sometimes there's a funny little smell, sort of like ammonia, and the tears run down your face. But they employ four hundred people, Trav. Big tax base. They gave 'em the keys to the county to move in here."

"But I thought this country had pretty fair zoning and pollution control and all that. I mean Broward Beach is a——"

"Don't you know where you are, boy?" he asked. "You're a good mile west of that county line. You are in Shawana County, Mister McGee. A garden spot. Go right over to Sunnydale, to the County Courthouse, and ever' one of those happy, smiling five commissioners will tell you a man couldn't pick a better spot to live and raise his kids and grow with the county." He astonished me. I had never thought of Tush as being capable of irony. He was a big, amiable, beefy man, with mild blue eyes and stubby pale lashes and brows, and a pink, peeling, permanent case of sunburn.

I heard a car drive in. He went to the window on the road side and looked out and said, "Oh . . . *no!*"

I followed him out. Janine had got out of the car, a very dusty pale blue sedan about two years old. At twenty paces she still had the gawky, leggy look and stance of a teenager. She stood in an attitude at once defiant and disconsolate, staring at the left rear corner of the car, which squatted expensively low. Their youngest, about two and a half, stood nearby, scowling, giving the intermittent snuffle of tears not long ended. Janine wore bleached khaki walking shorts and a yellow halter in a coarse fabric. The shorts were darkened with perspiration around her narrow waist. She had cropped her black hair very short. With her deep tan, and the length and strength and slender delicacy of her face, her dark eyes, she looked like a young man, Mediterranean, ready to guide you to the Roman ruins, pick your pocket, sell you fake heirlooms, send you out in a leaky gondola with his thieving cousin.

But the shape of the ears was girl, and the corners of the mouth, and the elegance of the throat, and from there on down no doubt at all, even were she clad in a loose-fitting mattress cover, no doubt whatsoever. And I knew her maiden name was Sorrensen, and she was Wisconsin Swede, and she birthed towheaded Swede kids, and so she was one of the improbabilities of genetic mathematics, of maybe one of the Scandinavian raiders who brought home from a far country a swarthy boy to be a kitchen slave.

Tush got down behind the car and rolled onto his back and wormed his way under it. She said, "It was just a half mile this side of the hard top. I guess the rains dug it out and then the dust drifted into it, and I swear, honey, nobody could have seen it."

He slid out. "Spring shackle."

"She *hit* me!" the little kid said. "She hit me awful hard, Pop."

"Were you going fast, Jan?" he asked her.

She stared at him. She raised a helpless arm and let it flap down. "Oh, good Christ, I was making better time than Phil

Hill, laughing and singing because the world is so sweet, and I was probably all boozed up, and I was trying to break the goddamn whatever it is!"

She spun and went by me, giving me a sudden and startled glance of recognition, but too trapped then in the compulsions of the quarrel to deviate from the planned exit.

He shouted after her. "You can say hello to my friend! The least you can do is say hello to my friend!"

She walked ten more strides, shoulders rigid, and then turned at the motel doorstep and, with no expression on her face or in her voice, said, "Hello. Hello. Hello. Come on, Jimmy. Come with mother."

The kid went plodding after her. The door closed. Tush looked at me and shook his head and tried to smile. "Sorry, boy."

"For what? There are good days, medium days and bad days."

"We seem to be getting a long run of one kind."

"So, for starters let's fix it."

He ran it down to the marina shed, where the tools were. We used the forklift to raise the back end. It took two gallons of sweat apiece to punch the busted pieces out, hacksaw some bar stock, clumsy it into place and peen the ends over. We set it down and it sat level, no longer looking like a spavined duck. I stepped on the rear bumper and it didn't come back up as it should. It oscillated, good proof the shocks were nearly gone, and from the way he sighed I was sorry I'd done it.

I got fresh clothes off the boat, and Tush gave me a motel unit to shower and change in. I was just buttoning the clean shirt when Janine knocked at the door. I let her in. She carried a clinking pitcher of iced tea, and her apologetic pride. She wore a little pink cotton shift and a pale pink lipstick.

She put the pitcher down, put her hand out. "Hello the right way, Travis. Like welcome. Excuse the bad scene." Her hand was long and brown and slender, and her grip surprisingly strong. She poured the two tall glasses of tea and gave me one and took hers over and sat on the bed. I counted back and realized that this would be the fifth time I had seen her. And, as before, the chemistry was slightly off, as it so often is with the friend who knew the husband before the husband met the wife. It can be a kind of jealousy, I guess, because it is a reminder of years she didn't share, and of an acceptance of the husband's friendship, which was in no way her decision. She seemed to relate to me with a flavour of challenge. Prove yourself to me, McGee. But you can't, McGee, because you aren't house-broken. Your life isn't real. You drift around and you have your fun and games. You make my husband feel wistful about the debts he has and the girls he hasn't. When you come near my nest, just by being here, you remind my man of the gaudy grasshopper years, and somehow you turn me into some kind of guard, or attendant, or burden.

With some of the wives of old friends I have been able to quench that initial antagonism. They soon find out that I am aware of what every single unwed person knows—that the world is always a little out of focus when there is no one who gives the final total damn about whether you live or die. It is the price you pay for being a rambler, and if you don't read the price tag, you are a dull one indeed.

Jan had obvious warmth. She seemed to have the empathy to realize that I meant her well. But the antagonism wouldn't melt. She could hide it pretty well. But it was there.

I toasted her with tea, saying, "That was a mere snit, Janine. One of the tizzies you get during the hot months."

"Thanks," she said, and smiled. "Tush gobbled and ran. He took over the child taxi service. Come on over in about ten minutes and I'll have a sort of a lunch."

She finished the glass of tea, then poured herself another to take with her. As she moved toward the door she shook her head slowly and sadly. "You know, I think it was guilt mostly. Poor darn little Jimmy kid. What's wrong, Mom? What busted, Mom? Will it run, Mom? So I swatted him a dandy. Much too hard, without thinking. Taking it out on him." Beyond the wry smile her eyes looked wet. "I don't know what's happening to me lately. Oh, how I hate that goddamn car. That goddamn stinking car. How I hate it!"

CHAPTER TWO

AS I waited, sitting in the full huff of the air-conditioner, gulping down the tea, I thought of the little dreamworld called Detroit, fifteen years behind the rest of America, as usual.

Janine had nailed it. People hate their cars. Daddy doesn't come proudly home with the new one any more, and the family doesn't come racing out, yelling WOW, and the neighbours don't come over to admire it. They all look alike, for one thing. So you have to wedge a piece of bright trash atop the aerial to find your own. They may be named after predators, or primitive emotions, or astronomical objects, but in essence they are a big shiny sink down which the money swirls—in insurance, car payments, tags, tolls, tyres, repairs. They give you a chance to sit in helpless rage, beating on the steering wheel in a blare of horns while, a mile away, your flight leaves the airport. They give you a good chance of dying quick, and a better chance of months of agony of torn flesh, smashed guts and splintered bones. Take it to your kindly dealer, and the service people look right through you until you grab one by the arm, and then he says: Come back a week from Tuesday. Make an appointment. Their billions of tons of excreted pollutants wither the leaves on the trees and sicken the livestock. We hate our cars, Detroit. Those of us who can possibly get along without them do so very happily. For those who can't, if there were an alternate choice, they'd grab it in a minute. We buy them reluctantly and try to make them last, and they are not friendly machines any more. They are expensive, murderous junk, and they manage to look glassily contemptuous of the people who own them. A car is something that makes you whomp your youngest kid too hard and then feel ashamed of yourself.

I had just been through the bit. My elderly Rolls pick-up, *Miss Agnes*, was as agile as ever, which meant about 40 seconds from a dead stop to sixty miles an hour. And she had the same reluctance to come to a stop once she was humming along. So she and I were slowly becoming a highway hazard, the narrow shaves getting narrower. So I had gone shopping, test driving, and found they all had fantastic acceleration, and they'd all stop on dimes, and they all bored me to hell.

So I went looking for a boat I could use as a car. I would keep *Miss Agnes* for back roads and the *Flush* for open waters, and use the *Muñequita* for errands, and if I had to have a car, there was Mr. Hertz trying hard, and Mr. Avis trying harder, and Mr. National hoping they'd run each other into the ground. Anything in Lauderdale that I wanted to buy, and I could lift, if I couldn't buy it right at Bahia Mar, I could go off in the *Muñequita* and buy it. And it was nice to poot along an urban waterway and hear the distant clashing of fenders, gnashing of bumpers, and the song of the ambulances.

Janine and I ate ham and cheese sandwiches at the breakfast bar, and every time Jimmy came stomping by, he got a couple of loving pats from his mother. I had forgotten the names of the older two boys and had to pick them up out of her conversation. Johnny and Joey. Joey was the big kid. Six. Johnny was four and a half.

I realized I hadn't seen Tyler around, the Negro who had been working for them the other times I'd been there, a tall, stringy, cheerful, ageless man, dark saffron in colour, and with a scholarly face, plus an uncanny knack of diagnosing the ailments of marine engines. I asked her if it was his day off.

"Oh, Tyler quit us . . . it must be eight months ago. Tush was very upset about it. You know how good he was around here. But now . . . it's just as well, I guess, because we couldn't afford to pay him anyway, the way things are."

"On account of the road?"

"And a lot of other things."

"Such as."

"I think if Tush wants you to hear the tale of woe, he better be the one to tell you. But I'll tell you one thing, Travis McGee!" Her eyes narrowed, and she thumped her fist on the formica counter top. "We are *not* going to be run off this place!"

"Is somebody trying?"

"You'd best talk to Tush about it."

"Can you get a sitter for tonight?"

"Huh?"

"Wear your pretties and the three of us will go run-abouting into Broward Beach and track down some booze and some meat and come home late, singing all the way."

Her narrow face lighted up. "I would *love* it!"

And when Tush got back with the other two towheads, he approved. The sitter was handy. Jan explained they had made a special rate on a houseboat rental to a couple. Young kids. About twenty-one years old. They were in the houseboat where the old yellow station wagon was parked. There was a retired couple in the one on the far end. Those were the only two rented at the moment.

"Arlie and Roger Denn, their names are," Janine explained. "They're a little on the weird side. Sort of untidy-looking. He makes little funny figurine things and he makes shell jewellery. She does handweaving and she paints these insipid little sea-scapes, and when they have enough, they fill up the station wagon and go around and sell them to gift shops. Sometimes it takes two days, and sometimes it takes a week."

Arlie Denn arrived for sitter duty right on time, and I could agree about the untidy part. She was a soft, doughy, pallid girl with a long tangle of dark blonde hair, wide, empty, indifferent blue eyes, a little sing-song voice and a mouth that hung open. She wore a man's white shirt, dirty. Pale blue denim walking shorts, ditto. Bare feet, also dirty. I could see why Janine had fed the kids before we left.

Once I had the little boat away from the dock, I turned it over to Tush. And with the sun lowering behind us, we skimmed down the long, broad curves of the Shawana River, past the mangrove and the white herons, and out into the big bay where, corny as any postcard, a ketch was moving northward up the Waterway, sun turning the sails orange, while a ragged flight of pelicans passed diagonally in front of her, heading for the rookery, pumping then soaring, taking the cue from the flight leader.

With his big paw on the twin throttles Tush raised a ques-tioning eyebrow, and I made a shoving motion with the heel of my hand. Janine sat on a life cushion on the transom engine hatch, in her pretty yellow dress, her short black hair snapping in the wind, her face alight with the pleasure of

speed and change and the rush of the soft evening air after
the heat of the day.

At the city marina Tush slowed and we went up the channel
and under the bridge, and along the bay side of the beaches.
I took it into a place called Beach Marine, where the man
said nobody would mess with it. We walked three blocks to a
good place I knew. Thirty feet from the restaurant entrance
Jan balanced herself with one hand on Tush's big shoulder
while she changed from the zoris to the high-heeled shoes
she was carrying in her straw purse.

The drinks were good, the steaks were good, the evening
was almost good. Every marriage at one time or another is
going to run through some heavy weather. Heavy weather
comes in all kinds of flavours. Slowly going broke, slowly
losing the whole stake instead of making it like you thought
you would—that can erode the happiest of hearts. With the
two of them it wasn't a continuous thing. It just kept crop-
ping up now and again, and clouding the fun and games.

There was just enough said for me to see the shape of the
running quarrel, or argument, or regret. Over a year ago, when
they had a chance to pull out, when they had a buyer for
the place, Jan had wanted to take the loss and get out. Only
about a ten per cent loss on what they'd put into it, but that
didn't count all the hours of their brute labour. But he'd
insisted it was just a run of bad luck. Nobody was really
trying to stack the cards against them. Things would get
better. Things always got better.

Except when they get worse.

Tush didn't want to talk about it at all. To him it was
like whining. He would let it go just so far, and then he would
reach out, grab the conversational ball, and throw it the hell
into centre field.

But they seemed to have a good time, on average. Maybe
a better time than in many months. It was overcast, and there
was pink lightning on three sides of us when we went hurrying
back across the bay. Tush picked up the markers for me with
the hand-held spotlight, with its 45,000 candles and its narrow
one-mile beam. We got the boat tied up and the first fat
drops were speckling the dust as we made it to the motel. The
rain roar was coming. The fat sitter went cantering and
bobbling off to her rented houseboat.

Maybe three inches came down in the hour we sat at the Bannon's breakfast bar and drank kitchen whisky and told lies.

Back in my borrowed motel unit, after starting to get ready for bed, I decided I'd better check the *Muñequita* and see if the automatic bilge pump had handled the heavy rain and turned off, as promised. The air was washed clean, and the hungry mosquitoes hadn't begun to roam. The wind was rain-fresh, and from the west. The boat was fine, and, as I turned, the bulk of Tush Bannon standing in the night startled me.

"I miss the sound of that old hump-back bridge when the wind's from upriver," he said. "Not much traffic over it, but the timbers would rumble. You get so you don't even hear a sound like that, and then you miss it after it's gone."

"They put a new one there?"

He sighed. "Not there. Three miles further upriver. That hurts. It lost me most of the business I was getting from the people that live on the other side. TTA wanted it taken out. They wanted the road to it officially abandoned. We went to the Public Hearing and made a lot of noise, but what TTA wants from this county, TTA gets."

"Tush, if you need any help hanging on here until things pick up. . . ."

"Forget it. Thanks, but forget it. It would just take that much longer to run down the drain."

"Is it all going to go?"

"Probably."

"Can you sell?"

"Sell what? Our equity? Go ask the bank what they think our equity is." He yawned. "Hell, I can always get a pretty good job selling. I can sell pretty good. Trouble is, I hate the work. 'Night, McGee. And thanks again. It was a good evening. It helped. We needed it bad."

I left the next morning. And that was in October, and I kept thinking about them and wondering about them, but I didn't do anything about it. I didn't run up there again. I wish I had. There are a lot of things in this life I wish I'd done, and a pretty gamey collection of things I wish I hadn't done—but the things you don't do leave the remorses around a little longer somehow.

The last time I saw Tush Bannon alive was the weekend

before Christmas, late on a Saturday afternoon. It was by the kind of accident so unlikely, one has the temptation to call it fate. My friend Mick Coseen was awaiting a very important phone call from Madrid, and he had given my phone number aboard *The Busted Flush*. So when it was delayed, he asked me if I'd take his car and run down to the Miami International and pick up his date, Barni Baker, a Pan-Am stewardess due in from Rio for a Miami layover. As I was the only other one in the group who knew her by sight, it was more efficient for me to go down.

For company I toted Puss Killian along in Mick's rental convertible. It was a cool, bright day, and the time of year when the gold coast is as empty as it ever gets. Nervous little men who own points in the big beach hotels brood about their fifth mortgages, and the retailers give fervent thanks that the Christmas pressure on the locals makes up for the lack of snowbird money. Puss is a big, stately, random redhead, a master of the put-on and the cop-out, who believes the world is mad, so she is the best of companions if you can keep up with the slants and shifts of her conversation, and merely irritating and confusing if you can't. A little herd was assembling, and it was shaping up party time.

We put the car in the lot and went in and checked the board, and the man said that 955 was just touching down. After the passengers had been herded off and aimed in the right direction, Barni, with her peer group, came brisk-clicking along, button-big, button-bright, a little candy-package blonde with eyes of widest innocent blue, eyes casting right and left, searching for Mick, finding me as I moved to intercept her. Big smile, gracious and wary acknowledgement of the introduction to Puss. I told her about Mick and his call, about an independent wanting somebody to take over the camera crew because their chief cameraman had racked himself up on a bicycle in Madrid traffic, and Barni Baker said to give her fifteen minutes, and I said we would be up at the bar on top of the International, and she said just fine and went tap-tapping away, moving firm and well in her uniform

In the big blue windowed room high in the air, the cocktail business was still thin, because of the hour, and a familiar face was working the quiet and elegant bar, and he remembered The Drink, and seemed so pleased with himself in remembering, that we each had one, sitting and watching the deftness with silent and respectful attention. Two ample old-fashioned glasses, side by side, filled to the two thirds line with cracked ice. A big, unmeasured slosh of dry sherry into each glass. Then swiftly, the strainer placed across the top of one and then the other, as with a delicate snap of the wrist he dumped the sherry down the drain. Then fill to the ice level with Plymouth gin, rub the lemon peel around the inside of the rim, pinch some little floating beads of citrus oil on the surface of the drink, throw away the peel, present with small tidy bow and flourish to the folk. "Two McGees," said he.

"Thank you, Harold," I said.

He had two new customers and when he moved away, Puss hoisted her glass, tinked it against mine. "The instant drink," she said. "Instant stupidity, or instant rape, or instant permission. Me, what I get is this instant numbness around the chops. Here's to flying quail."

"To what?"

"To stewardesses! You're slow today, lover. You're not relating now and again."

"It's just that I was looking at you. Then I don't hear so well." And looking by chance beyond her, I saw Tush Bannon sitting at a deuce against the wall, the shoulder bulk hunched toward a still-faced girl who sat across from him. She had long, straight auburn-brown hair, a pouty, impassive little face. She seemed to be listening to him with a thoughtful intentness, and she bit at the heavy bulge of her underlip and closed her eyes and slowly shook her head in a prolonged No.

That is not the point where one goes ambling over to the old buddy and whacks him on the shoulder and asks how Janine is. It was a private conversation, so private and intense they seemed to be inside an overturned bowl of thinnest glass, almost visible.

"Know them?" Puss asked.

"Just him."

"I'd say he's going to get called out on strikes. He's lost his cool. The hard sell makes a gal nervous these days."

"Hey!" said Barni Baker, and put her overnight case down and climbed up onto the stool on my right. She wore a little pale green sleeveless blouse with a high collar, a darker green short skirt, and she had little gold ladybugs in her pierced ears, and she wanted a bourbon sour.

Puss leaned forward and spoke across me, saying, "Gad, it must be the most marvellous, exciting, romantic thing in the world, jetting around to marvellously romantic places! It's really living, I bet. Those fascinating pilot types, and mysterious international travellers and all. I guess you realize how jealous of you all we earthbound females are, Barni."

There was just the slightest narrowing of Barni's eyes, gone in an instant. She leaned in from her side and said breathlessly, "Oh, yes! It's all my dreams come true, Miss Killian. To fly to all the lovely places in the world." She sighed and shook her pretty little head. "But it seems so . . . so *artificial* somehow to have to use an aeroplane, don't you think? But with my little broom, I can just barely get above the treetops. Have you had better luck?"

"I think having to carry that damned cat makes the difference," said Puss without hesitation. "And wear that stupid hat and the long skirts."

"And it's hard to enjoy the moonlight when you have to keep up that dreary cackling, don't you think?" Barni asked.

Tush came up behind me and said. "Talk to you a minute, Trav?" He turned and walked away before I could introduce him. The gals did not notice. I excused myself and followed Tush. Barni Baker moved over onto my stool. As I went out into the corridor, before the glass door swung shut, I heard the contralto bark of one of Puss's better laughs, in counterpoint with a silvery yet somehow earthy yelp from Barni. Knife-fighting among the females can spoil party time, and it was nice to know that this pair would get along.

I went with Tush past the elevators to the empty men's room.

"I would have said hello, but you had a friend."

"Friend! With friends like that, who needs, and so forth. She left. Look, I haven't got much time. I've left Jan along with the kids for three days and I want to get back. She said a year ago there was a pattern in this whole thing and we should get out, but I wouldn't believe her. Okay. I believe her now. It's a business deal. A land development deal. And we got in the way."

He was as big as ever, but his face looked oddly shrunken.

His big hands were shaky. His eyes had a starey look, somewhat like the eyes of people who wear glasses when they have their glasses off.

He tried to laugh. "I thought somebody wanted my marina. So I used money I couldn't spare to get a local lawyer to see what he could find out. Young guy. Steve Besseker. I thought maybe he was the only lawyer in Sunnydale who wouldn't scare. I told him everything that had happened to me, and he agreed it couldn't be coincidence. So he nosed around. Nobody wants the marina, Trav. They want to put together a parcel of four hundred and eighty acres. And my little ten acres is right in the middle of all that riverfront land they want."

"They?"

"All that area is zoned as an industrial park ever since Tech-Tex came in, across the river. Big high lines come in with all the power anybody would need. They're going to dredge the river and the channel so barges can come in from the Waterway. Some big corporation wants to come in, apparently, and they'd pay a nice price for the land."

"So who's putting it together?"

"A local real estate man named Preston LaFrance owns the fifty acres right behind me. Besseker found out LaFrance has an option on the two hundred acres just east of me, at a price of two hundred dollars an acre. It's owned by an old boy named D. J. Carbee, an early settler. On the other side of me, to the west, there's two hundred and twenty acres owned by something called Southway Lands, Incorporated. Besseker found out that Southway is one of Gary Santo's operations. Do you know him?"

"I know *of* him. Like everybody else in south Florida." A few years ago Santo had been the dramatic young swinger, with the touch of gold. Now he is the not-so-young swinger, moving in mysterious ways behind many scenes, behind barriers of privacy and money. The name in Miami has the flavour of penthouses, pipelines, South American playmates, mergers and acquisitions, private jets, and well-publicized donations to local drives in the art and culture areas.

"I don't know the exact relationship between Santo and Preston LaFrance, Trav. Maybe LaFrance is just acting as Santo's agent. Maybe it's a joint venture. Besseker heard a rumour that the plant location experts nosed around the area a year and a half ago and recommended that the big company that wants it could go as high as eight hundred thousand! Seventeen hundred dollars an acre. About the time I learned all this, an old friend came out and told me he couldn't help it, and didn't want to do it, but he had to pick up the houseboats. I still owed on them. He told me that one of the Shawana County Commissioners, Mr. P. K. Hazzard—they call him Monk Hazzard—had hinted that if my friend repossessed his houseboats, he'd get a favourable ruling on a zoning application. So when I told that to Besseker, he said that Monk Hazzard was Preston LaFrance's brother-in-law, and there wasn't any way to prove a thing. He acted funny. He said he had a lot of things coming up and he couldn't promise to give me any more time. They'd gotten to him too, I guess. He has to make a living there."

"All just folks," I said.

He stared at the paper towel rack. He shook his head. "You know my style, Trav. I don't like all this round-and-about stuff. Direct confrontation. I'd seen Hazzard at a couple of those public hearings where they'd messed me up, like about taking that bridge out, but I hadn't talked to him. So I tried to make an appointment and he kept stalling, and finally I took Jan with me and we sat there outside his office until finally he saw us. Smallish man, with a long neck and a little bit of a round head, and big goggly eyes behind his thick glasses. Face sort of like a monkey, and a squeaky voice. I said we were citizens and taxpayers and landowners, and he was a public official, and it was his ethical and moral duty to see that the machinery of government wasn't used to shove me into bankruptcy so his brother-in-law could make a few bucks. You know about humiliation, Trav?"

"I keep getting a little every once in a while."

"He strutted around and he squeaked and lectured. Folks come down from the north and think it's easy to make a living in Florida. Toughest place in the world. He wouldn't look at me. He looked out the window part of the time, and at Jan's legs the rest of the time. He said it wasn't the job of local government to save a man from his own mistakes and bad judgment. He said that the greatest good for the greatest number meant the best possible land use, and maybe a marina wasn't the best use when you think of the tax base and

employment and so on. He said he'd overlook the slur on his
honesty because a man in trouble says things he doesn't mean.
He said people just don't know how much talent it takes to
run a small business, and I'd probably be happier in some
other line of work. He said that he didn't know whether Press
LaFrance was interested in my ten acres or not, but maybe
if I could talk to him he might make me an offer, but I
shouldn't expect too much because the business was in bad
shape. He said that people in trouble get to thinking the whole
world is against them, and just because certain necessary
county improvements were hurting my business, it didn't
mean it was done on purpose. He said thousands of little
businesses go broke every year in Florida, and I shouldn't
think I was an exception. So we left and Jan was crying
before we got to the car. Humiliation and frustration."

"You're bucking the power structure, Tush. You can't
hardly win."

"I thought I could. When I saw LaFrance, I went along.
He gave me the same line, as if they'd rehearsed it. I told
him to make an offer. He said he wasn't interested. He said
maybe if it came on the market later on, he might make an
offer on a foreclosure price, but he didn't think it was worth
the mortgage balance. A little over sixty thousand, that is.
And we put fifty-one thousand in it. So I had to open my
big mouth. I leaned across his desk and told him he was
never going to get his hands on my property. I'd leave Jan
there to run it and go back to sales work, and put every
dime I could spare against that mortgage. So they squeezed
a little harder."

"How?"

"First they extended that road contract another hundred
days. Then they sent out inspectors from the County Bureau
of Services, and they condemned my wiring, and the septic
tank drain fields, and my well, and lifted my licence to do
business. With the licence gone, the bank said I come up with
the whole amount of the mortgage in thirty days or they
foreclose. It's way past due. We did well for a while there,
Trav. I didn't overextend. If they'd left me alone, I had
enough business to pay for the boat storage rack and the
motel enlargement. We were going to have one of the best little
operations in that whole area. I tried to see Commissioner

Hazzard again. I waited and a couple of sheriff's deputies showed up and said I could either leave or get picked up for loitering. So Jan and I talked it over and decided the best thing to do would be lay it all out for Mr. Gary Santo. We decided he was probably big enough so that he didn't even know what was going on up there, and would tell them to put a stop to it if he did know. We decided that probably LaFrance just got too eager to do a big job for Santo and do it as cheap as possible. I put it all down on paper. I guess that between us we must have rewritten that letter about nine times, and Janine typed it on the old machine in the motel office, and we sent it down here Special Delivery, marked personal."

"Any answer?"

"Verbal. From that girl I was sitting with. Her name is Mary Smith. I came down and tried to get to Santo. She was as far as I got. She said she'd meet me out here, because she had to catch a flight. Cold as a meat locker, boy. Yes, Mr. Santo had read my letter personally. Yes, he had an informal agreement with Mr. LaFrance. But Mr. LaFrance is not employed by Mr. Santo. Yes, Mr. France is under considerable pressure by Mr. Santo to produce the results promised insofar as land acquisition is concerned. Mr. Santo feels no personal responsibility for your plight. He is not running a charitable organization. I wanted to know if I could see him in person. No. Sorry. But no."

"Now what?"

"We lose it. That's all. The grace period is about gone. Janine is taking it hard. It's a lot of money and work and time down the drain, and nothing to show for it. I . . . I wish I'd come to you sooner, Trav, before it got to be too late. Maybe you could have figured out some kind of a salvage operation. Your kind of salvage. Squeeze them like they've squoze me." He gave me a strange, puzzled, thoughtful look. "You know, I keep thinking about how I might kill somebody. Hazzard, Santo, LaFrance. Somebody. Anybody. I never thought that way in my life before. I'm not like that."

He grimaced, whirled, kicked the big metal trash basket full of used paper towels. "Aaaah . . . Tush!" he yelled, and went blundering out.

I collected Puss and Barni. It was after six thirty when we got back to *The Busted Flush*. Mick had got his phone call, made his deal, and set up a Monday morning flight to Spain via New York. And so, though my mood was somewhat soured, there was song and sport, sunburn and music, beach time and nap time, old and new jokes, girls in the galley, new tapes on the music machine, lipstick and sand and the some-time kiss, and the long heavy look through curl of lashes.

Meyer trooped in and out from time to time with little groups of Meyer's Irregulars and Partisans. We had a slight overflow from the permanent floating houseparty aboard the Alabama Tiger's big cruiser.

Though it looked as it always looks—so informal you don't know who is tied up with whom—there is a protocol. There is a very real in-group unwritten list of things you do and things you don't do, things you say and things you don't say. And if you are the kind of person who can't case the scene and know by instinct what the rules have to be, then the blinds are closed, shades drawn, and the freeze is on. But sometimes, as in the case of one midday visitor on Sunday, someone is so obtuse the action has to be a little more direct.

This one was named Buster or Buddy or Sonny, one of those names, a big loud thirtyish jollyboy type, office-soft, overconfident, far from home on a business trip and out beagling for a broad, confident that he was twice the man any of these beach-bum types could be, ready for a nice little roll and scuffle that he could describe to the other JC's back in God's Country, and hide from li'l ol' Peggy staying back home there with the kids.

So he came up onto the sun deck and sprawled out next to Barni and told her she was cute as any bug in the wide world, and if she would just let him spread a little more of this here suntan juice on that cute little ol' back and this here cute little ol' tummy, why she'd be making him the happiest paper salesman in the southeast territory.

She sat up and frowned into his dumb, happy, smirking face, and as Mick started to get up to heave Buster-Buddy-Sonny over the rail she waved him back. "Music down and out," she said. Puss went to the speakers and turned the volume off.

In the silence Barni said, with a brutal clarity, "Puss? Marilee? Come here, dears. Come take a look at this one."

They came and sat close to her on her sun pad, all of them

staring at Buster-Buddy-Sonny. "The type I was telling you about," Barni said. "One of the charmers that make life hell for a stewardess."

"Now, don't you badmouth me, you purty thing," he said, grinning.

Puss said, scowling, "I see. Of course. All that fatty look around the middle. And that big voice and those dim, nasty little eyes."

"You funning me, you gals?" he asked, his smile fading a little.

Marilee tilted her head. "Mmmm. The kind you don't dare turn your back on when you're on duty. A real snatch-ass Charlie."

"They have this crazy dream, I guess," Barni said, "about how you're going to fall for all that meaty charm and go back to their hotel or motel and climb right into the sack. Can you imagine?"

Puss shuddered delicately. "My God, darlings, suppose we were call girls or something and we *had* to sleep with one of those."

"Ekk!" said Marilee.

Buster-Buddy-Sonny stood up and the three lovelies looked blandly up at him.

"Coffee, tea or milk?" asked Barni.

"You lousy little bitch!" said he.

Puss laughed. "See? Just like you said, dear. Typical reaction. Look at how red his face is! Let me guess. He'll be bald in five years."

"Four," said Marilee firmly.

"He needs glasses already and won't wear them," said Barni.

"He's going to grow an enormous belly," Puss said.

"And fall over dead of a massive coronary occlusion when he's forty-five."

"And when he falls over, it will burst his cigar and spill his bourbon."

"And some sorry wretched woman is married to him."

Barni shook her head. "No girl who ever spent any time as a stewardess would ever marry one of those. Look at that mouth on it! Imagine having to actually kiss something like that and pretend you were enjoying it!"

"And look at the dirty fingernails, will you!"

When Buster-Buddy-Sonny reappeared in view, he was eighty feet up the dock, walking briskly and not swinging his arms at all.

"You girls need your mouths washed out with gin," Mick said. "That was naughty."

"A little friendly castration never hurt anybody," said Marilee.

"Besides," said Puss, "we didn't touch on his *really* filthy habit. Given half a chance, do you know what that dreary bastard might do?"

Marilee, with a dirty chuckle, leaned close to Puss and whispered to her. Puss shook her head and said, "Congratulations, sweetie. You must be leading a full life. But I meant something much worse than that."

"Like what?" Barni asked, puzzled.

"If you were ever stupid enough to let him get just a little bit past first base, that utter spook would stare right into your eyes and he would kind of gulp and look like a kicked dog and his voice would quiver and he'd say, 'Darlin', I love you'."

"He would! He would indeed!" cried Marilee. "The lowest of the low. He's the *perfect* type for it. A real ratfink coward."

Meyer came out of a long and sombre contemplation, hunched like a hirsute Buddha, reached a slow ape arm and picked up his queen's bishop and plonked it down in what at first glance seemed like an idiotic place, right next to my centre pawn. A round little lady who was one of his retinue that week, beamed, clapped her hands and rattled off a long comment in German.

"She says you give up now," said Meyer.

"Never!" said I. I studied and studied and studied. Finally I put a knuckle against my king and tipped the poor fellow over and said, "Beach-walking, anyone?"

But before Puss and I went over, I tried once again to reach Tush Bannon at his Boatel by phone. Once again there was no answer. I felt irritation and depression. And, perhaps, the first little needles of alarm.

CHAPTER THREE

I AWAKENED at six thirty Monday morning thinking about Tush and his problem. If I hadn't awakened with that idea in mind, I could have gone back to sleep. But it snapped my eyelids up and held them there. And big as the bed was, the custom job that had been aboard the *Flush* when I won her in Palm Beach, Puss Killian had left me in precarious balance on the edge. She was curled, her back to me, and there was a solid and immovable feel to the warm and shapely rear that pressed against the side of my hip. She was deeply recharging all her redheaded batteries, in the deep, slow intake and humming exhalation of sleep of the heaviest and best kind.

So I gave up and got up and showered and came back, and tried to quietly get into a white sports shirt and khaki slacks. But in the muted light as I shoved my arm through the short sleeve I knocked a nightcap glass off the shelf and it smashed on the deck.

She rolled, rose up slowly, glowered indignantly at me and settled back down into her sleep, nestling onto her other side, a long, tangled tassle of red hair falling across her cheek and mouth, stirring with each breath.

I heard furtive galley sounds and found Barni Baker in a hip-length yellow robe, her hair in a kerchief, doing something to eggs. Her eyebrows went up when she saw me, and she whispered, "You too! What's *your* excuse? Don't answer. It's rhetorical. It's criminal to have to talk in the morning. I found this here good-looking roe and these here good-looking eggs, and what smells like good Herkimer County cheese, and if you want me to double the portion, just nod."

I nodded. I poured us some juice. She had the water on. I dumped the Columbian fine grind into the Benz filter paper and slid into the booth. She stared at me as I tried the egg invention. The question was in the lift of a little blonde eyebrow. The response was the circle of thumb and forefinger. When she started to tidy up, I told her to leave it until later, and I carried our coffee seconds in the white porcelain pot topsides, and she brought along the mugs.

The morning was almost cold. I dug a blanket out of the forward locker for her to use as a lap robe over her bare legs, and I put on an old grey cardigan I've had for seven hundred years. It could now be classified as a missionary barrel reject.

"I think we could have practised on the snare drum and tuba down there without bothering those two," I said.

"Mick needs all the sleep he can get. We'll have to leave by ten o'clock to make that flight. They're going to work him to death when he gets to Spain. The picture is behind schedule."

"When do you have to go back to work?"

"Tuesday noon."

"So come back."

"Thanks, but I don't think so. I think I'll turn the car in and hole up and try to do some thinking. You make damned good coffee, Trav. How good is your advice? Like to the lovelorn?"

"The best. But nobody ever takes it."

"So here is a hypothetical case about two loners, about this little ball of fluff who is an airline stewardess who is twenty-seven all too soon, and likes to be where the action is, but lately she wonders if the action isn't getting to be all alike. And there is this very special and talented guy who is a cinematographer, and who is a tough and sceptical thirty-two, who is gun-shy from a sour marriage, and who gets so hooked on his work he can't remember the stewardess's name, practically. And they are together maybe five times a year, maybe five days a time, and it is always the rightest of the right. The workingest of ever, even though they keep telling themselves and each other that it is going to wear off any minute now. So last time the camera guy wanted to marry the airline girl and she said hell no, so she thought about it a lot, and this time she brought it up and said okay and he said hell no, because he was hurt because she said no the last time. Can these two darling kids find happiness, McGee?"

"You get married when there is no other conceivable course of action, Barni-baby. You get married because you are both compelled to marry each other."

"Indeed?"

"Don't get frosty. I'm not putting down your romance. It

will either get inevitable or it won't. It won't hang where it is. It will get bigger, or it will start to dry up, and either way it goes will be the right answer at that time. Don't get pushy."

After a long silence she said, "Anyway, the coffee *is* good." She shrugged. "Change of subject. This Puss Killian of yours. I *like* her, Trav. I like her a lot. But there's a funny thing about her. You think she's telling you all about herself, and afterwards you know she hasn't really told you a thing. What about her, anyway?"

"I wouldn't know. Don't look at me like that. I've known her for four months. She goes away for a couple of days every few weeks. I could do some digging. But it's up to her. When and if she wants to talk, she can talk. I know that she's from Seattle, that she isn't hurting for money, that she's twenty-four or five, that she shed a husband not long before she showed up here, that I met her on the beach only because she stepped on a sea urchin and was cursing billy blue blazes and ordered me to come over and do something about it right now. I know she has enough energy for three stevedores, that she can eat three pounds of steak at a sitting, that she can hold her booze, and she would walk up and spit in a tiger's eye if she thought it would liven up the idle hour. And I know that once in a while she goes absolutely dead silent, and all she wants is for you to pretend she isn't there."

"She has a very soft look for you, Travis. When you're not looking at her."

"Troublemaker!"

I tried again and couldn't get an answer out of Tush. I had the long distance operator run a check on the phone up there, but it was reported in order. At a little after nine I thought I'd better see if Puss wanted to say her good-bye in person or let me relay it. I went in and sat gently on the bed. She was breathing faster. Her hand and arm were twitching as she dreamed, and she made a little whimpering sound. I gently thumbed the red hair back away from her face and saw a wetness of tears leaking out of the closed lids.

I put my hand on her bare shoulder and gave her a little shake. "Hey," I said. "It's not all *that* bad, is it?"

She opened wide blind eyes and snuffled and said in a little-girl voice, "But they keep saying. . . ." She shook herself like a wet red setter. She focused on me, snuffled again, smiled and said, "Thanks, pal. They were about to cut me off at the pass. Whassa time?"

"Nine fifteen."

"Hmmm. If I'm reading you, McGee, I admire your thinking. It's very good. Stay right where you are while I go brush my teeth first."

"Mick and Barni are taking off in a half hour. I wondered if you wanted to wave bye-bye."

She gave a leonine stretching yawn. "Yes I do indeed. And if you had any sense at all, you big brown knuckly idiot, you'd have come smirking in here at quarter of, not quarter after. Haste makes waste, and what I have is not to be wasted, lad. So set your little clock for siesta time."

"At siesta time we're going to be up in Shawana County visiting some old friends of mine with a problem."

"Really?" She sat up, holding the sheet to her breasts. "Hmm. Then hustle the lady some coffee while she showers. And set your clock ahead."

". . . on location like that," Mick was saying, "It's the time lag that drives you nuts, not getting to see rushes, and see how the colour values stand up until you're three days or four past that particular point."

And from the giant shower stall, above the sound of sloshing like unto that which a small walrus herd might make, the three of us could hear Puss in good voice: "With 'er 'ead tooked oonderneath 'er arm, she 'awnts the bloody tow'r. With 'er 'ead tooked oonderneath 'er arm at the midnight hour."

"So I turned around," said Barni Baker, "and there was that sweet little old man yanking away at the lever on the cabin door thinking it was how you get into the men's room, and we're at twenty-eight thousand feet over the Amazon basin. So I got to him at a dead run and steered him gently where he wanted to go. Then he came out and stared at the cabin door and the big lever and rolled his eyes up and fainted dead away. A passenger helped me get him back to his seat and I gave him smelling salts and then I explained to him how the doors are designed so the pressurization clamps them shut so tightly ten men couldn't open them. But he just kept shaking his head and saying O Dear God."

Puss appeared just in time, wearing her big white woolly

robe and carrying the half cup of coffee left from what I had taken her as she was stepping into the shower. The ends of her red hair were damp. She gathered little Barni into the big white woolly arms, hugged her, smacked her on the cheek, and told her she was all doll. We went out the aft door of the lounge and waved them off, and watched them get into the car and drive away.

"Nice ones," said Puss. "For such a raunchy old beach bum, you know a lot of nice ones. Like me, for example. I was nice enough to leave our coffee and my cigarettes right beside the bed." She went over to the phone and switched it off. She went frowning to the record bin, made a thoughtful selection of two and held up the sleeves so I could see what she had picked. George Van Eps guitar, and the Modern Jazz Quartet on Blues at Carnegie Hall. I took them from her, put them on the changer, fixed the volume where she said she liked it.

"Coming, dear?" she said with an excessive primness, and just inside the door of the master stateroom I had to step over the woolly whiteness of the robe on the deck just beyond the sill.

The day had warmed up. The *Muñequita* had run handsomely, with a deep drone speaking of a lot more power in reserve. When we had anchored for lunch in Fort Worth, well away from the channel, while we ate the thick roast beef and raw onion sandwiches and shared an icy bottle of dry red supermarket wine, I briefed her on Tush, on how long I had known him, and on Janine and what Tush had told me of his problems.

"No answer at all on the phone?"

"Not a thing."

"Seems odd."

"Seems very damned odd, Puss. The thing is, he isn't a devious guy. And he's caught in the middle in a very devious situation, with large money hanging on it, and old Tush may try to bull his way through, and he could get hurt twice as bad."

When we went up the Shawana River, there was a faint, drifting acrid stink. Our eyes watered. When I came around the last bend, I was shocked at the deserted look of the place. The cheerful white houseboats were all gone. All but one storage rack on the in-and-out boat shelter were empty, and the remaining boat was, at a hundred feet, worth perhaps fifty dollars, outboard motor and all. The moored boats were gone, except for a skiff so full of water there were only inches of freeboard left, and an old cruiser hulk that had sunk in the shallows. The forklift truck was gone.

I tied up and we went ashore. Near the cities, all the old highways of America pass businesses that have gone broke. End of the dream. The spoor of a broken marriage can be kept in a couple of cartons on a shelf in the garage. Broken lives can be tucked neatly away in graves and jails and sanitariums. But the dead business in a sub-marginal commercial strip stays right there, ugly and mouldering away, the frantic advertising signs of the final convulsive effort fading and tattering over the weeds. For every one of them was the big dream, the gala opening, the last dusting and arranging before the doors opened. "We're going to make it big, honey, Real big." Then there is the slow slide into doubt, into confusion, and into the terminal despair. "So we were going to make it real big, were we? Ha!"

It was a silent place. The acrid river slid by. Dry fronds rattled in the breeze. A sign creaked.

Even the two marine petrol pumps were gone. I went to the marina shed. The tools were gone. We asked each other questions in low, graveyard voices. There was a shiny new hasp and padlock on the marina building, along with a printed notification from the County Sheriff's Department. There was another on the motel office. I could find no note fastened to anything that told how to get in touch with the Bannons.

"Now what?" Puss asked.

"There's no neighbours, nobody here to ask. I suppose we could run upriver until we come to something."

She stared around. "Gives me the spooks," she said. We'd just reached the dock when I heard a car coming. We went back around in front and saw the phone company service truck lurching over the torn-up road. As I moved to wave him down, he turned in and stopped and got out and stared at us as we approached. He looked to be about fifty, a squatty, leathery man wearing silver-rimmed glasses.

"I'd like to find Mr. Bannon," I said.

"Why?" It was a very flat and very abrupt question, and there was something about the flavour of it that made me wary. So I reached into the old bag of tired tricks and pulled out the one labelled Real Cordial.

"Well, it's like this. Quite a while back, I can't remember how many weeks. I had a bilge pump acting up, and I stopped in here and Bannon pulled it and stuck in a loaner, the idea being he'd fix it if he could or sell me the loaner if he couldn't, but I didn't get back as soon as I thought. Now it looks like he's gone out of business or moved someplace else."

"You could say that. Yes. It surely does. Let me make the disconnect and check in first, then maybe I can tell you what happened."

He donned harness and spurs with practised ease and walked up the pole. He made his service disconnect at the lead-in terminals, clipped his handset onto the wires and called in. We could hear his voice but not what he was saying. He came down fast, showing off a little. He took off his gear and tossed it into the truck.

"Well, sir," he said, "you got here yesterday morning, you'd had some excitement for sure. You'da found Bannon right here. Promised myself I'd take a look and see where it was they found him. Maybe you'd like to come take a look, mister. Maybe the young lady should kind of wait on us."

But Puss tagged along. He went around in back and looked around, grunted and went over to a sturdy and rusty tripod made of heavy pipe, standing about fifteen feet tall. There was a manual winch with a crank, as rusty as the pipe, and a wire cable that went from the winch drum up through a pulley at the top of the tripod. A big, heavy old marine diesel, cannibalized down to little more than the ponderous block, hung from the taut cable about five feet off the ground.

The phone man sat on his heels and shook his head and said, "Sure a terrible way for a man to do himself. Look there! There's still hair and mess on the bottom side a that engine."

I had thought the stain on the packed oily dirt was merely more oil. Puss went trotting busily away about fifty feet. She stopped and bent forward and coughed shallowly a few times, then straightened up and went over and sat on a sawhorse with her back to us.

"What Freddy said this Bannon done—Freddy is one of Sheriff Bunny Burgoon's deputies and Freddy is the one that found him Sunday morning—this Bannon must have cranked that block up as high as he could get it, and then he fastened a piece of stove wire to that ratchet there on the side of the drum and lay out on his back right under that thing and give the wire a yank. The wire was still wound around his hand. Mashed him something terrible they say." He stood up, spat. "Well, you got to say one thing. It was quick and it was for certain. And I guess the poor fella didn't have much to live for."

"Because he went broke?"

"Maybe I don't have the straight of it. You know how people get to talking and every time they tell something, it comes out different. What I hear, he went off to try to raise some money fast to save the business. So when they come out here Friday with all the eviction papers and bankrupt papers and so on, just his missus is here with the youngest. She wanted them to hold off until Bannon got back, but all the legal steps had been took care of in proper order, and there was just no choice about it. They waited about an hour for her to pack up personal stuff and they helped her load the car. They say she was crying but she wasn't carrying on. She was crying without making any noise about it. She picked up the other two kids from school, and she left off Bannon's suitcase and a note from her to him with the Sherf, and she just took off. She must have had some travel money saved out, because they say that yesterday after they toted Bannon's body back to Ingledine's Funeral Home, Sherf Burgon opened that note to see where he could get in touch with her to tell her about her husband, but all it said was she was going to go stay with some girl's first name for a while, and Bannon would have known the whole name, but nobody else does."

He spat again and started to move toward his truck. I walked slowly with him and said, "He seemed like a bright, pleasant guy. He didn't seem like the kind who'd go broke. But you never can tell. Sometime it's booze, or the dog track, or other women."

He got into the truck and stared out at me. "Not this time.

They run this boy off. He was in the way, and they run him off. But you didn't hear me say that, mister."

"I didn't hear you, friend."

He headed back over the lumpy road. I walked around to where Puss still sat on the sawhorse. She looked up at me. With a small frown she said, "My heart bled for you the way you went reeling around in shock, McGee. You really took it hard. Your dear old buddy has gone to the big marina in the sky. The hard way. Came to get your bilge pump! God's sake, Travis!"

I sat on my heels and squinted up at her. Dark red hair and disapproval, outlined against a blue December sky. "Win a few, lose a few, honey," I said.

"What *are* you?" she asked.

I stood up and put my hands on her upper arms, near the shoulders and plucked her up off the sawhorse and held her. Maybe I was smiling at her. I wouldn't know. What I was saying seemed to come from a strange direction, as if I were standing several feet behind myself. I said some nonsense about smelling these things out, about sensing the quickest way to open people up, and so you do it, because if you don't, then maybe you miss one little piece of something you should know, and then you go join the long long line of the dead ones, because you were careless.

"And," I heard myself say, "Tush killed himself but not with that damned engine block. He killed himself with something he said, or something he did, and he didn't know he was killing himself. Maybe he didn't listen very good, or catch on soon enough. I listen very good. I catch on. And when I add up this tab and name the price, I'm going to look at some nice grey skin, honey. Grey and pale, oily and guilty as hell, and some eyes shifting around looking for some way out of it. But every damned door will be nailed shut."

I came out of it and realized she was making little hiccupy sobs and looking down and to the side, and her cheeks were wet, and she was saying, "Please, please."

I released her and turned on my heel and walked away from her. I went a little way up the road. I leaned against the trunk of an Australian pine and emptied my lungs a few times. A jay yammered at me. There were tree toads in a swamp somewhere nearby. Puss came walking very slowly up the road. She came over to me and with a quick, shy smile leaned her face into my neck and chest.

"Sorry," she whispered.

"For nothing?"

She exhaled. "I don't know. I asked you what you were. Maybe I found out, sort of."

"Whatever it is, I don't let it show, Puss. Ten more minutes and I would have been kindly Trav forevermore."

She pushed herself a few inches away and looked up at me. "Just smile with your eyes like kindly ol' McGee, dear, to kind of erase that other . . . that other look."

"Was it that bad?"

"They could bottle it and use it to poison pit vipers."

"Okay now?"

She nodded. "Sure." Her eyes were a sherry brown, almost a tan, and in that good light under the tree I could see the area right around the pupil, a corona of green. "He was a special guy?"

"He was that."

"But can't even a special guy . . . give up?"

"Maybe, but if that one ever had, it wouldn't have been like that."

We walked back toward the dead marina, my arm around her strong waist. "Call it enemy country," I explained. "He's dead, and it solves some problems for some people. And they'll want to forget all about it as fast as they can, and they won't know anything about anything."

I got the camera off the boat, a battered old Retina C-III, and put in a roll of Plus X. I hand-cranked the block as high as it would go before it wedged against the tripod poles. I got wire and pliers out of the toolbox aboard, fastened wire to the ratchet stop. I took pictures as I went along. When I yanked the wire, the great weight came down to thud against the hard dirt with a shock I could feel in the soles of my feet, while the drum clattered and the cable rasped through the rusty pulley. I craned it up and left it the way it had been.

She watched, and had the grace not to ask why.

I didn't rinse my hands in the river. I waited until we were well out into the bay.

Then I put it at dead slow, right at 700 rpm, and told her

to head down the channel. I climbed out onto the forward
bow shell and leaned back against the port windshield.

One approach: Go storming into Sunnydale, promising
stink and investigations and general turmoil.

Or: Find some kind of cover story that might open up
some mouths. See who can be conned. See who can be turned
against whom.

Or: Go in fast and quietly and come out with one Preston
LaFrance and take him to a nice quiet place and open
him up.

Or: What if some mysterious buyer picked up the Bannon
property? Then the boys couldn't put the whole two sections
together. And that might bring them out of the woodwork.

The last had the right flavour, if it could be worked.

But first there had to be a first thing, and it had to be poor
damned Janine. And if I couldn't get to her before the Sherf
told her the bad news, I could at least arrive shortly thereafter.

So I hopped down and took the wheel and ran at high cruise
to Broward Beach and tied up at the city marina. I left Puss
at the drugstore counter and shut myself into a booth and
made a person-to-person credit card call to Sheriff Bunny
Burgoon in Sunnydale. I yapped at him in the excited tones
of a whiter-wash commercial and told him that CBS news
had researched him and discovered he was a truly fine law
officer, and had they located Mrs. Bannon yet, and her three
kids, and it was a great human interest story and we might
do a little feature.

"Sure," he said, "Just before Christmas and all that. Yeh.
Locate her? Well, not exactly yet, but we're doing everything
that any human person could expect or ask for, and that's
the truth. We got aholt of her folks in Milwaukee, and they're
all upset as any human person could imagine, but they haven't
heard a word from her, and they don't know any friend of
hers of the name of Connie. Now if it was to go on national
television, she'd turn up right off, I imagine. The name is
Sheriff Hadley—that's an e-y, Burgoon, B-u-r-g-o-o-n. And
I've been elected here three times as Sherf of Shawana County
and——"

"Could you read me the note she left her husband?"

"Did you get the name wrote down with the right spelling?"

"I did, Sheriff."

"It's personal-like, but I see no harm in reading it to you, as any human person could tell it's a public service to find that poor lady. Just a minute. Let me see now. Here it is. It goes like this. 'Dear Tush, I'm sorry. This last thing was just the bitter end. Somehow it made me so ashamed. The boys are so upset and confused. I had to handle it alone because you weren't there, and it took the very last bit of strength and courage I had. Don't be angry with me. I'm worn out. I'm going to go stay with Connie for a while. I'm leaving this note and a suitcase with the things you'll probably need with the Sheriff. When you get the details and all straightened out, please phone me. Don't come charging up here, because I might not be ready to see you yet. I have some thinking to do, and then we have a lot of talking to do, about what's going to happen to you and me. Don't worry about me or the boys. We'll be fine. It was all so ugly, the way it happened. I suppose those men tried to be nice, and it wasn't their fault, but it was a terrible thing. Jan.' "

"I certainly appreciate your co-operation, Sheriff. We'll be in touch. Yes sir, we'll stay in close touch with developments."

I went back to the counter. Puss was sitting on the stool sipping her cola drink, eyes a bit narrow, and on her lips a dangerous little smile. A plump man with a vulgar shirt and a hairline moustache sat two stools away, blushing furiously. He tried to sip his coffee with trembling hand and spilled a dollop of it into his saucer.

"Darling!" she cried, turning toward me, her voice of such a penetrating clarity it reached all the way back to the remedies for iron-poor blood. "This dear little fat fellow wanted to show me all the sights. What's your name, dear little fat fellow?"

He clapped two bits onto the counter top. "Geee-ZUSS!" he muttered. He fled out of the cool into the midafternoon sunlight.

She gazed sombrely toward the door. "Seems to have turned chicken. Have you noticed the progressive emasculation of the American male, Travis? Present company excluded, of course."

She finished the soft drink with a rattling slupp amid the cracked ice, cheeks sucked hollow, and stood up in her sky-blue linen boat shorts, and her basque shirt, shook her hair back and smiled benignly up at me. "I counted myself in," she said in a low voice.

"How's that?"

"Since we left the river, I've felt like a bulky package you were tired of carrying around, and you were looking for a coin locker. I never knew Tush. I never met Janine. But I have a very hard nose, dear, and I don't scare, and I want to share."

"I'll give it some thought."

"You *do* that."

CHAPTER FOUR

I HAD to give a lot of thought right then and there to getting a good quick line on Connie. Janine's parents didn't know her. But somebody who had been close to the Bannons would know who she might be. I had to dig through the fragments of old memories and piece something together. I tried walking and thinking, Puss quietly, patiently trudging along beside me.

I found a dark little cocktail lounge, and a dark table in a corner. They had one cocktail waitress, and the small percentage of her that was not bare was cruelly bound and laced into the compulsory bunnyfication of tiny waist, improbable uplift and separation of breast, revelation of cleavages front and rear. She had a tired, pretty, sour little face, a listless manner. When she left with the order, Puss clamped her hand on my arm and stared after her, saying, "Santa Claus is coming to town."

They had their Christmas decoration up. It was a lush plastic spray of mistletoe, affixed exactly where the nubile legions of the Heffner Empire affix their fluffy white bunny tails. It expressed such a perfect comment on commercialized Christmas, it gave Puss a case of gasping chuckles that turned into hiccups, which were soon quelled by her big swallows from the steinkrug of dark beer on draft.

I shoved my memory back to the drinks at Tush and

Janine's breakfast bar two months earlier, when we had played what happened to who. And I finally came up with Kip Schroeder, the quarterback who, after seven years of high school ball, New Jersey All-State, and five years of college ball, a couple of All-American mentions, had been held together with wire, tape and rivets. He had been obsoleted by giant strides in nutrition. He was structured like a fireplug, and every year the line he had to see over was higher and wider. But where the hell was he? He and his wife, whose name I couldn't remember, had been best man and matron of honour at the wedding of Tush and Jan. I had to have a football buff, one of those nuts who know every statistic and what happened to everybody.

I tried the bald bartender, breaking up his murmured conversation with the mistletoe lass. His frown wrinkled the naked skull almost all the way up to the crown of his head.

"I think maybe Bernie Cohn. He does the sports on WBRO-TV. It ought to be a good time to catch him there at the station. Janie, look up the number for the gennaman, and plug the phone in over there, huh?"

It was a little pink phone with a lighted dial. She had to use a lighter to find the baseboard phone connection. She started to tell me the number, then shrugged and dialled it herself and handed me the phone.

I got the switchboard and then I got Bernie, who said, "Yes, yes yes?" with irritable impatience until I told him my question. Then he sounded pleased. "Let me see now. Schroeder. Schroeder. I'm not drawing a blank, buddy. You can put odds on that. I'm running through the career, up to the last thing I heard. Okay. Here it is. Two years ago Kip was athletic director, Oak Valley School, and that's in . . . just a minute . . . Nutley, New Jersey. Right?"

"Sure appreciate it."

"Did I win you a bet, fella? Express your appreciation by telling all your friends to watch the Bernie Cohn show at six fifteen every weekday on your Big Voice of the Big Bay, WBRO-TV. Right?"

Listless Janie came over when I signalled her, and I ordered two more draft and asked her if I could make a credit card call on the phone. When she came back with the beers, she said, "He says okay if I stand here while you make the call.

44 PALE GREY FOR GUILT

You know. On account of any long distance comes in on the
bill, it's a deduct on him."

Puss reached out with a foot, hooked a chair over from
the nearby table and said, "Rest your mistletoe, honey."

With her first smile, the waitress sat down, saying, "My
feet are like sore teeth, honest to God. I worked waitress three
years and no trouble, but in this costume the owner says high
heels, and now after three months I hurt all over, honest
to God."

I got through to area information on my station to station
call for anyone at the phone listed in Nutley for Kip
Schroeder. They didn't have one. They had a K. D. Schroeder.
I tried that and got a Mrs. Schroeder, and she said yes, she
was Kip's wife, Alice. Kip was out.

I said I had met her once, and she pretended politely that
she remembered me perfectly. I was glad she sounded so
bright. I said I was trying to locate a very good friend of
Jan Bannon, named Connie.

"Connie. Connie. Can you hold on a minute while I get
my Christmas card list? It's laid out even, but we haven't
got started on it yet."

She came back and said, "I think this is who you want.
Connie Alvarez. It used to be Tom and Connie, and he died.
I think she was one of Jan's teachers in school. Here's the
address I've got for her. To-Co Groves. That's capital To,
capital Co, with a hyphen. Route Two, Frostproof, Florida.
Frostproof! And you should see the sleet coming down here
today. It's worth your life to drive."

I thanked her and told her to give Kip my best, asked her
how he was doing. She said he'd had two good seasons in a
row and he was happy as a clam. So she asked how Tush and
Jan were. What can you say? I said that the last time I'd seen
the two of them, they were fine. It wasn't a lie. She said that
if I saw them soon again, to tell Janine she owed her a letter
and she'd write right after the holidays for sure.

I didn't want to make the next call from there, not with
tired Janie listening. So I paid her, and added on top of the
tip a little balm for sore feet.

Back toward the city marina, toward the drugstore, and
I briefed Puss en route. "She didn't need much travel money
to get there. Less than two hundred miles, I'd guess."

In the drugstore booth, on the off chance that Jan might answer, I made the call person to person to Mrs. Alvarez. I heard a maid answer the operator and say she would get Mrs. Alvarez. It was at least two minutes before Connie Alvarez answered, sounding out of breath.

"Yes?"

"Is Jan staying there with you?"

". . . I . . . I'm afraid I wouldn't be interested, thank you."

"Look, Mrs. Alvarez. This isn't Tush."

"Then, perhaps you could explain more about it, Mr. Williams."

"I get the message. She can hear your end of it. Now, listen very carefully. Please. Don't let her answer any phone calls, and keep her away from the newspapers and the radio and the television."

"I suppose there would be some reason for that."

"My name is Travis McGee. I'm going to try to get there this evening. And it might be a good idea if you could have a damned good tranquillizer handy. I'm an old friend of Tush's. I wasn't going to tell you this if you sounded bird-brained, Connie. But you sound solid. Tush is dead. And it was messy."

"In that case, Mr. Williams, I might be willing to listen. Perhaps if you could come out this evening? There's loads of room here. We can put you up, and it will give us a good chance to talk business. I know a little bit about the sort of proposition you mention, I mean, the background data. I'll look forward to seeing you. By the way, we're eight miles northeast of Frostproof. Go north out of town on US Twenty-seven and turn right on State Road Six thirty, and we're about five miles from the corner on your left. I'll turn the gate lights on at dark."

And then came the fat argument with Puss Killian as we walked back to the city marina. At last she said, "Old buddy, you are leaving out one ingredient. You say she was a steady one. Great. She can cope. So maybe she is one of those who can cope with all the mechanics of a situation. A real administrator. But maybe she can't hold people. Maybe it makes her feel itchy to try to hold somebody and hug somebody and rock somebody. I have this rusty nail for a tongue, and I kick where it is going to hurt the most, but I am a warm broad, like

in the puppy sense of touching and being touched. Contact
with flesh. That's where the messages of the heart are, McGee.
Not in words, because words are just a kind of conventional
code, and they get blurred, because any word doesn't mean
just the same to any two people. And I am very familiar with
that old spook with the scythe and the graveyard breath. And
I do *not* care to be sent back to Lauderdamndale to sit around
in that sexpot houseboat and crack my knuckles. Think of me
as a kind of tall poultice. Or a miracle drug. Part of your
kit. And if the lady administrator can supply the same item, I
will not enter a competition. I will stay the hell out of the
way. But this is women's work, and two are better than one,
and it is going to be ten times worse for her because she
ran for cover, and there will be guilt up to here."

So I scribbled her a list of my overnight needs and sent
her off to a shopping plaza winking and glittering in the dis-
stance. I checked the marina office and got the name and
location of a place that could lift the *Muñequita* out and
tractor it over and put it on a shelf. He phoned for me and
said they had space. I ran her over and took out all the stuff
I did not want to leave aboard. A boat you can check as if it
were a 4,300-pound suitcase is a vast convenience for people
who never know what they'll be doing tomorrow.

I watched them hose down the hull and put Little Doll
tenderly on her shelf, and soon a rental sedan arrived for
me, tow-barring the little three-wheeled bug that would get
the delivery man back to the rental headquarters. I accom-
plished the red tape on car and boat, locked the gear in the
trunk of the maroon two-door, and got back to the cavelike
cocktail bar ten minutes before Puss came striding in with a
new genuine imitation red alligator hatbox, a blue canvas
zipper bag advertising an obscure airline, two suitboxes and
a big shopping bag full of smaller parcels.

By five thirty we were making good time up State 710,
aimed like a chalk line at the town of Okeechobee, and Puss
was in the back seat, happily unwrapping packages, admiring
her own good taste, and packing the items in the oversized
hatbox. At last she came clambering over the back of her
bucket seat, plumped herself down, latched her belt, lit her
cigarette and said, "Now about a few little things aboard *The
Busted Flush*, friend. Like the little ding-dong when anybody

steps aboard. Like the way it is wired for sound, not the pretty music, but for tape pickup. And how about that cosy little headboard compartment with loaded weapon therein? Also, you have some very interesting areas that look as if you'd have a nice collection of purple hearts, if you got them in a war. And how about the way you go shambling mildly about, kind of sleepily relaxed, beaming at your friends and buddies, kind of slow, rawboned, awkward-like, and you were ten feet from Marilee Saturday night when she stepped on that ice cube on the sun deck and was going to pitch headfirst right off the top of that ladderway, and in some fantastic way you got there and hooked an arm around her waist and yanked her right out of the air? More? How about the lightning change of personality for the benefit of the phone man with the old-timey glasses, the way you turned into a touristy goof so completely I didn't even feel as if I knew you? How about this con you almost worked on me about being retired. How about the way I tried to pump Meyer about you, and he showed speed and footwork like you couldn't believe? How about that kind of grim professional bit with the camera and the hoist and the wire and all, so totally concentrated I could have been walking around on my hands with a rose in my teeth without getting a glance from you? How about my gnawing little suspicion that you aren't going up to Frostproof to comfort this Janine, but to go pry information out of her? Enemy country, you said. Maybe for you the whole world is enemy country, McGee. But somehow it would sort of fit one lousy guess, which would be a batch of official cars screaming up and the boys in blue jumping out, and a big loudspeaker yammering for you to come out quietly or they lob in the tear gas."

"You are a warm broad. You are a warm *nosey* broad."

"So I have this eccentricity, maybe. You know, a social flaw. Some kind of insecurity reaction or something. I started sleeping with somebody and I get this terrible curiosity about them."

"So? I could have the same trouble too. But I haven't asked questions. Or tried to find out things I could find out, without much trouble, probably."

She was quiet for a long time. I glanced at her. Her hands were folded in her lap and she was biting at sucked-in lips.

"Fair is fair," she said. "When it's time to tell you, I will tell you. Not in words, but in writing, so that I get it down exactly right. Not that it is so earth-shattering or anything. But for now, for reasons I think are pretty good reasons, I want to keep it to myself. Fair being fair, if you have good reasons, okay, I ask no more."

So I told her the retirement was accurate, except I am taking it in little hunks whenever I can afford it. "It's a tricky, complex, indifferent society, Puss. It's a loophole world. And there are a lot of clever animals who know how to reach through the loopholes and pick the pockets of the unsuspecting. Carefully done, the guy who has been plucked clean has no way of getting it back. There are a thousand perfectly legal acts that can be immoral, or amoral, acts. Then the law officers have no basis of action. Attorney's can't help. The pigeon might just as well have dropped his wallet into a river full of crocodiles. He knows right where it is. And all he can do is stand on the muddy shore and wring his hands. So I'm the salvage expert. And I've known a lot of crocodiles. So I make a deal with him. I dive down, bring it up, and split it with him, fifty-fifty. When a man knows his expectation of recovery is zero, recovering half is very attractive. If I don't make it, I'm out expenses."

"Or you are a dainty dish for the crocs, man."

"So far I've been indigestible. Now Janine Bannon is a client. She doesn't know it yet. Tush would have been. A client in the classic sense of the legal squeeze. I don't understand the killing. They didn't need that. I know one thing. I have to watch myself on this one. Strangers make the best clients. Then I can play the odds and stay cold. Here I'm too emotionally hung up. I'm too angry, too sick at heart. A dirty, senseless act. So I have to watch it."

She pondered it for a time. "Just one thing that bothers me, darling. How do you find . . . enough new clients?"

I told her how I had found the last one, by combing very carefully through all the local items in the fat Sunday edition of a Miami paper. Of the items I marked that looked interesting, one was an apologetic announcement from a stamp collector's club that Mr. So-and-So, a very long and complicated Greek name, the well-known restaurateur had, at the last minute, decided to withdraw from the exhibition and not show his complete and extremely valuable collection of Greek postage stamps, which had included the famous 1857 Dusty Rose, which had brought $21,000 at a New York auction house in 1954.

I'd called an officer of the Philatelic Society who said the old gentleman was not mad at anybody, that he took a lot of pleasure in exhibiting his collection and having it admired, and that though he had sounded upset, he had not given any reason for withdrawing.

It had taken a little more research to find out what company insured the collection. An agent who said he had never met the old gentleman gave me his card. So I took his card and his name and presented myself to the old gentleman and said we wished to make a new appraisal of the collection. He stalled. The collection was in the vault at the bank. He was very busy. Some other time. So I said we had reason to believe he had disposed of some of the collection.

He broke down. He had been remounting the collection under glass for the exhibition. He had to leave his home for a doctor's appointment. He returned. Twenty-two of the most valuable stamps, including the Dusty Rose, were missing.

"So he was the patriarch of a big family, all very close, all sensitive to scandal, and his wife had died, and he had been remarried for two years to something of the same colouring, general impact and impressive dimension of the late Jayne Mansfield, a lassy big enough to make two of the old boy, and he was so certain she had clouted his valuable toys he'd been afraid to make a report to the cops or claim insurance. So I followed the lady to an afternoon assignation with the hotel beachboy who'd blackmailed her into heisting the stamps, and after I got through shaking him up and convincing him that the old gentleman had arranged to have her last two male chums dropped into the Florida Straits wired to old truck parts, he produced eleven stamps, including the gem of the collection, and was so eager to explain where and how he had fenced the other eleven he was letting off a fine spray of spit. I helped him pack, and put him on a bus and waved good-bye and had a nice little talk with the big blonde about how I had just barely managed to talk two tough old Greek pals of her husband's from hiring local talent to write a little warning with a hot wire across her two most obvious endowments. A cop friend shook the missing items out of the fence, and I told the old man it hadn't been his wife at all, and he had every reason to trust her. So he hopped around and sang and chuckled and we went to the bank and he gave me thirty thousand cash, a generous estimate of half the value, and he gave me a note that gives me free meals for life in the best Greek restaurants in four states, and the whole thing took five days, and I went right back to my retirement, and maybe three weeks later one Puss Killian came along and enriched it considerable."

"Pull over," she ordered. I found a place where there was room to park on the grass between the two-lane road and the canal. She unsnapped the seat belt, lunged expansively over, a big hug, a big kiss from a big girl whose eyes danced and sparkled in the fading daylight.

"Drive on," she said, snapping the belt.

I did. "Whatever it was for, it was nice."

"Well, this is a very long day, and it was partly for way way back, having that coffee-with. And it was for getting so damned scarey furious—because maybe there isn't much real anger around any more. It's for appreciating mistletoe. It's mostly for being what you are, doing the nutty things you do, and letting me for once be . . . Sancho Panza."

"Please! Sanch*a*."

"Of course."

CHAPTER FIVE

T H E entrance gate was very wide, very high, with a floodlight shining on the clean white paint and on the sign that hung from chains from the top of the arch. To-Co Groves, Inc.

It was nine fifteen. We had stopped in Okeechobee for a hasty meal of some fresh bass, fried in corn meal and bacon fat. I turned into the gravelled drive and a figure stepped out of the shadows into the headlights, raising a casual hand to stop me. Ranch hat, faded blue denim work jacket and jeans.

She came to my side of the car and said, "McGee? I'm Connie Alvarez."

I got out, leaving the door open, shook hands, introduced Puss. Connie leaned in and shook her hand, then straightened again. In the glow of the courtesy light I had my first good look at her. A strong-looking woman, chunky, with good shoulders, a weathered face, no makeup, very lovely dark, long-lashed eyes.

"You would have helped them if they'd hollered, McGee?"

"All I could."

"Me too. Pride. Their lousy, stiff-necked pride. How many good people has pride killed? She's up there at the house thinking the roof has fallen in on her. She doesn't know it's the roof and the chimney and the whole damn sky, and it is a lousy time to have to tell her. What happened?"

"He was on his back on the ground and about five hundred pounds of scrap iron dropped on him from ten feet in the air. Head and chest, I'd imagine. I haven't seen him, and probably wouldn't know who I was seeing if I did."

"Jesus Christ, man, you don't tiptoe around things, do you?"

"Do you want me to?"

"I think already you know me better than that. Are they trying to call it an accident?"

"Suicide. He's supposed to have run a wire to the ratchet stop, lay down and yanked it loose. They found it still fastened and wound around his hand. Yesterday morning."

Suddenly her brown strong fingers locked onto my wrist. "Oh my dear God! Had he got the note she left him?"

"No."

I heard the depth of her sigh. "That could have done it. That could have been the one thing that could have made him do it. I think I got to know him that well. I think I know how much Jan meant to that poor big sweet guy."

"Not even that, Connie. At least not that way. He was murdered. But we've got to swallow the suicide story. All of us. We've got to act as if we believed it."

"Why?"

"Why do you think?"

"I think why use amateur talent when you can hire professionals."

"Rest your mind, Mrs. A."

"We'll talk after we get this sad thing done." She leaned abruptly into the car again. "You, girl. Do you dither? Do you bleat and snuffle and carry on?"

"Go grow yourself an orange, lady."

She threw her head back and gave a single bark of humourless laughter. "Maybe you'll both do." She pulled my seat back forward and scrambled into the back seat, rustling the discarded wrapping paper. "Let's go, McGee. The gate light turns off up at the house."

I wasn't prepared for a full half mile of drive, nor for the house at the end of it, big and long and low, with upswept drama of roof lines, something by Frank Lloyd Wright out of Holiday Inns. She had me park around at the side. "I'll have my people take care of the car and bring your gear in. You people use one bedroom or two."

"Two, please," said Puss.

"Well, at least the thundering herd is sacked out by now. Her three and my two." She looked up at the stars. And we squared our shoulders and went in to drop the sky down upon Janine, to change the shape of her world and the shape of her heart forever.

It was one thirty in the morning when Puss came walking slowly into the big living-room, yawning. Connie and I had been sitting for a long time in the dark leather chairs near a small crackling of fat pine in the big fireplace of coquina rock. We'd done a lot of talking.

"I think she's good until midmorning anyway," Puss said.

"But Maria better sit there by her just in case."

"She's there, Connie. If Jan wakes up, she'll wake us up. But it isn't likely."

Puss went over to the little bar in the corner, put two cubes in a squat glass, poured some brandy over them and then came over and shoved the footstool closer to me, sat on it and leaned her head against the side of my knee and yawned again. "She was trying to be so damn brave," Puss said. "She wouldn't let go, and she wouldn't let go, and then she did. And that's the best thing. Did you get the calls through, Connie?"

"I got that Sheriff and told him she knew and she was

resting, and I'd call him back tomorrow and let him know what she's going to do next. I got her people and got them calmed down. She'll have to phone them tomorrow. And the boys have to be told."

"Jan said not to tell them," Puss said. "She said it's her job. She keeps asking how we can be sure he never got her note."

Connie swirled the ice in her drink and then slugged it down. "Know what I can't forget? Can't and never will? Five years and it's still so clear in my mind. Every word that was said. Oh, it was a typical brooha. Tommy and I had hundreds of them. Yell and curse, but it never really meant anything. We both had strong opinions. What we quarrelled about that morning doesn't matter. After he went crashing out, I ran and yanked the door open and called after him. 'And don't be in a great big hurry to come back!' Maybe he didn't hear me. He had his jeep roaring by then. He never did come back. He didn't see the sinkhole and drove into it, and he stayed alive in the hospital two days and two nights without regaining consciousness, and he died there." She stood up, wearing a crooked smile, and said, "The guilts. That's what they leave you. Tomorrow is going to be a long rough day too, people. 'Night."

I was on the downslope into sleep when the bed tipped under Puss's stealthy weight and she slipped under the sheet and blanket to pull herself long and warm against me, fragrant and gentle, with some kind of whisper-thin fabric between my hands and her flesh.

"Just hold me," she whispered. "It seemed like such a dark, dark night to be alone." Her words were blurred, and in a very little while her breathing changed and deepened and her holding arms went slack and fell away.

The four of us arrived in Sunnydale three days later, at a little before noon on Thursday. Connie Alvarez drove the lead car, a mud-caked black Pontiac convertible of recent vintage and much engine. Janine was beside her. When the road was straight, I had all I could do to keep them in sight. Puss mumbled now and again about Daytona and Sebring.

"The whole thing sounds so nutty," she said. "Do you really think that funny-looking little old judge knows what he's doing?"

"That funny little old Judge Rufus Wellington knows what everybody is doing. And he'll have had the whole morning to pry around." I braked at the last moment, pulled the rental around a bend and peered ahead for the distant dot that would be the Pontiac. "Have you got any questions at all about your little game?"

"Hah! Can the gaudy redhead from the big city dazzle the young, earnest attorney with her promissory charms? Will Steve Besseker, the shy counsellor from the piney woodlands reveal the details of local chicanery to yon glamorous wench? I might have a question at that."

"Which is. . . ."

"You were a little vague about the details, McGee. Do I give all for the cause? Do I bed this bumpkin if it seems necessary, or don't you care one way or the other?"

I risked a high-speed glance at her and met the narrowed quizzical eyes of sexual challenge. I said, carefully, "I've always had the impression that if the string on the carrot was too long, and if the donkey snapped at it and got it, he'd lose his incentive and stop pulling the load."

"I resent the analogy and approve the sentiment, sir."

But challenges have to go both ways or there is no equality among the sexes. "On the other hand, I imagine that you're the best judge of your own motivations, and you would be the best judge of the appropriate stimulus and response. Such situations vary, I imagine."

"Are you trying to be a bastard?"

"Aren't we both trying?"

After a thoughtful silence she said, "Just for the hell of it, McGee, what would be your reaction if I said I'd keep the carrot on a mighty short string?"

"Killian, I would have to admit that I am just stodgy and old-fashioned enough to enjoy being the dog in your manger. I like a kind of sentimental exclusivity."

"Romantic exclusivity?"

"If you prefer."

"I prefer, thank you. So be it. I am now motivated to defend my honour. So suppose you watch yours."

The appointment had been set for twelve noon with Mr. Whitt Sanders, the President of the Shawana National Bank and Trust Company. I saw the empty Pontiac in the bank lot and parked near it and sent Puss on her way, wishing her luck. When I went into the bank, I could see Connie and Janine sitting in a glass-walled office in the rear, facing a big man across a big desk. The receptionist took me back, tapped on the door, and held it open for me.

Sanders stood up and reached across the desk and gave me a bully-boy handshake. He had tan hair and a big, sun-reddened, flakey face, a barrel of belly, a network of smile wrinkles and weather wrinkles, big red hands like ball gloves, and eyes that seemed to have the same size and expression as a pair of blueberries. "Mr. McGee!" he bellowed. "Pleasure! Sit right down and rest yourself."

I did and he said, "I was just telling the ladies that my sympathy goes out to Mrs. Bannon in this tragic time. You can rest assured, Mrs. Bannon, that the bank is doing every-thing in its power to liquidate the properties in question at the maximum figure obtainable. Of course certain unfortunate situations in that area have made it a difficult piece to move at this time, but we have negotiated something which I think anyone would agree is more than fair. As a matter of fact. . . ."

And in came little old Judge Wellington with his cream-coloured ranch hat shoved back, locks of white hair escaping in random directions, in his dusty dark suit and gold watch chain, carrying a briefcase that had perhaps first seen duty during the Lincoln-Douglas debates, his face remarkably like one of Disney's seven dwarfs, but I couldn't remember which one. "Hidey, Whitt," he said, "New panelling, eh? Purty."

"Rufus! I heard somebody say they thought they saw you over at the courthouse! *Glad* to see you."

"No. I'm not going to let you get aholt of my hand, Whitt. Not with my arthritis laying quiet for a change. So set."

Whitt Sanders looked confused. "Rufus, if you wouldn't mind waiting outside until I finish with——"

"Finish with my client? Now, even a jackass like you knows you can't keep a lawyer away from his client."

"*You* are representing Mrs. *Bannon*!"

"Why not? Mrs. Bannon is a dear friend of Mrs. Connie Alvarez here, and Miz Connie owns and operates To-Co Groves up to Frostproof, right in my back yard, which you may have heard of even down here in the wilderness, it being near three hundred thousand trees, prime Valencia on sour orange root stock, and she has enough legal battles going at all times with the Citrus Commission and the growers association and the concentrate plant she's got a stock interest in to keep me right busy in my declining years."

Watching the bank president, I realized it is possible for a big man to slowly come to attention while seated, and even give the impression of saluting. Connie had taken me on a tour of the groves, and I could see why Whitt Sanders reacted. For the first year after her husband had died, a management outfit had operated the groves on contract. Connie had spent every daylight hour with the crews and every evening studying, and at the end of the year she said she had been willing to take the risk of being able to do the job herself.

When we had come upon a trio of big spray trucks lumbering down the geometric lines, the nozzlemen garbed like astronauts, and I'd asked if bugs were a big problem, Connie had planted her feet, rolled her eyes skyward and chanted, "Kill off the burrowing nematode, the aphid, the rust mite, white fly, white fly fungus, Mediterranean fly, red mite, six-spot mite, rust mite, Texas mite, mealy bugs, cushion scales, black scales, soft scales, yellow scales, wax scales, snow scales, purple scales, dictyospermum, melanose, citrus scag, mealy bugs and orange-dog caterpillars, and keep killing them off, and if you don't get a hard freeze, you've got half a chance, man, of hitting today's market with a hell of a nice crop, which at today's prices costs me one dollar and sixty cents more per box to raise than I get for them." She had shrugged, scuffed at the sand. "I counted on the overproduction and set up a reserve. These prices are going to sink the half-ass operators and that'll cut production back to balance and bring back a fair price."

In the president's office the president said, "I didn't realize you were *the* Mrs. Alvarez."

"So I asked the judge if he could do anything to help my friend here, Jan Bannon."

Janine sat silent and motionless, dressed in darkness, and the blueberry eyes of Whitt Sanders seemed to slide uneasily past her.

Sanders said, at last, "I guess I don't know what you're

driving at, actually. The business holdings don't fall into the estate because there was an actual foreclosure before the time of death, with all proper advertising and notifications. So title passed. It's a standard first mortgage agreement, Rufus. Title passed to the bank."

"That so?" said the Judge. "Funny. I got the impression that when I turn over to you the certified cheque I got here for ten thousand dollars in the name of Mrs. Bannon, that is going to cover back payments on principal, plus interest, plus fees and expenses, and leave a little over which you can apply on the next payment, and I got the impression that title is going to ease right on back to her."

"But the grace period is up! It isn't possible now!"

Judge Wellington sighed. "Bullshit," said he. Then he swept his hundred-dollar ranch hat off in courtly fashion, nodded toward Connie and Janine and said, "Begging your pardon, ladies." He dropped the hat on the floor beside his chair and said, "Whitt, I can't remember you ever being admitted to the Florida bar, so there's no point in me citing the pertinent and appropriate cases where the courts have ruled that in the cases of widows and orphans, especially where the widow was one of the parties on the mortgage, foreclosure action can be set aside provided the bank has not yet passed title on to a third party in a liquidation of the recovered assets."

"But we've accepted earnest money from——"

"One Preston LaFrance in the amount of three thousand two hundred and fifty dollars, representing ten per cent of the agreed price on the foreclosed business property on the Shawana River, and the acceptance of that money did not constitute a change of ownership on the property, and here is the certified cheque for ten thousand, Whitt, and I request a signed receipt, with the date and the hour thereon."

"I can't accept it until I find out——"

"You take it and you make out the receipt saying you are taking it and holding it in escrow pending the decision of your legal people, or you and me are going to go around and around right here, boy. Besides, here is a situation where, by accepting the mortgage obligation and paying it up to date, Mrs. Bannon is putting that mortgage back on the books, sound and whole, in the amount originally owed and paid down to where this cheque puts it, and it would seem like a bank officer thinking of his stockholders—and thinking of the State Banking Commission—would snap at the chance to keep from showing a loss. Why do you seem to be holding back, Whitt?"

Sanders patted his red forehead with a handkerchief. "As you pointed out, Rufus, I'm not a lawyer. I don't know what our obligation to Mr. LaFrance might be."

"Absolutely no obligation, I can tell you, but you'll feel cosy hearing it from your own people, so we'll give you a chance to do just that. Suppose we come back at two thirty?"

"That . . . that ought to be time enough. Uh . . . Mrs. Bannon, do you intend to operate the business there yourself?"

"She's going to think about it," Judge Wellington said. "When her husband couldn't keep up on his insurance, he had the good sense to tell the company to apply the cash value to the premiums instead of drawing it out, so she has a little money to give her time to do some planning. We'll let you get on back to work, Whitt."

We left the bank and walked two blocks to the old Shawana River Hotel, and got a corner table in the dark-panelled, high-ceilinged old dining-room. Janine was at my right, and the judge across from me. Connie and the judge and I ordered drinks. Jan didn't want any. There was a yellowish look to the tan of her lean, Mediterranean-boy face, and the skin of her face and hands had a papery look.

I touched her hand and said, "Okay?"

She gave me an abrupt nod, a smile that appeared for but a moment. The judge seemed lost in private thought. Finally he gave a dry little cough and said, "McGee, you seem to know what you're trying to do for this little lady, and I know Connie well enough to know she'll go along with some pretty wild ideas. But I've heard a few hints around the courthouse, and a few rumours, and I can put things together, and I wouldn't be doing right by my client not to give advice, whether it's wanted or not."

"I want your advice, Judge," Janine said.

He sipped his bourbon and licked his lips. "These little counties all got what you could call a shadow government. These folks have known each other for generations. They

got to putting this land deal together, and there is a little
business right in the way and doing pretty good. Expanding.
So they use the county government to stunt that business
and knock it down to where the price is right. It doesn't take
all five county commissioners. Just a couple, plus the other
three needing favours themselves sometime, with no need of
anybody asking too many questions. You depended on highway trade and river trade, and giving service to local residents.
Now they could have kept that road open to traffic and in
pretty good shape too while fixing it, and set up a short-term
contract on it. There's pollution-control ordinances on the
books to keep that river in better shape. They could have
denied that Tech something outfit when they petitioned to
have the bridge taken out. When you didn't drop off the vine
as fast as they wanted, then they put those regulatory services
people onto you and really closed you down. Okay, Miz
Bannon, you got squoze bad. So what I say is this. I say
don't mess too fancy with these folk because in the long
run you can't win. You can lay the squeeze right back onto
them. I know how these folks think. You just say a hundred
and twenty-five thousand, plus the buyer takes over the
mortgage. No dickering. No conversations. Let them make
the offers. When time starts to run out on them, somebody
is going to get nervous and offer a hundred thousand, and
then you by God grab it and walk away, and you'll know
you've skimmed some good cream off their deal."

"That isn't enough," she said in a barely audible voice.

"But, girl, you'd be hurting them in the place that hurts
the most. What are you trying to get out of this? Lord
God, you can't make anybody *ashamed* of how they did
you, even if they'd ever admit it wasn't just kind of a series
of accidents. They just say it's dog eat dog and lots of
businesses fail all the time."

"But they had Tush killed."

That little embellishment had been kept from the judge.
He leaned forward, his old eyes wide. "You say killed? Now,
young lady, I can understand how you could come to believe
it was like that, but these folks just don't operate that way.
That man of yours worked hard and long and it was all going
down the drain, and sometimes a man gets to the point where
he——"

"You didn't know Tush Bannon," Connie said. "I did. And Travis McGee knew him longer than either Jan or me. We're not taking any votes, Rufus. We're not talking about probably this or probably that. We're telling you he was killed."

Judge Wellington leaned back, so upset he tried to drink out of the glass he had already emptied. "Well now! Then, it must have been some fool mistake. It must have been something else that went wrong. Then, by God, the thing to do right now is put it in the hands of the State's Attorney for this Judicial District and. . . ." He stopped suddenly and frowned at Connie. "By God, I must be getting old. He'd turn it over to the Assistant State Attorney for Shawana County, and the Shawana County Sheriff's Department would make the investigation, and the Shawana County Medical Examiner would do the autopsy, and all these folk are elected to office, and there'd be all the pressure to cover it over and forget it, and even if it went to a Grand Jury if it got that far, who'd get indicted? I'm getting so old I'm forgetting the facts of life. Second childhood. I'm thinking the world is like I thought it was when I was back in Stetson Law School." He scowled into his empty glass. "Maybe bring in somebody from the Attorney General's office to poke around?"

"Maybe," I said. "But first maybe we should blow some smoke down into the burrow and see what comes running out."

He thought and nodded. "Now I see why you want to do what you're doing. I won't say it has much chance of working. But it'll sure stir things up." He gazed at Jan. "Miz Bannon, I know it's a great and sad and tragic loss. And doing something about it can make a person feel better somehow. But don't aim all of yourself at that one thing, of paying somebody back. Revenge. Because it can turn a person sour through and through."

"I don't care what I turn into, Judge," she said.

He met her dark gaze, then opened his menu and said, "We better get our order in."

I went alone to Ingledine's Funeral Home and arrived at quarter of two. It was on a lateral street, and was a small version of Mount Vernon, set between a Savings and Loan branch and a used car lot. I asked for Mr. Ingledine and the stealthy, earnest, unctuous young man told me that Mr. Ingledine had retired, and that he was Mr. Farris, Junior, and that he and his father owned and operated the establishment, and how could he help me, sir.

We tiptoed past an arched doorway where, under a rose-coloured spotlight, a waxy pink and white old man rested, propped up in his bronze box, with floral offerings concealing whatever the box rested upon. Two old women sat on a couch on the other side of the room, holding hands and murmuring to each other.

Mr. Farris, Junior, opened a desk drawer in a small office and took a folder out, and extracted the death certificate signed by the County Medical Examiner.

"We obtained the vital statistics from available local records, sir. You might check them over for accuracy." Brantley B. Bannon, and the age looked right, and he had the next of kin right. The doctor had listed it as accidental death. I asked about it and he said that in the absence of any suicide note or any witnesses, and in view of the fact that he could have been working on the diesel engine, it would have been unfair to assume suicide.

"Would you care to . . . uh . . . view the remains, sir? I would not advise it. It's quite a . . . an extensive and nasty mutilation. There is absolutely no possibility of any reconstruction of the features. And I think it would be wise for you to discourage the widow from viewing the deceased. A memory like that would be . . . difficult to forget."

"What work have you done?"

"Well, a great deal of the blood was gone, of course. We trocared the rest of it as best we could, and the body fluids and so on, and by clamping some of the major vessels in the chest and throat area, we did manage to embalm to a certain extent. Let me see. Oh, yes, we were able to make positive identification so that we do not have to trouble anyone about that. They had at one time sold sandwiches and coffee at their marina, and the County Health Department requires a health card with a photo and thumbprint, and the Sheriff's Department verified the identity by taking a print from the body."

"You've been very efficient."

His smile was shy and pleased. "I am sorry, but I do not quite understand . . . what your function is in this, Mr. McGee?"

"Friend of the family, you could say. Here is a limited power of attorney, notarized, empowering me to make the arrangements in the name of the widow."

He looked at it with a faintly pained expression. "There'll be no services here, I would assume?"

"No. You can expect shipment instructions within the next few days." He led me back into the display room. The lids were propped open, the linings glossy, the handles burnished. They ranged from two twenty-five on up. I picked a three-hundred-dollar box. We went back into the office.

He said, "I'd recommend that we take the remains out of the storage vault and place the body in the casket and seal it, sir."

"I suggest you leave it right where it is, Mr. Farris, under refrigeration, until you get shipment instructions. And then please don't make a permanent seal. There could be an insurance question, on an accident indemnity clause."

"Oh. I see. But you should know that storage is costing eleven thirty-three a day. That's with tax, of course."

"Of course. Now may I see your statement on this?"

He took the statement from the folder and took it into the next room. I heard the slow tapping of unskilled typing. He brought it back and handed it to me. He had added the box and two more days of vault rental. The total was seven hundred and fifty-eight dollars and thirty-eight cents.

"Mr. McGee, I am sure you will understand our position when I point out that it is our information that the deceased *was* a bankrupt, and we will have to have some assurance that. . . ."

The certified cheque for a thousand dollars that I placed in front of him stopped him abruptly. I said, "Is this top copy mine? Just acknowledge the receipt of a thousand dollars on it, Mr. Farris, and when the body leaves here, deduct any further charges from the credit balance and mail your cheque to Mrs. Bannon, To-Co Groves, Route Two, Frostproof. And I see you have a photocopy of the death certificate, so you can let me have the original? Thank you."

He went with me to the front door, through the ripe smell of flowers in full bloom, through the muted organ music.

He put his pale hand out, smiled his pale smile, and said, "Please express our sympathy to the bereaved."

I stared at his hand until he pulled it back and wiped it nervously on the side of his jacket. I said, "Junior, you could make a tangible expression of your sincere sympathy."

"I don't believe I follow you."

"Before you send her the cheque for her credit balance, just refigure your bill. She's a young widow with three boys to raise. You padded it by at least two hundred and fifty dollars. I think it would be a nice gesture."

His face went pink. "Our rates are——"

"Ample, boy. Real ample."

Outside I took a deep breath of Shawana County air, but there was something vaguely industrial in it, some faint acid that rasped the back of my throat.

We were moving in, stirring them up with a blunt stick. The old judge, with good law and good timing, was snatching the ten acres right back out of the hands of LaFrance, just when he thought he had his whole deal lined up. And soon he would know a stranger was moving into the game, buying some chips, asking for somebody to deal. When in doubt, shove a new unknown into their nice neat equations and see how they react.

Hungry men think everybody else is just as hungry. Conspiratorial men see conspiracy everywhere. I strolled through industrial stink toward the bank.

CHAPTER SIX

WE gathered again in the bank president's office at two thirty. Sanders had the Bannon file on his desk, and a Mr. Lee, an attorney for the bank, sitting near his left elbow. Lee had a round, placid face and a brushcut. He could have been thirty or fifty or anything in between.

With obviously forced cordiality, Sanders said, "Well, Mrs. Bannon, the bank has decided to accept your payment and mark the mortgage account current and in good order."

Judge Wellington yawned. "You say that as if you had choice in the matter, Whitt. All right. My client is grateful. She thanks you." He opened his old briefcase and pawed in it and took out the papers that had been prepared Wednesday afternoon in the judge's law offices. He flipped them onto the desk in front of Whitt Sanders, saying, "Might as well get this taken care of too, as long as we're all foregathered here. Everything is all ready to record, but what we need is the bank's approval of the transfer of the mortgage from Mrs. Bannon to Mr. McGee here."

Mr. Lee hitched closer to the president as Sanders leafed quickly through the legal documents. He stared at Judge Wellington with a look of astonishment. "But . . . according to this, she's selling her equity in the property for fifteen thousand dollars, Rufus!"

"Wouldn't you call that a pretty good deal? Sixty thousand mortgage balance, and you were going to sell the whole kaboodle for thirty-two five and have a judgment against the estate, if any, for twenty-seven thousand five. So she pays the mortgage down to fifty thousand, then sells for fifteen thousand, which puts her five ahead instead of twenty-seven five behind. Why, this little lady is thirty-two thousand five hundred better off right this minute than she was when she walked in here. Or maybe you just look surprised she did so good. Remember, she's got a good lawyer."

"But we can't just . . . approve this transfer. We don't have enough information. Mr. McGee, we'll have to have a credit report on you, and we'll have to have a balance sheet and income statement. This would be *highly* irregular. I have a responsibility to——"

"The stockholders," the old judge said. "Whitt, you went through those papers too dang fast. Try it a little slower."

He did. He came to an abrupt stop. He stared at Connie. "You'll be the guarantor on the mortgage note, Mrs. Alvarez?"

"That's what is says there, doesn't it?"

"If you're still nervous, Whitt," said the judge, "go look up To-Co Groves in your D. and B."

"Oh, no. I didn't mean anything like that. It was just. . . ."

The judge sighed. "Could we just stop fumbling and get the red tape done so we can get this stuff recorded and set out for home?"

"Excuse me just a moment," Sanders said. He took Mr. Lee out of the office with him and over to a quiet corner of the carpeted bullpen. They held about a forty-second consultation. I hoped I knew exactly what it was about. I looked to the judge for reassurance, and got it in the form of a slow wink, an almost imperceptible nod.

Mr. Lee came back in with Sanders. He was apparently nominated by Sanders to put the matter into careful legal jargon.

"Mrs. Bannon," he said, "whether or not your sale of your interest to Mr. McGee is final at this moment, the bank feels that it is ethically obligated to inform you that shortly after two o'clock this afternoon a local attorney contacted Mr. Sanders here and asked him if the sale of the foreclosed properties had been consummated. When Mr. Sanders said that it had not, this attorney then said he was representing a party whose name he could not divulge, but who had directed him to inquire of the bank if, in the event the properties had not been sold, a firm offer of eighty thousand dollars would be sufficient to acquire it."

Sanders then interrupted, making Lee look exasperated for an instant. "It isn't a firm offer," he said to Janine. "But I don't think young . . . the local attorney would make a trivial inquiry. You see, if your arrangement with Mr. McGee isn't firm, or if he would like to withdraw, this might be a lot more advantageous for you. You would get back your ten thousand, plus the overage above the sixty thousand mortgage, or another twenty thousand."

Jan had been coached in how to react, by the Judge, if Puss had been successful in conning the young attorney, Steve Besseker.

"But couldn't this mysterious party be the same Mr. Preston LaFrance you were going to sell it to?" Janine asked.

"I don't think it would be very likely that Press would——"

"But haven't you told Mr. LaFrance he wasn't going to get my property?"

"Well . . . yes," said Sanders uncomfortably.

"Then, couldn't he turn right around and make a bigger offer through a lawyer, if he wants it bad enough?" she asked.

"It might be possible. Remotely possible."

"But don't you see," she said, frowning, earnest, leaning forward, "Mr LaFrance owns the acreage directly behind us. He's been after our property all along. He's schemed and plotted to drive us out of business, Mr. Sanders, so he could buy it, and so he's responsible for what . . . my husband . . . responsible for. . . ."

She snuffled into her handkerchief and Sanders, edgy and uncomfortable, said, "Now, there. Now, now, Mrs. Bannon. We all like to have some specific thing or person to blame when . . . when things don't go right. I'm sure Press LaFrance wouldn't——"

"My husband was convinced of it, and that's enough for me," she said spiritedly. "Why, I wouldn't accept any blind offer like that if it was . . . twice as much. Three times as much! I would rather sell it to Mr. McGee for eleven cents than see that man get it!"

Whitt Sanders fussed with the documents in front of him. He looked over at Rufus Wellington. "Rufus, I'd be way out of line, as you well know, if I made any comment about . . . about the resources of anybody doing business with us. All I can say is that . . . it is remotely possible the attorney is representing Press LaFrance. But it isn't very damn probable."

"You telling me, Whitt, it's pretty much a known fact around town this LaFrance couldn't scratch up eighty thousand?"

"I didn't say that."

"Around the courthouse this morning, Whitt, talking to the County Clerk, and passing the time of day with your Assessor, I got the feeling things are a little slow lately in the land business in Shawana County. Now if this LaFrance is up to his hocks in land deals, he might be like the fella with the itch who was juggling the family china and walking a tightrope, and a bee stung him right square on. . . . Sorry, ladies, we'll leave that one right there. Probably got a good-looking balance sheet, all considered, and you got some of his notes, but you won't go one more dime, and you're a little nervous about him." The judge laughed suddenly and slapped his thigh. "By God, Whitt, that explains how come you acted sorry as a skunked hound you couldn't sell off the foreclosure to this LaFrance. He must have some deal in the making that would get him free and clear. He into you a little deep, boy?"

"Now, Rufus," Sanders pleaded. "I haven't told you a thing, and I'm not about to."

"Not in words," the judge said. "But we've set in poker games together, Whitt, and I never had much trouble reading you."

So then the red tape was taken care of, and the necessary documents were recorded at the courthouse. I walked with the judge to his black air-conditioned Imperial and he stopped out of earshot of his driver, who had got out and opened the door for him.

"Son, we sure God rammed a crooked stick into the hornet nest and stirred it up. There'll be folk sitting up half the night trying to make sense out of it all, not knowing it doesn't make sense—not the way they're thinking. Make sure you keep back far enough from the hornets."

"I'll be careful, Judge."

"You tell that big sassy redhead she did good. That's as much woman as a man is likely to see in a long day's journey. Where are you meeting up with her?"

"Not anywhere near here," I said. "Back at Broward Beach. She said she could probably get Besseker to drive her over there, and if she couldn't, she could get there somehow."

He squinted into the late afternoon sunlight and said, "There's a gal like that so clear in my mind it's like yesterday, son. And that was nineteen twenty and six." He turned to me with a look of dismay. "And if she's alive any place in the world, she's somewhere in her sixties. Hard to believe. Know something? I wrote poems to that gal. First, last and onliest time in my life. You let me know how you make out with that old swamp rat, that old D. J. Carbee, will you? McGee, tell me one thing. Are you going to let the angries get in the way of pumping some cash money out of this for that widow girl and her kids?"

"The money first, Judge."

He looked at his watch and grinned. "The way Connie drives, they're probably halfway back to Frostproof by now."

It took me a long time to find anybody who could give me any kind of clear directions on how to find the Carbee place. He had no phone. He had a post office box in Sunnydale, and it was his habit to come in no oftener than once a week to pick up his mail.

In the end I had to go over the unending construction project that ran by my new property. Florida is full of long-range, unending road jobs that break the backs, pocketbooks and hearts of the roadside businesses. The primitive, inefficient, childlike Mexicans somehow manage to survey, engineer and complete eighty miles of high-speed divided highway through raw mountains and across raging torrents in six months. But the big highway contractors in Florida take a year and a half turning fifteen miles of two-lane road across absolutely flat country into four-lane divided highway.

The difference is in American know-how. It's know-how in the tax problems, and how to solve them. The State Road Department has to take the low bid, by law. So Doakes Construction says a half-year contract will cost the State ten million, and a one-year contract will cost nine, and a year-and-a-half deadline will go for eight. Then Doakes can take on three or four big jobs simultaneously, and lease the equipment from a captive corporation, and listlessly move the equipment from job to job, and spread it out to gain the biggest profit with the only signs of frantic activity can be two or three men with cement brooms, looking at first like scarecrows but, when watched carefully, can be perceived to move, much like the minute hand on a clock.

Of course if some brisk, hustling firm moved into the state and started bidding what the jobs are worth and doing them fast, it would upset the tax teacart. Some have been foolish enough to try it, and the well-established Contractor's Club has just taken round-robin turns low-bidding the interloper to death. When he has quit for lack of work, things settle down to the cosy old system whereby, through some miraculous set of coincidences, all the big boys have exactly the amount of work they need at all times.

A couple of governors ago, when too many road jobs were not up to specification, somebody ratted and there was a big hassle about the State Road Department engineers and inspectors getting envelopes with cash money therein from some of the club members. Those contractors were restrained from bidding for a little while, and the engineers and inspectors were suspended. But it died down, as it always does, and the companies were reinstated with authorization to bid on upcoming work, and the state employees were put back on the job also, with the governor explaining that men should not be judged too harshly for a "moment of weakness", even though it had been made quite clear they'd had their little moments of weakness every Friday afternoon for a long, long time.

The Shawana County project of repaving 80D was the same thing on a smaller scale. Though the workday was not over, the only sign of roadwork I saw was one bulldozer and one scraper parked and unattended off the side of the rutted road. I stopped at my dead business property, tore off the official notices of foreclosure, and decided against busting the shiny padlocks with a tyre iron. Near the far end of 80D I found the sand road I was told to look for. It wound through scrub toward the bay shore, and when I drove into the clearing at the end I saw the traditional old Florida shack of cypress and hard pine set high on pilings, so that looking under it I could see the bay water and a crooked little dock with a skiff tied up.

There was a twanging of dogs toenailing the wire of their run, and a heavy throated *Arooo, Arooo* of the indigenous hound. I was standing by the car looking at the hounds when the voice directly behind me said, "Evenin'." It gave me a violent start and when I whirled, I could see from the glint in his faded old eyes that he enjoyed the effect.

In the days before age hunched him and withered him, he could have been nearly my size. His sallow jaws were covered with long grey stubble, and his head was bald except for a sparse white tonsure. He wore torn, stained khaki pants with a narrow length of hemp line for a belt, and an old grey twill work shirt. His feet were broad and bare, and standing near him was like standing near a bear cage, but with a slight spice of kerosene amid the thickness of the odour.

I gestured toward the dog run. "Red Walkers?"

"Got some Walker in 'em. I don't sell no dogs this time of year. Got just one bitch carryin' but she got loose on me just the wrong time, so God knows what she'll drop."

"Mister Carbee, I didn't come by to look at dogs. I came on a business matter."

"Waste of time. I don't buy a thing except supplies in town and send for the rest out of the Sears."

"I'm not selling anything."

"They say that and I ask them to set, and it turns out they are after all."

"It isn't like that this time."

"Then, you come set on the stoop."

"Thank you. My name is McGee." When we had climbed the steep steps and were seated, Carbee in a rocker and me in an old kitchen chair that had several generations of different shades of paint showing, I said, "I just bought the Bannon place on the river from the widow."

"Did you, now? I seen her once and him twice. Heard he kilt himself last Sunday morning when he found he'd lost the place. Great big old boy he was. Him and that Tyler Nigra come on me one morning drifting on the bay. Year ago maybe. Heavy fog, and me out too deep to pole and the ingin deader'n King Tut. That Tyler knows ingins like he invented them. Spring thing busted on the little arm for the petrol feed, and that Tyler fixed it temporary with a little piece of rubber, got it running good. That Bannon wouldn't take a thing for it. Neighbourly. Couldn't been too much longer after that Tyler quit him. Heard Tyler is working at the motorsyckle place in town. Anywhere there's ingins he's got a job of work. Maybe Bannon knowed and maybe he didn't that when Tyler quit him, it was because no Nigra with sense like Tyler's got is going to stay in the middle of any white man's fussing. If you're going to run that place, Mr. McGee, the first thing you better do is get Tyler back, that is if you're peaceful with everybody."

"I'm not going to run it, Mr. Carbee. I bought it as an investment."

"Lease it off to somebody to run?"

"No. Just let it sit."

I let him ponder that one, and at last he said, "Excuse me, but it don't make good sense, unless you got it for the land value alone. The buildings are worth more than the land."

"It depends on who wants the land."

He nodded. "And how bad."

"Mr. Carbee, I've been checking land ownership at the courthouse. You own the two-hundred-acre piece that starts at my east boundary."

"Could be."

"Ever thought of selling it?"

"I've sold a little land now and again. I've got maybe seventeen, eighteen hundred acres left, scattered around the east county, and except for this hundred right here, my home place, I imagine it would all be for sale if the price was right. You thinking of making an offer? If so, you better come up with the best you can do right off, because I don't dicker. Man names a price, I say Yes or I say No, and that's it."

"Best offer, eh? I better tell you, Mr. Carbee, that I would be gambling on being able to pick up other parcels too, and gambling on being able to do it while my chance of resale is still good, resale of the whole two sections. And I'll tell you right now that if everything *does* work out, I'll make a nice profit, but if it doesn't, I'll have some working capital tied up until I can find some way of getting it back out. The best I can offer on an immediate sale—provided the title is clear of course—would be five hundred an acre."

He rocked forward and slapped his big bare feet on the boards and peered at me. "One hunnerd thousand!" he whispered.

"Less your share of the closing costs."

He got up and stamped over to the railing and spat. I knew the turmoil in his mind. He had wanted to check and see if he had optioned the two hundred acres to Preston LaFrance at a good figure. Two hundred dollars an acre had seemed like a good deal until I named my price. I could assume Tush's investigation was correct, and LaFrance's option was good until April. He wouldn't dare tell me about the option, for fear I would make my deal with LaFrance. And he was afraid that if he told me the land was not for sale, opportunity might move on to some other location and then he might not even get his two hundred an acre.

It was a pretty problem, and I wondered how he would handle it. He came back and sat down. The chair creaked. "Tell you what," he said placidly. "I have to think on that. And I should talk to the man that turns in the government figures for me when I sell things and see where that would put me on taxes and so on. Let me see now. This being Thursday the twenty-third day, that would mean two weeks from today would be . . . January fourth. Then I'll know more what I should ought to do. A man can't jump at a piece of money like that right off. He has to set and taste it a time."

"I understand. But you will have to tell me Yes or No when I see you again."

"One other thing. You said you were taking a gamble. What you might do is figure on maybe me taking some of the risk too, Mr. McGee."

"How so?"

"From what you said, if your deal doesn't work, then you got a hundred thousand tied up and it will take a long time to move that land at that price. But if it goes like you're hoping, you turn a good profit on it. Maybe double?"

"Maybe not."

"Let's think on it being double. One thousand dollars an acre, two hundred thousand all told. So maybe we could get a paper drawed up between us, a contract saying that you give me five thousand cash money in hand that says come next . . . oh let's say April the fifteenth . . . you got the right to buy the land from me for four hundred an acre if you're willing to buy and I'm willing to sell. And if it works out that way, then if you resell it any time inside two years or three, you agree to pay me half the difference between what you bought it for and what you get for it. So if it was for one thousand, you'd for sure clear three hundred an acre profit, and no chance getting stuck with it. Of course if I want to sell on April the fifteenth and you don't want to buy, I keep your five thousand. But if you want to buy and I've decided not to sell, you get it all back."

He looked at me, benign and gentle and O so eager to be agreeable and fair to all. Way up the coast from us were the little nests of the hideaway mansions of the international bankers, and to the south of us was all the trickery and duplicity of hotel and resort syndicate financing. He had the precise look of a man betting into a pair of kings showing, and him with a three in the hole and a pair of threes up, and a perfect recollection of having seen the other two kings dealt to hands that had folded, one of them a hole card inadvertently exposed when the hand was tossed in.

"Mr. Carbee," I said. "I think we'll get along fine. You might even sell me an undivided half interest for two hundred an acre, and we could make it a joint venture."

"It'll be a pleasure to do business with you, Mister."

It seemed to me that old Mr. D. J. Carbee could have floated very nicely in the tricky currents of Hobe Sound or Collins Avenue, and I had a sudden respect for the guile of Preston LaFrance. But I did not envy him the little talk he was going to have to have with the old man just as soon as the old man could catch up to him. There was a shaggy old high-sided International Harvester station wagon parked over near the dog run, and it seemed probable that D.J. would be going into Sunnydale either this evening or early in the morning.

It was full dark when I drove into the city of Broward Beach. The stores were open, because tomorrow was Christmas Eve. Hefty Salvation Army lassies in their wagon-train bonnets dingle-dangled spare change into their kettles, and fat foam Santas were affixed to the palm boles and light standards, high enough to keep the kids from yanking their foam feet off. "Adeste Fideles" was coming from somewhere, possibly a downtown church, electronic chimes that could rattle fillings in teeth, and overpowered the retail sound tracks of sprightlier seasonal music. I went through town and out to the beach and parked in the lot of the place I had told her to be, an expansive, glossy, improbable motel called Dune-Away, with a place pasted to it called The Annex, where food and drink was worth the prices they charge, even in the off season, and where if an attractive lassie wishes to be picked up, the hard-nose management will smooth the way, and if she doesn't, those same professionals can chill the random Lothario quickly, quietly and completely.

I looked at the lounge from the doorway and saw her alone at a banquette against the far wall. As I headed across toward her I was aware of a wary waiter also moving on an interception course. But he and I saw her quick recognition and saw her face light up in greeting. So he held the table out for me to sit beside her, and went off with our order.

"You missed our boy by ten minutes," she said. "He was very dear. Not my type. One of those narrow-boned dark ones, a bit stuffy. He wants to be with it, but he laughs a little too soon or a little too late, and he seems to sit and steer his car instead of drive it. Let me see. He's thirty-one and he's been married to Linda for five years, and they have two kids and she is a fantastic golfer, and her father owns the Buick Agency in Sunnydale, and he is worried about her drinking. He kept giving me a certain business with the eyebrows that maybe he learned in front of his mirror, and I made his hands clammy when we sat close. He didn't have the guts to take a hack at me right out of the clear blue. He'd have to be encouraged so that then he could tell himself he hadn't started it, and he's only human, isn't he? He's very nervous about the impression he makes, and he's steeped in all that radical right wing hoke about conspiracies and a bankrupt America and Chinese bombs, and it was a drag to listen big-eyed to that tired gunk and say Oh and Ahh and Imagine that! He does a lot of civic stuff and joins everything, and thinks of himself as being the fearless attorney, standing up for right and purity. As the dear judge would say—Bullshit. He tried to help Tush Bannon, and then when it got a little sticky, he dropped him. Know how he explained it to me? This is precious!"

She paused for the waiter to serve the drinks, then went into an imitation of Steve Besseker: "So long as we are operating under the Capitalistic System, Puss, and remember it is the best the world has yet devised, men will take business risks and some will win and some will lose. I won't deny there were certain pressures on Bannon, but he got so he thought everything was some kind of a plot. He started whining and stopped fighting. That's when I lost my respect for him and washed my hands of him."

"Yes," I said. "That is precious. That is very dear."

"I never met your friend Tush, Travis. But I don't think he ever whined."

"He wouldn't know how. Congratulations. You snowed him very nicely. Have any trouble with it?"

"None! I hitched my chair closer and closer to his and I kept my voice very low and full of secrets, and I kept my eyes wide and I put my fingertips on his arm. I told him that I was employed by Gary Santo and we had investigated him and it was Mr. Santo's decision that he could be trusted with certain delicate and private negotiations involving one of Mr. Santo's operations in this area, and could be trusted not to reveal the name of his client. I explained that it was so hush-hush that if he was foolish enough to even try to reach Mr. Santo by phone or in person, he would ruin everything for himself. But if things went well, then he could think in terms of a retainer of five figures annually. You know, when he began to swallow it, his eyes looked glazed and his mouth hung open. I almost started laughing. So he phoned the query about the eighty thousand to the bank like a good little fellow, and he was *so* upset when he met me later and told me that Mrs. Bannon had regained title and then sold it to some mysterious stranger named McGee from Fort Lauderdale. I thought he would cry. I told him I was sure that Mr. Santo would be convinced that he had done all he could. I told him he would get his instructions from me by phone or in person. I asked him if he would be willing to meet me sometimes, if it was necessary. In Miami, or even Havana or New York. All expenses paid, of course."

"Who told you to say that?"

"I made it up. It seemed like a good idea. I mean it makes him think more about me and not so much about it being a pretty funny way for a man like Santo to do business. Was I wrong?"

"No. I like it. And the final little hook? Did you remember to get that in?"

"Yes, but very casual, and not until he came in here to have a drink with me. I just said that I know the way Mr. Santo's mind works, and he would certainly wonder if there was any connection between a Mr. Preston LaFrance and Mr. McGee, any business connection, and if he could find out in advance of my phoning him about it, it might make a good impression on Mr. Gary Santo."

"Reaction?"

"Nothing in particular. He said he'd try to find out." She shrugged. "He's just a trivial little man, honey, really. And this is the first little whiff he's had of something big and important and kind of glamorous, and he can't hardly stand it. Feed me, please. I'm sitting here aching and gnawing, and

I keep looking at that door where the waiters go by with those steaks."

She ate with a savage and elegant precision, and an occasional little sound of contentment. I told her that as a reward for special sly services and for being a persuasive liar, I would stake us to the most elaborate accommodations the Dune-Away could provide.

"And go back in the boat in the morning?" she asked. "Would it be vulgar, dear, if I asked a special favour? So much has happened and I am so pooped, really, that all I can think about is that gigantic, fantastic, marvellous bed aboard the *Flush,* and it would be a nice place to wake up on the morning before Christmas, and I want to get to that bed faster than your pretty little boat can get me there. Possible?"

"Race you to the car, Red."

She was asleep by the time I hit the first stoplight, and slept all the way back, and groused about being shaken awake to walk from the car to the houseboat. I made her stand on the dock while I went aboard and, before unlocking the door, checked the little bulbs behind the sliding panel in the outside port bulkhead of the lounge. The bulbs were out, so I turned the knife switch below the bulb, turning off the little Radar Sentry that monitored the below-decks areas of the *Flush* while I was away from her. Had anyone broken in, their mass and movement would have closed the circuit that lighted the two hidden bulbs, or lighted one of them if by any chance the other had burned out. The gadget can be rigged if anyone wants, to turn on floodlights or sound a siren or even phone the cops. But I didn't want an alarm system that would spook the intruder. I just wanted to know if I'd had visitors, and then I could take the necessary steps to make them welcome if they happened to be still there.

I beckoned her aboard, and she came inside, stumbling and yawning. We shared a shower, and then we shared a lazy, easeful, gentled quarter hour of love, wherein she murmured she didn't think she could but don't go to any special trouble, darling, it doesn't matter that much, and then she murmured that if it wasn't too late for a lady to change her mind, sir, and it was just barely not too late to be able to wait just long enough, and so she rose, and caught, sighed long, and fell away purring. She called me back from my edge of sleep by gently thumbing my left eye open and saying, "Are you there? Listen, for making all these days and nights so full, the lady thanks you. Thanks for letting me come along for more than just the ride, McGee. Thanks for helping me cram three bushels of living into a one peck basket. Are you there?"

"You are O so welcome, lady."

CHAPTER SEVEN

M E Y E R came over on Christmas morning with a cumbersome vat of eggnog and three battered pewter mugs. We had a nice driving rain out of the northwest and a wind that made the *Flush* shift and groan and thump. I put on Christmas tapes because it was no day to trust FM programming. Sooner or later daddy would see mommy kissing Rudolph. Meyer and I played chess. Puss Killian, in yellow terry coveralls, sat and wrote letters. She never said who they were to, and I had never asked.

He won with one of those pawn-pressure games, the massive and ponderous advance that irritates me into doing the usual stupid thing, like a sacrifice that favours him, just to get elbow room on the board.

As we finished, Puss came over, shoving her letter into her pocket and said, "Should we call Jan and say merry merry? Which is worse, I guess, to call her or not call her?"

"There's one of Meyer's laws that covers it. Tell her, Meyer."

He beamed up at her. "Of course. In all emotional conflicts, dear girl, the thing you find the hardest to do is the thing you should do. So I guess you call."

"Thanks a lot. Trav? Will you do it? Please? Then you can turn it over to me. Okay?"

So I placed the call. Connie sounded too hearty. I guess it wasn't such a great day at the groves. Janine imitated the

requirements of friendship and holiday. But there was deadness under her tone of voice. I knew she would not break
up, not with that weight of the deadness holding her down.
After all the things to say I could think of, most of them so
trite I felt like both Bob *and* Ray, I gave the phone over to
Puss. She sat at the desk and talked for a long time with
Janine, in low tones. Then she said Connie wanted to talk
to me again. She said Janine had gone to her room, so she
could talk freely. She asked me when the body would be
picked up. I said I'd made arrangements and they would
come and get it tomorrow. The holidays had caused a delay.

"Any communication from sunny Sunnydale, Connie?"

"Nothing at all. Nothing yet."

As I hung up I turned and saw Puss leaving the lounge,
almost at a gallop, and heard her give a big harsh sob.

I looked at Meyer and he shrugged and said, "The tears
started to drip, and then she started to snuffle and then she
took off."

I filled our mugs and brought him up to date on my financial affairs in Shawana County.

He pondered the situation and said, "It's pretty flexible.
There's a lot of ways it could go."

"That's the general idea. To keep my skirts clean I have
to have a legitimate sale of my legitimate ownership in that
marina and motel. I think that's where I pick LaFrance clean.
If he could offer thirty-two five, I'll settle for forty thousand,
and he assumes the mortgage. He'll have to go for it because
that's the only way he'll have a package he can provide Santo
—his own fifty acres, my ten, and the option on old Carbee's
two hundred. Now this LaFrance is a greedy and larcenous
bastard. He was trying to make the deal as sweet as possible
for himself by driving Tush into the ground and getting those
ten acres cheap. I think he will continue to be a greedy and
larcenous bastard, and I think that if I can offer him a little
extra edge, for cash under the table, I'll get the cash somehow, and I hope it will be from that brother-in-law of his on
the County Commission." I went and checked the name in
my notebook. "P. K. Hazzard. Known as Monk. He—meaning
Preston LaFrance—is going to be very jumpy, so you and
I are going to work a little variation on the old pigeon
drop."

His big bushy brows climbed his Neanderthal forehead. "We are?"

"Meyer, I think you'd make a nice plant location expert, somebody with the authority to make firm recommendations to a nice big fat rich company."

"It is an exact science, my good fellow," he said. "We take all the factors—labour supply, area schools and recreation facilities, transportation costs, construction costs, distance from primary markets, and by adjusting these by formula before programming the computer, we can arrive at a valid conclusion as . . . Travis, what is a pigeon drop?"

"Unlike what might first come to mind, Meyer, this is something one drops *onto* a pigeon."

"You couldn't have made it more clear. One thing. Aren't you on a little dangerous ground on this body-snatching thing?"

"Body-snatching! Me? Meyer! A perfectly legitimate funeral home in Miami is going to pick up that body in a licensed hearse and bring it back to Miami and air-ship it from there to Milwaukee."

"And the place is run by a man who owes you a big favour, and that hearse is going to make a stop at a very well equipped and staffed pathology lab during the off hours, where two more of your strange friends are going to determine if there was some cause of death besides dropping an engine block on him."

"Meyer, please! It's just normal curiosity. Jan gave her permission. Is there an ordinance against it?"

"What about concealing evidence of a crime?"

"If you're nervous about evidence we don't even have yet, you don't have to help me play games with LaFrance."

"So who's nervous?"

"I am. A little."

We sat in silence. The tape had run out and turned off. I wondered if I should go in and give Puss a little comforting pat to cure the Noel blues. Too many pasts crowd in on you at mistletoe time. It's the good ones that hurt.

"Meyer?"

"At your service."

"On the sale of the marina thing to LaFrance, Jan will end up with thirty thousand, net. If we can work that pigeon drop, she'll get maybe fifty, maybe a hundred on top of that. Money won't buy what she's lost, but it would be nice to get her a really good big chunk. If I could find out that Gary Santo knew about what was being done to the Bannons, knew about it and didn't give a damn because he was pressuring LaFrance into assembling the adjoining parcels so she could buy them for resale, then it would be nice to take a slice of his bread too."

"Now *wait* a minute! This is not somebody that goes for your pigeon drop. This man operates very big, my friend. He has lawyers and accountants double-checking every move."

"I was thinking of something legitimate. Something in your line. Like some kind of an investment where you would know it was going to go sour and he wouldn't. Then couldn't there be some way of . . . funnelling money out of the same proposition into Janine's pocket? Hell, Santo is a plunger. With all the protection, he's still a plunger. Some kind of a listed stock, maybe, like those they were rigging on the American Exchange you were telling me about one time."

"So why should Gary Santo listen to Meyer?"

"Because first we build you a track record. You dig into those charts of yours and make some of those field trips and surveys and come up with some very very hot growth items. And I think I've got just the pipeline, once I develop it a little, to feed them to him. The pipeline is named Mary Smith. She has brown straight glossy hair. She is small, and stacked, and she looks sullen and hungry."

"So if the great Gary Santo knew nothing about your friend Bannon?"

"I know Tush tried to get to him and couldn't get past the girl-curtain. He didn't think Santo was the kind of man who'd want the little guy crushed under his wheels. Somehow Santo squeezed LaFrance and LaFrance squeezed various folk, which happened to include Tush. If Santo knew—and let the roof fall on Tush—for a lousy little crumb of the acreage he needs up there, then I would like to have him get it where it stings. And, if so, can you work up something?"

Meyer got up and plodded back and forth, all hair and simian concentration, and scowling little bright blue eyes. He stopped and sighed. "McGee, I don't know. I just don't know. The problem divides itself into two interdependent parts. First

I would have to get a line on a dirty situation like Westec before it leaks out. Those people falsified their earnings statements to keep the stock at a high level so they could pick up smaller companies on favourable merger terms. Then one executive put in for eight million worth of the stock, traded on the American Exchange, and he couldn't come up with the money to pay for the stock and that's when trading was suspended. Now *if* I could smell out something like that, heading for disaster, and then if I can pick a few legitimate winners to make him feel as if I——"

"Or as if you *had* picked some winners, Meyer."

He looked startled for just a moment, and then came that broad Meyer smile that turns one of the ugliest faces of the Western World into what one of the articulate lassies among the Meyer Irregulars one season called "a beautiful proof that someday, somehow, the human race is going to make it."

"Dated, official, machine-printed confirmations of stock purchases on official forms from a reputable brokerage house! Hindsight! Perfect! One day, maybe two, in New York, and I can come back with proof I'm such a genius I bought——"

"You had *me* buy. . . ."

"Yes. I see. I had you buy highfliers right at the point where they were taking off, and I don't have to go back far, less than a year in every case. Gulton, Xtra, Leasco Data, Texas Gulf Sulphur, Goldfield Mohawk Data. Fantastic performers! Listen, I won't make it too good. If every buy was at the bottom, there'd be suspicion. Like instead of Gulton at fifty dollars a share, you get on at sixty-five."

"Where is it now?"

"It went up to nearly a hundred and ten, split two for one, and the last time I looked it's maybe sixty dollars." He sat down and emptied the nog mug again. "Travis, how rich do you want to be? I can use an old and dear friend who will be delighted to help, so I can get you monthly margin account statements showing the security position, the debit and so on."

"Say I started a year ago with a hundred thousand."

"Congratulations! You are now worth a quarter of a million."

"Success hasn't spoiled me, Meyer. Have you noticed?"

"All I notice are your criminal instincts, my dear Travis, and how rash you are with your queen, which lets me whip you at chess, and how right now you are too tightened up over this Tush business. You are too close to this one. Be careful. I don't want to lose you. Some terrible people might take over Slip F-18. Nondrinkers, going around saying shush."

Puss Killian came drifting back into the lounge, looking wan. Her face was puffed, her eyes red. She snuffled and then honked into a Kleenex, and said, "Give me that Meyer's Law again, please? The exact words."

"In all emotional conflicts the thing you find hardest to do is the thing you should do."

"I was afraid that was what you said, Meyer. What we all do is make excuses why we shouldn't do the hard things. Like apologize. Like visit the dying. Like spend a little time with bores."

"Stop short of masochism, dear girl," Meyer said.

"I always have. Too far short, maybe. Gad! I feel as if I'd been pressed flat and dried out, like an old flower in a bad book. *Do* something, gentlemen!"

And so we did. Meyer and I went off in opposite directions, head-hunting. He had a quota of five—three female and two male. I went after two couples. It is an old contest. They can be friends, or acquaintances, or absolute strangers. After the festivities, we rate them on a scale of ten, the measurement being rather or not you'd be willing to spend a month on a small boat with them. We made a good Christmas bag, because there was a compulsion to have a good time. We unfastened all the umbilical devices affixing the *Flush* to her mooring space, and, with eighteen yuletide souls aboard, chugged down into the breadths of Biscayne Bay under clearing skies, edged the old girl as close as I could get her to good beach with good protection near Southwest Point, stayed the night in drink, argumentation, minimal sleep, beach walks, a touch of skinnydipping for those brave hearts who can stand the December waters, and came trundling back up to home base the next day.

Sometimes it doesn't work at all, but this time it had jelled. There had been some good minds, outrageous opinions, furious squabbles, laugh-till-you-cry incidents, games and contests, confessions and accusations, tears and broad smiles. But no sloppy drunks, no broken crockery, or teeth. We aimed homeward tired and content and, for the most part, friends.

Waterborne group therapy, Meyer calls it. It restored Puss Killian. Late on Tuesday afternoon as we were scoring our recent boatmates, with Puss as arbiter when we disagreed, she said, "Does anyone else have the feeling that little jaunt lasted at least a week?"

"When they don't seem to," said Meyer, "they haven't worked." Which could be another one of Meyer's Laws, but he says it is too close to aphorism to be significant.

CHAPTER EIGHT

WEDNESDAY, December 27th, before Puss and Janine and I had to catch the flight out of Miami to Milwaukee for Tush's funeral the next day, I had a chance to talk with Dr. Mike Guardina at the lab. I left the gals with the car and told them I wouldn't be long, so not to wander too far.

Mike took me into a small office and closed the door, and took a folder out of the locked file. He is thin, intent, strung on taut wires, totally intent on finding out why people die. He is qualified in about all the kinds of pathology they have.

"Trav, the first impression was of too much damage. Way too much to go with the way it was supposed to happen, from what we found on your roll of film once we made prints. So much damage that actually trying to locate any specific tissue damage or bone damage not likely to have been caused by the impact of that weight dropping on him would have been pretty iffy. About all we can say for certain is that there is a good chance he wasn't shot in the head first, nor much of a chance that there was any blow that struck him from behind. Now you *did* want a cause of death to a reasonable medical certainty, but I gathered from your conversation over the phone with me that you want suicide ruled out if possible."

"But if you can't——"

"This is another approach. Take a look at these." He put three 8 x 10 glossies on the desk top. He pointed with the eraser end of a yellow pencil. "This is a blowup of the central portion of one of your pictures, Trav, where you had that block cranked high and you aimed up at it. See these rusty hexagonal nuts along here, toward what we will call the rear end of the block? Look at this one in particular. Somebody apparently tried to knock it off with a cold chisel, and knocked off a third of it before they gave up. Now this next print is full frame, of the chest area of the subject. Note these three marks circled with a grease pencil, and marked A, B and C. This third print is actually a triptych, an enlargement of A, B and C. The area marked A shows a clear imprint or incised impression of that damaged nut. The encircled B area shows the same imprint exactly, and it is about four inches from the point marked A, in a lateral direction across the crushed chest, from right to left. Imprint C is, as you can see from the print of the whole chest area, another inch and a quarter or inch and a half further, going from right to left, from imprint B. But here, as it struck, or would seem to have struck a previously damaged area, we do not have as obvious an identical match. However, if you want me to project the thirty-five millimetre colour slides we took of points A, B and C, I think you will see that it is reasonable to suppose that impact area C represents the same deformed nut."

"In simple lousy English," I said, "you are certain that the engine block was dropped onto him twice, and you can make a case that it could have been dropped, cranked up, dropped again, cranked up, and dropped the third time."

"Yes," said Mike. "It wouldn't be consistent with suicide."

Long ago and far away I could see Tush Bannon under the needle spray in the long shower room that smelled of old socks, soap and disinfectant, rubbing up a suds on that barrel chest and bawling, off-key, ". . . and this is my storrrreeee, as you can plainly see. Never let a sailor put his hand above your kneeeeeeee."

"Spare me the slides, Mike. Can I have dupes of these?"

"Got them right here for you. Smaller. Five by sevens. Okay?"

"Fine. And what about a grand jury? Will it make you nervous if we don't do a thing?"

"What could you do with it? Somebody got clumsy. They found him crushed under that thing and so they cranked it up and it slipped and fell on him again and they cranked it

up again and locked it. He was obviously dead, so why make
a big statement about the crank slipping? We can't prove
the third drop, even though I feel certain it happened. You
understand what I'm saying, Trav. In a court of law any
neophyte defence attorney could set up an area of reasonable
doubt you could take a truck convoy through."

"But if there ever comes a time for affidavits?"

"Me and Harry Bayder, and the tape going as we worked,
and a resident in pathology taking notes. Time and place,
and an accurate identification of the body, and signed statements in the file from all three of us. Just in case. If and
when you ever get something else to go with it."

"You are a good man, Guardina."

"Beyond compare, surely. Keep in touch, hombre."

All I could tell Janine, or wanted to tell Janine, was that
any last faint possibility of suicide was long long gone. I
told her on the way out to the airport. She didn't say a thing.
I had my hands on the wheel at ten of and ten after. She
reached up and put her long fingers on the ten after wrist.
At the chapel in Milwaukee, when we bowed our heads in
prayer, I looked down at the underside of my right wrist and
saw the four dark-blue half moon marks where her nails
had bitten deep. Her parents thought she should have brought
her three young sons to the services. They thought Tush
should have been shipped sooner and buried earlier. They
thought she should come home with the boys and stay. They
thought her tailored navy-blue suit was not proper attire for
a widow. They thought it odd she had brought along this
McGee person and this Killian woman when there were so
many old friends who were—or should have been—so much
closer in a time of need. They resented not knowing Connie
Alvarez. They had remembered that she had been at Janine's
wedding, but they let it be known she had struck them as a
rather coarse and peculiar person, not at all the ladylike type
their daughter should cultivate. They made it clear that it
was an affront to them that poor Janine should go back
immediately to Florida with these . . . these *strangers*.

On the flight back we had three side by side. Janine was
in the middle. She said, turning her face from Puss to me and
back, "I'm sorry. They just . . . they aren't. . . ."

Puss hugged her and said, "Honey, if you put the knock on them you'll feel like a traitor. Everybody has people, and their people don't want to let them go or admit they're gone when they're gone. They love you. That's good enough. Right?"

"Should I have brought the boys? That's what I keep wondering."

"Ask each one of them when he gets to be twenty-one, dear. Ask them if they felt as if they had been left out of anything," Puss said.

So they sat, holding hands, and Jan fell asleep. Puss gave me a sleepy wink and then she was gone too. I looked out of the jet at December grey, at cloud towers reaching up toward us. Tush was gone, and too many others were gone, and I sought chill comfort in an analogy of death that has been with me for years. It doesn't explain or justify. It just seems to remind me how things are.

Picture a very swift torrent, a river rushing down between rocky walls. There is a long, shallow bar of sand and gravel that runs right down the middle of the river. It is under water. You are born and you have to stand on that narrow, submerged bar, where everyone stands. The ones born before you, the ones older than you, are upriver from you. The younger ones stand braced on the bar downriver. And the whole long bar is slowly moving down that river of time, washing away at the upstream end and building up downstream.

Your time, the time of all your contemporaries, schoolmates, your loves and your adversaries, is that part of the shifting bar on which you stand. And it is crowded at first. You can see the way it thins out, upstream from you. The old ones are washed away and their bodies go swiftly by, like logs in the current. Downstream where the younger ones stand thick, you can see them flounder, lose footing, wash away. Always there is more room where you stand, but always the swift water grows deeper, and you feel the shift of the sand and the gravel under your feet as the river wears it away. Someone looking for a safer place can nudge you off balance, and you are gone. Someone who has stood beside you for a long time gives a forlorn cry and you reach to catch their hand, but the fingertips slide away and they are gone.

There are the sounds in the rocky gorge, the roar of the water, the shifting, gritty sound of sand and gravel underfoot, the forlorn cries of despair as the nearby ones, and the ones upstream, are taken by the current. Some old ones who stand on a good place, well braced, understanding currents and balance, last a long time. A Churchill, fat cigar atilt, sourly amused at his own endurance and, in the end, indifferent to rivers and the rage of waters. Far downstream from you are the thin, startled cries of the ones who never got planted, never got set, never quite understood the message of the torrent.

Tush was gone, and our part of the bar was emptier, and the jet raced from the sunset behind us to the night ahead, and beside me slept the two women, hand in hand, their lashes lying against the high flesh of their cheeks with a heartbreaking precision, a childish surrender, an inexpressible vulnerability.

By Saturday, the next to the last day of the year, I was beginning to feel surly and uneasy. I held a slack line. I felt that I had deftly pulled the barbed hook through the underlip of one Preston LaFrance, and that boating him was inevitable. He had to come aboard the *Flush,* flapping, gills working. The name McGee had suddenly cropped up at too many points in his life. McGee at the bank with the widow. McGee at Ingledine's, making the arrangements about the body. McGee out at the old shack, souring his deal with old D. J. Carbee. McGee, the new owner of the property he wanted.

But the line lay slack on the water, without the slightest twitch or tension. Puss and I drove up to Broward Beach early Saturday morning, turned the car in, and came back down the Waterway in the *Muñequita.* I made a fast run, thinking I might find LaFrance when I got back to *The Busted Flush.* Nothing. Puss was withdrawn, remote, and did not help my mood by telling me she was going away Monday morning for a little while. A few days. No clue as to where or why. And be damned if I'd ask. As she packed a bag it seeemed a gratuitous affront that she should hum to herself. What was she so cheery about?

And why didn't Meyer phone from New York? Too busy having a fine time with old stockbroker buddies, probably.

At ten minutes after four the slack line twitched. I tested the tension cautiously. It was still through the underlip. I shooed Puss into the master stateroom and invited Preston LaFrance into the lounge. He came in, grinning, hesitant. A gaunt and ugly and sandy one. Maybe the young Sinclair Lewis, if the old photographs are accurate. Fifty per cent hick. Fifty per cent con artist. Cowlick. Long lumpy face. Lantern jaw. Nervous cough. Ploughboy hands. Brash sports jacket with the wrong button buttoned. A gangly diffidence overlaying a flavour of confidence. When he looked around the lounge, his expression vague, I had the feeling he saw everything that had any bearing on his own aims and motives, and could price the whole layout within plus or minus three per cent.

His big hand was warm, dry and utterly slack. "Mr. McGee, we seem to be aiming in kind of the same direction on a little matter, and what I thought, I thought it might be time to see if we can eat out of the same dish or spill the dinner."

"I guess that depends on how hungry we are, LaFrance. Sit down. Get you a drink?"

"Mostly I'm called Press. Short for Preston. Thank you kindly, and if you would have such a thing as a glass of milk, that would be fine. I had an ulcer and got over it, and they tell me sipping milk instead of kitchen whisky will keep me from having the next one. And I guess you've upped my milk bill by maybe half, Mr. McGee."

"Mostly I'm called Trav. Short for Travis. And we stock milk, because there is very little damn else you can put on cornflakes."

"You are so *right*!"

I brought him his glass of milk, and a beer for me. He sat on the long yellow couch. I pulled a chair a little too close, turned the back toward him and straddled it, forearm along the back of the chair, chin on the forearm, expression politely expectant and benign. It put my face two feet from his, and six inches higher, with the brightest window right behind me. Closeness is a tactical weapon. We do not like our little envelope of anticipated separation and privacy penetrated. It is a variable distance, depending on the needs and necessities of the moment. We endure the inadvertent pressure of the flank of the office worker in the crowded down-elevator at five o'clock. If we are alone with the office worker, if it is male—without overtones of fag—then it is insolent challenge, demanding action. Being jostled in a crowded airport is acceptable; on a wide and empty sidewalk it is not. A fixed stare is a form of penetration of the envelope, carrying different messages according to the sort-out of sex, station, race, ages and environment.

Always we want some separation, some tiny measure of distance regardless of how clumsily our culture mechanizes an inadvertent togetherness. The only exception time is when sex is good in all dimensions, so that even in the deepest joining there is the awareness of that final barrier, an apartness measured by only the dimension of a membrane, and part of the surge of it is a struggle to overcome even that much apartness.

The lounge aboard the *Flush* is a sizeable enclosure, and I positioned myself well inside the area of logical separation. Once you learn the expectations of distances, small and great, you can use them in tactical ways, watching for reaction, for a pulling back, a pained stiffness of expression, an awkwardness. Or position yourself beyond the plausible distance and watch for the forward lean, the advance, the slight what-is-wrong-with-me agitation. It is a kind of language without words, a communication, and incites a reversion to the primitive compulsion of the pecking order, the barnyard messages— You get too close so I peck you back to where you belong.

Press LaFrance sipped his milk, looking down into the glass. He looked to the side and reached and put the half glass on the end table. He then hiked one limber Ichabod leg up, heel on the edge of the couch cushion, long fingers of both hands laced around his ankle, slouching just enough to interpose the knee between us so that he looked at me over the top of it. With that interposition he increased the subjective distance between us.

"Fifty mortgage plus fifteen cash equals sixty-five thousand," said he. "And that is better than twice what any licensed appraiser would put on it."

"For the same use Bannon put it to. A man with his house on fire and a man dying of thirst would put a different value on a glass of water."

"Hard to put a value on 'if', Trav. Link three or four ifs

together and it comes out long odds, so you can't go very high."

"There are some men, Press, who get a little confused between greed and shrewdness. Maybe they are a little bit shrewd, and then they want to buy at the lowest dollar and sell at the highest, and finally it comes out as if they weren't shrewd at all. They end up doing the very same thing as if they were stupid to begin with."

The knobbly face coloured a little and the mouth stiffened then relaxed as the colour faded. "A fella could have made an offer way back, through a third party, and a fair offer, all considered, but somebody could have been too bullheaded to listen."

"Fair offer?"

"We aren't talking marina, McGee. We aren't talking motel. You know that and I know it. We are talking ten acres."

"Ten acres in the middle of the deal, smack in the middle of it, like a June bug in the birthday cake."

"So I was coming up with thirty-two hundred and fifty an acre for those ten acres."

"Which gives you sixty acres, if you'd got it. What did the fifty behind Bannon's place cost you?"

"A fair price."

"One thousand dollars in nineteen fifty-one, according to the tax stamps on the deed as recorded in the Shawana County Courthouse, which comes out to twenty dollars an acre. That was probably a fair price in nineteen fifty-one. We can do a little arithmetic, Press. When you pay me forty thousand for clear title to the Bannon place, and assume the mortgage, then you have a ninety-one thousand cost figure on the sixty acres, or just about fifteen hundred an acre. That will turn you a profit of five hundred an acre on resale, or thirty thousand, and because you are a reasonable man and because you are in a bind, you are going to be sensible and take it."

He was absolutely immobile for long seconds. I think he even stopped breathing. He dropped the knee, swivelled and got up and peered down at me. "Man, you lost your cotton-pickin' mind for sure! That would be two thousand an acre on resale! The deal with my buyer is for nine hundred. I couldn't pay you any forty thousand and take over a fifty-thousand mortgage! I'd come up with a loss of six hundred an acre. Where do you get this crazy two-thousand figure?"

"Why, Press! You'd make out just fine on nine hundred an acre! You've got old D. J. Carbee screwed. You pay him two hundred an acre, or forty thousand, and you resell it to Gary Santo for nine hundred, which comes to a hundred and eighty thousand. So deduct that thirty-six thousand you'll lose on that sixty acres, and there you are, fat and sassy, and a hundred and forty-four thousand ahead."

He picked up the glass and drained the milk, wiped a chin-drip on the back of his wrist. "D.J. told me he didn't tell you a thing about that option. So by God, you knew about it when you went and offered him five hundred an acre. You upset that old man something pitiful."

"Maybe I was trying to upset you, Press."

He sat down on the far end of the yellow couch. He shook his head like a sad hound. "What in the world are you after, McGee?"

"Money. Just like you, Press."

"You knew I had to show up here. You left a trail and you left loose ends. But you didn't do all this just to charge me forty thousand for something that cost you fifteen."

"That isn't much profit, come to think of it. What do you think I ought to charge you? Sixty? A hundred?"

"Oh, come *on*!" he wailed.

"You can't come up with much. You've got the shorts, haven't you? Overextended?"

"Don't you worry about *me*!"

"But I *do*! I'll tell you what I'll do for you, LaFrance. I'll pay you fifty thousand dollars in cash for your fifty acres *and* the option you've got on the Carbee acreage. Then you're out of the whole thing with a nice profit."

He stiffened. "Hell *no*! Then you got the whole two hundred and sixty acres Santo wants to buy."

"But I wouldn't sell it to him. The price isn't right."

"But you can't move it, McGee, unless you move Santo's parcel at the same time! Calitron has to have the whole four hundred and eighty acres. You know the rest of it, so you have to know that much."

"I know the Calitron Corporation will go as high as

seventeen hundred an acre to Gary Santo." It was nice to have the name of the corporate buyer.

Preston LaFrance brooded about it. "He never did let on what he expects to get. But there's not a damn thing anybody can do about that. Hell, Santo can just let his land sit there for ten years. He doesn't have to sweat these things out."

"In a smaller sense, Press, that's my policy too."

He looked startled, and then alarmed. "Now, you wouldn't squirrel up the whole deal by setting on that little ten acres forever, would you. Jesus, man, Calitron will go somewhere else if they get held up! Then where are we?"

"Maybe I've got a buyer who doesn't need that much room. I'm thinking of your health, Press. Fifty thousand and no more worries, and your ulcer will feel fine. You can pay off some of the notes at the bank and make Whitt Sanders happy."

His jaw firmed up. "I'll play it like a Mexican standoff, mister. I'll squat on my fifty and you squat on your ten."

"It's like what you said when you came in. Do we learn to eat out of the same dish or do we spill the dinner? Know what the difference is, Press? I'm not hungry and you are."

He cracked the knuckles of both hands, methodically, one at a time. "Now you said something about being shrewd and being greedy both and how it turns out stupid, Trav. I've been working on this thing one way or another for a year and a half, about. The way things are, I have to make it big, and that's the truth. Not big the way Santo thinks about money, but big for me. I'm levelling with you. I've got to come out of this six figures ahead anyway, or with the present timing I'm going to end up way the hell back where I started in forty-six when I got out of the service, and I don't want for that to happen. I had it within an inch of being home free, and you slipped in out of nowhere and bollixed it all up for me. Okay, it was smart business and you're pretty cute. So right now I think it's up to you to find some way to fix it so we get to eat out of the same dish, each to his need. I've got my good option out of old Carbee, even if he is thinking about shooting me since you went to see him. And I got the fifty acres behind your place."

"As long as you're levelling, you can settle one thing that bothers me a little. Back when you found out Bannon wouldn't sell and wouldn't budge, and if you had the shorts so you couldn't offer him enough, why didn't you turn the problem over to Gary Santo. With what he'd stand to make, he could have paid Bannon twenty cents for every dime he had in that business, and bought him a new location."

"I told Santo about that! I had that same idea. It took me a whole month to get to talk to him face to face, and then I had to chase him up to Atlanta, where they were opening up a hotel he's got money in, where he's got a penthouse thing he keeps for himself. I was up there drinking and waiting around maybe an hour and then he was ready to talk and we went back into one of the bedrooms and I told him these Bannons were a nice little family, working hard and doing pretty good, and if he could make them a good offer, which I wasn't in any shape to do, then we were all ready to move. So he said don't bother me with the details, LaFrance. He said that if he had to take care of all my problems, why should I have a slice of the cake. He said that come next May first he'd pay the full two hundred and thirty-four thousand for a clean, clear title to the two hundred and sixty acres to the east of his holdings, or I could forget the whole thing. And that was what I couldn't do, McGee—forget the whole thing."

"So you broke them. You busted them down to a price you could afford. You didn't have any other choice."

"No other choice in the world, excepting to go broke myself. I swear, if it had been my own brother running that place, it would have had to be just the same. But let me tell you, I never did count on Bannon killing himself. That never entered my head one minute. We were having a late Sunday breakfast in the kitchen when I got a phone call telling me what he'd done, and after I hung up and thought about it, I went right in the bathroom and threw up. I swear, it made me sick. I was in bed most of the day. Suzy wanted to call the Doc, but I told her it was just probably something I ate at the hotel Saturday night, at the testimonial dinner for old Ben Linder, retiring from the law, looking like a little old grey ghost the way the cancer is eating him up." He sighed. "You know, having you come out of noplace and snatch those ten acres away from me is like punishment for what Bannon did to himself. It's like getting the word that nothing ever is going to work out right any more for me, and things used to go so good there for a while."

"Maybe Bannon didn't kill himself."

His sagging head snapped up. "What are you trying to do now? What kind of new game are you playing?"

"Just a thought. I suppose it was pretty well known who was putting the pressure on Bannon and why. Maybe somebody wanted you and Monk Hazzard to be appreciative. Maybe they roughed Bannon up just to prove a lot of real diligence and co-operation and went a little too far. And if Bannon just happened to die on them, it would be a pretty good way of fixing it so that nobody would ever be able to find out that Bannon took a bad beating."

He chewed a crumb of skin off the corner of his thumb. "Suzy said if it was sure going to crush a man's head anyway, he might as well be face down so he couldn't see it falling. . . ." He straightened and shook his head. "No. There's nobody around who'd do a man that way. Nobody I know. Nobody Monk knows."

I looked at my watch. "I'll tell you exactly what you do, Press. I'll be up there on Thursday the fourth. I'll have somebody with me who can tell you something you might find interesting. But the only way you can get to talk to them is to have that forty thousand in cash or certified cheque all ready and waiting, and I'll have a deed and closing statement and so on. Show me the money and then you can talk to the man I'll bring along. Then you can decide whether you want to buy the Bannon place. Because that's the only way you're going to have any dish to eat out of."

He stood up. "Otherwise?"

"Otherwise I just wait you out, and I wait until the Calitron deal is dead, and then I make my own deal with Carbee, because he certainly isn't going to renew that option with you, and then I see if my buyer can get along without your land and without the Santo land, and I think it's quite possible that two hundred and ten acres might be enough."

"You wouldn't be running a bluff?"

"Prove you have forty thousand to get into the table stakes game, and we'll give you a little peek at the hole card. Believe me, it's the last and only chance you've got."

From the dock he looked back toward me, standing on

the afterdeck. He shook his head and said, "You know, damn it, McGee, it's almost easier dealing with that son of a bitch Santo. At least you know more about what the hell is going on."

I went back in and hollered to Puss that she could come out. I took a yellow cushion off the couch and lifted the little Sony 800 out of its nest and took it over to the desk. We'd used up two-thirds of the five-inch reel of half-mil tape and three and threequarters ips. I unplugged the mike and plugged in the line cord to save the battery drain and rewound it to the beginning. I stretched out on the couch and Puss sat cross-legged on the floor and we listened to it all the way through. I got up just once and held the rewind key down a few moments, and replayed the account of the talk with Santo in Atlanta, and let it continue on from there.

At the end, Puss got up and punched it off and came over and hip-thumped herself a little room on the edge of the couch. "Is that what we've got for a villain, dear? That weak, scared, sly, sorry man? Just scrambling and hustling and trying to keep his stupid head above water? So his stomach hurts all the time, and he threw up."

"Settle for Santo?"

"Maybe indifference *is* the greatest sin, darling. I'll settle for Santo, until a new one comes along. McGee, tomorrow is New Year's Eve."

"So it is. So it is indeed."

"How would you feel about no throngs, dear?"

"I was thinking about trying to prove two is a throng."

"I think two people could purely lang the hell out of auld zyne if they put their minds to it. Is it zyne, or syne or what?"

"It is old acquaintance ne'er forgot."

"New acquaintance ne'er forgot. What happens to people who start on Black Velvets and taper off on champagne?"

"They seldom remember their own names."

"Let's try for that."

A slow grey rain came down all day long on the last day of the year. We kept the *Flush* buttoned up, the phone off, ignored the bing-bong of the regulars who were drifting from boat to boat. It was a private world, and she provided a throng of girls therein. Never had she released all that mad and wonderful vitality for so long. She had come all the way out of the shell she had been keeping herself in for the last few days. We peaked at that point where the wine held us in an unreal place, neither drunk nor sober, neither sane nor crazy, where the funny things were thrice funny, where all the games were inexhaustible, where tears were part of laughter or sadness, and every taste was sharpened, every odour pungent, every nerve branch incomparably sensitized. The ones who are half alive can reach that place, perhaps, with their trips and their acids and their freaking, but reality truly felt, awareness made totally aware, is a magic they can't carry around in powdered form. She was a throng of girls and she filled the houseboat and filled the day and filled the long evening. Some of the girls were ten, and some were fifteen, and some were ten thousand years old. And, like Alice, I had to run as fast as I could to stay in the same place. HAPP-eeee New Year, my love. . . .

I awakened on Monday with the impression that I might have to get up and bang my head against the wall to get my heart started. The bedside clock was at seven after eleven. No hangover. Just that leaden heavy contentment of an expenditure so total the account was seriously overdrawn. I plodded my way into the vast shower stall, soaped and then stood swaying, eyes closed under the steaming roar, like a horse sleeping in the rain. Finally out of a sense of duty and character I fixed the heads to needle spray and switched it to cold. As I hopped and gasped, I thought dourly of how inaccurate are all the bridegroom jokes about window shades. A long and private holiday with a sizeable, sturdy, vital, demanding and inventive lass leaves you with the impression that you had merely rowed a couple of tons of block across a lake, then ran them up to the top of a mountain with a dozen or so trips with a wheelbarrow, then rolled back down the mountain into the lake and drowned.

As with sad and reminiscent smile I was reaching for my toothbrush, I noticed that hers was gone. Okay. So she had packed early. But while brushing, I reached my free hand up and opened the other cupboard. It was bare. She had taken everything of hers, for the first time in all these months.

I rinsed and spat and wrapped the big damp towel around

my waist and went in search of her. Of course there was nothing of hers left aboard. She was gone. She had scotch-taped a note to the side of the coffeepot. It was in her free-hand printing, using a red ballpoint.

And so, my scruffy darling, cometh an end to all good things. Endeth with a flourish, what? You are the best that could have happened to me. It isn't Killian and it wasn't Seattle, so don't waste time and money. And nothing you said or did. Your saying and your doing are a memorable perfection. I am just not a very constant type, love. For once I wanted to quit when I was ahead. Think kindly of the girl. Because she did love you, does love you, will love you from here on in. Cross my heart. (Say my good-byes to all the good ones.)

Instead of a signature she had drawn a circle with two little almond shapes for eyes, and a great big curved line for a smile. Three tears were dripping down out of each eye.

But, damn it, I wasn't *ready* yet.

Those were the words in my mind. I read them back and suddenly understood them, and I sat down in the booth suddenly full of self-understanding and self-loathing.

Sure, Puss-baby. We just hadn't reached the cutoff point where McGee would make the break on *his* terms. Which would have kept you from quitting while you were ahead. The key word is "Yet." So all that's hurt is pride, you sorry son of a bitch.

I could have done without that kind of self-revelation. I felt like a very trivial and tiresome animal, a sluggish animal sitting slumped in its tired slack hide—hide that bore the small and involuntary marks of fang and claw of the other-wise gentle she-thing now gone for good. Who is the user, Trav baby, and who is the used? And have you ever given anybody anything worth the having.

I clamped my jaw until my teeth squeaked and my ears buzzed. Why such a big hang-up over another promiscuous broad? Town was full of them. Go whistle up another one. Be the jolly old lover-boy, and be glad the redhead left before she turned into a drag, before she started bugging you about making it something legal and forever, and a-crawl with kids.

I like last year's McGee better.

CHAPTER NINE

MEYER was back on the second day of the new year, back on Tuesday at ten in the morning, and came over in his New York garments after leaving his suitcase off on his boat, so eager was he to display the fruits of his efforts.

There were two thin sheafs of brokerage house forms, paperclipped together. He sat across from me in the galley booth and said, "That batch is the monthly margin account statements."

The forms were printed in pale blue ink on a thin off-white paper. The name of the firm was but vaguely familiar. Shutts, Gaylor, Stith and Company. 44 Wall Street. New York 10004. Established 1902.

"And these are the confirmations of purchases and sales. The prices are correct for the date of sale. The monthly statement of account checks against the confirmations, of course. The monthly statements cover eleven months, including last month. I put in several where you bought at such and such a figure and then sold after they'd gone up just a few points. They went up further and then dropped like stones. I gave you two small losses, short term, on the same basis. In effect in eleven months you built a hundred thousand into almost two hundred and ninety thousand, so that according to the summary, right now you could sell two hundred thousand worth, pay a twenty-five per cent long-term gain, and pocket a hundred and fifty thousand, leaving almost your original investment in the securities you'd still be holding."

"What about anybody checking it out?"

"Your account number . . . that number there . . . oh-three-nine-seven-one-one-oh, that's in legitimate sequence. Somebody started an account eleven months ago, then cancelled out. It's a small, conservative, reputable house. I can tell you that there is not one other person in the world they would do this for. I had to make so many solemn oaths I've forgotten half of them. If anybody checks back to the margin clerk, he will say it is all legitimate. If anybody tries to go further, they will come upon either Emmet Stith or Whitsett Gaylor, who'll confirm."

"So how did I make payment to them?"

"Always by cheque on the Bank of Nova Scotia in Nassau."

It was beautiful. There is no way that even a Gary Santo could pry information out of the bank of Nova Scotia. It is a system some call Zurich West.

I leafed through the sheets. I had bought at the right time. I'd done very well.

"So what is wrong with you?" Meyer asked.

"I'm just great. Nifty peachy."

"You are stimulating. Like a dirge. Where's Puss?"

"Gone for good."

"So!"

"So?"

"So I don't think you drove that one off. So it was her choice. So she isn't the kind who says it is for good and then come back all of a sudden. With her, gone is gone. So if I were you, I would be just as bad off as you look. Or worse. So if I were you and one like that was gone for good, I'd miss hell out of her and wonder if maybe I'd handled things a little differently somehow, I could have kept her around permanently."

"That's enough about 'so'."

He got out of the booth. "When you want to be civilized, I live over there on a boat. *The John Maynard Keynes.* Fourteen hundred and forty a year, special annual rate, less a discount for paying the year in advance. Ask for Meyer."

"Okay, okay. These sheets are perfect. You did a hell of a job up there. You are intelligent, crafty, loyal, persuasive and diligent. Puss or no Puss, the job goes on. LaFrance showed. I'll play you the tape. It's interesting. He spilled the name of the company. Calitron. Mean anything?"

"A name only. Listed on the big board. A growth issue, going at thirty times earnings. Volatile. I'll check it out. Play the tape and I'll go away and let you sit and chew your hands and moan a little."

"I'm glad I depend on you for sympathy, Meyer."

"What sympathy should you get? A little arrangement, wasn't it? A sea urchin arranged the meeting. The urchin didn't wash up, she didn't step on it, what have you lost?

Don't answer! Your disposition you've lost. Play the tape before I start to cry."

I put it on. I stretched out on the yellow couch. I closed my eyes. If I opened them quick enough, turned my head quick enough, I would see Puss sitting cross-legged on the floor, scowling as she listened to Preston LaFrance.

When it was through, I turned it off. Meyer sighed. He said, "I think he will have the forty thousand. Even knowing I was hearing nonsense, I could believe you a little. Forty thousand is better than getting poked in the eye with a stick."

"You left something out. Did you find the kind of a company Gary Santo should invest in?"

After the first five sentences I was totally lost. I stopped him and told him to start over again, and give it to me in baby talk.

He sighed; pondered. "Try this. A company has only so many shares of stock issued. The number of shares is called the 'float'. When there aren't many shares, it is called a 'thin float'. Somebody buys ten thousand shares of General Motors, he might move it up an eighth of a point—twelve and a half cents a share—just by the effect of his demand on the floating supply. But if he put in an order for ten thousand shares of Peewee Incorporated, the demand might shove it right through the roof. It might boost it four or five dollars a share. Are you with me?"

"So far."

"Every day in every newspaper it shows you, with the two zeros left off the end, how many shares of every listed stock were bought and sold. People watch like hawks. Two kinds of people. One guy wants capital gains. He wants to buy something for twenty dollars a share, hold it for six months and a day, sell it for forty a share, pay Uncle twenty-five per cent of the profit in capital gains tax, or five dollars, and put fifteen in his pocket. Other characters are traders. They sit in brokerage offices and watch the tape. They want to buy a stock for twenty a share, sell it next week at twenty-five, when it drops down from twenty-six, buy it back at twenty-seven, sell at thirty, buy back at twenty-eight, sell at thirty-five and so on. They pay straight income tax on their net gain. Gary Santo is the first type, the capital gain guy, because all his income is being taxed at the maximum rate already."

"Still with you, Professor."

"Splendid! Now when something good is going to happen to a little company, the number of shares sold and bought every day goes up. It becomes more active. The price of the stock goes up. So it gets noticed. So more people want to get in the act and make a buck. That creates more demand. The demand pushes the price higher. In every trade, Travis, nobody can buy unless somebody is willing to sell. The more people who want to hang on, the fewer shares floating around, and the higher it goes, because the price has to go up to the point where somebody will say: Okay, I've made enough off this stock, so I'll sell it. I'll put in my order to sell it at two-dollars a share higher than it is right now. It is a big snowball rolling *up* the hill. Okay?"

"One thing. What keeps Santo from making a lot of money too?"

"Nothing, if he gets out in time. But look at the credentials I fixed you up with. All splendid values back at the time you bought them, at the time you apparently bought them. Stock prices go up because the company is *making* money, and has the look of making *more* money than before when they make their next earnings report. So the stock I found, Santo will think it has the same beautiful future like these, you made the capital gains out of. They are still all hanging up there pretty good. So why should he be nervous? I tell you, he would be nervous if he knows what a terrible lousy stock I found."

"What is it?"

"A dog called Fletcher Industries. I read maybe two hundred balance sheets and operating statements. I started with two hundred and weeded down and down and down, hunting for something that looks okay fine on the surface but is rotten underneath. It could win a prize for the worst stock. It has a thin float. It shows sales and profits going up every year. It has a nice profit margin, nice book value, big words in the annual financial report about a glowing future and so on."

"So what's wrong with it?"

"This I shouldn't even try to explain. Listen, there are

maybe eight perfectly ethical and legitimate choices a C.P.A. has when he is figuring profit per share. Each choice makes the profit higher or lower, accordingly. You could find some old conservative companies that make the eight choices so they show the lowest per share profit. Most companies make one choice one way, another, another way, so in general it cancels out. But this little Fletcher outfit, they use every chance they have to make profits look bigger. I reworked their statements. The stock sells right now for fifteen a share. Over the last twelve months the earnings reports say they made ninety-six cents a share. This was up from seventy-seven cents the previous year. Use the most conservative methods and you know what it is? It is a lousy eleven cents the previous year, and it is a four-cent loss this year. Such a statement they publish! The book value is all puffed up. The profit margin is nonsense. Even the cash flow is jiggered up."

"Book value? Cash flow?"

"Forget it. You don't have to know. All you have to know is that no matter how careful Santo is, the published trading volume will go up, the stock will go up, a lot of careless people will jump on the wagon and push it higher. They'll think a big increase in earnings is going on. Or a merger, or a new product. Like with the ones you are supposed to have bought. But this one has no substance. It will go up like penny rockets and when it starts down, it should maybe end up a two-dollar stock where it belongs."

"So we con him into buying it, Meyer. So it goes up and up and he makes a lot of paper profit, and then when it goes down, he sells out and keeps the profit."

"With everybody selling, with everybody trying to save out some profit, who will buy it? No buyers and they'll suspend trading, investigate the heavy speculation, and when it opens again, it will open in the cellar. Santo should lose most or all of his bundle."

"So how does Janine make the money you were talking about?"

"With the forty thousand from LaFrance we start her off, pick up three thousand shares. As it moves, I use the increased market value to pick up more for her. I watch it like an eagle, and then I start pulling her out of it very, very gently, and putting her into a nice solid little sleeper

I happened to find when I was looking for this Fletcher dog. It should give her a hundred-per cent gain in a year, along with a nice dividend yield."

"How much can you make for her if things work out right?"

"If? Did I hear you say if? You get Santo to bite at it, and I'll do the rest. End of the year? Oh, say the original stake plus a quarter million."

"Come *on*, Meyer!"

"Oh, that's before short-term gains tax on Fletcher. You see, that's what'll lock Santo into it. He'll be hoping to ride the profit for six months. Say a fifty to sixty thousand tax she'll pay."

"You kill me, Meyer."

"Make sure nobody else kills you. It would be boring around here."

For the first time since I knew Puss would never come back, I felt a faint and reluctant little tremor of excitement and anticipation.

Meyer, frowning, said, "You are going to see LaFrance the day after tomorrow? Does that give us time to do everything we have to do?"

"I was just making him sweaty, Meyer. I'll phone him Thursday night and say we'll have to change the arrangement. Don't call us. We'll call you. And I can get a pretty good indication of whether he has the forty all ready."

"You know, you look more like yourself, Travis."

"It's the sympathy that does it, every time."

"An obligation of friendship. What do you do first?"

"Find that little pipeline."

After a long conference Wednesday morning with Meyer about strategy and tactics, and the documentation he ought to have, I went down to Miami. The offices of Santo Enterprises were in an unimpressive six-storey office building on North East 26th Terrace, a half block east of Biscayne. Reception was on the sixth floor. A wide corridor, glass doors at the end, and beyond them a panelled room, thick blue rug, and elegant blonde desk-table on a raised dais and, behind it with a look of polite and chilly query, a slender princess with white dynel hair, glowing in the drama-light of

a little ceiling spot, who asked me in the beautiful clarity of
the English upper class if she might be of service.

When I said I would like to see Mr. Santo, she looked
remotely amused. "Soddy, sir, but he is out of the citeh.
Possibleh someone else could help you?"

"I'm inclined to doubt it."

"Praps if you might tell me the nature of your business,
sir?"

"I'd rather not."

"Ektually, then, there isn't much that can be done, sir. Mr.
Santo only sees one by appointment, and he would certainly
not relish having his secretary make an appointment . . . blind,
as it were. You see the problem, do you not?"

"Why don't I talk to his secretary, then?"

"But you see, sir, I would have to know the nature of your
business to know *which* secretary you should speak with."

"Does he have a super-special personal private one?"

"Oh yes, of course. But, sir, one must have an appointment
to speak with her. And to make the appointment I should
have to——"

"Know the nature of my business."

"Quite."

"Miss, we're both in trouble."

"I wouldn't really say *both* of us, sir."

"If you don't help me a little bit, and when I do get to
Gary Santo, which I most certainly will, he is going to wonder
what took me so long, and I am going to tell him that I
just couldn't get past that limey wench with the white hair
under the spotlight.

"But, sir! Really, I have——"

"Your orders."

"Quite!"

"Do I look like a con artist? Do I look like a salesman?
Do I look like a pest? Dear girl, aren't you supposed to
exercise *some* instinct and judgement about people?"

"Sir, one might possibly say . . . pest, should this go on
too much longer. Oh! My word! Are you a pilot? Is it about
that . . . currency matter?"

"I am not a pilot. But some currency might enter into it.
I just remembered something. Somebody said at one point
that to get to Santo with a certain suggestion, they had to

clear through Mary Smith. Is that a person or some kind of a code name for something?"

"Mary Smith would be a person, sir."

"A special personal private secretary, maybe?"

"Praps just private secretry, sir, might be suitable."

"Now, please don't tell me I need an appointment with her."

She studied me for a moment, tilted her head, looked slightly quizzical and inwardly—and possibly bitterly—amused. The appraisal was like unto that given a side of beef when the US Grade stamp is not easy to read.

"You could give me your name, sir?"

"McGee. T. McGee."

"This is teddibly irregular. Just a chawnce, y'know."

"Tell her I do card tricks, have never been completely domesticated, and show signs of having been struck sharply in the face in years gone by."

"At least you are amusing," she said.

"Quite!" said I.

"Please have a seat. I'll find out what she says, Mr. McGee."

I sat cautiously in a chair that looked like the slope-end of a blue bathtub resting on a white pedestal, and found it more comfortable than it looked. Windowless rooms always give me the feeling of having been tricked. Now they've got you, boy, and they're going to come through all the doors at once. I opened a mint copy of *Fortune* and a grizzled fellow looked out at me with alert and friendly squint of eye, advertising my chummy neighbourhood power company. I think I could remember having seen him on somebody's television set shilling an adenoidal housewife into squealing in ecstasy about suds.

The limey maiden murmured into the oversized mouthpiece of one of those privacy telephones. In a little while she hung up and said with a certain air of accomplishment and mild surprise, "She will be out in a few moments, sir."

A flush door, bone-white, off to the left of the receptionist opened, and little Miss Mary Smith came through and toward me without a glance at the receptionist. I put *Fortune* aside and stood up. She marched to within four feet of me and stopped and looked up into my face. At least it was not a

name they handed around the office. She was the one I had
seen with Tush Bannon in the bar lounge atop the International Hotel. The dark and rich brown-auburn hair fell in
a straight gloss. I had misread, across the room the last time,
the expression on her face. It was not petulance, not discontent. It was a total and almost lifeless indifference, a completely negative response. In a special way it was a challenge.
It said, "Prove I should relate to you, buddy." Her eyes were
the improbable emerald of expensive contact lenses, made
more improbable by just enough eye makeup to make them
look bigger than they were. And they were generous to start
with. Her skin texture was a new grainless DuPont plastic.
The small mouth did not really pout. It was just that both
upper and under lip were so heavy it was the only choice
it had. They were artfully covered with pink frost. White
blouse, navy skirt—that nunnery flavour of offices and hospital wards.

She looked up at me, motionless as department store wax,
with two millimeters of query in one eyebrow.

"The eyebrow," I said, "is the exact same shade of those
woolly bear caterpillars I remember from my childhood.
You'd look for them in the fall to see if they were heading
north or south. It was supposed to predict what kind of a
winter we'd have."

"So you've verified Elizabeth's claim you're mildly amusing. This is a busy office."

"And I just happened to come bumbling in off the street
to bother all you busy, dedicated people."

She took a step back, a quarter turn. "Then, if that's
all."

"I want to see Santo. What do I have to say to you? A
magic word?"

"Try good-bye."

"My God, you *are* a silly, pretentious little bitch!"

"That doesn't work either, Mr. McGee. The only thing that
does work is to state your business. If Mr. Santo did not
employ people of some judgement to screen out the clowns,
his time would be taken up with clowns . . . and eccentrics,
and clumsy con men. Do you want him to finance a flying
saucer?" She rested a finger against her small chin and tilted
her head. "No, you have that deep-water look. A bit salty?

This is probably more of that treasure-map nonsense. Spanish galleons, Mr. McGee? And you have some genuine gold coins minted in the New World? I would say we average eight or ten of you people a month. So either you tell me or you don't tell anyone here at any time. Is that quite clear?"

"All right. I will tell you. I will tell you enough so that you will open the door for me to see Santo."

"May we call him Mr. Santo?"

"But I am not going to talk standing here like the last guests at a cocktail party. I want to sit at a desk or a table and you can sit on the other side of it and listen to as much as I care to tell you."

"Or as much as I care to listen to." She turned to the receptionist and said, "I shall be in Conference D, Elizabeth."

"Thank you, Miss Smith," said the humble limey.

I pushed the glass door open for little Miss Mary Smith and followed her down the corridor. Her walk was engaging, as it seemed to involve a conscious effort to inhibit any swing and flourish of her solid little rear end, and was successful to but a limited degree.

Conference D was a ten by twelve cubicle. But the end wall opposite the door was all window, looking out across Biscayne Bay to the improbable architectural confectionery of Miami Beach, with a sunlit glitter and shimmer of traffic across the Julia Tuttle Causeway a little to the north, and the residential islands off the Venetian Causeway about the same distance south. It was a grey room with grey armchairs, six of them, around a Chinese red conference table. On one wall was a shallow grey case, glass-fronted, wherein a very diversified collection of white nylon gears and cogs and rods and bushings of various sizes had been arranged against a Chinese red background in simulation of some of the art forms of Louise Nevelson.

I could be reasonably certain that as we had walked down the corridor, Elizabeth had, as common practice, turned on whatever bug system was used in Conference D. After all, Elizabeth could look through the glass doors and see which door we had entered.

I had learned the right terms from Meyer. She sat across from me, radiating scepticism.

"I am a speculator, Mary Smith. I'm not a trader. My

speciality is in the maximized capital gains area. There is enough income from certain other sources so that the Fed hasn't, and won't, class me as a professional and cut it all back to straight income. Is this over your head."

"Hardly! In fact, you've almost run out of time, Mr. McGee."

"I do *not* want to sell Santo a hot item. I do *not* want him in any syndicate operation. I do *not* want any piece of his action, or even any knowledge of the details just so long as he *does* move in on it. This is not nickel and dime. It's a listed security. Now, usually, I operate in a sort of informal syndicate deal. Every man for himself, but we make the same move at the same time. But we've done so well we've got some security leaks. I dug this one out and it's too damned good to get the edge taken off of it by too many leaks. I could probably establish a position in it and then arrange a show of interest on the part of one of the aggressive funds. But they work out in the open, and the blocks they buy are too big."

I looked at her questioningly. "You haven't lost me. And your time hasn't run out," she said.

"So I have the word here and there that Santo will swing when something looks good. And I think he is smart enough to ease his way into it, because if he comes in too hard and fast, it is going to go up the ladder so fast I'm not going to have a chance to use the buying power on the margin account to keep doubling on the way up. He'll have to set it up to work through several accounts, and be willing to sell off blocks of it to kill the momentum if it starts to go too fast."

"You said something about it not being nickel and dime."

"So it would depend entirely on how far he wants to go with it. If he goes in, it will take a million to create the pressure it needs. I would say he could come in anywhere from one million on up to a tops of four. Over four and it would put it too far out of balance and attract too much attention in the long run. Frankly, I'd be hitch-hiking, using his buying pressure to get on for the ride up, and taking the chance he can keep the climb controlled. I could assemble syndicate money because the track record is good, but the leaks would hurt. If I had the million, I wouldn't be here. Let's say he can count on three hundred per cent long-term gains, if he doesn't plumber it. This is the kind of thing that comes along every three to five years, where all the factors fit like a beautiful watch."

"Mr. Santo has very little tendency to plumber anything."

"That was my evaluation. And when the ride is over, I should be where I won't have to fool with syndicates and Santo. I'll be where I can make my own markets."

"A listed security?"

"And a company in a potentially dynamic growth area."

For the first time I saw the suggestion of a smile on that heavy little-girl mouth. "And absolutely no point at all in asking you the name of it, of course. But I can ask you for . . . bank references?"

"That's a silly question. If he wants to dig around and check me out, lots of luck. He could find worms in the apple. All he'll be interested in is the track record." I took the envelope out of my inside jacket pocket and took out the brokerage account forms and flipped them over to her. "Take a look, if you can read them and interpret them, and then you can give Santo a nice verbal reference."

She went through the margin account monthly summary forms first, sheet by sheet. Midway through she gave me a sudden green glance of reappraisal. On the last one, the December one, I had pencilled beside each stock listed in the security position the January second market value. She checked those values against the purchase confirmations—not all of them, just a random few.

"May I hold these for a few days?" she asked.

"No."

"Can I have them Xeroxed? It would take just a few minutes."

I hesitated. "On one basis, and I can't enforce it. You see them and Santo sees them, and that's it."

"That would be up to him."

"So relay my humble request to the great man, sweetie."

"Do you have to be so sarcastic?"

"Am I supposed to be impressed by Gary Santo? He happens to be my number one on a list of three possibles. Whoever it turns out to be will make a bundle on their terms while they help me make a bundle on my terms. I didn't come to beg, sweetie."

"You *do* make that clear. I'll be right back."

"If you ever stoop to manual labour around this shop, I think it would be nice if you did the Xeroxing yourself."

"I shall, sweetie. And you just made a nice brownie point. Cautious is as cautious does. We treasure that around here."

She was back in under ten minutes. She did not sit again. I stowed the account forms in the envelope and in my pocket.

I said, "You see, Miss, there's all those chests of gold coin busted open and spilled out right across the white sand bottom next to Hustler Reef."

"That was clumsy, wasn't it? I must stop typecasting. Of course you realize I have no idea whether or not this will appeal to Mr. Santo. The idea, I mean. If it does, he will have to know the security you're talking about, and he will want to have it checked."

"Quietly, I hope."

"Of course."

"When do I get to see him?"

"How can I reach you?"

"I'm going to be on the move. Suppose I phone you to-morrow afternoon."

She shook her head. "Friday. Say at four in the afternoon. Ask for me by name and give my extension number or you won't be put through. Sixty-six."

"Just what *is* you job around here, Mary Smith?"

"You might call me a buffer zone."

"Have I gotten past you?"

"On Friday we'll both know, won't we?"

CHAPTER TEN

ON Thursday evening I reached Preston LaFrance by phone at his home in Sunnydale. I taped it so that Meyer and I could study the playback.

"McGee? Trav? I've been wondering all day——"

"Too much has been happening, Press. I might say that

things are shaping up a little better than I'd hoped. I might have some good news for you when I'm able to get up there."

"I need some good news, and you can believe it. When are you coming up."

"I'll have to let you know. That money we talked about. Have you got it set aside?"

"Let me get one thing straight. I get to know about what's going on before I have to go ahead and buy that damned thing for three or four times what it's worth, don't I? I mean I get a chance to make a decision based on what you tell me?"

"Naturally. But as you must realize, I'm not in this thing for *that* kind of a profit."

"I can figure that out for myself all right. Okay, I've got that money set aside, in case I want to go along."

"You will. I'll have the papers all drawn and bring them along. But one thing has come up which worries me a little, Press."

His voice tightened up. "What? What?"

"Have you had any recent contact with Santo?"

"No. No reason to. Why?"

"I think it would be a very good thing if you make certain he never hears about any kind of deal between you and me."

"I don't understand what you——"

"Did you hear anything about somebody topping your offer that same day title reverted to Mrs. Bannon, and I bought it from her?"

"I sure did, and it puzzled the hell out of me. It come through Steve Besseker here, and he won't say who made it."

"I have it on pretty good authority that Besseker was representing Gary Santo."

"What! The hell you say! Steve?"

"Santo sent some woman up to give him his orders, apparently. A tall redhead."

"By God, somebody was kidding Steve about seeing him over in Broward Beach with a big good-looking redhead sometime just before Christmas."

"It was probably the same day I bought the Bannon property. And it strikes me that the way things are going, Santo would want to know if there is any present or pending agreement between you and me, and he might have asked Besseker to find out."

I could hear him breathing, and then he said softly, "Well, I'll be a son of a bitch! The very next day he asked me if I knew you, and if maybe you were acting for me because, like Whitt Sanders said, that Bannon woman certainly wouldn't have sold to me no matter what I offered her. What's going *on*, McGee?"

"I'm afraid he's got wind of the deal I'm trying to pull off, and it would sting him a little. I suppose Besseker will keep him posted on every move you make. Well, we may have to move a little faster than I planned. Santo will hear about you buying the Bannon place from me as soon as the sale is recorded. Until then, keep your mouth shut because I wouldn't want to have it turn out that you end up with no share in either his deal or mine."

"Listen, I can't risk anything like that happen——"

"Sit tight, Press. Hang on. Keep the faith."

As he started to speak again I hung up on him.

About an hour later I played it for Meyer. He listened and then shook his head. "What's the point, Travis? Why are you confounding that dull boy with all this business of wheels within wheels?"

"For the variation of the pigeon drop, my friend. If suddenly the whole world seems more conspiratorial than he ever believed it was, then he'll be in a better mood to stand still for the sleight of hand. Confused people are less sceptical. I was going to use Besseker another way, but it had to be through Puss, and she doesn't seem to be around any more, so I salvaged a piece of the situation anyway."

"But one thing puzzles me," Meyer said. "Here you are worming your way into one kind of thing, directly with Santo. And up there you have your thumb in another kind of pie, but that is Santo's too, but not so direct. Up there you are Travis McGee, this address. And down there in Santo Enterprises, you are Travis McGee, this address. There is the chance that by some accident Santo or one of his people finds out you are in both things. That would immediately alert a man like Santo. He could find the relationship between you and Bannon, and he would smell mice."

"So?"

"Maybe I should have been the one to set up the investment thing."

"It would take the joy out of it. He might never make the connection. I need the chance to look him in the eye, laugh at his jokes, share some booze with him, and then sting him where it hurts. Then he can find out why it happened to him. I'll tell him, given the chance. For the rest of his life, the name Bannon is going to make him feel sick."

"Maybe he has some people who will make you feel sick in other ways."

"And sometimes they almost make it."

"This time they could."

"You always worry. It's nice. If you stopped, *I'd* worry."

He sighed. "Okay. So look at my expert, specialist, impressive kit. Meyer, the big industrialist."

He had the aerials of the Shawana River area, and the series of overlays marked as planned. He had soil surveys, water table data, labour supply data. He had business cards of expensive buff stock, engraved, turning him into G. Ludweg Meyer, Ph.D., Executive Vice President of Barker, Epstein and Wilks, Inc. Management Engineering Services.

"Let us sincerely pray," he said, "that one of these cards never finds its way back to that very sound and good firm."

"It might be therapeutic. It might stir them up. Let me see the correspondence file."

The letterhead startled me. It looked totally authentic. One of the giant corporations that have become household words in these days of electronic fantasy. I stared at him and he beamed at me and said, "It was a bit of luck. So wonder about it. Note that it is from the office of the President of the corporation. That is his name, truly. Note that it is marked confidential. Note the very impressive carbon ribbon type face. See the secretarial initials at the bottom. Those are the initials of his actual private secretary. The signature is not great. I copied it from a copy of their annual report. The top letters are background. The key letter is about the fourth one down. There. That's the one. Is it what you had in mind?"

The president called him *My dear Ludweg*: The first paragraph acknowledged the receipt of reports and recommendations, and then the letter went on to say, *I tend to agree with your appraisal of the competitive implications and possible danger to our industry position in that particular manufacturing division should Calitron establish a branch facility in such close proximity to Tech-Tex Applications, Inc. Though the branch facility we now have in the final planning stage is smaller, one could logically assume that proximity to TTA would benefit profit margin to the same extent percentagewise.*

In view of the necessity of moving quickly, and the favourable report our people brought back, you are authorized to make a firm commitment in the name of the Corporation for from 200 acres minimum or 260 maximum either in general area A, or general area B. A separate letter of authorization is appended hereto. In view of the other interest in these industrial lands, you are authorized to bid up to $2 thousand per acre, or a maximum of between $400 thousand and $520 thousand, at your discretion.

"Very nice," I said.

"What should my approach be up there? How should I act?"

"Self-important, influential, crooked, and careful of being caught at it. Great letters, Meyer. You are showing more and more talent every time you get into one of these things."

"And getting more and more scared. Isn't this a conspiracy to defraud?"

"Let's say to highjack. Now let me tell you how it is supposed to work."

He buried his face in his hands and said, "I can hardly wait to hear." After I explained it, it took him a long time to smile.

When I phoned Mary Smith at four on Friday, she said, "Mr. McGee, would it be possible for you to have a drink with Mr. Santo this evening at seven at the Sultana Hotel on Miami Beach?"

"I can arrange it."

"The Out-Island Room, then, at seven. Just ask for Mr. Santo's table."

I arrived at the arched doorway a few minutes after seven. A lackey with a face like a Rumanian werewolf slunk out

of the gloom and looked at me with total disdain, as if
Central Casting had sent the wrong type with the wrong
clothes. It was a cold day, and I had put on the Irish jacket.
After five or six years, twigs still occasionally fall out of the
dark, coarse weave.

"Mr. Santo's table, please."

"And your name?"

"McGee!"

He lit up with joy at beholding me. He popped his fingers
and a waiter trotted over, bowed several times, and led me
back through the labyrinths of partitions and alcoves to a
deep corner, to a semicircular banquette big enough for six,
and a semicircular table to fit. He pulled the table out,
bowed me in, put it back and bowed and asked for my drink
order.

At ten after he came on the run and pulled the table out
again as the Santo party arrived. Gary Santo, Mary Smith,
Colonel Burns, Mrs. Von Kroeder. I measured Santo as we
shook hands. He was not as tall as he looked in his pictures,
but with all the shoulders and chest so frequently mentioned
in his publicity. He was shading fifty, but fighting it and
winning the same way those more directly in show business
win it, with the facials, the luxuriant hairpiece touched just
enough with grey, the laborious hours in the home gym, and
the sessions on the rubbing table, and the hefty shots of
vitamins and hormones, and a hell of a good dentist. He came
on all virility, white teeth, wrestler's handshake, and the knack
of looking you squarely in the eye and crinkling his eyes as
if you and he shared a joke on the rest of the world.

In resonant boyish baritone he told me I knew Mary Smith,
of course, and presented me to Halda von Kroeder, who
had as much thin, pale, graceful neck as I have ever seen, a
small, pert head, a tall, slat-thin body, a cascade of emeralds,
and a set of breasts so awe-inspiring she gave the impression
of leaning slightly backward to keep herself in balance. "So
bleezed," she said in a Germanic rasp, then hiccupped.

Colonel Dud Burns had the look of eagles . . . defeathered,
earthbound, and worried about cirrhosis. Gary Santo
arranged the group with himself in the middle and, at his left,
first Mary Smith and then me at the end, and with Halda
and Burns in that order at his right.

Mary Smith was at that daring outer limit where style becomes comedy. There was more eye makeup, and the mouth more frosted. She wore a grey sweater with a great deal of complex stitchery and welts and seams. It came down to within six inches of her knees. Showing under the sweater was two inches of blue tweed skirt. Below the skirt were sheer blue stockings that were a perfect match for shoes with stubby heels and high, stiff tongues. On her head was a wide-brimmed hat shaped much like the hats the novilleros wear in the bullring. It was of a stiff eggshell fabric in a coarse weave. She had it perched aslant on the gloss of the brown-auburn spill of hair, with a white thong under her chin, a blue wooden thong bead at the corner of her little jaw. The sweater sleeves came midway down her forearms. Her gloves and purse matched the eggshell hat. When she pulled her gloves off, she uncovered nails painted a thick, pearly, opalescent white.

She sat bolt upright like a bright and obedient child and smiled at me with wide eyes and careful mouth, and told Santo she would have the regular, which turned out to be a straight shot of Wild Turkey with water, no ice, on the side. When she got it, she went at it with frequent little sippings, each of which must have been three or four drops by volume.

Santo turned finally, after some in-group jokes and conversation I couldn't follow, and faced me across Mary Smith, his back squarely toward the kraut lady.

"Our little Poo Bear here gives you a good mark, McGee."

"Poo Bear Smith?" I asked.

"It's an office thing," she said. "I have this instinct or something. He says what about this one and I say Poo. And that one, and I say Poo. Then the next one I say okay for brownie points."

"She's got a nose for it. Questions, McGee. If I go for it, if I like the flavour of it, how much do you have to know?"

"The day you start and how much you are going to spring for all together."

"Have you taken a position in it?"

"About the same way porcupines make love, but I'm nowhere near as far in as I want to be. It's been moving in a narrow range and I've been buying on the downs."

"Will you need to know my orders?"

"No. I'll have a man tape-watching it."

"There's one place where we have to be co-ordinated on it, and that's getting off it."

"As carefully as we got on, I hope."

"And the last thing, of course, is the name of it."

"Right here?"

"The other two can't hear, and Mary is the best you've ever seen at keeping her mouth shut. About anything."

"Fletcher Industries. American Exchange."

"Want to brief me a little?"

"Why should I? It's a duplication of effort. If your people can't see why it's as good as it is, you need new people."

"You have your full complete share of mouth, McGee."

"Have you got too accustomed to total humility on all sides, Santo?"

"Hush, now!" said Mary Smith. "You both hush. You're both right. Don't you two go all ballsy and wicked when you're going to be helping each other."

Santo threw his head back and laughed his boyish laugh. "Her biggest trouble is making sense. By Wednesday . . . that will be. . . ."

"The tenth," said Mary Smith.

". . . phone her and she'll have the Yes or No on it, and give you a probable figure."

"Will do," I said.

He smiled down into her face. He said to her, "I think I like your new friend, Mary. I think he's maybe brought us another winner." He took out his bill clip, slipped some bills out of it, and put them quickly into her purse. "I'm so sure, here's an advance on your bonus. Use it to take him to where the steaks are."

She looked at her watch. "Yes, you'd better start moving it, Gary. Ben will be out there with your luggage. Kiss Bonnie Bea for me."

He made the smallest of gestures and people came on the run to pull the table away, hand him the bill for signature, bow the three of them out and away.

We went up the beach in her little red car to what she called one of "her" places, a little bar dark as pockets. Once we were sitting across a very low and narrow little table from each other, so that we had to hunch over it in intimate arrangement, she figuratively rolled up her sleeves and went to work. She had awaited the pass, and for once there hadn't been one.

She had put the strange hat aside. She shook out her gleaming hair. A stray pattern of light rested on a long diagonal across her face, from eyes to lips.

She dipped into her shot like a moth, put it down, picked up the stray lip-drop with tongue tip. "Want to know, Travis? Want the crazy message?" It was half whisper, her voice dragging.

"Message by special delivery. Sure, Mary Smith."

She made her eyes very wide and solemn. Her lips parted. She reached and took my hand in both of hers and pulled it slowly to her side of the table. She turned my slack fist over, then put the nails of her right hand high on the inside of my wrist, and slowly drew her nails along my wrist and over my palm, uncurling my slack fingers as she did so. Holding my fingers down, she dipped her head suddenly, pressed the mouth moist against my palm, lifted her head very quickly and stared at me, her face both sly and fake-frightened.

"Is there more?" I asked.

She turned my hand over and formed it into a fist and, holding it in both her hands, lifted it, held it, her elbows braced on the table. She bumped her chin into the knuckles, closed her eyes.

"Pow," she whispered. "Like right off, the first minute. Pow. I'm *never* like that."

"Comes a time," I said.

"There does indeed, Mr. Travis McGee." She tilted my fist slightly for a better angle, and went across the knuckle ridge with her warm little mouth, taking a gentle little bite at each knuckle and kissing the space between each knuckle. With each kiss, her tongue tip flicked at the closed space between fingers.

"When it's going to be what it's going to be, there's that message, don't you think? An old-timey thing, way deep, that's been waiting for it special. So very rough crazy everlasting special. And you know it too. Don't you? Don't you?"

She sat back there some place behind those swarming eyes,

listening to herself pant, in such a soft little wondrous way. She watched herself work herself up, no doubt measuring the bra-tickle of the nipples becoming erectile, sensing the new softness of thigh and belly. This was one of the new breed who assist the manipulators. Gary Santo, being a manipulator in a large way could be expected to have one who would know her business backward and forward and upside down. He might have two, three or a dozen in the retinue. He would keep them loyal not only with money, but with the feeling of being part of an operating team and performing a function for the team.

Sex with a particularly skilled and desirable woman who could convince you that you were the greatest thing since fried rice was a marvellous gadget for one of the manipulators. The bedazzled male is incautious, mazed, thunderstruck. In that condition he can provide the maximum benefit to the manipulator and the least problem. He will come trundling along in the entourage just to be near his brand-new love-light. He will tell her all he knows and all he hopes, and in a frenzy of team spirit and accomplishment, she will bang him out of his mind and drop him right back where she found him when the manipulator has the last crumb of information he can use. But while he's getting the treatment, he tags along with the team, with the group but not really a part of the group, aware that the team knows the basis for the attraction, aware of a team attitude of kindly contempt for him but so enthralled in his doggy, lolling, bitch-trailing way he will endure the little humiliations to keep getting what becomes more instead of less necessary to him the more he gets of it.

The role requires a woman exceptionally confident and decorative, a woman of a hearty and insistent sexuality, a woman who understands that serving the manipulator in this way is part of the price of the ticket on all the best flights to the best places, and if you want to be coy, or choosy or chicken, you can drop right back to the posture chair and the old electric and the girl's room scuttlebutt about who might get promoted to what. It takes special gals to travel with the team, so dig in and enjoy the special assignments, because between the romps the guy will talk and you tote the crumbs back to Gary and he fits them together.

The manipulators are the brash gamblers putting little corporations together to make big ones, and they are the talent packages who stick a half dozen special abilities together and end up with the percentage off the top of the network serial show, and they are the showboaters who take on the tax cases of the mighty and fight the Fed to a draw—or a cheap compromise—and they are the inventive money men who direct the conversion of hoodlum funds into legitimate enterprise, and they are the whiz kids who tear down the honest old buildings and stick up the glittery new boxes on the lease-back, write-off, tax shelter kick, and they are the ones that boost the market price of a stock up and unload and then kick it back down and buy back.

They buzz around the country and the world in little groups, where everybody is always laughing, and at the resorts and airports and executive dining-rooms, at the padded bars and the swinging casinos, in the groups there are always the Mary Smiths, pert, tidy, high-style, voracious and completely with it, eyes a-dance, freed by The Pill to happily pull down the game the manipulator fingers for her, the new Gal Friday who has become the Gal Friday Night.

It is a new breed that did not exist a few years back, but cultures seem to have an uncanny way of spawning creatures to fill any need. So situation ethics, plus profitable manipulation, brought this merry regiment out of the wings, as if they had been waiting there all along. It would be pointless to conjecture about immorality or amorality, or make analogies about whoredom, that word with the ring of Biblical accusation. A Mary Smith would not even be upset, merely puzzled.

In the diagonal of light she rested her chin against my fist, her two warm and shapely little hands holding it there, elbow-braced, and made her eyes huge, then dipped and turned her head first one way and then the other, to slowly drag first one sheaf of the dense and fragrant hair across the back of my hand and then the other.

I remembered the shaggy and ancient joke of the young man in the strange city who had arrived with the phone number of a hundred-dollar girl. He called her up and was invited up to her luxurious apartment, where she cooked him a gourmet meal, recited French poetry, played the piano for him and sang with professional skill. She mentioned that she spoke six languages, had a master's degree in psychology, and had designed and made the gown she wore on her lovely body. At last as she led him in toward the canopied bed he had to ask. And so he said, "Please would you tell me how a girl like you got into . . . a business like this?"

She twinkled up at him and sighed and said, "Just lucky, I guess."

Mary Smith took a deep and shivering breath and said, "There is a steak, darling, and it is not frozen and never has been, and it is in the meat-keeper thing in my apartment, which is, God help us, a con-do-min-i-um, which will never cease to sound like a dirty word, and the apartment is twelve and a half minutes away, give or take ten seconds, and the steak will keep for us, darling, until three A.M., or until twelve noon tomorrow for a Texan's breakfast for us because I don't have to tend the store until Monday morning, and that twelve and a half minutes might just be the longest twelve and a half minutes in my life up till now."

The temptation was to accept the whole con. But there is an immense perversity in the male animal at the most unexpected times. And why *didn't* you climb Mount Everest, Sir Hillary? Because it was there, fellow. And I could see her in memory in another bar, by daylight, teeth set in that meaty little underlip, eyes half closed, listening to Tush, and turning her head slowly from side to side in a denial as definite as the slam of a door and clack of the lock. She would be exquisite in all detail, from earlobes to cute little toes to the dimples at the base of the spine. She would be fragrant, immaculate, prehensile and totally skilled, and she would ring all the changes, and pace herself beautifully, and draw me to her pace, and inflate my ego with her breathless astonishment at how it had been the most fantastic and lasting that had ever happened to her and how she had thought it could never even be equalled again, but lo and behold, when it had happened again, it was even more so, and if it ever got to be any more than that, she just couldn't stand it at all; it would blow her out of her mind, and how did we get to be so great, darling, so that really and truly it is as if it was the very first time ever with anybody.

The temptation was to take the man's Ferrari around the

track a few times, just to prove to yourself you couldn't get hooked on a great piece of machinery or on the whole speed competition bit.

But it was right there and it was buzzing with it, and how do you sidestep without creating some unhappy suspicions about the whole approach? It would have to be some fancy footwork, and it would have to be on her terms, something she could comprehend immediately.

I slipped into my elk-hide ring-shoes just in time, just as her eyes narrowed and she said, "You're not exactly overwhelming the girl with enthusiasm, old buddy."

"Decisions, decisions, decisions," I said. "I seem to have this hex lately."

She let my hand go. "What's to decide?"

"There is this very pigheaded man sitting in a hotel suite and looking at the phone and getting madder and madder by the minute. I have been trying to unload this and that for cash money so I can get the maximum out of our little gem of opportunity. And he flew down from Chicago because this particular item happens to be worth about twenty thousand more to him than to anybody else in the world, for reasons I will not go into at the moment. So I told him I had to delay our meet because of something that came up, and I would try to get there by eight. And right now it is quarter to nine, and he is the type who feels unsure of who he is right down in the gut where it matters most, the type who to prove he is who he thinks he is might wait about one minute more and cut off his nose to spite his face, or he may have cut it off already and be on his way to the airport. I have been looking at you and trying to get a little controlled piece of amnesia about him, but it doesn't seem to work so good."

She sat taller and gave a little shake like a toy poodle who has just been lifted out of her doggy-bath, and gave her hair a few pats, and gave a hitch at her complicated sweater and said, "Darling, you are an absolute idiot! Why didn't you *say* something? Didn't you think I'd understand? I'm all grown up and everything."

"Let's say I was enjoying myself. I was listening to the message of the Poo Bear Smith."

She reached and patted my arm and with a crooked little

smile and a bawdy wink said, "Let's put it this way. The twenty grand won't keep. You hustle and phone him. There's a phone at the end of that hallway over there that goes to the biff."

I went to the phone and lit a match and looked up a random number and dialled it and asked a nasal woman if I could speak to Mr. Bannon. She told me I had a wrong number and hung up, and so I talked for a while over the empty wire to Tush and told him the news of the moment, with a few comments on the weather. He didn't have a thing to say.

I went back to the table and told the chicklet that my man was very frosty, very frosty indeed, but still available for negotiation. She said, "Darling, if you'd lost him on account of me, I was sitting here deciding I was going to make one hell of a try at being worth the whole twenty big ones, but no broad in the world carries a tag like that. I might have choked up and blown the whole match."

"I like a practical woman."

"Can I drop you at his hotel?"

"Thanks, but I gave myself time to go pick up my car at the Sultana, if you want to drop me there."

"And wait for you, I hope, I hope?"

"I guess you better wait at your place, because I am not exactly together on price with this clown yet."

She lifted her purse onto her lap, opened it and dug around inside and took out a little flashlight. She gave it to me and I held it for her while she took out a little golden notebook with a snap fastener. She opened it and slipped the little gold pencil out of the little gold loop and said, "I just realized I'm absolutely starving, dear, so let's say it'll be ten before I get home. This is the unlisted number. And this is the address, on Indian Creek Drive, on the west side going north. Look for a raspberry-coloured thing with a white canopy and white awnings and white balconies. Call me first, love, because I want the delicious feeling you're on your way to me."

Again she drove the little red car. She whirred into the Sultana parking area, cutting off her lights as she did so to keep the front boys from noticing us and whistling her up to the entrance. She unstrung her bead, put her hat on the shelf in back, said, "Um" and splayed her little fingers on the nape of my neck and impacted a kiss with sufficient know-

how to leave my knees feeling loose and fragile as I strode
to my rental car after she had driven away.

At twenty to midnight, aboard *The Busted Flush*, after I
had washed up after my plate of scrambled eggs and onion,
I got the little sheet she had torn out of her notebook. It
was oyster-coloured parchment, thin and stiff, with tear-out
perforations down the left side. And in the bottom right-hand
corner was imprinted, in the plainest imaginable type face,
in gold: Love, Mary Smith.

I direct-dialled her number.

It rang five times, and then her muffled, silky voice said,
"Mmmmm?"

"T. McGee, ma'am."

I heard a small yowly yawn. "W'time zit, sweetie?"

"Quarter to Cinderella, almost."

"Mmm. I was having the most interesting dream about
you. And I have on this interesting little yellow night
garment I bought in Tokyo. And I dumped this and that in
the big hot tub, and so I smell interesting, sort of like between
sandalwood and old rose petals, and something else mixed
in. Some kind of spicy smell that makes me think of Mexico.
Do you like Mexico as much as I do? How soon will you
be here, my darling?"

"That's a very good question."

"I don't like the sound of that, somehow."

"That makes two of us."

"You sound so depressed. Troubles?"

"Out of the blue. Now we've ordered up some food and
we're waiting for a third party, and by dawn's early light
my guess is that we'll be a hundred miles from here looking
at the property in question, on the Tamiami Trail, just this
side of Naples."

"Oh poo!"

"I think I'd use a word with a little more bite to it."

She gave a long sigh. "Well," she said, "down, girl. Bear
me in mind, will you?"

"Get all the rest you need. And I will phone you precisely
at twelve noon tomorrow and we'll get out the old starting
blocks again."

"The old track shoes. Bang. They're off. Anyway, as long

as you might have some faint idea what you're missing, dear, drive a very hard bargain. You should be motivated. God knows."

After I hung up, I packed a pipe and took it topsides and stretched out on a dew-damp sunpad, down out of the bite of the breeze, and looked at the cold stars.

Where is the committee, I thought. They certainly should have made their choice by now. They are going to come aboard and make their speeches and I'm going to blush and scuff and say, "Shucks, fellas." The National Annual Award for Purity, Character, and Incomprehensible Sexual Continence in the face of an Ultimate Temptation. Heavens to Betsy, any American Boy living in the Age of Heffner would plunge at the chance to bounce that little pumpkin because she fitted the ultimate playmate formula, which is maximized pleasure with minimized responsibility. With a nice build, Charlie. With a lot of class, Charlie, you know what I mean. A broad that really goes for it, and she had a real hang-up on me, Charlie. You never seen any chick so ready, Charlie buddy, to scramble out of her classy clothes and hop into the sack. Tell you what I did, pal. I walked away. How about that?

There had to be a nice medal to go with the National Annual Award. With the insignia of the society. A shield with a discarded bunny tail, and an empty bed, and a buttock rampant on a field of cobwebs, with the Latin inscription, *Non Futchus*.

A nice pink and white old gentleman would pin the medal to the bare hide of the chest, as recommended by Joe Heller, while a violin would play, "Just Friendship, Friendship."

The ceremonial kiss on the stalwart, manly, unsullied cheek and. . . .

A huff of wind came and flipped the point of my collar against my throat. It ruffled the canvas laced to the sundeck rail. The collar was the tickle of the brisk red hair of Puss, and the canvas sound was her chuckle, and without warning I had such an aching longing for her it was like long knives in my bowels, and my eyes stung.

You never do anything for no reason at all, and you never refrain from doing something for no reason at all. Sometimes it just takes a little longer for the reason to get unstuck from the bottom of the brew and float to the top where you can see it.

I rapped the pipe out and went below. So it wasn't righteous denial at all. Or a lofty, supercilious disapproval. It was the monogamous compulsion based on the ancient wisdom of the heart. Puss had made of all of herself an abundant gift, not just the giving of the body or the sating of a physical want. And no matter how skilled the erotic talents of a Mary Smith, sensation would not balance out that privacy of self that she could not give, nor would want to, nor perhaps could ever give even if she wanted to.

And I knew just how it would have been with Mary Smith, because Puss was all too recent and all too sadly missed. All the secret elegancies of Mary Smith would merely have told me of wrong shapes, wrong sizes, wrong textures, wrong sounds from her throat, wrong ways of holding, wrong tempos and tryings and wrong oils of a wrong ungency. So it would have become with her a faked act of memory and mourning, to end in an after-love depression that would make the touch of her, the nearness of her, hugely irritating.

Puss was too recent.

After I was in bed, I went back and forth across the same old paradox: Then if Puss gave of herself so totally, opening up all the girl-cupboards in the back of heart and mind, how could she leave? Why did she leave?

There was a little chill that drifted across the back of my mind and was gone, as before, still unidentified.

There had been one cupboard unopened, all those months.

But at least I could now stop making wistful fantasies about the little garden of delights in its yellow garment from Tokyo.

Hogamus, Higamus. Mary's polygamous.

Higamus, Hogamus. Trav is monogamous.

For a while. It won't be any good until big Red wears off more. It will be a drag. And when it seems time to begin to expect something of it, and the opportunity comes along, don't risk it with a Mary Smith, whose involvement would be about on the same order as all other kinds of occupational therapy.

CHAPTER ELEVEN

ON Saturday before noon I looked through the stowage areas for fifteen minutes before I found my gadget. It is called the McGee Electric Alibi. The two D cells had expired, so I replaced them with fresh ones and tested it. Once upon a time it was a doorbell, but I removed the bell and replaced it with a piece of hardwood that has exactly the right timbre and resonance.

I direct-dialled my love and hunched over the desk top so I could listen to the earpiece and hold the mouthpiece at the pretested and precalculated distance from the mouthpiece. It only rang twice before she picked up the phone, but twice was enough to give me the duration and interval of the rings.

"Darling?" she said. It was exactly noon, as promised.

I pressed the button, transmitting the raucous clatter of a phone that keeps trying to ring after you've picked it up.

Between the first two imitation rings I heard her say, ". . . dammit to . . ." and in the next gap, ". . . stinking thing. . . ." I heard the clicking as she rattled the bar. ". . . n of a bitch. . . ." I gave it eight fake rings and that made ten in all, as they instruct you in the yellow pages, and hung up.

Poor guy calls up all steamed up, right on time, and she isn't even home. Fine thing. So he thinks maybe her clock is wrong and she ran out for a paper or a loaf of bread or something. Five minutes later I tried again, and she answered, and I rattled her eager, frustrated, infuriated, helpless little eardrum and this time heard her cry over and above the racket, "Goddamn it to hell!"

So on the off chance, the guy would call the office, so I phoned at once before she would decide I might, and a subdued voice said, "Three one two one."

"Is Mary Smith there, please? Extension sixty-six."

"Miss Smith is not in today, sir."

"Well . . . if she should come in or phone in, would you tell her that Mr. McGee has been trying to reach her, and he'll phone her at home again at three o'clock."

"Is there a number where she can reach you, sir?"

"No. I don't expect to be here much longer, thanks."

She would know I had the right number, as I had reached her before. I had the bell on my phone switched off. I could make outgoing calls, however. So I tried her at twelve thirty. She hung up on the second rasp. At one her line was busy when I tried it. I had been hoping for that. It would be a help. A few minutes later it wasn't busy. She caught it on the first ring. "Hello?" Raaaasp. Cry of pure respair. Clunk as she hung up.

Snoopy the dog wears a guilty and evil grin from time to time. I couldn't work one up.

Meyer and I were in the lounge going over final details when I suddenly realized it was exactly three. I had no time to prepare him for the Electric Alibi. I heard a distinct sob before she hung up.

He stared at me as I came back to the chair. "Sometimes you worry me, Travis. It's something about the way your mind works."

"I often find it depressing." I stood up again. "Hell, we're all set. I'm going to drive up and see Janine and Connie. I'll stay over, and drive down to Sunnydale early Monday. You get there about noon and get a motel room somewhere, and go to the hotel I told you about for lunch. I'll show up with our pigeon. I think that sometime about maybe five or six o'clock Miss Mary Smith will show up and beat on the doors. I think I've described her well enough. Keep an eye out for her and intercept her and tell her you think I'm on the Alabama Tiger's cruiser and point the way."

"Consolation prize?"

"Who for?"

He gave up and sighed and left. I phoned To-Co Groves and Connie's cry of pleasure at my coming was convincing enough. I buttoned up, switched the Sentry on, and put my gear in the car. Then I walked to the Tiger's permanent floating houseparty. Even with the boat closed up, the Afro-Cuban beat was loud. When I opened the door to the big main cabin area the sound nearly drove me backward. The big Ampex system was blasting, and the regulars were all around the perimeter because Junebug had herself a new challenger. She is a rubbery brown solid chunk of twenty-something-year-old girl, a sturdy mix of Irish, Gypsy and Cherokee. She wore a pink fuzzy bikini, and she was a go-going dervish, black short hair snapping, face and eyes a blur, body flexing and pumping to the beat, which Styles was sharpening with a blur of hands on the battered old bongos. The challenger was one of the king-sized beach bunnies, one of the big young straight-haired blondes about nineteen who look so much alike lately they should wear numbers on the side like stock cars. The money was in three piles on the deck by the Tiger's big bare feet. The big bunny was beginning to lag and flounder, miss the beat and catch up. Her mouth hung open. Her hip action in her zebra bikini was getting ratchety. The Tiger sat in a high glaze, swaying on the stool, smiling to himself, glass in hand. Muggsie Odell gave me her big smile, and I pointed at my watch and raised an eyebrow. She checked her watch, then flashed me seven sets of ten fingers plus four. Except for being so sweaty her body looked oiled, the Junebug looked absolutely fresh after seventy-four minutes of it. Maybe the challengers can go all day long to the beat they're used to, but they don't realize the additional demand on stamina of the Afro-Cuban tempo. One of them is reputed to have lasted over two hours before hitting the deck, but the Junebug wasn't even close to her own limit.

I crooked a finger at Muggsie. She nodded and followed me out and closed the hatch against the noise.

We sat on the wide transom and Muggsie said, "She's good for five more minutes, if that. I just as soon not be in there. They're waiting for her to fall down, and she's a stubborn kid and she'll keep going until she does drop. I just don't like to see them fall down like dead."

"A favour?"

"Depends. Probably yes, McGee."

"I'm going away for a couple of days. A very very nice little package is going to come right here looking for me. I'm having her steered here. The name is Mary Smith."

"No kidding!"

"Tell her I was here with the group but I went away and you think I said I was going to come back, so it would be best for her to wait. Meanwhile, has Hero been around?"

I was interrupted by a yell from the group. The door burst

open and somebody stopped the tape. The Junebug came out, yelling Ya HAA, Ya HAAA, and jumping into the air with every third stride. Through the open door I could see the bunny face-down on the deck trying to push herself up, with people reaching to help her. Junebug gave a great leap to the dock, spun the valve on the dock hose and held the nozzle aimed right at the crown of her head. After it had streamed down her face and across her smile and pasted her dark hair flat, she stuck the nozzle under her bikini top for a few moments and then under the elastic of the bikini bottoms and, with an ecstatic smile, worked it slowly all the way around to the back and around the other side of that muscular body to the front again.

"Anybody else?" she yelled. "Any new pigeon, step up and put your bread on the deck! The old Junebug is ready."

"I'd watch *her* fall," Muggsie said grimly. "I'd watch her fall and hope for a couple of good bounces. What's this with Hero? What are you asking about Hero?"

"Has he been around?"

"Who can stop him? You know Hero. Every hour, cruising in and seeing if there's any new stuff he hasn't seen before. With him it's a dedication. Are you saying aim Hero at this Mary Smith? What's the matter? You hate the girl?"

"Let's say they deserve each other. As soon as he starts trying to snow her, Muggsie, you go back to her and say you just heard that I came here in a bad mood and there was a girl who wanted to cheer me up and we went off together, so maybe there's no point in waiting."

"Why don't I just chunk her on the head and help Hero carry her back to his pad?"

"Because it is entirely possible she'll chunk him on the head and take him back to hers."

"Oh. One of those. Anyway, Hero certainly is a handsome guy, and he certainly has enough charm for a whole charm school, and he certainly has given an awful lot of lady tourists a vacation they'll never forget. I was saying just the other day, I could really go for that guy, if only he just wasn't a real rotten person through and through."

"You mean if you didn't know him."

"That's what I must mean. Wherever you're going, have

fun, Trav. I'll unite the happy couple and get her off your hands for good."

As I left I walked by Junebug on the dock, towelling herself dry. "Hey you, McGee," she said, with the big white mocking grin. "Hey, you never tole me when we're gonna start to go steady. How about it?"

I looked at all that brown rubbery, arrogant vitality. "I told you, Junebug, the very next time I get a death wish, I'll look you up."

"Some coward!"

"You can believe it."

"Aww. Poor fella. I wouldn't kill you. Just cripple you up pretty good, hah?"

"I think your trouble is that you're too shy. You lack self-confidence. Get out and meet people."

When I was a long way away I could still hear Junebug cawing with laughter.

I made good time and got to the Groves an hour after nightfall. We had drinks by the fire of fat pine, and a good dinner, and good talk. Janine got up and came over to me, hesitated, then leaned and touched her lips to the side of my face, and went off to bed.

Connie asked me what I thought of how Jan looked and acted.

"Listless. Thinner. More bones in her face."

"She's not eating well or sleeping well. She'll start to read or sew and end up staring into space. I hear her wandering around the house in the middle of the night. She's not coming out of it the way she should. I don't know what to do to snap her out of it. She's a damned fine girl, Trav. She's turning into a ghost."

"It's good of you to have her and the kids here."

"Don't be a jackass! I told her she can stay forever and I mean it. Those are three good kids. Five kids make a good kind of noise to have in the house. It's been quiet around here too damned long."

She asked about my redhead, and why I hadn't brought her along. When I said we'd called it off, she was suddenly furious, saying she thought I had more sense than that. I had to explain that it wasn't my idea and I'd been given no chance to make her change her mind. Then she was merely puzzled, saying it didn't make any sense at all.

On Sunday the three of us went fifty miles in Connie's Pontiac at her customary Indianapolis pace up to Rufus Wellington's law office. He had had his elderly secretary come in, and she was just finishing the typing of the deed and other documents pertinent to my sale of the Bannon property to Preston LaFrance. I had the power of attorney with me that Meyer had given me, which, when signed by Janine and witnessed, would authorize him to buy and sell securities in her name in the margin account he was establishing for her at the brokerage firm he used in Lauderdale.

Rufus eyed me and said, "You sure LaFrance will pay forty for an equity that isn't even there? Young man, do me the favour of not telling me what kind of persuasion you're fixing to use on him. I don't think I would like to know. I don't even want to know who this Meyer is, thank you. Any member of the bar is an officer of the court."

"If I have any trouble with the bank approving of the transfer of the mortgage to LaFrance, can you help?"

"I can phone Whitt Sanders and remind him of something that would make him approve transferring it to a little red hen. But I don't want to use it less I have to, just like I didn't have to when Connie went on the note with you. I have the feeling LaFrance is going to have trouble making those payments on the mortgage."

"If you don't want me to tell you anything, Judge, why do you make leading statements and then wait for me to explain?"

"Because I guess I figure you're not likely to tell me, son. But I do have a couple of clients here. You, Connie, and you, Miz Janine, and it would rest my mind to feel sure that nothing would come back on these ladies from anything too cute you are figuring on working on some of those folks down there in Sunnydale."

"Rest your mind, Judge," I said.

He leaned back, looked beyond us into the misty places of memory and said, "When I was a rough, wild young man, which seems like it was all in a different world than this one, I ended up down in Mexico one time, near Victoria, on a horse ranch. You had to prove you were all man. There was a thing they did, called the *paseo de muerte*. Maybe I don't have the lingo just right, but it's close. It was just riding full out, a full hard run over rocky land on half-broke horses, and the one who wants to test you, he comes up on you on one side, and he grins and you grin back and kick your feet free of the stirrups and you change horses right there, risking the way the footing is, and spooking one of the horses, or losing ahold. Once you'd show them you were ready to do it any-time, then they'd leave you be, because they weren't any more anxious deep inside to keep doing it than you were. Any fool could see that every time a man did it, his odds got shorter." He shook his head and smiled. "Long hours and short money, and one day out of noplace I could imagine came the idea I could start reading for the law. Why did I start all this? There was some point I was going to make. Oh. You keep in mind, Travis McGee, that the money game is one wild horse, and the vengeance for murder is another wild horse, and you try riding them both, you can fall between and get your skull stamped with an iron shoe. Bannon was your friend, and Connie's friend, and he was your husband, Miz Janine, daddy of your boys. Murder can come in when the money game goes bad. But don't think of it as being black dirty evil, but more of it being sick and sad, of some stumbling jackass that didn't mean it to come out that way, and he wakes up in the night and thinks on it and he gets sweaty and he hears his heart going like mad. Well, you folks have refused my kind offer to come on home with me for kitchen whisky and side meat and fancy conversation, so you will forgive me if I tell you all to be careful, and speed you on your way."

I phoned Press LaFrance in the late afternoon and arranged to meet him in Sunnydale the next morning. He sounded cautious and nervous and he gave me the impression of a certain evasiveness. He assured me the forty was still waiting, and he was anxious to listen, but I had the uneasy feeling that something had changed.

I went out to the sheds and sat on the truck dock, feeling dispirited. I finally admitted to myself that I felt guilty about Mary Smith. I could rationalize it as an adroit defensive manœuvre. Gary Santo had aimed her at me. Maybe the little code word had been "steak". He had evaluated me and decided there was enough chance of additional useful information to turn her loose. So I had sidestepped her and aimed her at Hero.

But, after all, she knew her way around. She was about as gullible, innocent and vulnerable as those limey lassies who had starred in the Profumo affair. It was a good chance that she would case Hero in about forty seconds and turn him off, because he could certainly never be a business assignment.

I wished, however, that one little comment about Hero had not lodged itself so firmly in my memory. He looked like the big, gentle, slow-moving, kindly star of a hundred Westerns, and he had the charm to make a woman feel admired, protected and cherished, until he could ease her back to his pad, or back to her place, or any nearby nest he could beg, borrow or rent.

And there he would tirelessly demonstrate that degree of satyriasis that stopped short of landing him in various kinds of corrective institutions. He cruised the festive areas and cut his quarry out of merry packs with easy skill and monomaniacal determination. The comment that lingered in my mind came from a weary man who came aboard Meyer's boat one hot Sunday afternoon and said, "Knowing Hero this long, I sure God should have had the good sense never to let him bring a woman aboard my ketch last evening, but with Myra and the kids off visiting her folks, and the forward cabin empty, and me a little smashed, I said okay and what he had was some young schoolteacher he'd found right over at the *Yankee Clipper* in a big batch of schoolteachers having a party before going on a five-day cruise to the Islands out of Everglades. The ship left this morning and she sure God isn't going to make that cruise. Giggly woman, kind of mousy and trying to get along without her glasses, and built real good, especially up front. His angle was showing her a Bahama-built ketch on account of she was going to the Bahamas. I left them aboard and that was nine or ten o'clock and I came back at midnight or later thinking they'd be gone. Honest to God, I'm dead for sleep, men. It would get quieted down and I'd be drifting off and it would start up again. With all that whinnying and squeaking and thrashing around, the nearest thing it sounds like, and it's still going on from time to time, is like somebody beating carpets with a shoat. One day Hero is going to nail him one with heart trouble and she just isn't going to last it out. I should have had more sense last night. Meyer, what would you say to me going below and getting a little nap?"

So maybe, I thought, Hero never came back to the Tiger's, or maybe Mary Smith never drove up from Miami to try to find me, and if she did, maybe Meyer missed her. Or little Muggsie could have decided she deserved better.

Janine came walking slowly from the house, hands deep in the pockets of a borrowed grey cardigan worn over white ranch jeans. She hadn't seen me, and when I called to her, she turned and came over.

"Have a good nap?"

"I slept a little." She sat on an upended cement block and reached and picked up a piece of lath and started drawing lines in the dirt with the sharp end. She tilted her head and stared up at me, squinting against the brightness of the sky.

"Trav," she said, "I keep wondering about one thing. It keeps bothering me. I keep trying to figure out what happened, but I can't seem to think of anything logical. It's sort of strange."

"Like?"

"How did Tush get out there? I had the car. He was going to come into Sunnydale by bus and phone me to come get him. Did somebody give him a ride, or what?"

"I never thought about that."

"Then, whoever gave him the ride could tell when he got there. They . . . found him at what time was it?"

"A sheriff's deputy found him at nine o'clock, approximately. The medical examiner estimated he had been dead from one to four hours at the time he was found."

"From five thirty to eight thirty, then. In there somewhere, somebody . . . killed him. But he was so strong, Trav. You know how powerful he was. He wouldn't just stretch out and let somebody. . . . He was dead when they put him there. Maybe whoever drove him out there saw somebody hanging around."

"We're going to get to all that, Jan. Believe me, we're

going to do our best to find out. But first we've got to do some salvage work for you."

She made a bitter mouth and looked down and drew a dollar sign. She reached a foot out and slowly scuffed it out. "Money. It got to mean so damned much, you know. Getting pinched worse and worse, and snapping at each other about it, and being so scared we were going to lose the whole thing we started with. And now it doesn't mean anything. Nothing at all."

"With those three kids to bring up? Shoes and dentists and school and presents?"

"Oh, I suppose it will be something I'll have to think about. But right now I'm just . . . nowhere. You're sure you can fix it so I'll end up with thirty thousand clear, and you seem so sure you can make me a lot more out of that stock stuff I don't understand at all. I ought to sound grateful and pleased and delighted and so on."

"Not for my sake. Or Meyer's."

"Everybody is doing things for me. But I ran. Everybody knows that. I'm a lousy person. I don't like myself. Trav, I used to like myself well enough."

I slid off the dock and took her hand and pulled her up. "Let's walk for a while." We walked and I gave her some dreary little sermons about how never quite matching up to what you want of yourself is the basic of the human condition. She heard, but I don't know if she believed. I was trying hard to believe my own hard sell, because I kept thinking of carpets and shoats and wide wide emerald eyes and a delicately provocative little pressure of teeth against the knuckles of my stupid right hand.

CHAPTER TWELVE

I ARRIVED in downtown Sunnydale at nine o'clock on Monday morning and parked in the bank lot, and walked toward the Shawana River Hotel, where I had arranged to meet LaFrance in the coffee shop.

When I went into the lobby, two men in green twill uniforms moved in from either side to position themselves with an unhurried competence between me and the glass double doors. A cricket-sized man of about sixty planted himself spread-legged in front of me and said, "Nice and easy, now. You just lay both hands atop your head. You're a big one, all right. Freddy?"

One of the others came in from behind and reached around me and patted all the appropriate pockets and places. I had recognized the sheriff's voice from having heard it over the phone. He wore a businessman's hat wadded onto the back of his head. Straight grey hair stuck out in Will Rogers style. He wore an unpressed dark suit with a small gold star in the lapel. The suit coat hung open, exposing a holstered belly gun small enough to be an Airweight. Small enough to look toylike, but in no sense a toy.

The legal papers, billfold and keys were handed to Sheriff Bunny Burgoon. From his voice I had thought he would be all belly, with porcine features. He opened the wallet, flipped through the pliofilm envelopes. He stopped at the driver's licence and studied it.

"Your name Travis McGee? You can put your hands down, boy."

"That's my name."

"Now we're going on over to my office and talk some."

"Can I ask why?"

"It's my duty to tell you that you got no obligation to answer any questions I or any of my officers may ask you without the presence of any attorney of your choice, and you are in your rights to request the Court appoint an attorney to represent your interests in this matter, and anything you say in response to interrogation, with or without the presence of your legal representative, may be held in evidence against you."

He had run all the words together, like a court clerk swearing a witness.

"Is there a charge?"

"Not up to this minute, boy. You're being taken in for interrogation in connection with a felony committed in the county jurisdiction."

"If I'm being taken in, Sheriff, then it is an arrest, isn't it?"

"Boy, aren't you coming along willingly and voluntarily like is the duty of any citizen to assist law officers in the pursuit of their duty?"

"Why certainly, Sheriff! Willingly and voluntarily, and not in the cage in the back of a county sedan, and with my keys and papers and wallet in my pockets. Otherwise it's an arrest, and if so, my personal attorney is Judge Rufus Wellington and you better get him on the horn and get him down here."

"Read his name in the paper, boy?"

"Instead of bothering the judge, why don't you just ask Whitt Sanders if the judge represents me?"

I was watching for a shift of uncertainty in his eyes and saw it. Apparently he had not anticipated any connection with the local power structure. He motioned one of the two deputies close, stood tall, and without taking his eyes off me, murmured into the younger man's ear. The deputy walked out. Burgoon asked me to come over and sit on a couch in the lobby. The deputy was back in five minutes and the sheriff went over and talked quietly with him, then came over and gave me back my possessions. With one of the deputies ten paces behind us, we walked through the morning sunshine to the Shawana County Courthouse and around to the side and into the entrance labelled COUNTY SHERIFF.

I was aware of a particularly avid curiosity on the part of the desk personnel and the communication clerk as he led me back into his office. The slats of the blinds were almost closed. He turned on the ceiling fluorescence and his desk lamp. He had me sit in a straight chair facing his desk and six feet from it. The sheriff looked at the papers on his blotter, put them aside and sat in his big black chair. A portly man in deputy uniform came in and sighed and sat in a chair back against the wall. "Willie will be bringing it along, Sherf."

Burgoon nodded. There was silence. I looked at the framed testimonials on the walls, and the framed pictures of Burgoon taken with various political notables, past and present. Some file drawers were partially open. The contents looked untidy, with documents sticking up out of the file folders.

"Make that deal with Harry?" Burgoon asked.

The portly one said, "He give me an estimate of over seventeen hundred. And it was supposed to be a twenty-year roof. I told Cathy we could buy a lot of buckets to set under the leaks for seventeen hundred."

"Harry does nice work."

"Wisht I'd used him when I was building."

Burgoon looked at me. "You made up your mind about a lawyer yet, mister?" I had been promoted from boy.

"Sheriff, I think it would be easier for me to make that decision if I had more information about what you think I did. It could be something we might be able to straighten out without bothering anybody."

"Maybe. Maybe not."

"When and where did the alleged crime take place? That might give me something to go on."

"It took place, mister, on the morning of December seventeenth last, and it took place at a marina on the Shawana River just about eleven miles east of here."

"That was a Sunday morning?"

"Yes it was."

"Would you be trying to make a capital case, Sheriff?"

"Murder first."

I remembered that Sunday with no trouble. Puss, Barni Baker, Mick Coseen, Meyer, Marilee, in fact a lot more people than we had needed or wanted aboard, and a dozen ways to refresh their memories that it was that exact day.

"Just one more question and I can give you an answer. Am I supposed to be connected with it in some way, or are you trying to say I was there at that time?"

"There at that time and did commit an act of violence which resulted in the death of one Brantley B. Bannon."

"Then, I don't think I need a lawyer to straighten things out."

It seemed to startle Burgoon. He said irritably, "Tom, what the hell is holding up that damn Willie?"

"Right here, Sheriff. Right here," said a thin young man who came in carrying a tape recorder. He put it on the corner of the sheriff's desk, knelt on the rug and plugged it in. "Sheriff, you just push——"

"I know, I know! Get on back to work and close the door." When the door was closed, Burgoon said, "We took this with the court reporter and on tape at the same time, and there hasn't been time to transcribe it yet. You get to hear it on account of now we've got that damn new law on full disclosure, and the defence would get a certified copy of the transcript anyways, and the State's Attorney said it was all right I should do it this way. You listen, and then you answer questions and make a statement, and then we hold you and this goes to a special meeting of the Grand Jury for the indictment so you can be arraigned proper."

He punched it on and leaned back and closed his eyes and rested his fingertips together. The tape had a lot of hiss. Apparently nobody ever bothered to clean or demagnetize the heads. But the questions and answers were clear enough.

I recognized the flat, insipid, dreary little-girl voice before she even gave her name, saying that she was Mrs. Roger Denn, Arlene Denn, and that she had been living with her husband at the Banyan Cottages, Cottage number 12 ever since the tenth of December, that she was twenty-two years old and that she was self-employed, as was her husband, making and selling art objects to gift shops. Prior to that time they had lived aboard a houseboat the Bannons had rented them, tied up at the Bannon Boatel on the river, and had lived there eight months.

"What were the circumstances of your leaving?"

"Well, they had to come and take the houseboats back. They owed on them and some men came and towed them off, I don't know where. That was . . . early in December, I don't know exactly what day."

"What happened then?"

"We put all our things in the two end units of the motel just for a while, until we could find something, because Mr. Bannon said it looked like he might lose the place. We went looking and we found a place at the Banyan Cottages and moved in on the tenth, and we were making trips in the station wagon to bring our supplies and so on back to the cottages."

As she spoke on the tape, through the hiss, I could picture her clearly, pallid and sloppy and doughy, with dirty blonde hair and a mouth that hung open, and meaningless blue eyes.

"What was the occasion of your last visit to Bannon's motel."

"It was because of missing some silver wire. We use it in the jewellery. On Saturday, that was the sixteenth, we

looked all over for it and it was just gone. We knew then
that the place was foreclosed out there, but we still had a
key to the end units on account of Roger forgot to leave it
off when we made the last trip. I kept thinking that maybe
what could have happened to it, we had a lot of supplies
piled on the beds and maybe the wire slipped down and
caught somehow like at the headboard or the footboard,
because I had crawled around looking to see if we'd left
anything on the floor the last trip we took. Roger kept saying
to forget it because it was real trouble going into a place
sealed off by the court, and maybe they'd changed the locks.
But it was twenty dollars' worth of wire and maybe seventeen
left on the roll, and we don't do so good we can just throw
away seventeen dollars. So we sort of had a fight about it,
and I said I was going to go out there whether he was or not,
so I went out when it was just getting to be daylight the next
day, which was Sunday. I drove right on by, slow, to see
if anybody was there and I didn't see anybody, so I went
a ways up the road and put the station wagon in a little kind
of overgrown place that used to be a cleared road once. I
backed it in. You know, kind of hiding it, and I went back
with the key and when I was pretty sure nobody was around,
I tried the key and it worked and I let myself in and started
hunting for that wire."

"What happened next?"

"I guess I was hunting for maybe ten minutes or fifteen
minutes. I don't know just what time it was. Maybe sometime between seven and seven thirty and I heard a car coming,
so I squatted down so nobody could look in and see me when
they went by. One of the windows, those awning kind of
window things, was open three or four inches. So I heard
the car drive in and it stopped and then I heard a car door
slam and then I heard another car door slam and I heard
men's voices."

"Could you hear what was said?"

"No sir. They were loudest near the car and then kind
of faded when they were walking toward the marina. I
couldn't hear words but I had the feeling they were mad at
each other, almost shouting. I think one word that was shouted
was Jan. That was Mrs. Bannon's name. Janine. But I couldn't
be sure."

"What happened next?"

"I didn't know what to do. I was afraid to leave. I tried to peek out the windows and see where they went to, to see if it was safe for me to sneak out."

"Could you see the car?"

"No sir. But I knew I would hear it if it started up."

"Then what happened?"

"Somebody shouted a lot louder, and further away, and I knew they were real mad. It sounded to me like Mr. Bannon. Then it was quiet. Then maybe five minutes later I looked out the back window that looks toward the river, and I saw a man dragging Mr. Bannon across the ground. He had his arms wrapped around Mr. Bannon's ankles and he was leaning forward and pulling hard and pulling Mr. Bannon along. I was kneeling and looking out a corner of the window, like with one eye. He dragged him right to that old hoist thing and then kind of rolled and shoved and pushed him under the motor. Mr. Bannon was real limp, like unconscious or dead. The man stood up and looked at him and then he looked all round. I ducked down and when I got up enough nerve to look again, he was walking toward the hoist thing again from the marina and he was carrying something small, some wire and something. I watched him and he kneeled down and did something to Mr. Bannon I couldn't see, and then he worked some more at the hoist thing. Then he turned the crank and the motor went up real slow. I could hear the clickety sound it made. Then he stood near the gear part and bent over and did something and . . . the motor fell down onto Mr. Bannon. There was a rackety sound when it came down and the wire ropes slapped around and hit those poles and made a ringing sound."

"And then?"

"He cranked it up halfway and looked at Mr. Bannon close, and cranked it up the rest of the way and let it fall on him again. When he cranked it up again, Mr. Bannon looked . . . kind of flattened out. He didn't put it all the way up again. He just let it fall from there and he left it there and picked up something off the ground and then kind of stopped and dropped it and then picked it up and wiped it on some kind of a rag and dropped it again. He was nearly running when he left. And then I heard one car door slam and after a little while the car started up. I stayed way down until it was gone."

"Which way did it go?"

"Back this way, toward Sunnydale."

"Did you get a look at the man?"

"Yes sir, I did."

"Had you ever seen him before?"

"Yes sir."

"Would you recognize him if you saw him again?"

"Yes sir."

"Do you know him by name?"

"Yes sir."

"What is his name?"

"His name is Mr. McGee."

"Under what circumstances did you first see Mr. McGee?"

"I only saw him two times before that, both on the same day. It was back in October. I don't know the exact day. He was a friend of theirs and he came in a nice boat to visit them. He took them over to Broward Beach in the boat that night for dinner and I sat with the little boys. So I met him when I came over to sit, and then I saw him again when they came back."

"Did they seem friendly, McGee and the Bannons?"

"I . . . guess so."

"You seem hesitant. Why?"

"I had the feeling it was Mrs. Bannon he came to see."

"What gave you that feeling?"

"Well, actually I saw him three times that day. It was an awful hot day. Mr. Bannon and Mr. McGee had fixed Mr. Bannon's car. Then Mr. Bannon went off to get the boys from school. I saw Mrs. Bannon taking a pitcher of iced tea to one of the units. I wanted to ask her about something she was going to bring me from town, to save a trip. I needed it in my work and I went down there to where she took the iced tea, thinking she would come right out. When she didn't, I sort of looked in the window. I didn't know his name then, not until later. But I saw Mr. McGee and Mrs. Bannon laying on the bed, kissing."

"Did you notice anything else that day in October that seemed odd or unusual to you?"

"No sir. Nothing else at all, sir."

"What did you do after McGee drove away?"

"Well, I thought I better wait a little while in case he forgot something and came back. So I looked for the wire some more and I found it. I left and made sure the door was locked and then I ran all the way to our car. I threw the key in the bushes when I was getting into the car, the room key."

"Why did you do that?"

"I was very frightened, I guess. I didn't want anybody to know I'd been in the motel."

"I show you a motel room key. Is this that same key you threw away?"

"I think so. Yes sir. That's the key."

"Did you relate all this to your husband?"

"No sir. I didn't tell him anything."

"Why not?"

"Because he said I shouldn't go out there, and even though I did find the silver wire, he was still right about that. I wish I hadn't gone out there that Sunday morning."

"Will you tell us why you finally came forward, Mrs. Denn?"

"I thought they would catch Mr. McGee. But they didn't. I worried and worried about it and the other night I told my husband the whole thing and he said I had to come and see you. I begged him not to make me do it but he said I had to. That's why I'm here."

Sheriff Burgoon turned it off. "There's more. But it covers the same ground. It doesn't bring up anything new. It's an eyeball witness, boy, with nothing to gain or lose. We took her out there and she showed us the window and you get a real good view from there."

He had demoted me back to boy, heartened by his evidence.

"I think she saw almost exactly what she says she saw, sheriff."

"Want to change your mind about a lawyer?"

"Motive, opportunity, weapon, and an eyewitness. Sheriff, don't you think it's all wrapped up just a little too neatly?"

"A man can be damn unlucky."

"How true. I wonder just who he is."

"Suppose you make a little sense."

"Okay. Here is something that the unlucky man, whoever

he is, had to take a chance on. He had to take a chance on there being some probability or possibility of my being in this area at that time, and my having no way to prove I wasn't."

"It's going to take a pretty good piece of proof."

"I can place myself aboard my houseboat where I live, *The Busted Flush*, Slip F-18, Bahia Mar, Fort Lauderdale, at nine o'clock that Sunday morning. Does the rest of the tape establish her best guess as to the time I'm supposed to have left after the murder?"

"Maybe eight thirty, give or take fifteen minutes," he said. "But let's get to just how you place yourself there and how come you'd remember it so good."

"Because I arrived at Bannon's place the following afternoon and found out he was dead. I found out he had died the previous morning. Somehow you remember what you were doing at the time a good friend died."

"And just what were you doing?"

"Socializing, Sheriff Burgoon. Being a jolly host, right out in front of everybody. I think that I could probably come up with the names of at least twenty people who saw me and talked to me between nine and ten o'clock that morning. Some of them are totally unreliable. I don't pick them for social standing and credit rating, and I wouldn't ask you or anyone to believe them if they swore on every Bible in Shawana County. But there are a half dozen well worth believing. Suppose you write down the names and addresses and pick a couple of names off the list and question them by phone right now any way you feel like. Try any trick or trap you can think up."

"What did you mean saying she saw almost exactly what she says she saw, mister?"

"She saw everything except me doing it. She saw somebody else do it, and that changes your theory about nothing to gain or lose."

"How do you mean?"

"Somebody prepped her pretty good, Sheriff. I might even have thought that she saw somebody she sincerely mistook for me. But the iced tea sequence was a little too much."

"Didn't happen?"

"I got hot and sweaty helping Tush fix the spring shackle

on his car. I showered in the motel unit they loaned me. I had just finished dressing when Jan brought the pitcher of tea and two glasses. We talked about the problems they were having. Maybe fat-girl even looked in the window. But no bed and no kisses. Nothing like that between us. Not even any thought of it on either side. At the moment I happen to own the Bannon place, Sheriff. I bought it from Jan Bannon. Why in hell would I do that?"

"*You* are the one who bought it!"

"I'm here today to try to resell it to Press LaFrance."

Burgoon looked very thoughtful. "He's surely been wanting it so bad he could taste it. Trying to put some kind of parcel together for resale. Don't he own a patch out there, Tom?"

"Fifty acres right behind."

Burgoon nodded. "Probably could move it if he had river frontage to go with it."

Tom scrubbed his snow-white brush cut and coughed and said, "Bunny, that Bannon woman didn't seem to me to be that kind of woman when I had to go out there and roust her and the kids out and seal it up. That's one part of this job I surely hate. We tried to make it easy as we could, but there isn't any good way to make it easy. She was one upset woman and you can believe it."

The sheriff asked me for the names of my witnesses and wrote them down.

I thought of something else. How come they had been waiting for me at the hotel? And did that have anything to do with LaFrance's evasiveness when I had phoned him?

"Who told you I was coming to the hotel, Sheriff?"

"Wasn't it Freddy dug that up, Tom?" Burgoon asked. When Tom nodded, Burgoon said, "Didn't you say you were coming here to see Press LaFrance? Then, that answers it, sure enough. Freddy Hazzard is Press's nephew, his sister's eldest boy. He's my youngest deputy, mister. You saw him at the hotel, the lanky one."

"Is he the son of one of your County Commissioners?"

"Sure is. Monk's boy. But that's got no bearing on me taking him on. Freddy came out of service with a good record in the M.P. and he earns his pay right down the line."

"Didn't somebody say that it was somebody named Freddy who found the body?"

"That's right. On a routine patrol at nine thirty. You see, I had a note for Bannon from his missus, and she'd left a suitcase here for him, and I didn't know but what Bannon might hitch a ride to his place or come by boat or something. She'd said he was planning to be back Friday or Saturday, so I had the boys keeping an eye on it out there off and on." He peered at me. "You getting at something?"

"I don't know, Sheriff. I'm going to check out all right. You have a hunch I will, and you hate to admit it to yourself because it's such a nice neat painless little case."

He slapped his hand on the desk top. "But why would some other damned fool, if somebody else besides you did it, why would they want to pick *you* for it? They should know there was a chance you'd be in the clear. Why not some description to fit somebody we'd look for and never find?"

"Suppose this person heard, second hand, that I had a theory somebody had done too good a job of working Tush Bannon over and killed him, then dropped the engine on him to hide the traces, and fixed the wire to make it look like suicide?"

"If you can prove you said that to anybody at any time, mister, it might be more help than this list of folks I wrote down."

"I told that same person that maybe it was somebody who was trying to do him a favour and do Monk Hazzard a favour, by trying to take some of the spunk out of Bannon so he would leave quietly. Because the person I was talking to has been trying to get that land."

"LaFrance?" Burgoon said, almost whispering it. "Tom, you think Press ought to come in for a little talk?"

"Can I make a suggestion, Sheriff?" I asked.

"You mean you've got another way to make things worse than they are right now?"

"Isn't the weakest place the fat girl? She lied and she'll know who made her lie. Don't you think she could be brought in to make a positive identification?"

"You ever been in this line of work?"

"Not directly."

"You got a record, mister?"

"Four arrests. No convictions, Sheriff. Nothing ever even came to trial."

"Now, just what would those arrests have been for, mister?"

"Assault, which turned out to be self-defence. Breaking and entering, and it turned out I had the owner's permission. Conspiracy, and somebody decided to withdraw the charges. Piracy on the high seas, dismissed for lack of evidence."

"You're not exactly in any rut, are you? Tom, send somebody after that Arlene Denn."

After he left, I said to the Sheriff, "When did she make that statement?"

"Saturday, starting about . . . maybe eleven in the morning."

"Did you try to have me picked up in Lauderdale?"

"Sure did."

"And Deputy Hazzard found out yesterday in the late afternoon that I would be at the hotel this morning?"

"He got the tip last night and phoned me at home."

"Did he have any objections to the way you set it up to take me?"

"Well . . . he did say maybe if I stationed him across there, like on the roof of the service station with a carbine, it would be good insurance if you smelled something and decided not to go into the hotel at all." He shook his head. "Freddy is a good boy. It doesn't fit the way you want me to think it fits."

"I'm not trying to sell you anything."

In twenty minutes Tom brought her in. She stopped abruptly just inside the door and gave me a single glassy blue look and looked away. She wore a paint-spattered man's T-shirt hanging outside her bulging jeans, and apparently nothing under the T-shirt.

"Move over near Tom and let her set in that chair," he said to me. She sat and stared at Burgoon, her face so vapid she looked dimwitted.

"Now then, Arlie," said Burgoon, "we had a nice talk day before yesterday and you helped us a lot and we appreciate it. Now, don't you be nervous. There's another part of it you've got to do. Do you know that man setting over there by Tom."

". . . Yes sir."

"What's his name, Arlie?"

"The one I told you about. Mr. McGee."

"Now, you turn and look at him and be sure and if you are sure it's the man you saw dropping that engine onto Mr. Bannon, you point your finger at him and you say, 'That's the same man'."

She turned and she looked at the wall about a foot over my head and stabbed a finger at me and said, "That's the same man."

"You had a clear view of him on the morning of December seventeenth? No chance of a mistake?"

"No sir."

"Now, don't be nervous. You're doing just fine. We've got another little problem you can help us with. It turns out Mr. McGee was way down in Fort Lauderdale that same identical morning at the same time you think you saw him, and he was on a boat with some very important people. A federal judge and a state senator and a famous surgeon, and they say he was right there at that same time. Now, Arlie, just how in the wide world are we going to get around that?"

She stared fixedly at him, her mouth sagging open.

"Arlie, are those big people lying and are you the one telling the truth, so help you God?"

"I saw what I saw."

"Who told you to make up these lies, Arlie?"

"I told you what I saw."

"Now, Arlie, you recall what I said before, about you having the right to be represented by a lawyer and so on?"

"So?"

"I'm telling you again, girl. You don't have to answer any questions. Because I think I'm going to hold you and book you."

She shrugged plump shoulders. "Do what you feel like."

Crickety little Burgoon glanced over at Tom and then looked at the fat girl again. "Girl, I don't think you rightly know just how much trouble you're asking for. You see, I *know* you're lying."

Tom, responding to his signal, came in on cue. "Bunny, why in God's name you being so kindly to this fat dumb slut? Let me run her on out to the stockade and turn her over to Miss Mary. Leave her out there three or four days and Miss Mary would purely enjoy sweatin' off fifteen pounds of slop and teaching her some manners. She'd have a nice attitude when you have her brought back in."

Arlene Denn turned and stared at Tom. She bit her lip and swallowed and looked back at Burgoon, who said, "Now, if we have to come to that, Tom, we'll come to that. But this isn't any ninety-day county case. And this isn't any one to five up to the state women's prison. What the law of the State of Florida says is that giving false testimony in a capital case, or withholding evidence in a capital case is punishable by a maximum sentence of imprisonment for the rest of her natural life."

She stiffened as much as her figure permitted, sat up straight and said, "You've got to be kidding, Sheriff!"

"You know how to read, girl?"

"Of course I know how to read!"

He dug a battered manual out of a desk drawer, licked his thumb and found the right page. He handed it across to her. "Second paragraph down. That there is sort of a short form of everything against the law. It's what new deputies have to study up on and pass a test."

She read it and handed the manual back. She looked over at me. The look of vacuous stupidity was gone, and I realized it was the mask she wore for the world she was in.

"Now, without me saying I *would* change my story, Sheriff, let's suppose I did. What would happen to me?"

"Would the new story be the exact truth, Arlie?"

"Let's say it would be."

"Would it have you out there seeing anything at all?"

"Let's say it would have me seeing somebody else instead of Mr. McGee. Let's say that when I looked in the window, Mr. McGee and Mrs. Bannon were just talking."

Burgoon said, "What do you think, Tom?"

"I think she ought to do some laundry work for Miss Mary for thirty days."

"Maybe. Maybe not. I'd say it's going to depend on *why* she showed up with those lies."

"Regardless," said Arlie, "would you bust me for any more than thirty days?"

"Only if it turns out you're telling more lies. We are going to check this new one out every way there is, girl."

"Okay, then, here is the way it really was. . . ."

The sheriff told her to wait a moment. He spoke into his intercom and got hold of Willie and told him to bring in some fresh tape, and told him the Denn girl was changing her story, and stop the transcript on the old story. Willie groaned audibly. He came in with the fresh tape, took the old one off the machine and set it for record.

"It's mostly all still good what I said before," Arlene said. "I just have to change some parts. I mean it would save doing the whole question bit right from the start, wouldn't it?"

"Then, save that tape, Willie," said Bunny Burgoon, "and close the door on the way out."

He started the tape rolling, and established time and place and the identity of the witness.

"Now, Mrs. Denn, you have told us that you wish to change portions of your previous statement."

"Just two . . . no, three parts."

"What would be the first change?"

"I didn't hear anybody say anything that sounded like Jan. The two men were mad at each other, but I didn't hear any word like that."

"And what is the second change you wish to make?"

"What if you decide to protect your own and throw me to the dogs, Sheriff?"

"What is the second change you wish to make?"

"Well . . . it wasn't Mr. McGee I saw. The man I saw did everything in the other statement the way I told it. But it was Deputy Sheriff Freddy Hazzard."

"Oh, God *damn* it!" said Tom.

"Hush up," said Bunny. "And the third change?"

"I looked in the window back in October but they were just talking. Drinking tea. That was all."

"Now, hold it a minute, girl. Tom, you go tell Walker and Englert to pick Freddy up and bring him back here and. . . . Damn it, tell them to take his weapon and put him in the interrogation room and hold him until I can get around to him. When does he come on duty, Tom?"

"I think tonight he's on the eight to eight again. But you know Freddy."

"Sheriff?" the girl said as Tom left the office. "You weren't having me on, were you? About how big I could get busted for telling something that didn't happen?"

"I never said a truer thing in my life, Mrs. Denn."

"Why box me?" I asked her.

The vacant blue look she gave me was a total indifference. "Every straight one looks exactly alike to me."

Tom came back in looking distressed. "Damn it all, Bunny, he was out there checking the skip list when you came over the box telling Willie this girl was changing her story. And he walked right out and took off. He's in uniform, driving number three. Terry is trying to raise him on the horn but no answer. All points?"

Burgoon closed his eyes and rattled his fingers on the desk top. "No. If he's running, there's eighty-five back ways out of this county and he knows every one of them. Let's see what more we've got here." He leaned wearily and put the recorder back on.

"Who induced you to lie about what you saw that Sunday morning, Arlie?"

"Deputy Hazzard."

"What inducement did he offer you?"

"Not to get busted for possession, and some other things he said he could bust us for."

"Possession? Do you mean narcotics, girl?"

"That's your word. That's the fuzz word. But all we had was acid and grass. Booze is a lot worse for you."

"Arlie, are you and your husband addicts?"

"What does that mean? We're affiliates with the group up in Jax. And we get up there now and then. We take trips sometimes here, but it's a group thing. You couldn't comprehend, Sheriff. We all have our own thing. We don't bug the straights, and why shouldn't they leave us alone?"

"How did Deputy Hazzard learn you'd been a witness?"

"Like an accident. Last Thursday night out at the Banyan Cottages there was a complaint from somebody, and I guess it would be on your records here someplace. I didn't even know Hazzard's name. But he was the one who came there. Five of the kids had come down from Jax, three of them gals, in an old camper truck in the afternoon, from the Blossom Group in Jacksonville, and they had some new short acid from the Coast that never gives you a down trip and blows your mind for an hour only. We had almost two lids of Acapulco Gold, and we just started a lot of turn-ons there in the cottage, relating to each other, that's all. At night, sometime, I don't know what time, maybe the music got too loud. An Indian record. East Indian, and the player repeats and repeats. Maybe it was the strobes. We've got one and they brought two, and each one had a different recycle time, so there was a kind of pattern changing all the time. I guess you have to know the way it was when Hazzard came busting in. We had the mattresses and the blankets on the floor, and one of the gals was a cute little teeny-bopper and I'd painted her all over eyes."

"Ice?" said the sheriff.

"Eyes," she said impatiently. "Like eyeballs and eyelashes. All colours. And one boy and girl were wearing just little bells and rattles. You do whatever. Who are you hurting? It was blossom-time. A love-in, sort of, and our own business. Just with the strobe lights and the samisen music and he came breaking in because maybe we didn't hear him. Him and his gun and his black leather evil thing for hitting and hurting. You can't turn off a high like in a second. So he found the lights and ordered things in a big voice and nobody did what he said or cared. So he starts yelling and chunking people. The teeny-bopper wanted to tune him in and turn him on I guess and she started throwing flowers at him and he chunked her too. Of the seven of us he chunked the four that were turned on to the biggest high, chunked them cold, and he chunked the record player, busted it all to hell and got the other three of us finally sitting in a row on the cold bare bed springs holding onto the backs of our necks. Not scared or angry or anything. Just sorry there's no way of ever getting through to that kind of a straight. All he thinks of is busting people and busting things. And he chunked all the three strobes and broke them up. They're expensive and hard to find ones that don't overheat and burn out when you keep them cycling a long time. In my high I understood all about him. He was breaking things and hitting heads because he hated himself, and I had seen him mushing Mr. Bannon with that heavy motor, and I knew that was why he hated himself. He collected up all the grass and the three little vials of powdered acid, and he picked up all the colour polaroids laying around that a boy had taken earlier to take back to Jax to the group on account of the girl painted all over eyes was a big turn-on for him."

"Lord Jesus God Almighty," said the sheriff in a hushed voice.

"He was going to radio for help and take everybody in and bust them, and I just felt sorry for him being so empty of love and so I said to him that he hated himself for what he did to Mr. Bannon. He looked at me and he picked up a blanket and wrapped it around me and took me out in the night. He shoved me up against his car and I told him the whole thing, just the way I saw it. I told him he could trade in his hate for love, and we could show him the way. I could feel myself beginning to come off the high, because I began to think about it being a lot of bad trouble, and it was a poor time to get busted because of orders Roger and I had to fill. He kept wanting to know who I'd told about it, and while I was coming off the trip I got smart enough to say maybe I had and maybe I hadn't. So he said he was going to keep the evidence and think about what he was going to do, and we should cool it and he would come talk to me the next day.

"So in the morning the kids headed on away in the camper truck and the first thing I did was tell Roger the whole thing. That was Friday, and Hazzard came out in the afternoon and sent Roger out of the place and talked to me. He said he'd put the evidence away in a safe place, and in the pictures he had proof on both Roger and me on the teeny-bopper on corrupting a minor, and lewd and lascivious conduct. Then he questioned me over and over on what I saw that Sunday. Then he brought up if I knew a friend of Bannon's named McGee. I told him about just that one day, and he made me remember every little part of it. So he walked back and forth and then he told me I was going to come in and make a statement and what I was going to say. I asked him why I should do anything he said, because if he left us alone, I wouldn't say anything about him. He said if I didn't do it, he would bust us both good, and he had enough proof and enough charges to get us both five to ten anyway. And I said if he tried to bust us that way, when he took us in, I'd tell what I saw him do. And he said then it would be pretty clear to everybody that I was making it up just to try to get him in trouble for doing his job and nobody would believe it because nobody ever believes an acid head about anything,

and those pictures would make a hog sick. He said if I did
my part, then after McGee was convicted, he'd give back
everything he took. Then he gave me a chance to talk it over
alone with Roger and for a while we thought maybe we ought
to just take off and go merge into a colony some place, but
we went that road for a while and we relate better like
plastics."

"What?" What?" asked the sheriff.

"Take the group thing now and then, and have a square
thing we do for bread. We take off and we lose the trade
we've built up that comes to maybe a hundred and fifty a
week on average, and then maybe that Hazzard could get us
brought back anyhow." She combed the fingers of both hands
back through the dark blonde stiffness of her long hair, shook
it back and said, "So we decided okay, only what we didn't
know is how I could get busted a lot bigger for the statement
than for what he's got on us, and I didn't know McGee would
be in the clear, because he said maybe McGee might not even
get to answer any questions at all. So where are we?"

"Where are you?" the sheriff asked. "Honest to God, I
don't even know *what* you are, girl."

I looked at my watch. It was just eleven o'clock. The sheriff
told Arlie he'd like to hold her and her husband in protective
custody on a voluntary basis, and she agreed. I knew that
part of the case against Freddy Hazzard would be Press
LaFrance's testimony about whatever conversation he'd had
with his nephew, triggered by my comment to LaFrance about
the possible reason why Tush had been killed. But had I
reminded Burgoon of that point, he was going to mess up
my timing, which was already two hours off. So I wondered
out loud if Tush could have come in by bus early Sunday
morning and if Hazzard, cruising around, had picked him up
near the bus station and driven him out there.

Arlie had been taken off to the female detention tank.
Tom, the chief deputy, said that if anybody could place
Hazzard and Bannon together in town at dawn on Sunday,
it would lock it up tighter.

"Tighter than the way he run?" Burgoon asked. "He was
a *good* boy. He worked harder than any two others I got.
Just a little bit too handy with that mail-order pacifier sometimes. But you take a county where you got some hard cases

back in the piney woods, a little head-knocking keeps things levelled off. He lived clean and straight. It must have shook that boy when he checked out that complaint, walking in on that. Like looking into a bucket of mealy grubs. What's going wrong with folks lately, McGee?"

I had neared the ultimate promotion, to Mr. McGee.

"It's a mass movement against head-knocking, Sheriff."

"What kind of a joke is that?"

"All kinds of head-knocking. Commercial, artistic and religious. They're trying to say people should love people. It's never been a very popular product. Get too persistent, and they nail you up on the timbers on a hill."

He stared at me with indignation. "Are *you* one of *them*?"

"I recognize the problem. That's all. But the hippies solve it by stopping the world and getting off. No solution, Sheriff. I don't seek solutions. That takes group effort. And every group effort in the world requiring more than two people is a foul-up, inevitably. So I just stand back of the foul line and when something happens that doesn't get called by the referees, I sometimes get into the game for a couple of minutes."

"Around here today," he said sadly, "it's beginning to seem to me like in my sleep last night I must have forgot half the English language."

"Can I go take care of my business matter?"

He looked at Tom, got some signal in reply, and said, "Stay in the area, Mr. McGee."

CHAPTER THIRTEEN

I SAW Preston LaFrance sitting at his desk inside his little real estate office in a converted store on Central Street. He had his head in his hands, and he was alone.

When he heard the door open, he looked up with the beginnings of the affable show-you-a-fine-parcel smile, and it froze there partially developed. He jumped and boggled and said, "McGee! You . . . you're alone? But I saw you with . . . you were. . . ."

"Sorry I couldn't keep the coffee date, Press. I had to go answer some fool questions the sheriff wanted to ask me."

"Bunny . . . let you go?"

"What's the matter with you? Are you disappointed?"

"No! Hell, no! Sit down! Sit down, Trav! Cigar? Take that chair. It's more comfortable."

I sat down. "Did you have the same weird idea Burgoon had? Did you think I killed Bannon?"

"But Freddy said an eyewitness had turned up, and they were going to grab you down there in Lauderdale and he was going to go down and bring you back."

"It would have been an exciting trip."

"What happened? What about the eyewitness?"

"Burgoon satisfied himself that she was lying and I wasn't."

"Freddy said everything fitted together."

"It did."

"What? What do you mean?"

"It worried you a little, Press, when I told you that maybe somebody was trying to give you and Monk Hazzard a lot of co-operation in rousting Bannon out of his property, and maybe they busted him up too much. And you said that there wasn't anybody involved who'd do a thing like that, but you hesitated a little. So you were thinking of Nephew Freddy, the head-knocker. So you came back and laid some very indirect questions on him and he convinced you he was absolutely innocent, and then you told him who had been feeding you such crazy ideas. So, lo and behold, the eyewitness was brought in and she changed her story and the sheriff let me go."

"I guess then we can . . . talk business?"

"Sure, Press. That's what I'm here for. By the way, the eyewitness identified Freddy as the killer. He heard about it by accident and took off. They're running a manhunt right now. So it was a pretty good guess."

"I got the money together, but first I have to. . . . What did you say? Freddy? Come *on*!"

"He ran, Press. He took off. Check it out. Call Burgoon."

He reached for the phone, hesitated, then picked it up

and ran a thumbnail down the typed list of numbers under the desk-top glass. He dialled and asked for Burgoon. "Okay, then give me Tom Windhorn. Thanks. . . . Tom? This is Press. Say, Tom, is Freddy in some kind of a . . . Huh? No kidding! But look, it couldn't really be that he would. . . . Oh. . . . I see. . . . Yeh. . . . Boy, some mess. Anybody get hold of Monk yet. . . ? Oh, that's right I forgot. . . . No, Tom, I don't even know what route they were taking. Monk said he was going to take his time and see the sights. Sis will be out of her mind. Tom, is everybody absolutely *positive* he. . . . All right. Sure. I'll be over later." He hung up and shook his head in bewildered fashion. "I just can't believe it. He's a nice clean-cut boy."

"I'm afraid you've got too much on your mind. This is no time to talk business. We've got another deal we can work out. So let's forget the whole thing. Okay?"

"But I . . . but I need——"

"Just hang onto your fifty acres and use the forty thousand to pick up that Carbee land. The way the area is going to go, you ought to make a nice profit in a couple of years. Just sit tight."

His smile was slightly ghastly in its attempt to be reassuring. "Listen: Trav. Believe me, I can keep my mind on your proposition. I mean this is a terrible tragedy in the family and all, but it isn't going to do anybody any good for me to lose out on something."

"Maybe you won't like it anyway," I said. "Give me a piece of paper and a pencil. I'll show you how it works."

I wrote down a little tabulation on the sheet:

```
Carbee          200 acres @ $2000 = $400,000
LaFrance         50 acres @  2000 =  100,000
McGee            10 acres @  2000 =   20,000
                                    ---------
Total purchase price                 520,000
Cost to LaFrance:
McGee 10 acres              $ 90,000
Carbee 200 acres              40,000
                            --------
                            $130,000   130,000
                                       --------
```

Total available for split		$390,000
To LaFrance	$265,000	135,000
McGee (+ 40,000 from LaFrance)		95,000
×		60,000
		390,000

"Who is this X? What does your ninety-five thousand come out of? I don't understand this."

"Mr. X is the man we're going to meet at the hotel for lunch. The point is, I don't trust him completely. But he has the authority to buy—from one single owner—those two hundred and sixty acres at two thousand an acre. And because he's going to the top limit authorized, he wants a cash kick-back, under the table. The trouble is, he wants it now. And I don't think we ought to turn it over until we get the full amount on the land. If something went wrong, we couldn't prove a thing. Right?"

"Yes, but——"

"Listen, can you get my forty thousand in cash instead of by certified cheque?"

"I . . . I guess so. Sure. But——"

"Then, maybe there's a way we can work it so we won't end up with the dirty end of the stick, Press."

"But what's this ninety-five thousand for you?"

"For putting this thing together. You are going to sell me a twenty-five per cent share of that option for five thousand."

"The *hell* I am! I can sell that Carbee land for——"

"Forget it. Forget Calitron. You'll see why when you see the correspondence X has. If X can't deal with us, he'll deal with Gary Santo and we'll be out in the cold. Why are you crying anyway, LaFrance? You get all your bait back, all hundred and thirty grand, plus a hundred and thirty-five on top. That's fifteen thousand over a quarter of a million."

We had lunch with Meyer at the hotel. He was superb. He told us where he was staying. I went to the bank with LaFrance and got the papers on our land sale signed and notarized, and he got the forty thousand cash. I drove him to the motel where Meyer was waiting, and before we went in, I unlocked the trunk compartment and dug out the little package of currency I had taped to a far dark corner. It was my total war fund, and it made me feel uneasy carrying it around. Meyer showed us the rest of the correspondence and the overlays. He took them out of the bulky despatch case. He was properly arrogant, properly shifty. LaFrance bought the con. I could read it on his face and in the sweatiness of his hands, leaving damp prints on the papers.

"So, if we can settle the last little detail, gentlemen?"

"Doctor Meyer," I said, "We get . . . I mean Mr. LaFrance gets the point five two million cheque or definite confirmation from topside that it has gone through, then you get the money we agreed on."

He stared at me with a heavy, convincing contempt.

"And sue you if I don't get it, Mr. McGee? Where? In Small Claims Court? You see the correspondence. You see the authorizations. It will go through. Believe me."

"And at the last minute they change their minds. What have we got to make you give it back, Doctor?"

"There will be nothing in writing. You understand that. You have my word."

"But you won't take ours, Doctor?"

"So forget it, gentlemen. Impasse. I'll resume the negotiations for the other tract."

"There's one possible solution, Doctor, that might satisfy both sides. It would be safe for both of us."

"Which is?"

I took out the two packets of money and dropped them on the coffee table. "Seventy-five thousand dollars, Doctor Meyer."

"So?"

"Let's seal it in an envelope and we can put it in the hands of a local attorney, and give him instructions about it."

"To do what?"

"I'll tear a dollar bill into three pieces. We each keep a third. The attorney is authorized to surrender the envelope to whoever shows up with the three pieces, or to any two who, between them, have all three pieces."

"Kid games!" said Meyer. "Nonsense games!"

"The extra fifteen, Doctor, is a bonus for doing it this way. Does the game sound better?"

He nodded. "A little. But you can save fifteen by giving me the sixty now."

"We'll pay the extra fifteen for insurance, Doctor."

"Sometimes being too careful is stupid," he said. "I'll play your game."

The good doctor had a fresh Manila envelope in his despatch case. He handed it to me. I put the money in it and sealed it and handed it to LaFrance, saying, "Which lawyer do. . . ."

"I think," said Meyer, "as long as we are not trusting one another, I will choose not to trust any lawyer of your selection, gentlemen. The old hotel where we lunched has a safe, no doubt. And some sort of claim check arrangement. The claim check could be torn into three portions, and the manager instructed not to surrender the envelope except for an entire claim check taped back together. Satisfactory?"

"Suits me," I said. "Press?"

"Sure." So we went back downtown in my car, Press beside me, Meyer in the rear. I parked and we went in. Meyer hung back while Press and I went to the desk. The girl greeted him by name and Press asked for the manager by name. He came out of his office.

"Can I help you, Mr. LaFrance?"

"Harry, this is sort of a wager. Can you put this in the safe for me and give us a claim check. We're going to tear it into three hunks, and don't surrender it unless you get the whole claim check."

Harry was affable about the whole thing. He took the envelope into his office and came back with the other half of the perforated tag he had affixed to the envelope. I had a five-dollar bill ready and reached and laid it on the counter and said, "For your trouble," and he gave me the tag, telling me it wasn't necessary to . . . uh. . . .

"Go ahead, Harry," I told him. I turned away, and walked over to Meyer, with LaFrance hurrying to keep up with me. I tore the tag into three parts, making them irregular, and ceremoniously put a third on each of their outstretched palms.

Meyer sighed. "Games for children. An expensive game for you, my friends." We walked out and stood by my car. I offered the doctor a ride back to his motel. He got into the front seat. I closed the door and turned and held my hand out to Preston LaFrance.

"Press, I think we're really in business. I'll be seeing you in a few days. You draw up the agreement on the Carbee option."

"Sure, Trav. I'll sure do that." His expression was doleful and earnest and anxious, like a dog hoping to be let in out of the rain.

"I hope you get your trouble worked out all right."

"What? Oh, that terrible business about my nephew."

"The boy just got too eager, I guess. He knew you and his father were using every legal means to run Bannon out of business. He probably tried a different way of discouraging him."

"That's probably it. And he tried to cover up. It was sort of an accident, I'd say. Freddy wouldn't want to kill anybody. When they find him, I think if he tells exactly what happened, they might agree on letting him plead guilty of manslaughter. Monk has got a lot of leverage in this part of the state. Trav, how . . . how soon do you think our deal will go through?"

"A matter of days. Don't worry about it."

"I think I'll go over to the sheriff's office and see what's happening."

He walked away. I walked around the car and got in and drove away. "Pigeon drop, smigeon drop," said Meyer. "How was I?"

"Like a pro. Great natural talent, Doctor."

I reached into my breast pocket and took out the intact green claim check and handed it to him. He took the little tin tape dispenser out of his pocket and tore the check in thirds and stuck it back together with the tape.

I made two right turns and parked on the side street behind the hotel. He gave me the claim check and said, "So soon?"

"Why not? While we know Harry is still in the office and we know where ol' Press is. Wait right here. Don't go away, pro."

I walked around the corner and went in the side door of the hotel and across the old-fashioned lobby to the desk. Harry was alone, sticking mail into the room boxes.

I handed him the check and said, "The winnah!"

"That was a quick one, sir."

"Wasn't it, though!"

He brought me the envelope and I said, "Harry, if you want to keep on being friends with Mr. LaFrance, you'd better not mention this little fiasco to him. He was so sure he was right he's going to be *very* grumpy about the whole thing."

"I know what you mean, sir."

I walked back to the car and drove Meyer to the motel. I gave him the forty thousand, and taped my emergency fund back into its inconspicuous place in the car trunk.

It was just three thirty. When I walked back into the motel unit, Meyer was on the phone talking with his Lauderdale broker. He hung up and looked at the figures he had scribbled down.

"I think the answer is right here, Travis. I don't think it has to come from Mary Smith. Fletcher Industries moved up one and an eighth today, to sixteen and three eighths on a volume of ninety-four hundred shares. So Janine Bannon has made eleven hundred and twenty-five bucks today."

"Today?"

"Well, so far. I mean the final returns for the day aren't in, but it will be pretty close to that. The Dow is off a little over five points. You look astonished. Oh, I see why. This morning before I left I opened her margin account with cash money, pending the power of attorney that you forgot to give me. I put in enough to buy her a thousand shares, and I got them at fifteen and a quarter."

I gave him the power of attorney. He put it in his despatch case, and took out all the fake correspondence to My dear Ludweg and the fake reports on plant location data.

"So," he said, "it was worth the chance and now I reimburse myself out of this money and put the rest into her account to cover the order I placed for the opening tomorrow. Another twenty-five hundred shares. That will commit her account up to maximum. Then I have to go sit and stare at the tape, day after day, ten in the morning to three thirty in the afternoon. Bring me sandwiches." He waved the sheaf of counterfeit letters and documents. "When these are confetti and flushed away, my heart might slow down some you think?"

He went into the bathroom with them and I placed a credit card call, station to station to the Santo offices, and after a short wait I got Mary Smith.

The approach, to be convincing, had to be that of the male who'd been brushed off.

"McGee here," I said. "What was Santo's decision?"

"Oh. Trav. I've been *so* impatient for you to call, darling."

"I bet. What did he decide."

"I want to tell you something else first, because I have the hunch that if I tell you first, you'll hang up."

"Can you think of any good reason why I shouldn't?"

"Darling, I can think of a *very* good reason. My darned telephone was acting up. I *knew* it was you, but it just kept making a horrid ringing sound in my ear when I picked it up." Her voice was intimate, cheery, persuasive.

"Nice try, kid."

"But I'm telling the *truth*! *Really* I am. What could make you possibly think I wouldn't *be* there? If you want to be such a grouchy old bear, you can call the phone company and ask them if a certain Mary Smith raised absolute *hell* with them Saturday afternoon. I got the message you left at the office, and I left one for you, hoping you'd call back."

"At least you make it sound good, Miss Smith."

"Travis, I *know* how disappointed and angry you must have been."

"How come the phone company couldn't fix the phone?"

"Actually they swore there was nothing wrong with it. They tested and tested, and when I made them come back the second time, they took out the instrument and put in a new one."

"Which didn't work either. Which didn't work on Saturday night."

"I . . . wasn't there."

"You said you had the week-end open. So why didn't you hang around? How about four o'clock Sunday morning, kid?"

"I . . . I was told you'd made other plans, dear."

"By who?"

"To tell you the truth, I drove up to Lauderdale just to find you. I saw that fantastic boat of yours, dear. It must be a marvellous way of life. A man told me you might be at a party on another boat and I went there, but a very odd-looking girl told me I'd missed you and you might come back. So I waited there. You can ask those people. A lot of them are your friends, I guess. It is quite a . . . lively group.

Then that strange girl came and told me that she found out you had left with another girl, so you probably wouldn't be back. So . . . you see, I really tried."

The persuasive lilt of her tone was dying away, fading back into the monotone of a deadly exhaustion.

"So even at four in the morning, you weren't home yet? I guess you had a good time?"

"Not terribly. But it was pleasant. I . . . called up an old friend and she invited me over, and it got to be too late to drive back, so they put me up for the night, dear."

"So when did you get home?"

"I think it was about . . . ten o'clock last night. I spent the day with them. Why, dear? You had a date, didn't you? There was hardly any point in roaring home and sitting panting by the phone, was there? Listen, dear, I don't *blame* you for having a date. After all, it was perfectly reasonable for you to assume I stood you up, and so you said the hell with Mary Smith and her lousy steak. Don't I get any points for driving all the way up there to find you?"

I said in a marvelling tone, "And all it was was a phone out of order. You know, there must be a hex on us."

"I guess there must be," she said. She sighed audibly and heavily.

"So expect a man at about nine tonight, honey. Okay?"

"Oh no, darling! I'm sorry."

"What now?"

"Well . . . I guess the hex is still working. I . . . uh . . . my friends have this little boat at their dock. They live on a canal. And they were going to take me out in the boat, and like a clumsy idiot I tripped somehow and fell headlong, right off the dock into the boat. Honestly, I'm an absolute ruin. I was waiting for you to call so that I could get out of here and go home and take a hot bath and go to bed. I've been tottering around here today like a little old lady."

"Gee, honey, that must have been a nasty fall. Where did you hurt yourself?"

She gave a tired laugh. "Where didn't I? There were a lot of . . . you know . . . fishing tackle things in the boat. I must have hit my mouth somehow because it's all puffed out, and when I looked at myself head to toe in my mirror this morning, I swear I didn't know whether to laugh or cry.

I'm battered and bruised from head to toe. I *couldn't* let you see me like this. I'm a fright."

"That could be dangerous, Mary, a fall like that."

"I know. I strained my back somehow, I think. It's such a shock I guess it takes a lot out of you. My bones ache even." She sighed again. "Darling, give me time to get all well again, just for you. Please?"

"Sure. Take care of yourself, kid. Sorry our luck was running bad."

"Friend McGee, you are not one tenth as sorry as I am," and there was total conviction gleaming through the drag of her words. "The decision was yes, by the way."

"Good. How much."

"He said it depends on how it goes. At least one and a half. Maybe up to three, or anywhere in between. He said to tell you he'll be doing it through different accounts, scattered across the country. He wondered if you mind the amount being a little vague."

"I expected that. If it gets too much play from the traders, he won't be able to slow it down enough."

"Dear, may I wish us better luck next time?"

"You may indeed. Hurry home to bed, honey."

I hung up and looked into the bathroom in time to see Meyer sprinkle the last of his confetti and flush the toilet.

"The evidence is destroyed," said Meyer, with big smile and big sigh.

"And Santo has climbed on."

"May he enjoy the trip in good health. May he have asked a few friends to join him even."

I gave him my third of the other claim check and he put it carefully into a pocket of his wallet. "So tomorrow," he said, "I drive up to Broward Beach and go out A-One-A and find a place called the Annex, and at seven I am sitting at the bar, waiting for the pigeon. Correct?"

"Looking important and shifty. Correct."

"Shouldn't you ask me what it is I checked when I arrived for lunch? Don't you care?"

"I do now. Now that I know it must be interesting."

"Here is the scene. Mr. LaFrance rushes to the desk at the hotel. He has the three parts of the claim check taped together. He is panting, right?"

"His hands are trembling." He can't wait for Harry to give him the money," I said.

"So Harry takes the check and he doesn't come back with a big brown envelope. He comes back with a small white envelope. Number ten. Greeting card size. The envelope I checked when I arrived for lunch, so I could get a claim check, so you could make the substitution and tear it up into three pieces and give him one."

"Meyer, remember me? I *know* all this."

"Shut up. Let me enjoy. So he asks Harry, where is the brown envelope? Where is the money? So Harry says the other fellow claimed it ten minutes after it was checked. Yes, Mr. LaFrance, he had the right three pieces stuck together. He said I shouldn't mention to you that you lost the bet. I *know*, Mr. LaFrance, this check is torn in three pieces too, but it isn't the check for the money. It's the check for this card."

"And so," I said, "stunned, bewildered, shocked, our Mr. LaFrance wobbles over to a lobby chair, falls into it and thumbs the white envelope open. Come *on*, Meyer! What does the card say?"

"Don't rush. It says on the front: 'Congratulations from the Gang at the Office.' You open it. Inside it says: 'It couldn't have happened to a nicer guy."

"That is very wicked, Meyer."

"But the signature. That's the good part."

"What did you do? Forge my name?"

"Not exactly. He saw your houseboat. He saw the name. Inside the greeting card he finds five playing cards I took out of a deck. I threw the rest of the deck away. The five, six, seven and eight of hearts. And the king of clubs. Right? A busted flush?"

I looked at him admiringly. "Meyer, you have great class. You have an instinct for this kind of work."

"It was nothing, really. Just innate good taste, a creative mind, and high intelligence. It will make a nice signature any time you want somebody to know who gave it to them good."

CHAPTER FOURTEEN

A T nine that evening Sheriff Bunny Burgoon sent word out from his office that he could see me.

His chief deputy, Tom Windhorn, was planted in the same chair against the wall as before. They both looked as if they'd had a very hard day.

"From the talk out front I know you haven't got him yet. But have you got any kind of line on him, Sheriff?"

"What I got doesn't exactly boost up my spirits, mister. And it's no joy having every newspaper and TV and radio station yappin' on and on about Shawana County having a deputy that turned bad. And it didn't help any to have Monk Hazzard chewing me up long distance and telling me I was crazy as hell. But when I told him about car number three, it slowed him some."

"Where was it? I heard you found it."

"Just before sunset. The Highway Patrol chopper spotted it way over in the southwest corner of the county, run off into a marsh and bogged up to the top of the fenders. I got a call from the boys that went to check it out. There's little places along the lake shore there, spread out. They were checking all the driveways and heard somebody yelling in one of the places. Retired couple, trussed up, scared, and mad as puckered owls. Seems that Freddy drove in, knocked, real polite, a little after two in the afternoon. Asked to come in. Said it was on a complaint on the fish and game laws. Head-knocked them both, tied them up, stuck dishtowels in their mouths. The boys say it's a big tall old man, so his clothes fit Freddy good enough. Left the uniform. Put on the old man's best suit, packed a bag with other clothes and toilet articles. Picked up what money they had around. Thirty or forty dollars. Drove off in the county car. Came back on foot and drove off in their two-year-old Plymouth station wagon. Said he seemed nervous. Told them he was sorry he had to do them that way. Seemed right sorry about it. The old man tongued the towel out of his mouth after a while. When he heard the boys drive down his drive, he started bellering. So we put the car and the clothes on the wire. From there he's twenty miles from the Interstate. If he pushed it hard enough, he could have crossed into Georgia before we got the word out."

"Once they calm down," Tom said, "if we get all their stuff back to them and fix up anything busted or lost, and talk nice, they might not press charges."

"We sort of reconstructed the thing with Bannon," the sheriff said. "I say he must have come across Bannon on the road, hiking out to his place and told him he'd been foreclosed and his wife had took off on him, and he must have wanted to drive Bannon back here, but Bannon just wouldn't believe him and wanted a look, so when he insisted, Freddy drove him the rest of the way out. That would account for the fat girl thinking they were talking ugly to each other. Now I'd say Bannon lost his head and tried to bust into the place that used to be his. Now that's against the law and Freddy tried to gentle him some, but that was a lot of man and if he didn't drop with the first knock, and if he rushed Freddy, that boy in his excitement just swung too hard is all. Caved his head bone in, maybe. And he knew Tom and me had chewed him for being too goddang quick with that mail-order pacifier, and I guess Freddy just lost his head is all. Having that girl see how he covered it up was just plain bad luck."

"And was he in line to be the one to come to Lauderdale and bring me back if I was picked up there?"

The sheriff looked uneasy. "That was what was planned, mister."

"I guess I would have tried to open the car door and jump out when we were going seventy-five or eighty. After I got through bounding along the pavement, nobody'd find a little extra lump on my skull."

"Now you can't be sure that would have happened that way."

"I wonder why he told anybody about hearing from his Uncle Press that I was going to be here this morning?"

"Because," said Tom Windhorn, "he knows I play golf Sunday mornings in a foursome with Press LaFrance every week of my life, and Press knew we were hunting you, and Freddy knew there was no way in the world of stopping Press from telling me. So he brought it in first. And the fool thing about it is that Press never did play yesterday. He phoned in he was feeling poorly, too late for us to get somebody to fill out, and so they stuck some old coot in with us that couldn't hit the ground with his hat."

"That poor boy just had plain bad luck all the way around," I said. "He never did get a chance to kill me."

"He's no killer," the sheriff said. "He just lost his head some."

"Nice I get to keep mine. Find the stuff he picked up out at the cottages?"

The sheriff nodded. "It was at his place, under his clean shirts. The narcotics we got packed up to mail in for analysis. No case on that because without Freddy we can't prove the chain of possession." He opened the shallow middle drawer of his desk and then held an envelope toward me. I reached and took it.

The colour prints were sharp and clear. I leafed through them. They did not leave the feral and cynical impression that the posed product of the hard-core studios induce. This was a tumble of ageing children, most of them rather badly nourished. In spite of their placid, dazed, beatific smiles and grimaces, they were a kind of curious sadness, in their weird, bright patterns of love-paint on the scrawn of flesh, in their protest bangles and their disaffiliated bells, crushing the flower blossoms in a dreamy imitation of adults acts that for them had all been bleached of any significance or purpose. The rites of the strobe, frozen in such a sharpness it caught forever a wistful dirtiness of knuckles, the calico of bad bleach jobs, the moles and the blemishes and the sharp, helpless angle of shoulder blade. This was not a rebellion against mechanization, or emotional fraud. This was denying life itself in all eras and all cultures, and instead of being evil or outrageous was merely empty, bland and slightly saurian somehow, as though in a vain attempt to warm the blood that had begun to turn cooler in some gigantic and total regression that would take us all back through geological time, back into the sea where life began.

Said Tom, "Ain't that Arlie the damndest sight a man would ever want to behold?"

"Unforgettable," I said, and put the envelope on the edge of the desk. "I've been waiting around to ask permission to leave your area, Sheriff. Here's the address where you can get me. I'll come back if you need me. But now I'd like to drive up to Frostproof and see Jan Bannon."

"Get your business done with Press?"

"Yes, thanks."

"Well . . . I guess there's no call to keep you waiting around. Thank you for your co-operation, Mr. McGee."

"Thank you for your courtesy and consideration, Sheriff."

When I phoned ahead, Connie said that Janine had heard the news and that she was very upset and puzzled. I said it would be well after midnight before I could make it, and she said that it had been too much of a long, hard day to wait up. I told her my day had been on the same order, and told her that everything had gone very smoothly so far.

It was ten after one when I got there and turned under the arch and through the glare of the gate light and drove to the big house. The night was cool and the stars looked high and small and indifferent.

Jan stood in the open doorway waiting for me. And she leaned up to rest her cheek for a moment against mine, with a quick, soft touch of her lips. "You must be exhausted, Trav."

"And you shouldn't have waited up."

"I couldn't have slept."

I went in and sat down into the depth and softness of a big leather couch. There were two red embers among the silvery ashes of the hearth. She wore a floor-length navy robe with a white collar. She said, "Connie left orders to give you a great wallop of bourbon to unwind on." I said it sounded great. She drifted out of sight and I heard the clink of cubes and the guggle of a generous dose.

"Water?"

"Just the ice, thanks."

She brought it over and fixed the cushions at the end of the couch and told me to lie back and put my feet up. She moved a footstool close. The light behind her from the corner lamp, the only one on in the room, shone through the fine ends of her cropped black hair. Her face was in shadow.

I sipped the strong drink and told her about Deputy

Hazzard. "That's what I couldn't believe," she said. "He and the older one, with the funny name. Not the sheriff."

"Windhorn?"

"Yes. They were the ones who . . . came out with the padlocks and the notices. And he, the young one, seemed so very shy and nice and troubled about everything. There was no point in taking it out on them. They had their orders."

"Had he been out there before?"

"Several times, yes. To serve papers, and the time they checked to see about the licences we have to have for the houseboats. A lanky boy with a long face, kind of a red, lumpy face, but sweet. But very official about what he had to do. All leather and jingling and creaking."

"That reconstruction of it doesn't fit," I said. "It doesn't fit Tush."

"I know. He never got mad that way. Not like me. I fly off the handle and want to hit everything I can reach. He'd just get very very quiet and sad-looking, and he'd walk slowly away. It's better for me to . . . to be absolutely positive once and for all that he didn't kill himself, Trav. But it just seems to be such . . . a stinking trivial way to die, to be killed by that harmless-looking young man."

"Most of the ways people die are kind of dingy and trivial, Jan."

"It just shouldn't have been that way for Tush. But how in the world did that Freddy person get Arlie Denn to tell such an ugly lie about you? She always seemed to me to be sort of dull and placid. She never seemed mean or vicious or anything. It must have been horrible for her—watching like that. I would think she would just . . . have never told anybody at all, ever."

And that took some explaining and finally I managed to make her comprehend it, up to a point. But comprehension was comingled with revulsion. "But we let that wretched girl sit with our boys a lot of times! She could have taken something . . . and hurt them."

"I doubt it."

"What kind of people were those others? How old were they?"

"I'd say Roger and Arlie were the oldest. The others looked nineteen and twenty. And the one girl about fifteen or sixteen."

"What are they trying to do to themselves?"

"Drop out of the world. Hallucinate. Turn on. Dig the sounds and colours and feels. Be at one with the infinite something or other. I can't lay too big a knock on them, you know. In another sense I'm a dropout. I don't pay for my tickets. I jump over the turnstile."

"I think I've *been* dropped out somehow. For good."

"Now I am supposed to tell you about how you're a young woman still in your twenties with most of your life still ahead of you."

"Please don't."

"A guy will need you in the right way sometime."

"Tell him not to *really* need me. That's when I run like a rabbit." She took my empty glass and said, "another?"

"No. That one is going to do it."

"I made you talk too long. There's more I want to ask. But I'll wait until tomorrow."

She got up and took the glass away. I decided I'd better get up and head for bed while I could. I closed my eyes for a moment and opened them again and a high sun was shining and her middle boy was standing holding a saucer with both hands, and he had his tongue sticking out of the corner of his mouth to help with the chore of keeping the coffee from spilling out of the cup.

"Everybody's been up a *long* time," he said disdainfully. "Mom said bring you this and if I stood here, the smell would wake you up. I think it's a lousy crummy old smell and I'm never going to drink that stuff. Oh. Good morning."

My shoes had been removed, belt loosened, necktie removed, collar unbuttoned. There was a blanket over me. The lady had given me bourbon and loving care. I hoped that it would be at least another full year before I had to put a necktie back on.

I sat up and took the coffee.

"*You* spilled a little bit," he said. "*I* didn't."

"Like it here?"

"It's neat. Today there's a teacher's meeting, so we don't have to go on the bus. Charlie's going to let me ride on the tractor again with him. It's real neat. I gotta go." And he went—at a full run.

I dialled Press LaFrance direct at twenty after ten. I wanted him to have a lot of time to make some collections. Just as I was ready to hang up, he answered, out of breath.

"Who? Trav? Where are you? What's up?"

"Miami, boy. And I'm getting a little sweaty. Maybe we're in trouble."

"How? My God, Trav, I thought everything was——"

"I've been making some long distance calls, Press. And it looks as if everything might go through okay. I was with Doctor Meyer a few minutes ago and he as much as admitted that he might wait until Roger Santo gets back from abroad and see if he wants to make a better deal on the side, a fatter deal for Meyer. I told you he's slippery."

"But what are we going to do?"

"If we play it his way, the way he suggested in the beginning, he'll move right ahead with it. But it has to be today. He's on his way up to Broward Beach. Do you know a place called The Annex?"

"Yes, but——"

"I had to take the chance, Press. I had to move fast. I gave him my third of the claim check. Now he's going to be at the bar at The Annex at seven o'clock tonight. I told him that you would meet him there and give him his damned sixty thousand in cash for the two thirds he's holding."

"Where am I going to get that kind of money before seven?"

"The minute after you get back to Sunnydale and walk into the hotel, you'll have it back, won't you?"

"Yes, but——"

"Scrounge it somehow. You could pay somebody a very fat amount of one-day interest out of that fifteen extra, couldn't you?"

"But, Trav, suppose he takes the sixty and then screws us and makes his deal with Santo? What can we do?"

"Absolutely nothing. But stop running around in crazy circles, man, and *listen* to me. I'm assuming the risk. Got that? It's my money sitting up there. Give me a week and I could scrape up three or four times sixty in cash, but I damned well can't do it today. If it falls through, what are you out?"

"There's . . . maybe one possibility."

"Now you're beginning to think. I'll phone you back. How long will it take you to find out?"

"I . . . I should know by . . . you phone me back right here at two o'clock?"

The shape of larceny is, in time, written clearly enough on a man's face so that it can be read. Constant greed and sharp little deals and steals had left the sign on Preston LaFrance. There is the old saying that God and your folks give you the face you're born with, but you earn the one you die with.

I went back into the house at two o'clock and phoned him. I knew just how he had probably worked it out in his mind. Get hold of sixty thousand cash to buy the claim check to seventy-five thousand in cash. Nobody ever gets hurt taking a profit. The small towns of Florida are peppered with old boys who don't like to have too much information on record about the deals they make. And they like to keep a little leverage around in the form of cash money. LaFrance would know a couple of those shrewd old hawks. He'd hunt one up, probably put up his fifty acres and the Carbee option as security, if the bank wasn't holding them, and pay the old boy a thousand dollars or five hundred for the loan of sixty thousand in cash for a few hours. Then he'd hike the interest rate as high as he dared when he reported to me.

"Trav?" he said. "I've been dreading this call, cause there's something I hate to have to tell you."

"You couldn't get the money!"

"No, no. I got the money. I got it locked up right here in my office. I got it from a fellow that keeps cash on hand. Trouble is, he knows I'm spread thin. Maybe I got too anxious. Anyway, he gave it to me good. The only deal I could make was to pay him the whole fifteen thousand. Honest to God, Trav, when a man gets the tights, all the money dries up on you. There just wasn't anybody else who'd give me the lend of it."

"Pretty damned steep, Press."

"Like you said, this is an emergency."

It was the perfect example of the philosophy behind all kinds of con, big and small: You can't cheat an honest man. I gave him a B in the course. B for Brass.

"When I get back," he said, "that old boy is going to

be right there in the hotel lobby with his hand out, and there won't even be any point in unwrapping it, except he'll want to count it slow and careful, and then go on rattling home in his old pick-up truck, smiling like a toad in the moonlight. Trav, it was the pure best I could do on short notice, and that's God's truth."

"Okay, then. Tote it over to The Annex and give it to Doctor Meyer, and don't lose it on the way. Then we'll just have to keep calm and wait for the corporation cheque to come through.

"How long will it take?"

"Ask the Doctor."

I hung up, knowing it was going to work. The secret of the big con is to move the victim, bit by bit, into increasingly implausible situations. At last, in the act of plucking him clean, you have him performing such a damned-fool act he will never understand how he came to do it, why he didn't see through it. He was blinded by the conviction he couldn't possibly lose a dime. And when he learned he'd been conned, he couldn't take it to the law. He'd have to tell them he had been taking a sixty-thousand-dollar bribe to a man pretending to be a field representative of a huge corporation. He would have to tell them he'd paid forty thousand dollars for a worthless equity in a defunct marina. If a story like that got out, every member of the Sunnydale business community would laugh himself sick. So he didn't have a chance. Poor LaFrance. Exactly the same situation he put Tush in. Smashed flat, plucked clean. No mercy for Tush. No mercy for LaFrance.

I walked out and found Connie by the equipment barn. We strolled over and sat on the mossy old stone bench under the huge banyan tree in the side yard.

I told her that our fish had gobbled the hunk of ripe bait, and the hook was perfectly set. A very greedy fish, that one.

Her weather-beaten face twisted in mocking amusement. "Maybe he's just greedy enough so your friend should be a little careful leaving that place, Trav."

"He's got a self-addressed envelope with him, and he walks right from The Annex through into the motel lobby and drops it in the slot. It's got more than enough stamps on it. It'll be solidly sealed with tape, and the money will have cardboard and a rubber band around it. Connie, again thanks. I'm going to head back."

"You come any time, hear? Are you going to make our gal rich?"

"Let's say reasonably comfortable, if all goes well."

"And you'll have sixty more to fool with?"

"Meyer wouldn't like that verb."

"Ahh, McGee, all those poor bastards who'll wish that Tush Bannon never had a friend like you. Anyway, when things get just a little quieter—if they ever do—please let me know because then I think would be a good time for you to phone Jan and tell her that there are papers to be signed or something, any excuse for her to come down there. I'll talk her into it and keep the kids here, and when she gets down, you make her stay awhile. She needs a change. She needs to get away from the kids and away from here. She ought to get a lot of sun, and walk on a beach and swim and catch a fish and hear music and be near happy people. Okay?"

"Okay, Connie. Soon."

At eight thirty that evening the bing-bong announced that somebody had stepped over the gangplank chain and come aboard. I looked out and saw Meyer. I let him in.

He had a grin like a piano keyboard. He fell onto the yellow couch and said, "Build me one of those death-dealing in-and-out jobs named after somebody who's name escapes me."

"You'll get maudlin."

"So?"

"Any trouble at all?"

"None. You know, I have seldom seen or touched a greasier, grimier wad of money. I didn't know hundred-dollar bills ever got so cruddy. They must have come from a fondler."

"LaFrance was calm?"

"He stammered and sweat and his eyes bulged and he spilled his drink and mine. Otherwise, a cucumber. By now he's got the greeting card. By now he knows how it was done, by you switching claim checks as you turned away from him to walk over to me. By now he knows you picked it up ten minutes after it was checked. By now maybe he has leaned across the desk and hit Harry in the mouth. What a pity not to see him read the nice card I bought him."

"You'll get to see a certain amount of agitation."

"You can arrange that?"

"The phone is turned off. He'll be here in the morning. Count on it. Come over early. We'll play a little chess."

"I should be down watching the board. Today it moved almost too good. Volume is picking up. Very close to two points. Seven grand, practically, for the widow. I've got a friend on the floor of the exchange keeping in close touch with the fellow who maintains the position in Fletcher, and he calls me at my brokers the minute anything starts to look sour. And I should put in some orders for her out of the sixty. We'll have five days to meet the margin call. I don't think the mail takes that long from Broward Beach to here. At least not usually."

"We could be having a little game on the sun deck. The forecast is warm and bright. We invite him aboard. We have a little chat. He goes away."

"So I could phone in the first order. So it isn't as risky now in the beginning as it is going to get. Also, there is a variation of the queen's pawn opening I think I can break your back with. You know, you don't look so great."

"I brood a lot."

He finished the last of the drink in one huge gulp. He shuddered and got up and said, "Now if I can be standing by the bunk when that hits me. . . ."

CHAPTER FIFTEEN

WE had placed the chess table and chairs near the rear of the sun deck so we could look down onto the dock. We surveyed the morning traffic between moves. At one point Hero went by, swaying his big shoulders. The usual lock of hair was combed to fall just right over his forehead. He was taking a morning saunter through the game preserves, just in case he might flush something even at an unlikely morning hour. His grey slacks were tightly tailored to his narrow hips, and the broad belt was cinched tightly around his improbable waist.

He crinkled up at us and said in his mellow bass-baritone, "Morning, gents. Nice day out today."

"Getting any?" Meyer said contemptuously.

"Can't complain, gents. It's the best season for it."

He came to a momentary point and then lengthened his relaxed stride. I turned and saw two girls in beach togs with pale northern faces and legs, heading from the dock area toward the shops. Just as they disappeared from sight beyond the palm fronds Hero was ten feet behind them and, I suspected, clearing his throat and checking the third finger, left hand. That was his quaint little conceit, his only concession to any rule of human behaviour. He proclaimed it often, with great conviction and emphasis. "I hold marriage sacred, and never in my life have I knowingly courted nor touched a lady united in the holy bonds of matrimony, no sir. It's something no gentleman would do."

A little later Meyer went below and phoned his broker and came back acting less restless. "It opened up a whole point, and then a couple of pretty good blocks came on the market and knocked it down to an eighth below yesterday's close. Insiders unloading, maybe. If so, in another week or two, they'll be slitting their throats at what they could have got."

At a few minutes before eleven, Preston LaFrance came along the dock at a half lope. He looked rumpled. He hadn't shaved. He came to a lurching halt and stared up at us.

"Doctor Mey. . . ." It came out falsetto, so he coughed and tried again. "Doctor Meyer!"

"Hidey, Press," I said. "How you, old buddy? Come on aboard. Ladderway up here is on the port side."

He came clambering up and came over and stood beside us. We studied the chess pieces. "Doctor Meyer!"

"Just Meyer," he said. "Plain old Meyer."

"But don't you work for——"

"Work? Who should work? I'm an economist. I live on a little cruiser that has a case of dry rot lately. If I decide to get out the tools and go to work on it, then I'll be working."

"Then there isn't any . . . offer for the land?"

We both looked up at him. "Offer?" I said. "Land?" said Meyer.

"Oh Jesus, you two were in this lousy racket together. You are a stinking pair of con men. Oh Jesus God!"

"Please!" said Meyer. "I'm trying to figure out why he moved his bishop."

"I'm going to have you two bastards thrown in jail!"

"McGee," said Meyer, "let's finish the game after the noise stops." He stood up and leaned against the rail. Meyer in his white swim trunks reminds me a little bit of a man who is all dressed to go to a masquerade as a dancing bear. All that is left to do is put on the bear head and the collar. He stared at LaFrance. "Jail? For what?"

"You two took a hunnert thousand dollars away from me! More than that! That Bannon place isn't worth half the mortgage on it!"

"Mr. LaFrance," I said, "the records will show that I paid a legitimate fifteen thousand for Mrs. Bannon's equity in the Bannon Boatel, and then I turned around and sold that same equity to you for forty thousand. And I think that your banker will remember how anxious you've been to get your hands on Bannon's ten acres on the river."

"But . . . but . . . damn it, that was because you said. . . ." He stopped himself and took a deep breath. "Listen. Forget the forty thousand. Okay. You suckered me. But the sixty thousand I gave this man last night, that's something else again. I've *got* to have it back."

"You gave me sixty thousand dollars!" Meyer said in vast astonishment. "Look. Stop standing in the sun. Get some rest."

He stood there, blinking, clenching and unclenching his bony fists. His colour was bad. He smiled what I would imagine he thought was an ingratiating and friendly smile. "You took me good, boys. Slick and perfect. You made a nice score off ol' Press LaFrance. And I guess you're not going to give it back just because I say pretty please with sugar. But you don't understand. I had to put up the Carbee option to get the sixty thousand. Now, if I had it back, I could go ahead and make my deal with Santo. That's what I got to trade with, boys. We'll draw it up legal. You'll get the sixty thousand back that you stole off me, and twenty more to sweeten the pot."

"If I had sixty thousand," said Meyer, "would I be hanging around with such riffraff? I would be riding around in a white convertible with a beautiful woman in furs and diamonds."

"How can you lose?" LaFrance said. "There's no way you can lose."

"No thanks," I said. "What shape does that leave you in, buddy?"

He wiped his mouth with the back of his hand. "I just plain can't afford to get left in the kind of shape I'd be in. Why, I would be worse off than dead broke. I would be a mile underground, boys. I would be attached and garnisheed the rest of my natural life. I would never have dime one to call my own the rest of my days."

"Now you know how it feels, Press."

"How what feels?"

"How some of the people felt who got in your way. Like Bannon."

He peered at me. "You bleeding for Bannon? That was straight-out business. He was squattin' right in the way of progress, and he was so dumb it took him a long time to catch on, is all."

"It would have helped him a lot if he'd had a brother-in-law on the County Commission."

"What in the wide world is eating on you, McGee? My God, there's a whole world full of Tush Bannons stumbling around, and they get et up left and right, and that's what makes the world go 'round. I put Monk onto some good things and he owed me a favour."

"And you and Monk let Freddy Hazzard know you'd appreciate him leaning a little hard on Bannon any chance he had?"

"Now, we never meant anything like *that*!" He smiled. "You're just trying to sweat me up a little. Isn't that right? Look, boys, it won't improve the deal any. Twenty more on top of the sixty is the best I can do."

He was such a weak, miserable, unsatisfying target. He still thought he was one of the good guys. I tried to reach him, just a little.

"If you could bring in a thousand per cent profit a day,

LaFrance, I wouldn't throw pocket change on the deck there in front of you. If I was on fire, I wouldn't buy water from you. I came prowling for you, LaFrance. If the thing you cared most about in the world was that face you wear, I would have changed it permanently, little by little. If your most precious possession was a beautiful wife, she'd be right down there below in the master stateroom waiting for you to leave so I could get back to her. If you juggled for a living, friend, you'd now have broken wrists and broken elbows."

"What the *hell* is the matter with you?"

"Get off the boat. Go ashore. Tush Bannon was one of the best friends I ever had. All you give a damn about is money, so that's where I hit you."

"Best . . . friend?" he whispered.

And I watched the grey appear. That grey like a wet stone. Grey for fright. Grey for guilt. Grey for despair. His mouth worked. "You . . . rooned me, all right. Ever'thing I worked all my life for is gone. You finished me off, McGee."

"Wait a minute," Meyer said. "Maybe I've got an idea."

LaFrance came to point like a good bird dog. "Yes? Yes? What?"

Meyer smiled at him benignly. "The answer was staring us right in the face all the time. It's so simple! What you do is kill yourself!"

LaFrance stared at him, tried to comprehend the joke, tried even to smile, but the smile fell away. Meyer's smile stayed put. But not one gleam of humour touched Meyer's little bright blue eyes. And I do not know many people who could have stared into that smile for very long. Certainly LaFrance couldn't. In the same soft persuasion a lover might use, Meyer said, "Do yourself a favour. Go kill yourself. Then you won't even know or care if you're broke. Maybe it hurts a little, but just for a split second. Use a gun or a rope, or go jump off something high. Go ahead. Die a little."

It is a kind of rat-frenzy I suppose, that dreadful and murderous fury of the weak ones when the door of the trap slams shut. With a mindless squalling he plunged at Meyer, long yellowed ridged thumbnails going for the meat of the eyes, knees jacking at belly and groin. The squalling and flailing and gouging lasted perhaps two and a half seconds before I clamped my forearm across his throat. I pulled him back away from Meyer, spun him and let go. He ended up against the far rail.

Obscenities are tiresome. He kept repeating himself. I cuffed him quiet and he went down the ladderway and I helped him along the way and onto the dock.

He stayed there perhaps three minutes. He was going to come back with a gun. He was going to bring friends. He was going to have my boat blown up. He was going to have it burned to the waterline. He was going to hire some boys from back in the swamps to come with their knives some dark night and turn us into sopranos. We were going to be awful sorry we'd ever messed with Preston LaFrance and you can by God believe it.

His eyes bulged and his voice had hoarsened and the saliva shone on his chin. And finally he hitched up his pants and walked away. His walk was that of a man wearing new bifocals and not being very sure of how far away the ground might be. Meyer was able to stand up straight without much discomfort, and I dabbed iodine on the thumbnail gouge under his left eye. He seemed troubled, thoughtful, far away. I told him LaFrance wouldn't make any trouble. I asked him what was bothering him.

Meyer, scowling, pinched the bridge of his nose. "Me! Did you hear me? On the sidewalk if there is a bug, I change my step and miss him. For me the business of the hooks almost spoils fishing. Me! I don't understand it. Such a rotten anger I had, Travis! Thick in the throat like a sickness. Oh, he won't kill himself. Not that one. He'll live on and on so he can whine. But it was like changing your step to squash the bug, not flat, just a little squash so he can crawl a little bit, slow, leaking his juices. McGee, my friend, I am ashamed of that kind of anger. I am ashamed of being able to do something like that. I said to myself when I first got into your line of . . . endeavour, I said—forgive me for saying this to you— I said I will go only so far into it. There are things McGee does that somehow hurt McGee, hurt him in the way he thinks of himself. I talked to Muggsie. This business of the pretty little woman who just somehow happened to go off with Hero, that wasn't pretty, and you were punishing something in yourself. Now I find myself a little bit less in my own eyes. Maybe this is a bad business you're in, Travis.

Is there this kind of ugly anger in a man that waits for some kind of virtuous excuse? Was it there in me, waiting for a reason only? Travis, my friend, is this the little demonstration of how half the evil in the world is done in the name of honour?"

He wanted help I couldn't give him. One does not pat a Meyer on the head and give him a lollypop. He had overturned one of the personal stones in my garden too, and I could watch leggedy things scuttling away into comforting darkness.

I said, "You still didn't figure out why I moved my bishop."

He sat down and fixed a total concentration on the board. He gave a little nod at last and pushed a pawn one space forward, spoiling the sequence I was planning. He pinched at the bridge of his nose again, then smiled across at me, a hairy Meyer-smile, and said, "You know, I think I must have taken some sort of a dislike to that fellow."

Two days later, Friday afternoon, Meyer came aboard the *Flush* at four thirty, just after I got back from the beach. A mass of that arctic air that Canada sends down free of charge had begun to change the day a little before noon. It had come down so swiftly I knew the grove people would be worried. There were frost bulletins on all the broadcasts. An edge in the crisp north-east breeze had cleaned the long beaches of everybody except diehard Yankees and one masochistic beach bum named Travis McGee. I had been taking out all the kinks, in the muscles in both body and brain, of too many sedentary days, swimming parallel to shore, in and out of the surf line, for all the distance, endurance and occasional speed sprints I could manage. It had been hard work to even stay warm, and I had ground away at it, breaststroke, backstroke, crawl, until on my chattering lope back to the *Flush* I felt as if I had pulled most of the long muscles loose from the joints and sockets and hinges they were supposed to control.

Any persistent idiot, like Hero, can strain away at the doorframe isometrics and build impressive wads of chunky fibrous muscle with which you can lift the front end of any sedan to make the girls say Oooo. But if you want the kind of muscle structure that will move you from here to there very very quickly, that will enable you to slip a punch, snatch a moving wrist, turn a fall into a shoulder roll that will put you back on the balls of your feet, balanced and ready, then you'd better be willing to endure total expenditure over long, active and dogged periods. I was going to be slowed down by time and attrition, and maybe it had begun, but not to a degree as yet for me to notice, nor to a degree to make me doubt myself—and doubt, of course, is more fatal than slowed reflexes.

I had the heat going aboard. Meyer drank coffee and worked on his investment figures while I hot-showered the salt away, dressed in ancient, soft, treasured, threadbare checked shirt, grey Daks, and a pair of Herter's Two-Point woodsman's shoes, of oiled, hand-treated bull hide, worn to a condition as flexible and pliable as an Eskimo wife. In the shower I had begun to raise tentative voice in song, but had remembered another day, another shower, when that same song had been interrupted by a lady named Puss handing me in a well-made sample of the drink known as a McGee. So that song clogged and died, and I dressed and made the drink myself and took it into the lounge.

Meyer looked up from his work and said, "You look grotesquely healthy, Travis."

"And your eyes look grainy, and you look tired, and how long do you have to go five days a week and sit and watch the board like a great hairy eagle?"

"Not as long as I thought."

"Indeed?"

"Sit and listen. Without a glaze in the eyes, please. Try to understand."

"Proceed."

"These Fletcher Industries earnings statements. Look, accounting is flexible. There are choices. Each one is legal. However, say there are fifteen ways to handle different things to make earnings look a little bit better. So this outfit uses all fifteen, right up to the hilt. The last published quarter, it looks like they made forty per cent more money than the quarter before that. I rework the statement and I come out with earnings not even flat. But down a little, even."

"So?"

"At fifteen dollars a share it *looked* as if Fletcher was a bargain for a growth stock, selling at maybe twelve times anticipated earnings for this year. So on top of that—which you call the fundamental picture, then there is the technical picture of the stock in the market. This buying pressure improves the technical picture. It becomes very desirable. Big volume attracts attention. Today I saw how it was going, how it was reacting, and so I took the risk, and I committed her all the way. Here is where her account stands. She's got seventy-four hundred shares. Average cost per share is eighteen dollars. Today it closed at twenty-four and a quarter. So, right now, a short-term gain of forty-six thousand dollars."

"Of what!"

"She holds shares worth right now a hundred and eighty thousand, less the margin account debit. The supply is shrinking and the demand is increasing. It is moving too fast. The *Wall Street Journal* yesterday had a statement from management saying they don't know why all the big interest in their stock all of a sudden. It got out of hand too fast. I made this projection about where it is going to go next week. I have a used crystal ball an old gypsy gave me. I say a minimum eight points next week, so it will close between thirty-two and a half and thirty-seven. Traders will grab profits and get out. Usually I would wait, buy on the correction, and ride up with it again. But we get a trading suspension, maybe an investigation of corporate books. I think they used all the accounting gimmicks they could, and then they lied a little. It went up too fast and next week will be faster. So I start moving her over into that nice one I found for her to keep."

"You're telling me or asking me?"

"Telling you. What else? You are the expert on pigeon drops. I am the expert on the biggest crap game in the world."

"But you have to talk to her and explain all this."

"I do? Why?"

"Because she ought to come down here."

He cocked his head. "Connie suggested?" I nodded. "I should discuss all this with her. It is only fair to her."

"And she should sign some papers, maybe?"

"Very important-looking documents." He scratched his chin, tugged at his potato nose. "One part of your thinking I don't understand. That lousy fellow, that LaFrance, it makes some sense he should go to Santo to see if he can get bailed out by maybe peddling him the option he's got on the Carbee land. So doesn't he mention you?"

"If he mentions me, it's the same as telling Santo that he was a damned fool. If he admits he's smashed and trying to salvage something, the price from Santo will go way down."

"How can you be sure of how that idiot will react?"

"I can't be sure. I just make my guess and live with it."

The freeze hit low spots well to the west and north of the To-Co Groves, hit them hard enough so that all the smudge pots and aeroplane propeller fans and bonfires of old truck tyres failed to save the dreams of a lot of the smaller growers. They expected the same on Saturday night, but the upper winds changed and a warm, moist breath began coming up from the lower Gulf and the Straits of Yucatán, moving across the peninsula from out of the southwest, and after some unseasonable thunderstorms, the afternoon was clear and warm and bright on Sunday when Janine Bannon arrived in the car Tush and I had fixed a quarter of a year ago.

I was watching for her, knowing when she had left the groves, and went and took her small suitcase from her and brought her aboard. She had been aboard before, when I had taken the *Flush* up the Shawana River, back when the Boatel was doing well, and they had told me their plans with an air of pleasure and excitement, so she knew the layout.

She looked trim and attractive in her green suit and yellow blouse, but thinner than she should have been. The difference in her was the way the vitality had gone out of her, deadening her narrow and delicate face, making her move like a convalescent, taking the range and lilt and expression out of her voice. Even her dark hair had lost lustre, and there were deep stainings under her eyes, fine lines around her mouth.

I took her back to the guest stateroom and she said, "I don't want to be a bother. I should have found a place."

"Which would be a very good trick right now. No bother. You know that. Get yourself settled in. Meyer will be over in a while for drinks and talk, and then we'll go out and find some beef, or Chinese, or whatever you feel like."

"Oh, anything is all right. Trav, it'll just be for overnight. I have to get back."

"That will depend on what Meyer has set up for you to take care of."

A little while later I heard some small clatterings in the galley and the chunk of the refrigerator door. I went forward and found her bending over and frowning into the little freezer. She turned and said, "I'd feel a lot better about all this if you'd let me earn my keep, Trav. Connie has all that help, and they have their own ways of doing things, and I feel like a parasite. You have lots of stuff here. Honestly, I *like* to cook."

"Never volunteer, lady. Somebody will take you up on it. So you're hooked."

She smiled. "Thank you. You know things, don't you? Like you know what people really want to do. Now go away and let me just potter around and find out where everything is and how everything works, all by myself."

I went in and looked at the tape labels and picked out one of a lot of classical guitar with Julian Bream and started it rolling, adjusting it to that level that is not quite background and not quite for listening only. It wasn't until Meyer was aboard and I called Janine in from the galley that it occurred to me that they had never met.

She put her slim hand into his paw, and she had that speculative reserve that women seem to have for the first twelve seconds when confronted with the rather outrageous presence of Meyer.

He peered at her, shaking his head slowly in a disconcerting way and then said, "Tricked again! Janine, my dear, if I had been told you were beautiful, I wouldn't have been working so hard to make you rich."

"Beautiful! Now *really*."

He turned to me. "See? A fishing expedition even. She protests so she can hear it again. Okay, Janine. You are a beautiful lady. I am very sensitive to beauty. A man who makes children run and hide behind mommy is very receptive to beauty."

"You should see the wolf pack of little kids," I said, "following this character up and down the beach, listening to his lies."

Suddenly her dark eyes looked lively. "Meyer, you too are beautiful. I do not know how you are doing it or why you are doing it even, but if you are making me rich, I will be very pleased and grateful."

"I am doing it because McGee nags me. That is a good guitar to drink by. And how long do we stand around with no drinks?"

She cooked up a great kettle of a delicious thing that she called "Sort of Stroganoff". I found some red wine that, for a change, Meyer approved of. After she had cleaned up, she and Meyer went into a huddle at the desk over the papers he had brought over. I sat on the yellow couch, reading and digesting, hearing them with half an ear.

At last she came over and plumped down beside me, sighing. I put the book aside. "That fantastic man keeps telling me fantastic things, Trav."

"Meyer is like that."

"He says you are supposed to tell me where so much money came from to start with. I *know* you somehow tricked Mr. LaFrance into paying such a price for our place. But there's a lot more."

"He made a donation, Jan. Press LaFrance made a nice gesture."

"But . . . if you stole it from him, I don't——"

"Meyer, did he give you that money willingly?"

"Willingly!" said Meyer. "He could hardly wait to get rid of it. That is the truth, dear lady."

"Okay. I give up. But apparently I might end up. . . . Tell him, Meyer."

"It's an estimate only. At the end of this year, after all taxes are paid, you should have, I think, about two thousand shares, free and clear, of G.S.A., General Service Associates, worth seventy dollars a share now, and more then. The dividend income will be six to seven thousand a year. All your eggs in one basket, but a very nice basket. Great ratios, great management, fantastic promise. Meyer will have his eye on the basket. With little kids, and you a young woman, you need growth and income. Tomorrow we see some people, start setting up some basic living trust structures."

"I have to stay over another night," she told me.

"Or more," said Meyer. "Depending. A three-year pro-
gramme and you will be on a five-figure income with a nice
reserve, with insurance trusts maturing for the college
expenses. The boys grow up, get married. You can go abroad,
go to Spain, rich and foolish, marry a bullfighter, buy fake
paintings. I'll be right here. A little trembly old man, feeling
terrible because I ruined your life."

And I wondered if it was the first time she had laughed
loudly and long since Tush had died.

CHAPTER SIXTEEN

ON the following Tuesday night at ten thirty, after Janine
had once again fed us well, I strolled with Meyer back to his
boat to check on the strategy.

"A piece of genius," he said, "that call from Connie."

I had arranged it earlier with Connie, while Meyer was
taking Jan to mysterious appointments with lawyers and trust
officers, and Connie had called back at six and asked Jan
if it was all right if she took the boys with her for a few
days. She would take Marguerita with her to look after the
kids. There was an Association meeting in Tampa, and then
she wanted to go up to Tallahassee for a few days, and stop
and visit some other growers on her way back. She'd be
gone a week, and why didn't Jan stay right where she was?

"Once she gave in," said Meyer, "you noticed the relaxa-
tion.. You noticed she ate better too? You noticed she laughed
a little?"

"Conspiracy."

"The best kind," he said. "Today I unloaded a thousand
shares of Fletcher at thirty-one and moved the funds into
G.S.A. It's the critical time right now. I don't know how
high the rocket goes. Ninety-two thousand shares traded
today. Suppose in the morning I call her and tell her the men
we have to see will be available Friday morning. No. Saturday morning. So you should move that hunk of ugly luxury
before it congeals to the slip. A nice little cruise some place."

"I'll try it. Don't count on it."

I went ambling back and went aboard and into the lounge. Janine was standing in the doorway at the forward end of the lounge, the companionway dark behind her.

"Trav?" she said, and her voice was all wrong. It was a sick sad scared voice, and the belt she was wearing was a sinewy, sun-reddened forearm. "Trav? I'm . . . sorry."

A knuckly hand appeared at her left side, at waist-level, aiming a short barrel of respectable calibre at my middle. "I'm sorry about this, Mr. McGee," he said. I could make out a tallness behind her, a relative pallor of the face against the gloom behind her.

"Freddy?" I asked.

"Yes sir."

"I'm sorry about this too, Freddy."

"Just you stand quiet," he said. The arm left her waist. A set of regulation handcuffs arched toward me, gleaming in the light, and fell on the lounge carpeting with a jingling thud.

The arm quickly clasped her waist again. "Now you move all the time like slow-motion movies, Mr. McGee. You get down on your knees and take those cuffs there slow, and you edge over slow and reach both arms around that pipe thing and put them on and press them nice and tight."

"Or?"

"I think you know the corner I'm in, Mr. McGee. It has piled up on me, and no way to stop it or change it. I couldn't stand being locked up any place even for one month without being turned into some kind of animal. So I've got no choice. I'm sorry about everything, but sorry doesn't help. So do it right now, start moving, or I'll lay one slug right through your forehead, Mr. McGee."

Freddy had been worn thin. He was on the edge, and the truth was in his voice. It made me very obedient. Very humble. I moved the way the specialists move when they are lifting the fuse out of a bomb. I snapped the cuffs snugly, taking a faint remote comfort in the knowledge that given ten seconds alone in the lounge I could brace myself, wrench the stanchion loose and get my hands on the revolver in the desk.

He walked Janine out of the doorway and into the lounge.

As he put the handgun away, I heard him sigh with the release of tension. He released her and gave her a litle push. She stumbled forward, her body slack, head bowed in her despair. "I'm sorry," she said in a low voice.

His hand went to his hip pocket, then reached out toward her quite casually. There was a barely audible sound of impact, a hairsoftened, leathery little thopp. She took half a broken step, face emptying. She started to lift her arms to break the fall, then pitched onto her face, jelly-slack, with a tumble of cushioned bone against the lounge carpeting.

I had seen something odd in his face just as he had flicked the lead against her skull. It had been a moment of change and revelation, showing a pleasure of erotic dimensions, of sensual pleasure. It is not an unusual way for the mind of a man to turn rancid. Cops fall in love with the hickory nightstick. Prizefighters forget to pace themselves, going for the sweet knockout. It is a pull that takes some twisted ones into anaesthesiology, or into preparing the dead for burial, or into scut-work in asylums. They are the dark brothers of the slackened flesh, turned on in some soiled way by a total vulnerability.

He looked down at her, stepped over her and sat in a chair just out of my reach. He yawned hugely. There was a faint family resemblance to LaFrance. He was a big, stringy, slope-shouldered boy, and he looked stone tired. He held the spring-handled tranquillizer in his right hand and gently bounced the leaden end off the open palm of his other hand. It was of black leather, intricately woven, greasy with much handling.

The only other time I had seen him was when he and another deputy had backed up Sheriff Burgoon when he had picked me up in the lobby of the old hotel.

I sat and hitched around to where I could lean my back against the bulkhead, the stanchion between my flexed knees, forearms resting on my knees.

"Why did you come here, Freddy?"

He was so exhausted his mind was moving slowly. "I remembered two days ago my Uncle Press telling me about this houseboat of yours. I was trying to sneak aboard one of the freighters heading out of Tampa. They watch them too close. I figure I can get out of the country somehow, I can get myself all sorted out and get some time to think what to do next."

"What you ought to do next is pick up that phone over there and call Sheriff Burgoon and tell him where to come get you."

"Too late for that."

"You've got a lot of friends in Shawana County. They'll work things out for you. They think you were defending yourself from Bannon and hit him too hard and got scared. They'll make sure that old couple where you got the clothes and car won't press charges."

"I tell you, Mr. McGee, it's too *late*. I had some more bad luck. That's the only kind I've had lately. There's a woman I killed not meaning to, over west of Dade City. I tunked her perfect, light and easy and just enough, and she took two steps more than she should have been able to and when she fell, it was right on a garden rake across her throat, and no way in the world to stop all that blood. God there was a lot of blood! He run into the brush and I don't know if I winged him at all. Anyway, I couldn't find him and I had to get out of there. No sir, it's too late for anything but running and hiding. Things start to go wrong, they just seem to keep right on."

"How did they do wrong with Tush Bannon?"

"I was patrolling and seen him at just about first light walking the shoulder of the road, carrying a suitcase. I stopped and he said he'd come in on the bus and phoned out to his place and no answer at all. He was worried about Miz Bannon. It's easy to know later on what you should have done. My daddy had said Mr. Bannon was sure a hard man to discourage. I should have taken him in where we were holding the stuff his wife left and the letter from his wife, and told him his place was all foreclosed and sealed up with the notices and all. Uncle Press had to have that ten acres, and he was sure going to get it. It had been a real quiet night, so I decided what I'd do was run him on out there so he could see with his own eyes, without me telling him, how he'd lost the whole works for good. I think I wanted to do that because he didn't act whipped at all. He acted like he had some way out of the mess he was in. So I said maybe the phone wasn't working and took him out. We got out there and he got ugly when he figured out I had to know that he'd been all foreclosed. Then I told him his wife had left him and left his stuff and a letter with the sheriff and he called me a liar. He walked at me, half yelling at me and I tunked him on the skull. It should have taken him down, but it just bent his knees some and he shook his head and kept coming. So I knew he had a hard skull, and he was big, and he felt ugly, so I made sure the next one would take him down. I put a lot of wrist in it and I figured to lay it right onto his forehead, but he was quick for a big man like that, and he tried to snap his head back." He sighed. "It hit him right square on the bridge of the nose, Mr. McGee. That's a real bad place because it drives two little thin bones right back into the brain. I squatted there beside him in the morning light, sweaty and cold, and held my fingers on his wrist, and felt his heart go slower and slower and softer and softer and then it stopped all the way and he shivered sort of, and after a while I figured out it would seem likely he had enough troubles to want to kill himself, and figured out how to make it look like he did and at the same time cover up the places I'd tunked him. You see, I knew if I had to tell what happened, I'd get run out of police work for good, maybe, and it's the only way I feel good, with the uniform and people listening when you tell them something."

"But Arlene Denn saw you."

He shook his head slowly. "All those weird kids. I thought I was in the clear on Bannon. Then she said she watched. I stood out there in the night trying to think of some way I could kill all of them. Like tunk them all on the head and an overdose of something. Or a fire. But I was on the despatch book because they gave me the complaint. I had those pictures, and I had that stuff I took off them. She didn't want trouble. I could give her a lot. So when she was off her high and made sense, I asked about maybe if Mrs. Bannon was playing around, or if there was some friend she could say she saw instead of me. So. . . ."

There was a stir beyond the yellow couch, a grunting sigh. Freddy got up quickly and went to Janine. When he bent down over her, he was out of sight. I heard the tone of his gentle voice but not the words. It sounded as if a lover were murmuring to his beloved, comforting her fears. I heard the tiny thud once more.

When he came back and sat as before, I said, "That isn't going to do her any good, Deputy."

"Or no harm, Mr. McGee. I know just where and how hard. It just kind of puts a jolt onto the brain, with hardly even a headache afterward. I'll be thinking on what I should do so I can get some sleep without worrying about either one of you. You know, if you'd only been right here on this boat when Shawana County made the request to have you picked up and held, everything would have been all smoothed over."

"Don't count on it. No matter how good you make it look, Freddy, the people I was with at the time you killed Tush would have come forward and cleared me and left you with a lot of explaining."

"By then there would have been no Arlie to change her story. It maybe would be a big mystery, but there'd be no way to get me mixed up in it."

"So Tush was an accident, and the woman with the rake in her neck was an accident, but Arlie Denn was going to be on purpose."

"You get pushed so far there's only maybe one little narrow way out of the corner. I better get you two. . . ."

I awakened lame and sore, with no knowledge of time or place. Daylight came from overhead, around the edges of a hatch cover that did not fit as well as it should. I had what I thought was a hangover headache, and when I realized that I was in the forward bilge area of the *Flush*, curled close to the anchor line well, the old frame members of the hull biting into my side, I thought that only a sorry drunk would pick that as a place to sleep. But when I tried to bring my right hand up and rub my face, it stopped with a jolting clink of chain. I turned my head and saw that my right wrist was handcuffed to one of the forward braces made of two-inch galvanized pipe, braces I had installed long ago to give her more forward rigidity in rough water. And I wasn't going to yank one of those loose, not without a chain hoist and a power winch.

I fingered my skull with my left hand and found a tender area above the right ear and a little behind it. I could not remember being "tunked," or where the conversation had stopped. My thinking gear was sluggish. It took me a long time to realize that my houseboat could not be moored at

Bahia Mar. The motion was wrong. She was at rest, bow into a gentle swell, lifting and falling. Sometimes she would get out of phase with the swell and I could feel the soft tug of the anchor line snubbing the left of the bow.

I sat up and shifted and found a better place to stretch out, where no white oak ribs dug into me. I kept telling myself that Janine was perfectly all right. There wasn't a thing in my pockets of any earthly use to me. And there was nothing I could reach. I managed to doze off a few times. The motion was restful. At eleven fifteen by my watch I awoke and heard the latch on the small hatchway entrance to the forward bilge click.

Freddy Hazzard came crawling through, wearing a pair of my fresh khaki pants and a clean T-shirt. He nodded and reached back through the hatch and lifted a half bucket of water through and put it within reach. He reached again and brought in a brown paper bag and put it beside the bucket.

"Mr. McGee, there's milk and bread and cheese in the sack, and a roll of toilet paper. You'll have to make out best you can with a bucket, because I'm not about to let you loose until there's a good reason."

"Where's Mrs. Bannon?"

"She's just fine. I found some chain and a padlock, and I got her chained in the head by one ankle, and I took her some food first."

"Where are we?"

"Anchored in the flats just off Sands Key, way east of the channel, maybe twelve miles south of Miami. I had me a time working this thing out of that big marina. The wind takes it. I fished commercial about every summer I was a kid in school. Mr. McGee, I found your fuel tables in the drawer next to the chart rack. With the fuel aboard it figures out to maybe four hundred miles range. Does that sound about right to you?"

"Why should I tell you anything, Freddy?"

He squatted on his heels, balancing easily to the motion of the hull. He looked at me in a troubled way. "I got that little runabout boat in tow. That's what gave me fits getting clear of the boat basin. I've been checking her over, and I think she's got maybe three hundred miles in her because the tanks are topped off full. Cuba would be easy, but I got the feeling it would be another kind of jail. I've been checking weather and there's a good five-day forecast. I think I could just about get to the Caicos Islands. There isn't much of any red tape or government there because, like a friend explained to me, they used to belong to Jamaica and when Jamaica went independent, the Turks and Caicos Islands weren't in that deal. I've got your papers and I can scorch them up some like this boat burned, and leave enough to read so I can pass for you where nobody knows you. I'm sorry about the way it has to be, but if I'm going to be you, I'm going to have to leave you and her fastened tight to this thing when she runs out of fuel and I open her up and let her go down. I thought of all other ways and there just isn't a one. Now, I'm telling you this, how it's going to be, but I'm not telling her because she'd come all apart. And you won't be telling her because you and she aren't ever going to see each other again. It's the only chance and I'm sorry about it, but I have to give it a try. Now you want to know why you should tell me anything. It's because when the time comes, I can lay one on your skull bone and hers too and you'll drown without knowing a thing about it. And I'll make you comfortable as I can meanwhile. Her too. But every boat has cranky ways, and when this thing isn't acting right, I want to ask you what to do and you tell me right. If you don't, you aren't either one of you going to be comfortable hardly at all. And you should know that when I was carrying her into the head and getting that chain fixed on her leg, I thought about how full-grown women like that always made me feel dumb and clumsy and afraid to even think of touching them. But since she's going down to the bottom anyways, it wouldn't matter what happened to her beforehand. I might mess with her and I might not. I couldn't say right now, but there's not so much chance of it if you act right. So right now I want to know just where to put those tacs to get the top range out of this thing."

"It isn't going to work."

"It's the only chance I've got. What rpm, mister?"

"Eleven hundred."

"Where's the switch on the automatic pilot?"

"Up on the topside controls, under the panel, over on the port corner."

"Where's your compass correction card?"

"Pasted to the inside lid of the box where the rule and dividers are."

He nodded. "I got a nap, but I need a lot of catching up. I'm going to sleep out the rest of the day and move on out of here about dusk. I'll bring you down some blankets so you can rest better, Mr. McGee."

"Don't knock yourself out with favours."

He left. It was just a wild enough idea to work, if I'd been alone aboard. But Meyer would know Janine had been aboard, and so would Connie Alvarez. They would never quit, not until they found out what happened. Small comfort.

So this had to be the time. During this long afternoon. Don't count on his getting careless later on. Because even when pooped, he wasn't careless. He'd been on the run. His two shipmates are latched up tightly. The bed is deep and soft. The sea rocks him. He may never sleep as deeply again.

So get to it, McGee. Get something working, mostly your dull head. Nothing in the pockets. Escape needs tools. Like a belt buckle? Ah yes. A careful young man. The old jail training. Belt and shoelaces were gone. What have you got that's made of metal, fella? Well, you have a corroded old bucket and you have a wristwatch, and you have some fillings in the fangs, and that is it.

And if you had metal, what could you do? You might try to pick the lock on the cuff. Think nothing of the fact that they are designed to be pickproof. Or if you happened to have a very thin and fairly narrow piece of spring steel, you could maybe work it into this little aperture where the cuff clasps together and maybe free the ratchets somehow. Except the good sets, like this one, have little knurled places designed to keep you from doing just that.

The hatch latch clicked and it opened and he shoved two blankets in far enough for me to reach them and slammed it again. Nice gesture, fella. Thanks a lot.

More appraisal. The cuff would slide along the heavy pipe bracing. They were in the shape of the letter X lying on its side, and I was cuffed to the one with its low end on the starboard side, the high end on the port. They did not quite touch at the centre of the X. There was room to get the cuff between them. I could stand up, if I kept pretty well hunched over. I gave myself very good grades in the handyman department, at least in that bracing chore. I had hacksawed them to fit snugly, then slipped the collars over them, each with a base about four inches across with four big bolt-holes. Even with the biggest wrench aboard, I would have had trouble. The rust looked as solid as the steel.

Suddenly I remembered that they were just friction collars. They were not threaded on. And the lip was about one inch deep. So, if a man could put his back into it, and put enough of a bend in one of them to make it an inch shorter, it would slip out of the bolted collar and that intelligent fellow would be free.

I made a blanket pad to protect my back. I hunched under the cross pipe, got myself nicely braced and tried to bend it. I tried until the world turned jet black with little streaks of red flickering through it. I tried until my ears were full of blood roar and my jaws ached and the pipe was grooving my bones, but it did not bend a quarter of an inch, if that.

I sat down and panted for a time. My eyes stung with sweat. Impasse. The only possible way I could get myself loose, other than chewing my hand off at the wrist, was to bend the pipe brace. And I couldn't bend it.

Give me a lever and a place to stand, somebody said. Or was it a fulcrum? Anyway, he was going to move the earth. If a reason had been given, I had forgotten it.

Sure. With a lever or a winch or a truck jack, no problem at all. I drank some milk and ate some cheese. Okay, McGee. Sit here and make yourself a truck jack out of some bread, cheese, a watch, a pail and two blankets. The old know-how.

And something went skittering across the back of my mind so swiftly I didn't catch it. A frail ghost of some kind of a frail idea. I lay back and tried to think of nothing at all, and when it appeared again I grabbed it. I shook it but it didn't have anything to tell me. It muttered something about a turnbuckle and I let it go.

There are two ways to move something Push it or pull it. I sat up and looked at my equipment. I took one blanket and, starting at one corner, I rolled it as neatly and tightly as I could. There was a squat thick short timber brace on the port side near the bulkhead, but it was a foot beyond my best reach. I soaked the ends of my blanket rope in the water bucket. I took off my shoes and socks and stretched out and fumbled the end of the blanket rope around the brace and clapped it between the soles of my feet and pulled it through and toward me. I looped the other end around the pipe brace to which I was fastened, and pulled it as tightly as I could manage and knotted the wet ends together. I poured the water out of the bucket, put my boat shoes back on and trod upon the bucket until the side seam parted and the seam that held the bottom on tore loose. Then I stomped and folded and grunted and sweated until I had a clumsy metal club about two and a half feet long. I wrapped that up in the other blanket as tightly as I could and tied it with strips torn off my shirt. Then I stuck six inches of the padded lever between the two strands of the blanket rope and began winding.

It was easy—at first. The blanket began to twist and knot like the rubber band in a toy aeroplane. The timber brace made alarming creaking sounds. Each full wind took more effort. I had wrapped my lever in the blanket to try to keep it from bending. But as I began to have to hold it right out at the end to get enough leverage, it began to take on a curve. When I noticed that the pipe brace was taking on a curve too, I began to worry about what might happen when all that accumulated force was released. The sweat ran. I turned my lever. The blanket was so taut I could imagine I could hear it humming. What is the breaking strength of the average blanket?

Suddenly it was like being dropped into the middle of a threshing machine. The pipe sprang out of the collars and banged me on the shoulder. The lever spun free and hit me on the elbow and numbed my forearm and hand. The pipe spun and rang against my skull and knocked me down and tried to twist my arm off by the cuffed wrist. It was an ungodly din, and Freddy was going to come charging down. I slipped the cuff off the end of the pipe. I clawed the shirt strips off my lever and knelt by the hatchway with the raw, flattened chunk of bucket held high, silently begging him to stick his head in, and wondering if he was on the other side waiting for me to stick my head out.

So I went creeping cautiously out, holding the loose cuff in my right hand with enough tension to keep the chain from clinking. I went up through the other hatch forward and moved silently aft. I stopped every few steps to hold my breath and cock my head and listen. At the mouth of the corridor I heard a buzzing snore, deep and slow and regular. The door of the master stateroom was ajar. The door to the head was closed, and I could hear a faint clinking of chain.

Procedure: Go to the lounge. Get the weapon from the desk. Go charging in and blow one of his kneecaps off just to be on the safe side. Liberate the lady. Head for Dinner Key and radio the police to meet us.

But again he was careful. He had shaken the place down. No 38. I checked the pilothouse and the shark rifle was not in the spring clamps where it belonged.

Revised procedure: Silently liberate the lady and get her the hell out there and into the *Muñequita* and when we had drifted far enough, start her up and leave in a big hurry.

Chain. So the quickest, easiest way would be with the great big nippers, a brute set with handles a yard long. And they were right where I hoped they would be, in behind the tool locker, wedged in place.

I enjoyed his snoring as I moved like a ghost past the door to the master stateroom. I opened the door to the head slowly. She was sitting on the floor. She snapped her head around and looked at me with a madwoman's face, eyes and mouth wide and round, breath sucking to scream. But comprehension came just in time and I eased in and closed the door just as silently as I had opened it. She had found some greasy medication in the medicine locker and she had greased her bare ankle and foot and had been trying to work the chain off of it. She had gouged through the skin and her greasy ankle and the floor was speckled with blood.

I slid one jaw of the nippers under the ankle chain and applied pressure. The jaws bit through and the chain fell away, rattling on the deck. I put the nippers down and helped her up. She clung to me. I whispered to her and told her he was asleep and we were going to go aboard the *Muñequita* and release her tow line and drift away. She bobbed her head in violent agreement.

When we had crept to within two feet of the partly open door we had to pass, I suddenly knew what was wrong. I couldn't hear him snoring. So I took her by the arm to try to make it a fast run, but the door swung open and there he was. I shoved her along the corridor and in the same violent effort I tried to jump him. But a big soft hot red hammer hit the meat of my left shoulder and that much impact at that close range spun me and drove me back through the open dor and the guest stateroom. The spinning tangled my legs and I fell heavily, remembering as I went down an old lesson painfully learned long ago. When you are shot, you are dead. Bang, you're dead! So be dead, because it might be the only chance you have left in the world.

I heard him come in to stand over me. "You damn fool!" he said. "You sorry pitiful damn fool." And he put his toe against my hip and nudged me to see how slack I was. I swung both legs and swept his feet out from under him and clawed my way onto him, yelling at the same time to Jan to get off the boat, swim ashore, run like hell.

It was very busy work. My left arm wasn't part of me, and he kept trying to work that revolver around to get it against me, and I kept trying to stay behind him and get the cuff chain around his throat. He managed to struggle up with me, which was a demonstration of an impressive amount of wiry strength, but I yanked him off balance and toppled back on the bed with him. It had taken only a very few seconds. I gave up the chain bit and got my right forearm across his throat, but he kept his chin tucked down well. I got the gun wrist with my left hand, but the left arm was getting worse by the moment, and slowly, slowly he was turning the muzzle to where he could be sure of putting the next slug in my head without even having to look back at me.

It was then that Janine came through the door screeching, and bearing on high, in both hands, the small red fire extinguisher she had apparently yanked out of the clips on the corridor wall. Screeching, face contorted, she ran directly at us, starting the great descending blow when she was at least three steps from the bed. He wrenched the gun wrist free and there was the great slamming sound of a shot in an enclosed place, and I saw her head wrench sideways as she struck her fearful blow, then a jostle of great weight made such a sickening pain in my shoulder and arm, the world shrank down to a little white thing and winked out.

I don't know how long I was out. Thirty seconds, fifteen minutes. I came struggling up aware of great urgency, aware of being pinned under great weight. Freddy Hazzard seemed very heavy. I fingered his slack throat with my right hand and couldn't find a thing. I wormed part-way out from under him and saw one good reason for the weight. Janine lay spilled across us, supine, the small of her back across his loins, her dark head hanging back over the edge of the bed.

I squirmed out from under both of them and stood up. I did not want to feel any more dead throats. The left side of her head was toward me. Her hair was clotted heavily with blood. I stared at her and when I saw the rise and fall of her chest, I risked the finger on the throat, found a place going bump, bump, bump.

Then I looked at him. Nobody was going to be able to feel any pulse. He had a grooved head. Diagonal. From one temple across to the opposite eyebrow. A groove as wide as the fire extinguisher and maybe an inch deep. The eye bulged with a blank astonishment greater than any astonishment in the living world.

The faintness came over me and faded away slowly. I stood three stories tall and I would sway in the slightest breeze. Toy fellow made of broomstraws and flour paste. My left arm hung there, and I looked down and saw the blood dropping busily from my fingertips.

Things to do, McGee. Got to take care. Got to tidy ship. Grab the buckets and brooms, men. Clean sweep fore and aft. So start moving, because you don't know how much time you have, and it might not be enough. I fingered Hazzard's pockets and found the cuff key and managed to turn it with numb fingers and get my right wrist free. The metal had rubbed it raw.

I could not make myself hurry. I felt thoughtful. It was a kind of faraway game. Amusing and not very important. I might be able to do what might keep me from falling off the edge for good, and I might not. Interesting.

On my slow way to the head I ripped my shirt off. I turned my left side toward the mirror. The entrance hole was three inches below the top of the shoulder and on the outside of the upper arm, but deep enough so that I couldn't tell if it had done bone damage. The slug had tumbled apparently, and torn one hell of a hole on the way out. I lifted my left arm with my right hand, braced the left palm against the wall and locked the elbow. I took my time putting the gauze pads on the wounds, winding it very neatly, tearing the surgical tape with my teeth.

"Nice," I heard myself say in a voice that seemed to come from the next room. "Very neat."

So I went floating blissfully to the galley. Shock. Loss of blood. Replace fluids. Use stimulants. There was a quart jar of orange juice in the icebox. I found an unopened fifth of Wild Turkey in the liquor locker. I put them on the booth table and eased into the seat and wondered what a good name would be. An Orange Turkey? A Wild Screwdriver? The white mist began moving in from the edges and I realized nobody was going to come along and serve me. I picked my left arm up by the wrist and put the arm on the table. It wiggled its fingers when I sent the message down the nerves. I drank a third of the quart of juice. I took four long swallows of the bourbon. Second third of the juice. Another deep drag on the liquor. Polish off the juice. Then enough bourbon to just begin to tickle the gag reflex.

Come on, white mist. Take another shot. Here is McGee.

But it had edged so far back I couldn't see it anymore out of the corners of my eyes. I got up without thinking of my arm. It slid off my table and flapped me on the leg. And I thought about Janine, and she had a slug in her skull, and the bump, bump, bump would be over. I picked up my left arm and turned it and looked at my watch. How had it got to be three in the afternoon?

Go find out. You have to find out sometime. So go take a look at her.

The throat was still knocking away like a good little engine. I tugged at her and got her off Freddy and straightened her out on the bed. I did not want to move her too much. But I did not want to take the chance of her waking up all of a sudden and finding herself right there side by side with what had been Freddy.

I got an old tarp and put it on the floor beside the bed, on his side, reached beyond him and got hold of the bloody sheet and yanked it out from under her, and tugged on it until it rolled him off and he fell onto the tarp with a lanky thudding, face-down. I left the sheet on him and flipped the ends and side of the tarp over him. I turned on the bright reading light and fingered her crusted hair apart and found where the bullet had grooved her skull in an area an inch and a half long and the same distance above her left ear. There didn't seem to be anything you could pull together or sew together. It had punched out a strip of scalp meat, hair and all, and had clotted over and stopped bleeding. I soaked gauze in antiseptic and patted the wound very delicately, then tied the pad in place with more gauze.

Then, in a moment of pure genius, I got a piece of sheeting and made a sling for myself, so my arm would stop swinging around and flapping at me. It was much better. I didn't want her to wake up and look in that tarp. I found the fire extinguisher in the corner where it had rolled. I wiped it off and put it back in the clips. I sat on the floor and put both feet against the tarp and shoved Freddy half under the bunk, where he was less noticeable.

I went above decks. We were riding well at anchor. Sea calm. Skies clear. I went below and stripped and cleaned myself up. I wasn't bleeding through the gauze. Good sign. I put a robe on. The empty sleeve flapping was less troublesome than the empty arm.

I made two giant peanut butter sandwiches and yonked them down and washed them the rest of the way with a quart of cold milk. What every healthy American kid needs after being shot.

At four thirty, after some mental practice, I warmed up the set and got through to Miami Marine and put through a credit card call to Meyer aboard his boat. She told him she had a call for him from the motor vessel, *The Bustled Lush*.

"Travis? Say, I see you must have talked her into it without too much trouble, huh? Over."

"It was spur of the moment, Meyer. Crazy wild kids taking off on a magic adventure. Over."

"Are you maybe a little smashed, old friend? Listen, I can't talk about the other thing, not with half this transmission open for anybody who wants to listen. Tell her things are going well. How about the next time you call me, make it from shore and I can tell you the news. Over."

"Will do. I don't know how long we'll cruise around. Maybe I can keep her out a couple of weeks. Over."

"It will be great fun for her, Travis. And it won't hurt you. Have some fun. Catch fish. Sing a little."

As soon as I signed off, the reaction began. Somehow you do what you have to do, and somehow the machinery accepts the abuse. But when you've forced your way through it, all the gears and wheels start to chitter and grind and wobble around on the pinions. I felt icy cold. I knew it was all sour. She would never come out of it. Something would be bleeding in her head and that would be the end of it. Or somebody had seen him coming aboard, or seen him taking the houseboat out. My arm would start to rot. The hook would pull out of loose sand and we'd drift aground.

I went back below and looked at her and went into the master stateroom and slipped out of the robe and into the giant bed and wished I wasn't too old to cry myself to sleep....

I heard her saying my name for a long time before I let it wake me up. She sat on the edge of the bed, facing me. She wore a short beach robe and she had fashioned a turban affair out of a pale blue towel. It was night. The light was behind her.

"Trav? Trav?"

"Mmm. How's your head, Janine?"

"I'm all right. I'm perfectly all right. Trav, how badly are you hurt?" She had bared my shoulder and she was looking at the bandage.

"It's just a scratch."

"Please. How bad is it?"

"I don't think it's too bad."

"I want to look at it."

"Let me wake up. I didn't mean to sleep so long."

"Get waked up, then. I'll be right back."

She came back with a towel, a first-aid kit and a basin of hot water. I rolled onto my right side. She went to the other side of the bed, spread the towel and equipment out, and snipped the bandage off.

I heard her insuck of breath, and said, "That bad?"

"I . . . I think it looks worse than it is. I'll try not to hurt you."

She busied herself. She was very gentle.

"Travis?"

"Yes, Jan."

"He was going to kill us both, wasn't he?"

"Maybe."

"I know he was. From the way he looked at me. After he . . . I thought when you came in and snipped me loose, it was him coming back."

"Did he give you a bad time?"

"Sort of. After he chained me up, he hit me on the head again. Very very lightly, and it was just enough so everything seemed to go far away and I couldn't move or speak or see. I wasn't awake or asleep. I could feel what he was doing. Just with his hands. Sort of . . . to see what a woman was like there. And when I could move, I grabbed his hands and pushed them away. And he looked at me and blushed and then sort of half smiled and shrugged and I knew he knew I wouldn't ever be able to tell anybody about whatever he decided to do to me. I knew he'd come back . . . but it was you. And then I was sure he'd killed you like he killed Tush and . . . I knew I could kill him. I knew he couldn't stop me. And so . . . I did."

"You didn't quite make it, honey. I took care of it."

"Don't try to be sweet and protective and all. I looked at him in there. I had to touch him and turn him over to make sure. I even felt it in my hands when it hit him, a kind of looseness, the way his head went. I'm not proud of it or full of joy or anything. But I can live with it. . . . There. I think that's better than the way it was, Travis."

"Thanks," I said and rolled onto my back. She took the basin and towel and gear away.

When she came back, she stood at the foot of the bed and said, "What do we do now?"

"I called Meyer while you were still out."

"And told him about this?"

"No. I said we might cruise around for quite a while."

"You did?"

"Until we're both healed up enough so people won't ask questions. If we go back, we make statements. Everybody will want to see how much front page space they can get, how many times they can get their pictures taken with us. What good will that do you or your kids?"

"No good at all."

"Or do Freddy's people?"

"They might as well think he's alive in the world, some-where."

"And I couldn't take that kind of hot publicity, Jan. I can't start wearing a public face. It would put me out of business. I don't need a lot of official interest. There's a little bit now. All I can handle. So we deep-six him and say nothing. Not a word, Jan. Not ever, to anyone. Can you handle that?"

Her face was quiet, her eyes thoughtful. In the sea-night there was the tangible presence of death aboard. A head-knocker whose luck turned very bad, who'd never make it to the Caicos, who'd had something rancid going on in the back of his mind, some warped thing all mixed up with darkness and helplessness and sexual assault. The sickness had begun to stir and move under stress, had begun to emerge, but his life had stopped before it had gone out of control.

She said, "What if you don't heal right? What if we have to find a doctor?"

"We have a story. We were potting at beer cans with a thirty-eight. The kick startled you. It slipped out of your hand, went off when it hit the deck."

"Does . . . anyone but us know he was aboard?"

"Not likely."

She nodded. "I'll be all right, Travis. I'll be fine."

I got up and went on deck and discovered I had com-pletely forgotten the anchor lights. We were well away from any course a small boat might take, but a darkened boat at night invites investigation. I put us back onto legal status. We were riding well. The night was soft, the stars slightly misted. Miami was a giant glow to the north.

I stayed topside a long time. When I went below, she was curled up on the yellow couch in the lounge, sound asleep. I looked down at her and hoped that she would have enough iron in her to help a one-armed man with some curiously ugly chores. She had dark patches under her eyes. I turned off the small dim lamp nearby and felt my way through dark and familiar spaces back to the master stateroom.

I didn't really know if she could last, if she could handle it, until the next morning when I sat on the edge of the freshly made bed in the guest stateroom and watched her using the curved sailmaker's needle and the heavy thread, sewing Freddy into his sea shroud. She had cleaned and dressed my wound afresh. I had wired a spare anchor snugly to the deputy's ankles, and tucked his gun and cuffs and the black leather sap in beside him.

When she ran out of the hank of thread, and clipped it off and took a fresh end from the spool and moistened it in her lips before threading the needle again, she looked up at me for a moment. It was a flat, dark look, and it made me think of old stories of how warriors dreaded being taken alive and turned over to the women.

At the end of day she wrested the anchor free when I ran the *Flush* up to it, and brought it aboard. We ran outside, creaking and rocking in the swell. I put it on automatic pilot at just enough speed to hold it quartering into the sea, and together we clumsied him up and out onto the side deck. She held the book and tilted it to catch the light from where the sun had gone down, and she read the words we thought would be appropriate to the situation.

She laid the book down and with my one arm and her two, we lifted the stiffened body upright, and as she held it propped against the rail, I bent and grasped the tarp at the feet and lifted and toppled it into the sea. It sank at once. And then I took the wheel and came about and headed for the buoy that marks the pass back into Biscayne Bay.

CHAPTER SEVENTEEN

ONCE she accepted the need to stay by ourselves, to heal in order to avoid questions, a strange new placidity came over her. She had long times of silence, and I could guess that now that she knew what had happened, and how it had happened, part of it was over and the part about finding an acceptance of Tush's death had begun.

She began to eat well and spend some of the sun hours

basting and broiling herself to the deep tan her skin took readily, and she began sleeping long and deeply, gaining the weight that softened her bone-sharp face, that filled out the long concave line of the insides of her thighs, that made her fanny look a great deal less as if it had been slapped flat with a one by six.

I called Meyer from shoreside phones. I wore the arm out of the sling for longer periods each day, reslinging it when the knitting muscle structures began to ache.

She phoned Connie when the trip with the kids was over, and Connie accepted the notion that a little more time cruising would do her good. She talked to each of the boys. They were fine. They missed her. She missed them.

Meyer eased out of the last of her holding in Fletcher on the Wednesday, the last day of January, at a good price, and when we talked again the following Monday evening—I had phoned him from Islamorada—he said with undisguised glee that Fletcher had got up to forty-six dollars a share at noon, and the Exchange had suspended trading in it fifteen minutes later, pending a full investigation of a tip that the earnings reports had been misstated, that a syndicate of speculators had been boosting the price, and that the company officers had been quietly unloading all their own holdings at these false and inflated values. The word on the Street was that it might be another Westec case, and it was rumoured that a Florida-based speculator named Gary Santo was deeply involved in the artificial runup of the price.

"If they ever approve it for listing again," Meyer said, "it will open at about six dollars, and even that is more than a realistic book value per share."

The next morning the *Flush* was tied up at the marina dock at Islamorada, and after breakfast I had Jan peel the final dressing off the wound. The entrance wound was a pink dime-sized dimple, vivid in the middle of the surrounding tan. She made careful inspection of the exit area, held the back of her hand against it to check for any inner heat of infection and said, "This last little piece of scab is going to come off any day now. If we could have had it sewn up, there wouldn't be so much scarring, Trav. It looks as if . . . somebody stabbed you with one of those wood rasp things."

"I got through the whole day without the sling yesterday.

And I can hold that smallest sledge out at arm's length for fifteen seconds. And so I keep a shirt on till the scars bleach white and match the old ones."

"You would make a very low-grade hide," she said. "They might find three or four sections that would make nice little lampshades, but they'd have to throw the rest away."

"Just accident-prone, I guess. And you pass inspection now, lady. Keep it combed that way and you're fine."

"You see, I was aboard this funny houseboat and it got rough and I lurched and took this great gouge out of my scalp on some kind of sharp thing sticking out."

"We can head back so Meyer can help you count your money."

Late that afternoon she went below and came up with two cold uncapped bottles of Tuborg and sat close beside me and said, "A sort of an announcement, Travis McGee. There won't be another chance to talk, probably. I wish to announce that you are a dear, strange, ceremonious kind of guy, and I didn't like you very much at all before Tush died and didn't know why he liked you, and now I do, maybe."

"Tell me. Maybe I can use it."

"It made me jumpy to be alone with you, because the way I had you all figured out, you were going to comfort the little widow woman. Life goes on and all that. Let me bring you back to life, darling. A woman always knows when a man finds her physically attractive, and I am flattered that you so do."

"I so do."

"I expected some of the gooey rationalizations of the chronic stud, including how Tush would approve, and besides it's so healthy. But you have been very stuffy and proper and dear. Thank you."

"You're welcome."

"Maybe I would have gone along with it, out of some kind of self-destructive impulse. I don't know. I don't know if I was a one-man gal. I sort of think so. Maybe that part of me—the privacy part—will come alive again. Anyway, I'm glad you didn't give me a chance to make any choice. Physically I'm a lot better than I was. Better nerves. But I'm still half a person. And so damned lonely, and the world is so . . . flattened out." She reached up and kissed me under the ear. "So thanks for not trying to be God's gift to the bereaved, dear."

"You're welcome aboard any time. You wear well."

She smiled a bitter little twisty smile and, eyes wet, took my hand and clenched it tightly. So we were a couple of kids in an abandoned barn and the big storm was hammering down, and we held hands for comfort. Tush was her storm, and perhaps Puss was mine.

On another Wednesday, the day of the Valentine, Meyer came over at high noon and interrupted my project of cutting and laying some Nautilex that was a clever imitation of bleached teak on a portion of the afterdeck.

"So I am here and I have brought you a Valentine," said he.

"Sometimes, Meyer, when you act like Porky, you make me feel like Pogo."

"Read the card."

I put down the knife I was cutting the vinyl with and thumbed his card open. Homemade. He had drawn a heart pierced by an arrow, with a dollar sign dangling from the end of the arrow. His verse said, "Roses are red; violets are blue. Unadulterated, unselfish, unrewarded efforts in behalf of even the grieving widow of an old and true friend are not like you."

"It rhymes," he said.

Inside the folded card was his personal cheque made out to me for twenty-five thousand dollars.

"What the hell is this?"

"Such gratitude! It hurt me to see you lose your professional standing, McGee. Like you were going soft and sentimental. So, through my own account, I put us into Fletcher and rode it up nicely and took us out, and split the bonus right down the middle. It's short-term. It's a cheque. Pay your taxes. Live a little. It's a longer retirement this time. We can gather up a throng and go blundering around on this licentious craft and get the remorses for saying foolish things while in our cups. We had a salvage contract, idiot, and the fee is comparatively small but fair."

"And you are comparatively large but fair."

"I think of myself that way. Where did the cheque go? Into the pocket so fast? Good." He looked at his watch. "I am taking a lady to lunch. Make a nice neat deck there, Captain." And away he went, humming.

And not over four minutes later a half-familiar voice said, "McGee?" I looked up from the tricky bit of fitting the vinyl at the hatch corner and saw the three of them lined up on the dock, staring at me without much affability or enthusiasm. Gary Santo on the left. Mary Smith in a bright orange minitent and a little-girl hat standing in the middle. A stranger on the right, medium tall, of that hunched, thin pallor that looks like sickness, even to the little watermelon pot, with a face like a bleached mole, glasses with massive black frames, a briefcase in hand.

"Howdy do there, Gary boy," I said. "Miss Mary."

"And this is Mr. D. C. Spartan, one of my attorneys. May we come aboard?"

"Why, surely. Please do."

I took them into the lounge. There was no handshaking going on. I excused myself and went and washed the grime off my hands, pulled the sweaty T-shirt off, swabbed chest, neck and shoulders with a damp towel, put on a fresh white sports shirt and rejoined them, saying, "Coffee, folks? Booze?"

"No thanks," said Santo.

Spartan said, in a voice like a talking computer with a slight honk in the speaker system, "It might be advisable for you to have your attorney present, if you could reach him quickly."

"Now what would I need lawyers for? Somebody suing me?"

"Don't get so damned cute!" Santo said. His face looked slightly mottled and puffy, as if the facials weren't working well lately.

"Please, Mr. Santo," Spartan said. "Mr. McGee, we are facing what might shape up into a very exhaustive investigation of Mr. Santo's role in the speculation in Fletcher Industries. And it may well become necessary to have you testify as to your part in bringing this . . . uh . . . investment opportunity to Mr. Santo's attention."

"Why?"

"There seems to be an unfounded opinion that Mr. Santo knew of the precarious condition of Fletcher Industries and conspired to run the stock up, and then short it, and that this scheme was interrupted by the suspension of trading in Fletcher common. To show Mr. Santo's good faith, we will have to subpoena your trading records and show that you had taken a position in Fletcher and then went to Mr. Santo to elicit his interest, and that Mr. Santo then made a cursory investigation of the company's condition before beginning a very active trading in the common stock."

I shook my head. "Mr. Spartan, you lost me there some-where. I never bought a share of Fletcher. I don't own any stock at all. Never have."

"Come off it, friend," Santo said in an ugly way. "You better be able to show me you took a real good bath in Fletcher. You better be able to show me you got stung."

"I've never owned a share of stock in my life!"

Spartan looked sad. He dug into the briefcase. He took out the stapled Xerox copies of the fake margin account with Shutts, Gallor, Stith and Company. "Come now, Mr. McGee. Surely you know that your account records can be subpoenaed from the brokerage house."

I looked at them and handed them back. "I'd say that's going to be a very confused bunch of brokers, folks. If I had to guess, I'd say these were Xerox copies of some kind of forgery, or there's somebody else with my name. I just don't know what the hell you're talking about."

"But Miss Smith can testify to what you told her and to you giving her the originals to Xerox. Do you actually want to deny that you went to Mr. Santo's offices and talked about this whole matter to Miss Smith?"

"Oh, I went there all right. I didn't have any appointment, and I had a hard time getting to talk to anybody, even this pretty little quail. Now, I suppose whatever we said was taped, just as a matter of convenience, you know, for reference. But I don't think you can introduce that kind of a tape, and even if you can, it would have to be the whole tape, not just some edited parts of it."

"There is a tape, of course," Spartan said, "And we can prove it predates Mr. Santo's interest in Fletcher common."

"Spartan," said Gary Santo, "I think this son of a bitch is too cute. I think he was working for somebody. I think he was setting me up."

"Sometimes I work for people," I said. "But not for long. Mary, you remember the long talk we had about that Gary's parcel he holds up there in Shawana County under the name of Southway Lands, Inc.?"

"What?" she said. "There wasn't anything like that."

"But, honey, you confirmed the rumour that Southway was going to sell out to Calitron for a nice price, if a fellow up there by the name of LaFrance could assemble the rest of the acreage."

"But what are you trying to *do* to me?" she asked.

"Say! If I've spilled the beans and got you into some kind of trouble or anything . . . I guess we didn't talk about it up in the offices. That was later, honey."

"We *never* talked about that!"

I shook my head. "But you told me how Bannon got through to you, and you had a drink with him at the airport, and he told you how he was being squeezed and wanted Santo's help, and you decided you couldn't take a little thing like that to Mr. Santo and waste his time with a little guy who got caught in the middle."

She caught her little lip in her teeth the same way she had when talking to Tush.

I continued. "Remember, honey? You said that you thought Mr. Santo had mentioned how, up in the hotel penthouse in Atlanta, LaFrance had tried to get Santo to buy Bannon out and Santo told LaFrance that it was his problem and he should handle it? That was the same night you told me you'd give me a clean bill with Santo."

I moved just fast enough. Santo got up and got over to her and got his hand back for a slap that would have loosened her teeth. I caught his wrist. The position gave me very nice leverage. I swung the wrist back and over and down and ended up in about the same position as a pitcher after letting go of his best fast ball. Santo boomed into the yellow couch hard enough to snap his head back, and then bounced forward onto his hands and knees on the rug.

"Now just a minute. Gentlemen! Just a minute!" Spartan said.

Santo shook his dazed head. I picked him up by the nape of the neck and sat him on the couch.

I stood in front of him and said, "Fun time is over, Gary baby. I didn't get a damned word of this from pretty-bit over there. She's devoted. She's energetic. She just never got a chance to get close to me. I made sure of that. Tush Bannon was a damned good friend. Your pressure, second-hand, drove him into the ground. And it went a little wrong up there and they went further than they had to and killed him."

He stared up at me, very attentive.

"I squashed LaFrance. I would have squashed you too if I could have figured a way. But you're too big and too spread out. All I could do was sting you a little."

"A little?" he said wonderingly. "A little? You cut my venture capital right down to the nub, friend. You fixed me so I'm associated with any new stock issue and it never gets off the ground. Sting me a little! God damn you, I might never take up the slack you put in me. And all of this was over some . . . dreary little small-time buddy of yours?"

I leaned over and slapped his face sideways and back-handed it back to centre position.

"Manners," I said.

I moved back to give him a chance to come off the couch. He thought it over. Then he took out a frosty-white handkerchief and patted the corner of his mouth and examined the dappling of blood.

I turned to Spartan. "Tell him how he stands if it checks out that I've never owned a share of Fletcher."

"Well . . . it would eliminate one possible way to ease the present situation."

I turned back to Santo and looked for that tinge of grey under the barbered, lotioned, international complexion. Saw a little. Not like LaFrance. Saw enough of it, and enough slump of resignation. He dabbed at his mouth again and got up.

"Come on, Spartan," he said. He stopped so close in front of Mary Smith's chair there was not room for her to get out of it.

"You're fired, you stupid bitch!"

"But you heard him say I didn't——"

"You didn't do what you're overpaid to do, which is to

stick close and check every little thing out. You could have saved me going into the tank for enough to buy five thousand of you for a lifetime. And that makes you too damned expensive. I'll have your office stuff packed and dropped off at your place. I'll have your cheque mailed. I couldn't look at you again without feeling sick."

"Gary, you just don't know how mutual that feeling is."

His arm came halfway up. "Uh uh!" I said. He lowered it and left swiftly. Spartan hurried behind him, and gave me a single despairing glance as he left.

She slumped in the chair. "Hooo, boy," she said wearily. "They told me there'd be days like this." She gave me a look through the emerald lenses. "Thanks heaps, McGee."

"I didn't exactly intend it that way, Mary Smith."

"But that seems to be the way it is. In many respects that was a very very very nice job, lad. It did have its cruddy intervals. You know, I didn't realize how much enjoyment I'd get out of seeing the great Gary Santo get clouted around. Funny. In three years he's popped me in the face three times. And I told myself that one more time, brother, and that's it. Would I have quit, though? I wonder? I am going to believe I would."

"Will he send any muscle around to teach me I can't do that?"

She looked at me, head cocked, wearing a little frown. "I'd say not. I mean if he thought you were absolutely alone in this, I think he would. But when he thinks it over, he's not going to believe that a person of your type could con him so completely. He'll think you're a front man, and I think he'll leave well enough alone. Besides, he's got a lot to think about.

"Do you think I'm a front man?"

"I am inclined to doubt it somehow. How about buying an unemployed girl a drink and then some lunch? You know. Like no hard feelings. You know, this is quite a setup you've got here, McGee. I couldn't tell much from the outside that time."

"Bourbon straight, water with no ice on the side?"

"Exactly."

As I was fixing the drinks Johnny Dow hallooed and stuck my mail under the corner of the deck mat. I gave her her drink and went out and brought the mail in, flipped through the customary junk and came upon an airmail one from Chicago in Puss's broad, round scrawl.

"Excuse a little mail-reading?"

"Sure. I'll just sit here and plan my future."

Old dear darling, I said one time that I would write it down to get it straight for you, and so I have and even have the eerie idea you might be able to read all the words between the words. The name was right. I lied about that. But the town wasn't, and Chicago isn't the town either. And there was no divorce. And I love Paul very dearly and have all along, and love you too, but not quite as much. That lousy Meyer and his lousy Law. Get a pretty girl to kiss Old Ugly and tell him he was absolutely right. You see, my dear, about six months before you met me on the beach with that living pincushion stuck into the sole of my foot, they took a little monster out of my head, maybe as big as an English walnut almost, and with three stumpy little legs like a spider. Half a spider. And the men in white dug around in my head to try to find every little morsel of the beast, because he turned out to be the bad kind. So . . . I got over confusions and got my memory all straightened out again, and my hair grew back, and I pinned an old buddy of mine to the wall of his office and he levelled because he has known me long enough to know I have enough sawdust to keep me solid. His guess was one chance out of fifty. No treatments possible. Just go off and get checked every so often, bright lights in the eyes, stand and touch the tip of your nose with your fingertip while keeping the eyes closed. That stuff. And pens drawing lines on little electric charts. I could accept it, my dear, because life is very iffy and I have busied up my years in good ways. But I could not accept the kind of life that went with the waiting. Dear as Paul is, he is a sentimental kraut type, and we had the awareness of the damned time bomb every waking moment. So life became like a practice funeral, with too many of our friends knowing it, and everybody trying to be so bloody sweet and compassionate during a long farewell party. I began to think that if I lucked out, I'd be letting them down. So I finally told Paul that if it was the end of my life, it was getting terribly damned dreary and full of violin music, and I am a random jolly type who does not care to be stared at by people with their eyes filling with tears. So I cashed in the bonds for the education of the children I'll never have, and I came a-hunting and I found you. Was I too eager to clamber into the sack? Too greedy to fill every day with as much life as would fit into it? Darling, I am the grasshopper sort, and so are you, and, bless you, there were dozens of times every day I would completely forget to sort of listen to what might be happening inside my redheaded skull. Be glad you jollied and romped the redheaded lady as she was coming around the clubhouse turn, heading for the tape. She loved it. And you. And how good we were together, in a way that was not a disloyalty to Paul! He is one of the dogged and stead-fast ones. Can you imagine being married, dear, to Janine, great as she is, and having her know you could be fatally ill? She would mother you out of your mind until you ran. As I ran. But there was the little nagging feeling I was having it all too good. I kept telling myself, Hell girl, you deserve it. And then hairy old Meyer and his damned Law about the hard thing to do is the right thing to do. I suppose you have been wondering about me and maybe hating me a little. I had to run from you exactly when I did and how I did, or I couldn't have left at all. You see, the dying have a special obligation too, my dear. To keep it from being too selfish. I was depriving Paul of his chance of being with me, because it is all he is going to have of me . . . all he did have of me, and I was forgetting that I had to leave him enough to last him long enough to get him past the worst of it at least. The darling has not done the interrogation bit, and if he thinks or doesn't think there was a man in the scene, I couldn't really say. You would like each other. Anyway, the female of the species is the eternal matchmaker, and I have written the longest letter of my life to Janine, all full of girl talk, and about living and dying, and I have, I hope, conned her into spinning a big fancy pack of lies about the Strange Vacation of Puss Killian, because I am leaving her name and address with Paul, saying that she could tell him how I was and what happened among people who didn't know. It is a devious plot, mostly because they would work well. He is a research chemist, and perhaps the kindest man alive. Anyway, last week all of a sudden the pupil of my big gorgeous left eye got twice as big as it should, and they have been checking and testing and giving me glassy smiles, and I am mailing this en route to the place where they are going to open a trap door and take another look. So they may clap the lid back on and say the hell with it. Or they may go in there and without meaning to, speed me on my journey, or they may turn me into a vegetable, or they may manage to turn me back into me for another time, shorter or longer. But from the talk around the store, the odds on that last deal make the old odds seem like a sure thing bet. Do you understand now? I'm scared. Of course I'm scared. It's real black out there and it lasts a long time. But I have no remorses, no regrets, because I left when I had to, and Meyer got me back in good season. Don't do any brooding, because if I can try to be a grownup, you ought to be able to take a stab at it. Here's what you do, Trav my darling. Find yourself a gaudy random gorgeous grasshopper wench, and lay aboard the Plymouth and the provisions, and go fun-timing and sun-timing up and down the lovely bays. Find one of good appetite and no thought of it being for keeps, and romp the lassie sweetly and completely, and now and again, when she is asleep and you are awake, and your arms are around her and you are sleeping like spoons, with her head tucked under your ugly chin, pretend it is . . .

Puss, who loved you.

"Is something wrong?" a voice said.

I looked at Mary Smith, realizing that it was not the first time she had asked me. "Wrong? No. Just a letter from an old friend."

"You looked funny."

"I guess it was . . . because the old friend decided to cancel an old debt." I got up and got the bottle and refilled her shot glass.

She lifted it in toast. "Here's to vacations without pay. Oh, Christ, that was such a great job! Such a sweet lush life, dear. But you know, sometimes you get an instinct. I think other things are going to go bad for Santo. I think he's going to strain too hard to catch up, and he'll choke, and he'll lose his style, and in a couple of years he'll be one of those whatever-happened-to people."

Puss's letter said, *"It's real black out there and it lasts a long time."*

I could feel my heart fall. It dropped a certain distance and there it would stay.

I could look at Miss Smith as if I'd never seen her before. She sat with a little inward smile of satisfaction, thinking of what she wished for Gary Santo. She dipped at the shot glass for her little butterfly sips. The edge of the minitent came to mid thigh. Exquisite legs, honey-tan and matte finish, were crossed. The light of early afternoon came through the window ports, highlighting the lustrous brown-auburn fall of hair, a healthy pelt. The secretive lashes half veiled the vivid plastic green, the secret half smile curved the corners of the plump mouth.

She got up and wandered over to look at the titles on the sleeves of the records on the shelf by the player. "Do we get music with the booze," she asked.

I went over dutifully and when I stood beside her, I realized she had suddenly fixed her attention elsewhere, so totally that she was unaware of me and unaware of the music. She was standing looking diagonally through the starboard aft port toward the dock, and following the direction of her intent gaze, I saw Hero ambling along, looking for fresh game, the meat of his shoulders slowly rolling, one thumb hooked into the tightness of the broad leather belt.

I looked down at her face, saw that the lips, now parted, looked almost swollen. Breathing deeply and slowly through parted lips, eyelids heavy, head nodding slightly, she watched Hero.

Then she turned to me and it seemed to take her a moment to remember who I was. In a voice pitched lower than usual, and with a huskiness, she said, "Darling, forgive me if I uninvite myself for lunch? Thank you for drinks and entertainment. Thank you for saving me from a shot in the mouth. I think I'll . . . look up those friends I have here. Some other time, dear. You have a lovely boat."

She put on her huge black sunglasses and put the empty shot glass down, and smiled and left. I went out on the afterdeck and watched her go hastily in the direction Hero had taken. Swing of the purse. Quick clip-clap of the sharp little heels on the cement. Rapid bouncing of the weight of the rich brown mane. Unseen, tented hips swinging. And, I could guess, a crawly butterfly awareness of the silky brushing of the softening thighs together, awareness of the prickling tickle of erectile tissues, of labial weights and thickenings, and a feeling of being unable to take a breath quite deep enough— as she went tocking and bobbing in her scurry to fall under the brutalizing, tireless, impersonal hammer of the Hero, to be once more the bed-beaten shoat, to be spent and lamed and emptied as before.

So I walked slowly to Meyer's boat and sat on the bunk with my head in my hands while he read Puss's letter. He finished it and coughed and honked and wiped his eyes. So I told him that we were going to take his little cruiser because it could take more sea than a houseboat, and we were going to take the *Muñequita* in tow, and we were going to go as far down the Exuma Cays as the range of his boat would allow, and then we were going a lot further down in the Little Doll. I told him I was sick unto death of miniwomen, mini-clothes, miniloves, minideaths and my own damned minilife. I wanted empty cays, gaudy reefs, hot sun, swift fish, and maybe some talk when it was time for talking.

And Meyer said, "So give me a hand with the lines and we'll take this crock over to the gas dock and top off the tanks."

One Fearful Yellow Eye

Glory Doyle had been one of the broken birds. McGee had
taken her aboard *The Busted Flush*, patched her up, and
turned her loose to make another try at life. Now she was
calling for help again. Someone had very quietly, very
skilfully, extracted six hundred thousand dollars from her
husband during the last painful year of his life.
Blackmail? Obviously. But the how and the why of it
baffled McGee until he began to detect the lingering,
unpleasant odour of sadism; until he began to turn up the
nasty little bits of evidence left by someone who preferred
to maim rather than kill, someone who like to watch and
savour the agony of his victim . . .

ONE

AROUND and around we went, like circling through wads of lint in a dirty pocket. We'd been in that high blue up yonder where it was a bright cold clear December afternoon, and then we had to go down into that guck, as it was the intention of the airline and the aeroplane driver to put the 727 down at O'Hare.

Passengers reached up and put their lights on. The sky had lumps and holes in it. It becomes tight-sphincter time in the sky when they don't insert the ship into the pattern and get it down, but go around again. Stewardesses walk tippy-dainty, their colour not good in the inside lights, their smiles sutured so firmly in place it pulls their pretty faces more distinctly against the skull-shape of pretty bones. Even with the buffeting, there is an impression of silence inside the aircraft at such times. People stare outward, but they are looking inward, tasting of themselves and thinking of promises and defeats. The busy air is full of premonitions, and one thinks with a certain comfort of old Satchel's plug in favour of air travel: "They may kill you, but they ain't likely to hurt you."

It is when you say, "What am I doing here?"

I was here because of the way Glory Doyle's voice had sounded across the long miles from a Chicago December down to a balmy morning aboard *The Busted Flush* at Slip F-18, Bahia Mar, Lauderdale.

"Oh Trav," she said, a wan voice, deadened and miserable, "I guess there's only one word. I guess the word is help. It's a lousy leverage, huh?"

"But I'd use it on you if I had to, Lady Gloria."

"You'll come up here? You really will?"

It was a valid assumption she was a few thousand feet below me, below layers of snow flurries and pockets of sleet. And then we dipped a sickening wing, leaving my stomach back up there at ten o'clock high, stood precariously still on big flaps, then steadied down into the runway lights streaming by, bumped and squeaked, brake-blasted, and everybody began smiling at everybody for no special reason, and began gathering gear, as

5

the hope-you-enjoyed-your-flight-aboard-the speech came on, articulated by one of our stewardesses over a PA system which seemed to be constructed of an empty tomato can and a piece of waxed string. The speaker systems, and the interior bean-wagon plastic décor seemed planned to give the air passenger the minimal confidence in the unseen parts of the mechanism. As if the brass did not expect the fad to last.

The sludge upstairs was rain by the time it settled onto Chicago. When I was ten feet into the scurrying cross-traffic of the terminal building, amid fluorescence and PA instructions, Glory Doyle—correction—Glory Doyle Geis, or alternately Mrs. Doctor Fortner Geis, or acceptably, widow of Dr. Fortner Geis, came flying at me, to hug and hiccup and make glad sounds, lift a mouth up as high as she could get it, which is perhaps a little over five feet off the ground when she is in four-inch heels.

It had been four years for us. She was thinner than she should have been. Deep vertical creases between black brows, lines bracketing the mouth, smile lines deep at the corners of the eyes. But even so, looking younger than the thirty-four I knew she had to be. After the kiss, I held her off a half-step, hands on her shoulders, to look at her. She tilted her head, made an upside-down smile, and her brown eyes filled quickly with tears.

"McGee, McGee, McGee," she said. "God, it's so *good*!"

Hers is a moppet face, mostly eyes and a mouth made for laughing, helter-skelter crop of black hair, tidy little figure, and remorseless energies.

She looked at her watch. "Let's talk over a drink before we have to plunge into the damned traffic." She guided us into a three-deep bar, and moved around to the far side, around a corner, and while I was putting our order in, she managed to ease onto the last stool as it became vacant, hitched it close to the wall to give me a leaning space, my back to the neighbouring stool.

"Your luggage?" she asked.

"Just what I carried off. Just this."

"Always simplify. Peel it all down. One of the rules of McGeeism." I could see what four years of marriage to Geis had done for her. She had far more assurance. She wore a dark green knit suit under a tweedy rain cape, and a frivolous little Sherlock Holmes hat that went with the cape. The diamonds in the wedding ring winked in the backbar glow as she lifted

6

the Irish and Soda to touch the rim of my gin over ice, and said, "To crime, Travis dear."

"And little women."

She drank and smiled and said, "But you had eyes for all the great huge broads, sweetie. What was that funny name everybody called that dancer? The one named McCall?"

"Chookie. She married one Arthur Wilkinson, who builds spec houses and makes her very happy indeed."

"And Meyer?"

"Sends his love. He's as hairy and bemused as ever."

"And the Alabama Tiger?"

"The party still rolls on, never really quits."

"It's a lot cosier aboard the *Flush*, Trav. Golly, I miss that whole bit, you know? If Fort hadn't come along just when he did, I could have turned into a beach girl forever, and ended up as one of those nutty old biddies who go pouncing around after seashells. It was just right, you know. My whole damned life fell all to bits and pieces, and you helped me put the pieces back together, and then I had to have somebody who needed me instead of the other way around, and Fort came by. But . . . it was too short. Four years. Not enough, Trav. Very good years, but not enough by half."

"I would have come up, but I was over in the Islands, and when I got back your letter was two weeks old at least."

"He was buried on October tenth. My God, a beautiful day, Trav. One of the greatest you could ever see. A real sparkler. We knew. Right from the first night I dated him, he levelled with me. I went into it knowing. But you kid yourself . . . when you're that happy." She lifted her shoulders slowly, let them fall, then grinned at me and said, "You are certainly a pretty spectacular sight, man, around this pasty old town. I never saw you out of context before. You're a little startling. I was aware of people looking at you, saying with that size and that much tan, he's a TV actor hooked on sun lamps, or from an NFL team in Texas or California, or some kind of rich millionaire playboy up from Acapulco, or you have this big schooner, see, and you go all over the Pacific. Hell with them. Let them wonder. Now let's go home."

The rain had stopped but it seemed darker. The highways were wet. She had a very deft little hunk of vehicle, a Mercedes 230 SL, in semi-iridescent green-bronze, automatic shift. I am no sports-car buff. But I enjoy any piece of equipment made to highest standards for performance, without that kind

7

of adornment Meyer calls Detroit Baroque. She said, "I better drive it because I'm used to the special ways they try to kill you here, and the places where you've got to start cutting out of the flow or get carried along to God knows where."

"Fine little item."

"Fort's final birthday present, last May. It's a dear thing. If I do anything that bothers you, McGee, just close your eyes."

Glory and the car were beautifully matched. They were both small, whippy, and well-made, and seemed to understand each other. There was that good feel of road-hunger, of the car that wants to reach and gobble more than you let it. We sped north on the Tri-State, and she had that special sense of rhythm of the expert. It is a matter of having the kind of eye which sees everything happening ahead, linked to a computer which estimates what the varying rates of speed will do to the changing pattern by the time you get there. The expert never gives you any feeling of tension or strain in heavy traffic, nor startles other drivers. It is a floating, drifting feeling, where by the use of the smallest increments and reductions in pedal pressure, and by the most gradual possible changes in direction, the car fits into gaps, flows through them, slides into the lane which will move most swiftly. She sat as tall as she could, chin high, hands at ten after ten, and made no attempt at chatter until the stampede had thinned.

"We jump off this thing at Rockland Road," she said, "and take a mess of shortcuts you couldn't possibly find again, and end up at Lake Pointe, with the terminal E, twenty-five bitch miles from O'Hare, where awaits a shaggy house, shaggy beach, shaggy drink in front of one of the better fireplaces in the Western world."

"Will I be staying near there?"

"In there, stupid. Not in the fireplace. There's a ton of room, and help to run it. And a lot of talking to talk, dear Travis."

On some of the curves of her shortcuts she showed off a little, but not enough to break the rear end loose. She knew the route through the curves and laid the little car on the rails through each one, steady as statues.

She laughed, and it was a fond laugh. "That man of mine. That Fort. Do you know what came with this thing? Lessons from a great old character named Kip Cooper who raced everything on wheels on every course there is. When old Kip finally approved, then and only then was this my car. Have you still got that absolutely ridiculous and marvellous old Rolls-Royce pickup truck?"

"Please, you are speaking of Miss Agnes. Yes, but lately I'm feeling wistful about her. She's becoming obsolete. You have to be up to speed when you bust out into the turnpike traffic, or you're a menace, and the old lady just hasn't got enough sprint. She accelerates like the average cruise ship. I'm going to have to save her for back roads, lazy days, picnic times."

We slowed and went between fat stone columns. Private. Slow. Lake Pointe. Residents and guests only. In the grey light through the branches of the bare black trees I saw fragments of houses, a wall, a dormer, a roof angle. When the leaves were out it would be impossible to see them from the smooth curves of wide private asphalt road.

Glory drove to the far end of the area, by a sign that said Dead End, and into a driveway. She parked by garages. The house faced the dunes and the lake. It was a long house, of grey stone, pale blue board and batten, dark blue tile roof. We went in through a side door into a foyer, and a big broad smiling woman in an apron came to meet us.

"Anna, this is my old friend Mr. Travis McGee. Anna Ottlo."

"I am please to meet," Anna said, bobbing her head.

"Trav, you're in the east wing. Anna will show you the way. This is going to be just the two of us, informal. I'm going to change to a corduroy jump suit, if that clues you."

"Miss Glory, the Mr. Andrus was phoning again. Best thing, I told him, you phone him in the morning, yes?"

"Perfect, Anna. Thanks."

I started to contest Anna to see who would carry my flight bag, but she looked so distressed I had to let her have it. I was put in a fine room, more apartment than room. There was a hidden unit of stove, sink, and refrigerator for breakfast. She showed me the button that rolled the panel back to expose the built-in television set. She showed me where the light switches were, and where I could find more clean towels.

After she left me, I unpacked, changed from the suit to the pair of slacks and grey flannel shirt I had stuffed into the bag as an afterthought. An ancient and treasured shirt, that good Limey wool that turns softer as it grows older. French

9

doors opened on to a planked deck facing the expanse of dunes and wind-twisted dwarfed trees between the house and the lake shore. The temperature was dropping, the wind increasing out of the north, and in the last greyness of the day I saw a full line of red in the west, like distant cities burning. The cloud cover was breaking up and I saw the first star. Wish I may, wish I might . . . I found myself wishing that Glory Doyle Geis would find some good and rewarding thing to do with her life from now on in, find someone who would sense how much she had to give, and how badly she needed someone to need her—as Fort Geis had.

The wind began to search out my tropic bone marrow, and I could smell a sourness in the wind. I remembered that it blew across a dying lake. For a hundred years the cities had dumped their wastes and corruptions and acids into it, and now suddenly everyone was aghast that it should have the impertinence to start dying like Lake Erie. The ecology was broken, the renewing forces at last overwhelmed. Now the politicians were making the brave sounds the worried people wanted to hear.

Now they were taking half-measures. Scientists said that only with total effort might the process be slowed, halted, reversed. But total effort, of course, would raise havoc with the supposedly God-given right of the thousand lake-shore corporations to keep costs down by running their poisons into the lake. Total effort would boost the tax structure to pay for effective sewage disposal systems.

So in the night wind, the lake stank, and I went back in out of the wind, and thought of the endless garbage barges that are trundled out of Miami into the blue bright Atlantic. People had thought the lake would last forever. When the sea begins to stink, man better have some fresh green planets to colonize, because this one is going to be used up.

I found my way to the big living-room. High beamed ceiling. Low fat lamps with opaque shades. Off-white walls, with good strong paintings. Islands of furniture, demarked by bright rugs, and between those areas, a floor of pale planking in random width, polished to semi-gloss. Slate fireplace big enough for an ox roast, with a broad hearth raised two feet above the floor level. Bookshelves on either side of the fireplace, and built into the shelves on the right, a high-fidelity installation, doors open, reels turning on the tape deck, making a sound of indolent piano in the room, at a volume just high enough to be audible over the crackle of logs and the wind sound around the corners of the house.

Glory sat on a crimson cushion on a corner of the hearth away from the direct heat of the fire. She wore a pale blue wide-wale corduroy jump suit, silvery where the nap caught the light.

She sat huddled, drink in her hand, looking into the flames. I stood and looked at her for a few moments. By some trickery of firelight, I could see how she would look when she became very old. She would become one of those simian little old ladies, wrinkles leathery against the round bones, eyes bright with anthropoid shrewdness.

So I put a heel down on the polished wood as I approached, and she snapped her head around, her brooding look gone in an instant. She motioned toward a chair which had been pulled close. "Did I say it was a great fireplace, McGee?"

"It's a great room."

The drink tray was on a low table between my chair and where she sat. Into a heavy half-sphere of Swedish glass she dropped three ice cubes, then with a knowing, mocking look showed me the label on the bottle of gin before pouring it over the cubes.

"Good memory," I said.

"What do you mean? For heaven's sake, remember how we had to practically go on an expedition from that crazy cottage on Sanibel so the lord and master could restock the Plymouth gin supply? I remember that day so well. When we got back, finally, you walked me so far along that beach that before we got back I wanted to sit down in the sand and cry. I've never been so pooped in my life. I thought you were being cruel and heartless. It wasn't until later I realized it was one of your ways of putting the jumbled jangled lady back together. And then I wondered why you bothered. I certainly wasn't much good to you or anybody until later."

"I used to wonder too."

Four and a half years ago I had gone dawn-walking and found Glory Doyle sleeping on the public beach. She was twenty-nine. She was broke, loaded with flu virus, hysterical, suicidal, and mean as a snake. I packed her back to the *Flush* like a broken bird. As she was mending, reluctantly, I pried the story out of her, bit by bit. She had no intention of telling anyone her troubles. She had no people. At twenty-two she had married a man named Karl Doyle. He was a chemist doing

11

industrial research for a firm in Buffalo. He was handsome, amiable, competent, and an emotional cripple. He was not capable of love because of his deep feeling of insecurity. The more she gave, the more he demanded. His jealousy of her was like a terrible disease. They had a daughter, and he resented the child deeply because it took some of her attention from him. After their son was born, he became worse. As he became ever more violent and unpredictable, she begged him to get professional help. She fought to make the marriage work, and she was a fighter, warm, understanding, gutsy. One night after he beat the little girl for a minor infraction of his ever more stringent rules, she took the kids to the home of her best friend and stayed there with them. When he called she said that when he started going to a psychiatrist, she would come back to him. One Saturday morning when it was her turn to do the marketing, she came back to the house to find that her husband had broken in, had killed the friend, both children, and himself. She could not remember very much about the next few weeks, but finally, after everything was settled, all she had was the car, her clothes, and a few hundred dollars. She headed south. Somewhere in the Carolinas the car got low on oil and the motor burned out. She sold it for junk and continued by bus. She had planned to get a job in Florida. But when she got to Lauderdale and rented a cheap motel room a few blocks from the beach a strange lassitude came over her, the end product of her conviction of guilt. She slept twenty hours a day. The money slowly dwindled away. She began to hear voices, and she knew that when she went out people nudged each other and pointed at her and told each other of the terrible thing she had caused. She was warned about the rent until one day she came back and found a new lock on her room, found that they were holding her possesions. She was feverish and dizzy. I found her on the beach the following dawn. She had fallen asleep while awaiting the necessary energy to walk into the sea and swim out as far as she could.

Somehow you can tell the real crazies from the broken birds. This one was pure bird. She'd had just a little more than she could handle. She had to have somebody to hang on to, somebody who could make her see that her disaster was as much her fault as is that cyclone or flood or fire which takes all but one of a family. Her nerves were shredded, digestion shot, disposition vile. She was without hope or purpose,

12

and she had gone a dangerous distance along the path toward despising herself. But in the end it was her sense of humour which saved her. There was a compulsive clown carefully hidden away, who had almost forgotten tricks and jokes and absurdities. When I got her weary enough and healthy enough, the clown part began to make tentative appearances, and the good mending started. After it had turned into a physical affair between us, another danger arose. She began to become too emotionally dependent on me. She was a very affectionate woman, needing and giving the casual touches and pats which to her were as necessary a part of communication as words. I felt too fatuously delighted with myself for bringing her back into reality to let her slip into another kind of fantasy. So, after helping her get a job as a dining-room hostess in a Fort Lauderdale hotel on the beach, I firmly, gently, carefully disentangled myself.

It was through her job she met Dr. Fortner Geis. He was staying alone at the hotel.

A log shifted in the fire. She sighed audibly. The music ended and she went over and punched the button to reverse it, so that it would play the other half of the tape.

"I love this house," she said.

I looked at a large painting on the opposite wall, the colours vividly alive, the composition very strong. A small gallery spot shone on it. I got up and went half-way to it, and then made out the artist's signature and went back to the chair.

"An incredible old man," I said.

"Fort and I picked that out in New York three years ago. It had just come into the gallery. Fort met Hans Hoffman once, years ago. He told me that Hoffman had such an almost childlike quality of enthusiasm, that youthfulness that comes from being eternally inquisitive. I told Fort he had exactly the same thing. He looked so startled I had to laugh at him. Golly, I'm going to miss that painting."

"Do you have to sell it?"

"In November, two weeks after Fort died, a very polite and considerate man showed up with a perfectly legitimate bill of sale for that Hoffman. He's a Chicago collector, and he paid Fort seven thousand five for it. He said that he had added it to his fine arts rider on his insurance policy, and he insisted on leaving it here until I decide what I'm going to do. It wasn't a shock, Trav. Not by then. By then I knew I couldn't consider anything mine. Not even the house."

"I don't understand."

She took my empty glass and said, "The lady yelled help. Remember?"

TWO

I KNEW she must have planned how she would tell me, but when she started, I could see that it seemed wrong to her. She stopped and hopped up and began pacing around.

At last she stopped in front of me and said, "Okay. Look at it this way. Look at me and Fort from the outside, the way his son and daughter saw us. Their mother, Glenna, died eighteen years ago, when Roger was eleven and Heidi was seven. So they were the privileged children of Dr. Fortner Geis. Money *and* prestige. Money in the family from their mother's side, plus what Fort added to it by becoming a great neurosurgeon —and the prestige of being the children of a man who'd made himself an international reputation. Fort told me he'd made a lot of mistakes in his life. but the worst one of all was the one he made five years ago, after the diagnosis was absolutely certain, after the prognosis was definite, deciding to tell Roger and Heidi that he probably had not more than three more years left. Damn it, Trav, he wasn't looking for sympathy or being dramatic. He was a doctor. He knew a fact pertinent to their lives. So he told them. He'd always worked too long and too hard for the relationship with his kids to be terribly close. They set up a death watch, practically. They started dropping in on him, full of brave and noble cheer. And it started depressing him to the point where finally he had to get away by himself. He cancelled out everything for a month and came down to Fort Lauderdale and didn't let anybody know where they could find him. He told me he had some adjusting to do. He said he had been too busy to think about dying. And if a man was going to die, he should have some time for contemplation, so he wouldn't die without coming to any decision about what it had all meant. He wanted to walk on the beach, look

14

at the birds, read something other than medical journals. And he started coming into the dining-room at odd times for coffee when I could sit with him and we could talk. Dammit, Trav, I had *no* idea he was important. I knew he was a doctor. I knew he was a widower. He said he was taking his first vacation in twenty-five years. There was that wonderful . . . simplicity about him."

"I know," I said. "That long nobbly face and the spaniel eyes and the slow grin."

"Loneliness," she said. "Both of us. We never talked trivia. We started talking from the heart right off. He'd loved Glenna deeply. He still missed her. And when we finally had a date, he told me what was wrong with him, and how long he probably could keep operating, and how soon he would die. We'd each taken our lumps. I told him . . . what had nearly sunk me without a trace. He was fifty, Travis. I was twenty-nine. Something in us responded to each other. He said it was because we knew what some things cost, and why other things were worthless, and too many people never found out. Then he asked me to marry him, and he said that if I felt squeamish about his being sick, I'd better not, because he desired me, and that was the kind of marriage he wanted with me, along with being friends and in love. He said he would have two years anyway before there was any outward sign or feeling and it would get bad, but not too bad, when the medication stopped working. So I thought it over for two days, and knew I wanted him, and proved there was no squeamishness, and married him with the idea we'd be going back to some sort of old frame house with a downstairs office and waiting-room in front, and some old dragon of a nurse. We had three and a half good years, Travis. We laughed a lot. I tell you, we laughed a hell of a lot. The pain started last April, but it didn't get as bad as he thought it was going to. And in September, he just started . . . dwindling away. Very quietly."

She sat down again. "Anyway, he was like a kid when he brought me back here to Chicago. I'd been too dumb to know who he was. He had this house designed and built for us, and sold the one in town. He cut his work back to just the experimental part. He didn't do any routine operations. It gave us more time. But you can guess what his friends and his kids thought. They made him so mad. They looked at me as if I was some kind of a bug. They acted as if marriage was some act of senility or something. I was the smart little operator, a waitress type, who nailed the poor guy when he was depressed about knowing he wasn't going to get anywhere near three score and ten. And the inference was that I probably liked it better that way. Roger was the worst. He's twenty-nine. He's a market analyst. He's a self-satisfied fink. He had the gall—and the stupidity—to go to Fort and suggest that inasmuch as I'd married him so late in his life, it would be a lot fairer to his kids to just leave me a reasonable bequest in his will. Fort had made a new will by then. It was pretty complicated, with trusts and so on, but the basic idea was he'd leave me half and them each a quarter. I told him I didnt want to make that kind of hard feeling, and he got so annoyed I had to drop the whole thing. I had to go to the bank with him a few times to see Mr. Andrus, the assistant trust officer, and sign things. He's very nice. I decided that after it was all over I could talk to him and see about some way of taking just what I'd need to get settled into a new life, and let his children have the rest of it. As it turned out, there was no problem."

"How do you mean?"

"He just didn't leave anybody anything. There wasn't anything left to leave."

"What do you mean? Had he been kidding people?"

"No. Starting about a year ago in July, he started changing things into cash. Mr. Andrus is going to bring the list around tomorrow. You see, he didn't have things actually put away in trust where he couldn't get at them. Mr. Andrus can explain all that. And his lawyers had no way of knowing what he was doing. He just . . . sold the stock and the bonds and everything and kept putting the money in current accounts. Then he kept drawing cash. Nobody knows where it went. He mort-gaged this house right to the hilt. He cashed in his insurance policies. All but one. I'm the beneficiary on that. And it pays me f-f-four hundred dollars a m-month as long as I . . . as long as I . . . l-l . . ."

"Whoa, girl."

She rubbed the corduroy sleeve across her eyes. "Damn! I'm not the crying kind. It's just that everbody has been so damned ugly to me."

"How much has disappeared?"

"A little over six hundred thousand dollars."

"In a little over a year!"

"He did it in such a way it wouldn't attract attention. He opened other current accounts, and he'd make deposits to other banks by cheque and then draw the cash. There was enough for the funeral, and enough to run this house for . . . oh, until February or March. Roger and Heidi seem to think it's some kind of cute stunt I've pulled. They act as if I'd drugged him or hypnotized him or something. The Internal Revenue people and the state tax people started treating me like a criminal or something. They came with a warrant and they searched every inch of this whole house and made inventories of everything. They kept coming back and asking the same questions. I told Mr. Andrus I couldn't stand it, and he took me right down to Fort's attorneys. Waldren, Farhauser and Schrant. Old Mr. Waldren kept asking me questions. He looked as if he was taking a nap all the time I was answering. But finally he said he would see that I was not bothered anymore, but I had better stay right here at the house, for the time being. I know I'm being watched. I think it's Roger or Heidi though, paying someone to keep an eye on me. I yelled help, Trav. I don't *want* the damned money. But I don't want people following me for the rest of my life trying to catch me with something I haven't got."

"Was there any change in Fort's attitude or manner?"

"When he started selling things? I didn't notice a thing different. He seemed happy. That's what I wanted. I mean we couldn't be all the way happy, knowing the time was growing short. But we could give it a good try. And we did. That's another thing. I don't think he was trying to cheat on estate taxes or anything like that. I don't think he wanted to cash in those things. So somebody was making him do it somehow. And so that *was* making him unhappy, but he kept it from me. He hid it from me. And I would like to get my hands on somebody who'd do that to him when he had so little time left, damn them."

"Would the illness affect his mind in any way?"

"Absolutely not!"

"Could he have been planning some . . . easier way of handling his estate and died before he had a chance to tell you?"

"They kept asking me that, sort of. No. Those last days before he went he went into a coma, I sat by him all day long. Held his hand. We'd talk. He'd nap and we'd talk more. He had a chance to say everything to me. He knew he was going. And . . . God, how he hated to leave me. He wasn't afraid of death. He was a man. It was the same way he used to hate to leave me when he had to go to a meeting. That's all. How much in love do you have to be before people believe it? I would have burned every inch of all that money to give him one more day."

She stopped looking fierce and glanced at her watch. "Medium rare? Butter on the baked? Garlic dressing?"

"Your memory is still working, kid."

She trotted out toward the back of the house to tell Anna to serve as soon as it was ready. When she came back I asked her how well-fixed Fort's children were. She said that Heidi seemed to be doing just fine. She was twenty-five—married at twenty-two and divorced at twenty-four. It had been a second marriage for her husband, Gadge Trumbill, usually referred to in the society pages as a prominent sportsman. When Heidi had tired of Gadge's fun and games on the side, it was rumoured that she employed people thorough enough to make an iron-clad list of positives which had included eleven wives of fellow members of the Harbour Yacht Club, but that the generous settlement and alimony had been the result of the respondent's unfortunate carelessness in not hiding more successfully his occasional penchant for willowy young men. Heidi Trumbill was living in a studio apartment at 180 East Burton Place, was busily painting very large abstracts, and was showing and selling them at a gallery four blocks away on East Scott Street called Tempo East. Gossip of the more rancid variety pointed out that her partner in the gallery operation, Mark Avanyan, was one of those who had made Gadge's second divorce considerably more expensive than his first. It made for interesting speculation.

"She is one very icy dish indeed," said Glory. "Take Grace Kelly like ten years ago, and give her a little more height and heft, and put her in a part where she's a nun who has to dress in civilian clothes to smuggle the code to the French army, and you'd be close. She's really beautiful, but she's one of those people you can hardly believe they have even a digestive system. She's a lot brighter than Roger, I think. He lives in Evanston, where else? He'll be thirty soon. He works downtown in one of those big new office buildings. He's a specialist in the commodities market, and his father-in-law is very big in the commodities market. Jeanie, his wife, seems nice enough. She's one of those brown tennis-playing ones, and they have three kids, and they go to horse shows and eat off the tailgate and talk about hocks and fetlocks and all that.

"Neither of them are hurting a bit, but you'd think I'd

18

pulled some tricky thing to get them tossed out naked into a blizzard. From everything Fort told me about Glenna, she must have been a doll. How could those two have such dreary people for their children?"

We ate busily and finally she looked over at me and said, "What I really had the most need of, Trav, was somebody to be my friend and take it for granted I haven't stolen money, and who'd know I didn't know anything about the money when I married Fort. I didn't make friends here. We wanted all our time together. There wasn't enough to share. But I thought, too, it *is* a lot of money and it *does* have to be somewhere. And I remembered the way you . . . make a living. Maybe I'm crazy to think you or anybody could ever find out where it went."

"It went somewhere. It's a nice jackpot. He had to have a good reason. Let's just say I don't have the feeling I'm wasting my time. If I can get some kind of line on what happened, then I'll see if my fee formula grabs Sonny and Sis. If the only way they can possibly get what they had coming is through me. . . ."

"Expenses off the top and cut the rest down the middle. You know that is okay with me on my share, dear. When I think it even entered my mind to turn mine over to those two . . . I'd rather give it to a home for . . . old television comedians!" She looked so totally outraged and indignant I had to laugh. She put her plate aside and I saw she had not eaten much.

"Where's that wolf-like appetite I remember from old?"

"I don't know. It's fine for five minutes and then gaah. I guess I could have expected some kind of crazy thing happening, like the money. What is it, Travis? Why in the world should *my* life be some sort of continuous soap opera? I think I had six uneventful years. The first six. Gloria Anne Ridgen. Then all hell broke loose. Is there such a thing as drama-prone? You know, *you* go *hunting* for the action. My daddy bought me a ride on a merry-go-round, and that was the time the man running it had to be drunk and decided he wasn't going to stop it. When they died I had to live with my nutty old aunt, and if my astrology tables were wrong any given day, she wouldn't let me go to school. The boy I went with in high school was walking by a building and somebody dropped a can of paint, and when he woke up from the coma a year later, he had the mind of a two-year-old. In college my room-mate was a secret klepto and hid the loot in my luggage and when they began to narrow it down, she turned me in, and six months later she got caught and they apologised and asked me to come back to school and the day I was due to leave I got infectious mononucleosis and my dog was run over. All I want is a plain, neat, ordinary, unexciting life. But what happens? In Buffalo one day I got off the bus downtown on a hot afternoon and the bus door closed on my wraparound skirt and drove off and left me spinning like a top in my little yellow briefs on the busiest corner in town. You know, I dream about that. There I am, and everybody is applauding and I can't stop twirling."

Anna Ottlo had gone to bed. We took the dishes out to the big bright kitchen and she rinsed them and put them in the dishwasher. I was aware of the wind, and of the emptiness of the stretch of dunes and winter beach outside, and of the comfort of the house.

"Was this whole thing in the news?" I asked her.

"No. From what John Andrus says, it isn't news until there's some kind of legal thing that goes on, the probate or something. He can explain."

"I decided it would be better not to tell her what had entered my mind. If a man, before dying, had converted his holdings into over half a million in cash, there would be a certain number of dim minds in a city of this size who would be inspired to pay a night visit to the little woman and see if she could be persuaded in ugly ways to tell where the deceased had hidden it away. It would be a clumsier variation of Heidi's and Roger's incorrect suspicion.

She turned lights off, and when one was left, we said good night by the embers of the fire. "You're so good to come," she said softly, standing close, hands holding my wrists, head tilted back to look up into my eyes.

"Beach bums have to take care of each other, Glory."

"But it's never your turn."

We were smiling, and then there was that awkwardness born of a simultaneous remembering of a special closeness of long ago. Her gaze slid away, and I bent to her quick kiss, and we said good night. I took one glance back into the big room after she had turned the last light out, and I could see her small brooding silhouette in front of the ember glow.

THREE

THERE was a watery sunlight when I got up, and a diminishing wind. I found the bright and cheerful breakfast alcove off the kitchen. Anna said Miss Glory had gone walking along the beach and should be back soon, and I should eat.

"Eat like the bird, Miss Glory is. Too thin, ya?" Anna said.

"She looks healthy."

"Need some fat. Better in the winter some fat."

When she brought my bacon and eggs to the breakfast booth I asked her if she had worked long for Dr. Geis.

"From I was thirty only," she said proudly. "Refugee. Only the German language I had. My little girl eleven. Husband had one grandmother Jew. He got us out, was to come later." She shrugged. "The Doctor Geis helped looking for him after the war. Never found. Then it was the house in the city we were in, ya? Heidi has only one year then and Roger has five years. All happy. Three years I am here and the lady then has the bad sickness of the heart. A very sad thing for the house. Weaker weaker weaker, and the last year in bed. Nurses. Even such a man like the Doctor Geis, he cannot the lady save." Her broad heavy-featured face looked tragic, but then as she looked beyond me out the window, she smiled suddenly, "Here comes Miss Glory."

Gloria came striding through the loose sand and stamped her feet when she reached the flagstone walk. She had on winered wool slacks, a stocking cap with a red topknot, her hands shoved deeply into the slash pockets of a short leather coat. She smiled at me through the window, and came in, yanking the stocking cap off, shaking her black crisp hair out, shedding the leather coat. As she slid in opposite me, Anna brought her a steaming cup of coffee. Glory had red cheeks. She wore a black lightweight turtle-neck sweater. "My word! Can we afford to feed this creature, Anna?"

"Good to cook for a big stomach."

"Sleep well, Trav? It's going to be glorious later on. There's that feel in the air. It's going back up into the fifties, I bet."

She had a toasted English muffin, and we took our second coffees into the living-room where she called John Andrus and told me he said he would try to get out to the house by ten-thirty.

"Who does he think I am?"

"Sort of an appointed big brother. An old friend. Somebody I trust. I told him I wanted him to explain the things I don't quite understand, so you can advise me and help me."

"What does he think I do for a living?"

"Well, I said you're in marine supplies. Okay?"

"It's nice to know what you said," I told her. "And after we get into it, could you sort of remember something you have to go do?"

"Darling, it will be a pleasure. When he talks about that stuff, it makes my head hurt."

John Andrus was a likeable guy in his late thirties. He was stocky, dark-haired, well-tailored, with the strong features of a character actor. We talked in Fort's study. Andrus had brought along the documents in a black dispatch case.

"This report summarizes an awful lot of leg work," he said. "He had thirteen months of activity. It would average a little under fifty thousand a month converted into cash. He didn't want to attract attention, obviously. He opened up current accounts in six other banks. He fed the money through the seven accounts. Apparently he also, in addition to cashing cheques at the banks, cashed cheques at clubs, restaurants, and hotels where he was well-known. He cashed in his securities holdings at at least four different brokerage houses. I think this summary by month of the assets converted to cash and the cash withdrawals through the current accounts is very close to actuality. See, here is the biggest month for sale of assets, over two hundred thousand. He converted seventy-two thousand into currency last January, and that was the biggest month. The smallest was last June. Twenty-one thousand. He was a very respected—and respectable—man, Mr. McGee."

"Strange behaviour."

"We're a little dazed, frankly. We had the estate set up so beautifully. Residuary trusts, insurance trusts, beautifully drawn instruments. And when the time comes to put them into effect, we can't find anything except some very minor asset values. It wasn't really big money, of course. But it's enough to be worth handling properly. We've been through all his personal papers and records, and there isn't a clue. It's distressing."

"To you and the IRS too."

22

He frowned. "Unfortunately the man assigned to it was not too experienced. He got very agitated. He was going to attach everything in sight, the small equity left in the house, Mrs. Geis' insurance, the cars and so on. So we elected, as executor, to have the estate appraised one year from the date of death, as is our option. I imagine the IRS man thought it was some sort of attempt to evade estate taxes."

"But you don't?"

He looked shocked. "Of course not! Fortner Geis was not a stupid man, and I think he was an honest man. I think he would . . . weigh all the alternatives, and do what he felt he had to do."

"Which one of us is going to say the nasty word, Mr. Andrus?"

He shrugged. "Okay. Blackmail. I investigated that possibility with Mrs. Geis, and with the daughter, Mrs. Trumbill, and with young Mr. Geis. I also checked with . . . some of the doctor's associates. It is a complete blank. Well, not exactly a complete blank. Mrs. Trumbill was very distressed when her father married a woman so much younger, and a woman . . . not quite on the social level of the Geis family, let us say. She suggested that her father might be paying out large sums to protect Mrs. Geis."

"From what?"

"When her father brought her back here, Mrs. Trumbill thought it would be wise to . . . have her stepmother investigated. She got a report on what had happened to Mrs. Geis' first husband and her two children in Buffalo over six years ago." He hesitated, looked troubled, and said, "I have a lot of respect for Gloria. I like her a great deal. And I do not like Heidi Geis Trumbill. Mrs. Trumbill suggested to me that perhaps Gloria in a jealous rage had killed her neighbour and her first husband, and the two children who witnessed it, and then someone who could prove that's what happened showed up and the doctor was paying that person to keep silent."

"Heidi seems to have a nasty mouth."

"She thinks Gloria had her father hypnotized. I felt duty-bound to .check out her murder theory. Nonsense, of course. According to the Buffalo police reports, a neighbour saw Gloria turn into the driveway and get out of the car with a bag of groceries about two minutes after the woman had phoned the police about hearing the shots. When I told Mrs. Trumbill about that, she gave me a strange little smile and said perhaps

23

if we kept on digging we'd probably find something sufficiently nasty in Gloria's background to account for where the money went. And, if not, it was obvious that she had talked the Doctor into putting his estate into cash and turning it over to her. How could we be sure, she asked, that Mrs. Geis hadn't already taken it out of the country?" He sighed. "I suppose I shouldn't let it bother me. Estate work gives you a chance to see people at their worst."

"How much would Heidi have got?"

"The way it was set up, and you must understand that there were insurance policies cashed which would have built the estate up to over seven hundred thousand. Once the estimated taxes and expenses were paid, Gloria would have got three hundred thousand, and his children a hundred and fifty thousand each. Three trust funds. Heidi's was the most restrictive. She was limited to the income only, say seventy-five hundred a year, and at the time of her death the principal amount was to be divided equally among her children, if any, and her brother's children. Roger was to be given the right to withdraw in any year up to ten per cent of the amount originally placed in trust for him. Gloria was to have the house and all physical property, and the right to withdraw all or any part of the monies in trust at any time. When he learned of this provision, Roger said it proved that his father was not of sound mind at the time the instruments were drawn up, because it did not make sense to give a woman untrained in the handling of money complete freedom of access to three hundred thousand dollars, while restricting the son, who was in the business of handling money, access to not more than fifteen thousand a year of the principal amount."

"Great kids, those two."

"Unfortunately I'd say they were about average."

"If nobody ever finds out where the money went, what happens? Can Gloria lose that insurance money?"

"No. There'll be no estate taxes at all. The government can't merely assume she has the money, and proceed against her on that basis. I imagine they'll keep careful track of her, and if she seems to be spending more than her income, they would ask awkward questions."

"She thinks she's being watched now."

"She might be. If it bothered her too much, I'd arrange to find out who is behind it. Oh, there was something else I discovered when I was asking Mrs. Geis about the possibility

24

of blackmail. She said that there was a clumsy attempt to blackmail the Doctor over two years ago, nearly three years ago in fact."

"On what basis?"

He looked uncomfortable. "I think it would be more proper if Gloria told you about it."

"Sure. I understand."

"Mr. McGee, I think it would make sense if you would advise Mrs. Geis to close this house and let us put it on the market. I think we might be able to clear fifteen out of it, possibly a little more. I hate to see her run through what she has in her own current account so quickly."

"She said Fort's attorney, Mr. Waldren, advised her to stay put."

"It was my impression he meant she should stay in the Chicago area. Well . . . I have other reports here, but they don't help us much. He died on October seventh. It wasn't until early November we began to realize most of the capital asset value had disappeared. By then the trail was cold. He'd wound it all up four months earlier, in July. If he was turning the money over to someone, we have no way of telling when or how or who."

"Gloria said he seemed happy that last year—as happy as you could expect a man to be under those circumstances."

"That's puzzling, Mr. McGee. He would have had to be under strain no matter what the reason behind it was."

"Strain," I said. "I guess it's relative. I remember a story about him in *Time* magazine. I can't remember the details. It must have been at least ten years ago. He flew over to some place in the Middle East and took a benign tumour out of some politician's brain. He operated for nine hours, and he could have lost the patient at any minute of those nine hours, and there was a chance that if he did lose him, some of the wild-eyed members of the party would have gunned him down when he left the hospital in spite of the troops they'd assigned to guard him. There was some background in the article on him too. In World War II in Europe he went AWOL from the General Hospital where he was on the neurosurgical team, and they found him at a field hospital trying out and getting good results with a nerve graft technique that had to be done as soon as possible after the wounds happened. He'd made his request through channels and nothing happened, so he reassigned himself. The only time I knew him was when he was in Florida and married Gloria. Okay, a very mild and gentle guy. But he had that look. The ones who get past the the point of ever having to prove anything to themselves or anyone else have that look. We laid on the bachelor brawl bit for him. By two in the morning there were just the three of us left, Fort, a friend named Meyer, and me. Fort started telling doctor stories. He talked until dawn. Meyer said it had been a long time since he'd had anything shake him up that much, anything that started him thinking in a different kind of pattern. I have this feeling, Mr. Andrus. Anybody who tried to lean on that nice mild guy would do better trying to pat tigers, I think."

"So what did happen?"

"Somebody as essentially tough as Fortner Geis found some leverage that would work on Fortner Geis, and they were smart enough to stay back out of range while they squeezed him. And he was fatalist enough to adjust, to accept a lesser evil. Next step: accepting Fort as the kind of man he was, that leverage had to come from something in the past, some place where their lives crossed. Somebody has a very large and nervous amount of cash. If they were hard enough and smart enough to squeeze it out of Fort, they must have some very good idea of how to get the juice out of it without alerting the IRS computers."

John Andrus nodded slowly. "The more you have, the easier it is to add more without atrracting attention."

"And if you can't do it that way, you have to have a lot of patience and control. You have to sit on it and then have some logical reason to pull up stakes and go elsewhere. Then, if you can get to Brazil or Turkey, and move very carefully, you can dig yourself in as a rich man without creating too much suspicion."

"Yes. It could be done," he said.

"Another thing interests me. The man applying the squeeze apparently knew or had some way of knowing how much Fort had. Otherwise I think Fort would have come up with, say, a quarter of a million and then made the squeezer believe he had it all."

Andrus began staring at me with a curious expression. "Mr. McGee, a lot of people have done a lot of wondering about this whole thing. And I've sat in on most of it. So you come along and for the first time I am beginning to get some kind of an image of what the person or persons had to be like. A very vague image, of course. But somehow . . . things seem to be narrowing down for the first time. Did Gloria tell me you're in the marine supply business?"

"Supply and salvage. Maybe I have a talent for larceny. A great parlour trick, thinking like a thief."

"Are you going to . . . pursue your theories?"

"I might look around a little, sure. Just as a favour for an old friend."

He put his papers away and snapped the catches on the dispatch case. "Is there any way I could make things easier for you? Unofficially."

"Did you have something in mind?"

"I don't think any friend of Mrs. Geis' is going to get any casual conversation out of Heidi Trumbill or Roger Geis." He took out two calling cards and with a slender gold pen wrote on the back of each, "Any co-operation you can give Mr. McGee will be appreciated—John Andrus."

"Thanks. Little talent for larceny yourself?"

"If there is, I hope to God they never notice it down at the Trust Department. Or run across one of those cards."

After we'd said good-bye to him, I went walking on the lake shore with Glory. She told me it was turning into a beautiful day. I told her that twenty-five more degrees would make a Floridian happier. Then I told her what John Andrus had said about cutting her expenses by giving up the house.

"Oh, I suppose that's very logical and bankerly," she said. "But Fort built it for us. The happiest time of my life was right here. Fort is here too, when I wake up, in those minutes before I remember he's gone. And he's in the next room, or around a corner, or on his way home. Those things hurt, Trav. They sting like mad. But when I leave here, then he's really gone forever. How else could I . . . buy the feel of having him near? The first insurance cheque came December third, last week. One every month for the rest of my life. Four hundred dollars. I'll put that into the kitty to hang on to the house a little longer. I'm not even going to think of what comes next, or plan anything, until I am all packed and on my way down the road. Don't expect me to be practical and logical, dear. Okay?"

"Okay. John Andrus seems fond of you."

"I know. In a very nice and special and, thank God, unsexy way. He has an adored wife and teen-age daughters. I think

I was a refreshing experience to him because he finally realized I was absolutely sincere in not giving a dang about money, really. Oh, it's kind of delicious to have it. But too many of the things I like best don't cost a thing. At first poor John seemed to think I was trying to knock the Establishment. We were standing in the yard a month ago. One of the last leaves came off the maple. So I picked it up and made him look very closely and carefully at it. I made him *see* it. Then I asked him what it was worth, without cracking a smile. I could almost see the lightbulb going on in the air over his head, like cartoons. Then, bless you. I fed him that speech you made a lifetime ago on Sanibel Island. If there was one sunset every twenty years, how would people react to them? If there were ten seashells in all the world, what would they be worth? If people could make love just once a year, how carefully would they pick their mates? So now John thinks I am very nice in spite of being quite mad."

"I had to hold the world out to you the way you held the leaf out, Miss Glory, and make you look at it. Question. Does this hotel serve lunch?"

"Anna wouldn't miss the chance. She goes around smiling, she's so happy to have somebody around here who eats."

"What will happen to her when you close the house?"

"From what has happened so far, I imagine you will see the most noted socialite hostesses from the entire lake shore skulking around in the brush and crawling across the dunes, with money in one hand and leg irons in the other, wearing fixed glassy smiles. Anna Ottlo can name her own ticket."

It wasn't until cocktail time in front of the fireplace that I got around to the blackmail attempt John Andrus had thought more fitting for Glory to tell me.

"Heavens, he could have told you! He's really very circumspect. But . . . I'm glad he didn't really. Because I think that you might not understand just how it happened. Fort, all his life, was very attractive to women. I guess he made every woman feel . . . valuable. He listened. He was interested. He liked them.

"Travis, I have to go way back to what life was like for him with Glenna, the things he told me about their marriage. They were very close. They were very important to each other. It was wretched timing for them that as soon as he got out of the army—he was about the same age then that Roger is now—

and he and Glenna were just one month apart, they found out Glenna had congestive heart disease, and had maybe had it for some time without knowing it. Let me see now, Roger was eight and Heidi must have been four, because when she died three years later, Roger was eleven and Heidi was seven.

"Because Glenna had some money, they'd been able to marry and have children when Fort was going through the intern and resident thing, and they'd been able to have a nice home in the city, with Fort devoting more time, both before and after the war, to staff surgery and instruction than to surgery for private fees. He came back to find that Anna Ottlo had become indispensable to Glenna, and that her daughter Gretchen, who was fourteen then, had become almost an older sister to Roger and Heidi."

She turned her glass slowly, then held it and looked at the firelight through what was left of her weak highball. She gave me a small and humble smile. "I'm not as objective as I sound, you know. I'm still jealous of Glenna for having so many more years of him than I did, and I resent her, sort of. That's kind of lousy, isn't it?"

"No. It's kind of nice. It's part of the human condition."

"The human condition isn't very logical. When Fort married Glenna, I was spilling pablum. Anyhow, as more background, I have to give a little sex lecture. Sex and the doctor. It's something Fort explained to me. There are all those doctor-nurse stories, and there is a certain basis of truth in them, and here is one incident Fort told me about that explains that strange kind of truth. He said that when he was operating in the General Hospital, doing more operations in one day than he ever had before or ever would again, he had the luck to get hold of a great operating-room nurse, a big severe steady tireless girl named Fletcher. First Lieutenant Lois Fletcher. He said you have to acquire some kind of emotional immunity to all that terrible waste, all that young battle-torn meat. He said you get a kind of black humour about it, and a good team, like he and Fletcher were, get in the habit of saying things to each other that would make a layman think they were heartless monsters. Fletcher's husband was a sergeant with the First Marine Division in the Pacific. He said that he and Fletcher were not promiscuous types, even in that permissive and demanding place. But one week they had, he said, a run on paraplegics. A terrible incidence of them, and not one of what he called the happy ones—where you could go in and take out a splinter of metal and relieve the pressure and know that the feeling would return to the lower body. After several days of that he said they finished one night, took off the bloody gowns, and went and sat in silence having coffee. They were both beat. Suddenly he said they were looking into each other's eyes, and they just got up without a word and went off to an empty room and closed the door and with a kind of terrible exhausted energy they made love. He said she clung to him and cried almost soundlessly, and they made love again and again. A despairing affirmation, he said. That was his phrase. And he said it was transcendent. That's the important idea, Trav, the one to remember. He said it was a way of turning the mind off, where all the horrible wheels are going around and around, and losing yourself in sensation for a little while. He said that was the only time for them, and the team was a little awkward the next day or so, getting signals slightly crossed, but from then on they were okay again, and they never spoke of it to each other."

She stopped and sat, scowling. "What's the matter?" I asked.

"I talk too much. Maybe now it's going to sound like a bigger deal than it was. Anyway, here's the scene. They have tried everything for Glenna. But the heart just does less and less of its job. She has been in bed for ten months. He has been back home for three years. Now it is suddenly necessary to have nurses around the clock. He does not know how long she will last. Actually, she lasted about six weeks more. She would not benefit by being put in a hospital to die. It would frighten her. Circulation is so bad the organs are not able to function properly. There is a danger of gangrene of her feet. But worst of all, because the brain is not properly supplied, her mind is failing. She moves from lucidity to fantasy and back, sometimes thinking he is her father. He is in hell. To provide better accommodations for the nurses, he moves to a small bedroom in the back of the house above the kitchen and pantry and service areas, the area where Anna and her daughter sleep. Both Anna and her daughter Gretchen are terribly worried about him. Their hearts go out to him. Anna cooks his favourite things so he will be tempted to eat. Gretchen's feelings toward the doctor are complicated by two factors. First, she has such a fantastic crush on him, she can think of nothing else all day long. Second, she is not really very bright. She is not a retarded child. Just a little slow of wit, with a short attention span. She has romantic dreams of sacrifice, for the sake of love. She is seventeen, intensely physical, completely mature, and healthy as a plough horse. The doctor is thirty-five, suffering, miserable, wanting Glenna to die before she becomes a total vegetable, yet unable to comprehend how he can make a life without her.

"And now, Trav, the final little factors that made such a weird thing possible. An old house, thick walls, heavy doors. He has found that he can sleep if he drinks a great big slug of bourbon as he is going to bed. The infatuated girl is in the next room, her mother in the room beyond. Fort awakens, half-stoned, with the naked girl snuggled against him in darkness, hugging him, gasping into his throat, her body all hot velvet, smooth as a seal he said, her blonde hair long and perfumed, her hands damp and cold with nervousness. There is a perversity about the tempted animal, Fort explained to me. First you say you are imagining it or dreaming it, and then when it begins to become all too real, you tell yourself that in a moment you will wake up all the way, register shock, and end the self-indulgence before it goes too far."

"But there was the word you told me to remember. Transcendent."

"Yes. Turning off all the awful engines in the mind. He said that only when the child began orgasm did he suddenly realize what a shocking and fantastic and inexcusable thing had happened. Afterward he told her that he was as guilty as she, and they would talk to her mother about it the next day. She wept and begged him not to, and said she would never tell, and said she loved him, she would die for him, all she wanted was to please him a little, to make him happier, to make him forget a little bit.

"In the morning it seemed very unreal to him. And he could not imagine how in the world he'd tell Anna Ottlo that the master of the house had romped the housekeeper's more than willing daughter."

As she told what happened I could see just how he could have been in the emotional condition to get into such a bind. The girl had come sneaking back the next night, of course, and then he knew he couldn't tell Anna. He knew after it had happened again. He made her promise never to come back again, and never to tell. So she stayed away one night and then she came back saying she couldn't help herself, couldn't stay away from him, loved him and so on. Fort was, from my candid appraisal, a thoroughly masculine type. He was thirty-five, and he certainly hadn't had any sex in his marriage for a long time. From what Glory was telling me, I could see how it could happen even with a man like Geis, to whom you could apply the adjective good without feeling self-conscious about it.

The girl Gretchen, from Glory's second-hand description, was a sturdy fräulein, extremely blonde, big breasts, big hips, China-blue eyes, who'd blush so furiously every time she ran into Fort during the day he wondered how soon somebody would guess what was going on. So each day the beloved wife faded further toward death, and each night Fort would lose himself in that firm, eager, abundant young flesh. I could guess that she was not sensuously complex, just hearty and lusty, and it was very probable that as they became closely attuned, they would find the joining becoming almost ritualistic in its sameness, the hands, heads, mouths, legs always placed just so, the bodies becoming like one entity, so that no matter which one began the completion first, the laggard would be brought quickly along by the body's awareness of it being the time of climax. It would be ritualistic and hypnotic, and a man like Fort would feel guilt and shame, but it would be cushioned by his knowing that no matter how wretched the inevitable ending of it would be, the bad ending of marriage and the bad ending of his wife's life was just as inevitable. In such a situation there could be almost a compulsion to find a guilt-feeling. When the beloved is dying, we want to be blamed and punished. Without that there seems to be nothing left but an indifferent malevolence of fate.

She fixed new drinks, handed me mine and said, "Fort told me it all became unreal to him. And then Glenna died. He moved back to the bedroom where she had died. He'd become so . . . habituated to Gretchen he could not comprehend not wanting her. But suddenly he didn't. She couldn't risk sneaking through the house. Two days after the funeral she was waiting in the garage when he came home from the hospital. She told him she was pretty sure she was pregnant. He gave her a test. She was. She said there was no reason why he couldn't marry her. Now if Fort had been a weak, silly senti-mental man, he might have done just that. But he was always able to look at things objectively. A marriage that grotesque would have been as bad for her as for him. So he told her it was ridiculous to even think of such a thing. He came home in the middle of the morning the next day, when his kids were in school. He had told Gretchen to stay home from school. She was slow in school. She was in the tenth grade, and kept asking her mother to let her drop out. Fort brought Anna and her daughter into the living-room and had them sit down and he told Anna what had happened and what the situation was.

"That must have been a dandy morning."

"Fort told me that it had to be done. When something has to be done, you do it. You have no choice. Gretchen tried to lie, and say that Fort had seduced her. Anna knew Fort better than that. She got in about three good whacks, and Gretchen, bawling, told the whole truth. Fort said Anna was very pale. She asked questions about exactly how the affair had begun, and then sent Gretchen off to her room. Fort said Anna was eminently practical. She blamed him only for not telling her the first time it happened. She said it was best to assume the girl had been impregnated that very first night. Then there was less guilt. A man was a man. The girl was very ripe and eager. But the girl's idea of marriage to Herr Doktor was, of course, impertinent. Arrangements could be made if it was known how much the Doctor would settle on the unborn child. She said that if Gretchen were a bright girl and doing well in school and deserved more education, perhaps an abortion would be best. But a girl like her daughter would be much better off married, and with children. Fort said that as soon as Glenna's estate was settled, he would arrange very quietly to buy a single payment annuity which would provide the child with approximately a hundred dollars a week for life, and in the interim, he would turn over a hundred dollars a week out of pocket to Anna to give to Gretchen. Anna said that was more than enough, much more. Fort said he would not feel right about making it any less. Two weeks later Gretchen was married to a twenty-year-old boy named Karl Kemmer. Karl's mother was, like Anna, a refugee, an older woman than Anna. She had lost two older sons in the war. She had got Karl out and into the States less than a year earlier. He was an apprentice, learning sheet-metal work. Fort said he seemed like a very decent kid. Gretchen gave birth to a girl. They named her Susan. Through his lawyer, a man who has since died, Fort arranged the annuity in the name of Susan Kemmer with the money to be paid monthly to her parent or guardian until she reached eighteen, and then paid directly to her."

"How did Gretchen react to that?"

"Not so great. She blamed her mother for not siding with her to get Fort to marry her. Fort said that while Anna and Gretchen were still getting along. Anna enjoyed being a grandmother. Then the marriage started to go bad. Maybe Karl Kemmer resented the bargain he made. Gretchen started going with other men. Fort said she and Anna had battles about it. When Susan was three, Gretchen had a little boy. When the little boy was a year old, Karl Kemmer was killed in an industrial accident. After another quarrel, Gretchen left town suddenly with a married man, taking both children with her. Fort said Anna was grim and remote and unapproachable for a time, and then she became herself again. But she would not mention Gretchen. She told Fort she did not have a daughter."

"So it had to be Gretchen who tried to shake Fort down a couple of years ago?"

"Three years ago next month. She waylaid him at the hospital. She said she didn't want to come here because she didn't want her mother to know she was back in Chicago. She'd been back three months. She didn't want her mother to know that things hadn't gone too well for her. Fort said she was heavy and coarsened, but sexy in a full-blown blowzy way. She said she was doing waitress work in a restaurant on West Lake Street, and living with her five kids in a fourth-floor walkup in the Maywood section. She had married somebody out West. I can't remember the name he told me. And she'd had three children by him and one had died, and she had married another man and had one child by him who was then three years old. I can't remember the third husband's name either, but she told Fort he was in prison. She said that even with the money coming in for Susan, she couldn't seem to make ends meet, so she'd come to tell him he had to start sending her another hundred a week."

"Just like that, eh?"

"It irritated Fort and it puzzled him that she should put it in the form of a demand, and look so perfectly sure of herself. So he asked her why she thought he'd do that. So she said she'd found out he'd just moved into a fine new house and he had a new young wife and probably the new young wife thought she'd married a great man, but she wondered how the new young wife would react if Gretchen paid her a little visit and told her that while his first wife was on her death bed, the big famous Dr. Geis was busy knocking up a young dumb kid, his house-keeper's daughter, right in the same house,

34

every night for weeks. Fort said he wasn't irritated anymore. Just sad. So he told her about how he and I had no secrets. and he had told me the whole thing, so there wasn't any way she could put that kind of pressure on him. Then in that gentle way of his he asked her why she would try such a thing, and why she would make what had happened between them, foolish as it might have been, sound so much dirtier than it had actually been. So she began to cry and she told him that her husband had told her to try it. He realized that she was basically unchanged. She was still a slow-minded, amiable, romantic kind of person. He said he would look into her situation and see if he could give her some help if she really needed it."

"I would guess she did."

She explained that Fort hired investigators to make a full report, and asked them to go into detail about the daughter Susan, age fourteen then. He showed Glory the report. It said she had been the common-law wife of the man out West and she was the common-law wife of the man in prison in Wisconsin. She was a sloven, but good with her kids, affectionate with them like a mother bear, hugging them and whacking them. But not much sense of responsibility. She'd get off work and go to a beer joint, and Susan would be the sitter for the littler ones. She apparently could be picked up without too much trouble, but she never took men back to her place. Susan sounded pretty special. Bright and blonde and pretty, and very earnest about seeing that the kids got proper food and were dressed adequately. And she kept the apartment clean. It looked as if they could get along on the four hundred from the annuity and the two hundred and fifty or so that Gretchen was making in wages and tips, but Gretchen liked to play the numbers and the horses too well. If there was more money, she'd just bet more.

"Fort and I talked over what if anything he ought to do. In the end he got in touch with Gretchen and told her that if she stopped gambling, all her kids would be better off, and he had no intention of giving her any money. Then he had the same investigators get word to Susan that if any emergency ever came up that she couldn't handle, she was to contact them, but it would be best not to tell her mother about it. We wondered what we should try to do when Susan became eighteen and began getting her own money directly. We talked about it as if . . . Fort would still be around. She'll be eighteen next year. We wanted to make sure she'd go to college and not get cheated out of it by having to look after the other kids. She certainly wasn't any threat—Gretchen wasn't—to Fort. It was just sort of dreary and sad. I'd half decided that after Fort died, I'd go to Susan and explain everything and see if I could sort of . . . look after her. After all, I guess I'm only a couple of years too young to be her mother. So that's all it was. Look how long it took me to tell it. That's what comes from living alone. Dinner now?"

"Unless you want to see a grown man cry."

When we were eating I asked her if Anna knew about Gretchen's attempted shakedown. She said Fort hadn't told Anna about it, but he had told her about Gretchen being in town with five children. At first Anna hadn't wanted to do anything about it, but Fort had sensed it was pride and bull-headedness. She had visited once when Gretchen was there and it had ended very badly, so from then on she had visited when she knew the kids would be there and Gretchen would be working.

"Did you go see Susan yourself?"

"I waited too long. I had . . . a sentimental idea, Trav. I thought I would find out very carefully if she knew Fort was her father. If she did, I wanted to find out if she had any bad feeling about him. If she did, I was going to try to make her see how it was, how it happened, how Fort had done what he could, and then, if she was willing, bring her out here to see him, I know he wanted to see her. I mean from the report I guess he had the feeling he had fathered at least one pretty good kid. But he had made. I went there in September and they were gone. I felt reluctant to upset whatever adjustment the girl had. They'd been gone a couple of weeks. I asked Anna about it. She looked pretty bleak. She said that if she'd known I was going there, she would have told me they were gone. She said it was her idea Gretchen didn't want Anna buttering up the kids, so she just moved, maybe somewhere else in the city, maybe out of town. No forwarding address. Probably some new man, Anna said, looking as if she wanted to spit."

"Glory, have you got that investigator's report?"

"No. I thought they'd find it when they went through everything. But I guess Fort destroyed it."

"I wonder why he'd do that?"

"I guess he had a good reason. Trav, Fort had a lot of . . .

wisdom. I guess that's the word. He thought things out and did what he felt would be best for everyone Like when. . . ."

"When what?"

"Nothing."

"From the expression on your face when you stopped yourself it wasn't exactly nothing, girl."

"It was just a personal thing, between Fort and me."

"And has nothing to do with anything else?"

"Nothing."

But I knew she was troubled, and so I decided not to take her off the hook. Again I went to the kitchen with her whilst she stowed the dishes. Again we had a nightcap by the last small tongues of flame in the glowing bed of embers. She talked trivia, and kept lapsing into silence, and finally out of a silence she said a bad word.

"Hmmm?" I said.

"Okay, okay, okay. That personal thing. Maybe it does have something to do with something. Trav, Fort and I had kind of let ourselves drift into a fool's paradise. We'd begun to believe it wouldn't end, and then the pains began. And when they did, neither of us were as good about it as we thought we were going to be. We disappointed ourselves. Depression and irritability and restlessness. It looked as if it was going to be totally lousy from then on in. We just didn't seem to be able to handle it . . . and get any good out of the time we had left. So Fort got something from a friend of his. Dr. Hayes Wyatt. He'd told Fort one time about the good results he'd been having with terminal patients using psychedelics. As Fort explained it to me, when there is pain, after a while the patients begin to identify the pain with death. Then the pain becomes like something that's after them, trying to take them away, and that makes the pain worse because there's fear there too. So he talked our problem over with Hayes Wyatt and Hayes thought it would be a good idea for both of us and told Fort what kind of a procedure might work best, and gave Fort a tiny little vial of it. LSD-25. Do you know about it?"

I did not tell her how it could still give me the night sweats to remember one Doctor Varn and the Toll Valley Hospital where they had varied the basic compound and boosted the dosage to where they could not only guarantee you a bad trip, they could pop you permanently loose from reality if you had any potential fracture line anywhere in your psyche. As a part of mending the damage they did to me, a bright doctor gave me some good trips and had given me in that special way the ability to comprehend what had happened in my head during the bad ones.

"I've been there," I told her.

She lighted up. "Then you *know!* You can't tell anybody what it's like."

"I haven't taken the social trips with a batch of acid heads who want to freak around. It was a medical thing, controlled."

"Oh, it has to be!" she said. "Fort measured the dosages on to little wads of surgical cotton. He gave me four hundred micrograms the first time, and stayed with me. It took about eight hours before it began to wear off. I watched over him after he took five hundred micrograms. It's spooky, you know. It was much too much to get the kind of good out of it we wanted. It took us too far to let us make any good bridge between here and there. But then we knew. And then, twice, we took a little less than a hundred micrograms at the same time. We could talk. We could talk with a closeness we never had before, and we'd thought we were as close as two people could get. What you learn is that you are . . . just one part of the whole human experience, part of a great rhythm of life and death, and when you have that insight, there's no fear. I knew the ways we would always be together, and I knew the ways we would have to part and I could accept that. Twice was all we needed. It gave us peace. It gave us a special happiness, not *more* than we had before, but different. It made us able to understand and accept . . . our identities."

"And you found out why you were so badly racked up when I found you on the beach?"

"Of course! Because I was wishing he'd die without letting myself know I was wishing it. And when he died and the kids died with him so horribly, losing the kids was the penalty I had to pay for wishing him dead. And Fort, to his utter astonishment, found out that he had secretly resented Glenna. She was one of those terribly terribly sweet women who never raise their voices, and who are fantastically strong and tough and aggressive underneath. He discovered that he had pretended love and created a myth-woman to fit that love, and that underneath she was maybe not a nice person at all. So he could not ever let himself comprehend he was glad she was dying. Accepting Gretchen's silliness gave him a guilt he *could* admit."

"So after the LSD, you could both handle the situation."

"He died damned well, and I helped him die well, and . . . those insights are still with me, Trav, still helping me. But I had never thought of how . . . it could relate to the money. Psychedelics give you an acceptance of inevitable things. Sort of—'so be it.' It would have given him the chance to weigh the difference in importance between death and money, and money is so . . . kind of insipid compared to true identity. Without that experience, Trav, I couldn't stay here. It would smash me to stay here. Now I wouldn't want to be anywhere else."

There is, I thought, almost no useful thing the human animal will not in his eternal perversity misuse, whether it be alcohol, petrol, gunpowder, aspirin, chocolate fudge, mescaline, or LSD.

I once helped a baffled father get his daughter out of an acid party in downtown Miami. She went from the party directly into a private sanitarium. She had been a mildly disturbed personality before she got into that cult group. There were nine kids in that small room, aged eighteen, nineteen, and twenty. They had taken the trip together and they were about three hours into it, and had taken a heavy dose, so heavy there was no relating or identity between any of them. They brooded over the infinite in separate silences, isolated, somnambulistic, while the record-player needle made a hissing sound where, at the beginning of a record, it was trapped in a locked groove. Only two of them were having a bad trip. One boy sat in yoga position in a corner, facing into the corner, beating wearily at the side of his head with his fist and weeping hopelessly. The girl we were after was on her belly, creeping slowly backward, her shift hiked high above her waist by the friction, her eyes full of terror. The kids had not picked anyone to be the gooney—that wingless bird which never flies—to see that no one took a bad trip and harmed himself. The girl we took out of there had chewed her fingers to bloody ragged ruin. The others dreamed, swayed, smiled—and we left them there.

FOUR

THE next day was Saturday, and after breakfast I had Glory drive me into town and drop me. I told her I would poke around and be in touch. It was another one of those days Chicagoans have no right to expect in December, bright and balmy. My topcoat was more than adequate. I decided a large impersonal commercial hotel would make sense, so I took a cab to the Drake, checked into a single, found Mrs. Heidi Trumbill in the book at the 180 East Burton address, and phoned her. It was ten-fifteen.

After four rings a female voice said with considerable impatience and exasperation, "Yes? Yes?"

"Mrs. Trumbill, my name is McGee and. . . ."

"*Please* try again at eleven-thirty, will you? I'm working with some acrylic paints, and they're drying so fast I'll lose what I'm after if I keep answering this goddam phone!" She hung up. Forcefully.

I went out and walked south on Michigan Avenue. In nice week-end weather it is one of the specialties of the house. Chicago is a strange one. It is not on my list of favourite places. Insofar as restaurants and lounges and hotels are concerned it is strictly hinterland, strictly hick. And as you go down the scale it becomes more shabby and shoddy than rough. I do not know why anyone should expect anything special in that line from a place where the Hefner Empire seems to represent some sort of acme of sophistication, based as it is upon fantastic centrefold mammalians for the pimpled self-lovers, upon a chain of bunny-warrens styled to make the middle-class sales manager feel like a member of an in-group, and upon a laborious philosophical discourse which runs interminably in the ad-happy magazine and in the polysyllabic style of the pseudo-educated, carrying the deathless message that it is healthy to screw and run if everybody is terribly sincere about it.

A great university they have indeed, but if you take a train there from the centre of the city, you pass through whole areas of the South Side which make the worst of Harlem look like Scarsdale. It is a gigantic shameful tinderbox everybody is trying not to notice. If you are a stranger and want to leave the university area after dark, they insist on getting you a cab.

The best of Chicago, I think, must go on quite privately, and it must be very fine indeed. Private homes and private clubs, and a lot of insulation and discretion, because as I hiked along Michigan I saw and admired what I had come to see, strolling, window-shopping flocks of women of that inimitable smartness, style, loveliness, assurance, and aroma of money which will make headwaiters and captains all over the Western world leap, beaming, to unhook their velvet ropes before they even hear the name. I feel that they live in Chicago in very much the same spirit the early settlers lived in the wilderness full of Indians. They keep the big gates closed. They consort with each other, and they import those specialities their rude environment cannot supply, and when they need relief from that nerve-twanging combination of unending drabness and glittering boosterism, they take their ease at the truly smart spots of the world and, when asked where they are from, tell the truth with that mocking inverted pride of the fellow pinned to the sod with a spear who said it only hurt when he laughed.

Statistically it is probably the one city in the world where the most people have been killed in arguments over professional athletes. The middle of the city, where nine bridges cross a large sewage canal called the Chicago River, is beginning to look as if Martians had designed it. For untold years the city has limped along under what might well be the most arrogant, ruthless, and total political control in the country. In a kind of constant hysterical spasm of self-distaste, the city uglifies itself further each year by chopping away more trees and paving more areas for all those thousands of drivers who seem to have learned their art at Daytona.

So I walked in the sunlight, and appreciated all the lovely ladies, and looked at the rich goods in the rich store windows. They had strung their Christmas lights, thousands and thousands of tiny white transparent bulbs festooning the bare branches of the trees which, by some oversight, still remain standing along Michigan Avenue. At the corner of Huron something that was entirely girl came swinging along, and wrapped the whole thing up for me. Nearly six lithe feet of her, and unmistakably great handloomed tweeds in conservative cut, lizard purse and walking shoes and hair chestnut-brown and gleaming with health, styled with no trickery, bobbing to her resolute stride, and one gloved finger hooked through the string of a parcel wrapped in gold foil paper, and on her mouth

41

a lovely secret smile, perhaps part memory, part anticipation, and part appreciation of the day and of the good feel of taking long strides, and part being lovely and young. There is something about seeing one like that which tries to break your heart. You will never know her, but you want it all to be great for her, all the parts of it, the wine, the weather, the food, the people, the beds, the kids, the love, and the being old.

I walked all the way down to Monroe and then over to Wabash and into one of the great pipe stores of the Western world, Iwan Reis, across from the old Palmer House, and celebrated my luck at having seen so marvellous a girl at so marvellous a moment by gifting myself with a pale Ropp with a birds-eye grain, comfortable bite, and generous bowl.

Then I took a cab back out to East Burton, to a quainty old pile of red stone squatting close to the narrow sidewalk. There were four mailboxes and push buttons in the small foyer. Over the tube when I gave her my name, her voice, reduced to a frail buzzing sound, demanded to know what I wanted. So I said I had a note from John Andrus. She said she was on the second floor in the back and the door catch made a sound like a rattlesnake as she pressed the release.

Her heavy door was Chinese red, and when she pulled it open I saw how accurate Gloria's description of her had been. She was a tall slender golden-blonde, features so coin-cut, so classic and clear she had an ice-maiden look.

She looked at Andrus' card, front and back, handed it back, and said, "You're not exactly my picture of a banking type, Mr. McGee. Come in, please."

I followed her into a high-ceilinged living-room. She wore white canvas coveralls, too big for her, man-size, the pant cuffs turned up. She had fashioned a belt out of a red scarf rolled to narrow width, and cinched the baggy garment around the narrowness of her waist. She had appraised me with blue-grey eyes which told me nothing, merely looked at me and made a record and filed it under McGee. Minimum makeup, no jewellery of any kind. She had that rare and contradictory look of being both slender and substantial, a look which I suspect comes from a certain breadth of shoulder, fruitful width of pelvic structure. Though the coveralls were spotted with stains of paint old and new, she looked groomed and immaculate.

She turned and leaned against a table edge, crossed her ankles, crossed her arms under her breasts and said, "So?"

Personal chemistries have not yet been isolated and analyzed

42

by the physiologists. Here was a specimen in her twenty-five-year-old prime, in full bloom. Certainly the female of my species, beyond question. She had walked with a promising curl of power in the haunch. Her arms were crossed under a hammocked roundness of breast, and her mouth was of an understated sensuality in shape and dimension.

But we were saying no to each other without any words. In my out-sized, wind-weathered, semi-battered, loose-jointed way I seem to get the right responses for my full and fair share of the fair ones, but I could not see any signs of impact, or experience any. Maybe Old Lady Nature sets up some kind of over-riding counterirritant when the genetics are a bad match. I knew this could be a heady package for somebody, but not for the McGee. I had caught the smiling eye of the girl at the corner of Huron for a half-second, and it had been a resounding yes, both ways. A conditional yes. Yes, if it wasn't too late for us by the time we met. Yes, but I'm sorry it can't be.

I wondered about the No which Heidi Geis Trumbill and I were saying to each other. I know when you can hear that large No: when they are too wrapped up in exactly the right guy to even be aware you are alive, when they are one of the cool voyagers from the Isle of Lesbos, and when they are seriously thinking of killing you. I could not fit Heidi into any pattern.

"Sometimes," I said, "the banking types get some help from non-banking types."

"Let me say I think they need it. Talk about impartial. Hah! It's perfectly obvious John Andrus has let that sweet demure elfin little bitch sell him down the river. Any slight suggestion that she might not be a hundred and ten per cent perfection, and he gets furious."

"Kind of a strange marriage, I guess."

Suddenly she approved of me. "Do take off your coat, Mr. McGee. Care for a drink?"

As she went and fixed herself a beaker of dry sherry and some gin over ice for me, I wandered over and looked through a wide arched doorway into her studio. It had a lot of tall windows for good north light, and it was painted a good off-white. It had at least the look of a working artist's studio—work tables, easels, bouquets of worn-out brushes in old paint pots, new work on easels and on the walls, deep painting racks, scabs of paint on the floor, stacks of paintings leaning against the walls.

43

She came up and handed me my drink and stood beside me looking into the studio. "Please don't ask me to explain my work."

She had a rare talent for irritating me. So I said, "I doubt if you could, Mrs. Trumbill."

With a cold smile as she turned toward me, she said, "And what is that supposed to mean?"

"Sorry. I don't think you know what you're doing."

"My dear man, abstract expressionism has been around so long that it. . . ."

"That it gets imitated too much. You've got some colour sense. You go too far in setting up weird composition. But that doesn't mean you are setting problems or trying to solve them. It's glib stuff, Heidi. It hasn't got any bones. It hasn't got any symbol values, any underlying feeling of weight or inevitability. It's just sort of shock-pretty, and you certainly get some satisfaction out of doing it, but just don't start taking it or yourself too seriously."

Fury drained the colour out of her face. She went striding away, whirled so quickly she slopped some of her sherry on to the living-room rug. "Just who the hell are you? My work *sells*! I've been in damned good juried shows. I've had some fantastic reviews."

"I'm just a guy who buys a painting once in a while."

"Then what could you possibly know about it? You jack-asses learn a couple of stock words and voila! you're a critic yet."

"There's nothing wrong with decoration, Heidi."

"You will call me Mrs. Trumbill if you don't mind."

"I mind, Heidi. Your stuff will melt right into the wall after a week. Nobody will see it. That's no disgrace. It's decorative, but it ain't art."

"Get *out* of here!"

"You can call me Trav, or Travis." There was a piece of paper on a table beside a lamp. I saw a pencil on the coffee table. I took the blank paper over and put it beside the pencil. "Just make me a sketch of that lamp and the window beyond it, girl, and I'll go quietly."

"Oh, you mean draw you a cow that looks like a cow?" she said with a poisonous and knowing smile.

"Go ahead. Funny, but everybody I can think of right off the top of the head could sure God draw a fat realistic cow if they ever happened to want to. Hans Hoffman, Kline, Marca-

Relli, Guston, Solomon, Rivers, Picasso, Kandinsky, Motherwell, Pollock. And you know it, baby. If you can't stand the heat, stay out of the kitchen. You dabblers bug me. You want the applause without all the thousands of hours of labour learning how to draw, how to make brush strokes, learning all the things that give painting some bite and bones even when you don't use any part of it. Go ahead, draw the lamp. Quick sketch. Prove I'm a jackass."

She trotted over, flounced down, took the pencil and made some quick lines, then stuck her tongue tip out of the corner of her mouth and drew a more careful line, then she got up and threw the pencil at the paper. It went bouncing under a chair. "Shit!" she said. "So I fake it. Everybody does. And I get away with it."

"Suddenly I think I like you a little better, Mrs. Trumbill."

Her smile was wan and strained. "I'm overwhelmed, Mr. McGee. People don't talk to me like that often."

"Drenches out the glands, they say."

She studied me. "I suppose it's an approach, actually. You get nasty to a girl and it shocks her so she gets hung up. Nice try."

I gave her my most amiable grin. "Miss Pussycat, I have the feeling if some jolly experimental giant crammed us both buck naked into a one-man sleeping bag, we'd apologize to each other, get back to back, and try to get a little sleep."

"And that too is an absolutely transparent pass, damn you."

"Try me. You turn on my lights not at all, Miss Heidi."

"I damned well could if I should ever develop a taste for huge dull muscular men, but I'm afraid I put all that behind me when I reached sixteen. Can't we please finish whatever it is you came for and break this off?"

"Pleasure. We're checking out Gloria Doyle Geis very carefully."

"It's about time, wouldn't you say?"

"I know you made some suggestions to Andrus."

She sat on the couch again. "But he won't really see what a cheap little adventurer she is. I think I've figured it all out. Of *course* there isn't anything on her record. I think she had an accomplice. They worked out some kind of a story about something she was supposed to have done, and then the accomplice blackmailed all that money out of my poor sick confused father. She had him on drugs, you know. I think that could be proved in court. Now all she has to do is just sit tight and pretend she doesn't know a thing. Believe me, that money is hidden in some safe place and when the fuss dies down, she and her unwashed friend will disappear with it."

"Makes sense, I guess."

"You *know* it does. My God, he denied his own children, his flesh and blood, by leaving that grubby little waitress a whole half of his money anyway. But oh no, that wasn't enough for her. There's no limit to the greed of that kind of person."

"Pretty tough to prove that was the way he was cheated."

"You people should track down all her old boy friends, and you can tell just by looking at her that there are plenty of them and they weren't very carefully selected either. Did you know she knew Daddy was dying when she married him? What kind of a person would be so eager to marry a dying man who was pretty well-off? Ask yourself that."

"I guess she didn't get a very warm welcome from the family when he brought her back here from Florida."

"You can say we made it very clear to her how we felt." She shook her head, slowly. "And to think that Roger and I used to think what a shame it would be if Stanyard's husband died and Daddy made an honest woman of her. But we would certainly have settled for Stanyard a dozen times over rather than darling Gloria."

"Stanyard?"

"Chief OR nurse on neurosurgery at Methodist Hospital where Daddy did most of his operations. Her husband was hurt about the same time Mommy passed away. It was a fishing accident and they resuscitated him, but he'd been out too long and because of no oxygen going to the brain, there was a lot of damage. I guess he's sort of half in a coma. He's in an institution near Elgin. He sort of wanders around, I understand, and he can say a few words, and he seems glad to see her in a vague way. They had a little boy and he drowned when the boat was swamped. Stanyard has some kind of a thing about getting an annulment or a divorce. She was at the funeral. I hadn't seen her in years and years. I don't know when she and Daddy started having a thing. Probably not a very long time after Mommy died. I'm not censuring them, you understand. Two lonely people with the same interests. She's still fairly attractive—as nurse types go. And they did make a big effort to be discreet, at least. But the summer I was twelve, one evening after dark she drove him home

46

because his car was being fixed, and I looked through the hedge and saw them kissing. You know how kids are. It made me feel quite ill and wretched and confused. I told Roger and he said to keep my mouth shut. He said he'd known it for a year at least. I guess it really must have shaken her up when he married that Doyle person. Poor thing. When he had to go off on trips to do special operations he'd arrange to have Stanyard go along as OR nurse. She was—is—very good, I guess. I mean nobody would question his wanting her right there for tricky operations. But I guess it was . . . quite a handy arrangement for them."

I said nothing. She realized how patronizing she had sounded. She coloured slightly. "I'm not really a prude, Mr. McGee. When it's your own father . . . somehow it's more tawdry. You expect more. Mommy was such an absolute angel. I guess I should realize that Daddy was a man, with a man's . . . requirements. But it seems like such an insult to my mother's memory, the affair with Stanyard and then marrying the Doyle person. I guess that because a man is famous in his field, it doesn't mean he can't be foolish and gullible about women. Of course, I didn't exactly make one of the world's best marriages."

"Better luck next time."

Her smile was cold. "No need for a next time, thank you."

At that moment the red door swung open and a young man came hurrying in, saying, "*Really*, it's too *much*! Darling, that wretched Kirstarian is absolutely *intent* on ruining the entire exhibition, and I just. . . ."

He stopped and stared at me, eyebrows arching in surprise. "Well, excuse *me*! I didn't know anyone was. . . ."

"Mark," she said wearily, "you've promised and promised not to come charging in here. If you ever do it again, I'm going to make you give me that downstairs key back."

"I was just terribly excited, Heidi. This is really a *crisis*! Wait until you *hear*! But shouldn't you introduce us?"

"Mr. Travis McGee. Mark Avanyan. Mark and I run a little gallery on East Scott Street."

"The Tempo East," he said. He wore a shaggy green turtleneck and skinny jeans in an almost white denim. He had the build of a good welterweight in peak condition. His hair was a half-inch length of dense black pelt that began about an inch and a half above his dark heavy brows. He smiled approvingly at me. "It's so marvellous to see somebody who looks

47

really *outdoors*." He sat on a bright blue hassock and tucked his sneakers under him and scowled and said, "Kirstarian is absolutely *adamant*, darling. He brought in a new piece and he says it goes in the show or there won't be any show. And I can't *endure* it. It is absolutely *ghastly*."

He turned to me and explained, "Kirstarian calls his latest work Stappenings. For static happenings. He makes these marvellous life-size wire armatures of people and objects and wraps them with muslin and then sprays them with some sort of hardener. They have tremendous *presence*, they really do. And I have been working myself into exhaustion since dawn, practically, making the most effective arrangements, and then he comes in with his . . . impossible *thing*."

"What's in it, dear?" she asked.

"It's two large dogs—uh—copulating like mad. They are sort of vaguely dogs, you know. Kirstarian just *stands* there, saying it is one of the statements he wishes to make in this show, and he is not going to let anyone censor his work. And there are those fat white terrible beasts, and it is the *only* thing people are going to look at, and it seems like some sort of terrible vulgar joke he's trying to play on us. Actually, he *hates* me. I'm just becoming aware of it. Heidi, darling, we're not *ready* to show something like that. I mean you could say that *Chicago* isn't ready. And the preview is *tomorrow*. And we've *publicized* it. Darling, you have to *do* something."

"He's *your* friend, dear."

"Not any longer, believe me."

"Run along, Mark, dear. Run on back and tell him to wait and I'll be by in a little while to take a look."

As he started to leave he looked into the studio at the new painting on the easel. "Heidi! he cried. "It's *stunning*. And I believe it's transitional. Your work is getting so *strong*!"

After saying he hoped we'd meet again, he went hurrying off.

"Poor Mark," she said. "Everything is always a crisis. But he does work very hard. Had we finished?"

"There's a couple of questions. I'd like to get a look at those problem dogs. If you want to change, I could ask the questions on the way."

She changed to a grey flannel suit worn over a pale green sweater, and agreed it would be pleasant to walk the four blocks or so to the Tempo East Gallery. I did not have to shorten my normal stride very much to stay in step with her.

I said, "Did you have any idea the bulk of the estate had been liquidated before the bank told you?"

"I had no idea! Roger and I knew he'd changed his will and was cutting us each from a half to a quarter. Roger even had his attorney look into it, but there was nothing we could do. I suppose we could have guessed the woman might be capable of some sort of trickery."

"How was your relationship with your father the last year of his life?"

"Unfortunate. The Doyle person poisoned his mind against his own children. We saw him a few times, of course. He seemed pleasant but . . . remote. Not terribly interested in what we were doing. Oh, he was a lot of help to me with the wedding, and later with the divorce from Gadge. Actually, Jeanie— Roger's wife—seemed to get along with him better than we did. She'd stop with the kids. Daddy enjoyed seeing his grandchildren."

"Gloria Geis claims that all she gets from the estate is the insurance policy that brings her in less than five thousand a year."

"A lovely smokescreen. That's what I think."

"Maybe that nurse blackmailed your father."

"Stanyard? Janice Stanyard? Nonsense!"

"Actually, since you couldn't have touched the principal, your inheritance would have been just the seventy-five hundred a year, right?"

"Meaning I shouldn't care so much about it? Mr. McGee, I do not like to be cheated. The amount is not the point at issue. I *can* get along without it, of course. My alimony is four times that, and I do sell many of my paintings, regardless of your opinion of my work."

"And there's an income from the gallery?"

"A small one. My divorce was final about . . . fourteen months ago. There was a settlement and the alimony agreement, and at Daddy's suggestion John Andrus advised me on handling the settlement money. I bought the building where my apartment is, and I bought some good blue-chip stocks, invested in the gallery, and put what was left in a savings account. I can get along nicely, thank you. But why should that make me feel indifferent about someone else having something Daddy intended I should have?"

"Is Roger doing as well?"

"Better, if anything. Jeanie has her own money. And Roger

49

is very good with money, very shrewd. But he doesn't like being cheated any better than I do. Here we are."

The sign on the door said the gallery was closed. As she was looking for the key in her purse Mark Avanyan opened the door for us. When we went in, he gestured toward the dog tableau, gave a loud theatrical sigh, and turned away. Though small, the gallery was well-lighted, attractive, pleasantly designed not to detract from any work being shown. Kirstarian stood with his back toward us, arms folded, and he was as motionless as all his white muslin people. They made an eerie effect, white mummies frozen at some moment of action. The form was entirely derivative, of course. A movable spot on one of the ceiling tracks shone down upon the large dogs. Mark had not reported inaccurately.

Kirstarian turned very slowly to face us. I was astonished to see how young his face and his eyes were in that small area not obscured by the huge, untrimmed black beard. He wore the kind of black suit favoured by European intellectuals, and I had thought from the shape of him that he was at least middle-aged. But he was merely a plump young man with bad posture.

"Avanyan," he said in a slow and heavy voice, "is incurably middle-class. He is a silly little tradesman and this is his silly little shop. Perhaps, Mrs. Trumbill, you have more integrity."

Heidi stared at the muslin sculpture, fists on her hips. "This is a necessary statement?" she asked.

"An expression of eternal relationships. Yes."

"Dear Jesus," whispered Mark Avanyan, rolling his eyes toward the ceiling.

I broke the impasse by saying, "I think it's fabulous, Mr. Kirstarian." I caught his hand and pumped it.

"Thank you, sir. But, please, not mister. Just Kirstarian."

"Let me give you my card," I said. I had managed to turn him and position him perfectly. I fumbled in my wallet and dropped several cards. "Ooops!" said I, and ducked for them as they were still fluttering down, and put my right foot crosswise, an inch behind the heels of his shabby black shoes. As I straightened up, I managed to nudge him in the chest with my shoulder. He teetered, waved his arms wildly, then sat solidly upon his dogs. As I had dared hope, the hardening agent made the structures brittle. Muslin love ended in a huge Nabisco crunching, a spanging of wires, a rattle of dog-fragments across the floor.

With loud sounds of apology and dismay, I lifted him up out of the unidentifiable ruin. As he sputtered I turned him and heartily whacked all the white powder off the back of his shiny black suit. He was in despair at the tragic accident. He kept picking up parts and dropping them. We all tried to comfort him. He said he hadn't even photographed it. He went trudging sadly off, a blackness marching through the brightness of the Saturday mid-day.

At one point during the helpless laughter I learned something about Miss Heidi. She clung to me, tears rolling down her face, and then suddenly became aware of my hands on her waist. She froze at once, and turned rigidly away, taking a tissue from her purse and dabbing at her eyes. She said she had some errands, and left so abruptly it was very much like flight.

After she left, when Mark wanted to know how I knew Heidi, I explained that I was investigating the disappearance of Fortner Geis' estate. He had no ideas. He wanted to be helpful, because I had extricated the gallery from an idiotic impasse. There is a delicate protocol in such relationships. He was carefully flirtatious, lookng for any subtle encouragement. So I managed to drop into the conversation quite casually those clues which turned him off for good. His acceptance of the inevitable was philosophic.

I am always sceptical of the male who makes a big public deal out of how he hates fairies, how they turn his stomach, how he'd like to beat hell out of them. The queens are certainly distasteful, but the average homosexual in the visual and performing arts is usually a human being a little bit brighter and more perceptive than most. I've had the opinion for a long time that the creative work of the homosexuals tends to be so glossy and clever and glib that it has a curious shallowness about it, as though the inability to share the most common human experience of all makes it all surface and no guts, and when there is an impression of guts it is usually just another clever imitation.

But once he knows that it is absolutely no dice, there is no persistence. They know how to keep their worlds separated. And most of them are wryly aware of the ugly fact that the overly male type who thinks he hates them so thoroughly is the man who is, deep in his heart, unsure of his own masculinity. The man who knows that his preferences are solidly heterosexual has no need to go about thumping everybody who lisps.

That outraged and muscular attitude always reminds me of a curious aspect of the Negro problem in the South. It is something seldom if ever touched upon in learned surveys of the situation, but the intelligent Negros have been sourly amused by it for many years. When you see photographs of violence directed against Negro civil rights workers, photographs in newspapers and magazines and on the television screen, it is inevitable that among the most hate-filled and violent faces on the whites you will spot an interesting incidence of a touch of the tar brush a few generations ago. Through ugliness and violence they are trying to overcompensate for that inner awareness of an ancestor who studied himself in the mirror one day and decided he could pass and get away with it, and who—young man or young woman— went underground and reappeared a hundred or five hundred miles away as a white, married white, and prayed to God almighty that every baby would be fair enough. And, because the dark skin of the Negro is genetically a recessive characteristic, the babies were fair—unless, of course, by cruel chance both parents carried the recessive gene. Other characteristics of race are there, exposed these days by the impartial lens.

So, sitting in the back of the gallery, drinking cold beer from a small refrigerator, I asked him what made Heidi tick. I knew that in the close associations of work they would have been like girls together, exchanging confidences.

"Poor Heidi," he said. "She's blocked. She's all tied in knots. She can't make out. Gadge had sort of a snow-maiden complex, I guess. But the kiss didn't awaken the virgin, the way it says in the books. To her it was just a lot of terrible senseless nastiness. *Heavens*, Gadge Trumbill would have been one of the *least* likely anyway. He's a possessor. He's a brutalizer. *Horribly* demanding. I met him through Heidi, of course. And I rue the day. I suppose it does give Heidi and me some kind of sick something in common. Disaster victims. A dear friend of mine, Anna VanMaller, the cellist, you must have heard of her, took a great interest in Heidi last spring, but poor Heidi can't go either way. She sublimates every bit of sexual drive into her work, and she uses the most *fantastically* subtle erotic symbolism without even *realizing* it. I keep telling her psychiatry might help, but she says she is perfectly happy the way things are. I think it is some sort of a father thing. When she was little, she adored him. Once I tried to tell her that she married an older man because the father had betrayed her by marrying the Doyle woman, and I *actually* thought she was going to scratch out my eyes. I will tell you this though. It is a damned good thing Dr. Geis brought some good tough lawyers into that divorce action last year. I think Heidi would have settled for peanuts, just to get out of Gadge's bed forever. Funny, though, if Heidi had turned into what Gadge thought she might become, he wouldn't have had to go catting around after everybody in sight."

As I trudged back to the hotel for a late lunch, I decided there was no point in trying to sort out the fragments of inference and information until I had more.

In many ways life is less random than we think. In your past and mine, there have been times when we have, on some lonely trail, constructed a device aimed into our future. Perhaps nothing ever comes along to trigger it. We live through the safe years. But, for some people, something moves on the half-forgotten path, and something arches out of the past and explodes in the here and now. These are emotional intersections, when lives cross, diverge, then meet again.

Rational examination of the specifics, like Janice Stanyard, Gretchen's disappearance, Heidi's coldness, Anna's denial of her daughter, would do me no good, not yet. I had to get more of the feel of Fortner Geis' life before I could understand how he could accept so blandly a condition which caused him to steal the inheritance his heirs expected and then die without leaving any explanation, though he knew that it would create a curious kind of emotional and legal chaos. It is almost impossible to bully a dying man, particularly one with the inner strength of Fortner Geis.

FIVE

AFTER lunch I rode up to my floor in an elevator-load of very noisy jolly fellows wearing nickname badges and smelling of sour mash.

I sat on my bed and checked the big phone directory and found several Stanyards. One was Mrs. Charles Stanyard. The others were male. It was a number on Greenwood. I had picked up a city map. Apparently the address would be reasonably handy to Methodist Hospital. Glory had given me Roger Geis' address in the Evanston area off Glenview. I wasn't interested in Roger. If there was anything he could add, Heidi would have known it. I was more curious about his wife, Jeanie, who'd got along well with Fort. Most of all I wanted to talk to Gretchen, to Susan, and again to Anna Ottlo.

I arranged for a rental Ford and drove out to the Roger Geis home, red brick with stubby white pillars, some fine old trees. I got there a little after three. The maid was there alone with the youngest child. She wouldn't take the chain off the door, and told me through the opening that the mister was playing golf, and that Mrs. Geis was at the Countryside Tennis Club with the two older children. When I asked her how to find it, she closed the door.

I got my directions at a gas station. The day was turning colder, but most of the dozen courts were in use. In a large play area noisy platoons of small children were keeping two young girls very busy. I asked a big winded lady carrying three rackets if Jeanie Geis was on the courts, and between pantings, she pointed to a game of mixed doubles and told me she was the girl on the far court. I moved over and watched them. Jeanie was a sturdy woman nearing thirty, not tall, a bit heavy in the leg. Brown legs, arms, face, hair. The heavy legs were the hard, muscular, springy legs of the athlete. She covered more than her share of the court. Her partner was a spry old man with white hair. They were playing a boy and girl in their early twenties. It was very respectable tennis, craftiness against power. Jeanie's little white pleated skirt whipped around as she twisted, cut back, dashed to the net. They weren't jolly about saves and misses. It was a blood game. On set point, Jeanie banged a cross-court shot to the young girl's backhand, and the girl took a nasty fall trying to get to it, but missed it. They gathered around her. She had taken some hide off her arm. She said she was all right.

As they all started back toward the small clubhouse, I asked Mrs. Geis if I could have a word with her. The others went ahead.

"Yes? What about?" she had that husky semi-drawl of the better finishing schools, an effective delivery styled to give equal and additional impact to witticism, cattiness or love words.

"Excuse the expression—money," I said. And there, for a

few moments, was the jackpot, and I couldn't bet my hand because I didn't know what cards I was holding. Jackpot in the sudden draining of all blood and colour from under the tan, in a sudden sickness of pleasant green eyes and in the shape of the mouth, and in a rigid kind of stillness. These are the parts of a terror almost animal in its intensity, when the body aches to spin and run blindly. But before I could find any way to make any use of it, I saw the swift return of control. It seemed almost as if control had returned through an exercise of logic. She had looked more carefully at me and had decided I did not fit into the pattern of fear, and so it had to be a mis-understanding on her part.

"Pretty broad topic to discuss, Mr. . . ."

"McGee. Travis McGee."

"I've heard that name before. Where? I have a fantastic memory for names. Faces mean nothing. Could we move along? I don't want to get chilled." As I began walking beside her she said, "Got it! Daddy Fort and Gloria were talking about you . . . oh, at least three years ago. I'd taken the kids by. He was kidding her, in a nice way. Something about her Florida boyfriend. You? The tan would fit."

"Old friend, yes."

"Wait just a moment, please." She went quickly over to the playground. As she was speaking to one of the girls in charge, two kids, a boy and girl perhaps seven and five, came running to her. She squatted and gave them a simultaneous hug. They went racing back to their group and she spoke to the girl again and then came back to where I waited. "I had to make sure we had the signals right. The sitter is going to pick them up here and take them home. And I go from here to join Roger at a cocktail thing. We'll have time to talk after I shower and change. You go through that door and turn left for the lounge. You could wait for me there. Order yourself a drink, please."

The lounge was comfortable. The healthy tennis set was noisily taking on a small Saturday night load before heading off to do the serious drinking elsewhere. The lounge had seen a lot of hard use, and the drinks were substantial. I picked a corner table where there seemed the most chance of privacy. After a half-hour Jeanie Geis joined me, looking more elegant in dark green cocktail dress, high heels, mink over her arm, than I'd expected. As I was seating her, the barman brought her a Gibson, straight up. "Thank you, Jimmy, and another whatever he's having for my guest, Mr. McGee. How's Skippy making it?"

"You know. Drifting and dreaming. Twenty times maybe she's tried on the wedding dress, her mother telling her she's going to wear it out."

"She's a dear doll and she's getting a nice guy."

When he was out of earshot she looked speculatively at me and said, "As a friend of Glory's, it has to be Daddy Fort's money you wanted to talk about. But why me?"

"I talked to Heidi. I don't think your husband could add anything. Incidentally, Heidi doesn't know I'm Glory's friend."

"How could I add anything Roger couldn't? I mean it is all terribly mysterious, and Heidi and Roger are furious, and it puts Gloria in a very odd position. But if she asked you for help, if she asked you to come and see if you can find out what *did* happen, I can understand but I don't have to approve."

She hesitated as Jimmy put the new drink in front of me, continuing as he moved away. "It's over, isn't it? If Fort thought anything should be explained to the family, he would have. And maybe you should explain why you came to me? Are you implying I'd keep anything from my husband?"

"I am not concerned exclusively with what people know they know, Mrs. Geis. From what Heidi told me, you were getting along with the Doctor better than his own children. So you saw him oftener. So you could have pertinent knowledge you don't realize *is* pertinent."

"Are you some kind of a detective?"

"Me? No. Just a friend of Glory's. You come in from the outside, sometimes it's easier to see the shape of things. You must have had some guess as to why Fort did what he did."

Her mouth firmed up. "Mr. McGee, the only thing I can tell you is what I have told my husband. And though I do not think it good taste to tell this to a stranger, Roger and I have come closer to . . . very real trouble in our marriage over this than anything. Heidi is in no financial pain. Neither are we. Gloria is the worst off, but if people would just leave her alone, I think she'd be quite content. We're not close friends. We don't have enough in common. But I realize how good she was for Fort. And certainly she'll marry again, and she should be able to marry quite well. She has a special style of her own, and a capacity for loyalty, and a very personal kind of warmth,

56

and the urge to take care of a man and please him. I have told Roger that I think it is shameful and vulgar and disgraceful to keep prodding at this whole thing. It isn't a financial motive at all, really. It took me a long time to understand it. Fortner Geis was a very strong personality. When his wife died, he lost himself in his work. Roger and Heidi thought he was rejecting them. It turned them into emotionally insecure people. Heidi is a crashing neurotic. I've had to work twice as hard as anybody knows to make this marriage of mine work. I think that all the time they hoped that one day he would . . . accept and cherish them. What happened? An affair with a nurse that lasted for years. That was a rejection. Then, after they learned he had a fatal illness, he came back here from vacation with a bride. That hurt them. It was a symbolic rejection when he changed his estate arrangements in her favour. They hate her. The final rejection was to find that he had somehow arranged to leave them nothing. They talk about money but they are really looking for some proof of love. Heidi is far worse than Roger, God knows why. I feel this way. Fortner Geis must have had a very sound and good reason for not telling Gloria and Heidi and Roger what he was doing and why he was doing it. To me that means that if they do ever find out, it might be worse than not ever knowing. They should trust him, accept it, forget it."

Had I not seen the earlier and more extreme reaction, I might have missed this one. It was just a hair too much intensity, too much edge in that hoarse social voice.

"Did you make any guesses why he did it?"

"It doesn't matter to me why he did it."

"You liked him?"

"I think . . . he was the finest man I've ever known."

"But he fouled up his kids, didn't he?"

"Did he? Maybe their mother did. They were eleven and seven when she died. She had enough time. And, believe me, I have heard far too much talk from Heidi and Roger about how sweet and brave and noble she was. She's assumed the stature of a mythological being, Mr. McGee. She's hard to believe in."

"Mrs. Geis, I'm a little puzzled by one thing. Who did you think I was when I stopped you and said I wanted to talk about money?"

"I had no idea who you were."

"Then why were you terrified?"

57

She frowned and smiled at the same time. "Terrified? Oh come now, really! Why should I . . . Oh!"

"Oh what?"

The green dress made her fine green eyes greener, Though they had shifted about during all the previous conversation, now they were very steady on mine, and she had widened them a little bit. "They kept us on the run for two long sets, trying to wear the old man down. When I stopped to talk to you, I suddenly felt quite faint. The world had a swimmy look and my ears were ringing, and then it went away, or I would have had to sit down right in the middle of the walk."

"Son of a gun!" I said. "That must have been it." It was more gallant than telling the lady she was a lousy liar. "I guess I should tell Gloria she shouldn't let all this bother her so much. Having Fort's children hate and resent her so much confuses her. She's one of those people without malice. Did you ever tell her your rejection theory?"

"Yes. She seemed to understand how it could be that way."

Night had come. The lights were on. She craned her neck to look at the clock over the bar. I walked her out to the parking lot to her car. After she got in, she looked out at me and said, "I think it would do Gloria a lot of good to get away now. Maybe she could go back to Florida with you, Mr. McGee. You'd be doing her more good that way than by . . . trying to find out why the Doctor did what he did."

"It's an idea," I said.

I found my way, after several wrong turns, to Lake Pointe, the handsome house, snap and hiss of logs aflame, chunky glass in my hand, Glory Doyle Geis in wine slacks and white sweater sitting on a cushion on the raised hearth, dainty, bittersweet, semi-sad in the firelight.

"Not so good of a day for me," she said, "and I don't really know why. I couldn't settle down to anything. Kept roaming. I'm supposed to be inventorying the books. They go to the university library. What did you do? Who did you talk to?"

"Heidi. And Mark Avanyan. And a fat boy named Kirstarian. Jeanie Geis. I saw the happiest girl in Chicago, but I didn't meet her. I busted hell out of some very advanced sculpture. I nearly ran over a black cat wearing a red collar."

"Tell me all!" she cried, her face lighting up.

58

"First you tell me about Janice Stanyard."

She studied me for a few moments. "You mean you're annoyed I didn't tell you about her before?"

"Didn't you think it was pertinent?"

"Not particularly."

"You sound as frosty as Miss Heidi."

She looked dismayed, then grinned. "I didn't know I could. Anyway, when I tell you you'll understand. Fort told me about her while we were still on our wedding trip, before we came back to Chicago. We were talking about different kinds of love. And he just sort of casually mentioned he'd had a long affair with a nurse. He said it started a year after his wife died. And it ended two years before he met me. When I realized that was nearly eleven years, I was *furious*! And he laughed at me. He didn't explain for a while because he said he wanted to prolong the pleasure of having me so jealous of another woman. He said it was marvellously flattering at his age. But when he saw I was really getting upset, he told me just how it was."

"About her husband's accident and the little boy drowning?"

"Yes. He said she had worked with him long enough by that time so that she was like an extension of himself, like having another pair of hands. She knew his procedures, knew the instruments he would want at each stage, and also knew what to have ready to hand him when things went wrong this way or that way. She did not disturb his concentration the way other surgical nurses did. He said she seemed glad to share the enormous work load he had shouldered after Glenna died. After a year had gone by he knew he was changing in some way he did not like. He was thirty-six. He had not been with a woman for a year. He was putting so much of his total energy into his work he did not feel any particular tension because of physical desire. As a doctor he knew that continence does an adult no particular physical harm. He told me that the idea of regular sex as a necessity for health is something young men use as part of their persuasion technique. Fort told me he began to feel remote. He said that was the best word for it. He had less feeling of involvement with his patients, less triumph when things went well, less regret when they didn't. He couldn't chew out people who made foolish errors the way he used to. It didn't seem worth the effort somehow. And he knew his praise was becoming half-hearted, which is worse than no praise at all.

59

"So he went to his friend Doctor Hayes Wyatt with the problem. Dr. Wyatt gave him a complete physical, and then listened to Fort describe the remoteness. Then he told Fort that no matter how much he might try to deny it or ignore it, he was still a mammal. By questioning him, Dr. Wyatt showed how much warmth there had been in Fort's childhood. He'd been breast-fed, hugged, patted, cuddled, kissed and spanked. People with austere childhoods could adjust to the life Fort was living. But for Fort, some essential assurance-area was being starved. He felt remote because his body, untouched, was beginning to doubt the reality of its own existence. Hayes Wyatt told Fort that casual sex relationships would not do very much to help him. He said Fort should marry an affectionate and demonstrative woman."

"Like Glory Doyle."

"Sure. What was I then? About fifteen? Great. Fort didn't want marriage, not then. For weeks he wondered what he was supposed to do, what would be best for him. One day, after they scrubbed, there was a long delay in setting up the proper anaesthesia for a complicated spinal disc operation, and he realized that Janice Stanyard was once again talking about her two Siamese cats, and it was a little bit too much like the way people talk about their children. He watched her and thought about her for days. He knew she admired and respected him, and he knew they liked each other. She was twenty-seven, nearly twenty-eight. He said he would like to meet those most unusual cats. He went to her apartment a few times. One night, like a fatuous pretentious damned fool—Fort said—he asked her what she thought about the sort of 'arrangement' he had in mind.

"She was puzzled, hurt, offended. She still loved Charles and always would. It was ugly to think they could enter into that kind of thing without love. It would not hurt anybody else, she agreed. but it would cheapen both of them. A month later they were in Atlanta on an emergency, a small calibre bullet lodged in the frontal lobe of a young girl, pressing against the optic nerve. It was long and precarious, and it went well. They had dinner together at their hotel, with wine, feeling good about the day's work. He seduced her that evening in her room. He spent the night in her bed. When he awoke in the morning he found himself looking into her sleeping face not a foot away. Her arm rested on him. Her round knee was against his thigh. Fort said he had a terrible sinking of heart, a dread about the inevitable scene when she awakened. He remembered all the tears, the protestations, and even, after she had been at last aroused, the small dead voice in which she had begged him not to. He said her face looked as calm and unreadable as the face of a statue. Her slow warm exhalations brushed against his lips. At last she stirred and her eyes opened. At first they were blank and unfocused. Then they focused on him and she gave a great start and pulled her arm back. She looked into his eyes, half-frowning, and he told her that it was a mistake, all a mistake, all a mistake, and he was sorry. He said the corners of her mouth turned up, she stretched and yawned, then put her arm around him, hitched close, put her face in his throat, made kind of a little purring sound of contentment and in moments went back to sleep. Fort said it was a kind of love, always gentle, always placid, always kind. He said that the sexual release was less important to them than the nearness of someone, the warm flesh and the breathing and the beating of the nearby heart when you woke up in the night. Once it had begun, he said she accepted it undemandingly, and with the enormous practicality of which most women seem capable. He said they tried to be discreet, taking the chances which came along rather than trying to make chances. Remoteness went away. As a team they functioned as perfectly as before, no better and no worse. He said that once again his work came alive, and the intense involvement with it returned. So, I'm grateful to her, Trav. She kept him whole and alive for all those middle years of his life. He said there wasn't any decision to end it. They just seemed to need each other less often and finally not at all, without jealousy or suspicion or regret. He said that it was an affair without the words people say during affairs. When they were together, when they talked, it was not about their work, or about Glenna or his children, or her husband. It was easy, homely talk, he said, about the cafeteria coffee, and it was the right time for her to trade her car, and what the cleaner was doing to his suits, and how she had liked Kup's show the other night, and who to vote for this time, and how the weather was hotter or colder than usual. That's what it was, Trav. An arrangement. It was a good thing for them. Heidi told you about her?"

"To say it would have been bad enough if he'd married that nurse person, but it would have been better than marrying you."

"What a disastrous marriage!" she said bitterly. "I made the poor man so miserable. *Damn* her!"

"Don't let it get to you. She isn't worth it. Did you ever meet Janice Stanyard?"

"Oh yes. While Fort was still operating. She must be about forty-five now. She is . . . attractive in her own way. You don't see it at first. She grows on you, sort of. You see, she knew Fort's bad prognosis before his children did. He handed her the results of the tests moments after he read them. Then when he came back from Florida married to me, the first time I met her was in the staff lounge at Methodist. Fort introduced us and then made out like there was something he had to go and do. She wasn't antagonistic, just very curious about me, about what sort of person I am. Finally she decided in my favour, we were sitting on a couch. She took hold of my hand and held it so tightly it went numb. She told me to help him. I knew what she meant. She said he was great and good, but he might be scared. I said I loved him with all my heart. And so we sat there with goofy smiles and the tears running down our faces. She's nice, Trav. She came here a few times toward the end. She was at the funeral. We had a few minutes alone, afterward. She hugged me and said nothing better could have happened to him than me. I haven't seen her since."

"And it didn't occur to you, Glory, that if he had a very tough decision to make, if he was in a real bind, he might go to the person he had worked with for years, whom he liked and respected and trusted, and to whom in a strange way he had been in effect married."

After a few moments of round eyes and parted lips, she said, "But he was closer to me!"

"Which could have been his reason for not bringing you into it."

"What do you mean by that?"

"I don't know yet. Maybe he said nothing to her. Maybe she knows the whole thing. I have to talk to her."

"Of course."

"So call her and I'll get on an extension."

But when nine rings brought no answer, as we went back to our places by the hearth, Anna came in and said proudly that the kidney mutton chops she had were so thick, maybe she should start them now. I knew that with absolutely no trouble at all, Anna could balloon me up to a mighty two fifty, and it would take me months to fit back into my clothes.

62

When I said I hadn't planned to stay to dinner, she said with a kind of contemptuous sadness that if I hadn't stopped by, Miss Glory would have insisted on some cold cereal and a piece of dry toast.

With icy gin replenished I told Glory about the rest of my day. I pointed out the significance of learning that Fort had taken direct steps to improve the terms of Heidi's divorce. "He'd already started liquidating the previous July. He knew Roger was pretty well set. He knew then he wasn't going to be able to leave them anything, so he made sure Heidi got some security out of Trumbill's money."

"Which didn't exactly pinch Gadge Trumbill," Glory said. "He had an ancestor who homesteaded two hundred and forty acres. The Chicago Civic Centre is right smack in the middle of it, and the old boy believed in leasing instead of selling."

"Next item. Neither Heidi nor Jeanie brought up the Gretchen thing. And they had their chance."

"They never knew about that."

"Now to get back to Jeanie Geis. She was terrified, and then she lied about it. Why?"

"I think I can answer that, Trav." She explained that nearly two years back, when their eldest child was five, there had been an attempt to kidnap him. The boy, Branton Fortner Geis, named after both grandfathers, had actually been taken, but the kidnapper had evidently lost his nerve because after he had driven the boy all the way into the city, he had abandoned him in Grant Park near the fountain. The boy had been driven around for some time, because it gave his parents about three hours of terror before a park policeman took him in and he was identified.

"Since then it has been a thing with Jeanie. She takes the kids wherever she can, and doesn't let them out of her sight. She even got a pistol permit, and she spent hours and hours on the police range, and she's an expert now. Their home has all kinds of burglar alarms and floodlights, and their sitter is a retired cop. He has a licence to carry a gun too, and he takes them back and forth to school. I think she goes a little too far. I don't think it's what you could call a normal childhood for them. Roger is just sort of . . . tolerant of Jeanie's precautions. I guess you can't blame her too much. But it's such a twitch with her, I guess that's the first thing that would enter her mind if you walked up to her and said you wanted to talk about money. You aren't exactly a clerical type, Mister

63

McGee. You are huge and it is obvious you have been whacked upon, and you look as though you damned well enjoyed returning the favour."

"An obvious criminal type?"

"To Jeanie, for a couple of seconds. Until her mind went to work on it, and she got a better look at you. Nobody would walk up to her in broad daylight with all those people around and say, Lady, I got one of your kids."

"So why did she lie later?"

"A white lie, dear, to avoid telling you what she thought you were. It wouldn't be terribly flattering. Besides, she's a little punchy about the precautions. She gets a certain amount of snide comments from the other mothers."

"It explains why the maid wouldn't unchain the door or answer the questions. But, baby, it does not explain her earnest sales talk about lets all forget the whole thing. Why don't you take Glory to Florida, and so forth and so forth."

"How do you explain it then?"

"I don't know. When I get reactions I don't understand it's like an itch I can't reach. I have to make the logical or illogical connection between six hundred thousand gone into thin air and somebody being kidnapped. When did the boy get grabbed?"

"Let me think. I have to remember what we were . . . oh, we'd just come back from New York. Fort read a paper at a medical convention. It was quite warm. . . . May. That was it. A year ago last May."

"Two months later Fort started cashing in his securities. What about this? Suppose sombody got a message to Jeanie. Come up with lots of cash or we'll take one of your kids. So she comes running to Fort. And . . . no, there's two big holes in that."

"Like what?"

"One. She'd tell Roger. He'd know that's where the money went, and he wouldn't be making such a jackass of himself about it. Two. Fort was certainly smart enough to know it would be an awful lot cheaper to get Jeanie and the kids out of reach. Fly them to Switzerland for example, and put the cops to work on the problem. I suppose the kid was too little to give any description of the person or persons who took him riding, or the car they took him in."

"Branty said it was a nice man who sang a lot."

"That doesn't sound like a nervous type."

"Somebody saw the car driving away. They said it was a blue Dodge. I think it was about a week later they found what could have been the same car, but they couldn't be sure. It had been stolen from a shopping centre the morning of the day the boy was taken, and they found it in a big used-car lot out near Midway Airport with no plates on it, and no fingerprints or anything. Nobody could say how long it had been there."

"It doesn't fit."

"What doesn't?"

"The car is clouted in a very professional way, from the kind of place where the pros work, and it is unloaded in a very professional way, as if it had been iron they'd used in a bank job. But the man gets nervous and changes his mind and leaves the kid off. It couldn't have been the same car, Glory. That's the only thing that makes any sense."

Her mouth trembled for a moment and then she smiled. Her eyes were shiny. "We better face it, McGee. Nothing about this whole thing is ever going to make any sense, and for the rest of my life people are going to keep an eye on me, just in case."

At quarter to ten after Glory had stashed the dishes, we tried Janice Stanyard again. She picked up the phone on the first ring.

"Janice? This is Gloria Geis."

"Hello! I've been wondering about you, dear. I was wondering if I should ask you to come in and have lunch with me some day."

I'd like that, I really would. I tried to get you earlier."

"Today? I was over in Elgin."

"How is he?"

"Fine. He had a bad cold but it's nearly gone now. What did you call me about, dear?"

"Well . . . I want to introduce you to a friend of mine from Florida. He's on the line too. Travis McGee. Janice Stanyard."

"Hello, Mrs. Stanyard."

"How do you do, Mr. McGee." Her voice sounded puzzled. It was a good voice, a firm and nicely articulated contralto.

"Trav would like to come and talk to you, Janice."

"He would? What about?"

Gloria started to explain, but I broke in and said, "It's just

65

a little confusion about Doctor Geis' estate, and Glory thinks you might have some answers."

"But I wouldn't know a *thing* about that!"

"Sometimes the way these things work out, Mrs. Stanyard, you can help out without realizing you can. I'd just like to drop by anytime tomorrow at your convenience for a few minutes."

"But. . . ."

"We'd both be very grateful to you."

"Well . . . would three tomorrow afternoon be all right?"

"Just fine."

"Will you come too, Gloria?" she asked.

"Just me," I said quickly, "and now I'll hang up and let you people fix up that lunch date."

As I was leaving, I remembered my other question. I asked Glory who had done the investigation work for Fort when Gretchen had asked him for more money. "He dealt with a Mr. Smith. But I don't know the name of the company." We went to his study and looked up Smith in his address book and found a Francisco Smith, hyphen, Allied Services, in the Monadnock Block on West Jackson. I checked the yellow pages and found Allied Services under Investigators.

A funny thing happened to me on the way to the hotel room. I was a long way from the elevators. When I approached the last right-angle turn before my room, I came upon a couple standing and talking in low tones. I heard her say in wheedling tones, "Whey-ya-yuh room key, honeh? It hey-yuv the nummah on to it."

He peered at me and said in surprisingly articulate tones, slightly Bostonian, "Sir, I have a distressing concept worthy of scholarly research, and it should appeal to anyone of conjectural turn of mind. Have you a moment?"

I stopped and said, "Conjecture away, friend."

"Is there a sense of entrapment in being locked into your own century without chance of escape? What is the effect on the psyche? Those of us born in the first two decades of this century are subliminally aware, my good sir, of that marker on the grave which will say nineteen hundred and this to nineteen hundred and that. Do you follow me?"

He was fifty-something, excellent suit, topcoat, shoes, hat, shirt. But the hat was dented and sat askew, stubble on the jowls, necktie awry. His face had the slack sweatiness of heavy drinking, and he had trouble focusing his eyes on me.

And he was being tugged this way and that way by the girl who was going through his pockets with great energy, muttering about the room key and saying, "You wah somepin, honeh. Somepin for shu-wah."

"I follow you," I said.

"But this lovely child is going to break through into the next century, at exactly the age I am now, and the prospect makes me desperately envious. You, sir, could well manage it too, I suspect, but in the fullness of your years and with dimming. . . ."

With a little squeal of satisfaction she yanked the key out of one of his pockets, stared at the tag, then looked at the nearby room numbers. She wore a bright red cloth coat over a very short white dress that was cleft almost to the navel. Her pouty, saucy, cheap little face peeked out from between the two heavy wings of white-blonde hair that hung straight from centre part to collarbone.

In the corridor light I noticed their hands were dirty. It is impossible to drink all evening without ending up with dirty hands. It is one of the unsolved mysteries of our age.

"Raht they-yahs youwah nummer, sweetsie pah!"

He put a soiled hand against the wall. "I don't believe I . . . I think I'm going to. . . ." He slid slowly and fell on his side with a small thudding sound against the carpeting.

I offered to help her with him. She refused so very sweetly. She couldn't trouble me none. She said she could manage all raht. So I went around the corner and began humming just loudly enough so my voice would carry to where she was. I unlocked my door and opened it and then closed it again without going in, closing it audibly and cutting off the little tune just as it clacked shut.

I went back to the corner and put one eye around carefully. His topcoat was pulled out of the way. She was kneeling, just pulling his wallet out of his inside jacket pocket. Her thick white hair hung forward as she bent over him. Her underlip had fallen away from her teeth and I could hear how her excitement and fear was making her breath fast and audible. She kept snapping her head around to look the other way, toward the elevators. She shoved the currency into the slash pocket of her red coat, put the wallet back in his inside pocket. She picked his arm up and started to take the wristwatch, hesitated, let the arm fall. She picked the key off the carpeting, stood up, and, biting her lip, looked at him and at the door to his room. I could guess what she was thinking of. Would it be worthwhile to unlock the door, drag him in, and go through his belongings? She stood crouched, fingers hooked, her stance ugly. It was a posture feral as any carnivore. It was the hunting stance, and it made me think of Fortner Geis' money, and the far cleverer beast who had gone after it and taken it from him.

I saw her decide to settle for what she had, and cut her risk by getting away quickly. She straightened, shook her hair back, and I pulled back and flattened against the wall, realizing she would come my way, heading for the fire stairs.

The only sound she made was the quick whisking of fabric. She came around the corner in a hurry, saw me out of the corner of her eye, gasped, tried to run, but I caught her from behind, my left arm around her waist, right hand snaking into the right pocket of the coat and coming out with the folded wad of bills as I released her.

She spun, felt in the pocket, came cautiously toward me. "Hay-yuff, huh?" she said in a husky whisper. "Gimmie hay-yuff."

"Give you nothing, dear girl."

"Oney a feeyiffteh then, huh? Pitcher a Gen'l Grant for lil ol' Cinny Lee?"

She spread her coat, wet her mouth, arched her back. "You room raht close by, innit? Less you'n me tote that ole man inna his room so as nobody gets agitated bout him lyin inna hall, then it give me time, I go inna your room, given you a ride like you never had-yud afore, worthen at fifty plusen a tee-yup for sure, lahk to pleasure me a big size may-yun all the whole naht long, honeh pah."

"Run on back to your cotton patch, corn pone."

She had the heels of her hands on her hipbones, fingers spread on her thighs, pointing to the floor. I saw the hemline of the narrow skirt of her white dress climbing as she stealthily worked it up with her fingertips. I knew what she was going to try. If the kick had landed where she wanted it to, she could have plucked the cash out of my nerveless hand and gone tripping happily down the stairs, leaving me there making goldfish mouths, and sweating into the carpet. When it came I turned sharply and, as she missed, got my palm under the back of her ankle and gave the kick a lot more elevation than she wanted. The skirt ripped up the side and she went tumbling back, rolling up on to her shoulders, legs scissoring. I noticed with academic appraisal that she wore nothing under the dress, that she was an unpleasant soft white, almost blue-white, and that she was by no means a natural blonde.

"And the accent is fake too," I said.

She sprang up, looked as though she might try for the eyes, and thought better of it. And in the brisk and nasal flatness of the pure Midwest accent, the kind you hear in the small towns of Indiana and Iowa, she suggested I perform an anatomical impossibility and categorized me as an indulger in several of those specific practices most frowned upon in our culture. Somebody behind one of the closed doors yelled to knock it off for chrissake, and she stopped abruptly, ran to the stairway door, yanked it open, and disappeared.

I found the key on the carpet beside sweetsie pah, unlocked his door, scooped him up, carried him in, and dumped him on his bed. I went out and got his hat and brought it in, closing the door behind me. Turned a light on, worked him out of topcoat and suit coat. Hung them in the closet. Put money in billfold, billfold in suit coat. Loosened tie, belt, removed shoes. Turned out light. Stood for a moment looking down at him, hearing his steady snore. Poor honeh had slipped through the fangs of the cat, and he wasn't the type to give them a chance at him again. I had fanned the currency before putting it back where it belonged, didn't make an exact count, but saw it was over four hundred. We were both locked into this single century. As Fortner Geis had been. So help the fellow traveller, McGee. The Cinny Lees spring at you every chance they get.

If this man could be a four-hundred-dollar fool, Fort could have been one too—at fifteen hundred times the cost. I set his night latch and closed the door behind me and went back to my own leased cave.

After my light was out I made a better identification of Cinny Lee's emotional climate after she knew she'd lost it all. Outraged indignation. She had invested time, training, and experience, had cut him out of the pack, softened him perfectly, had slipped by the hotel security patrol, and had got the chloral hydrate into him at just the right moment. If he had not gone into that talking jag, if he'd had the room key in his hand instead of an inside pocket, if the big stranger hadn't come along, she would have got inside the room with him minutes before it hit him and knocked him out. Then, in

69

privacy and safety she could have plucked him clean of every valuable from his gold wedding ring and cuff links to the change on his bureau. Then, if she was the cool hardened operator I guessed she was, she would sneak out with his key, stash the loot, sneak back into the room, strip him to the buff, take all her clothes off, rip the cheap dress in strategic places, tip a chair and a lamp over—quietly—and get into bed with him and get some sleep and be ready, when he awakened with a savage and blinding headache and total loss of memory, to be crying hopelessly and pitifully. She had no idea where his money was. He could search her if he thought she had it. All she knew was he had forced her. He had torn her pretty new dress, see? Her father and her brothers would be frantic. She'd never been away from home all night before. She was really only fifteen. He'd been like some kind of crazy horrible animal. Oh, oh, what was she going to do. Oh boo hoo wah haw hoo, oh God. She'd better k-k-k-kill herself. Th-Throw herself out of the windowwwwww. . . .

The timing would give her all day Sunday to work on his fears, with the Do Not Disturb sign on the room door, food and drink ordered up, and she would hide in the bathroom when it was brought in. She would have learned every scrap of usable information about him from what she could find in his billfold and elsewhere in the room and in his pockets. He could cash cheques, couldn't he? He could have his bank wire money, couldn't he? She would have to leave town. She would remember a girl-friend in New Orleans. Monday morning he could go out and buy her some clothes and luggage for the trip, and get the money in cash. She would have to have money to live on until she could get a job. At least fifteen hundred over the airline fare to feel really safe. If he dragged his feet she could wonder out loud if maybe she ought to go back to Boston with him and see if his wife could help her get a job. Her name is Frances, isn't it, honeh? Once he agreed, she would become very happy and excited and affectionate, and with any luck she could seduce him, a shameful confirmation of his guilt, and good for at least five hundred more for the poor dear girl. It wouldn't work on a man who had been down the mean streets and seen the dark places. It would work on just such a man as honeh—bright, good, and decent and, in this first and last wild oat, gullible as the youngest sailor in the Navy.

It made me realize with what exquisite care, caution, and

patience Fortner Geis had been cleaned. A man will let his money be taken only when the alternative is something he cannot endure.

What was it Fort could not face? And how much more dangerous was the predator who hunted him down than was this faked-up Cinny Lee?

SIX

Nurse Janice Stanyard lived on Greenwood in one of those standard six-storey apartment houses of yellow brick which were built in such profusion after World War II. They were planned to do an adequate and durable job of housing people, and were designed with the idea of minimum maintenance and upkeep, and with all the grace and warmth of the Berlin Wall.

She was on the fifth floor toward the rear, with windows that looked out over a tarred roof of a neighbouring building to the Sunday emptiness of the broad asphalt parking area of a shopping plaza a half block away, the grey paving marked in the yellow herringbone pattern of the parking slots.

I had not known quite what to expect. My first impression as she let me in was certainly not of a femme fatale. She was a sturdy woman with a big-boned look, a broad and pallid face without animation, dark brown hair turning grey. She wore scuffed loafers, white ankle socks, a baggy herringbone tweed skirt, a loose-fitting brown cardigan. The impression was that of an enduring and stolid woman with no interest in self-adornment. The furniture was plain, heavy, and not new. But it looked comfortable. The decor was a monotone of greys and browns without pattern or touches of colour except for the dust jackets of hundreds of books in long low shelves, and the covers of the magazines in racks and stacks.

"Do sit down, Mr. McGee. I'm afraid I'm not going to be much help to you." She sat at the corner of a couch and I sat in a facing armchair. I suspect that it was the quality of her voice, the earthy richness of the contralto modulation that made me look at her more closely. Her hands were large, and beautifully formed. Her throat was long and solid and grace-ful. Her eyes were particularly lovely—large, the iris a deep clear blue, the lashes naturally dense and long. Once I had seen that much, I could then see the gentle contours of her mouth, and the rich curve of the strong calves.

What had seemed drabness, both in her and in the room became merely understatement. I had the feeling this would be a comfortable room to be in, a comfortable woman to be with. She had the indefinable quality of restfulness, of making no trivial demands upon others or upon herself.

"You worked with Fort a long time and knew him well. I need to know more about him, and maybe then I can figure out why he did what he did."

"Did you know the Doctor well enough to call him Fort?" There was cool surprise in her tone.

"Well enough so he asked me to. In Florida. I stood up with Fort and Glory when they were married. I didn't know him long. I liked him. I was suppose to come visit them here after the house was built. It didn't work out. I wish it had."

"He was a good man," she said. "I miss him. But why did you sound as if he did some inexplicable thing? Fort usually had reasons for what he did."

"Would you have any idea about what sort of estate he left? The size of it?"

"I wouldn't know, really. When Glenna died he got her money. I don't think it was really a lot. I think he used it on Heidi and Roger. They seemed to get anything they wanted at least, cars and sailboats and trips to Europe. Money wasn't particularly important to Fort. I don't mean he was indifferent to it. He would bill a patient according to what the patient could afford. From ten dollars to ten thousand. He didn't spend much on himself. It wasn't because he was stingy. He just didn't have expensive hobbies. He invested his money after taxes and living expenses into good stocks mostly, I think. If I was forced to guess, I'd say he probably was worth half a million dollars when he died. Another man with the same ability and reputation could have been worth . . . three or four times that, possibly."

"When was the last time you saw him?"

"Ten days before he died."

"When was the last time you worked with him?"

"Last January, almost a year ago. The last operation he did. Craniotomy for a neurofibroma, extensive. He started it but he didn't finish it. By then he had good people backing him up every time. His fingertips went numb. He couldn't get the feeling back into them. It's one of the symptoms of what he had. So he turned it over to his assistant. He stood by and watched. It went well. Outside, afterward, he told me that was the last he'd try. He thanked me for putting up with him in all those hundreds and hundreds of operations. At least I held the tears back until I was alone. Everybody who ever worked with him felt the same way."

"Did you have any kind of contact with him between that time and when you visited him at his house?"

There was a little flicker behind the blue of her eyes, a half-second delay. "No, Why?"

I wondered if with a wicked needle I could penetrate that placid manner. "I suppose like all the rest of them, the reputation was a little larger than the man."

Her eyes narrowed. "What is that supposed to mean?"

"There can be twenty or fifty men with the same ability, and one seems to get the good publicity."

"You don't seem to know what the hell you're talking about!"

"Cutting is cutting, no?"

"And some of them are so concerned about setting records they go in there like a whirlwind, and some of them are so picky and cautious the patient is under for six hours when it could be done in four. Then there are people like Fortner Geis who are as quick as they should be and as careful as they should be, but there's something else, too, something that isn't in the books, and you can't describe what it is, and damned few surgeons in any generation have it. It's an instinct for the living flesh under the knife. Two surgeons can make two cuts that look identical, and one will bleed like a pig and the other will be almost dry. One surgeon can cut to where something is supposed to be, and it isn't there, and another will somehow guess that the patient doesn't quite match the anatomy lessons and, without knowing how he does it or what clued him, go right to where he wants to be. Surgeons who worked beside Fort have a right to make comments about his ability. You don't!"

She sat glaring at me. I smiled and said, "I gave you a cheap opportunity to put the knock on him, Mrs. Stanyard. Just checking."

Anger changed to a puzzled indignation. "Why do that? What's the point?"

"I guess the point is that he would have left around seven hundred thousand and something, but he cancelled out his insurance for the cash value, and he cashed in everything else too, except a small equity in the house and a life annuity option policy for Gloria that'll bring her ninety something a week. It took him thirteen months. He finished the job last July. He did it on the sly and covered his tracks. The money is gone and everybody is upset, each one for his own reasons. So when I find out that the Doctor and his favourite nurse had an affair going for ten or eleven years and then he married somebody else, I want to see if there is enough hate left for the nurse to leap at the chance to lay a little bad-mouth on the famous surgeon."

"She told you about Fort and me?"

"She did."

"She had no right!"

"Heidi mentioned it first. I think she said she was twelve years old when she saw you and the Doctor necking. And just how much poking around would I have to do, amid the medical brotherhood and sisterhood, before somebody mentioned old times?"

"You make it sound dirty!"

"Do you know how it sounds to me?"

"I can't imagine caring."

"It sounds as if it was a very good thing for two lonely people to have. I think you are much woman, Mrs. Stanyard. I know where your husband is. I know Gloria *thinks* the affair ended a year or two before she met Fort. If he could change six hundred thousand in assets into cash and put the cash where nobody can find it, keeping you on the string would be no special problem."

"He wasn't that kind of man. I'm not that kind of woman. I didn't even know if he told her about me. But from the way I acted toward her when they came back from Florida, she certainly would have had to guess something. I like her *very* much."

"He told her. In detail."

"And she told you. I don't think I care at all for her telling you."

"After what Heidi said, she had to tell me something. And the detail was so I'd understand. She was anxious to make sure I didn't think less of Fort or of you. Of course, I go around making these moral judgments all the time. Meaningful

74

relationship. That phrase has sure God been worked to death. Like constructive and sincere. What it is, Janice, it's a curious, confusing bitch of a world, and you don't get a very long ride on it, and it is hard to get through to anybody merely by making mouth-sounds. So we all do some taking, up to the point where we don't gag on it. And we all do some giving, because taking doesn't taste right without it. With any luck we can sneak through without crapping up too many other lives, and with a little more luck we can make things shine for somebody sometime."

As she was staring at me, a chunky Siamese cat, a pale one like tea with cream, came in through the door that probably led to the bedroom. He stretched each hind leg separately, gave me casual inspection with eyes as blue as his mistresses', though slightly crossed, came over and snuffed at my shoes, and went on out to the kitchen, indolently purposeful.

"Who *are* you?" Janice asked me.

"T. McGee. T for Travis. Friend of Glory." I motioned toward the kitchen. "Who was that who went through?"

"Ralph. Maybe I made things shine for Fort. My husband will be a four-year-old child as long as he lives. There was that much damage. I visit Charlie every week. I'm a quiet person. I don't require much of life. After Fort and I became lovers, I couldn't understand why I'd put up such a desperate fight for my so-called honour. Maybe I thought that if someone made love to me, I'd start to resent Charlie. I didn't want that. Fort needed me. My God, there was a man I would have crawled through broken glass for, jumped out of windows for. And I couldn't willingly give him something . . . nobody was using and Charlie wouldn't miss. But Fort made it happen anyway, bless him. And then all of a sudden it was just something two people could have. Closeness and pleasure, and all the ordinary little things. Socks and shaving and reminding him of haircuts, and waking up and hearing somebody breathing beside you, feeling the warmth of their body near you. When he wanted me, I wanted him *because* he wanted me. It was like a voyage, I guess. We travelled from one place in our lives to another, and then what we needed from each other was over. I never made any demand on him after it was over. Sometimes I would wish he was with me so I could tell him some dumb thing, like how my alarm clock finally quit—he hated it. It had a terrible ring. I'm a heavy sleeper. Once, after he was married, I *did* ask him to come here. He came as soon as he could. He knew it wasn't . . . what some small-minded man might have guessed it could be. It was a year ago last May. On Memorial Day. I didn't know if I should report it, or what I should do."

"Report what?"

"I went to see Charlie and I got back at ten-thirty at night. When I went into the kitchen there was my poor old Ethel cat dead in the middle of the floor. She was Ralph's mother. Somebody had put a big meat skewer out of the drawer right through her, just behind the shoulder, right through her heart, and left it in her. It was such a horrid, pointless thing to do. A very sick mind, certainly. There was still some warmth in her body, and all the blood was not clotted on the tile floor. I'd left a kitchen light on, knowing it would be after dark when I got back, and they like a light to eat by when they get hungry. Ralph is like Ethel was. They leave a little in their dish and go back and have a little snack every now and then. There's a ladder that is fastened to the outside of the building and it passes right by the kitchen window. The weather forecast said no rain, so I'd left the bottom sash all the way open. Somebody had kicked the screen out and come in through the window in the night. It wouldn't be hard to do. Poor Ralph was all scrunched down in the back of my closet on my shoes, still growling, and terrified. Fort answered the phone and he got here at eleven-thirty. I was a mess, of course. It upset him terribly too. Ethel had been very fond of him."

"Did you report it?"

"We decided not to. I'm not a sissy usually, but I was all shaken up. I packed an overnight bag and Fort dropped me at a hotel. He had wrapped poor Ethel up in an old sheet. I couldn't find any damage beyond the broken screen, and nothing seemed to be missing. He put Ethel in the trunk of his car, and the next day we buried her at a place down on Marley Creek where we used to have picnics sometimes. I had the super come and look at the broken screen. He was upset. But he wasn't going to do anything about it. I had people come and put steel mesh on that window and I told the other people who had windows close to that ladder what had happened and what I'd done about it, and what it had cost."

She stopped, frowned at me, shook her head. "What in the world could the Doctor have done with six hundred thousand dollars in cash? It wouldn't be like him to do something like that."

"Could his illness affect his mind?"

"Oh no. And the few times I saw him, toward the end, he was perfectly all right. He knew he'd never get out of that bed. The pain was bad and getting worse, but he decided he'd rather fight it than be so drugged he couldn't communicate with anyone."

"And he was an honest man?"

"Certainly. Oh, he didn't make a big thing of it, and go around glowing with righteousness—you know the type."

"Mrs. Stanyard? Janice?"

"Janice is fine."

"You didn't know a thing about the missing money. But you can count on other people getting around to you before very long."

"I don't understand."

"Excuse the bluntness, but when the wife and children get dealt out, they dig up the past, and you are the ex-mistress, the trite old triangle of doctor, wife, and nurse."

"But it. . . ."

"I know it wasn't like that. But for seven of the thirteen months he was cashing things in, you were working with him."

"Not anything like the way we used to work, though. No routine things at all, no matter how intricate. He was sort of . . . . wrapping up what he knew and what he was still learning. His post-operative dictation was about twice as long as it had ever been, because he was making suggestions about alternative techniques he knew he was never going to have time to attempt. He wanted to leave something other surgeons could use. And he wanted to spend as much time as he could with Gloria and his grand-children."

"Do you remember anything at all strange during those seven months? Any mysterious letters or visits or phone calls? Did he seem troubled?"

"No. But he didn't trouble easily, you know. He had his own philosophy about worry. He always told me that people spend so much time fretting about what they did yesterday and dreading what might happen tomorrow, they miss out on all of their todays. He said that when you realize you can't change the past or predict the future, then you come alive for the first time, like waking up from half-sleep."

"You might be questioned by people who are better at it than I am, and a lot more merciless."

"Why do you say that?"

"They'll catch you up a lot quicker when you lie about having no contact with Fort from January to when you visited him at his home."

"Lie! I swear to you I did not see him once during that time."

"That isn't what I said. A contact is not necessarily a confrontation."

"I don't have to take this, you know."

"Phone? Letter?"

"*Damn* you!" She stood up and went to the windows, stood there with her back to the room. Her anger made a pink tint on the pallor of her neck below the greying hair. I went over and stood behind her and to her left. The sky above the distant parking plaza was as grey as the asphalt. Three kids were running diagonally across the lot, a big yellow dog loping along with them.

"Use your head, Janice. If you don't know how to handle it with me, how can you expect to handle it when the cold winds really start to blow?"

"He had reasons for everything he did."

"And never miscalculated? Never made an error? Do you really believe that he *wanted* Gloria to be persecuted, treated as a suspicious person and watched and followed the rest of her life?"

She turned and stared up into my eyes. "Will it be like that?"

"Not if it was six thousand or sixty thousand. It's six hundred thousand. It hasn't hit the news yet. The bank and the lawyers and the tax people have kept the lid on it. Fort's mind was clouded in one way. I can draw pictures for you. There have been people killed in this happy village for forty cents. No matter how carefully the missing money is reported, there are going to be some types sitting around wondering which way and how soon they'll pick up the bride and take her to a cosy place and treat her pretty little feet with lighter fluid. They'll think that either she knows or she doesn't, but that much cash is worth the try. She'll end up in the river wrapped in scrap iron either way."

Her eyes widened and her throat bulged as she dry-swallowed twice, and, with her colour going bad, she braced a hand against the window frame and closed her eyes for a moment. I asked her if she was going to faint.

"No. I don't faint. It was just the idea anybody . . . could do that to Gloria Geis."

"And if she doesn't know, there's always Heidi and then Roger and then you. It's big loot, and it is in the handiest form loot comes in. You don't have to fence it."

Her colour was better. She swallowed again. "I . . . I guess I do have some of it. Not here. It's in my box at the bank. The letter is here. But I don't think it will mean anything, and it says not to tell anybody. But, as you say, I don't think he realized what could happen. . . . Excuse me."

She went over to a desk and opened a drawer and sorted through a half-box of new stationery, rifling it with her thumb until she came to the letter. She looked at it before she handed it to me. She shook her head. "I hate what happened to his muscular control. His hands were so good."

It was small, shaky, uncertain writing, but reasonably legible. It was dated the previous August eleventh.

Janice, dear
Put this in your lock box at your bank.
I have got word to someone to come to you in case of emergency. You will find out what might have to be done. Use the money for that purpose. You will understand why I couldn't ask G for this kind of help. If no one comes to you within a year of my death, please get the money to G. I would write more, but it is hard to write. I know I impose. Thanks for many things, and thanks for this.

Fortner

"It's ten thousand dollars," she said. "In hundred-dollar bills, mostly. It was in a manila envelope wrapped with rubber bands inside another manila envelope. I think he thought it was ten thousand even, but it was a hundred dollars short. It came in the regular mail."

"You saw him after that. Did you mention the note and the money?"

"When I started to, he closed his eyes and shook his head. Gloria was out of the room just then."

I read it once more and gave it back to her to put away. "Not a clue," I said. "Some unknown person may or may not come to you for help, and if they come, they'll tell you what kind of help they need. Isn't that just dandy? Only five hundred and ninety thousand to go."

79

"I wish I could help. I really do."

She meant it. Sincerity and conviction, and a great directness. But I had to come to the usual screeching halt. I didn't have her lashed up to a polygraph with a good man watching the styluses or styli or whatever the hell the proper plural might be. Pen points, maybe. And I didn't know if she was one of the small percentage who can fool the polygraph every time. In a world of plausible scoundrels and psychopathic liars, hunch can take you only so far.

I have to keep remembering at all times that sweet little old lady on the verandah in Charleston, South Carolina, the one who told me the story of her life in a sighing little voice, a story so sad that my eyes were misty and my voice thick by the time she shot at me with the Luger she was holding in her lap under the corner of her shawl. The slug took a little bite out of the side of the collar of my white shirt and exposed a dime-sized piece of blue necktie.

"Maybe," I said, "the money's for Gretchen."

"For who?"

"For Gretchen. I guess you could call her an indiscretion. Long ago. Way back when Glenna was dying."

She looked puzzled. "I don't know anything about that, It doesn't sound right, somehow. He worshipped his first wife."

"At least he always thought he did. Until he took a little acid LSD, provided by a buddy."

"Dr. Wyatt? Hayes Wyatt?"

"Glory took the trip too. I guess they were both getting a bad hang-up on his situation being terminal."

She nodded. "Dr. Wyatt has had a lot of success with it with terminal cases, where the pain is bad and they're terribly frightened, or terribly depressed. It's disassociative, you know. It gives them a breathing space to kind of sort out what it all means."

"And he sorted Glenna out and found out he didn't like her at all. Glory says it surprised him."

"Who was Gretchen?"

There was no reason not to tell her. There was even the chance it might knock loose some useful memory. But I told her and it didn't. The tale intrigued her. It gave another dimension to her hero, Fort Geis. But at the same time it diminished her. She had thought of herself as one third of the women in Geis' maturity—Glenna-Janice-Gloria. News of hearty little Gretch made it a foursome. It complicated her mental biography of the great man. It put two little vertical lines between her eyebrows, and I no longer had her full attention.

So, with promises to get in touch if either of us learned anything, I went back out into the last grey fading of the daylight in the damp and windy streets. I knew the sun was still shining way down there at Bahia Mar in the bottom right corner of the map, and *The Busted Flush* would be creaking and sighing when the dying wash from the incoming charter-boats got to her. The sandy little brown broads would be ornamenting the sunset beach, casting the swift sidelong glance, trying not to blow their cool with the slightest trace of smile, and other kids would be playing the big game of pretending to be surfers, as they rode their bright boards in the gigantic, savage, towering breakers—two feet high that break for twenty feet and six whole seconds sometimes.

Surfers of the World, save your money and dream long dreams of getting to that one unspoiled beach that makes both California and Hawaii look like a sometime thing. Two whole miles of ocean straight out from the beach, six feet deep on the median tide, all sand, and flat as pool tables. On the prevailing wind out of the southwest, girls and boys, those rollers start to build way down by Mozambique and Madagascar, and have a two-thousand mile run across the Indian Ocean before they crest white two miles off the great beach at Galle, Ceylon, and run all the way in with such a perfect symmetry and geometry that when you look down on it from twenty thousand feet it is like looking at a swatch of fabric, a pure pinstripe white on a pale tan-green background. As a special added convenience, just a bit south, toward Dondra Head, the deeps are close to the beach, so that after you get beyond the first few, you have nothing to fight on the way out.]

But I was too far from a softer sunset and a better beach. I knew that with a little luck I could either get part of my path smoothed for me, or find out something that would convince me it would make a lot more sense to head south right away. In the premature fading of daylight, I drove my rental car back through the damp and windy streets to the hotel and went up to the room, practising a glassy smile to see if it would help lift me out of a mood turning as grey as day's end. See, brain-pan? The mouth is smiling. Feel the smile muscles? Hi ho, hi ho. The eyes are squinching too. McGee is one happy fella. Right?

I think I was trying too hard with the smile. When the

elevator door opened at my floor, a substantial matron in a fur hat was waiting to board. When she glimpsed me, she sprang back a good distance and then waited until I was four strides away before scuttling into the Otis-Box.

I turned on the lights in the room and emptied all the cards out of my wallet on the bed. You may charge me, dear people, with being a Card-Carrying American. I find these little tickets to perpetual consumption distasteful. I do not like to see my name on them, deeply embossed into everlasting plastic. They make me feel as if I should wear a leather collar and hang them all thereon. When there is a mistake in the billing on any of them, if you persist, you can fight your way past the icy and patronizing indifference of the electronic computers and reach a semi-human who can straighten things out. It only takes a year or so.

Yet in our times the thick wad of credit cards is a cachet of respectability, something more useful to me than any questionable convenience. When a cop lays upon you the white eye, and you stand there hunting for a driver's licence as identification, and he watches you fumble through AmEx, Diners, Carte Blanche, Air Travel, Sheraton, Shell, Gulf, Phillips, Standard, Avis, and Texaco before you find it, he is reassured. You may have thirty-seven cents and a dirty shirt, but you are completely on record and in good standing with the Establishment. If all you have is the licence and a bale of vulgar cash money, it piques his curiosity. Who is this bum who can't get credit cards like honest people?

I found Maurie Ragna's personal card among the seldom used credit cards tucked into a side pocket of the wallet. He had written his unlisted phone number on the back of it. An East Chicago number, over the line in Lake County, Indiana, where as I understood it, the authorities were still as co-operative and hospitable to Ragna and his playmates as they had once been in Calumet City and Cicero. The Outfit, as it is known along the lake, had responded to the roust by moving over the line into Gary and East Chicago.

I had come along once at the right time and, down in the Keys, had pried Maurie out of an exceptionally ugly situation, wherein he had no future at all to speak of. Grateful as he was, he was astonished any bystander would voluntarily involve himself. As it was, he couldn't put any weight at all on his feet for days, and walked in a very tender way for much longer. But that is an old and complex story, and he had tried

82

to show appreciation by gifting me with cars, broads, and vacations on the cuff, but I had settled for a dozen mohair cardigans and passed along eleven of the twelve to friends. So this was the first time I was making a call on an old obligation, and if he was not yet buried out in the desert near Vegas or chained to the bottom of lake or river, it might hearten him.

The number answered. A sceptical fellow who spoke in grunts took my name and where I could be reached and said if Ragna never got back to me he was maybe out of town or something.

It took an hour and a half. He was bursting with hospitality. He offered a car and driver, a choice of any kind of action I felt like, a certified stupendous broad, baby, name the age you like, the size, the build, the colour, Swede, Jap, Spic Polski, call it, McGee baby.

His voice sagged when I said maybe later, that right now I wanted information. When I said important information he brightened. I went into the indirect and elliptical phraseology of those whose lines are ninety per cent certain of being permanently bugged.

"You are so right," he said. "It hasn't come to my ear but it can be checked. If say some associate of some associate built the action on the Doc, then you scuffle around too much, I got enough going here and there you should get maybe only roughed up some, a three-day rest with nice nurses. But you could not clout any of it back, so scuffling would be a waste, right? Now on the little guy Smith, I will find out who owns how much of him. Hang easy, Mister M. Give me one hour, two tops."

I ordered up some ice. Long long ago a lass had gifted me with a solitary drinker's kit. It is a squatty pewter flagon, cylindrical and with a king-sized old-fashioned-shaped drinking cup in pewter, which fits upside down over the flagon, with threads at the midway point of the flagon so that assembled it is a perfect cylinder. With a nice regard for the emotional climate of the man who, when it is necessary, can drink alone without feeling degenerate, she'd had a single word engraved upon both flagon and glass: Mine. I had thought it all too elfin, thanked her too effusively, and put it away in a locker, and had come across it when packing for this trip and suddenly realized her instincts had been better than mine. It was not elfin. It was factual, and a derisive comment on all the His and Hers items in this chummy civilization. So I had filled it with Plymouth and brought it along, and it was indeed Mine.

I lounged and brooded and sipped and awaited Maurie Ragna's report. Sober sociological evaluations of the genus Hoodlumae americanus leave out their capacity for compulsive friendship. Once one accepts you he will lay gifts upon you like a potty rich uncle. You can do no wrong. You are forever his big great friend and buddy and chum and pal. If you get big-mouth disease, it is to him a disease, and he will have you gunned down, and he will cry, and send a whole truck of flowers. There are various levels of ethical values within the genus. I knew Ragna had a high contempt for those who deal in hash and grass, or schoolgirl recruitment, or housewife call circuits. He concentrates on such moral areas as bootlegging liquor and cigarettes, setting up casinos, operating resort properties here and there where he can supply a complete line of wheels, booze, hookers, and blue entertainment, as well as the more mundane items—such as vending machines, kitchen equipment, bed vibrators, and intercom equipment.

At last the call came back. "Took me too long, buddy boy, on account of a party I had to be sure of, he's at Acapulco and the call didn't go through so easy. It is no part of our action in any way, and though attractive, we stay off it, so go ahead and scuffle and stay lucky, you bum. I don't want you dead. About this Franky, he is owned like up to the throat and the word has gone to him to bust his ass doing any small thing anybody with your name wants done."

"It is a big help and a load off my mind, friend."

"Some phone calls, some lousy sweaters. Ask for something big so I can get even, will you?"

"When I need it, I'll holler."

After I'd said good-bye and hung up, I thought of a possibility which this contact with Ragna had suggested. The gambling itch was in many cases like other forms of addiction, a search for an excitement which turns the mind off. Maybe Geis had found a poker table. A big game would know just how high they would let the Doctor go on markers, and it was possible to lose six very big ones. It has been done before and will happen again. In some London clubs the biggest chip in play is worth twenty-eight thousand, and there are some in play every night. And if Geis had been expertly plucked, they would collect on the markers ruthlessly.

But I had to give that up. If the score had been made that way, Maurie would have come up with the information.

I rubbed my thumb across misted pewter and read the name again. Mine. That was the name of the problem. All mine.

SEVEN

FRANCISCO SMITH cut me off when I tried to tell him over the phone what I wanted from him. The agency offices were in the Monadnock Block on West Jackson. He named a lunchroom a block and a half away. I said I was six four, Florida tan, grey topcoat, no hat.

I got there within the half-hour, and had a six-minute wait over bad coffee before he arrived at quarter to ten, came directly to the booth and sat opposite me.

"Smith," he said to me. "Coffee black," he said to the chubby waitress. When she went away he said, "With everything in the shop bugged every way those sons of bitches can dream up, I couldn't take a chance you might say too much about what you want."

He was on the short side of medium height, stocky, balding, mottled red face, rimless glasses with gold bows and nosepiece, and lenses strong enough to magnify the size of his weak-looking blue eyes. Medium blue suit, dark blue topcoat, light grey felt hat. He talked with very little lip movement, rather like an unskilled ventriloquist. You would have to glance at him a dozen times in a dozen places in one day before you'd begin to wonder if you had ever seen him before. All the cities of the world are stocked with innumerable replicas of Frankie Smith. They are clerks, fry cooks, building inspectors, watch repairmen, camera salesmen, estimators, adjustors, civil servants, church wardens, florists.

"I want to know all about the job you did for Dr. Fortner Geis."

He looked puzzled. "Keeping an eye on that Gretchen Gorba and her kids? It went on quite a while. Better than two and a half years. Just a spot check to see how they were making it. He pulled us off it last summer. Early July? No. Early

85

August. He died a couple of months later. Big play in the papers."

"He was a big man."

Smith studied me. He nodded abruptly. "I think I get the picture. The contract with us would be sort of proof the kid was his. Susan. The oldest. Hell, copies of all the reports are in the dead file. The court can make us turn them over if it comes to that. There could be a nice piece of change in it for an eighteen-year-old kid, enough to split it a lot of ways."

"Did he tell you Susan was his daughter?"

"Hell no. Look, if you tell us to run a complete check on Joe Blow, we'll do it. But to keep our own noses clean, we'll want to find out why you're so interested in Joe. We got the contract three years ago next month. Gretchen Gorba is a big good-natured slob. She likes the horses and draft beer and shacking up, in any order they happen to come along. So I put a big old boy in our shop on to it. He's the kind women tell things too. He took a furnished room in a handy neighbourhood, and as soon as he started laying her, she started telling her sad story, about how she was the housekeeper's daughter, and when the Doctor's wife was dying, the Doc knocked her up when she was just a dumb kid, and the Doc and her mother arranged to marry her off to somebody, and the Doc set up a lifetime annuity of a hundred a week for the kid named Susan. Gretchen whined to our boy that she had braced the Doc to improve the income, on account of having five kids, and her husband in prison, but he didn't scare and he didn't give. But from talking to him, I got the idea that if we'd reported they were having a hard time, he would have done something. She was making between sixty-five and seventy-five a week depending on the tips, and averaging maybe thirty a week to the bookies, so that if she was getting more, the bookies would get more. She bets the doubles and the parlays, a guaranteed way to stay busted."

"So Doctor Geis asked you to keep checking?"

"To keep an eye on them. I would have thought that Gretchen's mother, Mrs. Ottlo, could have done it just as well and saved him the fees. But I guess Mrs. Ottlo wasn't getting along so good with her daughter. She'd pick times to visit when Gretchen was working and the kids would be there. She'd bring food and presents. It could have been that the Doc was afraid Mrs. Ottlo would be too proud to let him know if Gretchen and the kids were having a hard time. After about five or six months he asked me to set something up with Susan. I handled it myself. Fifteen years old. Hell of a good kid. Smart. I gave her a phone number she could call day or night in case of any trouble where she needed help. She agreed to keep it from her mother. But she wanted to know who had this big interest in her family. I found out she had the idea she was adopted. Kids get that idea. Mama had got slopped a few times and said just enough so Susan thought the annuity was probably from her real parents. So I didn't say yes and I didn't say no. I left it the way I found it. Once it was set up that way, the Doc was able to cut down the expense of our checking them out so often. But I think it was the next January or February, two years ago minus a few weeks, he phoned me and said he'd heard through Mrs. Ottlo that Gretchen's husband had been released on parole and had rejoined the family, and he wanted to know what effect that would have on Susan. So I had a friend pull the file on Saul Gorba and give me a nice long look at it."

Smith had a good memory for details. Gorba had served over four and a half years of a six-year sentence in Wisconsin. Gretchen had lined up a job for him in a body and fender shop through the shop foreman who was a friend and a regular customer at the restaurant where she was working. Through a reciprocal arrangement on parole supervision, a duplicate file was sent along to the Cook County authorities, and that was the one Smith had examined. Gorba had been just past thirty when he had been tried, convicted, and sentenced. He and Gretchen had been living as common-law man and wife in Milwaukee. She claimed that during the two years they had been together, she had thought he was a salesman. They rented a small frame house in a quiet lower-middle-class area. She thought he sold novelties and specialty items and office supplies. He had a small hand press in the basement and he told her it was for sample letterheads. He had a large supply of the different colours of safety paper used for bank cheques, and he had a perforator, cutting board, several styles of cheque-writers, several typewriters.

His business trips lasted a week or two, and he would take a week off between each trip. His trips took him into Iowa, Minnesota, and Illinois. His procedure was to acquire legitimate cheques made out for commercial payroll purposes, or for payment on small accounts. One source was through mail order, where he would, using a false name and a post office box, send in an overpayment by money order and get a company cheque back representing his refund.

Once he had acquired, for example, a cheque from the XYZ Company in Madison, Wisconsin, he would take it home and, in his basement shop, make a dozen acceptable duplicates of it, in size, paper stock, imprint, cheque-writer patterns, typing, carefully traced signatures, and even to the careful duplication in India ink of the magnetic ink symbols used by the automated sorting equipment in the banks. With the dozen cheques made out in varying and plausible amounts, usually in odd dollars and cents between one hundred and two hundred dollars, he would hit Madison with them, using a falsified driver's licence as identification, and cash them without great difficulty as payroll in a dozen different places, clearing up to two thousand dollars. He was neat, personable, and careful to make significant alterations in his appearance for each job.

Shortly before he was arrested, he had told Gretchen that he was getting a chance at a better territory soon, and they would probably be moving to eastern Ohio.

An alert supermarket manager in Racine thought the cheque he had just cashed did not look quite right somehow. He compared it with another payroll cheque from the same company and discovered that the cheque paper was a slightly different shade of green, and that the cheque-writer numerals were larger. He ran out and caught Gorba as he was getting into his car. After he grabbed Gorba, the next thirty seconds cost the manager over three weeks in the hospital. An off-duty cop was trundling a wire basket of week-end groceries out to his car, and it took him a long and painful time to subdue the suspect.

Smith said, "A loner. A real weird. They confiscated twenty-eight grand he had squirrelled away in hidey-holes in that basement. Previous arrests and convictions were not in any kind of pattern like you expect. Assault with a deadly weapon. Conspiracy to defraud. Impersonating an officer. Attempted rape. In and out of four colleges. An IQ like practically a genius. Emotionally unstable, they said. She had the youngest by him after they put him away. Tommy."

"He doesn't sound like the kind who'd be attracted to Gretchen."

"Why not? Those jumpy ones, sometimes what suits them best is some big dumb happy broad. No demands. No arguments. And also you have to figure it made a nice cover for

88

him for those two years, the wife and family, quiet neighbour-hood, just another salesman. Anyway, I had to report to the Doc on how it was going to work out, and it didn't look so great to me. But it was the longest stretch he'd pulled, and it settled him down, apparently. His record on the inside was good. The parole officer said his attitude was good. Gretchen was clam-happy to have him back, and at the suggestion of the parole officer, they made it legal. The fore-man was satisfied with him. He kept to himself but he did his work at the shop. Gretchen kept on with the waitress work. With more pay coming in, they got an apartment in the same building but down on the second floor, with one more bed-room, three instead of two. I wouldn't say the relationship with the kids was real close, but it was workable. And I guess Mrs. Ottlo, the kids' grandma, approved, maybe because it was legal. I guess she started getting along better with her daugh-ter, because she took to going there Sunday afternoons when everybody was home, having dinner with them."

"And now she has no idea where they went. No forwarding address."

He stared at me. "You kidding?"

"They moved out last August, apparently."

Frowning, he counted slowly on his fingers, lips moving. "He was going to be on parole sixteen months, so it would run out last August, about. Maybe the brightest ones are the biggest damned fools. Maybe he kept his head down until he had his clean bill, then headed for someplace where he could go back into business for himself. Want me to try to trace them for you?"

"What are the rates?"

"Very funny! Expenses only, and on my own time, as you damn well know. And no written reports."

"Just checking," I said.

"Nothing has changed, and never will." He took his glasses off and wiped them on a paper napkin.

I wondered what hold they had on him. He apparently thought I knew about it. "See what you can do," I said. "I'm in 944 at the Drake. Meanwhile, I'd like some specific infor-mation out of your records on Susan and her brothers and sisters."

He returned in less than half an hour, sat across from me, and said, "Had to wait until the file girl went for her coffee break. Want to write this down? Susan Kemmer will be eighteen on January fourth. Gretchen had one kid by Kemmer. Freddy. He's fifteen. She had a common-law set-up out in California with somebody named Budrow. She had two by him. Julian is twelve and Freda is ten. The last one, Tommy, was by Gorba, and the kid is six now. The annuity is with Great Lakes Casualty Mutual. Their Chicago office is in the National Republic Bank Building on South La Salle."

"What happened to Budrow?"

"Just took off, I guess."

"Can you get on this right away, Smith?"

"All I can tell you is I'll do the best I can. It shouldn't be hard. I'll see what I can turn up at the places they worked, and see what happened with the kids' school records, and see where the annuity cheques are going. Saul Gorba is maybe foxy enough to slip out of sight if he was by himself. A whole family is something else. I could get shot with luck and hit it the first try and know by tonight. Or it could take a week of leg work."

"Find out if they left owing."

He looked slightly contemptuous. "The *first* thing I would do is check the Credit Bureau. There could be a tracer request and the new address already."

It took me four dimes to track down Martin Hollinder Trumbill the Fourth. In a brassy bass rumble he said he was too damned busy getting ready for a trip to see anybody about anything. I pulled a gentle con on him by saying that if he could see me, then maybe I wouldn't have to spoil his trip. After we went around and around on that for several minutes, he asked me to meet him at twelve-thirty at the bar of the Norway Club atop the Lakeway Tower.

I was five minutes late and he was ten minutes late. He didn't come in from outside. He came in from some nearby area where the club members evidently worked out. His hair was damp and he had the glow of sauna and sunlamp. He was fifty, bronzed, about five nine, with most of his hair, a ruggedly handsome face, a body like a bull ape, as broad and thick through the shoulder as any NFL tackle. Arrogant little simian eyes stared out at me from under great grizzled black tangles of eyebrow. Tufts of black hair grew out of nostrils and ears, and his big hands had a heavy pelt on the backs and on the backs of the fingers down to the middle knuckle. A shetland sports jacket, perfectly tailored to his broad, long-armed, bandy-legged build, softened somewhat the brute impact of him. But I wondered what he was trying to prove by making his barber leave the nostril and ear hair alone.

An attendant had pointed me out to him as the man who was waiting for him. A drink appeared on the bar and he took it and walked away toward the view windows. A powder snow was falling, and the wind whipped it against the curved glass. I followed him as he expected I would.

"In thirty seconds make me believe you could spoil anything for me, or I'll have you thrown out." He spoke without turning to look at me.

I said, "Golly, sir, gee whiz, now you've got me so terrified I can't hardly think straight."

He pivoted and stared at me. "What the hell *is* this?"

I smiled upon him. "I guess I don't like jackasses. I guess I don't like rich jackasses. I guess I don't like rich, rude, double-gaited jackasses. Now would you like to try again? You got off on the wrong foot, Gadgey."

"I didn't realize he could get those eyebrows so high. "Who the hell do you think you *are*!"

"T. for Travis McGee. I know. You'll buy the ground I'm standing on and have me torn down. I am an old buddy of the Widow Geis. Doctor Fort shoved the first legal team into the fray and Miss Heidi got very well. Am I getting past that hair in your ears? I wouldn't want you to leave town without answering a question. Are you a miserable enough bastard to have found a way to gouge Heidi's winnings back out of her poor old dad's hide?"

"Gouge? Gouge?"

"There's no estate left."

"I know."

"Now how would you know, Gadgey?"

"Her brother Roger was wringing his hands about it. He's a goddam stuffed shirt and. . . . What gives you the right to ask me questions anyway?"

"Because I am helping the Widow Geis find out where all the money went."

"All the money? For God's sake, McGee, sure Heidi took a pretty good cut. I've still got eleven million in tax-exempt municipals, if you can comprehend what I'm talking about?"

"You're talking about at least three hundred and thirty thousand a year you don't even have to report on the good old ten forty. Cut the shit, Trumbill. If it was a hundred and ten million, you still couldn't impress me. You can afford to buy me a drink in your own club, can't you? A double Plymouth gin on ice, plain. I'll wait right here while you go make the arrangements."

I watched him head for the bar and I wondered how far he could be pushed. He did not lumber. He had a springy and youthful stride. As he approached bearing my drink, I heard him chuckling. He handed it to me, bowed, and said, "Golly, sir, gee whizz, now you've got me so terrified I can't think straight."

"Thank you for the drink, Mr. Trumbill."

"My pleasure, Mr. McGee," he said. "Let's sit in the lounge and get acquainted. There's no particular reason why I give a goddam about your opinion about anything, but there's one thing that needs correcting."

I followed him to two wingback chairs with a small table between them, angled to look out at the scenery and provide privacy for conversation. "You have met Heidi?" he asked.

"Yes."

"The ice queen. The snow maiden. But when you look at her, everything points the other way. When I married her three years ago, I thought I had the optimum solution. McGee, I am not a locker-room sex hero. I just happened to be born with a hell of a lot of sexual drive and capacity. Sleeping around is a damned bore. Everything about her looks as if she was made for it. Fantastic body. Healthy as a field hand. The way she walks, the timbre of her voice, the shape of her hands, it's all provocative and invitational. I thought to myself, hell, Gadge, there's the answer. She was twenty-two and I was forty-eight. She'd be thirty-five when I was sixty-one, and she'd be getting ready to slow down a little when I damn well had to. But finding out she was a twenty-two-year-old virgin should have told me something. Let me tell you, I worked like a slave on that damned girl. The harder I tried, the nastier she thought it was. Finally I could practically see her flesh crawl when I touched her. The only response I ever got was a goddam martyred sigh. Sexual frustration is a hell of a sorry condition, McGee. So I went out to get what I couldn't get from her. I think I was a little out of my mind. I grabbed on to anything warm and breathing that came within reach. And a couple of times when I was pig-drunk it happened to be her willowy little art-class boyfriends who wanted a way to get a hand in the till. When I gave no

92

big gifts of money, they went whimpering to her about her gross, horrible brute of a husband. Now I give her this. She knows she's frigid, and she knows that her condition had a lot to do with the situations I got into after I gave up with her. So she wasn't going to try for a big settlement and big alimony. But her darling daddy egged her on and got her some hot legal talent, and they gave me a pretty fair bruise. It could have been even bigger if she'd really wanted to take it all into court, but they still had enough pressure to extract a generous agreement. Those months were the only time I ever went the AC-DC route, and it isn't going to happen again because I'm never going to get into that kind of desperate mood again. So drop back on the double-gaited. I like girls. Always have. Always will. And I prefer girl-girls with all the girl-girl equipment to the girl-boys with the long locks and the squeaky voices. I don't know why I should give a goddam about your opinion. . . ."

"You're repeating yourself. There's another question I want to. . . ."

He looked at his watch. "Okay. Come down to the apartment and ask it there. I'm expecting some people and I want to be there when they get there."

I got my coat from the attendant and we rode down to the sixteenth floor and got off. He explained that quite a few of the members kept an apartment in the building as a convenience, and if they were going to be away for six months or longer, the club management would arrange a sublet.

He unlocked it. It was as impersonal as a decorator's advertisement.

As soon as I had a chance I asked my question. "Mr. Trumbill, last year, in April or May or June, while you and Heidi were still together. . . ."

"I moved out the last week in May."

"Okay. During those last two months did anything happen which seemed odd?"

"Odd?"

"Any kind of accident which could have been dangerous, or any near-accident, where Heidi was involved?"

"Why?"

"It could be important and the reasons would take too long to explain."

"Important to whom, McGee?"

"Does it matter? Come on."

93

"There wasn't anything . . . unless you mean something like that damned candy."

"Candy?"

"Oh, there was a kind she was nuts about. Chocolate cherries. A lot of juice inside. She never bought them for herself. Her father would bring her a box or have them sent over on special occasions. Birthdays, anniversaries. Sometime in early May—we'd had a big scrap—I walked through the living-room. She was watching the news on television. I was going out, and I knew she damned well wasn't going to say good-bye dear have a nice time. The way she ate them, she didn't nibble. She'd lift one out of the box, pop it into her mouth, and mash it. The box was half gone. She was down to the second layer. Suddenly she began making the damnedest noises, gasping and whoofing and spitting pieces of chocolate all over. She went to the kitchen on a dead run, scaring hell out of the maid. She kept rinsing her mouth in cold water. Her eyes were running and her nose was running. She couldn't say a word we could understand. Finally after she ate some crackers and rinsed her mouth out some more, she started chewing me out for pulling such a nasty trick. I finally convinced her I didn't know what the hell she was talking about. She had got a chocolate that instead of having a cherry and cherry juice inside had apparently been filled with about a quarter ounce of straight Tabasco. She was furious. I was running late, so I left."

"How did it happen?"

"She never found out. She opened all the ones left in the box. They were all perfect. She phoned her father and told him about it. He said it must have happened after the box was opened, because he had bought it one day, and brought it over to our place the next day in person, and the shop was certainly reliable. He said maybe it was some friend of mine who knew her habits. I guess you could classify that as an accident. It made her very uncomfortable, but I guess there are things you could put in candy that would do more than. . . ."

The phone rang and he answered it, then hung up and told me his people were on the way up. I thanked him and said I'd run along. He said, "Meet the group, McGee. Highly talented people. We're going to Guadeloupe and make a motion picture. Highly unusual script. Be released in France. Some of the crew is there now, picking locations."

There was a brisk rap on the door, and he went and let four of them in, two young women, two young men. They were laughing and gay and all a little tight. One was a Limey lass, the height of mod exhibitionism, her little-girl skirt a good four inches above the knee, and a metallic golden serpent wrapped around her left leg just below the knee. While she was saying, with little chopping motions of her hands, "What a fantastically gawstly city, Gadge darling, ectually!" he was introducing her as Pansy Perkins, certainly I'd heard of her.

"Certainly I haven't, sorry," I said. "I live a quiet life."

With a speculative glint she started appraising me, but Trumbill put a huge paw on her slender shoulder, and as he introduced a busty Italian girl whose name *was* vaguely familiar (she took a slender cigar out of the centre of her considerable mouth to acknowledge the introduction) and then a Pierre something, talented director, all in black, even to little black onyx buttons in his pierced ears, and a Willy something, fat, pasty, scruffy, with too blatant an Irish accent. Gadge was at the same time stroking the throat of his Pansy with a spatulate thumb, an attention which unfocused her eyes, loosened her mouth, and sagged her head like a wilting poppy.

"We are going to go down there and do something true," Trumbill said. "We are going to work hard and we are going to work well, and get it all down the way it happens."

Suddenly I realized who he was trying to be. "For God's sake, Papa, don't forget the wineskins. Catch a brave and true marlin. But if this curious quartet has conned you into backing some feelthy movies, why bother trying to snow me? I don't care who reels you in, Pansy or Pierre. Papa never had that kind of problem."

Pierre hissed like a pooty tat, and the Italian gave an evil grin around her cigar, and Irish belched loudly, and Pansy murmured a few gutter words. Martin Hollinder Trumbill the Fourth gave a tight grin and rolled his big shoulders, clapped his hands like a gunshot, and came at me very Black Belt, springing and landing this way and that, paws in chopping position as he yelled, "Huhh!" and "Haaah!"

His quartet backed out of the way, looking expectant. Their imitation Papa would defend the honour of the group and throw Bigmouth all over the place. I pointed beyond him at Pierre and yelled, "No knives you!"

Gadge turned quickly to see the imaginary knife, and opened up his left side just enough. I screwed my heels down into his gunmetal carpeting, pivoted hips and shoulders like Palmer needing an eagle on a par five, and bombed him on the left side, just above the belt, slightly around to the rear, straight punch, hooking slightly at impact, good snap, lots of follow-through.

He groaned, arched, grabbed at the impact point with both hands, and stood with his face screwed up like a little brave boy on the playground trying not to cry.

As I headed for the door I said, "Get it looked at before you leave, Trumbill. I may have tore up that kidney some."

The four rushed to him with little coos and murmurings and cries of compassion. I left as they were leading him to a chair. As I was going down in the elevator I realized that my appraisal of the relationship was not quite accurate. Those four might be under the impression they had a captive placid beast and if they kept scratching it behind the ears, it would moo with joy and give milk indefinitely.

They would discover eventually that it was much more like the relationship of shark and remora fish. The four remora fish would suck hold of the shark for the ride. Sharks are messy eaters. Remora are sustained by the bits of torn meat afloat when the shark feeds. But when any remora becomes too greedy and a little careless, he becomes a part of the very meal he is trying to share, an accident seldom noticed by the shark.

I did know that I wanted no judo or karate games. The expert can whip you with no fuss, and the amateur can kill you without meaning to, if you give them a chance to play their Asiatic game. The mystique of judo is based upon an irrationality. It supposes that the opponent is going to play by their rules. The way to meet it is with a hefty glass ashtray smacko in the chops, or knocking a kneecap loose with a leg off a chair or coffee table, or faking them out and giving them enough bright and sudden pain they forget their trick art. The gutsy dramas on the mass media tend to make us forget that the average urban male is so unaccustomed to sudden pain that if you mash his nose flat, he'll be nauseated for hours, spend two days in bed, and be shaky for the rest of the week.

The temperature had dropped. Snow was bounding like wedding rice off the pavements. It stung my tropical nose, and the wind yanked at my topcoat, congealed my blood, and made my bones feel like old icicles wrapped in freezer bags. Santas dingle-jangled their street-corner appeals, hopping from foot to foot, changing the bell from hand to hand, saying thank you sir with a huff of frosty breath, and the department stores sang "Ave Maria" in stereo high-fidelity while stocky ladies whomped each other with purses and elbows as they competed for Bargain Gifts Galore, and the stone-faced virgins who staff the toy areas drove away the urchins who had come to play with the trains.

I found a warm and tranquil place where they put beef in the beef stew, and ground their own Colombian coffee beans, and even had a waiter who expressed a certain tender anxiety that I should be content with what he brought me. In the darkness of the afternoon when I left the car lights were on, the snow was horizontal, the girls hugged and scuttled, and I couldn't get my rental car started.

EIGHT

THE phone was ringing when I unlocked my room door at the Drake. It was Maurie Ragna phoning to see if I had talked to Smith and if he had been co-operative.

I'd say he was very anxious to please, Maurie."

"Good. Good. Kid, what I wanted to tell you, I suddenly have to make a little business trip. Three days, four days. But what I am going to do, I'm going to have somebody stand by this number with the word if you call for any help you get it."

"Don't go to all that trouble."

"Right now I'd be dead a long time and he talks about trouble! Look, I worry about you. It's a big piece of money you're working on, sweetie. I can give you some top quality walkaround muscle for as long as you want. Looks like a bond salesman. Drives like Phil Hill. Knows the fastest route from anywhere to anywhere. Licensed to carry. Quick as a cat, with a left hook you got to see to believe. Kid, I would feel a lot better about you, and I swear to God, which you should know anyway, it isn't a way of moving in on your action."

I assured him that such a thought would never enter my mind, and I managed to refuse the offer without hurting his feelings too much.

My full and rightful share of Chicago's pollution had fallen on to me all day, A Monday fallout, rimming my collar with grey. It was four in the afternoon, but from my hotel window it looked like midnight. I ordered up a jug of ice, broke out my travel-keg of Plymouth, and built a tall one. I showered first, then drew a tub as hot as I could stand it, and once I had made a gingerly descent into it, I reached and gathered up the icy glass and took one long draw upon it and put it back, away from the steam.

Some of the small sybaritic enhancements of life are worth far more than they cost, and one of them is the very hot tub combined with a sup of dry and icy gin which goes freezing down the throat, bombs the gut, then spreads its inside warmth in pleasant counterpoint to the tub water. To hell with all their hot rocks, whipping each other with greenery and diving into snowbanks. McGee will take a hot hotel tub and a very cold gin.

This is when the mind works. There is a hairy chimp caged in the back of the mind. The bananas hang out of reach. If you can make him stop leaping and chittering and clacking his angry teeth, make him settle down and look around the cage, usually he can find some boxes which he can pile on top of each other, and some sticks, and some string to tie the sticks together. Then he can climb on to the top box and knock down some bananas.

The biggest box in my cage was the concept of how very busy that month of May had been, nineteen months ago. A singing fellow had snatched Branton Fortner Geis and let him go loose in a downtown park. Ethel the Cat had been skewered by a prowler and left in her blood puddle on the nurse's kitchen floor. Heidi, the snow virgin, had chomped tabasco candy and sprung into considerable activity.

Symbols of violence. Demonstration. Kindly note, Dr. Geis, that I could have strangled the kid instead of letting him loose. I could have skewered the nurse instead of the cat. The candy could have had the bland and deadly flavour of almonds instead of the heat of tabasco. So let us start negotiations, Doctor, sir, and you can give me six hundred thousand arguments as to why I should not ugly up your last year or so of life.

So I sipped of coolness again, and became Fort Geis. Okay, I have dealt in the very basic life-and-death business for many years. I have stuck my fingers into the brain-meat after lifting off the sawed lid of bone and laying it aside. Had I been hooked on money. I would have laid away a lot more. Now here is a crazy who wants to take away what I *have* put aside. Pay off, Doc, or you'll die absolutely alone, because everyone who loves you and whom you love will go first. I'll wear you out with funerals, man. Dying alone is a dreary bit.

But, I say, as the Doctor, how did *you* know I was dying? And, second question, how do *you* know how much I can come up with?

Drop that for the moment, chimp. It won't hold your weight.

So as the good Doctor Geis, I look around. Nurse Stanyard can make it. Heidi is married to a lot of tax-free municipals. Roger is doing well. But what about the new wife? So negotiations are in order. Look here, old chap, I can't leave Glory without a bean. You'll have to cut the demand a bit so that I can leave some of the insurance intact. so she'll have an income. Money is not important to her. It doesn't have to be much. A little security for the girl.

Then, as I have begun the payoff routine, I find my daughter Heidi is divorcing Trumbill. She will need money. She depends upon it. I find out she is going to let Gadge off lightly. But if she can't get it from me, she better get it from him, so I run in a legal team to pluck him pretty well.

So why did I send ten thousand to Janice Stanyard with such a vague note? Why did I refuse to talk about it to her when she came to the side of the deathbed? Who has Janice's name and address to use in case of emergency? The signs pointed to Susan, the daughter he had fathered by the housekeeper's daughter during his first wife's final fatal illness. Susan had been given a place to turn, but that had ended when the Doctor had cancelled his arrangement with Francisco Smith and Allied Services.

But why Susan? Why would *anyone* be in danger if Geis was paying off like a good pigeon? I might guess that the insurance saved for Glory was by arrangement, but that the ten thousand for Susan—if it was Susan—had been palmed and tucked aside, without permission of the fellow turning the thumbscrew. Again, a box that would crumple if I put any weight upon it.

So let us see how well Saul Gorba fits. A very meticulous, sly, clever, unbalanced fellow. Arrives in the city four or five months before Geis begins the thirteen-month span of Operation payoff. Leaves a month after the payoff ends. A nice stick, but too flimsy to whack loose any of the bananas tied to the top of the cage.

Last sip of the ice-diluted gin. Cubes clicked against my teeth. I came sloshing and wallowing up out of water gone tepid, all long brown hide flawed by the healed places which marked old mistakes in judgment and reflexes, pelted moderately with sun-baked hair. Wiped misted mirror with the corner of a bath towel. Stared into my spit-pale grey eyes as I slowly dried myself. What are you doing here, laddy buck? This is a dirty one. Something is twisted. Something has gone bad. You are going to lift the wrong rock, and something is going to come out from under it as fast as a moray, aiming right for the jugular.

And, bless us every one, wouldn't *that* be a dingy way to die, in one of the greasy twilights of Chicago in December, a page 40 paragraph in the World's Greatest Newspaper.

"Look, Maurie, old sweetie buddy of mine, you are so right about stumbling around alone, my solo gig, white knightism. The ladies have discovered that it stings too much to dangle the tresses down the tower wall for some idiot to use as a climbing rope.

And all the dragons go around looking just like anybody else.

On this kind of a Monday I know I'm going to get killed in this line of work. It should interest the statisticians. As I am the only fellow in my line of work, it would give a rating of 100 per cent mortality. Just as, until we lost an astronaut, travel in orbit was the safest travel man ever devised with 0 per cent mortality for millions upon millions of passenger miles. Safer than wheelchairs.

Maurie, baby, make me the resident muscle at one of your island operations, with all the beach and broads and booze a man can use, and I shall have cradles built and the *Flush* deck-loaded on to a freighter and let you guarantee all the rest of that retirement I am taking in instalments every time I get well enough.

But in the cage the chimp was looking at the big box and scratching himself like a Red Sox outfielder. No bananas yet, so I called Glory Geis, who chortled happy welcome, and I fenderfought my way to the lake-shore fireside, where once again in the blue jump suit the graceful ragamuffin lady in her second widowhood plied me with a potion which sharpened the taste buds for what the kitchen would provide.

The snow had stopped. The wind still blew, whining around

the house corners, intruding upon fire-crackle and music off the tape. When I asked my key question about accidents she looked blank. "Heavens, I can't think of anything like that. We had such a quiet life, Trav. Just being together. It was all we wanted or needed. No, there was nothing."

"Okay. Not here then. You went shopping and a truck nearly ran you down. Something fell off a high building and nearly hit you."

"Nothing like that! Really! What are you trying to get at? What does it mean?"

"Maybe nothing. I look for patterns. Did anybody bully you off the road in that hot little job Fort bought you?"

"No. I've never put a scratch on it. The only time it had to go in for repairs was when somebody played a joke."

"A joke?"

"Oh, one of those fool tricks that kids send away for. They put one on my dear little car. The yard man was edging the driveway and he came in to get the keys so he could move it. I left it in his way. Actually, I'd left it out all night. It was a Friday night, and I was going to go out again so I didn't put it away, and then I didn't go out and I forgot it and left it out and in his way. He used to come Saturdays. It was warm and the house was open, one of the first warm days, and Fort was here, and we heard this funny siren sound. It went up and up and up, and then there was a bang, and we went hurrying out and the yard man was standing about fifty feet from my car staring at it with horror, and there was white smoke pouring out from the hood. You know those silly torpedo things they sell to play tricks on your friends. Some of the neighbourhood teen-agers had put one on my little car."

"It damaged it?"

"It buckled the hood a little and blew some of the wiring loose. But that isn't the kind of thing you mean."

"No, it isn't," I said, Doc, I could have put the skewer through the nurse, drowned the grandson, poisoned the candy, and wired the little Mercedes so it would blow her into the tops of several of your tall trees, a little here and a little there. "When did that happen?" I asked casually.

She scowled into her weak drink. "Hmm. Let me think. Memorial Day came on Sunday last year. So it was the following Saturday which would be. . . ."

"June fifth."

"I remember he didn't expect to be home that morning.

He had surgery scheduled. It was a primary cancer of the spine, which is very rare and supposed to be inoperable. It was a twenty-eight-year-old woman, and she seemed very strong, but they phoned from the hospital Friday and said she had died. Fort was depressed. The husband wouldn't give permission for an autopsy."

"So I suppose the smoke bomb was the final straw?"

"He was upset. Not too badly though. He went for a long walk down the beach. I remember I wanted to go with him, but he wanted to be alone that time. It wasn't like him. I was hurt, sort of. But I guess you aren't doing a husband any favours by smothering him, by hanging on to him every second."

"Glory, I know you kept pretty good tabs on him. When did he have a chance to pick up the cash and leave it somewhere?"

"It must have been done at the same time. That's the only thing I can figure out. When he got it at one bank or another, he must have got rid of it right away. He must have mailed it. Even if I had seen him mailing it, I wouldn't have paid any particular attention. He was always mailing things in heavy manila envelopes to doctors all over the world. Case histories, notes, things he was going to publish, film strips of operations. And the mail he got at the hospital was always full of things like that. Later that kind of mail came here."

In the artsy-fartsy tales of intrigue, the pigeon has to tote the bundle of bread to the city museum and stuff it under the tunic of the third mummy from the left, whistle the motif from "Lazy Bones," stick his right thumb in his left ear, and walk out sideways. A real live thief will go to the main post office, lay down cash, and rent a box under any name which happens to strike his fancy. If he does not want to take any chance on handwriting or latents, he will take the order form away and have somebody else fill it out for him, and bring it back in gloved hand. If it is a one-shot payoff, he will get a hungry bell-hop to go open the box with the key, and then he will tail the kid through the streets until he is certain the kid is not under observation. If it is on the instalment plan he is going to be certain enough that his pigeon will not get restless so that he can risk a bus ride to the main post office to clean out the box whenever it seems convenient. Otherwise the cleanest one I ever saw took place in a big busy New York restaurant during the lunch rush on a weekday. He was carrying the package as directed. He got a phone call. A muffled voice told him to take his package to the checkroom and ask the girl to put it with number 308, and go right from there to the men's room before returning to the dining-room, and not to fake out because he was being watched. I got to the checkroom girls perhaps ten minutes after one of them had given the coat, hat, and parcel to number 308. They could not remember one single fragment of description. They were indignant to think I expected them to. Obviously he had checked his coat and hat, then used a pay booth to phone the restaurant number and have my pigeon paged. At Shor's you can see the check counter from the pay phones. He timed it right, when whole flocks of lookalikes were heading back from lunch to the Big Media. And he needed the money.

"Penny?" said Gloria Geis.

"Do you think you could make a chance for me to have a little chat with Anna Ottlo?"

"Why? What about?"

"Maybe I want to see if she'd like to cook aboard a houseboat for a single gentleman, quiet, respectable, appreciative."

"Oh, go to hell, McGee. Okay. I'll remember a phone call I have to make."

I went sauntering towards the good smells. Anna Ottlo looked anachronistic in that mechanized, stainless-steel kitchen. Broad, hefty, florid, with white hair and blue apron and twinkling eyes, she looked like a television commercial grandmaw who was going to tell me how to get the stains out of the sink, or grow coffee on mountains, or get rid of that oily taste. Real grandmothers don't look quite like that anymore. I think it is the water-skiing that keeps them firmed up.

"You like roast pork, sir? Yah?" she said beaming.

"I think you could make old floor mats taste good, Anna."

"To the big strong man, all taste vunderful the foods."

I leaned against a hotel-sized refrigerator, drink in hand. "Had any word yet from Gretchen?" I asked.

She stopped slicing a tomato, turned and stared at me, her smile still there, but without meaning.

"*Nein!*" she said. "Nothing. No Gott damn goot, that girl. Trink beer, throw away money, play with mens. Years I hear nothing. Not even how many babies. Gone off someplace. Some man, yah?"

"She's got a husband, hasn't she?"

"This Gorba? From Jails? Hah! Best she can get. Another

103

mans wink the eye, off she goes, babies and all. Now I forget. All done. Over. I said give me the babies. I can take care, raise goot. More time you have for beer and betting money and boyfriend. Big fight. No goot, my only child, that one. Bad life." She tapped her temple, shook her head sadly. "Not much bright."

After dinner Glory told me that she wouldn't be staying there as long as she had planned. "I'd be completely alone. Anna wants to leave, after Christmas."

"New job?"

"Not right away. Later, probably. She says she wants to go and visit an old friend. Mrs. Kemmer, the mother of the boy Gretchen married. She's somewhere in Florida, and Anna wants to spend the winter with her, and maybe stay down there if she can find work, after she's had a rest. All this hasn't been exactly easy on her either. I guess I'm going to have to find an apartment, and something to do. I'll have to stay in Chicago until . . . things are settled. But when I can leave, I'm never coming back. I don't think Heidi and Roger will miss me dreadfully, do you?"

"They'll brood about it."

"Trav? Are you finding out anything?"

"It's at the point where I don't really know. I don't want to talk about it until I have something worth telling you. Or asking you."

She tried to smile. It was a ghastly grimace. "I dreamed you were dead, Trav. It scared me."

"It scares me too, but nobody has figured out a good way to avoid it. The guy who does will clean up."

"Fort knew when. You and I don't. I guess that's the big difference. All we know is Sometime."

"That's what you know when you've grown up. The ones who never grow up keep thinking. Never. Not me, boss. Take those others, but don't take me."

She hunched her shoulders. "Yesterday wasn't so great. I couldn't find any meaning in anything. I felt lost. I kept thinking I could find my way back if I took just a little more of that. But I didn't know how it would hit me. It might be too strange. I even thought of trying to get you to come out and be with me."

"Don't go freaking around alone, Glory. Ever. How much of that have you got left?"

"Just a little bottle. It's in a diluted form so that each drop out of a medicine dropper is fifty micrograms. If I had to guess I'd say there's a hundred drops in the bottle."

"Flush it down the toilet."

"Maybe I will. A little later. When I know I won't need it ever again."

"Why would you need it?"

"Because yesterday I thought it would be easier to be dead than be alive."

"I guess it would be a lot easier. No decisions. No headaches. No constipations."

"Sometimes you make me feel just as silly as I very probably am."

Fifteen minutes after I left to drive back to the city I felt as silly as a girl myself. It can happen when you get too cute. It can happen when you have a memory a little too fresh in your mind of disillusioning a muscular and hairy karate expert. I saw a movement in the bushes where there should have been no movement. I saw it in my side view mirror as I drove out of the driveway. So I drove briskly off into the curving maze of Lake Pointe, circled, left the car in a dark place near a house without lights, and went skulking back.

Bare-handed hero. But I cannot think of any kind of weapon small enough to lift that would have done me much good. I cased the empty bushes. I made a slow circle of the house. From out in the dunes I saw Glory move past an uncurtained window. I stood up and somebody hit my head on a line drive to third, where it was fielded on one hop and hurled across to force the base runner at second, but he came in spikes high to break up the double play, and the second baseman threw my head over the first baseman and smack into the wall in front of the box seats along the first base line. My head rolled dead, eyes turned completely around so that they looked back into the blackness of my brain where fireworks were on display.

Then I was in a pocket in the dunes with a mouth half full of damp cold sand, my hands fastened behind me with something, and with something tied around my eyes. Somebody of considerable muscular weight and with very hard knees knelt on my back. They put a hand on my forehead and lifted my face out of the sand. They lifted it too far. They lifted it until my neck creaked.

"Hey!" I said, and spat sand. "Wait!" I said and spat sand.

A whisper came from lips close to my ear. It seemed to be a whisper with an English accent. "If I tell him to snap your neck, he will snap your neck."

"I believe you."

"What is your interest in this, Mr. McGee?"

"Interest in what?"

"Are you trying to find out if I will actually tell him to pull your head back another. . . ."

"No! I was visiting Mrs. Geis. I'm an old friend. I saw something move in the bushes when I drove out."

"You are a big man. You are in very good shape. You move very well through the night. With professional competence."

"They put me in a brown suit and taught me a lot of things like that. Could he ease the tension a little? I'd hate to go through life looking straight up."

"Terribly amusing," he said. He spoke in a language I could not identify. The fellow on my back lowered my forehead a generous inch and a quarter.

I said, "Did you fellows squeeze a lot of money out of Doctor Geis before he died?"

"No."

"Do you know who did?"

"It would be a matter of no interest to us."

"Gloria Geis asked me to come up from Florida and see if I could find out. It's sort of a hobby with me, helping my friends."

"A profitable hobby?"

"Once in a while. Not real often."

He was silent for a time. I listened to the surf. I ran my tongue over and around my teeth, collecting sand.

"I shall require you to accept certain assurances, Mr. McGee. We have no interest in any friends of yours, to do either good or harm. We are very careful people. You will gain nothing by reporting this to anyone. We examined everything you are carrying, and have replaced everything, exactly as we found it. If you had seemed overly nervous or hysterical about this, we would have been forced to execute you. In simplest terms, you go your way and we will go our way. Keep your mouth shut. We are not likely to meet one another again."

"I am glad to hear that."

They did not hang around to say good-bye and shake hands. A terse and guttural order was given. My face fell into the sand. The weight was lifted away, and a quick nip at my wrists freed them. I rolled over slowly and sat up. I worked at the small hard damp knot at the back of my head. My fingers were cold, and the tightness of the binding had numbed my fingers. When I at last uncovered my eyes, I was alone in the dunes. I was further from Gloria's house. Her house was completely dark. I massaged my neck and rolled my head around to loosen the kinked muscles. I found the strip of fabric which had been around my wrist, and put it with the fabric which had been tied around my eyes and stuffed them into my top-coat pocket. They were going to be very valuable clues. I found out later that one was my necktie and the other was the entire tail off my shirt.

I could find no specific impact point on my skull. The whole right side of it, from front to back, felt slightly tender.

The hideous and unspeakable bruise was upon my ego. I had been taken on open ground with a contemptuous efficiency, dropped, trussed, dragged, inspected, and dismissed. It had been done without giving me the slightest chance of any kind. Yet it was not because they thought me particularly dangerous, but because they were what the Limey whisper had described—"very careful people." And, I could add, very skilled people. Very well-trained and conditioned people.

They worked with military precision, spoke of execution as if it was their right by nature of their trade, and left me without a clue as to age, description, dress—or even how many there were.

At the end of a fifty-mile hike I got into the rental car, and as I started it up, I realized I was perfectly willing to take the word of the whisperer. They were not interested in Gloria Geis. Or in me. Or in the Doctor's money. On the drive back into the city I could come up with only one wild guess—that the piece of empty lake beach was some kind of rendezvous point for transhipment of something, import or export, by boat from beach to ship or ship to beach, or even beach to beach.

I knew one thing without having to guess. I did not want to try my luck against them in groups of two or more. Just as I had no interest in finding out if I had hands as fast as Cassius Clay, or if I could stop one James Taylor coming down the sidelines, all by myself.

There were two phone messages at the desk for me. A Mr. Smith had phoned, and would phone back in the morning before nine. A Mrs. Stanyard had called and left her number.

I got back to the room a little past eleven-thirty. I phoned Janice Stanyard immediately, and after it rang ten times I hung up. I showered again to get the sand and grit out of my scalp and limber up the muscles in my neck and shoulders. My head had begun to ache. It was that kind of dull traumatic throb which sets up echoes of queasiness in the gut and makes the eyes hypersensitive to light. And it makes you wonder if some little blood vessel in the brain might be ruptured and bleeding.

I sat on the bed and just as I reached toward the phone to try Nurse Stanyard again, it rang, startling me. It was Janice Stanyard.

"I called you back fifteen minutes ago, Janice, but there. . . ."

"I'm not home. And . . . I need help." Her voice was very tense, very guarded.

"Help you get. Any flavour."

"Thank God! The person I'm supposed to help is with me. I have to get back to her. We're at the Oriental Theatre. It's a movie house on West Randolph, just west of State. We're in the middle of the last row downstairs on the left. Please hurry."

I hurried. The box office was closed. I told the ancient ticket taker I wanted to catch the end of the feature. He pocketed my dollar, put a fist in front of a huge yawn, and waved me in. On the huge screen was an extreme close-up of a blonde singing about Trooo Laahv to an enchanted throng of about twenty-seven widely scattered customers, singing through a mouth big enough to park a pair of Hondas in. An usher bird-dogged me with wary flashlight until he heard Janice greet me, and then he moved away.

I sat beside Janice, A blonde sat on the other side of her, hunched and still, head bowed, hands covering her face. There was no other customer within fifty feet of us.

"She phoned me from the Trailways bus station. It's in the next block east. She said Doctor Geis had written her to contact me if she needed help."

"Susan Kemmer?"

"Yes. How did you. . . ."

"Why wouldn't she go home with you?"

"She's afraid to. She's been terribly beaten. She won't tell me who did it. She seems . . . dazed. I phoned you before I left for the bus station. I've been phoning you from here. It seemed like . . . a good place to wait."

I got up and squeezed past them and sat on the other side of Susan. When I put my arm around her shoulders she flinched violently and moved one hand enough to peer at me. In the reflected light of the noisy movie I could see that her eye was puffed and discoloured.

"I'm a friend," I said. "We want to help you, Susie. Doctor Geis told Mrs. Stanyard to give you any help you might need. Why won't you go to her apartment?"

"He'll look there," she said in a very small voice.

"If someone hurt you, we should report it to the police."

"No. Please. All I asked her for is some money, so I can go to a hotel. That's all. I can't stay with her."

"She shouldn't be alone," Janice said.

I thought of a wry possibility and said, "If she'll have you, Susan, will you stay with a friend of mine, a woman who lives alone?"

"Who?" Janice asked.

"If she knows, I can't stay there," Susan said. "I've been telling Mrs. Stanyard. I don't want her to know where I'll be."

"Don't be idiotic!" Janice said crossly.

"He could make her tell," Susan said to me.

"Maybe it isn't exactly idiotic," I told Janice. "Sit tight. Let me check."

I found the phones and looked up the number. After the fifth ring, Heidi Trumbill answered in a blurred, irritable voice.

"Travis McGee, Heidi."

"Who? Who?"

"I saw you Saturday. John Andrus wrote a note to you about me on the back of his card."

"Oh. Yes, of course. How could I forget? Dear Mark has been babbling about you ever since. He was very taken." I heard her yawn, a very rich, gasping, jaw-creaking yawn. "This better not be a social call, McGee."

"It isn't. I'm making a little progress with our problem."

"Really!"

"And because what I'm doing is in your interest, I have to ask you for a little help."

"Such as?"

"A young female is involved. She's been roughed up. She needs a safe place to hide out, to hole up and get some rest

109

and recuperation. She has some information I want and I won't be able to get it out of her until she feels safe and unwinds a little. Miss X. No names. No questions. No answers. You have room for her there. Okay?"

"Are you drunk by any chance?"

"Not noticeably."

"What do you think I am? Some kind of rest camp? Some kind of a house mother?"

"Heidi, I think that in many respects you are a silly, arrogant, pretentious bitch. But I also think you are probably a patsy for starving kittens and busted birds."

"And painters who can't paint? And sculptors who can't sculpt? Say it all, McGee."

"If the spare bed isn't made up, make it up. We'll be along in a bit."

"You are so *sure* of yourself, damn your eyes. How soon?"

"Half an hour."

"See you," she said and hung up. I got back to the mouth of the aisle just as the marching-into-the-sunset music swelled strong, and the thin grey line of customers began getting up to walk through the spilled popcorn and paper cups toward their shrunken realities outside. My two females got up and we headed out of the palace. Susan was in a blue cloth coat and she kept her mouth and chin ducked down into a concealing billow of blue knit scarf, and kept her face turned away from the public as much as possible.

Before we went out into the icy night I stopped them and said, "You've got a car, Janice?"

"Yes."

"If you have any company, what happened was you got a call from the Trailways station. It was a girl. She told you Dr. Geis had said you would help her. She didn't give her name. You went there and she was gone. You waited around, then decided to see the movie. You thought she might be one of the Doctor's patients."

"Where will she be? Where are you taking her?"

"A safe place, where she'll get rest and care. I'll be in touch."

She hesitated, then touched the girl on the arm. "You can trust me, dear. I'll help you any way I can. And you can trust Mr. McGee. You have to tell someone what kind of trouble you're in." When Susan Kemmer did not answer, Janice gave a helpless little shrug and walked out. I gave her thirty seconds, then pushed the door open for the girl. I'd parked a block away. I held her upper arm, and walked her into the wind. She was limping.

Heidi buzzed the downstairs door open, and when we got to the red door at the second-floor rear, she was standing in the open doorway, the lighted room behind her silhouetting her. She took Susan's coat and scarf and laid them aside. I had Susan sit in a chair and I said, "For reasons I won't go into, we'll keep this whole thing anonymous. Friends helping friends. Miss Brown, meet Mrs. Jones. Let's get a good look at you, dear."

I tilted the opaque lampshade to put the full light on her, and with my fingertips I lifted her reluctant chin. Heidi, looking in from the side, made a little whimper of concern. Young lips mashed, puffed, and scabbed. Nose intact. Eggplant bruises on the cheekbones, a quarter-inch slice of one blue eye visible between puffed flesh, and a slightly wider segment of the other. They looked out at us calmly enough. Left brow slightly split. Forehead bruise shaded with saffron.

"Yesterday?" I asked her.

She nodded. "Yesterday morning. Real early."

I put one hand behind her head and with the fingers of the other hand prodded at her cheekbones and at the brows to see if there was any give or shift of broken bone. She winced but endured.

"Double vision? Any nausea today?"

"No sir."

"Are you hungry?"

"I . . . don't know. My teeth are loose over on this side."

"Open wide."

I wiggled them with a fingertip. Four in a row on the lower jaw, right side. "You won't lose them. They'll tighten up again, kid."

Heidi said she had the ingredients for an eggnog, and she brought me some cotton pads and rubbing alcohol along with adhesive tape and scissors before she went to mix it. I had the girl stretch out on the couch and I knelt beside her. I loosened the caked blood on the split brow, wiped it clean, dried it, then used the strips of adhesive scissored to narrow widths to pull the split together. She sucked air a few times, but she was pleasantly stoical.

Heidi was able to produce a mild sedative. The girl took it with the tall eggnog. When I was able to look past the battered face I saw that she was practically type-cast, an almost perfect fraülein type, fair and blue-eyed, plump as a little pigeon, round sweet face. She should milk cows, and hop around in the Bavarian village festival in her dirndl to the accordion music while her boyfriend blew foam off his stein and slapped his leather pants and yodelled once in a while.

I decided it was no time to question her. Heidi took her in to bed her down and came back in about ten minutes. She wore a navy-blue floor-length flannel robe, starkly tailored. Again I wondered about that total lack of physical communication and awareness between us. It was incredible that a mouth curved thusly, eyes placed so, body with that look of slenderness and ripeness and power, hair and eyes gleaming with animal health, provocative grace in every movement—incredible that it could all add up to absolute neuter.

"I think she was asleep before I closed the door," Heidi said. "The child is exhausted in every way. Her body is terribly bruised. The worst bruise is on her thigh. It looks as if she was kicked. I asked her who did it and she just looked at me."

"No questions. Part of the deal. It's good of you to take her in. But what's with this child thing? How much older are you? Seven years?"

"Seven hundred. How long will she be here?"

"Two days, three, four. I don't know. Just don't let her take off before I get here in the morning. She might want to."

She drifted about, touching small things, straightening them. She turned and looked at me. "You're really strange, Travis McGee. You took it absolutely for granted I'd take her in. I just don't *do* things like that."

"Hardly ever. I know. How did the opening go yesterday?"

"As expected. Well, more people than I expected, actually. Poor Mark was darting about like a mother hen. One too many people compared Kirstarian to Segal, so he made a fantastic scene and stalked out. Mark sold three pieces, and it made him so happy he drank all the champagne we had left and I had to put him to bed." She sat on the arm of the couch and looked across at me. "It's so strange. That girl. I have the feeling I knew her long, long ago. But I couldn't have. She's too young for that. Who is she, Travis?"

The temptation was to drop the bomb and say it was her half-sister. But that wasn't going to do anyone any good. I said, "You don't know her. She very probably knows something about where your father's money went. But she might not even know she knows. She is a good and staunch girl."

"I sensed that about her."

"The problem is the money."

"Oh yes, the money. And poor elfin little heartbroken Gloria, the waitress type, knows absolutely nothing about it, Right?"

"As far as anyone can tell."

"Well, she certainly fooled John Andrus without any trouble. And she sold my father a bill of goods. So I guess you don't present any special problem."

I smiled at her. "Heidi, she had to be lousy and crooked and dirty because she had the unholy impertinence to marry the daddy. She cast an ugly spell over him. She even seduced him physically, fornicated with him, and made him think he was enjoying it. What a degrading thing for the big wise important daddy to be doing! Didn't he know it made darling daughter feel actually ill to wake up in the night and think that right at that moment that woman was making him do that sick ugly animal thing?"

She turned ice-pale, jumped trembling to her feet and said, "Stop that! Stop it!"

"Where do you think you came from, Heidi? Did they find you out in the cabbage patch? There's only one known way he could get to *be* your father."

She wiped her mouth on the back of her hand. In a thin prim little voice she said, "It killed her. She died."

So I got out of there after suitable apologies. Two swings, two hits. Anybody who wanted to find a woman under that luscious structure was going to have to tear it down and start over. Marriage to her had been as exciting as two years of root canal treatments, on a dead fang.

I knew that Francisco Smith had better find me Mother Gretchen, and fast.

NINE

FRANCISCO SMITH woke me up with his phone call at quarter past eight on Tuesday, that thirteenth day of December.

"Got something to write on?" he asked.

113

"Hold on," I said, and got set and told him to go ahead.

"Okay, here's the number of the annuity policy. GLC 085-14-0277. Four hundred thirty-three dollars and thirty-three cents gets mailed out the first of every month. The guy at Great Lakes is named Rainey. T. T. Rainey. The September cheque came back, addressee moved, no forwarding address. They tried a trace. The Gorba family left last August 22nd. A Sunday. The couple and the five kids, in a big grey Cadillac sedan, towing a U-Haul. Licence 397 110. Dropped the apartment keys in the super's box. Rent paid to the end of August and a month deposit in advance. Mrs. Gorba was paid by the week. She picked up her pay at the restaurant when she left work Friday evening. He was paid twice a month. His pay is still sitting there at the body shop. They left the apartment in good shape. They didn't pick up the utilities deposits. They left clean. At least there's no judgments filed against them."

"Is Great Lakes still trying to find them?"

"No. They tried it on the cheap and gave up quick. They weren't like somebody trying to collect. They sent out the cheque for a double payment October first and it came back too. So they put it and the November and December cheques in an interest account. The January cheque will go in the same account, the one made out to her mother like the cheques. But she turns eighteen in January, so if nobody shows up, they'll start a new interest account in the name of Susan Kemmer."

"Car payments?"

"No dice there. You see, it was a two-year-old Cad that the owner totalled, and the place Saul Gorba worked bid three-fifty for it. Then they found more wrong than the estimator thought there was. Gorba put down two hundred on it and agreed they could take another two-fifty out of his pay. That was back in April, I think. It was with the idea he could work on it in his spare time when he'd put in his regular hours, and buy the parts from them at cost or scrounge them from the yards, and they'd let him use the shop tools. A lot of those guys work it that way for a personal car. They don't like them trying to fix iron up for resale as it puts them in competition with the shops they're working for. But Gorba didn't have a car so it was okay with the boss. So for about nine hundred, plus all the hours he put into it, he came out of it with a pretty good automobile. I understand he's handy with tools and catches on fast."

114

"When did he finish it, Smith?"

"August sometime."

"What would be the chance of tracing them in a hurry?"

After a short silence he said, "I wouldn't say it was real great, not if Gorba doesn't want to be traced. School records, medical records, IRS refunds, Social Security—he'd be more careful than most. He had to rent the trailer someplace and he had to turn it in someplace, but he could unload it, drive it three hundred miles empty, and turn it in. With the car registration, he could cover up best by unloading it on a cash deal and buying something else under another name. My hunch would be check close on the daughter's friends. You tear a seventeen-year-old kid away from all her friends, she is going to find some way to drop them a card. But I don't like the feel of it, not with those cheques unclaimed. What is it now? Thirteen hundred bucks. Listen, they're going to keep me on the run all day. This evening I maybe get a chance to cover a couple of other angles. I'll be in touch."

The day was like a dirty galvanized bucket clapped down over the city. When you swallowed, you could taste the city. All the trees looked dead, and all the people looked like mourners. Happy Christmas. Bingle jells. Brace yourself for hate week.

Heidi opened the red door with a fractional smile of cool welcome. She was in one of her painting suits. This one was yellow, like shark repellent. It had forty-three pockets with flaps and zippers. "How's our patient?" I asked, very jolly.

"I made her go back to bed. She was shaky."

Heidi had a blue smudge on the back of one hand, two speckles of bright red on her chin. The door to her studio was open. She was dressed for air-sea rescue, visible at thirty miles.

I glanced through the doorway into her studio. She said, "Kindly do not express an interest in my work. I already know your opinion."

"Look, I did not mean to rawhide you last night. I'm sorry."

"It isn't something new, Mr. McGee. Men try to shake me up by saying ugly things. It's a sort of an erotic compulsion, I guess."

"Maybe you're an example of conspicuous waste."

"Don't try to make phrases. You're not the type. She's in the second bedroom on the left."

115

Susan Kemmer was propped up on two pillows. Her face was turned toward the grey light at the window, and tracked silver with tears. She looked at me, dabbed in gingerly fashion at the tear marks with a tissue, snuffled, and hitched the pale blue blanket higher. The gestures had the flavour of bracing for ordeal. It looked to me as though some of the puffiness was gone. But the areas of discolouration were larger, and the hues more varied.

I pulled a chair over and sat by the foot of the bed, facing her. "Saul work you over?"

"I'm not going to answer questions, Mr. McGee."

"Why don't you just think the questions over, and answer the ones you feel like answering? I won't try to trick you. Take your time."

"Who are you?"

"A friend of yours. I might have some answers to some of your questions. If you have any."

"Why should I want to ask you anything?"

"You might want to know why Dr. Fortner Geis was anxious to help you. I guess he had the feeling you might get in a real jam. A ten-thousand-dollar jam, Susan. That's the amount of cash he sent Mrs. Stanyard."

"Ten . . . thousand . . . dollars!"

"If you didn't contact her in a year, then she was to give it to Mrs. Geis."

"But . . . wouldn't it be mine anyway?"

"How come?"

"I mean it would have been money he got from my. . . ." She stopped abruptly. I could guess at what was going on in her mind. Storybook stuff. Afternoon soap opera. There could be a dozen versions. Famous surgeon has a friend who has a daughter dying of a brain tumor. She is pregnant. Unmarried. Influential family. They don't want a scandal. The Doctor keeps the girl alive long enough so that she can have her baby, and then he arranges with his housekeeper for the housekeeper's daughter and her young husband, Karl Kemmer, to raise the baby as their own. So the money that had always come every month came from the annuity her real mother's people had bought for her, and the ten thousand is some kind of emergency fund entrusted to the Doctor long ago. I did not want to reach into her head and wrench any of her dreams loose. They had sustained her. One day she would be able to jettison them herself, after they had served their long purpose. There

116

was strength in this girl. But very strong people can break when there is too much all at once.

"How did Dr. Geis get word to you about contacting Mrs. Stanyard in case of trouble?"

"I don't want to answer questions."

"Take your time. See if there is any harm in answering that one, Susan."

"But if I don't want any help, why should I answer anything?"

"You have an orderly mind. But I gave you some help last night. You needed it and took it."

She thought that over. "He wrote me a letter last August. The writing was shaky. We knew from Grandma he was going to die. The Sunday before I got the letter she told us he was failing. It just said if I needed help I should go to Mrs. Stanyard. I was to write down her phone and address and destroy the letter, and not tell anybody. I thought it sounded sort of . . . crazy. He said Mrs. Stanyard was a nurse and a nice person and I could trust her. I did like he said in the letter even if I didn't expect anything to happen, and sort of forgot it until. . . ."

"Until the day before yesterday."

"But you wouldn't go to her apartment with her because you said they'd look for you there. What did that mean?"

"Nothing."

"Okay. Now then. You're in some kind of a jam. You can call on me, and I can be just as rough as I have to be to get you out of it. And you've got ten thousand to finance the operation. I am yours to command, kid."

She turned her face toward the window. The tears started again. "But I can't do anything," she said hopelessly. "Nobody can do anything. She went away once in California and they put us in a place. There was just three of us then and we were little, and we almost didn't get Freddy back. The judge said he was disturbed."

"Gretchen has gone off someplace?"

Defiant eyes stared at me through the slits. "I don't know what you're talking about."

I stood up. "I'm going to leave you alone for a little while to think something over. Let me see if I have the names right. Freddy, Julian, Freda, and Tommy. Christmas vacation is coming up, Susan. I don't think it would be too difficult for an obviously respectable type like me to go gather up the kids. I know a crazy wonderful couple in Palm Beach. House as big as a hotel. Pots of money. Cook, maids, housekeeper, yard men. And scads of kids. They adopt them. Five more over Christmas would hardly be noticed. I could set it up with one phone call, and you've got the aeroplane money. Think it over."

I walked out without giving her a chance to respond. Heidi did not hear me. I leaned against the studio doorway. She was reworking the bottom corner of a big painting, standing bent over with her back to me. Her air-sea rescue costume was clinched tight around the slender waist, and stretched tightly across the pleasantly globular rear. I had always thought it fallacious to make an erotic speciality out of any particular portion of the form divine. When it is good it is all good, and some days some parts are a little better than others, but you need the entire creature to make any segment of it worthwhile. In three silent steps I could grab a double handful of all that and see if she could manage a standing high jump over the top of the painting.

"Ah Hem !" I said.

She straightened and whirled around. "Oh ! Did you find out anything?"

First I broke it to her that her patient was Gretchen's kid, and was the eldest granddaughter of Anna, the housekeeper, and briefed her on Gretchen's home life, hubby and sudden departure.

She looked thoughtful and troubled instead of startled, and said that she guessed that subconsciously she must have had some hint. She had dreamed about Gretchen last night for the first time in years. So I went back to her specific question. Had I found out anything?

"Just enough to make some guesses, and they are probably wrong. She thinks any kind of help is going to make things worse. I have a hunch the Gorba family moved well out of town. Fifty miles, a hundred miles. Mama Gretchen missed the lights and the action, so she took off. So Saul Gorba took a little hack at the ripening daughter, maybe to get even with Gretch for taking off. I would think she'd put up a pretty good scramble, so maybe she got her nails into his chops, or a solid little knee into his underparts, and he lost his temper and hammered her. I think he would know she wouldn't blow the whistle on him. With his record they would tote him off gladly, and the social workers would, in the absence of the old lady, stuff the kids into the handiest institution. I think she

118

is hooked on being the little mother hen to these other four. I think she is worried to death about them right now. If she goes back, the stepdaddy tries again. And if she stays away and Gretchen is away, who looks after the little ones? Not so terribly little, actually. Fifteen, twelve, ten, and six."

She nibbled the wood end of a paint brush, frowning. "That sounds so ugly, the whole situation. It's so strange. really. Roger has such clear memories of Gretchen when she lived with us. Of course he's four years older. But I must have been almost eight years old when Gretchen got married. I can remember a lot of things from a lot earlier than that. But Gretchen is sort of dim. I can't see her face at all, or remember her voice. Roger says she was good to us. He says she was good-natured and sort of dumb and sloppy. But would she just walk out on her kids?"

"Apparently she's done it before."

"Poor Anna. She deserves a more reliable daughter. Couldn't Anna take her own grandchildren for a while? Maybe not. Probably Lady Gloria wouldn't want brats from her own social level cluttering up her illusions of grandeur."

I started to speak and then let it stand. We could not head in that direction and get anywhere. She was blocked. So I made some unimportant small talk and then went back in to catch Susan's reaction. It was a firm shake of the head— from side to side. No more questions and no more answers. She didn't want to be any trouble to anyone. She would leave as soon as she felt well enough. Thanks a lot.

I talked with Heidi again before leaving. She promised she wouldn't try to pump Susan Kemmer, but if the girl said anything useful, Heidi would get in touch with me right away.

I went to the nearby Ambassador for some midmorning coffee and some midmorning thought. A trio of high-fashion models, young ones, were gathered there for some do. They chittered and squeaked at each other. Their starved faces were painted to a silver pallor, their tresses shaped by men who hate women, using only soup bowls and hedge clippers, their clothing created by those daring little hanky-stompers who vie with each other in seeing how grotesque they can make their clients. It is an in-joke with them, and it gives them hysterics when they get together. They whinny, fall down, and spill their money. I think they would do a lot less harm sculpting pop-art dogs.

I ordered more coffee and went and phoned Janice Stanyard.

No answer. I tried the hospital. She was in surgery, and scheduled through until at least four in the afternoon. I went back to my coffee and dug through the scrap paper in my side pocket and found the phone slip on Nurse Stanyard's call. It had come in at nine. So I went to the bus depot on East Randolph. It was to buses what Miami International is to aeroplanes. They had American, Continental, DeLuxe, Indiana, Santa Fe, Suburban, American Coach and so on—big inside ramps and stations, gates and callers.

In order to get anywhere I had to make certain assumptions. With her face in that condition, she wouldn't hang around waiting to make up her mind about calling Janice Stanyard. Give her ten minutes to get from the platform to a phone. Give Janice five minutes before calling me. So I was interested in anything arriving from, say, eighteen minutes before the hour to five minutes before the hour. After studying and crosschecking the printed schedules and the arrival boards, I came up with five possibles, all based on the assumption she came in from out of the city somewhere. My only prayer was her very memorable condition. When you see a young girl with the kind of a face Dick Tiger could give any contender back in his better days, it can stick in your mind. But I was at the wrong end of the day. Depot personnel on duty this Tuesday morning wouldn't have been around on Monday night at nine. If she was on one of the five arrivals, she would have used one of three gates to come into the terminal.

Mark time. Futz around. Scratch. Fret. Watch girls. Wonder what the hell you are doing in this huge damp cellar full of three or four million people. Between announcements the speaker system in the depot was telling everybody about we three kings of Orient are. Damn you, Fort Geis, why didn't you leave a message in a hollow tree? Why didn't you realize what a pot of trouble you were leaving behind? It was an example of the terrible innocence of men who are superb in their own fields. Einstein had some grotesque political opinions. Jack Paar knew how we should get rid of the Berlin Wall. Kurt Vonnegut keeps losing aeroplane tickets.

Fortner Geis had not the slightest idea that people representing a dozen different interests and points of view would compete for the chance to drag the widow into their particular cave and gnaw her bones clean. Six hundred big ones brightens the eyes, sharpens the taste, bulges the muscles. O speak to us from beyond, Great Surgeon.

I trudged out into the hooing of damp and grisly wind, into the kind of gunmetal day when you wear your headlights turned on, and think of a roaring fire, hot buttered rum, a Dynel tiger-skin, and a brown agile lass from Papeete. I took my dismals to the Palmer House and traded them to a sad-smiling man for a C-cup of Plymouth. We stood on either side of the bar and sighed at each other in wistful awareness of our mutual mortality, and I left half the drink and went off and phoned Heidi.

When she answered I said, "Is the battered bird responding?"

"Not so that anyone could notice. She's taking a bath and washing her hair. If it's any use to you, her clothes are from a cheap chain with about ten thousand outlets in Chicago, and her shoes seem to be a very good grade of cardboard, and her total of wordly goods comes to four dimes and four pennies, a red comb, half a pink lipstick, and one wadded-up bus schedule."

"What bus line?"

"Hmm. Let me go look. She's still sloshing in there." she came back and said, "North Central. I looked to see if she'd marked anything on it. She hasn't."

"Thanks. It could be a help. You make a good secret agent."

"Secret agent hell, McGee. It's pure female nosiness."

I went back to my drink in better humour. I separated the North Central timetable from the others I had picked up. Bus Number 83 arrived every week-day night at 8.45, back at the point of origin from where it had left at 8.20 that morning. Elgin, Rockford, Freeport, Clinton, Moline, Galesburg, Peoria, Peru, Ottawa,, Joliet, and home to the barn. I could guess the union wouldn't let them load that kind of a run on one man. Probably one man took it to some mid-way point, possibly Moline, and his relief brought it on in and took it out the next morning and traded off again at Moline.

So the driver who had brought her in Monday night would be bringing her in again on Wednesday night, The company ran shorter routes and longer routes, and the Chicago office address was printed on the timetable. I signalled for a refill, left money as my surety bond, and went off and called North Central.

"Give me somebody who knows your driver roster," I told the girl.

"Herbison speaking," a man said, moments later.

"State traffic control," I said. "Sergeant Ellis. Who brought your 83 in last night?"

"Anything wrong, Sergeant?"

"Just a routine check. Trying to pin down the time we lost some intersection lights."

"Oh, Hold on." It took him twenty seconds. "Daniel D. DuShane, Sergeant." He explained I could contact him after two o'clock at a Galesburg address. He gave me the phone number. He said DuShane would be in again on 83 tomorrow night, that he was a good man, held a schedule well, and would probably be able to help me.

I felt reasonably cheery through the first half of my second knock, then I began to realize how rickety was my structure of hunch and logic. There were too many things wrong with it. If Gorba had cleaned out the Doctor's estate, and if he was as bright as Francisco Smith had reported, it seemed to me he would have done one of two things—either stayed put, kept his job, bided his time—or gone too far for North Central Transportation Company to get anywhere near him. Also, if he had made that big a score, it didn't seem like a very good idea for Gretchen to go off rambling.

True, one of the kids was his, the youngest one, but it seemed out of character for a type who could score so cleverly to saddle himself with even one, much less five. He did not seem to be the homebody sort.

In that mood, you can lose the whole thing. Okay. So a happy singing drunk had been charmed by the happy face of a small boy and taken him for a ride, got timid—or sober—and dropped him in the park. Neighbourhood teen-age clowns had wired the joke bomb on Glory's little car. Some twitch maniac, turned on with some kind of bug juice, had come looking for people to scrag and had settled for Ethel cat. One of Gadge Hairynose Trumbill's countryclub wives had booby-trapped the candy box as a sick little vengeance. Susan Kemmer had been bashed about by a hulk of a boyfriend.

Go home, McGee. It's too big and too scrambled and it happened too long ago. Smuggle Glory out of the polar regions. Take her home. Boat her, beach her, bake her, brown her, and bunk her. You too are a sucker for busted birds, starving kittens, broody broads. Healer McGee, the big medicine man. She's got that big fireplace out there, right? A stock of sauce, right? A fantastic grocery department, right? So go lay it all out and cry a little. She might even come up with an idea.

So in the endless twilight of noonday I went northward, locked into the traffic flow, listening to ghastly news from all over. Premier assassinated tax boost seen Wings lose again bombs deemed defective three coeds raped teen-age riot in Galveston cost of living index up again market sags Senator sues bowl game cancelled wife trading ring broken mobster takes Fifth bad weather blankets nation. . . .

The announcer was beginning to choke up. I turned him off. I couldn't stand it.

As I felt my way down through the Lake Pointe area, the wind was coming off the lake, bellowing and thrashing, and taking little plucks at the steering wheel. The driveway and the lighted house beyond was safe haven, and I slammed my car door, put my head down, and plunged through tempests. Anna Ottlo let me in.

"Ach! Thank Gott! Thank Gott!" She cried. She kept winding and unwinding her plump red hands in her napkin.

"What's the matter? Where's Mrs. Geis?"

It took me long minutes to piece it together. Anna had cleaned up after breakfast, and after she had finished the house-cleaning, she had asked Gloria if it was all right if she went to her room and lay down for a little while. She had bad pains in one hip. She thought it was the dampness. The doctor was giving her cortisone. Her hip would stop hurting if she could get off her feet every now and then. She had dropped off to sleep. A little while ago, maybe fifteen minutes ago, she had awakened with a start and been shocked to find it was almost twelve-thirty. She had gone hunting for Gloria to ask her what she would like for lunch. Gloria was not anywhere in the house. Her car was in the garage. She thought perhaps she had gone walking on the beach. But she had never gone walking when the weather was this bad. She had been acting very strange. Anna Ottlo had been wondering if she should call the police when I had arrived.

"The wasser," she said, her eyes miserable, her mouth sick. "I keep thinking of the wasser."

So I took off into the whirling gloom. I would guess the temperature at thirty degrees, and the wind seemed to take the whole thirty points off it. The wind, hard and steady, but with sudden gusts of greater violence, picked sand off the lips of the dunes and dry-lashed my face with it.

I loped and bawled her name, shielded my eyes from the sting of sand, and stared up and down the shelving beach.

Beyond the sand belt the spray whipped at me. There was no colour in the world. Grey sand, grey water, grey beach, grey sky. I was trapped in one of those arty salon photographs of nature in the raw, the kind retired colonels enter in photography contests. Through watery eyes I saw somebody waving a flag at me, a hundred yards away. The somebody turned out to be a twisted and barren bush a hundred feet back from the smack of the lake waves. The flag, however, was a pair of pale green nylon briefs. Ladypants. Elasticized waist, some dainty bits of machine lace. Fresh clean new—sodden with spray.

Twenty feet beyond the bush was the touch of colour in the grey world. Patch of dark red. Ran to it. Pulled it out of the sand. More than half of it was covered by the drift of sand. Dark red wool dress. Glory's size. Damned little fool with the broken heart. I wondered if the waves would shove her back on to the beach. As I started toward the beach I caught a movement out of the corner of my eye. I turned quickly and saw Gloria crouched on the crest of a small dune thirty feet away. Her posture was like that of a runner waiting for the gun. Her knuckles were in the sand. I could see a glint of her eyes through the sodden mat of hair. Her mouth hung open. The small row of bottom teeth visible. She was egg-naked.

I called her name and hurried toward her. She whirled and ran from me. It was the dreadful reckless run of absolute and total panic. She would stumble and fall and roll to her feet and as I closed on her, she would dart off in another direction. When I could get near her, I could hear the horrid sound she was making in competition to the sound of waves and wind. I was as desperate as she. That wind had to be sucking the heat and the life out of her. Finally I feinted one way and as she cut back I dived and got one hand on her slender ankle and brought her down. She kicked me in the face with her free foot.

She had fantastic strength. Her face was madness. As I struggled with her she suddenly snapped at my hand and got it between her teeth, right at the thumb web. With her eyes tight shut she ground with her jaws, making a whining and gobbling sound. I put my other hand on the nape of her neck and got my thumb on one side and my middle finger on the other in the proper places under the jaw corners and clamped, shutting off the blood supply to the brain. She slumped and rolled on to her back. I stripped my topcoat off, laid it down, put a foot on it so it wouldn't blow away, and lifted her on to it. As I did so I remembered long ago at Sanibel when I had first been surprised at how her small body which looked so trim and lean and tidy in clothes could have such a flavour of ripeness and abundance. I guess it was the ivory smoothness of her combined with a dusky, secretive, temple-magic look to the contours of breasts, belly, rounded thighs. Now perfection was abraded by sand, gouged and torn by the falling. I wrapped her up and ran for the distant house.

Once I got what I hoped was the right routine going—electric blanket turned high and heaped with other blankets, brandy forced past clenched teeth, I remembered who would have the biggest stake in giving her every attention she should have. I looked him up in the book and used the bedside phone. Her lips were blue. She made grunting sounds.

The office nurse said that Dr. Hayes Wyatt was with a patient and if I would leave my name and number. I have no idea what I said to her. I have absolutely no memory of it. I do know that the next voice I heard was that of Dr. Wyatt.

I got through it and he kept saying, "What? What? What?"

"Now goddam it, Doctor, pull yourself together. Gloria Geis had been freaking up and down this beach bareass naked God only knows how long, and I think it was the acid you let Fort Geis have, and she tried to chew my hand off and it scares me to look at her, so having you keep saying what what what isn't doing anybody any good at all."

Once he moved, he moved well. He got to the house ten minutes before the ambulance did. He took her to Methodist Hospital where the widow of Fortner Geis would get every attention in the book. I waited an hour before he came down and sat beside me in the lounge. He was a spare dusty tall remote man. He took off his glasses and pinched the bridge of his nose and sighed.

"We'll wait and see," he said. "She was all right last night and all right at breakfast. So as it wasn't repeated dosages we have to assume a massive dose. No matter how much or how little you take, it wears off in twelve hours at the outside. By ten o'clock tonight I should know a little more. She's in restraint now. She's being treated for shock and exposure. Did you notice her hands?"

"Yes."

"She chewed her arms and her knees badly, but the hands are the worst. I don't like that. It sounds as if the disassociation was total. Do you understand what I'm saying?"

"That she could stay out in left field from here on."

"Or come back in two days. Or two years. I should have got it back. I shouldn't have taken her word she'd got rid of it."

"She dumped it out. She must have found a new source."

He looked at me with surprise, started to protest, and then understood. "But I don't want to evade moral responsibility, Mr. McGee."

"Maybe Fort should have made sure it was dumped. Maybe he did. Maybe she found a wandering Mexican and bought mushrooms."

"Psychedelics have a legitimate scientific. . . ."

"So does alcohol. And Demerol. And every day they pump out some little kid who eats all the aspirin in the house."

"You should be . . . an assurance salesman." He looked mildly pleased with himself. It was a joke. I do not think he had made many jokes in his lifetime.

"Doctor, with the best response you could hope for, how long would she be in?"

"At least ten days. At the very least. I'm going to stay right with her. I'll leave word at the switchboard that I will accept calls from you."

I phoned Anna Ottlo. I could hear her snuffling after I told her the score. I told her that as far as I could see, she could start closing the house, and packing up all Glory's personal gear. I said I would relay the news to John Andrus at the bank and to Roger Geis and Heidi Trumbill. She wanted to know how soon she could come and see Gloria at the hospital. I told her I'd let her know.

After I hung up I remembered I had forgotten lunch, and it was almost three-thirty.

TEN

I HAD a sandwich and coffee at a twenty-four-hour place near enough to the hospital to get the random hours business of nurses and interns, clerks and dieticians, Grey Ladies and residents. There was a gabble of young nurses in a corner. The ceiling fluorescence was as bright as any operating room. My Formica tabletop was white as a surgical dressing. One young nurse had a lovely curve of temple brow, cheek, jaw.

I tried to contrast them with the spidery moon-painted fashion racks I had seen at the Ambassador, thinking that nursing seems to attract young women structured in a curious way—pretty and slender from throat to waist, and there swelling into sedate and massive hips, hefty peasant legs. Debutante riding along in an ox cart. Or, by analogue, some variant of the myth-man who, from the waist down, was horse.

Try as I might, I could not keep my mind twisted away from that great grey howl of beach where the pursuit still went on, the tall sunbronzed man made clumsy by the scuttling and dartings of the little naked woman. That look of madness is ugly beyond belief when you see it on the face which once had shown you love. And, in my arms and hands, I had the tactile memory of how the total panic of the inner beast felt.

Once, long ago, I went drift fishing with friends for small-mouth black bass in the St. Lawrence River near Alexandria Bay, using live minnows, and fly rods, pulling in the lines to run upriver, then drifting down again over the good places. At noon we beached the boat on a small island and cleaned and cooked some of the catch over a driftwood fire. One man cast a minnow from the shore and hooked and brought in a river eel perhaps two feet long, maybe a little more, and in the thickest cross-section no greater than the average banana. My friend lived on the river, and he hauled the eel on to a bit of hard ground and told me to stand on it. I thought he was out of his mind. Two hundred and twenty pounds of man on two pounds of eel. I'd crush it flat. He insisted. I pinned it with one foot, then put the other and my full weight on it. As it writhed it kept lifting me an inch or so. I stepped off. It was undamaged.

In her induced terror, Glory had that same incredible mus-cular tension, so that if I held her too tightly, the muscles would break her bones, unhinge her joints, as sometimes hap-pens under shock treatment. We use only the smallest part of the power of both brain and muscles. Even our senses are dulled in the state we call consciousness. Under hypnosis the good subject can read a newspaper across a room, hear sounds otherwise inaudible, detect differences in the weight of seem-ingly identical objects.

Perhaps it is merely sentimentality—that strangely unearned emotion—which makes us want to have the fates and fortunes of life favour the good guys. Glory was a good guy. She had had more than her share already. There is a grotesque and continuous tragedy about some lives which would be too extreme for even a soap-opera audience to stomach.

So I white-eyed a nurse into receptivity across forty feet of plastic restaurant, chomped down a plastic sandwich, gulped down acid coffee and plastic pie, and with accelerating stride got to the men's room just in time to whonk and brutch the belated lunch into a toilet. Homage to a one-time love. A sick heart makes a sick stomach. They had cleaned and dressed my hand. They do not give you a series of shots for girl-bite. Wasn't she the lucky one to think of asking you to fly up here and help her, T. McGee? You did great.

I shed coat and jacket and rolled up my shirt sleeves and drew a lavatory bowl of cold water. I wallowed and scrubbed and made seal sounds, and then found out that the management had thoughtfully provided one of those warm air tubes for the drying bit, the special kind that leave you feeling coated with grease rather than water. Small children think they are fun. Every adult in the land hates them. They are part of the international communist conspiracy. A nation forced to dry itself in a machined huff of sickly warm air is going to be too irritable, listless, and disheartened to fight. Americans unite! Carry your own towels. Carry little sticks with which you can wedge those turn-off faucets open so you can get two hands under the water at the same time. Carry your own soap so you need not wash your paws in that sickly green punch-button goo that leaves you smelling like an East Indian bordello. Carry your own toilet paper, men. The psychic trauma created by a supply of the same paper stock used for full-colour adds in *Life* magazine cannot be measured.

The cold-sweat sensation ended. I reassembled the hero, stared into his deadly mirrored eye, nodded reassuringly at the poor suggestible slob, and strode out into a blackening world where the wind had ended, where great slow flakes the size of quarters and half-dollars came falling down to melt into a black sticky slime on the sidewalks and on the fourteen million tons of scrap paper that littered the city.

At a drugstore full of games, toys, and sporting equipment, I downed a fizzing nostrum for ugly-gut, and from a booth got Heidi first. The fraülein was napping. I told her that Gloria

128

Geis was hospitalized, that she had suffered a little bout of nervous exhaustion.

"Is my heart supposed to go out to her?" asked the ice maiden.

"I don't think that's what she had in mind. But tell your brother. Maybe you two can have a good chuckle over it. Mrs. Ottlo will be leaving for Florida when she gets the house closed. I imagine John Andrus will be in touch with you about odds and ends."

"I hope you and John Andrus understand that the little bitch is probably faking."

I quoted her word for word to John Andrus when I phoned him at the bank. He was shocked and concerned about Gloria, and I didn't tell him any more than I had told Heidi. I said Hayes Wyatt was on the case and any reports on her condition would have to come from him. John Andrus said he would swing into action about the house, the furnishings, storing Gloria's possessions, and finding her a place to live. Then he said, "Are you making any headway?"

"I wish to God I knew, John. I'll be in touch."

I got more change and went back to the booth and phoned the bus driver, Daniel D. DuShane in Galesburg. A woman answered and told me to hold on while she went to get him.

When he came on I gave Sergeant Ellis a new job. I put him in Missing Persons investigating a female juvenile runaway.

"Five two, about seventeen, blonde, about a hundred and twenty pounds, blue coat, blue scarf. She could have come into the city on number 83 last night. She might have had facial contusions and abrasions."

"Sure thing. She was on my load, Sergeant. You know, I been thinking ever since maybe I should have reported her as soon as I got in. No luggage, no purse even."

"Where did she board you?"

"It's a crossroads. From Peoria I'm routed up 29 on the west side of the river to Peru and LaSalle. There's a kind of village name of Bureau, where 26 comes in from the left. There's a crossroads gas station and lunchroom there name of Sheen's. It's like a hundred miles from Chicago, so I must get there usually about I'd say six o'clock, give or take some, depending. Once in maybe ten times I get a pickup there, and what Sheen does, he's got an amber blinker he can turn on and I can see it way down the road, so when it's on I hit the air horns and swing in and the fare comes running out, so it isn't too much time out of my schedule. I had the inside lights out, and she boarded and I turned on the front lights to take the money. She said Chicago and gave me a dollar and the rest of it all in change, and I gave her the ticket and looked up and the first thing I thought was she'd busted up a car and had to take the bus home. The light kind of shone on to her face and it gave me a real jolt. She went back and took an empty, and later when I had the inside lights on at Ottawa, I saw her back there with her head kind of wrapped up in the scarf so it hid most of the damage. Runaway, huh?"

"Looks like her old man beat her up."

"Sergeant, I hope you locate her. It's no town for a kid like that to be wandering around in. And I hope you bend her old man a little. A guy who hits his kid like that is some kind of animal."

"Thanks for your help, Mr. DuShane." ·

"I guess I should have turned her over to the cops at the depot."

Back in my rental when I got the engine going and the heater on high and the wipers knocking the snow off, I dug an Illinois map out of the glove compartment and finally located Bureau. It was half-way between Joliet and Rock Island, and lay about eight miles south of Interstate 80. The legend said that from the size of the circle marking it the population was between zero and two hundred and fifty. The idea of a town of zero population bemused me. Should it not have been from one to two hundred and fifty? My eye, sliding, picked up the name of a town of the same size on the other side of the river. Florid. It looked like a typo. Florid, Illinois. The Florid Hotel. The Florid Bank. A community of fat happy little people suffering from high blood pressure.

So I had enough leverage now, properly used, to unlock Miss Susan Kemmer. And I knew I was sitting in a snowy automobile playing map games because I was reluctant to go use the leverage. Respect for the sanctity of the individual is a terrible burden in my line of work. I have seen cops whose greatest jolly is in taking your head apart and spreading all the pieces out on the table, under the interrogation lights. The totally dismembered personality can be put back together again, but the pieces never fit quite the way they did. And they come apart easier the next time. The old field strip.

Five o'clock and blundering old mother night had come

130

in ahead of time to squat upon the city, upon two hundred thousand hair-trigger tempers clashing their way back toward good old home-heated television dinners, steam heat, the headachy little woman, the house-bound kids, and the dreadful feeling that Christmas was going to tear the guts out of the bank account.

I found the parking slot around the corner from Heidi's place, and as I was going to enter the downstairs foyer, I turned on impulse and looked upward and picked out a big fat drifting flake, stuck my tongue out, and manœuvred under it. Consumer report: The snow is still pretty good. Cold as ever. Melts as fast. You can't hardly taste the additives.

She let me in through the red door, into lamplight glow. Her creative day had ended and she was austere and queenly in a white knit dress with long sleeves—an off-white, neckline, prim, shift-like in the loose beltless fit of it, hemline just above the knees in that third-grade look which gives women with legs as good as hers an innocently erotic flavour, and gives women with bad legs the clown look of Baby Snooks.

"What a Christly ghastly depressing day," she said. She hiccuped. Astoundingly, she giggled. She looked appalled at herself, turned with careful stateliness, and said, walking away from me. "Don't think you've discovered some kind of secret vice, McGee. I felt chilly and I had some sherry. The work was going well and I kept drinking it and I didn't realize how many times I'd filled the glass and suddenly I was quite drunk. It isn't habitual."

"I'd never tab you as a wino, honey."

She revolved like a window display, hiccuped again, and said, "I shall be perfectly all right in a few minutes."

"How's your house guest?"

"Still sleeping. She must have been exhausted. Let's go see, shall we?"

I went down the short hallway with her. She turned on the hallway light. The room door was closed. She turned the knob carefully and swung the door open, hand still on the knob. I was right behind her. The wide vague band of light from the open doorway reached to the bed on the far side of the room. The young girl froze and gasped. She was standing beside the bed, and had obviously just taken off the borrowed nightgown and laid it on the bed and had been reaching toward the chair where her clothes were. The light was too shadowy to expose the facial damage. She had a ripeness, a pale heartiness in the light, and she quickly clapped one arm across her big young breasts and shielded her ginger-tan pubic tuft with her other hand.

A sound came from Heidi which turned every hair on the nape of my neck into a fine wiry bristle, crawled the flesh on the backs of my hands, and turned the small of my back to ice.

It was a tiny little-girl voice, thin and small, with none of the resonances of her maturity. It was a forlorn and sleepy little question. "Daddy? Daddy? Daddy, I'm scared. I had a bad dream. Daddy?"

Then she backed into me, banged the door shut. She stepped on my foot, turned into my arms, shuddered, and said, in that same infinitely pathetic little voice, "I'm going to tell on her. I'm going to tell on Gretchen! She was all bare!"

I held her. She was breathing rapidly, breathing a warm sherry-scented breath into my throat. Suddenly she slid her arms around my neck and held me with all her strength, crushing her soft and open mouth into mine, rocking and grinding her hips into me. There was so much frantic hunger from such a delicious direction. I was at least two-tenths of a second catching up to her. Suddenly she sagged, fainting limp, and groaned, and would have fallen.

I helped her into the living-room. She coughed and gagged. She stretched out full-length on the couch and rolled her head from side to side. I turned out the lamp shining down into her eyes and sat on the floor beside her and held her hand.

"What happened to me?" she asked. The little-girl voice was gone.

"Listen to me, Heidi. I want to tell you a sad story about a sensitive and complicated little girl in a silent house. She must have been about seven years old, and there were nurses and the smells of medicine and the adored mother was dying, and she felt frightened and alone, and had nightmares."

She did not move as I reconstructed it for her. Her hand lay cool and boneless in mine. I finished it. There was no response.

"How vile!" she said in an almost inaudible tone. "How ugly and terrible."

"Sure. A lonely man, wretchedly depressed. A young girl with a terrible crush on him. A slow-witted, amiable romantic girl with all the ideas of soft surrender out of the love pulps and confessions. So she crept into his dark room and into his

132

bed after God only knows how many nights of thinking about it. Soft, loving, willing young flesh and he took her. You came in on one of those nights to be comforted. She was just climbing out of his bed. There is a sexual undertone to every little girl's love for her daddy."

"No!"

"It must have terrified them to think that you might tell. But you went back to your own bed in another part of the house. And the doors slammed shut. It was too terrible a betrayal for you to endure. So it got pushed into a back closet of your mind, and the door was locked. But Heidi, you had to push other things in there too, and lock them away. The love for the father. And your own sexual responses. Slam the doors. Forget. The way you've forgotten how Gretchen looked, forgotten her voice. It turned you off, Heidi. Sex is vile. The world is vile. Love is ugliness."

"Amateur diagnostics. Christ! It's the parlour game I'm most sick of."

"Look at me! Come on. One more little minute before you run and hide. You reverted all the way back. You regressed to seven years old. Then you slammed the door. Then you came at me like a she-tiger. Like rape. You couldn't have made it plainer."

"No. No."

"Don't lie, damn you! Don't hide! Who was I?"

She closed her eyes. Her lips moved. "Daddy."

"Who were you?"

"I was . . . me. And I was Gretchen too. All in one."

"How did you feel?"

". . . Aching. Empty. Wanting. As if something secret and delicious was starting to grow, something that could grow and burst, over and over. Then everything went dark and dead."

"Poor chick," I said. "It's all bottled up. It's all twisted and strange. So that everything he did was a denial of you the way you denied him. Janice Stanyard. Gloria. For about twelve fantastic seconds you started to break through. And you lost it. But it proves you could."

"No!"

"You want to enjoy your hang-up? You want to live a half-life in a half-world?"

She rolled her head from side to side and her hand tightened on mine. "No, but. . . ."

133

"But. . . ."

"It's no use. Gadge tried everything. Drinks, pills, different ways. It was just nightmare. Just all that terrible poking and jostling. So ugly." Her voice trailed off. "So stupid and degrading and . . . vile."

"Heidi, in that hallway shock turned your mind off, and your body came alive, and your body knew what it wanted."

"I don't want to be turned into an animal,"

"Like Gretchen? You damn fool, do you know why that girl in there triggered it? Because she looks like her mother did eighteen years ago. She's your half-sister."

She stiffened, yanked her hand away, sat up and stared down into my face. "Oh . . . my . . . God! . . . Oh . . . my GOD!"

"You sensed it, didn't you?"

"I could feel . . . something strange. Like an echo, like a memory I never had."

I moved up on to the couch beside her and took hold of both her hands. She looked at me, solemn and troubled, and extraordinarily lovely and alive. "And that girl in there is an animal?" I asked.

"No. No, of course not. She's a good person."

"So is Gloria. So is Janice Stanyard. So was your father. All this priss-prim condemnation act of yours is a by-product of what happened to you when you walked into that room at the wrong time, at the wrong time in your life and in your father's eighteen years ago."

She frowned. "It could be. Maybe. I don't know."

"Want to find out?"

"What do you mean?"

"After this is all over. After I'm through here, I'm going to find a place where the sun is hot and lasts all day. Come along with me. I'm the world's worst setup for screwed-up broads. I hate waste. You're worth special effort."

She bit her lip. "All that again? No."

"You responded to me once."

"That doesn't mean anything."

"You must have some strong motivation to break out in some kind of direction or you wouldn't have let your pretty partner, Mark Avanyan, buddy you up with his musician friend—VanSomething."

She gave a delicate little shudder. "Anna VanMaller. She finally started to arouse me. It was creepy and terrible. I kicked her and I ran and threw up. She was furious. I'd rather be . . . the way I am, even."

"Even?"

She tilted her head, then blushed deeply and looked down and away, but she didn't pull her hands away. "I guess that was a little too significant, Travis. Okay, I'm aware of the deficit. It's probably lousy, but I don't know how lousy because I don't know what it could be like."

"Just one rule. If you say yes, you can't call it off. You endure it, until I give up."

"Gadge gave up."

"I'm not Gadge. You're twenty-five. You are a beautiful woman, Heidi. What if this is the last chance?"

She pulled her hands away, shook herself as if returning to reality and stared at me with a little curl of contempt on her lips.

"So you'll make this terrible sacrifice, huh? Wow! I'm impressed. If you're the great lover who finds out how to turn me on, it gives you an ego as big as the *Tribune* Tower. And I can learn a wet smile, pose for a centrefold, and become a happy bunny. And if you try and try and I never make it, then you've had the loan of what I'm told is very superior equipment for God knows how long, and you can trudge away shaking your head and feeling sorry for the poor frigid woman. Tails you win, tails I lose, buddy. If foul-ups are your hobby, go find a different kind. I'm too bright to buy that line of crap, my friend. I'm not a volunteer playmate."

I got up and ambled around the semi-darkened room, scrubbing at my jaw with a thoughtful knuckle. She took very dead aim. She got inside. She made it sting. I will not fault my talent to kid myself.

I wandered, making bleak appraisals, and ended up standing behind the couch talking down at the top of her bowed blonde head.

"The first step has to be absolute honesty, Heidi. Okay. You are flat right, and you are flat wrong. Here's how you are right. I've got a plain simple old elemental urge to tumble you into the sack, on any terms. You have that cool remote princessly look in total contrast with a very exciting body and exciting way of moving and handling yourself. It intrigues. Man wants to possess. He wants to storm the castle, bust down the gates, and take over. But I think—I'm not really sure—but I think that if that was my total motive, I'm enough of a grown-up not to try to get to you by sneaking up on your blind side. Grabbing something because it looks great is kind of irresponsible. Life is not a candy store.

"Likewise, dear girl, life is not a playground full of playmates where all good men are supposed to come to the aid of old Hooo the Hef and dedicate themselves sincerely and with a sense of responsibility and mission to liberating the maximum number of receptive lassies from the chains and burdens of our Puritan heritage.

"I think my shtick, Heidi, is that I enjoy all the aspects of a woman. I like the way their minds work. I like the sometimes wonderful and sometimes nutty ways they figure things out and relate themselves to reality. I like the arguments, the laughs, the quarrels, the competitions, the making up. A nearby girl makes the sky bluer, the drinks better, the food tastier. She gives the days more texture, and you know it is happening to her in the same way.

"How this relates to Heidi Geis Trumbill is that I have the feeling it is a damned shame you stand outside the gates with a kind of wistful curiosity about what it's like inside. I want to be sort of a guide, showing off new and pretty country to the tourist. Life is so damned valuable and so totally miraculous, and they give you such a stingy little hunk of it from womb to tomb, you ought to use all the parts of it there are. I guess I would say that I want to be friends. A friend wants to help a friend. I want to peel away that suspicion and contention because I don't think it's really what you're like. If we can get friendship going, then maybe we can get a good physical intimacy going, and from that we can fall into a kind of love or fall into an affection close to love. If it happens, it adds up to more than the sum of the two people, and it is that extra part out of nowhere that has made all the songs and the poetry and the art.

"So it wouldn't be a performance. No great-lover syndrome. No erotic tricks, no Mother McGee's home-cooked aphrodisiacs. The only trick would be, I guess, to get you to like yourself a little. Then the rest would come.

"So you know what's wrong with the whole statement, just as I do. Why doesn't he get his own true permanent forever girl? Maybe it is some kind of emotional immaturity. Somehow I don't think so. I have a theory I can't prove. I know this. If I became one woman's permanent emotional stability and security, there would be a moral obligation on my part

136

to change the way I live, because I'd have no right to ask her to buy a piece of my risk-taking. Yet risk is so essential to me —for reasons I can only guess at—giving it up would make me a different kind of man. I don't think I'd like him. I don't think she would. I don't know if all this is excuse, explanation, sales talk or what. I really don't know. It's what I *think* I think."

I stood there. She did not move or speak. I heard a deep sigh. Then in a lithe movement she turned, rolling up on to her knees, and stood on her knees looking up at me across the back of the couch. Her eyes were evasive. She put her hands out and I took them.

"So I'll try friendship," she said. "I've tried everything else. I don't even know very much about being a friend, Travis. I should make some gesture to seal the bargain, I suppose."

She uplifted her face, eyes closed, mouth offered. But I could tell that she was steeling herself. Her hands had a clammy feel of nervous tension. So, briefly and lightly, I kissed one closed eye and then the other, I released her hands and said, "Contract confirmed."

She looked startled, stepped backward off the couch, and said, "You kind of lost me a little with that risk-taking part."

"I conned John Andrus into giving me that card. I knew Gloria before your father did. They met down in Lauderdale. I stood up with them when they got married. She phoned me in Florida and asked me to come up and help. You could say I'm in the salvage business. Suppose some very sly, slick, sleek operator worked on you and suckered you out of the settlement Gadge made on you. The statutes are full of gimmicks. Semi-legal theft. I might be induced to give it a try. Whatever I could recover, I'd keep half. Half is better than nothing. No recovery, and I've gambled my expenses and lost. Make a recovery, and expenses come off the top before I split. Somehow people on a dead run with a jaw full of stolen meat react badly to having it taken away from them."

She sat and stared at me. "Half? Half of six hundred thousand?"

"Half of her end of it, and that would be subject to adjustment. The circumstances are always different. You can see how far I would have got with you if I told you who I was trying to help."

"She sent for you?"

"Surprise?"

137

"I want to be able to keep hating her, Travis."

"Then don't get to know her, if there's ever any chance left for you to get to know her."

"Do you know where the money went?"

"I might. I don't know. Susan Kemmer could be the key." She looked toward the bedroom. "She *knows*?"

"I don't think so. But she knows things I have to know."

"Poor little doll. I must have frightened her." She got up and went to the bedroom. There was a line of light under the door. I hung back. Heidi knocked and the girl said to come in.

In a little while Heidi came back out and left the door open and beckoned me back into the living-room. "She was just sitting in there in the chair all dressed. Quiet as a mouse. I apologized for walking in on her before. I said I thought she was sleeping. She just shrugged and said it didn't matter. I told her you want to talk to her. Do you want me to be there?"

"It might help. But it might get ugly. Don't try to step in unless I cue you. The cue word is hell, said loudly. Then you hustle to her and hug her and comfort her and chew me out. You're the guy in the white hat."

I went in with her. Heidi sat on the bed. The girl had made the bed. I leaned against a chest of drawers. "Well, Susan, I guess we'd better start levelling with each other."

"There's nothing I want to talk about, Mr. McGee."

"I know that. But you have to."

"I don't have to."

"It won't keep me from finding out. It will just save me a lot of time and effort. I know you caught that North Central bus at Bureau, at the crossroads, at a place called Sheen's, a hundred miles from here. I know that Saul and Gretchen and you five kids left Chicago on Sunday the 22nd of August in the car Saul bought at the place he worked and fixed up. You were towing a U-Haul trailer. So the little family holed up a hundred miles west of here almost four months ago. Saul's parole period was over. That's just a sample, honey. I'm not going to tell you all I know. I'm going to hold back so that I can tell if you're lying to me."

She stared at me, startled, wary, worried. "*You* don't want to help me. You fooled Mrs. Stanyard too. You're after *him*!"

"The easiest way to atrract attention would be to keep you kids out of school. And he apparently wanted to lay low. So all I have to do is drive over there with you in the morning and hit the high schools in the area and find out which one you've been going to. Then get the home address from the school."

"No. Please. *Please* don't."

"Why the *hell* are you being so stubborn, girl?"

Heidi hurried to her on cue, sat on the arm of the chair, and put an arm around Susan and glowered at me and said, "Stop bullying her!" Susan had begun to cry.

"Stubborn is bad enough without being stupid too."

"She's *not* stupid!"

"Sure she is. She takes after her mother. She takes after Gretchen."

"She's not my real mother!" Susan declared.

I shook my head sadly. "Honey, Gretchen is your real mother and Dr. Geis was your father. And your friend and protector there is your big half-sister. Say hello to Sister Heidi."

And Heidi stopped faking it. "Damn you!" she yelled at me, her face pink. "What are you trying to *do* to her!"

"Shake her up. She needs it."

"Leave her *alone*!"

I smiled. "Okay, sis. You tell her the tender love story." I closed the bedroom door on my way out. I sat in the living-room and picked up an art magazine and began leafing through it. I was a great guy. I did things to people for their own good. It gave me that nice warm righteous glow.

The art magazine told me that when abstract expressionism reflected utter disenchantment with the dream it still reverted to rhetorical simplifications even in its impiety, and that it is not a unified stylistic entity because of its advocacy of alien ideas on the basis of a homiletic approach to experience.

Funny I'd never realized it.

After I spent twenty minutes admiring my sterling charac-ter, Heidi came out red-eyed and wan and said, "It's tearing her to ribbons. She's had all she can take."

"Loan me your white hat and stay here," I said, and went in. The girl looked at me. It's the look the caged things have in small roadside stands.

I sat on the bed and said, "Growing up hurts, kid."

"You made everything awful."

"Your father was a fine man. Possibly a great man. Your mother was a sweet dumb sexy kid and she caught him at the wrong time or the right time, and there you sprouted. Miracle of life. Ah, sweet mystery. Et cetera."

"But why didn't he ever want to see me?"

139

"Let me see now. Could it be because he thought you might not be old enough to take that kind of a jar? And maybe you aren't old enough yet. He made the deal he thought best for you long ago. It didn't turn out so great. But he knew you did. He paid to have you checked out. He liked the report. I think it would be safe to say he was proud of you. But I have the feeling that his little affair with the housekeeper's daughter cost him a lot more than the annuity and paying to have reports made on you, and the ten thousand he left with Mrs. Stanyard. I have the feeling his little bout with statutory rape eventually and indirectly cost him just about everything he ever saved. Six hundred thousand dollars. And I think Saul Gorba got it."

"No! Oh, no, it wasn't anything like that. Honest. They explained it all to us kids. Saul tried to go straight, really. But there was a man at the body shop. He knew Saul had a prison record. So he started stealing. It was some way of putting the wrong amount on the bills and receipts. Saul explained it. Then the man put some forms in the back of Saul's locker and he found them and he knew what was happening, and he was going to be framed. Momma was so upset. Saul said that with his record he didn't have a prayer. He said he'd be sent back to prison and he said that he was pretty sure the welfare would take over and split us up and call Momma an unfit mother on account of they'd picked her up twice in Chicago on D and D and let her off with a fine, but it was on the record. He said our only chance was to just leave. He said he'd found us a nice place in the country, and we weren't to tell anybody we were leaving."

"It sounded logical to you?"

"It was the only way we could stay together as a family." She frowned. "I would be all right, but it would be terrible for Julian and Freda. I don't think Freddy cares one way or another. And Tommy is only six. He needs the rest of us."

"Where did you go?"

"Saul rented a farmhouse. It's RFD 3 Box 80, Princeton. It's off the Depue Road, all by itself at the end of a little dirt road. It's about two and a half miles from Bureau cross-roads."

"Nice place?"

"Kind of shacky, but there's lots of room. Forty acres. Everything had grown up weeds and bushes. It had been empty a long time. They said we couldn't attract any attention. Our name was going to be Farley. And we had moved there from Chicago for Saul's health. We were going to farm it. We all had to practise the name. He put the Cadillac in one of the sheds and nailed up the door. He walked out and hitch-hiked and came back the next day with an old pick-up truck. He made a kind of workshop in another shed. When it was time to go back to school, he had our school records. He came back to the city and got them and he changed the names so you couldn't tell. They had drivers' licences and he fixed up birth certificates for us and everything. He said we were going to be the Farley family for the rest of our lives, and we shouldn't ever tell."

"Did you mind that?"

"Nobody minded much. Anything is okay with Momma, the way she is. It made me feel bad that I couldn't write to my friends. They'd never know what happened to me. It was hard to get used to it being so quiet all the time. But after a while it didn't seem so quiet. You just heard other things. Wind and birds and bugs."

"Did your mother or Saul try to find work?"

"No. Saul would go away once in a while and be gone overnight. He'd go in the old truck. We all worked fixing the old place up for the winter. Then one day when we came home on the school bus there wasn't anybody there. That was . . . just three weeks ago today. We thought they'd gone off in the truck. Saul came back alone in the truck and he wanted to know where Momma was. We told him she was gone when we came home. I looked and found that a suitcase and a lot of her clothes were gone. Saul cursed and stormed around. He said we'd just have to all sit tight and wait for her to come back. It bothered him a lot. I'd wake up in the night and hear him walking around downstairs."

"He did beat you up?"

"He was upset and he'd been drinking. All night maybe. He came into my room before daylight and he woke me up and handed me my coat and told me to come along and not wake the other kids. He said he had something to tell me about my mother. We went out to his workshop place. He had wired it for lights and he had a space heater going. He acted strange and he kept looking at me in a funny way. He had me sit down on the cot and he sat and put his arm around me and he was kind of half-crying. He said he was pretty sure that she had been gone so long now, she was never coming back.

141

"I told him I thought she'd be back and he told me she had threatened to go away for good because they hadn't been getting along. He kept rubbing his hand up and down my arm. He said there were just the two of us now to take care of everything. He said I was just like a regular mother to the other kids. He said I was a better mother in every way than she was. He said we had to stick together. I said I'd better go back to bed and I started to stand up, but he got my wrists and pushed me down flat on the cot. He lay down beside me and put my wrists around behind me and held them there in one hand, hurting me.

"In a funny whispery little voice he said everything was going to be wonderful. He said he loved me, and we were going to be a little family, just him and me and little Tommy, and we were going to leave soon and drive to Mexico in the Cadillac, just the three of us, and he was going to divorce Momma and marry me and we'd live in a big house with a swimming pool and have servants. He said that on the way out of town when we were fifty miles away he'd call the welfare to take care of the other three and they'd be in good hands. He kept stroking me with his free hand and I was starting to cry and begging him to stop. He kissed my neck and told me I was his little darling and he had been watching me ever since we'd left Chicago, and he had just one more little thing to take care of and then we would go on a wonderful trip. Then he opened my coat and pushed his hand up under my pyjama top and started squeezing and rubbing me. It scared me so I yanked my wrists loose and I hit at him and kicked him and he fell backward off the cot. I tried to get by him and get out but he grabbed me and pulled me down and then he got up and picked me up and threw me back on to the cot. He said I was old enough and big enough for it, so I better relax and enjoy it, because I was going to have a lot of chances to get used to it. I remember scratching and biting and kicking at him and all of a sudden he was on the floor again, kneeling, all hunched over, looking up at me and holding on to himself.

"His eyes are funny. They're sort of pale brown but when he gets mad they look yellow. Golden almost. He stood up slowly and when I tried to dodge around him he hit me in the mouth with his fist and knocked me down. He picked me up and hit me a lot more times, holding me with one hand and hitting me with the other. It all got blurred. He let go of me and I fell down and he kicked me a couple of times and went away and left me there. It was getting light. Pretty soon I could get up and I went back to my room. I didn't see him. I locked the door. Mr. McGee, I knew that if I went down to the road and hitched a ride into Princeton and told the police, he'd go to jail and the welfare would get us. And I knew if I stayed there, he'd keep at me until he got what he wanted. When the kids knocked on the door to find out about breakfast I said I was sick and I told Freda and Julian to help Freddy get breakfast for everybody. I stayed in there all day. After everybody was asleep, I sneaked down and got something to eat. I knew I was safe because I could hear Saul snoring. You can always hear him all over the upstairs part after he's had a lot of beer. I took food up to my room. Monday morning when Freddy knocked at my door I said I was better but I wasn't well enough to go to school. I'd remembered about Mrs. Stanyard. He reminded me, saying I better not go to her. I had the money I'd been putting away to buy baby chicks in the spring. I heard the truck go rattling out about two o'clock, so I got dressed and left and cut across lots and came out on the Depue Road and followed it to Route 26 and walked to the crossroads where I'd heard you could get a bus to Chicago.

"The waitress at Sheen's was nice. She let me lie down in back on a couch in a room off the kitchen, and she brought me things to eat even though I couldn't pay for them. I told her I fell downstairs. She said her boyfriend had a bad temper too. I think that when . . . Momma comes back everything will be all right again. But he couldn't have stolen all that money you said."

"He had to steal something."

"What do you mean?"

"What did seven of you live on for four months?"

"Oh, it was hardly any rent way out away from anything in that shacky place, and we've always had that four hundred and thirty-three dollars every month."

"Not since August first, Susan. The company is holding four cheques right now. The January one will be the last one made out to your mother. In February it starts to come directly to you, if they can manage to find out where you are."

She stared at me and even with the puffed lids she opened her eyes as wide as I had seen them. "But . . . I thought that was where she got the money to . . . to go on a vacation!"

"Did Saul quarrel much with her?"

"Oh yes. But it. . . ." She stopped and put her hand to her throat. "No! He *wouldn't*!"

"Let's hope it's a lousy guess."

She said, "I have to get back there! I left Freddy a note. I said I was going to go off to get Momma and bring her home and not to worry, and be good, and help each other and not fight. If he . . . if he. . . ." She could not continue.

"Sit tight, honey. Draw me a map so I can find the place. I am a registered licensed sneak. I'll go check on your clan, gather them up, and haul them back here. You've got more friends on your side than you know what to do with. Me, Heidi, Mrs. Stanyard. And there's always your grandmammy, Mrs. Ottlo."

"She doesn't like children very much," Susan explained. "I think they make her nervous."

Heidi spoke from the doorway, startling me. "She's right, you know. When we were little if we got in her way in the kitchen when she was busy, she'd do things that would hurt like fury, like snapping your ear with a finger-nail, and giving a little pinch and twisting at the same time. She'd laugh but it was . . . kind of a mean laugh." She tilted her head and frowned. "I remember once Gretchen showing us her back. She took her blouse off. She must have been about thirteen, and that would make me about four and Roger was probably eight. Anna had thrashed her with a belt. I can remember the marks still, the dark places and the little streaks where it had broken the skin."

"Please hurry," Susan said to me.

ELEVEN

I TOOK Heidi into the outside corridor beyond her red door and said, "Settle her down. Get a sleeping pill into her. I'm not going to go fumbling around in the boonies in the black black night. And I don't think he's going to do any harm to those kids. I've got a hunch they might be there alone, and Saul

Gorba may be rocketing south with the loot. The boy is fifteen. He should be able to cope."

"When are you going out?"

"In time to pick a nice observation post and see who gets on the school bus. I'll report by phone. Like having a sister?"

"I don't know how I feel yet. I like her."

"A staunch one. The kind that knows how to cope. Go in and be family. She needs it."

"Okay." She gave me a nervous smile. I guess it is the smile dentists see when the patient walks in and looks at the chair and the drills and then at the dentist. "I could need it too."

"So cosy each other, Heidi. Everybody has days like this."

The smile turned wry. "That's a little hard to believe."

I had noticed a change in her. The little provocative animal grace of her movements was gone. She had taken to walking like a stick doll. But at the same time she had stopped saying no. I knew she kept remembering the bargain she had made. But there was a certain little awareness mixed with trepidation. I had the feeling that if I made a sudden movement she would make exactly the same protective gestures Susan had made when we had looked into the room and seen her in the light from the hallway.

I rested my hand on the warm shoulder under the off-white knit and felt her tense up, and saw her throat work in a convulsive swallow.

I leaned and kissed her just to the starboard of the right eye and gave her shoulder a little pat and said, "Walk out there on that stage and give it all you've got, Gwendolyn, and I'll make you a star."

"Oh God, McGee, am I that obvious?"

"It's only terror, honey. No worse than a bad cold."

I drove famished to my hotel, ate hugely and well, and found no messages waiting. It was nine-forty-five when I got to the house that Fort built, out at Lake Pointe. Bits of light shone through the cracks in the drawn draperies and closed blinds.

Anna called through the door. "Ya? Ya?"

"McGee again, Anna."

I heard the rattle of chain and the chunking of the bolt, and she opened the door part way and said, "Comen in, please sir."

I slid through and she rebolted and rechained the door. She was concealing something in the folds of her dress and when she saw that I was aware of it, she held it out, a big ugly Army issue Colt ·45 automatic pistol. She held it clumsily.

"Are you frightened of something?"

"Hear noises, maybe. Herr Doktor's gun."

I took it from her. Full clip, a round in the chamber and the safety on. I put it on the table beside the door.

"How is she? How is the dear little missus?"

"I'll phone from here in a little while and find out. Anna, we have to have a heart-to-heart talk. And it might make you very unhappy."

She accepted the formality of the situation. She invited me into the kitchen into the booth. She served us coffee and little cakes and eased herself shyly into the booth across from me.

I had to start by saying that I knew Susan had been fathered by Fortner Geis. It distressed her that I should know. She acted as if it was her own guilt, her own shame. She kept telling me how "goot" the Doktor had been, and what a "bat" girl Gretchen was. Very stupid girl. You have to do your best. Some people are "veak." Gretchen had a veakness for men. Five children, four fathers.

Yes, she said, she had made it a habit to go visit Saul and Gretchen every Sunday. If a daughter tries, it is a duty, *nein*? They had married officially at her urging. True Saul Gorba was a criminal, a veak man, but brilliant. A pleasure to talk to. In prison he had studied many things. Languages. German. He had learned German so quickly. She helped him with his accent, with the idioms. She had the Germanic reverence for the erudite mind. She said she would take along small gifts for the *kinder*, help Gretchen cook the dinner, mend the clothes of the *kinder*, of them all a family to make.

Then poof. Shrug. Cast eyes heavenward. What goot is it? They are gone. No message, no word, no letter. Like animals of the forest. No consideration. It is never to try again with such a daughter, you can believe.

Key question. Anna, did you talk about Doctor Geis? Did you talk about Gloria and Heidi and Roger to Saul and Gretchen?

Deep blush, bowed head, contrite little nod. What is harm to talk? It is her life more with this family than that one, *nein*? A good man dying slowly, the dear wife trying to hold death back from him by love, his own children hating the wife, it is a sadness, and who else to talk to?

Did Saul encourage such talk? Did he ask questions?

Oh yes. Why asking?

And you know of the missing money?

She said with a firmness that whatever the Doktor did, it was right. One should trust.

So it was time to pull the pin. "Anna, I am convinced that Saul Gorba used the information he got from you to extort all that money from Dr. Geis."

Much the same effect could have been achieved by cleaving her open from the crown of her head to the brow line.

"*Lieber Gott!*" she whispered. "Can not be. Can not *be*! The Doktor would not give to him!"

"I don't think the Doctor knew who he was giving the money to. Someone gave him some little demonstrations. Someone said, in effect, you are dying and you know it. Dying is at best a lonely thing. If you want to hang on to all the money that won't do you any good anyway, you can really die alone. I have shown you how easily it can be done. Your grandson, your second wife, Nurse Stanyard, your daughter Heidi, and the daughter you had by Gretchen will all predecease you. I think he made a logical decision. I think he sensed he was dealing with somebody merciless and perhaps a little mad. And I think he was strong enough to make his decision and then not let it bother him. He made sure Heidi got a good settlement from Trumbill. He saved out a single insurance policy for Gloria. Susan was already taken care of."

She mumbled and groaned about the cruelty of it, about how she could not believe it. Then her eyes widened and she said, "Ah! With the money he left. They ran far."

"Not very far. Now I have to ask you if you will take the responsibility for your five grandchildren."

"How do you mean, sir?"

"Gloria told me you plan to go to Florida and stay with your old friend Mrs. Kemmer. Let me see. Her son Karl fathered one of the tribe before he died, didn't he?"

"Freddy. Strong boy."

"Suppose I bring all five of them to you tomorrow and drop them in your lap. Susan's cheques haven't been cashed for four months. There's a sizeable emergency fund too. They are going to need stability and order. Susan is responsible and mature and devoted to the younger ones. There'd be money to set up a place here or in Florida. I couldn't promise anything, but I think there might be some financial help from Heidi to make college possible for Susan. How about it?"

"But there is Gretchen!"

"I don't think so. It's only a hunch, but I better tell you. I don't want to, believe me. I think she's dead. I think Saul killed her. She disappeared three weeks ago. And Saul has the hots for Susan. He gave her a very bad time. Gretchen drank. She wasn't smart. She was too friendly. She talked too much."

Anna Ottlo got up with astonishing agility and pulled her apron up over her head. It was a gesture I had heard of but never seen. She trotted into a sort of pantry arrangement off the kitchen and I could hear her in there whuffling and snorting and moaning. I ate a little cake. It didn't swallow readily. I washed it down with cooling coffee. She came trudging back, knuckling her eyes like a fat child. She plumped herself down and sighed and shook her head.

"I'm going to go jounce Gorba around some. He's going to get a real good chance to work on his languages if they don't electrocute him. He can pick up Croatian, Tasmanian, and Urdu. He can have a ball. But even with what all those kids have been through, this will shake them badly."

She sighed again. She looked down at her hands, at the palms and then the backs. "All the life," she said. "Verk, verk, verk. I have the arthritis. I have the high blood. Cook, clean, sew, scrub for children? Six years is the little one. How much more years of that? Nerves make the heart flutter like a bird and the eyes go black. No. I am sorry. After the long verk there is rest. I must have. Susan is eighteen years soon, ya? With those cheques I think the judge says she can have the brothers and sister, take care. Maybe the welfare comes and looks sometimes to make sure. She is young. She can do it. I know that one. She would want it. A good lawyer could fix, *nein*? Maybe I am a selfish old woman. Too bad. Did I ask Gretchen to have five *kinder*? Life is too hard. Time to sit on the porch now. Rock the chair. Warm in the sunshine. Don't blame, please sir."

"Okay. I don't blame. W. C. Fields had a thing about children too."

"Who? Who?"

"Skip it." I looked at my watch. "Want to get on an extension while I find out about Gloria?"

"Oh yes!"

The operator at the hospital had me hold. I had a two-minute wait before Hayes Wyatt in his dusty, reedy voice said, "Mr. McGee?"

"Yes, Doctor."

"Bad news, I'm afraid. Pneumonia. Pulmonary edema, and we can't seem to hit it with antibiotics. Did a thoracotomy. Got her in a tent and a good team doing everything indicated, but we can't seem to make a dent in the fever. Almost a hundred and five, and if we get another three-tenths we're going to pack her in ice. So I haven't the faintest idea how much residual disturbance we've got from the dose she took, and the question may be academic. The first thing is to try to get her through the night. I better get back there, but here's someone who wants to talk to you."

"Travis? Janice Stanyard. I'm on the case with Dr. Wyatt."

"Is she going to make it?"

"If she's tough enough. I wondered how. . . ."

"Everything is just fine. How would you respond to my dumping five kids on you tomorrow for an indefinite stay? Buy you some rollaways. Bedding, chests of drawers, cardboard closets."

"I would love it!"

"Go back to work, woman."

"Yes sir!"

"I'm just checking possibilities. Don't count on the kids for sure."

"All right, but really I would. . . ."

"I believe you. When should I phone back to check?"

"It will go one way or another by dawn, I would guess."

Anna let me out. She was snuffling. She said Mrs. Stanyard was a nice lady.

I placed my dawn phone call long-distance, from a red brick Georgian motel just off the Interstate west of Peru, Illinois. My heart sank when I was told that Dr. Wyatt had left the hospital. I asked for Janice Stanyard. She came on, her voice blurred and dragging with exhaustion. "She was tough enough, Travis."

"Thank God!"

"She's sleeping now. I'm about to go home and do some of the same. She's going to be very weak. And we don't know about the other yet."

I went out into a bright grey Wednesday world to find that

149

a warm wind was blowing in from somewhere. Maybe all the way up from McGee country. I had driven through inches of sticky snow, but it had all been transformed into busy water, hustling down every slope it could find. I had no idea how early the school bus picked up the kids. I had forgotten to ask Susan. I did know that the coming Friday was the last day before Christmas holidays, And I knew the kids walked out to Depue Road and caught the bus there. The place was marked on the map Susan had drawn for me.

I knew that getting into position was more important than my morning stomach. It was flat lands, with a few gentle rolls and dips and hollows. It all looked bleak in the overcast morning light. There were some substantial farms, all trimmed and tended, and there were deserted places with tumbled buildings, fencing rusting away, leafless scrub tall in the silent fields, and it made you wonder how this one had made it and that one hadn't.

I parked by a produce stand on Route 26, shuttered and vacant. I was there a little before seven, and I had a forty-minute wait before I saw the yellow bus in my side mirror, coming around the bend. I let it get out of sight before I started up. I hung well back and then picked up speed after it made the turn on to Depue Road. Susan had said their dirt road was a mile from the corner and came in on the right, and I could tell it by the bright red paint on the post that held up the mailbox. There was no name on the mailbox.

I saw the red post all right. The bus didn't even hesitate. It rolled on by. I looked up the muddy rutted road and, half-obscured by a knoll, I saw what had to be the house, set way back, two storeys, steep, swaybacked roof, stingy little windows and not many of them, clapboards painted a dirty grey white. Two shutters crooked, one missing. A cheerless and isolated place.

Once well past it I dropped back and kept the bus just barely in sight. I tried to figure it out. Okay, the procedure would be to slow down, maybe look up the road to see if the kids were coming on the run. Stop and blow the horn maybe. So the driver knew they weren't going to be there. So I'd better know what he'd been told.

Seven miles further, at the big central school complex, I found out the driver was a she, a brawny, likely, and clear-eyed lass in ski pants, mackinaw, and stocking cap, with shoulders like Arnold Palmer.

"Excuse me," I said, with my best civil-service smile and patronizing manner. "District survey. A little spot check on percentage of equipment utilization. Hope you didn't get nervous to have me following you."

"Nervous? What about?"

I glanced at Susan's map and put it away. "My route sheet shows that your first stop on Depue Road is a mile from the corner. Five children. Farley."

"Got on at Shottlehauster's. Four. One's sick Oldest. High school senior."

"Got on where?"

She raised her voice as though addressing the deaf, and enunciated more clearly. "Shottlehauster's. Shottlehauster's. The big place on 26 three mile afore Farley's. They're staying there a time."

"Oh. I see. Thank you."

"Don't mention it."

So I went back a lot faster than I had come. I guessed that when she said three mile she meant three mile. But she had been wrong. It was three miles and one half of a tenth of a mile to the giant wine-red mailbox, "Shottlehauster" lettered in white in elegant script to a broad gravel drive, a long low white ranch-style house, and beyond, the quonset equipment shed, white barns, triple silo standing against the wide march of rich and pampered farmland. I turned in, parked and got out, hesitating over whether to go to the front of the house or the back. I could hear a loud twanging and thumping of folk-rock. A bakery truck was parked at an angle near the back entrance. Darling Bakery. "Fresh as a stolen Kiss." "Darling Bread is Triple Enriched." Bright blue and lemon-yellow décor.

At this time of day the back door would be more customary, I decided, for a hardworking credit-bureau fellow. To get to the back door I had to pass the kitchen windows. In the dingy morning the fluorescents were all on, bright enough so that it was like glancing through the tied-back café curtains into a stage set, the floor level in there maybe three feet higher than the level of the gravel driveway. I would say I was opposite that first window frozen in midstride for a second and a half. It took half a second to figure out what I was looking at, and half a second of confirming it, and half a second to get my direction reversed and get out of the way.

The Darling Bread Boy was bellied up to a long efficient counter top. Blue work shirt to match his truck. "Darling"

151

embroidered in an arc across chunk shoulders. But the "a" and the "n" in "Darling" were covered by two gigantic vertical fuzzy pink caterpillars. Then beyond the edge of the centre island in the kitchen I saw the lady feet in fuzzy white socks, clamped and locked together, pressing quite neatly the tail of the blue shirt against his butt. Saw one hairy straining leg with his trousers puddled around the ankle. Caterpillars became her sweatered forearms, her hands hooked back over the hanging-on place of the trapezius muscles, as though trying to chin herself. And over the Bread Boy shoulder was her effortful jouncing bouncing face, eyes squinched tight shut, mouth raw, like indeed with the struggle to chin herself on that horrizontal bar of muscle. The twangity-thump of country git-ar with electronic assist came from the truck radio (paternalistic bakery management) and from the kitchen radio in unison, and for a couple of micro-seconds before I sorted the scene out I had thought he was attempting a crude, vulgar, unskilled version of some contemporary dance. But it was busy old rub-a-dub-dub, humpety-rump, dumpety-bump, with the counter-topped farm wife all wedged and braced.

I fled bemused to my rental. The idling truck made little pops and puffs of exhaust smoke. Where the hell did they think they were? Westport? Bucks County? Didn't they know this was the heartland of America? Didn't she know Jack LaLanne was the only acceptable morning exercise for the busy house-wife?

I started the car engine and put the automatic shift into drive and kept my foot on the brake pedal. I wondered if maybe it was the architecture which had debauched her. I could not conceive of it happening in the traditional old farm kitchens. But she could see slightly glossier versions of her own fluor-escence, stainless steel, ceramic island, rubber tile, pastel enamels, warm wood panelling in the Hollywood product on both Big Screen and home tube, so there she was on the set, and she had to say the lines, but after you said the lines enough times all of a sudden you'd get interrupted by some-thing a little more direct than a commercial message from your sponsor. But it didn't count too much because it was as un-real sort of as a giant hand coming up out of the suds, or a washer going up like an elevator, or a nut riding a horse through the back yard and turning everything radiant white.

The instant Darling Boy came trotting into view I started

ahead so that he could be certain he had glimpsed my arrival. Chunky redhead, with a freckly good-natured, clenched-fist face, carrying cheerfully wrapped bakery items in his big blue alluminium home-delivery basket. He gave me a glance, a happy morning nod and grin, and swung aboard his service van and rolled on out, a thousand loud guitars fading down the road, but still playing faintly inside the house.

The incident had decided me in favour of the front door. Storm door, then a big white front door with a narrow insert of vertical glass. Brass knocker shaped like the American eagle. Brass and pearl bell button which, when pushed, set off the biggest and most complicated chime set in the Sears catalogue. When it had played through to its finish, faintly heard through the doors, I felt like applauding. I waited and then thumbed them into encore, and when the presentation number was half over I saw her coming toward the door, patting her hair, hitching at her clothes, giving that sucked-in bite that goes with fresh lipstick.

She opened the door inward, pushed the storm door open six inches and with a cheery smile, said, "You want Harry, he had to go up to Moline again early, but he ought to be home by supper."

She was weathering the downslope of the thirties very nicely, a small sturdy woman with a wide face, pretty eyes, network of grin wrinkles, mop of curly dark hair with a first touch of white ones over her ears. Fuzzy pink sweater, denim ranch pants in stretch fabric. White moccasins, white socks. A shapely and durable figure, breasts rather small and abrupt under the pink fuzz.

"You're Mrs. Shottlehauster?"

"Yes, but honest to Betsy, if you're selling something I just haven't got the time, and you can believe it."

"I'm not selling anything, and you can believe it. I'm trying to get a credit report on some people named Farley on Depue Road, and I'm not having much luck. I found out their kids know your kids. I don't want to bother you, but if you could spare just a minute or two to answer some questions. . . ."

"Heck, I can spare time for that. You come right on in, Mr. . . ."

"McGee. Travis McGee, ma'am."

"Well, I'm Mildred Shottlehauster," she said, leading me through the entrance hallway into a two-level living-room decorated in too many colours and patterns, and too densely populated with furniture, some of it good, and most of it borax.

"You sit right there and be comfortable," she said. "We've got those four Farley kids staying with us, and I certainly would like to know how long, not that they're any special problem or anything. I've got my six, and once you get up to six I guess it doesn't make too much difference if you have six or ten. And they're really good kids. They're almost *too* meek and quiet and polite. They make mine seem like wild Indians or something. Mine are sixteen, fourteen, twelve, eleven, eight and seven so. . . ."

"I'd never believe it, Mrs. S."

"Well *thank* you, kind sir, she said. Anyhoo, the Farley children seem to fit right in and actually there's less fighting and squabbling when they're here. Harry and I are just doing the neighbourly thing. Monday night it was, just on toward dark, you remember how raw and nasty it was, Mr. Farley came to the door and wouldn't come in. He hemmed and hawed and said that his wife had to go to Chicago, and Susan, the oldest—a perfectly darling girl she'd gone off to join her mother and he suddenly found out that he had to go on a business trip for a few days and he didn't want to leave the other four alone and could we give them bed and board for a few days. He said he could pay for it. Well, we forgave him for offering money for a neighbourly deed because . . . well, that family is right off the city streets and they can't be expected to know how we do things here in the country. When we said he certainly could bring them over, he said they were out in the truck, and so they were, chilled to the very bone. They came shivering in with their little bags and bundles of clothes and toothbrushes. I must confess I had qualms about my pack getting too friendly with those kids when they first came here. I mean they are sort of underprivileged, and you don't know what nasty tricks and habits children can pick up in the slums, and pass along, do you? It was last August my Bruce came racing home to tell me some family named Farley had moved into the old Duggins place. It's been empty three years since old Sam died, and he must have been older than God, and his only kin a sister in Seattle who couldn't care less, and nobody knew she'd even put it up for rent with that Country Estate Agency over in Princeton, but it's plain to see it's the kind of run-down place you could get for practically nothing, not like when you're nearer the city and they get

154

picked up for vacation houses and so on. But you can believe it, those Farley kids, Freda and Julian and Freddy and Tommy, they're dandy kids. What did you want to ask me? Ooops, I've got to go check the pies. I got stuck again. Four cherry pies for the Mission Aid supper and my dang oven thermostat is screwjee. Would you like some coffee, Mr. McGee? It's on the stove. Come on along."

I followed her out toward the whomping of the music, and she twisted the dial down to background size with a single expert tweak as she went by the radio. "I caught the coffee thing from Harry," she said. "He was in the Navy, so it's always on the fire, grind our own beans, never let it begin to bubble, like some people are about wine, I guess." And as she spoke she deftly assembled tall white cup and saucer, poured it steaming rich, slid it into position at the end of the centre island which was a breakfast bar, put sugar and cream within reach. She went over and stood at her eye-level wall oven, all copper and chrome, and peered in through the glass front at her pies.

"The only way I'm going to be able to tell is from the colour of the crust. Lousy thermostat. Hey, want a cinnamon pecan roll? The bakery just delivered fresh, and they're the special this week."

She poured coffee for herself, got out the butter and the rolls, and sat around the corner of the bar end of the island at my left.

"Marvellous coffee, Mrs. Shottlehauster."

"Speciality of the house, thank you kind sir she said. What is it the Farleys want to buy?"

"I don't know. We're a service organization and we work for a lot of different client companies. The point is are they a good credit risk up to such and such an amount."

She munched slowly, frowning. The pad of muscle at the corner of her jaw bulged with each bite. There was a flake of cooked sugar on her narrow underlip and her tongue slipped cleverly out and hooked it in. "I like to try to be fair to everybody. So I just couldn't say. It just depends on how much they can put into the spring planting, if they know what to plant, if they know how to go about getting help from the county agent and the state, if they're all willing to work like Arabian slaves. . . . I just don't know, honestly. Mr. Farley is well-spoken. You can tell he's had some advantages. I tried to be neighbourly, and so did a couple of other women, but we spread the word that nobody else need waste their time. I stopped there last September and didn't even get invited in. They just stared at me, and I had the idea they were laughing at me somehow. You know? She's a big heavy woman, coarse-looking, and I don't want to hurt their chances, but she smelled like a brewery, and it was a hot day and she wasn't . . . properly covered up. I guess that kind of thing doesn't mean much on a credit report."

"It's very helpful, really."

"I've been noticing what a wonderful tan you've got, Mr. McGee."

"I just got transferred up here from the Southwest. We get moved around a lot."

"I guess you must think I'm some kind of a nut, inviting you in and all, and being absolutely all alone here until the bus brings the kids back, but I've got a sixth sense about people, and there's a 16-gauge automatic shotgun standing in the corner there by the front door and you wouldn't have got a foot over the doorstep if I hadn't known right off you were perfectly all right, if I hadn't known I could trust you."

"I do appreciate that."

She smiled at me, and her pretty eyes had a slightly glazed look and they seemed to go in and out of focus. Her hand shook as she lifted the coffee cup. As she put it down she took a high quick shallow breath, shuddered, and her tongue hooked at crumbs that weren't there. Under the brightness of the artificial daylight I saw a little sheen of perspiration on her forehead and upper lip. A gentle sweet steam seemed to be rising from her. She hitched her hips on the stool and said in a huskier tone, "Since my littlest one started school and Harry took to being away politicking here and there, these winter days do seem to get awful long for an outgoing-type person like me."

No trouble diagnosing the problem. She was a little bit scared, and a little bit excited, and she wasn't accustomed to making a pass at a total stranger and she didn't know exactly how to go about it, but Bread Boy had not taken the edge off her and the only thing she could think of was how, without a total loss of all pride and dignity, she could hop back on to that counter top, sans moccasins, stretch jeans, and plain, practical briefs, and get rid of that aching weight, that burden teetering on the brink. She shivered again and gave a high

156

tense artificial laugh and said, "Somebody keeps walking across my grave, I guess."

I looked at my watch and said, getting up quickly, "Holy Maloney, Mrs. Shottlehauster, this has been so pleasant I lost track of the time. I certainly do appreciate your kindness."

"Don't you have time for just one more cup of coffee?"

"I wish I did."

As I drove away from the impressive farm, I tried to tell myself I was a very decent and restrained chap, quite above the shoddy device of rationalizing it as an act of mercy. But I knew I was lying to myself. I knew from a little sense of heaviness in my loins that had I not had that startled moment of peeping tomism, I might possibly have succumbed to the environment, realizing for the first time the grotesque eroticism of a kitchen deed, amid rich good smells of coffee and pies baking and country woman, as if desire had a curious link with the homely processes of hearty food. A brisk and staunch and amiable little woman, fruitful as the land, her needs earnest and simplified and swiftly and with abundant energy gratified, without residual obligation or accusation. Trot off and set herself to rights and come back with the grace to blush a little, then pay off with a pat, a sisterly kiss, more good coffee and another thickly buttered cinnamon pecan roll.

So it had not been restraint after all, not a moral hesitation. It had been just my supercilious sense of my own dignity. McGee could not take over the morning chore where Darling Bread Boy had left off. Fastidiousness. A stuffy sense of social stratum, and of course no chance to exercise that jackassy masculine conviction that the lady would not have yielded to anyone less charming and persuasive.

Every day, no matter how you fight it, you learn a little more about yourself, and all most of it does is teach humility.

I knew something about her too. In any other part of the house it would be a horrified No. What do you think I am? The rest of the house gave her the sense of her value, wife of Harry, mother of six, doer of good deeds. The kitchen was her domain. There any little clinging web of guilt could be swiftly scrubbed away, like a thousand other things spilled and broken. Kitchens took care of simple hungers. Stir, mix, bake, and serve, then clean up the litter, polish, and scrub, and it is bright and new again—as if you hadn't cooked a thing.

I turned the nose of the car into the third of a mile of

muddy ruts that led to the Farley farm. I stopped and stared at the road. I patted the slash pocket of the topcoat, feeling the little lump of the Airweight Bodyguard. Six rounds of 158 grain ·38 Special. I travelled with it wrapped in a washcloth and tucked into a slightly oversized soap dish. This will not delude professionals. It escapes casual snoopers.

I fed the gas evenly and fought the eagerness of the back end to swing itself into the ditch on either side. Mud slapped up into the fender wells, but I kept the momentum all the way up the gradual slope, speedometer saying thirty and thirty-five, car going about eight or ten. Once over the slight rise the speed began to catch up with the reading, and I eased off and ran on into the dooryard and found a slightly less soggy place to swing around and aim it back out before stopping. I got out and with the motor dead the wet landscape had a silence like being inside a huge grey drum. The air tasted thick. I could hear the hum of my blood in my ears. There was no smoke at the chimney, no face at the window. An old pickup truck stood beside the house. Road salts had rusted fist-sized holes in it.

I squelched my way to the front stoop, stepped up, knocked on the door and said, loudly, "Mr. Faaaaarley! Oh Mr. Faaaaaaaarley!"

Cheery and jolly. Mr. Faaaaarley your kindly insurance agent has come to call, heigh ho.

Nothing.

And so I went around the side of the house prepared to see the empty shed where the salvaged Cadillac had been hidden. I got into mud that grabbed and held. Ruined the shoes. Added ten pounds to each foot and made me walk like a cautious comedy drunk doing the chalk-line bit, and made me sound like a hippo in a swamp. A shed was open. Boards had been ripped away, the door pulled back, hanging at an odd angle from one hinge. It revealed the pale luxury sedan, a front view, the hood up and the doors open.

"Oh, Mr. Faaaaarley! Yooo hoooo!"

My voice seemed to wedge itself into the heavy air, then fall into the mud. I got to the shed and stepped inside, stamped my feet, and had considerable cause for thought. Tools lay about. Somebody had undone, with very little finesse, most of Saul Gorba's work. Interior door panels levered off with pry bars. All the seats ripped loose, dumped out, slashed open. Overhead fabric slashed open and pulled down. The trunk was

158

open. The front end of the car rested on the hubs and the back end was jacked up. All the wheels and the spare lay around, tyres deflated, pulled half-way off the rims. The big air filter lay in parts nearby. There was a ripe stink of petrol. The petrol tank had been hacksawed open.

The car was a dead animal. Somebody had opened it up to see what it had been feeding on. There was a sadness about the scene. I could see that Gorba had been working on the car prior to its demolition. He had a set of body and fender tools. He had quart cans of enamel (Desert Dawn Beige), and baking lamps. He had two cans of that plastic guck they use these days to fill the dents. It is cheaper and quicker than beating them out with a rubber mallet and leading the rips and grinding the job to smoothness with a power wheel before sanding and painting. He had packs of sandpaper to smooth the goop down after it hardened.

He had been making it very pretty. There was some masking tape on the back window yet. Everything in the shed had been given the same complete attention as the car. I squelched my way to the house and peered through the windows. Everything I could see had been pried open, broken open, ripped open, and spilled widely. The kitchen was left the way the Three Stooges leave kitchens.

Total silence.

I tried the only other outbuilding with an entire roof on it. The door was open an inch. I pulled it open the rest of the way, using my fingertips on the wooden edge of it, avoiding the metal handle. That kind of silence and that kind of total and ruthless search can teach you a spot of caution.

The door squeaked as it opened. There was a grey and dusty daylight in his little work chamber. And an elusive stink.

He sat on a chair placed against the wall, erect as an obedient child. Hands high, the backs of the hands against the wall, Head up. Can that be you, Mr. Faaarley? How straight you sit! But of course, sir! That leather belt around your chest has been nailed to the studding on either side. And your ankles are wired to the chair legs. And that other band of leather around your forehead has been nailed to the old wood too, with the same kind of galvanized roofing nails, one over each ear, the same ones they drove through your wrists and palms before all the unpleasantness. My goodness, they dropped the cold chisel among your poor teeth, sir. And ripped away your pants for further intimate attentions which have left that faint

159

stink of burning on the silent air. And there is just an ugly crusted paste in one eye socket, poor Mr. Faaaarley, but the other one is whole, a-bulge, and I saw an eye like that when I was very small, and crept on my belly to the edge of the lily pond intending to entice the grand-daddy bullfrog to bite on the scrap of red flannel concealing the trout hook.

From the nightly ga-runk, I thought he would be gigantic, and he was, but I was not prepared to part the last curtain of the pond-side grass to find him not eight inches from my face.

And, Mr. Farley, then as now, I stared with awe into one froggy yellow eye. It was not the yellow-predator eye of the great blue heron or the osprey, or the intractable black panther. Its fierceness was not as aimed, not as immediate. Like yours it was a golden eye, and like yours it was a bland and diffuse venom, a final saurian indifference from across the fifty thousand centuries of the days of the great lizards.

One fearful yellow eye. A terrible hatred, so remote and so knowing and so all encompassing that it translates to mildness, to indifference.

Oh, they used you badly, Farley Saul Gorba.

I found myself leaning against the outside of the shed, breathing deeply, my face sweaty in the fifty-degree day, and with an acid taste of coffee in the back of my throat.

I made myself go back in. I made myself touch him. Death had stiffened his body. I could find no wound that could have caused death. But enough pain can burst the heart or blow the wall out of a blood vessel in the brain. And he had been in the hands of someone who enjoyed that line of work.

"Did you tell?" I asked him.

What do you think? said the stare of the froggy eye.

It was a good thing he was stiff, perhaps twelve or more hours dead. But I still had the problem of foot tracks, tyre tracks, the motel registration, plenty of soil on shoes and car for analysis, testimony by the brawny bus-girl and the itchy farm wife.

I plodded to my car, only then noticing that the farm truck had been given its share of the attention too.

I put my hand on the door handle and wondered what it was in the back of my mind that was trying to claw its way out. Something did not make any sense. I had seen some contradiction and I did not know what it was.

I moved along the car and, in irritation, thumped a body

panel with my fist and felt the metal skin give and spring back.

The thought got through and it brought me up on to my muddy toes like a bird dog. The body and fender tools and the loving care expended on that Cadillac did not jibe with the use of that plastic goop. And somebody must have had some feeling the money was in the car somewhere. I went back to the car in a muddy noisy lope. I saw canvas work gloves on a nail and put them on. I picked a big screwdriver off the floor and with the metal end played a tune along the curve of a front fender. Pang pang pang pank pock tunk. Grab a rubber mallet. Dig the screwdriver end in. Whack. The hardened goop chipped away. It flew out in large chunks. It exposed, barely visible through heavy pliofilm, an oval etching of General Grant. The packet was almost an inch thick.

Pang pang pang pank pock tunk. I got better at it. I put the packets aside. I whistled between my teeth. Lordy me o my, I said. Treasure hunt. Here's another. And another.

Admirable idea. Take the rubber mallet, put a careful ding in the tailored metal wide, long, and deep enough to fit the pliofilmed money-package into it. Pack in the plastic glop and let it harden to hold the money in place. Then sand off the roughness of that first shaping of it to the curve of the metal, paint, and bake.

Gorba had the brains and I had the luck. I worked as hard and fast as I could, dug out eleven packets, couldn't find another place on the body that went tunk instead of pang. I'd had the luck to watch the process one day while roaming around a repair garage, and then to tell the manager what a cheap-ass system it was. He had the kindliness and patience to tell me some of the facts of life. Costs were going up so fast anything more than a gentle nudge would total a car. So be glad there was a new system that would keep the insurance cost from going out of sight a little while longer. If I wanted to complain about something, he said, I should complain about the shyster operators who'd buy one for dimes that had been in a head-on, then scour around for the same year and model that had been crunched hard enough in the rear end to be a total, saw both in half, weld the two good halves together, repaint and sell it a long way from home plate. The plastic just didn't fit the personality of a painstaking man very good with his hands.

I whacked the crumbs of hardened goo off the packets, stowed them in my pockets, ran to the car, carved the mud off my shoes with a sodden piece of wood, and made as good time as I dared driving over to Peru, a small city of about 9000. I put the car in a big petrol station in town, told the man to fill it and see if he could hose the worst of the mud off. I bought myself a pair of shoes and, in the dime store, some wrapping paper, twine, tape, and mailing labels. I parked on a quiet street, put on the new shoes, dropped the muddy ones on to the floor in back, packed the money and the gun into the shoe box, wrapped it neatly and solidly, filled out the label, drove to the post office, and mailed it to myself at the Drake. Parcel post. Fifty dollars' insurance. Special handling.

I was hurrying through the things I knew I ought to do because I couldn't find any good handle on the main problem.

The main problem was all too vivid. Country areas have their own kind of radar, and it is as old as man, old as the first villager after he got tired of being a roaming hunter and sleeping in a different tree every night. Once Gorba's mistreated corpse was found, Mildred Shottlehauster would leap into the act, grabbing her little moment of importance, and she would call the sheriff, maybe calling him Ted or Al or Freddy or Hank darling, and tell him about this great tall suntanned pale-eyed fellow driving a such and such, calling himself McGee and talking about a credit investigation and finding out there was nobody at the farm, but maybe he went up there and somebody was there, huh? And when this got around, Brawn-Baby, the gauntleted girl bus driver with the shoulders, would connect and come up with something else, and the ripples in that little pond would finally lap at the doorstep of my Georgian motel where Hank darling would get the licence number off the registration.

There was some merit in stopping it dead right at the source, right in Milly's kitchen before she started to make waves. I could hustle back there and make it before lunch, and play it cool, and tell her she'd been so helpful I thought I'd tell her I'd had to turn down the Farley family, and even though she had very probably been slowly turned off by the passage of time, with just a little firmness and insistence she would come back with a rush, and I could finish what Bread Boy had left undone, and later save her face with some sincere and solemn hoke about a sudden attraction so strong we really couldn't help ourselves. And then when she all of a sudden had an overwhelming urge to call Sheriff Darling Dear, doubtless a political buddy of her husband, she would yank her little competent hands back from that phone as if verily it were a

162

snake. They could bring McGee back and he could answer the right question in the wrong way, and the earth would open and the Shottlehauster's farm and hopes would slide slowly in.

Could do. Even had she known Bread Boy for years, the very basic rationalization was the same, the first hurdle overcome.

Listen, guys, let me tell you about the time I was up in Illinois and there was this little farm wife, six kids, and I'm telling you, I set her on to a counter top and she was as hot as a . . . .

Not today, fellows. Not to save the McGee skin. Had I taken the opening being so tentatively and warily offered when I had been with her before, it would have left a tired taste in the mouth and bad air in the lungs and a sorry little picture in the back of the mind. But this was too cold-blooded to be even thinkable.

So, okay, stop off and see Mildred and tell her that I'd gone to the farm and Farley was dead in a very ugly way, and I didn't want to be brought into it, and if I was I'd have to account for all my time in the area, and I'd spent some of that time looking in her kitchen window and reading the legends and persuasions on the Darling truck. Sure. Rub her nose in it. Grind her right into the dirt. She who play kitchen game pay big price sooner or later, hey?

Think a little, you big stupid beach bum!

I finally got the rusty gears working upstairs, popped thumb and finger, and hightailed it for the Shottlehauster farm, rehearsing my end of the dialogue en route.

She was surprised to see me. I exuded total confidence. Something had come up. I needed her help. I'd lied about the credit investigation. Sorry. Have to do that kind of thing sometimes. Line of duty. I sidestepped her questions, borrowed her phone, and made a collect call to Heidi and, with Mildred at my elbow, I asked Heidi to put Susan on.

"Susan? McGee here. The kids have been staying with the Shottlehauster family since Monday evening. They're okay, and they're in school right now. But I think I'd better bring them back to Chicago. I just stopped at the farm. He's there all right. And somebody has killed him Very unpleasantly."

At my elbow I heard Mildred give a gassy squeak. "Susan?" I said. "Are you all right?"

"I . . . I'm trying to be sorry about him. But I can't."

"Now would you do me a favour? Please talk to Mrs. Shot-

163

tlehauster and ask her to help me get the kids out of the school here. This can be a very ugly thing and they ought to be well out of range. Don't tell her anything about me except she can trust me. Okay?"

I handed Mildred the phone. She stammered and said, "It's a t-terrible thing, dear. I'm so sorry." She listened for a little while and then she said, "Of course, Susan dear. You can depend on me. I'll pack their things and Mr. McGee can bring them along."

After she hung up I ordered her to sit down in her own living-room. She was big-eyed and solemn. She said she knew who to call in the school system. She said she was a past president of the PTA.

"Here is what I want you to do. I know you have no training in this sort of thing, but you seem very understanding and intelligent. Here is your story. Susan called you from Chicago. She said a friend would stop by about noon to pick up the things her brothers and sister brought over here, and then go to the school and get them, and would you please arrange it, tell the school it is an emergency. Then she began to cry. You thought Mrs. Farley might be very ill. Mr. Farley had told you both of them were in Chicago. So you asked about Mrs. Farley. Susan then told you that her mother has been missing for three weeks and she thinks something terrible happened to her. So you did as the girl asked. A man came by and picked up the children's things. Just a man. He didn't give a name. But you knew he was all right because of having talked to Susan. Now, do you have a car here that you can use to get up that muddy road at the farm?"

"Harry's old Land Rover will go through anything."

"Do you mind seeing something pretty horrible?"

"I'm not a sissy, Mr. McGee."

"Back to your story. You will go to the farm because you thought Farley acted peculiarly Monday night. You wonder if he is there or Mrs. Farley is there. And you are a little uneasy about having made the arrangements on the word of a seventeen-year-old girl without consulting the parents. You'll find him in the first shed beyond the foundations where the barn was. I think he's been dead since sometime yesterday, but that's just a guess. You will notice that the whole place is ransacked. So you will go to a phone and report it."

She nodded. "To the sheriff. Jimmy Tait. He's an old friend."

"Good. Now then, by the time he gets around to questioning you, I'll be well on my way to Chicago with the kids. You don't know where Susan phoned you from. Suddenly you will remember running into Mrs. Farley a month ago. Think of a logical place. She was tight. She seemed very upset. She talked strangely. It didn't make any sense to you. Something about the Outfit, and something about her husband thinking she was going to find out, and something about Pushers."

Solemn as a library child she said. "Outfit. Fink out. Pushers."

"And then she said something about old farms having their own graveyards and laughed in a crazy way."

"But why do you want me to say all that?"

"Mrs. Shottlehauster. Mildred. If you were trained in this work you could go ahead without question. But I am going to take the chance of telling you what we think. Believe me, it will cause me serious trouble if you tell anyone this. Your husband, anyone at all. We believe Farley is a known criminal. We have no I.D. yet. Last Sunday Farley made advances to Susan."

"His own daughter!" Scandal made her eyes sparkle.

"Only the smallest one is his."

"Tommy."

"Yes. When she resisted him, he beat her badly. She didn't let the other kids see her condition. She took a bus to Chicago Monday evening. She came to us and told us she believed Farley had killed her stepmother three weeks ago and buried her somewhere on the farm. She said Farley was hiding out there, and she had no idea why. I was sent to look things over. You know the rest."

"It's so terrible. Those nice kids!"

I looked at her with a firm official frown. "When you know things other people don't, Mildred, it's a terrible temptation to tell so that you can feel important. I trust you to resist that impulse. Your only reward will be the knowledge that you lived up to your obligation as a good citizen. That will be in our files, but we can't thank you in any public way."

"Pusher means about drugs, doesn't it?"

"Please don't ask me any more questions because I've already told you more than I'm authorized to tell."

She glowed with her new responsibility. Her little jaw firmed up with resolve. She would hug her secret closely, cherishing the knowledge she was in our files. In my flush of success with her, I had the eerie temptation to tell her I was the man from

A.U.N.T. Association Uncovering the Narcotics Traffic. But there is a limit to what you can make them buy.

She jumped to her feet. "I'll phone the school and then I'll pack their things, sir."

"Forgive me for lying to you the last time I was here?"

"Oh yes! You've got a *job* to do."

TWELVE

FIVE days later, on Monday morning a little after ten, I sat in John Andrus' office at the bank. A quiet panelled room. We were alone. The door was closed. He had told his girl to hold his calls. He was troubled. He frowned, sighed, shook his head.

"It's a very awkward situation," he said for the third time.

"It doesn't have to be. Just keep it clear in your mind what we keep on the record and what we keep off the record."

"As a trust officer I have certain. . . ."

"I know, John. Fiduciary responsibilities. I gave you every last dollar I chipped out of that damned car."

"One hundred and seventy-eight thousand, six hundred and fifty dollars. How am I supposed to account for it? How did I get it? Where's the other four hundred and twenty thousand?"

"You worry too much. Let's take it one at a time. I told you Janice Stanyard will lie beautifully if she has to. Geis gave her a package to hold for him. She forgot about it. She found it the other day on her closet shelf, opened it, found all the money, contacted Heidi at once, and Heidi said to bring it to you."

"Fine," he said wearily. "Wonderful."

"And when the estate is appraised next October, if the tax boys get sticky about it, you call that number I gave you, and you will get three characters who'll swear that for over a year the Doctor was going over to Gary once or twice a month and playing high-stakes poker in a fast game and losing very very heavily. That is, if we don't turn up the rest of the money somehow in the meantime. Which doesn't look likely. Those three will give you an expert performance, and nobody will break them down."

Staring at me he shook his head in mild wonder. "Where did you develop contacts like that, damn it? How can you so blandly and so confidently come up with people perfectly willing to perjure themselves about something that doesn't concern them at all?"

"I did a favour for a local operator once. He's the type who stays grateful. Maybe local is the wrong word. This is home base. He operates in a lot of areas. John, if nobody comes up with any more of Fort's money, how does the estate thing stand?"

He hesitated and then said, "Rough estimate. Seventy-five for Gloria and half that for each kid, Heidi and Roger.

"Nice if I could have picked up the whole thing out there. Or if they had found anything when they took the place apart, inch by inch. Of course it would have been a rough go proving it was Fort's money if they'd found the rest of it, but you could have swung it."

"Vote of confidence. Hah!"

"John, there's just too many possibilities. He took a lot of little trips. So he was stashing it elsewhere. Or whoever came after him, maybe because he talked just a little bit too much about making a nice score, found everything except what I found. I think it's over. They identified him as Saul Gorba. They know he had an aneurysm that blew under the high blood pressure pain gives you. They assume that whoever worked on him left with what they'd come for. It is obvious Gorba was hiding out. And it is a safe assumption he strangled Gretchen and buried her five feet under, suitcase and all. And they know the kids don't know anything about anything. Murder first, felony murder, by person or persons unknown. We got a little back. We pick up the pieces, the world goes on."

"Wonder why he killed Gretchen?"

"Maybe because she kept wondering where the money was coming from, and even though she wasn't too bright, she had been given enough twos to add to twos over a long time, and when the answer began to show, she didn't like it. She was an amiable earthy slob, but she wasn't crooked. And putting leverage on a dying man is pretty ugly. Or maybe he just decided the daughter looked a lot better. We'll never know."

"One comment, Trav. It really surprised me to have Heidi pick up the tab for that double funeral."

And one of the eeriest ones I had attended. Saturday afternoon. Two boxes. One floral piece on each one. Select little group. The five towheads. Gretch must have had muscular genes. The kids all looked alike. Fair, blue-eyed, round-faced, sturdy. Seeing them together it was an astonishment that Susan had been able to sustain her personal myth of a different parentage. In dark glasses, dark hat and veil, Susan's damages were obscured. So it was the kids and Janice and Heidi and John Andrus and Anna Ottlo and me, and a sonorous voice reading a standard service, and a tired woman diddling with the keys on a small electric organ. Anna whuffawed and snuffled and grunted her anguish. Some tears were shed for Saul Gorba, the tears of Tommy, his natural child. Most of his were for Gretchen, but he had some for Saul. There had been a relationship between them not shared by the others.

"Maybe Heidi Trumbill is mellowing. John, thanks for getting the law boys on to it and getting that money turned loose for Susan."

"She should get it by tomorrow."

"And thanks for getting the court order set up to have the kids stay with Janice."

"On this money, Trav, I have to escrow it until the estate appraisal is firm next October, but Gloria can borrow against it right here if she needs to. She ought to know that."

"When I see her this afternoon I'll see if I can get it through to her."

In a lounge at the hospital, in a low voice, Dr. Hayes Wyatt explained it in layman's terms. "Think of the senses of sight, touch, smell, hearing, taste as being receptors, Mr. McGee. They have no analytical function. Think of a bundle of wires running from each receptor to the part of the brain which acts as a computer. The psychedelics are disassociative in that they loosen these customary connections between receptors and the analysis function. Messages become false and the analysis unreal. Hallucination. As the period of disassociation ends the connections grow tight again and the subject comes back into his familiar reality. The massive overdose she took tore all the wiring loose. It has to be fitted back, slowly and carefully. To continue the analogy you can say the wiring is hanging free and it is in aproximately the right areas, so it touches and brushes the proper connection quite often. But there is a continual hallucination which of course creates terror, so it is best

168

to keep her mildly tranquilized. There are motor defects. She will say a nonsense word when she means to say something quite different. This alarms her too. I think there is a certain amount of progress. I don't know how long it will continue, or if she will ever get all of the way back."

"Why did she do it?"

"She remembers wanting to take some. She can't remember the actual act. Possibly she is a semi-addictive, and even though LSD-25 is not physiologically habit-forming, the addictive personality has a tendency to overdose himself with any escape drug when depressed. She would be dead, of course, if you hadn't found her when you did. Even then it was terribly terribly close. Try to be perfectly natural with her. Cheerful. Confident. Ignore anything she says or does which seems out of line."

So I saw her, and her smile came and went too quickly and her eyes were strange. She called me Trav and she called me Howie, and she got scared of something on the bed I couldn't see. She dug her nails into my wrist and told me in a weak voice, "The cliffs are crooked near the edge. They wouldn't be that way home. They don't stop them here. They don't care."

I smiled my cheery way out and stopped a little way down the corridor and leaned against the wall, feeling more years than I had, more sourness than I was due.

I hunted up Hayes Wyatt and said, "So wouldn't she be able to hook those wires up faster where she knew what the hell she was looking at, where she knew the smells and the way things feel, and the sounds?"

"Home? Yes, of course, that would be useful, I think. But I understand that as a practical matter she can't afford the care she'd need there, much less maintain the house, so I haven't. . . ."

"But you'd approve it?"

"Certainly, but not right away. A week from now perhaps, with a guarantee she'd be taken. . . ."

So I hauled Janice Stanyard and Susan down to John Andrus' office. I gave my pitch. "The house is up for sale. Glory's personal stuff is in storage. Anna Ottlo has gone to Florida. Okay. The court recommended to Mrs. Stanyard here that she find a bigger place. Susan here has the annuity income. Gloria has the insurance income, and she can borrow against the seventy-five she's got coming if she has to. And Mrs. Stan-

169

yard has certain . . . resources. Financial. Aside from being a trained nurse."

"Which I insist be used for Susan and the others," Janice said with great firmness and dignity.

"And," I continued, "Dr. Hayes Wyatt says that Gloria's chances are going to be a lot better in familiar surroundings. The house is big enough. It's a fine house, a fine location. So it makes a crazy menage any way you look at it, but what I say is that Janice and Susan and Glory dump everything into the pot and dig in there, and everything has a lot better chance of working out all the way around."

So Susan scowled and scowled and then slowly lit up. The last strains of brutality were almost faded away. "Hey!" she said softly. "Hey now!"

And Janice said, "It just might. . . ."

And John said, "I could see my way clear. . . ."

Hayes Wyatt fudged the estimate of time by one day so we could bring her home in the early afternoon on Christmas day. Heidi and Janice and I and the kids had trimmed the tree the night before. And on the previous day, on Friday the 23rd, I had lost my wits, my judgment, and my self-control in Carson, Pirie, Scott.

She sat in a big chair, blanketed and feet up, and smiled and smiled and smiled, and had some bad times but not as many as we had been told to expect. John Andrus and wife stopped by, gift-bearing. So did Hayes Wyatt and wife. So, to my surprise, did Roger and Jeanie Geis and their kids. But Heidi told me on the side that she had gone and roughed brother up pretty good. He didn't like it, but he was there. He endured it. He wore a little obligatory smile.

Janice and Susan and Freddy, the oldest boy, had done a great job of settling them all in.

And so, all turkeyed up and tuckered out, I took the thoughtful snow maiden back to her shelter at 180 East Burton Place, and when she tried to end the evening with a friendly social handshake, I dug her private and special gift out of the car trunk and said that he who bears gifts gets a nightcap. And then she looked even more thoughtful and said she had a gift for me, so I should come on up, but give her a minute or two to wrap it.

Drinks made, she went off and came back in no more than

a minute with a plain white envelope. In red ink on the front of it she had written, "A Merry Christmas to Travis McGee." In green ink she had drawn a small Christmas tree the way children draw them, in jagged outline.

She sat with brandy snifter in hand, my gift to her on her lap, and said, "You first. It wasn't going to be a gift. Maybe it isn't a gift, really."

I thumbed my gift open. Pale blue bank cheque. Certified. Eighteen thousand seven hundred and fifty dollars.

"What the hell, Heidi!"

"Why don't you just say thanks?"

"But you're under no oblig. . . ."

"Hush. You explained it all to me. Half is better than nothing at all. You made the deal with Gloria, but you didn't go through with it. And Roger certainly wouldn't let go of twenty cents of his when he finally gets it. And out of family pride I just couldn't have you going around thinking of this as the Geis disaster. Please don't get all stuffy and noble and turn it down."

"Okay. So I accept it. Thank you very much. But only on condition that I lay a very good morsel of it on our little venture, yours and mine."

She went pale and her mouth trembled and she said, "But we aren't really going to. . . ."

"Open your present, girl."

Her hands shook as she loosened the ribbons and the metallic paper. She stared down into the box. After she had unwrapped in turn, the sun lotion, the giant beach towel, the big black sunglasses, the little beach coat, she had begun a dangerously hysterical giggling. And when she undid the last item, a bright bawdy little bikini that could probably have been packed into a shot glass without too much of it protruding, she stared at me and said, "But I couldn't ever wear . . . ever wear . . . anything . . . anything like. . . ."

So hysteria was suddenly tears. Hands to the face. Gifts spilling, The wrenching hopeless hoohaw of vocalized anguish. Went to the lady. Brushed gifts out of the way. Picked her up by the elbows, sat in her chair, lowered her back down on to the lap, hiked her long legs over the chair arm, wedged resistant head into side of my neck, held tight. Said, "There there. There there now."

No gossamer she. Respectable girl-weight, bearing down on cushiony-warm bottom, all misty, humid, solid, sweet that bundle of tears, sob-time, fright. All unresponsive flesh, like those store-window dummies now fashioned of some kind of yielding plastic which you can bend slowly into a new position which they will maintain. No answers in the flesh. No questions. Dull plastic acceptance.

So as she slowly quieted there on that Christmas night, I graded my own final examinations in my own version of a severe Calvinistic morality. Maybe we all mete out to ourselves our little rewards and punishments according to our very private and unique systems of guilt and self-esteem. I had the fatuous awareness of having earned this lovely and inhibited bundle thrice over, by not slipping up on Gloria's blind side in a parody of comforting the widow that evening after I had first arrived and when in the ember-light we were both aware of all the small ways of saying yes, and by not accepting the full measure of Maurie Ragna's total hospitality and by not counter-topping the intensity and diligence of little Mrs. Shottlehauster as had been inadvertently observed, an act which came complete with rationalization.

So when you skip the cream pie and pass up the chocolate shake and deny yourself the home fried, you begin to think that, by God, you have a right to the Cherries Jubilee.

Tears ended, she rested apprehensive upon me with all the nervous tensions of a jump-club recruit as the aeroplane makes its circling climb, and I knew that this was the wrong time and the wrong place and a certain guarantee of failure. So I set her on her feet, kissed the salttasty cheek, looked into evasive eyes, and said, "Sleep well. Get up and pack."

"But. . . ."

"Pack !"

The tenth day of February. Three o'clock in the afternoon. Beach cottage. St. Croix. Sun coming through yellow draperies into the bedroom. Rental Sunbeam outside the door. Little sailboat pulled up on to the private beach. Excellent hotel a ten-minute walk away.

I awoke from the nap which was getting to be an almost insidious habit with us. Eyes half shut, I did some sleepy arithmetic and discovered it was our forty-sixth day of residence.

In the subdued golden afternoon light, Heidi came into my range of vision, elegantly nude, smoothy beach-browned, swim-browned, sailing browned, topdown browned except for the narrow bikini areas which, when she had decided they were a sickly white, she had toasted to gold on the little walled patio off the living-room. She started to walk past the full-length mirror set into the closet door, caught sight of herself apparently, stopped, and inspected herself solemnly, carefully, from head to toe. She faced it head on, and then without moving her feet, turned to present left profile and then right profile to the mirror. The tension made long firm flowing lovely lines, a complexity of curves from earlobe to delicate ankle.

There is an elegance of total unity, and an elegance in the smallest physical details of a truly great pussycat, a truly fantastic bird. Fine-grained texture of the skin everywhere. Little fold of the upper lid, curves and pads of the fingers, jeweller's precision of eyelash and brow. It is an elegance that makes for mystery somehow, so that finally the most complete intimacy merely hints at intimacies beyond, at promises unreachable.

She faced herself squarely again, brushed pale hair back with both hands. Sun and salt and wind had bleached it and coarsened the texture of it. She frowned at herself, underlip protruding. She patted her tummy and sucked it in. She squared her shoulders and, still frowning. cupped a hand under each breast, lifting it slightly. She took a step back, dropped her hands, tilted her head slightly, and then nodded at herself and gave herself such a broad delighted, fatuous grin I nearly laughed aloud.

"Great merchandise," I said.

She whirled and stared aghast at me, mouth open. "Peeping tom!" she said. "Lousy peeping thomas!" Then came at me in a swift hippy hoyden run and pounced. After taking a certain amount of cruel punishment I managed to pin her wrists. She lay panting and grinning at me. The grin faded. I knew it was safe to release her. She nestled close and said, "It's what you kept saying, you know. About liking myself inside and out. Because if you can't there's nothing you can be proud of to give anybody, or share. It always used to make me feel crawly in a funny way to look at myself like that. Now I say Hey look! He likes it. It gets him all worked up. So it must be pretty good. And I own it. But, my God, Trav darling, I gave you a wretched time. Bless you. You are an infinitely patient man."

I held her quietly and thought once more of that descriptive cliché of comparing women to sports cars and violins and such, responsive to the hands of the master. What she reminded me of was the old yellow Packard phaeton with the Canadà goose on the radiator and the wire wheels which I had bought for sixteen dollars, a single shot ·22, and a block of Lindberg airmail stamps during the year before I was going to be old enough to get a permit to drive. My father raised such hell about having that piece of junk in the yard, I spent all my time at first giving it the coats of paint, rubbing them down, fixing the rotten canvas, mending the torn leather seats, haunting the graveyards to find replacement parts.

I had thought that with the service manual on that year and model, I could get it started without much trouble. I finally got it to the point where everything was in order. Valve springs, fuel pump, coil, distributor, spark plugs, carburettor, jets, clutch plate, air filter. I'd sit in tense anticipation behind the big wheel, turn the key, step on the starter, fiddle with the choke, and it would go wheery-yurry, wheery-yurry, wheery-yurry, wheery-yurry. Not a cylinder would fire. And finally it would go yurry, yurry, yurry . . . yug.

Then I would walk up the hill behind the house and sit alone and stare desolately out over the valley and suck my barked knuckles and quietly despise the whole concept of the internal combustion engine. Then I would take the battery out again, put it in the red tin wagon of my younger days, and wheel it three blocks to the petrol station for a slow charge, and endure stoically the gibes and taunts of the cretins at the petrol station.

Then one day when I least expected it, she fired and turned over. For maybe eleven magical seconds she popped, banged, shuddered, and gasped before she stalled out. The next day it was almost twenty seconds. I was able to stop hating her because it seemed to me that that yellow Packard had a personality and that it had astonished her as much as me, and she was saying, in effect, "So *that's* what you've been after." When I had begun to despair of ever keeping her running, or ever getting her out of the back yard on her own power, I found that the firing order was wired up wrong, and after fixing that, I found that a lubricant with graphite in it had hardened on the bakelite outside of the distributor cap and some of the impulses were shorting down the outside of the cap.

Then came the day when I tried and thought it had not caught and then became aware of the deep hum of vibration

I could feel through my fingertips on the steering wheel. Foot on accelerator pedal, I ran her up through the rpm's to such a roar of even, full-throated power it awed me. From then on, perfectly tuned, she would start at the slightest touch on the starter. I drove her when I passed my test. She and I went humming through many nights on the small back roads, taking the curves and grades in a perfect harmony. . . .

But now in all that golden light the holding had become nothing that could be called quiet, and in the strong and languid grace of sensuality totally aroused she turned and arched in presentation of self, her eyes huge in that listening look that measures the great slow clock of the body, and in the first taking of the gift her eyes closed, her mouth opened askew with tongue curled back, and she made a long soft vocalized exhalation, the haaaaaaah of small triumph, of search and finding. Then with growly little she-lion chuckle, she shifted and settled and braced herself for the journey.

That night we drank, we ate, we danced one dance at the hotel, and came walking back along the beach, hand-holding, shoes in the spare hand, walking in the wet where the tide had run out.

We sat on the fibreglass deck of the canted sailboat and looked at the stars. "What can scare you," she said, "when you squeak through, when you know how narrow the escape was, is all the crazy accidents and coincidences that got you to where you are. You let me out of a dark room. I'd have stayed in there thinking it was just as dark everywhere. Son of a gun! If you hadn't found Gloria long ago and put her back together, if she hadn't got a job at that place where Daddy was staying. . . . It can drive you out of your mind. There were so many choices and you don't know why, really, they went one way instead of another way. Even take something like Daddy not marrying Gretchen. It could have gone either way. Oh, how all the tongues would have flapped! But that wouldn't have bothered him. He was too busy to care what people thought."

I got up restlessly and walked about ten feet, sat on my heels, scooped up sand, and drifted it through my fingers.

"Is something the matter?"

"I don't know."

"Travis, for a week at least you've been going off somewhere. I have to repeat things I say. May I say something?"

"Why not?"

"If you're getting broody about this girl, don't waste yourself. I love you and I always will, in a special and private and personal way that is sort of . . . off to one side of what the rest of my life is going to be. One day this ends and I go back and I tear my painting all the way down to bedrock, and then I put it together again with some life and juice and fire in it, and I am going to look up and there is going to be some great guy there who wants the kind of life I want, and we are going to breed up some fat babies, and laugh a lot, and get old and say it was all great right up to the end."

"I wasn't worried about you turning into an albatross, kid. I'm worried about all the little things that didn't fit right. That Gorba thing is over and it isn't over. I got some answers. I got some salvage. I missed part of it. When you said that your father might have married Gretchen, I got a little resonance off that. Maybe she would have made him a good little wife. She got along with you and your brother. And she had her mamma there to keep things to rights. Anna Ottlo had her widower employer in a great bind. But she worked out an alternate choice, the Kemmer boy. Why?"

"Well, wouldn't you say it was just that sort of . . . humility of the Old-World German? Respect for the learned doctor?"

"But she was in the New World where things are not the same. And you will always want a better deal for your kids than you got."

"She was very harsh with Gretchen."

"And damned indifferent to her own grandchildren. It doesn't fit that . . . kind of hearty, hausfrau cook-up-a-storm image. Flour on the elbows, goodies in the oven, house clean as a whistle."

"Maybe she knew Daddy would never stand still for it."

"That's not my image of him. I think he had quite a load of guilt out of pronging that girl-child while your mother was dying, and the pregnancy meant more guilt, and marriage would have cleared it all off the books."

"Does it really make any difference?"

"With no life of her own really, except through your father, who was a damned busy man, and probably used the house the way other men use a residential club, you'd think Anna would want to be closer to her own daughter and the grandbabies."

"Oh, I think she had *something* else going for her."

"What do you mean?"

"I hadn't thought of it in a long time. Roger was home from school on vacation. He went to some kind of a party and then he went to a place where people parked and smooched. When he left he turned his lights on too soon. That's bad form. Lo and behold, they shone into a car and right on Anna. He didn't see the man. The next day he tried to kid her about it. She took such a clout at him it scared him. He barely got his face out of the way. She had a grater in her hand and he told me it would have taken the hide and meat off right down to the bone. He said it scared her too. She cried and said it was because she was so insulted. She was a decent woman. She did not do things like that or go to such places. He told me he was positive it was Anna. But he didn't try to argue the point or kid her about it, not after that first time. She was very upset. We agreed that she'd probably been out there. It seemed pretty hilarious that she should have a boyfriend. I'm just telling this to show that . . . she could have had other emotional outlets. I know *we* weren't one. She kept us warm, clean, and fed, and that was it."

"She was apparently very fond of Gloria. But she didn't tell Gloria that Gretchen and Gorba had made it legal, and she didn't tell her that better relations had been established and that she was visiting the family almost every Sunday."

"She was never one for talking about herself. I remember when we were studying World War II and the rise of National Socialism I tried to get her to tell me about Germany when Hitler took over before the war started and she just wouldn't talk about it. She said it was too sad and terrible. She said that she and Gretchen had been in a camp for a while and it was better to forget such things. Her husband and all her other relatives were dead and she wanted to foget it, not talk about it."

So I dropped it, admired the stars. We stacked our clothes on the sailboat and went skinny-dipping, and then went into the dark cottage and rinsed off the salt in a shared shower, and scrambled into the hasty bed.

As I was bobbing along in that dark current toward sleep Heidi walked her fingers along my chest and said, "Mister? You awake?"

"Oh, come *on* !"

"Don't leap to conclusions, friend. You haven't got the

strength. I just remembered something. When we were helping to get the house shaped up for Gloria to come back from the hospital, I was talking to Susan about the young kids, about relatives and so on. I asked about Freddy's grandmother Kemmer in Florida and if she'd let her know that her ex daughter-in-law had died. And Susan said that Karl Kemmer's mother had died back in nineteen sixty or sixty-one. So I said I was positive that was who Anna had gone to visit in Florida, her old friend. Susan said it must have been some other Kemmer. I was going to ask Gloria about it if she seemed up to that kind of talk, and then I forgot it completely until now."

So I was awake. Awake a long time. She drifted off. She purred into my throat. Her arm twitched and she muttered something. When I made the decision, I fell asleep. I told her in the morning over second coffee. Her face fell, but she tried to whip up a gallant smile.

"No, dear girl. Just because we check out of here doesn't mean you're going to get away just yet. I've got a shamefully neglected houseboat sitting up there in Fort Lauderdale, neglected mostly on account of you. You're going to earn your keep. You're going to learn how to chip and scrape and sand and paint, and when *The Busted Flush* looks brand-new, you can go back to Illinois."

The smile became real. "I work cheap. Board and bed."

"So okay. Start packing."

"You know, you keep saying that."

THIRTEEN

COMMUNICATION was far simpler back on the mainland.

I phoned Glory from the lounge of the *Flush* on Sunday a little before noon. She sounded a little more like herself, but uncertain, subdued.

"But where are you, Trav?"

"Back aboard the *Flush*. Taking my ease. There's a tall exhausted blonde puttering around in the background scouring the copper pots and muttering about mildew on the cabin curtains."

"We've all enjoyed her crazy . . . postcards. Darn it, I have to keep reaching for words."

"Otherwise?"

"Not so bad. Some bad little spots. Like the other day I was looking in the bathroom mirror and my face just started to sort of melt and slide off. It's like . . . parts of nightmares happen in the daytime. Heidi sounds happy as a clam."

"I beat her when she gets out of line. I'll let you say hello in a minute. Look, what I called about, where did Anna go?"

"That's a strange thing, Travis. I just don't *know*. I had an address she left, care of Mr. Hans Kemmer in Winter Haven, and I wrote there and it came back address unknown, and then Susan said that Mrs. Kemmer died years ago. It's weird, isn't it?"

"Very."

"I have a nightmare about her, over and over. She keeps clapping her hands in front of my face and telling me I'm burning up, that my skin is getting so hot I'm going to set fire to anything I get near."

"Maybe it was the fever you ran. How's your group there?"

"Great. Really great!"

I summoned Heidi on to the line. She took the phone and, talking, slid on to the long yellow couch and ended up in a teen-age posture, on her stomach, propped up on her elbows, sheaf of pale hair obscuring the phone, upright calves slowly scissoring. She wore white work pants with old paint stains there on. The soles of her bare feet were dusty. One of the two snaps was undone on the back of her bandana halter. She and Glory compared climates, and she told Glory that St. Croix was the absolute of all time. I sat and watched her and pondered the disappearance of Anna Ottlo. When I paid attention again, Heidi was talking to Susan. I looked at her slender brown back between halter and waistband, at the almost invisible sun-whitened fuzz along that graceful curve that deepened and then lifted to the bisected heartiness of the splendid bottom. I felt the inner wrench, the sideways slide, the feeling there was not quite enough air in the whole lounge to fill the lungs of McGee. I moved over and wedged beside her and she slid over to make room. I ran a slow thumb down the crease of the strong back across the little knots of the vertebrae. Her breath caught and broke in the middle of a word and picked up again and when I rested my hand quietly upon her I felt that inner humming that had begun, like the inaudible idling of the great engine of the yellow car of long long back.

Keep this one, I thought. It'll keep well. It has one hell of of a shelf life.

At the final good-bye, I popped the single snap with my thumbnail and the two halves of the halter slid away. She faked collapse, face down. "Nothing but work, work, work," she grumbled. "Jeez!" Then rolled around grinning to reach out with both arms, and the phone bumped on to the rug and was tugged toward the desk by the coiled accordion phone wire.

Monday morning I phoned Dr. Hayes Wyatt and he phoned back in a half-hour and I found out he had not heard Glory's dream about Anna Ottlo. He said she was coming along nicely and if she could keep on coming back at the present rate, she should be quite herself by June. The dream interested him. I asked some questions.

"Yes, Mr. McGee, under any of the psychedelics the subject is extraordinarily suggestible. If she could be made to believe that her body heat was such that her clothes and the things around her were beginning to smoulder, she might very well run out on to that winter beach, shedding her clothes."

"What about the hand clapping?"

"Yes. Acceptable technique to capture and hold the attention long enough for the suggestion to be made and accepted."

I looked down at my brown hand at the two pale little puncture marks, still visible, the scars from the bite of the terrified thing in the howl of wind on that beach. I explained the curious thing we had learned about Anna. I asked him if he could find out if Gloria could remember anything that could have happened the morning of that day or the evening of the day before which might have given Anna some cause. He said he would try, but if Gloria began to get agitated he would have to wait for another time.

When the call came through at four o'clock, Heidi was over on the beach with a hairy friend of mine named Meyer. The wind had died and the Florida day had warmed up, but not enough for swimming. When Meyer had first seen her he had shaken his head slowly from side to side. He had clucked. He had sighed. He had said, "Now if *Vogue* only used a centre-fold girl." He pointed a thumb at me, his eyes still on hers. "That one. He shouldn't have such luck. He shouldn't have such good taste. He brings you around and all of a sudden I am a bitter old man."

In resignation he had put his hand out, and she had laughed, moved in, kissed him a good hearty smack, and said, "I hate shaking hands with bitter old men, Meyer."

"I swoon," he had said. He offered his arm. "Come with me to a saloon. I need sustenance. Let this ageing beach boy here stew in his own jealous venom." And off they had gone, laughing, the best of friends. Instant Meyer.

Dr. Hayes Wyatt called back and apologized about being tied up and not getting to me sooner. "But I don't have much. It's all pretty shadowy in her memory. Seems she got up very early that morning. Much earlier than usual. And she found Mrs. Ottlo in Fort's study, sitting at his desk, just putting a handwritten letter and some kind of legal document into an envelope. As she was holding it, running her tongue along the flap, the envelope was toward the doorway, a pre-printed business address, quite gaudy. All she can remember is something like Mark Bay or Macko Bay, and a palm tree, and a row of airmail stamps. When she saw Gloria, she started violently and slapped the envelope face down on to the desk. She seemed agitated. That's all. I'm sorry."

"Not much to go on."

In the middle of the night something came sliding into my mind and slid right out again before I could grab hold of it. At breakfast I caught a glimpse of an edge of it in the back of my mind and caught it before it could get away and pulled it into sight.

Your retirement paradise! A planned community for the senior citizen. Live the golden years in the golden way. And it wasn't Mark or Macko, but she had been close. Marco Bay and Marco Bay Isles, between the mysterious Everglades and the glorious Gulf. Marco Bay Development Corporation.

"What's with you?" Heidi demanded. "Something wrong with the eggs, dammit?"

"They are beautiful eggs and you are a beautiful girl and I think I can lay a hand on Anna Ottlo. We're going for a nice long ride."

"But we were going to go fishing with Meyer, honey."

So we stopped and told Meyer it was off. I said we were going over to Marco Bay, between the mysterious Everglades and the glorious Gulf, to see if, perchance, a good cook I had met in Chicago had settled herself there to live the golden years in the golden way.

We took a cab over to the garage. Heidi was enchanted with my old stately transportation, name of Miss Agnes, one of the really big old Rolls-Royces. She had suffered a curious trauma, perhaps during the Great Depression, when somebody had converted her into a pick-up truck and painted her bright blue.

In the bright clear cool morning we struck west across the Tamiami Trail, sitting high above the squatty and more frangible products of later years, Miss Agnes going along with stately rumble and faint wind-hiss, floating up to her mild and amiable eighty miles an hour when I had clear pieces of road.

And so at eleven-thirty I parked in a broad lot next to the sales office of the Marco Bay Development Corporation. I left Heidi by the truck and went into the office. It looked like functional slices of three kinds of jet aircraft fastened together with aluminium windows. The salesmen weren't in. A Miss Edgerly was. She was all wrists, eyebrows, and big rabbity teeth, and determined to be helpful if it killed both of us.

"Gee now. From Chicago in late December." She went trotting from file to file. She was about eleven inches across the shoulders and forty inches across her secretarial butt, making the pink blouse and madras shorts less than totally attractive.

"With a thick German accent? Gee now. Well, heck, I can check it by date but that's about the last way left." She rifled through more files, pulled out a sheet. "Gee now, actually the only sale from the Chicago area was Mr. and Mrs. Hennigan, and that was just on account of our handling the resale of the Torbadill house at the end of Citrus Lane. Poor Mrs. Torbadill had . . . well, catering to an older group we often have to handle the resale of some very excellent properties."

I knew why she looked distressed. It's the old sun-city syndrome. Instead of fun in the sun in the golden years the oldsters find they've locked themselves into a closed society with a mortality rate any combat infantry battalion would find impressive. You have to make friends fast because they aren't going to be around long. Spooks in the sunshine. Change the club rosters once a week. For Sale signs sprout as fast as the pretty tropical flowers and trees.

"I guess that's it," she said. "I'm terribly sorry. Over here

182

are some pictures of the Welcome Party. Everybody who moves into Marco Bay has a Welcome Party at the Golf and Tennis Club. I think this is . . . yes, this is Mrs. Hennigan." And with the eraser end of her yellow pencil she tapped the fleshy smiling face of Anna Ottlo. "But of course she just doesn't fit the sort of person you are describing." She leaned close, squinting to read the typed legend taped to the bottom edge of the glossy colour print. "Perry and Wilma Hennigan are retireds from Chicago, all right."

"I suppose there's the off-chance they might know where the other lady is, if they know her at all. Long as I'm here I might as well ask. How do I get to. . . ."

"Well, hey, come look here at our wonderful map that's just been brought up to date!"

It was so big I hadn't seen it. Vivid green plaster for the grass. Blue mirror glass for water, in the bay, the canals, the community pools, the private pools. Some kind of grey flexible strip for the roads, complete to yellow centre line.

I followed the pencil eraser. "Right down Mainway all the way to Grapetree Circle, and then three quarters of the way around it and down Osprey Lane to the end where it runs into Citrus Lane, and then take your right and go to the end." She bounced the eraser off the roof of an L-shaped house on a point of land that jutted into the bay. Most of the houses sat shoulder to shoulder. The one she indicated, and a very few others, had a lot of lateral privacy. "You can't miss it!" she cried, spinning toward me, beaming, and smelling of peppermint.

"Looks pretty elaborate."

"Oh, it is! It's one of our Adventure in Living series, the biggest one. Tropic Supreme. It's thirty-one thousand nine hundred and ninety-nine, plus the lot, but including closing costs and title insurance, and the poor Torbadills added the Kingway pool, a second Florida room, and marvellous, absolutely marvellous plantings. They picked one of the choicest pieces of land, and they bought these three additional lots for privacy. They furnished it beautifully too. Why, I would say they had at least, at the very least, sixty thousand in it. It's really the nicest home in the entire development. And just when they had it exactly the way they wanted it, poor Mrs. Torbadill . . . well, that's another story, isn't it?"

"The Hennigans must be pretty well-heeled too."

"It was a fantastic bargain, actually. Forty-nine five for

183

everything, even including the boat poor Mr. Torbadill bought and only used twice."

"It still adds up to a big monthly bite though."

"I heard they paid a *considerable* part of it in cash."

"You've been very helpful, Miss Edgerly."

"That's what we're here for. To be of service."

When I went back out to the lot, Heidi was standing leaning against Miss Agnes, hands in her skirt pockets, ankles crossed. When someone has become very dear it is rare that you get a chance to see them anew, as though for the first time. I saw her before she saw me approaching. She stood there in her relaxed and slender elegance, chin up, expression cool, looking perfectly capable of buying the entire project and moving everybody out and building herself a castle.

I told her the whole bit. "Darling," she said, "are you quite certain it was Anna?"

"Positive."

"But how absolutely *weird*!"

"So we find out what goes on."

I drove the route pointed out to me. a pick-up truck means a service call, even if the basic vehicle happened to cost three thousand pounds back in the days when a pound was worth five dollars. So the glances were casual. The separate generations belong together. No matter how lush the flowerbeds, how spirited the bridge games, the shuffleboard competitions, the golf rivalries—nor how diligently the Hobby Centre turns out pottery waterbirds, bedspreads and shell ashtrays, this kind of isolation still makes a geriatric ghetto where, in the silence, too many people listen to their own heartbeats.

I had noticed a small community bayfront park at the intersection of Osprey Lane and Citrus Lane, so I pulled in there and turned Agnes off and reached across Heidi into the back of the shallow shelf under the glove compartment and took out the little canvas zipper case, extracted the Bodyguard, and worked it into my right-hand pants pocket.

"To see Anna Ottlo?" she said incredulously.

"Hear dem bells. In the back of my head. Better safe than sorry. A stitch in time. A penny saved. Hell, dear, I'm cowardly."

"But clean."

"You wait here. Think pretty thoughts. Paint a painting in your head."

Circular drive. Double carport. Dark blue Buick station wagon in one stall. Power mower and golf cart in the other. Drops from the sprinkler pattering off elephant ear leaves. Birds yammering. Blue bay beyond. Sizeable cinderblock house, awning windows, Bahama grey with white trim, glaring white roof.

When I pressed the button the chimes came loud and clear through the screening of the door. They were not as ornate as the Shottlehauster set. When I heard a female voice call, "Coming," I moved a little to one side, turned my back toward the door.

"Yes?" she said. "Yes? What is it?" I heard the spring creak on the screen door and I turned and caught it and faced her.

"Hello there, Anna!"

She had been somewhat thinner in the Welcome Party picture, and since then she had lost a great deal more weight. Her white hair had been dyed a peculiarly unpleasant shade of building-brick red, and cut into a style that would have looked cute on a young girl, the bangs curving down to eyebrow level. She wore dangling gilt ear-rings, a yellow blouse, purple pants, and zoris. It was a grotesque outfit for a woman in her middle fifties. The meaty face had lost no weight, and the pottery-blue eyes were the same.

"Anna, what happened to the vaudeville accent?"

She frowned and shook her head. "Young man, you apparently think I am someone else."

"I think you're trying to be someone else."

She turned and shouted into the sunny vistas of the house. "Perry! Sweetheart! Come here, dear. There's a man here saying the strangest things. Hurry, sweetheart!"

"Cleverness isn't enough," I said. "It takes luck too."

"You must be insane, young man." I realized how perfect a place she had picked. Guaranteed respectability. Immediate group identification. She was wearing the uniform of the day. Again she turned and shouted over her shoulder, "Will you please come out here at once, Perry, and help me with this. . . ."

It covered any small sound he might have made when he came up behind me. Something flickered in front of my eyes and then as I gasped with surprise, the standard reaction, something was yanked to a fatal tightness around my throat. I spun to grapple with whoever had sneaked up behind me, and I saw a plump bald man hop nimbly backward. But the pressure on my throat did not lessen. I could not take a breath. My ears began to roar. I tried to get my fingertips under whatever it was, but it was sunk too deeply into the flesh. I reached to the nape of my neck and felt some kind of a clip device and felt of the free end that dangled down my back. I fumbled with the metallic-feeling clip. The screen door had shut. She stood watching me through the screen. He stood with the same expression—interest and mild concern. Vision began to darken. I thought of the gun and I willed my hand to go down and take it out of the pocket and put one through the screening and one into the plump belly. But my hand was more interested in trying to dig enough meat out of my throat to get to the tightness and pull it free. Roaring had turned to a siren sound. I felt a jolt and a faraway pain in my knees. The world went from dark grey to black and I pitched from my kneeling position, face forward over the edge of the world, spinning down and down and down. . . .

Brightness shone through my eyelids. My chin was on my chest. I tried to swallow the gravel packed into my throat but I couldn't budge it. I opened my eyes and tried to sit higher in the chair and saw at once why I could not. It was a tubular aluminium lawn chair, the kind with a double bar for the armrests. My forearms were fastened with wide white surgical tape from wrists to elbow to the chair arms, wrapped around arm and armrest, tight and overlapping, so that my hands had darkened and puffed. My legs were straight out, heels resting on terrazzo, pants cuffs hiked up by the same kind of tape which had also been used to fasten my ankles together.

I lifted my head. I was on the sort of jalousied porch locally called a Florida room. Anna sat ten feet away and a little off to my left. Behind her was a picture window from ceiling to floor and ten feet wide, framing the swimming pool beyond. There was a row of little white sea-horses on the glass to keep the unwary from trying to walk through it. I could see a dense hedge of punk trees, tailored grass, concrete pool apron, redwood picnic furniture, a stone barbecue, a wall of pierced concrete block painted white. A blow-up duck, big enough to ride, floated high on the pool water, being drifted in random turning patterns by the light breeze.

On the table beside Anna was my undersized ·38 special. She was using yellow needles and knitting something out of bright blue yarn.

She gave me a merry little glance and said, "You're very heavy, Mr. McGee. It took both of us to drag you."

I started to speak, but it was a rusty whisper. I cleared my throat and managed a guttural rasp. "Was the code word *sweetheart*?"

"Hoping we'd never have to use it. You certainly had good luck. But when you add stupidity, what good is the luck?"

"Where *is* sweetheart?"

"Taking a little stroll. He wants to know how you got here and if you brought anyone along."

"Nobody important. Some state cops."

"I hardly think so."

"Not a trace of accent. You're very good."

"Thousands and thousands of hours, Mr. McGee, in my room, listening to your damned dreary radio programmes, practising into a tape recorder, playing it over and over and over, correcting it each time. Discipline. Endless self-discipline. Endless patience. And now, you see, we are quite safe. You are an annoyance only."

"You dosed Gloria, didn't you?"

"I knew where it was and what it was, and knew it would not change the taste of her morning orange juice. It was interesting, but it was just a little bit careless. I indulged myself. When she asked me what I was mailing to Marco Bay, I should have made quite sure, don't you think? Perry is very annoyed. The silly sentimental little bitch was quite amusing, gasping and panting and slapping at her clothes to put out imaginary fires."

"Anna, wouldn't it have been a lot easier to live the lush life by marrying your daughter off to the Doctor?"

The needles stopped clicking and she stared at me. "My *daughter*! If I'd ever had children, my dear man, I can assure you they would have had considerably more intelligence than Gretchen. But then again, had she been brighter, perhaps she couldn't have been persuaded to believe I was her mother. I had her on my hands only seven years, thank God. A tiresome child. Oh, you asked about the marriage. If the man in that untidy situation had been very rich and very obscure, it might have been an acceptable solution. But Fortner Geis was somewhat of a celebrity, and it would have been a treat for your dirty-minded newspapers, and I could not risk their prying into my personal history, of course."

"What are you wanted for?"

She saw me start and look beyond her. She turned and saw the bald man bringing Heidi around the house. He had her hand in his and she walked quite rigidly, with a twist of pain on her lips.

"Heavens!" said Anna Ottlo. "What a small world it is after all."

The man opened a jalousied door and pushed Heidi in and followed her. Heidi massaged the hand he had been holding and she stared at me and then at Anna and then back at me. "Trav, what are they. . . . He walked me and said such terrible things to me. Anna, my God, what are you trying to. . . ."

"I asked her name and she told me," Perry said. He stood beaming. His bald head was sunburned and peeling. He wore a sports shirt of pillow ticking, dark blue walking shorts, white canvas boat shoes. He wore his stomach high. It looked solid. He had meaty and muscular forearms, and spindly, hairy, pipe-stem legs. He had little brown eyes, a broad flattened nose, and a heavy sensuous mouth. "She made it too easy. I see you're breathing again, sonny," he said, turning toward me and giving me a quick little wink.

Anna shook her head. "How perfectly delicious, Perry. Dear Heidi. The arrogant bitch of all time. Why make her bed when old Anna could do it? Drop the clothes where you take them off. Never carry a plate to the kitchen. The cool, golden, superior princess."

"Anna! You don't have any accent at all."

"What a marvel! What a miracle! Stupid housekeeper. What a treat to have you here, Miss Heidi."

Heidi lifted her chin. "Stop this nonsense at once and take that tape off Mr. McGee."

Anna faked vast astonishment. "Is that an order?"

"I think I made it quite clear."

"Perry, if you could teach this child to sing us a little song, I think her manners would be better."

"My pleasure," Perry said, with a little bow. He moved over in front of Heidi, his pudgy back toward me. He hooked one arm around her and yanked her close and busied the other hand between them. I could see the elbow turning and working.

Heidi gave a harsh gasp of shock and outrage, then her eyes and mouth opened wide and she flapped her arms weakly at the plump shoulders of the man and gave a squalling sound of pain and fright.

188

He let her go. She staggered, going so pale her tan looked grey-green. Her face was shiny with sweat. She took two weak steps to an aluminium and plastic chaise and half fell on to it and bowed her head all the way to her knees, flax hair a-spill.

"A pretty little song, dear," Anna said. "Now mind your mouth." She spoke to Perry in a fast guttural rattle of German. He answered and seemed to ask her a question. She thought, shrugged, gave a longer speech and he nodded, gave a short answer, gestured toward Heidi. Anna responded and he went beaming to her and picked up one hand and hauled her to her feet.

He put an arm around her and led her into the house proper. She gave me a grey, lost, hopeless look as he led her by me. In a cooing little voice he said, "Tender little dearie. Dainty little dearie."

"Hardly little," Anna said. "She's a half-head taller than he is. You couldn't have made him happier."

"Look. She got a case of the hots and I made the mistake of letting her come back to Florida with me. She doesn't know anything about anything. She's a clumsy lay, and she's a bore."

"Perry won't be bored."

I heard a sharp thin high scream from somewhere inside the house. Anna looked irritated and yelled some kind of an order in German. He answered in a placating tone.

"Now he'll go get your truck and bring it around," she said. "All he was supposed to do was secure her in there. They have a charming little practice here in Marco Bay, Mr. McGee. We all have these little round signs on sharp sticks that we can stick in the ground out at the end of the driveway to show we are taking naps. They say *Hush, Friend* on them. Nobody ever violates the rule. Perry stuck ours in when he went to get Miss Heidi."

"Did both of you work on Saul Gorba?"

"Just Perry. Saul was a fool. Very smart and very sly, but careless and impulsive. Hard to control. He couldn't see why it was best he should marry Gretchen. We did not wish to alarm him by telling him that if the Doctor became stubborn it would be necessary to arrange certain accidents so that in the end Susan would be the only heir. Perry is very skilled at such things. But the Doctor decided not to be stubborn. I knew how much money there would be. I knew how long he thought he might live. I knew his warm feeling for Mrs. Stanyard, and knew when she visited her husband. I knew many useful things. Perry found that farm for them, a place good for our purposes. We needed Saul Gorba for certain risky things, like taking Branty for the ride, like breaking into Mrs. Stanyard's apartment to do the thing with the cat. And he was very good at documents. Perry and Wilma Hennigan are very well-documented people. Saul had a great greed for money. It was amusing to discuss it with him in German. Stupid Gretchen had lost almost all of her German. Saul taught me how to wire the noisemaker to Gloria's little automobile. And, of course, when the gift of candy was in the house, I opened it carefully and fixed a special treat for Miss Heidi."

"Why did Dr. Geis set up Mrs. Stanyard for Susan to go to if she needed help?"

"There was a certain threat made against the girl, a nastiness to be done to her. This was over the telephone, you understand. That is how negotiations were handled. A whisper over a pay telephone, by Saul, of course. We told him what to say. We frequently . . . encouraged the Doctor in that way." She bit her lip. "I could not say. Perhaps Saul was a little too convincing when he spoke of the girl. At any rate, I saw the letter before it was mailed to Mrs. Stanyard. I told Saul about it, and the fool told Susan he knew where she'd go for help, after he had beaten. . . ."

Perry came out on to the sun porch from the main part of the house. They carried on a lengthy conversation. I got the impression she made a suggestion he did not like, and he made a series of alternate suggestions. She turned every one down, firmly. He pouted like a fat child. She gave him a little lecture, a teasing tone in her voice. He shrugged, smiled, brightened up and went back into the house.

Anna said, "Poor disappointed man. He has all the rest of the day and into the night for both of you, and I have told him that under no circumstances must you be marked, either of you." She got up and came over and bent to peer at my throat. She rubbed it briskly with the flat of her hand and went back to her chair saying, "That will not be noticeable." She sat down and picked up her knitting. "We have decided to hold your faces down in a basin of salt water from the bay so that the lungs will be proof of death by drowning. And tonight late we shall undress you both on a quiet beach we found that is twenty miles from here, and put your clothing on the seat of that truck of yours and push you into the sea and drive back in our car together. A blanket on the beach and perhaps some beer, that will add conviction."

I heard Heidi's voice whimpering and pleading.

Anna smiled. "I told him it is a test of his ingenuity. Many things can be managed. At least he has time, not the way it was with Gretchen when Saul called up in panic to say she had guessed what he had been up to and was threatening to take the children and leave. He had only one hour with her."

A sudden hoarse cry of anguish from Heidi sickened me. It sounded effortful enough to tear her throat.

"His little bird sings well for him. You understand, of course, about people like Perry. I like a bit of it, for amusement. But to him it is necessary. A sexual orientation, I suppose. First there must be the gross humiliations, the unthinkable violations of the precious citadel of self, with pain as the spice and fright as the sauce. But he will have to do with what variations he can invent on that theme, because he cannot have what he likes best, to create those moments of ultimate hopeless horror when his companion experiences damage she knows cannot be undone, cannot be mended, and then begins to wonder how long he or she will be forced to sustain the burden of consciousness and of life itself."

Out of the silence Heidi began to make an explosive sound, a kind of squealing grunting sound repeated over and over in abrupt jolting rhythm, then dying slowly away.

Anna listened with tilted head, half-smile. "Ah, he is a rascal, that one!"

My heart was breaking for Heidi. All the silky luxuries of her, and the sense of fun, and all her quick sure hungers. . . .

"Listen, Anna. Make him stop. Please. I'll make a deal. I got to the farm before the police did. I found what Perry couldn't find. Maybe the figure is proof enough. A hundred and seventy-eight thousand, six hundred and fifty. I kept it. I'll make a deal. If she has to die, okay, but no more of him. Make it easy for her and I'll tell you where it is and how you can get it in absolute safety."

She put the knitting aside, next to the revolver on the table beside her chair. "Poor Saul thought he would keep that money. He could not know he was only holding it for us until it was time to leave. Then he lost his silly head over that juicy little wench and after beating her in a temper, let her sneak away. So when he found out she was gone, he went to a pay phone and called me late that Monday afternoon and I told him to get the children out of the house, to leave them with friends."

"God! God! God!" Heidi cried, her voice rusted almost shut.

"Stop him," I yelled.

"Where was the money, Mr. McGee?"

"Hidden in dings he put into the fenders and body and covered over with plastic and painted. Stop him. Please!"

With half-smile and half-frown she said, "But I'd have to give him a reason. Saul died after just a few hours. Perry was furious. He searched as long as he dared and then came back. It would be nice to have that money, but not really essential. I think you must have given it to Mr. Andrus anyway. If I called Perry and told him such nonsense he would just say that when he finishes with her and gets to you, you will tell him everything you know anyway, so what is the point? I wouldn't think of spoiling his pleasure."

Then came a cry from Heidi more horrid than anything which had gone before. It was a wild straining, climbing, gargling croak that stopped with a sickening abruptness.

Anna pushed herself to her feet, scowling. "Now I don't think he could get *that* much effect unless he has. . . ."

The blackest anger and total despair can give you what you need for superhuman effort, if you can focus it and direct it. I yanked my feet back, lunged up, and stood in precarious balance, hunched in the aluminium embrace of the chair. And I went at her, hoppity-hop, grunting, fighting for balance. I had the vague idea of charging into her, knocking her down, and getting my teeth into her fat neck. With a look of alarm she turned to reach for the pistol. I had lost my balance on the last hop and as I started to fall forward, I gave a final thrust and felt my head ram the softness of her belly, heard the air grunt out of her. I fell on to my side, the aluminium clattering on to the terrazzo and saw her stagger back, turn half around to catch her balance, trip as one foot came out of a zori, take two little running steps, head down, and then dive.

Her brick-red head hit the window wall section perhaps two feet from the bottom. It punched a huge shard of glass out onto the grass, and ran diagonal cracks all the way up to the top corners. Small pieces sprinkled down on to the terrazzo. She lay face down with her throat across the sill where the plate glass had been puttied in. The top section was suspended. It shimmied. It creaked. Pieces of dry putty fell, then suddenly the great plate of glass worked loose and fell like a great blade, straight down.

She humped her purple hips high and smacked them down. The final grind and bump. The falling glass had made an enormous sound. The brick-red hair did not go well with the spreading puddle of bright red blood.

I hitched myself with frantic effort toward the small table by her chair. I hooked my feet around a table leg and yanked it over. I could hear him coming. The gun spun to a stop five feet away. More lumpy hitching spasmodic effort, like a legless bug.

"Fredrika! Fredrika!" He called in a voice of anguish and loss. He was behind me. I could not see him. I got my fingers on the gun. I could barely feel it. My hands were numb. I fumbled at it and my right hand would not pick it up.

Something yanked my chair back. He bent and picked up the gun. He was bare to the waist, oiled with sweat, his chest hairless, his breasts fatty as a woman's. His mouth worked and he sobbed and he aimed the snub barrel at the centre of my face. He was bending over me. There was a strange sudden sound, a damp, smacky little chunking sound. He straightened up and stood very still as if listening to something a long way off. The Airweight slid out of his hand and clanked on the floor. Then he puddled down slowly, with a tired sigh, and stretched out on his back, his head lolling toward me, eyes half-open, only the whites showing, and with a small, very neat, very very round hole punched through the bone of brow an inch above the left eyebrow, and on the curve of fore-head into temple. A single blood-drop ran an inch away from the hole and stopped at the end of its pink snail-trail. Belly gas rumbled and then made a little snore sound as it came out through the flaccid throat.

I had a view of the lawn beyond the broken glass from a vantage point about as high as a rabbit's eye, and I saw two men come across from the direction of the punk-tree hedge. It was an arty director's angle at combat technique. They came toward the house, running swiftly, widely separated, constantly varying both direction and speed, weapons held in a familiar readiness. The ultimate and grotesque contrast was in the way they were dressed—neat dark trousers, dress shoes, white shirts, neckties.

"It's okay!" I shouted. "It's safe."

They dived and disappeared. "What is your name?" one of them called. Veddy British.

"McGee. Travis McGee. They're both dead."

They appeared suddenly, much closer, standing upright, stepping through the great hole where the glass had been, avoiding the blood. Trim-bodied men in their early thirties. Tough and watchful faces, an air of special communication between them. As they quickly checked the bodies of the man and the woman, I said, "The girl needs help. She's somewhere in the house."

One gave the other an order in a language I did not understand and then went into the house. The order-taker set his weapon aside and righted the chair with me in it with an effortlessness that shocked me. He took out a pocket knife, inserted the blade near the aluminium arm, and with one keen stroke sliced the tape open from elbow to wrist. He put the knife down, paused, shrugged, gave me a gold-toothed grin, and said, "No Englitch," and ripped the tape loose in a single yank that took the hair and felt as if it had taken the skin too.

As he was slicing the other arm free, the other one came out of the house on to the porch and said, "D'you know the lassie quite well, McGee?"

"Yes. How is she?"

"Bit hard to tell. Better see if you can settle her down."

I winced as the other arm was ripped loose. I massaged my hands and a painful prickling began to penetrate through the numbness. The gold-toothed one squatted to slice my ankles free.

The one standing gave the dead man a causual kick and said, "I suspect the old sod merely scuffed her up a bit. The Captain here had to take the clean shot before he blew your face off with this silly little weapon. Too bad. We wanted a chat with Wilhelm."

"Captain?"

"On leave. From the Israeli Army. Spot of sightseeing here and there." He helped me to my feet. I wobbled and then steadied. "Tend the lady while we look about," he said. "She's in the bathroom."

Heidi lay naked on her side in the corner beyond the shower stall, on a floor of yellow and white octagonal tiles. Her knees were pulled up to her chin, fists hugged between her breasts, smudged eyes closed, hair matted with drying sweat. There

194

were two doors into the bathroom. Her clothing was on a hanger on the hook on the closed door, arranged with a deadly Germanic neatness. Damp towels were strewn about. The man's pillow-ticking shirt was on another hanger.

I squatted beside her, touched her shoulder, and said, "Honey?"

She gave a convulsive start and scrabbled her way into the corner and kept scrabbling as though to push her way through the wall. With wide blue-grey eyes focused on me but not seeing me, she said, "Please not any more, please, oh God, please no." It was a sugary sweet little gamin croak, a humble little voice for begging, and it sounded like the husk of a long-ago movie star whose name I could not remember.

"You're all right now, honey. It's me. It's Trav."

She looked very dubious. Very sceptical. Her teeth chattered. Incongruously I remembered the fate of the Packard phaeton after my dear old buddy Buzzy borrowed it and didn't make a curve. He took me out the next morning and showed me. He had missed a tree and a telephone pole by narrow margins, had gone down a forty-degree slope and torn a swathe through scrub alder and then hit the almost dry creek bed. It had gone a hundred feet along the creek bed. The water-smooth boulders were the size of peck baskets and bushel baskets. The sturdy old car had re-arranged a few dozen of them. Everything that could possibly be shaken loose had flown off the car including both sides of the foldback hood. Axles, driveshaft, frame, engine block, and all four wheels broken.

"It's like a miracle all I got was just this one little bump on the head," said Buzzy.

We salvaged the parts worth salvaging. It squatted there among the stones and during the spring torrents from the snow melting up in the hills, it disappeared completely.

She let me take her by the wrists, and she did not resist very much as I pulled her to her feet. She leaned against me and in her tiny croak said, "He kept. . . . He made me. . . He put. . . ."

"Easy, honey. It's all okay."

"It hurt so," she said. "It hurt so bad."

It was like dressing a child who is just learning about buttons and sleeves. She would help a little and then forget. I took her into a bedroom. She walked like a convalescent taking the first trip down the hospital corridor without the wheelchair. I sat her on the edge of a neatly made bed, lifted her feet up on to the spread. She lay back and looked at me out of child-eyes and I said, "Rest a little while, honey. Then we'll go."

"All right."

I found them in the living-room, the Captain watching while the Englishman went through each drawer, looking at each piece of paper.

He looked up and said, "How is she?"

"Shaky. I made her lie down and get a little rest. Suppose you start with the beach that night in December. Who hit me and what with?"

"My dear chap, we don't have to start with anything and go anywhere."

I stood over him and said, "I have been goddam near choked to death. I have been tricked by two old folks, and I have listened to that girl screaming when I could not do a damned thing about it. With pure courage and brute strength and great skill I managed to kill a fifty-six-year-old woman in purple pants. Now stop the secret-agent act, buddy, and give me the score."

He spoke to his friend, the friend shrugged and said something, and they both laughed.

The Englishman went back to his search. He began speaking, stopping for a few moments when he came to any piece of paper that interested him. "I was eight years old, thereabouts, when our dead friends out there made the list. The names won't mean anything to you. Fredrika Gronwald. Wilhelm Vogel. He was one of the Munich bully boys. When The Thousand Years began, they became an interrogation team. They sifted the camp lists, picked up people who looked useful, worked the last crumb of information out of them, and made confidential reports to Himmler. I can assume they were ambitious, but their methods turned too many stomachs, Gestapo stomachs even, a very considerable accomplishment. Both of them would have given a clinical psychiatrist weeks of good fun. Aberrant types. Opportunity reinforces the aberrations.

"The list grows very short these days, McGee. Those two eased out so cleverly it took a long time to piece it all together. They fell out of favour in late 1942, and they were sly enough to sense how the war was going. While they still had interrogation privileges they searched the camps—not the death camps—for new identities. She found an Anna Ottlo, same age and build, some facial resemblance. She'd been in since thirty-seven. Her child, Gretchen, was in another area of the camp and hadn't seen her mother in the whole five years. From what we can gather, they took the Ottlo woman and extracted a complete personal history from her before finishing her off. Maybe she had remaining relatives who had to be done away with also in order to be safe. Perhaps the test was the reunion with the daughter, not a terribly bright child. When the daughter bought it, Fräulein Gronwald knew the child was her ticket through the interrogation by the other side. We suspect that Vogel did much the same sort of thing. They duplicated the camp identity tattoos, slipped into one of the underground escape routes, and made it all the way to the Land of Liberty.

"Four years ago we got a recognition report on her from Chicago, and it moved her name up to the active list. There was a certain clumsiness a year later which alerted her. We debated bagging her then before she made a run, but the move swiftly, unfortunately. Limited resources. No phone taps possible. One must have a taste for the hunt. Once they knew, or sensed, they had been spotted, I imagine they thought it powers that be are far more interested in Vogel. We can't essential to extort funds from her employer. Vogel's work on the Gorba chap was as unmistakable as a signature. Incidentally, you did a respectable job of work tracing them here, McGee. I imagine you have a good amateur instinct for it. We traced it through the shipping arrangements she made for her two crates of personal possessions. An intricate pattern, but not intricate enough. In earlier years she would have had the sense to abandon such things. Ah! This looks promising."

He showed it to me. It was a receipted statement for almost two hundred dollars for installation of a barrel safe in the utility room.

It had been installed in the floor. The circular cement lid with recessed lift-ring was hidden by a grass rug. The Englishman gave an order when the safe was exposed, and the Captain went out and came back quickly with a tool case. He opened it and took out a little aluminium chassis case with a speaker grill, toggle switch, and volume dial. The single lead was a suction-cup mike. He pressed it against the safe above the dial, turned the rig on, turned the volume high. It made a continuous hissing sound. He turned the safe dial slowly to the left. There was an amplified grating sound and then a sharp clack. He turned the dial to the right until it clacked again, then to the left until the third clack.

He tried to open it but it was still sealed. He went the second time to the right. After the fourth clack he tried again and opened the safe. As he turned the amplifier off and pulled the suction mike loose, the Englishman knelt and began reaching down into the safe and taking the contents out, examining each item. He opened a thick manila envelope, thumbed a double sheaf of currency over three inches thick, slipped the red rubber band around the envelope, and flipped it to me, saying. "Your affair, I believe."

I caught it, hefted it. "But shouldn't you take some of it, at least?"

He smiled up at me. "My dear chap, there would be a positive wilderness of forms and reports to complete, absolutely weeks of desk work. If you do feel some intense obligation, suggest to your principals they send some over as a contribution to the Irrigation Plan, or some such."

I made protest but he didn't hear me. He had found a little tattered pocket notebook. Their heads were close together as they turned the pages slowly. They made excited comment to each other.

He stood up. "Bit of luck. Seems to be some five-number groupings that could be what we call the Argentina code. Still a few of them holed up down there. Getting quite old. Sly as old foxes. Constant condition of fright, and bloody well justified. I think you'd best gather up your lady and be off. We have a spot of stage management to do here." His smile was the coldest I have ever seen. "Rearrange the meat, plausibly."

"But won't they. . . ."

"Don't worry your downy head, dear fellow. After all, it's our game, isn't it?"

With Heidi in a huddled silence on the seat beside me, I passed their parked car after I turned out of the drive. It was a pale green sedan with New York plates. Gold lettering on the side door said, "Freddy's Exterminator Service" with an Albany phone number.

I drove Eastward through the bright day, in tourist traffic. Herons and egrets fished the canals, as did people with cane poles. I had never thought that an ugliness of so long ago could ever reach into my life. I had thought it was all history-book stuff, and that all that Eichmann hooraw had been an anachronistic after-echo of it.

It gave the same feeling as if I looked over across the saw-grass flats dotted with cypress hammocks and saw one of the great carnivorous lizards rise up on to his steaming haunches, with scaly head big as a Volkswagen, scales gleaming like oiled metal in the sunshine, great tearing fangs of the flesh eater, and the cold yellow savagery of the ancient saurian eye.

I could not have guessed that any fragments of that old evil were still around, and still claiming victims. Gretchen, Gloria, Saul Gorba, Fortner Geis, Susan, and the silent, wretched violated girl beside me. Know-it-all McGee. I'd been a damned fool prancing in total naïve confidence around the edges of disaster, like a blind man dancing on a roof.

"Hungry at all?" I asked her.

Out of the corner of my eye I saw her shake her head no. I drove on, contemptuous of myself and my comedy automobile and my sybaritic nest of a houseboat, and all my minor skills, and all the too familiar furniture of my life and my brain.

FOURTEEN

THREE days later, after making the necessary phone calls to set it up, I got an early jet to Chicago from Miami International with a firm reservation for a flight back that would get me in at ten that night.

It was three below zero at O'Hare. Janice Stanyard met me and I drove her car out to Lake Pointe. All the kids were in school. Big logs were crackling in the fireplace. Jeanie, Roger Geis's wife, had come over to be with Glory while Janice went in to get me.

Gloria hugged herself to me, and laughed, and tears spilled at the same time. She looked better than I had been led to hope. John Andrus arrived ten minutes after I got there. I had given him the total of the second piece of salvage over the phone, and he brought along a work sheet of the probable estate-tax bite.

Gloria and John and I closeted ourselves in Fort's study. I

took the money out of the briefcase Meyer had loaned me and put the banded stacks on the desk. Personally counted and banded by McGee.

Gloria sat in Fort's leather chair. She studied the work sheet. "So, in round numbers. John, it makes an additional hundred and twenty thousand for me and sixty each for Roger and Heidi."

"Approximately. We're still way short of what's missing."

"But there won't be any more," I told him.

"As I told you on the phone, John, Travis gets sixty thousand of my share. Half."

"Just a minute, Glory. . . ."

"Minute nothing. You wouldn't take any of that first part. I know your rules, Trav. I knew them when I yelled for help. And even if I didn't, it's worth more than sixty thousand to know that . . . that damned woman gave it to me, that I didn't take an overdose. I don't care how you arrange it, John. Just arrange it."

I said I would take absolutely nothing. She said she would force me to take it all if I made her any angrier. Impasse. So I reached over and took one slender packet with $10,000 printed on the band and tucked it into the inside pocket of my winter jacket and said, "I must have made a mistake counting it. Pretty stupid, I guess. What I actually recovered is ten thousand less than I told you, John. Count it and see."

He looked at me in horror. "But you can't just pick up ten thousand dollars and put it in your pocket, man!"

"I didn't see him do that. Are you out of your mind, John? Did you pick up any money, Travis?"

"Certainly not! Do you think I'm low enough to steal from a poor little woman who has five kids to educate?"

"But," he said. "But . . . oh, the hell with it! I am going to take this to the bank. I am going to put it in the vault. Then I am going to the club and I am going to sit at the bar for a long long time."

After Andrus left I showed the women the clip from the Naples paper. Tragedy at Senior Centre. Wife dies in freak accident during quarrel. Husband slays self, leaves note.

I didn't answer their questions very well. I didn't know too much about anything, just that it seemed she was some kind of war criminal or something and she'd been in hiding for all those years, and Gretchen wasn't even her daughter. We'd been there when a couple of men appeared to settle old scores.

"But why wouldn't you let me talk to Heidi on the phone?" Gloria demanded.

"It was all pretty sudden and pretty violent and it shook her up badly. Sensitive, you know. Artistic temperament. She's started going to a good man. Talk it out. Get steadied down." I patted my pocket. "When she gets a clean bill, I think I'll tote her back down to St. Croix on this money."

"Have you ever considered making an honest woman of my sister-in-law?" Jeanie Geis asked sweetly.

Gloria snorted and said, "If she was honest they wouldn't have anything in common, dear. And I believe she did try marriage once."

"Dear Gadge," Jeanie sighed. "Well, do have fun. I have to run. Give Heidi a hug for me. Keep well, Glory. Jan, dear, I'll try to remember to phone about Tuesday, but if I forget, you call me. Let's all see if we can't settle down into some kind of nice quiet predictable life, shall we? Ciao, everybody."

We flew over and settled into a two-bedroom cottage on a Thursday, the second day of March. We were a couple of miles closer to Christiansted, the cottage not as attractive or as well furnished, the beach narrower. But the sea was the same, and the flowers and the smell of the air. And I managed to rent the same kind of car and lease the same breed of small sailboat.

The doctor had recommended that I try to create the same scene as closely as possible. It is both unpleasant and difficult to sit across a desk from a grave and bespectacled man and tell him in clinical detail just how one had managed to introduce the repressed lady to enjoyment and untie the knots that had kept her so hung-up. There is a temptation to skip parts of it, and to go into an aw-shucks routine. He solemnly told me the obvious as though it were news, saying that her previous sexual repression with its neurotic basis was what was now preventing her from recovering from the emotional damage of being abused in crude fashion. He said that I should not, under any circumstances, make any direct or indirect sexual advance to her.

And no matter how deliciously lovely she looked on the St. Croix beach or on the sailboat, or how painfully and often I would be spitted by a shaft of pure aching old-timey lust, sharpened by the bursting health of beach and sea, sailing and swimming, and one of my periodic programmes of physical conditioning—easy on the sauce and groceries, push-ups, sit-ups, duck walks, sprints on land and in the sea, I was not going to lay a hand on the damosel, not after two gestures of physical affection back aboard the *Flush* before I knew how deep the fright was. Each response was a convulsive leap. Once she spun into the wall, hands upraised, face sweaty and drained of blood, staring at me but without any knowledge of who I was or where she was. The second time she ran headlong over a chair and finished on her hands and knees, facing me, backing into a corner and trying to keep backing after she got there.

It is difficult to describe properly what our relationship was like during those weeks of March. We used separate bedrooms. Perhaps the best analogy is that we were like the only two passengers on a freighter. Because we were sharing meals and the long voyage, it would have been ridiculous not to go through the polite ceremonies of acquaintanceship. We could share the sea view, relish the weather, play deck games.

She was often listless, lost in her thoughts, looking up from a book to stare for a long time at the far edge of the sea, white teeth pinching into her underlip. At other times she had energy to spare. She was ripe with health, her hide taut and glossy, a blue tint to the whites of her eyes.

And then, one night, as the world was gathering itself to roll on into the fragrance of April, I was slowly awakened by her. I had been asleep on my back. She was beside me, braced to look down into my face, angled so that there was the warm silk of her against the side of my leg. Her face was in the steady silver of the moonlight, unreadable eyes pockets of shadow, the two sheafs of hair hanging to brush the sides of my cheek and neck. Moon made a single catch-light on the curve of underlip.

A scalding tear fell on to my upper lip near the corner of my mouth, and with tongue tip I hooked in the small taste of her salt. When she leaned slowly down and lay the soft acceptance of her mouth on to mine, I did not dare touch her. Each time she bent to kiss, I felt the weight and sweetness and warmth of her bare breasts upon my chest. Slow kisses and slow tears, and I dared hold her, but there was no start, no tension, just a slow and dreamy sensuousness, turning gently for me, with small urging pressures, to be as I had been and lift in a waiting readiness, fingertips on my shoulders bearing no more weight than the moonlight, and in the slowness of joining her catch of breath was almost inaudible, and the following sigh as soft and fragrant as the night breeze.

In one lifetime how many times can it be like that, be a ceremony that becomes so unrelated to the flesh that I had the feeling I floated disembodied in the night sky, halfway between sea and stars, looking down upon a tiny cutaway cottage, at two figures there in the theatre of moonlight caught in a slow unending dance to the doubled heartbeat, a counterpoint in offstage drums. But there is a time to fall out of the sky, and a fall from that height makes long moments of half-light, of knowing and not knowing, of being and dying.

When I felt her beginning to leave me, I caught at her to hold her, but she whispered, "No." I let my fingertips trail down her arm as she went out of moonlight into the darkness and back to her own bed. That single whispered monosyllable was the only word she had said. I could feel my mouth smiling as I slid toward sleep. Total and unflawed smugness. Patience, understanding, and self-control had done it, boy. She has turned the corner. And now day by day and night by night we would build it all back, into all our old moods and manners of making love, of hearing her little soft chuckling laugh of pleasure as she felt herself beginning to begin.

I slept later than usual and when I came yawning out in swim trunks, with a piece of tissue pasted on to a razor nick, she was just finishing her packing. I asked what the hell. She looked very groomed and brisk and competent. She said she had phoned and made flight reservations. If I'd put on a shirt and slacks we'd have time to drive to the hotel and have breakfast with a comfortable margin to get to the airport for her flight.

I kept saying Why often enough to sound like some kind of rotor that needed greasing. She looked pale. She snapped the catches on her second suitcase and looked around with that Got-Everything? look. Then she marched to me and stuck her hand out like a lady ambassador.

"We'd better say good-bye here, Travis."

I tried to pull her into my arms but she begged and demanded and I gave up. "Then answer the question," I said. "Why?"

"Because I have to have my own life."

"Oh, great!"

"I'll never never forget you. You'll always be . . . part of me, part of whatever happens to me."

"Thanks a lot."

"Don't scowl so, darling. Please. Remember when you told me in Chicago I was standing outside the gates looking in, wistfully? So you opened the gates. Huge heavy gates with rusty hinges, and you led me in to where all the gardens are. I thank you with all my heart. Darling, if it had stopped there, I could have survived beautifully, and kept my own identity. But don't you understand? I got thrown out into the darkness again. I nearly lost my mind. And you had it to do all over again, but differently, because I knew the second time what it could be. And, bless you, the gates are open again, just a little way. I squeezed through. I'm standing just inside the gates. But I can't see all the gardens with you."

"Why not?"

"Because then you would own me, every atom of heart and soul and body forever, and life would have no meaning except as it related to you. It would be a total dependency as long as I might live. I do not want that kind of life or that kind of love. But if you want me on those terms, Travis, if you want that responsibility for another human being forever, say so, and I'll cancel the reservation and unpack. I am fighting like hell for emotional survival, and I'm right on the edge of surrender. I think if I am going to be a whole person, now that I am inside the gates again, I had best go the rest of the way with some man I have yet to meet, but know in my heart I will meet. Shall I phone?" Her stare was intent, direct, searching. Her mouth was trembling.

So I put on shirt and slacks and put her bags in the car.

Meyer keeps telling me that I did exactly the right thing. He keeps telling me that she knew how a dependence that total would have suffocated me. But when he looks at the painting she sent me, his voice loses conviction. A small painting. She sent it air express from Chicago. It is an enchanted picture. At close range it is an abstraction, an arrangement of masses and light and colour. But when you get back from it you realize you are looking through the black bars of an ancient iron gate, into a place where there are black limbs of old and twisted trees. The sky is a heavy dreary grey, but there is a shaft of sunlight shining down on a vivid brightness of gardens, a small place you can see beyond the gate and the trees.

I think that when he looks at the painting Meyer has the same suspicion I have, that maybe all along this was the one, and that she got away. I am outside the gates and there is no one to open them.

So then he tries to lift our mood and he makes his jokes and when I sense that he is trying too hard with the jokes I manage to laugh a little.

Otherwise he'd just stand around looking like Smokey the Bear watching all the forests burn down.

A Tan and Sandy Silence

Until Harry Broll turned up out of the blue, waving a gun
and accusing McGee of spiriting away his wife, Travis was
blissfully contemplating the well-rounded bikini-clad joys
of life aboard *The Busted Flush*. Now all those sun-warmed
lazy days of love and leisure would have to be scrapped.
Because he had to find Mary Broll.
Mary was someone very dear to McGee. They had been
close once. Very close. And now, according to Harry, Mary
had disappeared. Vanished without a word to anyone. It
wasn't like Mary to run away. Especially without telling
Trav. A cold, ugly shudder of fear snaked through his
stomach. Wherever Mary was, she was obviously in
trouble. Bad trouble. And in need of a special friend—
namely one Travis McGee.

In northern Manitoba
a man saw a great bald eagle—
hanging from its neck,
teeth locked in skin and feathers,
the bleached skull of a weasel.

by Jim Harrison
(From "A Year's Changes")

one

On the most beautiful day any April could be asked to come up with, I was kneeling in eight inches of oily water in the cramped bilge of Meyer's squatty little cabin cruiser, the *John Maynard Keynes,* taking his automatic bilge pump apart for the third time in an hour.

The socket wrench slipped, and I skinned yet another knuckle. Meyer stood blocking out a sizable piece of the deep blue sky. He stared down into the bilge and said, "Very inventive and very fluent. Nice mental images, Travis. Imagine one frail little bilge pump performing such an extraordinary act upon itself! But you began to repeat yourself toward the end."

"Would you like to crawl down in here and—"

He backed up a hasty half step. "I couldn't deprive you of the pleasure. You said you could fix it. Go ahead."

I got it apart again. I spun the little impeller blade and suddenly realized that maybe it turned too freely. Found the set screw would take a full turn. Tightened it back down onto the shaft. Reassembled the crummy little monster, bolted it down underwater, heaved myself up out of the water, sat on the edge of the hatch, and had Meyer flip the switch. It started to make a nice steady wheeeeeeng, gouting dirty bilge water into the Bahia Mar yacht basin.

Meyer started to applaud, and I told him to save it until we found out if the adorable thing would turn itself the hell off like it says in the fine print. It took a good ten minutes to pump the water out. Then it went weeeeeeng-guggle-chud. Silence.

"Now cheer," I said.

9

"Hooray," he said mildly. "Thank you very much and hooray." I looked at him with exasperation and affection. My mild and bulky friend with the wise little blue eyes, bright and bemused, and with the bear hair, thatch black, curling out of the throat of his blue knit shirt.

"Another half inch of rain last night," I told him, "and you could have gone down like a stone."

He had stepped out of his bunk in the dark after the rain stopped and into ankle deep water. He had sloshed over to my houseboat, *The Busted Flush,* and told me he had a small problem. At three in the morning we had toted my auxiliary pump over and set it on the dock and dropped the intake hose into his bilge. His home and refuge was very low in the water, the mooring lines taut enough to hum when plucked. By first light the *Keynes* was floating high again, and we could turn the pump off and carry it back. Now the repaired automatic bilge pump had taken out the last of the water, but he was going to live in dampness for quite a while.

"Perils of the sea," he said.

I stepped up onto the dock and squatted and began to rinse the grease and bilge water off my hands under the hose faucet. Meyer shaded his eyes and looked toward the *Flush.* "You've got a visitor, Travis. Isn't that what's-his-name?"

I stood up and stared. "It sure is. Good old what's-his-name. Harry Broll. Do you think that son of a bitch has come to try me again?"

"After the showing last time. . . . Was it two years ago?"

"At least."

"I think he's at least bright enough not to try again."

"Not the same way. But he did catch me with one very nice left. True, he broke his hand, but it was one to remember."

"Want company?"

"No thanks."

Harry turned and saw me when I was about fifty feet away. He was big, and he had gotten bigger since I'd seen him last. More gut and more jowls. Not becoming. He

wore a pale beige suit, a yellow shirt, and he had a choco-
late-colored neckerchief with an ornate, gold slip ring.

He raised his hands in the most primitive gesture of reassurance. Palms out. Sickly smile to go with it. As I came
up to him he said, "Hi, McGee." He put his hand out. I
looked at it until he pulled it back. He tried to laugh.
"Jesus, are you still sore?"

"I'm not sore, Harry. Why should we shake hands?"

"Look. I want to talk to you. Are you busy or anything?"

"What about?"

"About Mary. I know you've got no reason in the world
to do me any favors. But this concerns . . . Mary's well-be-
ing."

"Is something wrong with her?"

"I don't know. I don't really know."

I studied him. He seemed concerned and upset. He
had the pallor of desk work. His black hair had receded
since I had seen him last. He said, "I couldn't think of
anybody else to come to. I can say please if it'll help.
Please?"

"Come on aboard."

"Thanks. Thanks a lot."

We went into the lounge. I had on an old pair of denim
shorts and nothing else. The airconditioning cooled the
sweat on my shoulders and chest. He looked around, nodding and beaming, and said, "Nice. Real nice. A nice way
to live, huh?"

"Want a drink?"

"Bourbon, if you've got it."

"Got it."

"On the rocks."

I put out the bottle and the glass and said, glancing
down at my soiled hands, "Ice is in the bin there. Help
yourself while I clean up, Broll."

"Thanks. You sure keep yourself in shape, McGee.
Wish I had the time. I guess I better make sure I have the
time one of these days."

I shrugged and went forward, dropped the shorts into
the hamper and stepped into the oversized shower, think-

ing about Mary and wondering about her as I sudsed and
scrubbed away the rest of the grime from the repair job.
Miss Mary Dillon when I had known her. Then abruptly
—maybe too abruptly—Mrs. Harry Broll. When I put my
watch back on I saw that it was nearly four o'clock. Meyer
and I were invited for drinks at six aboard the *Jilly III*. I
put on fresh slacks, an oyster-white sailcloth sports shirt,
my ancient Mexican sandals. On the way back to the
lounge I stopped in the galley and put some Plymouth on
the rocks.

He was sitting on the yellow couch, and he had lit a
small cigar with a white plastic mouthpiece. "It must really be something, being able to just take off any time you
feel like it."

I slouched into a chair facing him, took a swallow of my
drink, and put it on the coffee table. "You've got a problem, Harry?"

"About that time I made such a damn fool of myself . . ."

"Forget it."

"No. Please. Let me say something about that. Like
they say, the first year of marriage is the hardest, right?"

"So they say."

"Well, I knew you and Mary were old friends. I
couldn't help knowing that, right? I mean, you and Meyer
came to the wedding and all. I wondered how good friends
you had been. I couldn't help wondering, but I didn't want
to really know. Do you understand?"

"Sure."

"The way it happened, we got into a hassle. It was the
first real one we'd had. People shouldn't drink and fight
when they're married. They say things they don't want to
say. I started saying some pretty ugly things about her and
you. You know Mary. She's got a lot of spirit. She took it
and took it, and finally she let me have it right between the
eyes. I deserved it. She blazed right up at me. She said
she'd been cruising with you alone aboard this houseboat,
down through the Keys and up the west coast to Tampa
Bay, and she'd lived aboard for a month and cooked your
food and washed your clothes and slept in your bed, and

you were kind and decent and gentle and twice the man I am. So that Sunday afternoon I slammed out of the house and got in the car and came over here to beat on you. I could always handle myself pretty good. I wasn't drunk enough for that to be any excuse. Jesus, I never hit so many arms and elbows and shoulders in my life."

"And the top of my head."

"That's what popped the knuckles. Look. This knuckle is still sort of sunk in. How many times did you hit me? Do you know?"

"Sure I know. Twice."

"Twice," he said dolefully. "Oh, shit."

"I waited until you ran out of steam, Harry. I waited until you got arm weary."

He looked at me in an appraising way. "I wish I'd done more good."

"I had a pair of sore arms. You bruised me up, Harry. And a three-day headache."

"I guess I had to get it out of my system. Do you understand it's still pretty hard for me to come to you to ask for anything?"

"I suppose it might be."

"Mary kept telling me to grow up. Okay. I'm trying to grow up. I'm trying to be a mature, rational human being. Like they say, I've been examining my priorities and my options."

"Good for you. But where do I fit in?"

"Here's what I want you to tell Mary."

"But I—"

"Give me a chance. Okay? Tell her that as soon as the SeaGate project is all set up, I think we ought to get away, just the two of us. A cruise or fly over to Spain, whatever. And tell her that the Canadian girl didn't mean a damn thing to me, that I didn't bring her back down here or ask her down, that she came on her own. And tell her to please get in touch with me so we can talk."

"Hold it! I don't know where Mary is."

His face turned red. "Don't give me such crap. You willing to let me search this houseboat?"

"She isn't here, you damn fool."

"I'll find something of hers. Clothes, lipstick, something."

"Harry. Jesus. Look around all you want."

He settled back in the chair. "Okay. You and Mary knew I'd come here sooner or later. So you haven't been having your fun aboard this boat."

"That's called paranoia, old buddy. When did she leave you?"

"January fifth."

I stared at him in disbelief. "This is the fourteenth day of April. You have a slow reaction time."

"I've been hoping she'd come back or get in touch. Tell her how much I've been hoping. She caught me dead to rights. She went around the house with a face like a stone for nearly two weeks, then when I got home that Tuesday, she'd packed and left. No note, even. I went down the list of her friends and called them. It was humiliating for me."

"I bet."

"Now just one damn minute—"

"What makes you think she'd come to me?"

"I thought about it. I mean, back in January. It seemed like the most likely thing for her to do. I spent a whole weekend hanging around here. You had . . . another friend. So I decided if Mary had come here, she'd found you were busy, gone someplace else."

"She didn't come here, Harry."

"Not right away."

"What is that supposed to mean?"

He leaned forward. "Okay. Where were you at ten o'clock on Friday morning, April second?"

"I haven't the faintest idea."

"You and Mary came off this houseboat at ten that morning, and you went out to the parking lot and got into a white Ford LTD convertible with rental plates. A friend of mine happened to be here and happened to see the two of you get in and drive off. This friend followed you. You went over to the Parkway and turned south toward Miami, and he came back, and he phoned me about it."

"Are you willing to listen a minute? Are you willing to try to listen?"

"All I know is my wife left me and she's sleeping with you, McGee, and I'd like to see you dead."

"The woman I was with is about Mary's height, and her figure is just as good, at least as good as Mary's used to be. Her hair is dark like Mary's. The woman is an old friend. That's her rental convertible, and it's still out there on the lot. With her hair in a scarf and dark glasses, she was all prepared for a trip in an open car. She's here aboard her boat. Her name is Jillian Brent-Archer. I haven't seen Mary since the wedding. Not once, Broll. And that was better than three years ago."

He looked at me. "You're real cute, McGee. Jesus, you're cute. Most of the damn fools in this world would believe you. Are you going to tell Mary what I told you to tell her, what I've begged you to tell her?"

"How can I, when I don't even know . . ."

And the dumb little weapon came out from under his clothes somewhere, maybe from the waist area, wedged between the belt and the flab. A dumb little automatic pistol in blued steel, half-swallowed in his big, pale, meaty fist. His staring eyes were wet with tears, and his mouth was twisted downward at the corners. The muzzle was making a ragged little circle, and a remote part of my mind identified it as .25 or .32 caliber, there not being all that much difference between a quarter of an inch diameter and a third of an inch. There was a sour laugh back in another compartment of my skull. This could very possibly be the end of it, a long-odds chance of a mortal wound at the hand of a jealous husband wielding something just a little bit better than a cap gun. The ragged circle took in my heart, brain, and certain essential viscera. And I was slouched deep in a chair facing him, just a little too far away to try to kick his wrist. He was going to talk or shoot. I saw his finger getting whiter, so I knew it was shoot.

I shoved with my heels and went over backward in the chair. The weapon made a noise like somebody slapping shingles together. My left heel went numb. I rolled to my right, knocked over a small table, fielded the chunky glass ashtray on the first bounce, rolled up onto my knees, and slung it underhand at his head as he came up out of the depths of the yellow couch. I missed him shamefully, and was caught there too close to him as he aimed at the middle of my face from five feet away and tried to pull the trigger. But the slide was all the way back, the clip empty.

I got slowly up onto very wobbly knees as Harry Broll lowered the gun to his side, relaxed his hand, let it fall. My heel tingled. A slug had grooved the hard leather on the bottom of the heel. The lounge smelled like the fourth of July.

Harry's big face wrinkled like a slapped baby, and he took a half step toward me, arms half reaching out for comfort and forgiveness, and then he plumped back down on the couch and bellowed once, a walrus on a lonely strand.

My drink was gone, spilling when the table went over. I moved cautiously, checking myself for any area that might feel dead and damp. That is the bullet feel, dead, damp, and strange, before the torn nerves and muscles catch up and begin screaming. No such areas. I made tall careful steps into the galley, made a new drink. I went back in. Harry Broll sat with face in hands, snuffling drearily. The paper had kept me aware of him over the years. Broll plans new condominium complex. Broll given zoning board exception. Broll unveils shopping plaza concept. Chamber lauds Broll.

I sat opposite him again after putting the chair back on its legs. Looking around, I could count five ejected cartridge cases.

"How old are you, Harry?"

He sighed and mumbled it into his hands. "Thirty-five."

"You look fifty."

"Get off my back."

"You're too soft and too heavy. You sweat a lot, and you're short of breath, and your teeth need cleaning."

He lifted his mottled face and stared at me. "Why are you saying these things?"

"Maybe if you hadn't gotten so sloppy, Mary could have given you a second chance. Or maybe it was already a second chance."

"Oh, no. I don't play around. Jesus, I haven't had the time or the energy. This was the first time, I swear."

"You don't play around, and you don't go around killing people."

"You pushed me too far and—"

"You always carry that thing?"

"No, I—"

"You brought it along in case you felt like killing me?"

"Thank God, I missed you. I'm not thinking right lately. Everything would have gone down the drain. Everything."

"It would sort of spoil my day, too."

"You know, when a man takes a good look at himself, he begins to wonder why. You know? I've been pushing myself hard. Drinking too much, smoking too much. Late nights. Conferences. For what? Damned if I know. For the sake of winning? How did that get to seem so important? But you shouldn't have tried to lie to me, McGee."

"Your friend is an idiot. Mary never came near me. She hasn't phoned me or written me. I didn't know she'd left you. Look, I knew her a long time ago. She was at one of those crisis points in her life. She'd never met you, Harry. Never seen you, never heard your name, never knew she'd marry you. We were friends. We took a cruise down through the Keys and up the west coast, and she got things sorted out. We made love. Not for the first two weeks of the cruise. That wasn't the purpose of it. Once all the knots and springs began to loosen up, then it seemed like a natural thing to have happen. It made pleasure. It was a way of saying hello. Nobody was a victim. She was a very sweet lady, and what I remember best is that we laughed a lot."

"I . . . I have to talk to her before the thirtieth."

"Why the deadline?"

"It's a business thing. Some things to sign. To protect my interest in SeaGate. Of course, if I'd shot you, what difference would it make whether I kept my share of Sea-Gate or not?"

"Will it make a lot of difference when I sign the complaint against you?"

"Complaint?"

"Assault with a deadly weapon. Attempted homicide?"

"You wouldn't!"

"What's to stop me? My undying affection for you?"

He pulled himself together visibly. He wrapped up the emotions and put them on a high shelf. I could almost see the nimble brain of the entrepreneur take over. "We'll both have versions of what happened here, McGee. I'm essentially a salesman. I think I can sell my version far easier than you can sell yours."

"What's your version?"

"I'll let that come as a surprise to you."

I could think of several variations that could leave him looking pretty good. And, of course, there was the usual problem of believability. Does one believe Harry Broll, pillar of the business community, or a certain Travis McGee, who seems to have no visible means of support, gentlemen?

"A man as shrewd as you, Harry, should realize that the guy who gave you the bad information made an honest mistake."

"I know Mary. She'd get in touch with you."

"Would that she had."

"What?"

"A troubled friend is a friend in trouble. I'm right here. She could have come around, but she didn't."

"She made you promise not to tell where she is."

I shook my head. "Broll, come with me. I will show you that rental convertible, and I will show you the lady who rented it and who went to Miami with me and came back with me."

"It's a nice try. You've got a lot of friends. They'd all lie for you. Every one. Think it over. Tell her what I said. She has to get in touch with me."

We stood up. I picked up his little automatic, released the catch and eased the slide forward and handed it to him. He took it and looked at it, bounced it on his big hand, and slipped it into his side pocket. "I better get rid of it," he said.

"If you think you might get any more quaint ideas, you better."

"I was going to scare you. That's all."

I looked him over. "Harry. You did."

"Tell her to call the office. I'm not living at home. It was too empty there."

"If after all these years I should happen to see your wife, I'll tell her."

two

Meyer came aboard *The Busted Flush* at twenty minutes to six, five minutes after Harry Broll left. He was dressed for the small festival at six o'clock aboard Jillian's great big motor-sailer trimaran. He wore pants in a carnival awning pattern and a pink shirt that matched one of the myriad stripes in the awning.

"Goodness gracious," I said.

He put a hand on a bulky hip and made a slow 360-degree turn. "Plumage," he said. "And have you noticed it's spring?"

"If you'd carry a camera around your neck and walk fifty feet ahead of me, nobody would know we were together."

"Faw," he said. "And tush." He went toward the bottle department, saying, "About Mr. Harry Broll . . . ?"

"Who? Oh, yes. Of course. Mr. Broll."

"McGee, don't try me, please."

"You are supposed to walk in here, and instead of giving me a fashion show, you are supposed to snuff the air, look about with darting glances. Then you are supposed to find those six cartridge cases in that ash tray and snuff at them. Then you prowl around and find where all six hit, including the one that's hard to find. It hit right smack in the middle of my model 18 Marantz and killed it as dead as Harry tried to kill me."

Meyer backed to the nearest chair and lowered himself into it. "Six shots?"

"Six."

"With serious intent?"

"Damn well told."

20

I explained the situation. Meyer listened, looking very troubled.

"Don't sit there looking like an old beagle," I told him. "Harry won't be back."

"Maybe somebody else will."

"What is that supposed to mean?"

"Travis, are you just a little slower than you were a few years ago? Half a step, maybe?"

"I don't know. Probably."

"Why should you get slower and get careless at the same time?"

"Careless?"

"Don't try to kid yourself. You would have stumbled against him or spilled something on him and brushed it off. You would have checked him out and located the gun and taken it away from him."

"This was just old Harry Broll."

"And you are just old T. McGee, trying to pretend you don't know what I'm saying. You could be on the floor with a leaking hole in your skull."

"I can't go around acting as if everybody was going to—"

"You used to. And you are alive. What has given you this illusion of immortality of late?"

"Lay off, Meyer."

"Staleness? People are very good at things they are very interested in. If you lose interest, you are dead. If a Harry Broll can damned near kill you, Travis, what about somebody with a more professional attitude and background?"

"Wouldn't I be more alert?"

"Don't some of them look and act as innocuous as Harry Broll?"

"What are you getting at?"

"If you just go through the motions, Travis, maybe it's time to give the whole thing up. What good is a way of life if it turns out to be fatal?"

"Are you going to support me?"

"Not a chance. Anyway, isn't Jillian first in line?"

"Come *on!*"

"There are worse ways to live."

"Several hundred thousand worse ways, Meyer, but just because Harry Broll. . . . Consider this. Six shots in a very confined space. What's the matter with my reaction time?"

"The trouble is that they were fired at all. He came here once to try to beat your face flat. So two years later he comes around again, and you invite him in to try his luck with a gun. What are you going to dodge next time? A satchel charge?"

"I have to depend on instinct. I did not sense any kind of murderous intent on his—"

"Then your instincts are stale. Listen. I don't want to lose a friend. Go where I can visit once in a while. Exchange Christmas cards. Better than putting a pebble on your gravestone."

"Just because—"

"Don't talk. Think a little. And we should be going."

I shrugged and sighed. When he gets into one of those moods, there is nothing one can do with him. He smells doom. I buttoned up the *Flush,* making certain my little security devices were in operation. The sun was low enough to make a yellow-orange glow across all the white gleam and brightwork of a vulgar multimillion dollars' worth of seagoing toys. Hundreds of millions, in truth. As we walked over I saw the sixty-plus feet of a big new Bertram, grumbling, bubbling, sliding elegantly into a slip. Six thousand dollars a foot. It doesn't take too many of those, too many Matthews, Burgers, Trumpys, Huckins, Rybovitches, and Strikers, to make a row of zeros to stun the mind.

I stopped and leaned my crossed arms atop a cement piling and looked down at a rainbow sheen of oil on twilight waters.

"What's the matter now?" asked Meyer.

"Harry is right, you know."

"To try to kill you?"

"Very funny. He's right about Mary getting in touch. I get the feeling she would. Emotional logic. The last time her world ruptured, I helped her walk it off, talk it off, think it off."

"So maybe she had enough and said the hell with it."

"She is one stubborn lady. Harry is no prize. She married him a little too fast. But she would really bust a gut to make the marriage work. She wouldn't quit. She wouldn't run."

"Unless he did something that she just couldn't take. Maybe it got to her gag reflex. Wouldn't she run then?"

"Yes. I guess so. And maybe she's a stronger person than she was back when I knew her. All Harry said was that he had gotten mixed up with some Canadian girl, a first offense. I know that wouldn't make Mary give any ringing cheers. But I think she's human enough to know it wouldn't be the end of the world or the marriage. Well, he has to locate her before the end of April, or he has big business problems."

"Hmm?"

"Something about signing something so he can keep his interest in SeaGate, whatever the hell that is."

"It's a planned community up in the northeast corner of Martin County, above Hobe Sound where there's no A-1-A running along the beach. It's a syndicate thing, way too big for anybody like Broll to swing by himself."

"How do you know all that stuff?"

"There was a feature story about planned communities in the *Wall Street Journal* a month ago. The local papers have had articles about it for over a year. I believe *Newsweek* had a—"

"Truce. Could a guy like Broll do well in a deal like that?"

"Depends. The ownership structure would be the important consideration."

"Could you find out where he fits and how, and why Mary would have to sign something?"

"I imagine I could. But why?"

"Harry's nerves are bad. He looks bad. He has a money orientation. If he misses out on large money because Mary runs and hides and won't sign, it somehow doesn't sound like Mary. It would be a cheap shot and a dumb shot. She isn't dumb. Whether she stays with him or leaves him, it would be better for him to have money. She's been gone for two months. If he was so certain she'd run to me, where has he been for two months? Time is running out in two weeks. So he comes around with shaking hands and a sweaty shirt and a couple of places he missed while shaving. Time is running out not on the marriage, on the money. It makes me wonder."

"I'll look into it," he said as we walked.

End of discussion. We had arrived at the area where they park the showboats, the ones too big to bring around inside, and thus have to leave them on the river, not far from the fuel pumps, where two out of every three Power Squadron types who cruise by can whap them against the cement with their curling wash. The *Jilly III* is a custom motor-sailer trimaran out of St. Kitts, owned by Jillian, the widow of Sir Henry Brent-Archer. It is seventy feet long with a beam that has to be close to fifty feet. It rides a bad sea with all the stability of a brick church. Minimal superstructure to emphasize an expanse of teak deck as big as a tennis court, with more than half of it shaded by the big colorful awning tarp her crew of three always strings up as soon as they are at dockside.

The bar table was positioned, draped in white damask. A piano tape was playing show tunes with muted discretion over the stereo system I'd helped her buy the last time she was in Lauderdale. There were a dozen guests assembled, three conversational groups of elegant folk sipping the very best booze from the most expensive glasses. Jilly saw us approaching the little gangplank and came a-striding, beaming, to welcome us aboard.

A lady of unguessable years, who made damned well certain she gave you no clues at all. If she turned up as a Jane Doe, DOA, traffic, a hasty coroner could not be blamed for penciling in the apparent age as plus or minus twenty-seven. Tall, slender brunette of such careful and elegant grooming, such exquisitely capped teeth, it seemed safe to assume she was in some area of entertainment. But she had such a much better tan and better physical condition than most show business people, one might safely guess her to be, perhaps, a model for beachwear? A lead in a commercial water ballet?

But a coroner less hasty, more sophisticated, who searched the scalp and elsewhere for the faintest of traces left by superb Swiss surgeons, who slipped the tinted plastic lenses off and studied the eyes closely as well as the backs of the hands, base of the throat, ankles, wrists. . . . He might add a quotient of years in direct ratio to his quality of observation and his experience.

Jilly had a lively and animated face peering out from the careless spill of black hair, all bright questing eyes, black brows, big nose, broad and generous mouth. Ever since I had known Jilly, her voice had cracked like that of a boy in early adolescence, changing from the piercing, songbird clarity of the Irish upperclass countryside to a burring baritone honk and back again. It was so effective it seemed contrived. But a small sailboat had foundered one night in a bad sea, and she had clung to a channel buoy, permanently spraining her vocal cords shouting at the boat traffic until finally she was heard and she and her injured friend were rescued.

"Meyer!" she cried. "My *word,* darling! You're of a surpassing radiance. Travis dear, what happened to him? Did he molt or something?" She linked her arms through ours and croaked, "Come on, dears. Meet the ones you don't know and get smashed soon as you can because I am gallons ahead of you."

The introductions were made. Jillian slipped away to greet more guests. We drank. The sun went down. The night breeze was gentle but cool, and ladies put their wraps back on. The party lights strung from the rigging were properly dim, flatteringly orange. The buffet materialized, as if the table had risen up out of the teak. The music tape was more lively, the volume louder than before.

I found myself inadvertently paired with a smallish, withered Englishwoman with a shrunken face the color of weak tea and hair dyed the color of raspberry ice. A Mrs. Ogleby. I had seen Meyer talking to her towering and cadaverous husband, pumping him about the latest Common Market difficulties. We carried our buffet plates forward

where she could sit on a narrow shelflike bench built out
from the bow where the rail was solid. I sat crosslegged on
the deck with my plate atop the massive bow cleat.

"I understand that you are one of dear Jillian's very favorite Americans, Mr. McGee."

She managed to load the comment with sweetly venom-
ous insinuation. I beamed up at her. "And she's one of my
favorite foreigners."

"Really! How terribly nice for her. Actually, Geoffrey
and I were old friends of poor Sir Henry long before he
married Jillian."

"Then Jillian isn't one of your favorite people, eh?"

She clinked her fork against the plate and leaned forward and peered down at me. "Whatever gave you such
an odd idea? She is *very* dear. Very dear to both of us."

"I knew Sir Henry, too."

"Really! I wouldn't have thought you would have
known him."

"I was a house guest at St. Kitts for a few weeks."

"But that would have been after he was quite ill, I take
it." Her smile was thin and knowing in the light of the
nearby party lantern. A truly poisonous little woman.

"No. As a matter of fact, Mrs. Ogleby, Henry and I
swam our three miles every morning, went riding or sailing
every afternoon, and played chess every evening."

She paused and regrouped. "Before he became ill, Sir
Henry had really fantastic energies. How strange we all
thought it that he would marry someone that young, after
being a widower so long. It seemed odd. But, of course,
that was so awfully long ago it is rather difficult to think of
Jillian as—"

"Just think of me, dears, no matter how difficult it may
be," said Jilly. "Hmmm. What is this you have, Lenore? I
didn't see it at all. May I? Mmmm. Shrimp, and what a
deliciously fiery sauce! Difficult to think of me as what,
Lenore darling?"

When Mrs. Ogleby hesitated, I said, "She was about to
pinpoint the date when you and Sir Henry were married."

"Were you, dear? It slips my mind, you know. Was it

just before or just after that fuss with the Spanish Armada?"

"Don't be absurd! I was only—"

"You were only being Lenore, which is part of the trouble, isn't it? Travis, I was married to Henry long long ago. Matter of fact, I was but three years old at the time, and most of the people in the church thought it was some sort of delayed christening. There was talk that it was an unwholesome relationship, but by the time I was fourteen— eleven years later—I looked twenty, and everyone said that it had probably been all for the best. And it was, of course. Lenore, you seem to be finished. Dear, come with me and show me just where you found the shrimp, will you please?"

"But if there is any left, it should be quite obvi—"

"Lenore!"

"Quite. Of course. I shall be happy to show you, my dear Jillian."

"I knew it would make you happy to have a chance to be nice to me, Lenore."

Off they went. Old friends, smiling and chattering.

Twenty minutes later as I was moving away from the bar with some Wild Turkey straight, instead of brandy, Jilly intercepted me and moved me into relative shadow.

"Travis, if you are a truly thoughtful and understanding man, you have your toothbrush hidden away on your person."

"I had the idea the party girl would need her eight hours."

"Have a little mercy, dear. There's but one way to settle down from this sort of bash. You shall divert me."

"I can leave and then come back. You know. Like a house call."

"Is its tender little romantical pride bruised because the party girl thinks love making is therapeutic? To say nothing of being a hell of a lot of fun. Just stay on, dear. Stay by me. Smile like a tomcat with a little yellow feather caught in his whiskers, and soon now we can smile them off and sing out our merry farewells."

"Giving Lenore more food for thought?"

"Thought? Christ, that poisonous bitch doesn't think. She slanders, because she has her own terrible hunger she can't ease in any way. She burns in fire, my darling, and hates and hates and hates. Poor thing. Brace yourself, pet. I want you horribly."

three

_____

I drifted in and out of a placid and amiable doze. Water slapped the triple hulls, whispering lies about how big the seas could really get. I cocked an eye at an upward angle at the battery digital clock fastened to the bulkhead over Jillian's bed. Watched 4:06 turning magically to 4:07. There was a single light on in her stateroom, a rose-colored globe of frosty glass, big as a cantaloupe, standing next to its twin reflection in the dressing table mirror.

It was warm in her stateroom, not unpleasantly so, just enough to leave a humid dew, rosy highlights on our entangled flesh, sprawled and spent, atop a wrinkled dampness of custom sheets in a pattern of green vines with yellow leaves against white.

Jilly lay oddly positioned, her upper torso diagonally across my chest, face in a pillow, cheek against my right shoulder, her slack right arm hooked around my neck. Her long tanned legs were sprawled down there, off to my left. My right arm was pinned, but my left arm was free, my hand resting on the small of her back.

I traced the velvet geographies of that small concave area of the country of Jilly and then made a coin-sized circle of fingernails and thumbnail and made a slow circling motion against her there, a circle as big as a teacup. In time the pattern of her breathing changed. She shifted. She exhaled though slack rubbery lips, making a sound like a small horse.

"Is someone mentioning my name?" she said in a sleepy voice.

"Pure telepathy."

She raised her head, clawed her hair out of the way, and peered up at the clock. "Gawd! What year is it? Don't tell me."

She heaved herself up, tugging her arm out from under my neck. She sat up and combed her hair back with the fingers of both hands, yawning widely as she did so. She shook and snapped her head back, settled her hair, then curled her limber legs under her and smiled down at me. "Been awake long, Travis?"

"Off and on."

"Thinking? About what?"

I hitched myself higher on the pillows. "Random things. This and that."

"Tell me about them."

"Let me think back. Oh, I was wondering how it's possible to make this bed up. It's shaped to fit perfectly into the curves of this middle hull right up at the bow and—"

"There are little lever things on the legs down there, and when you push them down, then you can roll the bed back and make it up. You certainly think about fascinating things."

"Then I heard a motor go on, and I was wondering if it was a bilge pump or a refrigeration compressor or—"

"You are trying to be tiresome. Didn't you think about what I asked you?"

"Maybe I did. A little bit. Like wondering why it has to be me."

"If one could know why a person settles upon a particular person, one would know one of the mysteries, wouldn't one? I think it was because of four years ago. I think it started then."

A friend of a friend had put Sir Henry Brent-Archer in touch with me. A problem of simple extortion. I had gone down to the British Virgins and spent three weeks at their spacious and lovely home and found exactly the right way to pry the two-legged lamprey loose, file its sharp teeth off, and send it unhappily on its way. And during the three weeks I had become ever more sensuously aware of Sir Henry's handsome and lively wife. She made sure of that awareness.

"Because I kept it from starting?"

"Was I all that distasteful to you, my darling?"

"Not you. The situation. I liked Sir Henry. In spite of the fact I was working for him on a special problem, I was still a guest in his home. In a man's home you live by his code. It does not have to be typed out and glued to the guest suite door. He did not want me to kick his dogs, overwork his horses, bribe his servants, read his diary, filch his silverware, borrow his toothbrush, or lay his wife. I accepted the obligation when I moved in."

She snickered. "Would you believe that was the only time in the years I was his wife that I ever tried to be naughty?"

"There's no reason not to believe it."

"I was very grateful to Sir Henry. He came along at just the right time in my life. My whole dreadful family was sliding into the pit, and through him I could save them, so I snatched him up quickly. I liked him well enough for half the marriage, liked him a great deal for the rest of it, and started loving him after he was buried. Anyway, on that stupid night I lay and listened to my heart going bump, bump, bump. Then I got up and drenched myself with that lovely scent and put on the little froth of nightgown and crept through the night like a thief and slipped into your bed. And suddenly got lifted out bodily, carried to the door, given a great whack across my bare behind, and shoved out into the hall. I did not know whether to laugh or cry. I did both."

"It was closer than you'll ever know, Jilly."

"So it's you, dear man. The chosen. Relax and enjoy it. Why not? Am I trying to nail you down permanently? Of course, but through your own choice and decision. I give you full disclosure, dear. I have something over eight hundred thousand pounds, carefully managed by nice little Swiss elves. The income is about a hundred and fifty thousand of your dollars a year, and taxes take hardly any. There is the lovely house with the beach, the bay, and the view, and the boats and cars and horses. I am not exactly a junior miss, but I work very hard at myself, and I come from healthy stock. I suspect I shall go on about the same

for years and years and years and suddenly one morning
wake up as a shriveled, cackling little old witch. All I ask
of you is that you come back home with me, darling. Be
my houseguest. Be my love. We laugh at the same things.
We enjoy the same things. Last trip and this trip we've
certainly established . . . physical compatibility. Darling,
please! We'll travel when you want to and go where you
want to go. We'll be with people when you want to, and
they will be the people you want to be with. Please!"

"Jilly, you are a dear and lovely lady—"

"But! I know, dammit. But! Why *not?* Do you even
know?"

I knew but did not want to tell her. You see many
such couples around the yacht clubs and bath clubs and
tennis clubs of the western world. The man, a little
younger or a lot younger that the moneyed widow or di-
vorcee he has either married or is traveling with. The man
is usually brown and good at games, dresses youthfully
and talks amusingly. But he drinks a little too much. And
completely trained and conditioned, he is ever alert for his
cues. If his lady unsnaps her purse and frowns down into
it, he at once presents his cigarettes, and they are always
her brand. If she has her own cigarettes, he can cross
twenty feet in a twelfth of a second to snap the unwavering
flame to life, properly and conveniently positioned for her.
It takes but the smallest sidelong look of query to send
him in search of an ashtray to place close to her elbow. If
at sundown she raises her elegant shoulders a half inch, he
trots into the house or onto the boat or up to the suite, to
bring back her wrap. He knows just how to apply her suntan oil, knows which of her dresses have to be zipped up
and snapped for her. He can draw her bath to the precise
depth and temperature which please her. He can give her
an acceptable massage, brew a decent pot of coffee, take
her phone messages accurately, keep her personal check-
book in balance, and remind her when to take her medica-
tions. Her litany is: Thank you, dearest. How nice, darling. You are so thoughtful, sweetheart.

It does not happen quickly, of course. It is an easy life.

Other choices, once so numerous, disappear. Time is the random wind that blows down the long corridor, slamming all the doors. And finally, of course, it comes down to a very simple equation. Life is endurable when she is contented and difficult when she is displeased. It is a training process. Conditioned response.

"I'm used to the way I live," I told her.

"The way you live," she said. With brooding face she reached and ran gentle fingertips along the deep, gullied scar in my thigh, then leaned, and touched the symmetrical dimple of the entrance wound of a bullet. She hunched closer to me, bent, and kissed the white welt of scar tissue that is nearly hidden by the scruffy, sun-faded hair at my temple. "The way you live, Travis. Trying to trick the tricky ones. Trying to make do with bluff and smiles and strange lies. Filching fresh meat right out of the jaws of the sharks. For how long, dear, before finally the odds go bad and the luck goes bad once and for all?"

"I'm sly."

"Not sly enough. Maybe not quick enough anymore. I think you've been doing it for too long, darling. Too many years of getting things back for silly, careless people who should not have lost them in the first place. One day some dim little chap will come upon you suddenly and take out a gun and shoot you quite dead."

"Are you a witch? Do you so prophesy?"

She fell upon me, hugged me tight. "Ah no, dear. No. You had all the years when that was the thing you had to do. Now the years belong to me. Is it such a sickening fate you can't endure the thought of it?"

"No, Jilly. No, honey. It's just that . . ."

"Give us a month. No. One week. One insignificant little week. Or else."

"Or else?"

She burrowed a bit, gently closed her teeth onto the upper third of my left ear, then released it. "I have splendid teeth and very strong jaw muscles. If you say no, I shall set my teeth into your ear and do my best to tear it right off your head, darling."

"You just might at that."

"You love to bluff people. Try me."

"No, thank you. One week."

She took a deep breath and let it out. "Lovely! Time in transit doesn't count, of course. Can we leave . . . day after tomorrow?"

"I don't know."

"Why don't you know?"

"I just found out that an old friend might be in trouble. It just seems to me that if she was in trouble, she'd come to me."

Jilly wiggled and thrust away from me and sat up. "She?"

"Frowning makes wrinkles."

"So it does. She?"

"A respectable married lady."

"If she's so respectable, how is it she knows *you?*"

"Before she was married."

"And I suppose you had an affair with her."

"Gee, honey. I'd have to look it up."

I caught her fist about five inches from my eye. "You bahstid," she said.

"Okay. An affair. A mad, wild, glorious liaison which kept us in an absolute frenzy of passion."

Her look was enigmatic. "You are perfectly right, of course, darling. It is none of my business. What's she like? I mean, what physical type?"

"In general, a lot like you, Jilly. Tall, slender brunette. Dark hair, takes a good tan. Long legs, short waisted. She would be . . . twenty-eight or -nine by now. Back when I knew her, she didn't race her motor the way you do. More of a placid, contented person. She really enjoyed cooking and scrubbing and bed-making. She could sleep ten or twelve hours a night."

"You damned well remember every detail, don't you?"

I smiled up into her leaning, earnest face—a small face but strong of feature in the black, bed-snarled dangle of hair. I looked at her limber, brown body in the rose glow of the lamp ten feet away, noting the way the deep tan above and below her breasts decreased in ever more pallid horizontal stripes and shadings down to that final band of pale and pure white which denoted her narrowest bikini top.

"Why are you laughing at me, you dull sod?"

"Not at you, Lady Jillian."

"I am *not* Lady Jillian. That usage is improper. If you are not laughing *at,* then you are laughing *with.* And if you are laughing *with,* why is that I am not amused?"

"But you are, darling."

She tried to keep her mouth severe but lost the battle, gave a rusty honk of laughter, and flung herself upon me.

"I can't stay angry with you, Travis. You promised me a week. But I'll punish you for that dark-haired lady."

"How?"

"On our way to St. Kitts there will be at least one day or night when we'll spend hour after hour quartering into an ugly, irregular chop."

"I don't get seasick."

"Nor do I, my love. It would spoil it if either of us became ill."

"Spoil what?"

"Dear man, when the chop is effective, one cannot stay on this bed. You are lifted up, and then the bed and the hull drop away from you, and when you are on your way down, the bed comes up and smacks you and boosts you into the air again. It is like trying to post on a very bad horse. When that happens, dear, you and I are going to be right here, making love. We'll see how well you satisfy a lady in mid-air. I shall have you tottering about, wishing you'd never met Mrs. Whatever."

"Mrs. Broll. Mary Broll. Mary Dillon Broll."

"You think she should have come to you if she's in trouble? Isn't that a little patronizing and arrogant?"

"Possibly."

"What sort of trouble?"

"Marriage trouble. Her husband cheated, and she caught him at it and left him back in January."

"Good Lord, why should she come galloping to you?"

"It's an emotional problem, and when she had one sort of like it years ago, we got together, and she worked her way out of it."

"And fell in love with you?"

"I think that with Mary there would have to be some affection before there could be anything."

"You poor dumb beast. You're *so* obvious."

"What do you mean?"

"You can't for the life of you comprehend why she doesn't come scuttling back to Dr. McGee's free and famous clinic. Your pride is hurt, dear. I suspect she's found some other therapist."

"Even if she had, I think she'd have let me know the marriage had soured. I get the feeling something happened to her."

She yawned and stretched. "Let me make one thing abundantly clear, as one of your grubby little political types says or used to say. Once we have our design for living, if we have any doleful visits from one of your previous patients, my dear, I shall take a broom to them and beat them through the garden gate and down the drive."

"Don't you think you ought to type all these rules up and give me three copies?"

"You're so damned *defensive!* Good Christ, am I some sort of dog's dinner?"

"You are a lively, sexy, lovely, sexy, well-dressed, sexy, amusing, sexy, wealthy, sexy widow lady."

"And some *very* tidy and considerate men come flocking around. Men with all the social graces and very good at games. Not knuckly, scabrous, lazy, knobbly old ruins like you, McGee."

"So grab one of those tidy and considerate ones."

"Oh, sure. They are lovely men, and they are *so* anxious to please me. There's the money, and it makes them very jumpy and nervous. Their hands get cold and damp. If I frown, they look terrified. Couldn't you be more anxious to please me, dear? Just a little bit?"

"Like this, you mean?"

"Well . . . I didn't exactly mean that. . . . I meant in a more general sense . . . but . . . now that you bring it up.

... god, I can't remember now what I did mean. ... I guess I meant this. Yes, darling. This."

The narrow horizontal ports above the custom bed let a cold and milky morning light into the stateroom at the bow of the center hull of the *Jilly III*. As I looked up, 6:31 became 6:32. Jillian's small round rump, her flesh warmer than mine, was thrust with a domestic coziness into my belly. My chin rested against the crown of her head. Her tidy heft had turned my left arm numb. My right hand lay upon the sweet inward curve of her waist.

Worse fates, I thought. A life with Jilly Brent-Archer wouldn't be dull. Maybe it is time for the islands. In spite of all good intentions, all nervous concern, all political bombast, my dirty two-legged species is turning the lovely southeast coast into a sewer. On still days the stinking sky is bourbon brown, and in the sea there are only the dwindling runty fish that can survive in that poisoned brew.

It happens slowly, so you try not to notice it. You tell yourself it happens to be a bad day, that's all. The tides and the winds will scrub it all clean. But not clean enough anymore. One life to live, so pop through the escape hatch, McGee. Try the islands. Damned few people can escape the smudge and sludge, the acids and stenches, the choking and weeping. You have to take care of yourself, man. Nobody else is going to. And this deft morsel, curled sleeping against you, is a first-class ticket for all of the voyage you have left. Suppose you *do* have to do some bowing and scraping and fetching. Will it kill you? Think of what most people have to do for a living. You've been taking your retirement in small installments whenever you could afford it. So here's the rest of it in her lovely sleep. The ultimate social security.

I eased my dead arm out from under her and moved away. She made a sleep-whine of discontent. I covered her with the big colorful sheet, dressed, turned out the rosy light, and made sure the main hatchway locked behind me when I left.

Back aboard the *Flush* I put on swim trunks and a robe to keep me warm in the morning chill. The sun was coming up out of the sea when I walked across the pedestrian bridge over the highway and down onto the public beach. Morning birds were running along the wet sand, pecking and fleeing from the wash of the surf. An old man was jogging slowly by, his face in a clench of agony. A fat girl in a brown dress was looking for shells.

I went in, swam hard, and rested, again and again, using short bursts of total energy. I went back to the *Flush* and had a quart of orange juice, four scrambled eggs along with some rat cheese from Vermont, and a mug of black coffee.

I fell asleep seven and a half inches above my oversized bed in the master stateroom, falling toward the bed, long gone before I landed.

four

Thursday, when I got up a little before noon, the remembered scene with Harry Broll and his little gun seemed unreal. Six loud whacks, not loud enough to attract the curious attention of people on the neighboring craft. The *Flush* had been buttoned up, the airconditioning on. No slug had gone through glass.

I found where five had hit. At last I spotted the sixth one in the overhead. It had hit tumbling and sideways and had not punched itself all the way out of sight, so by elimination it was the one that had grooved the leather sole of my sandal and numbed my heel.

I had rolled to my right after going over backward in the chair. It gave me the chance to kick a small table over, creating more distraction and confusion, and it also forced him, being right-handed, to bring his arm across his body to aim at me, which is more difficult than extending the arm out to the side. Two into the deck, one into the chair, one into the table, one into the overhead, and one into my stereo amplifier.

So maybe the clip held six, and he had not jacked one into the chamber until he got to the parking lot at the marina. If he'd put one in the chamber and filled the clip all the way, there would have been one left for the middle of my face.

Dead then or a long time in the institutional bed with the drains in place and the pain moving around under the sedatives like a snake under a blanket.

Don't give yourself any credit, Mr. Travis McGee. The fates could have counted to seven just as easily. You had

39

an easy shot at him with the ashtray, but your hand was sweaty and the fingertips slipped. You missed badly.

Meyer could be right. I had depended on instinct. It had been my instinct that Harry Broll had not come to kill me. Then he had done his best, and I had lucked out. So was instinct becoming stale? When it stopped being a precision tool, when it ceased sending accurate messages up from the atavistic, animal level of the brain, I was as vulnerable as if sight or hearing had begun to fail. If soft, sloppy, nervous Harry Broll could almost do me in with a pop gun, my next meeting with professional talent could be mortal.

There was another dimension to it. Once I started doubting my survival instinct, I would lose confidence in my own reactions. A loss of confidence creates hesitations. Hesitation is a fatal disease—for anyone in the salvage business.

There are worse careers than house guest. Or pet gopher.

Too much solitary introspection started to depress me. I was ready for Geritol and cortisone. I pulled all the plugs and connections on the Marantz and lugged its considerable weight all the way to where I'd parked Miss Agnes, my ancient and amiable old blue Rolls pickup. I drove over to town to Al's Musicade. He is lean, sour, and knowledgeable. He does not say much. He took it out back himself and found bench space in his busy service department. I watched him finger the hole in the front of it. He quickly loosened the twelve Phillips screws that hold the top perforated plate down, lifted it off, found more damage, reached in with two fingers, and lifted out the deformed slug.

"Somebody didn't like the programing?"

"Bad lyrics."

"Week from today?"

"Loaner?"

"Got a Fisher you can use."

We walked out front, and he lifted it off the rack, a used one in apparently good condition. He made a note of the serial number and who was taking it out.

I put the borrowed amplifier on the passenger seat beside me and went looking for Harry Broll's place of business. I had seen it once and had a general idea where to find it. I had to ask at a gas station. It was west of Lauderdale, off Davie Road, over in an industrial park in pine and palmetto country. All of it except the office itself was circled by high hurricane fencing with slanted braces and three strands of barbed wire on top. There was a gate for the rail spur and a truck and equipment gate. I could see a central mix concrete plant, a block plant, big piles of sand, gravel, and crushed stone. I could see warehouses, stacks of lumber, piles of prestressed concrete beams, and a vehicle park and repair area. This was a Thursday at one thirty in the afternoon, and I could count only ten cars. Four of those were in front of the office. The office was a long, low concrete-block building painted white with a flat roof. The landscaped grass was burned brown, and they had lost about half the small palm trees planted near the office.

There were too many trucks and pieces of equipment in the park. It looked neat enough but sleepy. BROLL ENTERPRISES, Inc. But some of the big plastic letters had blown off or fallen off. It said:

ROLL E   TERP   ISES, Inc.

I cruised slowly by. I was tempted to turn around and go back and go in and see if Harry was there and try once more to tell him I'd had no contact whatsoever with Mary for over three years. But he was going to believe what emotions told him to believe.

I wondered how Meyer was doing, using his friends in the banks, brokerage houses, and investment houses to find out just how sweaty Harry Broll might be. The tight-money times and the over-building of condominiums and the pyramiding costs had busted quite a few able fellows lately. Harry probably hadn't come through that bad period without some ugly bruises. I could tell Meyer how idle Broll's place of business looked, if he hadn't found out already.

When I got back to Bahia Mar, Meyer was still missing. I felt restless. I set up the Fisher, hooked up the tape decks, turntables, and the two sets of speakers. It checked out all right. I turned it off and paced. The itch you can't quite reach. Familiar feeling. Like the name you can't quite remember.

I looked up the number for Broll Enterprises and phoned. The girl answered by reciting the number I'd just dialed.

"Maybe you can help me, miss. I'm trying to get a home address for Mrs. Harry Broll."

"In what regard, please."

"Well, this is the Shoe Mart, and it was way back in November 'we special-ordered a pair of shoes for Mrs. Broll. It took so long she's under no obligation to take them, but they're more a classic than a high-style item, so I figure she probably wants them, but I been drawing a blank on the home phone number, so I thought maybe they moved or something."

"Will you hold on a moment, please?"

I held. It took her about a minute and a half. "Mr. Broll says that you can deliver them here to the office. Do you know where we are?"

"Sure. Okay. Thanks. It'll probably be tomorrow."

I hung up, and once again, to make sure, I dialed the home phone number for Harry Broll, 21 Blue Heron Lane. "The number you have dialed is not in service at this time."

I scowled at my phone. Come on, McGee. The man is living somewhere. Information has no home number for him. The old home number is on temporary disconnect. The new number of wherever he's living must be unlisted. It probably doesn't matter a damn where he's living. It's the challenge.

Okay. Think a little. Possibly all his mail is directed to the business address. But some things have to be delivered. Booze, medicine, automobiles. Water, electricity . . . cablevision?

The lady had a lovely voice, gentle and musical and intriguingly breathy. "I could track it down more quickly, Mr. Broll, if you could give me your account number."

"I wish I could. I'm sorry, miss. I don't have the bill in front of me. But couldn't you check it by address? The last billing was sent to 21 Blue Heron Lane. If it's too much trouble, I can phone you tomorrow. You see, the bill is at my home, and I'm at the office."

"Just a moment, please. Let me check the cross index."

It took a good five minutes. "Sorry it took me so long," she said.

"It was my fault, not having my account number, miss."

"Broll. Bee-are-oh-el-el. Harry C.?"

"Correct."

"And you said the bill went where?"

"To 21 Blue Heron Lane. That's where I used to live."

"Gee, Mr. Broll, I don't understand it at all. All billing is supposed to be mailed to Post Office box 5150."

"I wonder if I've gotten a bill that belongs to someone else. The amount doesn't seem right either."

"You should be paying $6.24 a month, sir. For the one outlet. You were paying more, of course, for the four outlets at Blue Heron Lane before you ordered the disconnect."

"Excuse me, but does your file show where I am getting the one-outlet service? Do you have the right address?"

"Oh, yes sir. It's 8553 Ocean Boulevard, apartment 61. I've got the installation order number. That *is* right, isn't it?"

"Yes. That's right. But I think the billing is for eleven dollars and something."

"Mr. Broll, please mail the bill back in the regular envelope we send out, but in the left bottom corner would you write *Customer Service, Miss Locklin?*"

"I will do that. I certainly appreciate your kindness and courtesy, Miss Locklin."

"No trouble, really. That's what we're here for."

Four o'clock and still no Meyer, so I went out and coaxed Miss Agnes back to life and went rolling on up Ocean Boulevard. I kept to the far right lane and went slowly because the yearly invasion of Easter bunnies was upon us, was beginning to dwindle, and there was too little time to enjoy them. They had been beaching long enough so that there were very few cases of lobster pink. The tans were nicely established, and the ones who still burned had a brown burn. There are seven lads to every Easter bunny, and the litheness and firmness of the young ladies gamboling on the beach, ambling across the highway, stretching out to take the sun, is something to stupefy the senses. It creates something which is beyond any of the erotic daydreams of traditional lust, even beyond that aesthetic pleasure of looking upon pleasing line and graceful move.

It is possible to stretch a generalized lust, or an aesthetic turn of mind, to encompass a hundred lassies—say five and a half tons of vibrant and youthful and sun-toned flesh clad in about enough fabric to half fill a bushel basket. The erotic imagination or the artistic temperament can assimilate these five and a half tons of flanks and thighs, nates and breasts, laughing mouths and bouncing hair and shining eyes, but neither lust nor art can deal with a few thousand of them. Perceptions go into stasis. You cannot compare one with another. They become a single silken and knowledgeable creature, unknowable, a thousand-legged contemptuous joy, armored by the total ignorance of the very young and by the total wisdom of body and instinct of the female kind. A single cell of the huge creature, a single entity, one girl, can be trapped and baffled, hurt and emptied, broken and abandoned. Or to flip the coin, she can be isolated and cherished, wanted and needed, taken with contracts and ceremonies. In either case the great creature does not miss the single identity subtracted from the whole any more than the hive misses the single bee. It goes on in its glistening, giggling, leggy immortality, forever replenished from the equation of children plus time, existing every spring, unchangingly and challengingly invulnerable—an exquisite reservoir called Girl, aware of being admired and saying "Drink me!," knowing that no matter how deep the draughts, the level of sweetness in the reservoir remains the same forever.

There are miles of beach, and there were miles of bunnies along the tan Atlantic sand. When the public beach ended I came to the great white wall of high-rise condominiums which conceal the sea and partition the sky. They are compartmented boxes stacked high in sterile sameness. The balconied ghetto. Soundproof, by the sea. So many conveniences and security measures and safety factors that life at last is reduced to an ultimate boredom, to the great decisions of the day—which channel to watch and whether to swim in the sea or the pool.

I found 8553. It was called Casa de Playa and was spray-creted as wedding cake white as the rest of them. Twelve stories, in the shape of a shallow C, placed to give a maximum view of the sea to each apartment even though the lot was quite narrow. I had heard that raw land along there was going at four thousand a foot. It makes an architectural challenge to take a two-hundred-foot lot which costs eight hundred thousand dollars and cram 360 apartments onto it, each with a view, and retain some elusive flavor of spaciousness and elegance.

Economics lesson. Pay eight hundred thou for the land. Put up two hundred thousand more for site preparation, improvement, landscaping, covered parking areas, swimming pool or pools. Put up a twelve-story building with 30 apartments on each of the floors from the second through the eleventh and 15 penthouse apartments on top. You have 315 apartments. The building and the apartment equipment cost nine million. So you price them and move them on the basis that the higher in the air they are and the bigger they are, the more they cost. All you have to do is come out with about a thirty-three hundred net on each apartment on the average after all construction expenses, overhead expenses, and sales commissions, and you make one million dollars, and you are a sudden millionaire before taxes.

But if the apartments are retailing at an average forty thousand each and you sell off everything in the building except ten percent of the apartments, then instead of being a million bucks ahead, you are two hundred thousand in the red.

It is deceptively simple and monstrously tricky. Meyer says that they should make a survey and find out how many condominium heart attacks have been admitted to Florida hospitals. A new syndrome. The first symptom is a secret urge to go up to an unsold penthouse and jump off your own building, counting vacancies all the way down.

As I did not care to be remembered because of Miss Agnes, I drove to a small shopping center on the left side of the highway, stashed her in the parking lot, and walked back to the Casa de Playa.

On foot I had time to read all of the sign in front.

NOW SHOWING. MODEL APARTMENTS. CASA DE PLAYA. A NEW ADVENTURE IN LIVING. FROM $38,950 TO $98,950. PRIVATE OCEAN BEACH. POOL. HOTEL SERVICES. FIREPROOF AND SOUNDPROOF CONSTRUCTION. SECURITY GUARD ON PREMISES. NO PETS. NO CHILDREN UNDER FIFTEEN. AUTOMATIC FIRE AND BURGLAR ALARM. COMMUNITY LOUNGE AND GAME AREA. ANOTHER ADVENTURE IN LIVING BY BROLL ENTERPRISES, INC.

The big glass door swung shut behind me and closed out the perpetual sounds of the river of traffic, leaving me in a chilled hush on springy carpeting in a faint smell of fresh paint and antiseptic.

I walked by the elevators and saw a small desk in an alcove. The sign on the desk said: Jeannie Dolan, Sales Executive on Duty. A lean young lady sat behind the desk, hunched over, biting down on her underlip, scowling down at the heel of her left hand and picking at the flesh with a pin or needle.

"Sliver?" I said.

She jumped about four inches off the desk chair. "Hey! Don't sneak up, huh?"

"I wasn't trying to."

"I know you weren't. I'm sorry. Yes, it's a sliver."

"Want some help?"

She looked up at me. Speculative and noncommittal. She couldn't decide whether I'd come to deliver something, repair something, serve legal papers, or buy all the unsold apartments in a package deal.

"Well . . . every time I take hold of something, it hurts."

I took her over to the daylight, to an upholstered bench near a big window which looked out at a wall made of pierced concrete blocks. I held her thin wrist and looked at her hand. There was red inflammation around the sliver and a drop of blood where she had been picking at it. I could see the dark narrow shape of the splinter under the pink and transparent skin. She had been working with a needle and a pair of tweezers. I sterilized the needle in her lighter flame, pinched up the skin so that I could pick a little edge of the splinter free. She sucked air through clenched teeth. I took the tweezers and got hold of the tiny end and pulled it out.

"Long," I said, holding it up. "Trophy size. You should get it mounted."

"Thank you very very much. It was driving me flippy," she said, standing up.

"Got anything to put on it?"

"Iodine in the first aid kit."

I followed her back to the desk. She hissed again when the iodine touched the raw tissue. She asked my advice as to whether to put a little round bandaid patch on it, and I said I thought a splinter that big deserved a bandage and a sling, too.

She was lean, steamed-up, a quick-moving, fast-talking woman in her late twenties with a mobile face and a flexible, expressive voice. In repose she could have been quite ordinary. There was a vivacity, an air of enjoying life about her that made her attractive. Her hair was red-brown, her eyes a quick, gray-green, her teeth too large, and her upperlip too short for her to comfortably pull her mouth shut, so it remained parted, making her look vital and breathless instead of vacuous. She used more eye makeup than I care for.

"Before I ask question one, Miss Dolan—"

"Mrs. Dolan. But Jeannie, please. And you are . . .?"

"John Q. Public until I find out something."

"John Q. Spy?"

"No. I want to know who you represent, Jeannie."

"Represent? I'm selling these condominium apartments as any fool can plainly—"

"For whom?"

"For Broll Enterprises."

"I happen to know Harry. Do the skies clear now?"

She tilted, frowned, then grinned. "Sure. If a realtor was handling this and you talked to me, then there'd have to be a commission paid, and you couldn't get a better price from Mr. Broll. There used to be a realtor handling it, but they didn't do so well, and I guess Mr. Broll decided this would be a better way. Can I sell you one of our penthouses today, sir? Mr. Public, sir?"

"McGee. Travis McGee. I don't know whether I'm a live one or not. I'm doing some scouting for a friend. I'd like to look at one with two bedrooms and two baths just to get an idea."

She took a sign out of her desk and propped it against the phone. "Back in ten minutes. Please be seated." She locked her desk and we went up to the eighth floor. She chattered all the way up and all the way down the eighth floor corridor, telling me what a truly great place it was to live and how well constructed it was and how happy all the new residents were.

She unlocked the door and swung it open with a flourish. She kept on chattering, following a couple of steps behind me as I went from room to room. After quite a while she ran out of chatter. "Well. . . . Don't you want to ask *anything?*"

"The floor plan is efficient. The equipment looks pretty adequate. But the furniture and the carpeting and the decorating make me feel sort of sick, Jeannie."

"A very expensive decorator did all our display apartments."

"Yeck."

"A lot of people are really turned on by it."

"Yeck."

"We've even sold some with all the decor intact, just as you see it. The buyers insisted."

"Still yeck."

"And I think it is absolutely hideous, and it makes me feel queasy, too. It looks too sweet. Cotton candy and candy cane and ribbon candy. Yeck."

"Got one just like this that hasn't been messed with?"

"Down on five. Come along."

We rode down three floors. The apartment was spot-lessly clean and absolutely empty. She unlocked the sliding doors, and we went out onto the balcony and leaned against the railing.

"If the answers to the other questions make sense, Jeannie, my friend might be interested, provided you don't show her that one up on eight."

I asked the right questions. Was it long-term leasehold or actual ownership with undivided interest in the land? How much a year for taxes? How much for the maintenance contract? What were the escalation provisions in the maintenance contract? How much did utilities run? Would the apartment be managed, be rented if you wished when you were not using it?

"How many apartments are there all told?"

"Counting the penthouses—298."

"How many unsold?"

"Oh, very few, really."

"How many?"

"Well . . . Harry might cut my throat all the way around to the back if I told anybody. But after all, you are my surgeon, and I have the scar to prove it. We've got thirty-six to go. I've been here a month and a half, and I get free rent in one of the models and a fifty-buck-a-week draw against a thousand dollars a sale. Between the two of us, Betsy and me, we've sold two."

"So Harry Broll is hurting?"

"Would your friend live here alone, Travis?"

"It would just be more of a convenience for her than anything. She lives in the British Virgins. St. Kitts. She comes over here often, and she's thinking about getting an apartment. I imagine she'd use it four times a year proba-bly, not over a week or two weeks at a time. She might loan it to friends. She doesn't have to worry about money."

Jeannie Dolan made a small rueful face. "How nice for her. Will you be bringing her around?"

"If I don't find anything she might like better."

"Remember, this floor plan is $55,950. Complete with color coded kitchen with—"

"I know, dear."

"Wind me up and I give my little spiel." She locked up, and we rode down in the elevator. She looked at her watch. "Hmmm. My long, exhausting day has been over for ten minutes. I read half a book, wrote four letters, and got operated on for a splinter."

"There's some medication I want to prescribe, Mrs. Dolan. If there's an aid station nearby, I can take you there and buy the proper dosage and make sure you take it."

She looked at me with the same expression as in the very beginning speculative, noncommittal. "Well . . . there's Monty's Lounge up at the shopping center, behind the package store."

five

Monty's was no shadowy cave. It was bright, sunny, and noisy. Terrazzo floor, orange tables, a din of laughter and talk, shouts of greeting, clink of ice. Hey, Jeannie. Hi, Jeannie, as we found our way to a table for two against the far wall. I could see that this was the place for a quick one after the business places in the shopping center closed. There was a savings and loan, insurance offices, a beauty parlor, specialty shops all nearby.

The waitress came over and said, "The usual, Jeannie? Okay. And what's for you, friend?" Jeannie's turned out to be vodka tonic, and friend ordered a beer.

In those noisy and familiar surroundings Jeannie relaxed and talked freely. She and her friend Betsy had come down to Florida from Columbus, Ohio, in mid-January to arrange a couple of divorces. Their marriages had both gone sour. She had worked for an advertising agency, doing copy and layout, but couldn't find anything in her line in the Lauderdale area. Betsy Booker had been a dental hygienist in Columbus but hated it because no matter what kind of shoes she bought, her feet hurt all the time. Betsy's husband was a city fireman, and Jeannie's husband was an accountant.

She seemed miffed at her friend Betsy. There was tension there, and it had something to do with Harry Broll. I tried to pry, but she sidestepped me, asked me what I did. I told her I was in marine salvage, and she said she knew it had to be some kind of outdoor work.

Finally I took a calculated risk and said, "If my friend likes the apartment, then I'll see what I can do with Harry

51

Broll. Hope you don't mind hearing somebody badmouth him. Harry is such a pompous, obnoxious, self-important jackass, it will be a pleasure to see how far down he'll come on the price."

"You said you were friends, McGee!"

"I said I knew him. Do I look like a man who needs friends like that?"

"Do I look like a girl who'd work for a man like that?"

We shook hands across the table, agreeing we both had better taste. Then she told me that Betsy Booker's taste was more questionable. Betsy had been having an affair with Harry Broll for two months.

"Betsy and I were in a two bedroom on the fourth on the highway side, but she has gradually been moving her stuff up onto six into his one bedroom, apartment 61. I guess it hurt her sore feet, all that undressing and dressing and undressing and walking practically the length of the building."

"Bitter about it?"

"I guess I sound bitter. It's more like hating to see her be so damned dumb. She's a real pretty blonde with a cute figure, and she just isn't used to being without a guy, I guess. It isn't a big sex thing going on. Betsy just has to have somebody beside her in the night, somebody she can hear breathing. She makes up these weird stories about how it's all going to work out. She says he's going to make a great big wad of money on some kind of land promotion stock and because Mrs. Broll deserted her husband, he's going to be able to get a divorce and marry Betsy."

"Couldn't it happen like that?"

"With him? Never!" she said and explained how she hadn't liked Harry's looks and had checked him out. Her best source had been the housekeeper at the apartment building. Last November when the place had been finished, Harry Broll had taken over apartment 61. He had an unlisted phone installed. He did not get any mail there.

"It's obvious what he was setting up," Jeannie said. "The world is full of Harry Broll-type husbands. The housekeeper said some Canadian broad moved into the apartment a week later. Harry would take long lunch hours. But he must have slipped up somehow, because Mrs. Broll arrived one day about Christmas time and went busting in when Harry was leaving, and there was a lot of screaming going on. His wife left him, even though Harry had gotten rid of his girlfriend. Then Harry moved out of his house and into the apartment. Betsy saw his house once. He took her there and showed it to her. She said it's big and beautiful. She won't ever get to live there. He'll dump her when he gets tired of her."

She said two drinks would be plenty. I paid the check and took her out and introduced her to Miss Agnes. Jeannie was so delighted with my ancient Rolls that I had to drive her up to Pompano Beach and back. I let her out across from the Casa de Playa. I wondered if I should caution her about mentioning my name to Betsy, who might in turn mention it to Harry Broll, and turn him more paranoid than ever. But it seemed to be too long a chance to worry about and too little damage from it even if it did happen.

She gave me an oblique, quick, half-shy look that said something about wondering if she would ever see me again. I discovered that I would like to see her again. We said cheerful and conspiratorial goodbys. She walked around the front of Miss Agnes, waited for a gap in traffic, and hastened across the highway. Her legs were not quite too thin, I decided. The brown-red hair had a lively bounce. From the far curb she turned and waved, her smile long-range but very visible.

It was dark when I parked Miss Agnes. I walked to F Dock and on out to Slip 18 and made a ritualistic check of the mooring lines and spring lines, then checked to see how the *Muñequita* was riding, tucked in against the flank of *The Busted Flush,* fenders in proper placement to prevent thumps and gouges.

"Don't pretend you can't hear my foot tapping, you

rude, tardy son of a bitch," Jilly said with acid sweetness. She was at the sundeck rail, outlined against the misty stars with a pallor of dock lights against her face.

I went aboard, climbed up, and reached for her but she ducked away. "What did I forget, woman?"

"The Townsends. I told you I accepted for both of us. Don't you remember at all?"

"What did we accept?"

"Drinks aboard the *Wastrel* and dinner ashore. They're over at Pier 66. Old friends, dear. She was the heavy little woman with the good diamonds."

"Oh."

"You're drawing a blank, aren't you?"

"I seem to be."

"Hurry and change and we can join them at dinner. And, dear, not quite as informal as you were at my little party, please?"

"Is she the woman who kept talking about her servant problem? No matter what anybody else was talking about?"

"Yes. That's Natalie. And Charles is hard of hearing, and he's too vain to admit it or buy one of those little electronic things. *Please* hurry, Travis." She eeled into my arms, pressed herself close to me. She smelled very good, and she felt springy and useful. "The sooner we go, dearest, the sooner we can leave their party and come back and have our own little party."

I gave her a good solid whack on the behind and said, "You go ahead and make excuses."

"Ouch! That was too rough, really. You'll be along soon?"

"Jilly honey, I don't know those people. I can't talk to them, and they can't talk to me. I could use up my life with people like that and never know where it went."

"They're my *friends!* I won't permit you to be rude to my friends. You accepted, you know."

"*You* accepted."

"But I expect you to have some consideration for—"

"Don't expect anything from me, Jillian. Sorry I forgot.

Sorry you had to hang around waiting for me. Now go to your party and have a good time."

"Do you mean it?"

"Why shouldn't I want you to have a good time?

"I have *had* it with you, you bahstid!"

"Sorry, Jilly. I just don't go to parties unless I like the people."

She went clicking down the outside ladderway and clacked her way aft and off the *Flush* and down the dock and away into the night. I went below, turned on a few lights, built a drink, ran a thumb down the stack of tapes, picked Eydie, and chunked her into the tape player and fixed volume.

Eydie has comforted me many times in periods of stress. She has the effortlessness of total professionalism. She is just so damned good that people have not been able to believe she is as good as she is. She's been handed a lot of dull material, some of it so bad that even her best hasn't been able to bring it to life. She's been mishandled, booked into the right places at the wrong time, the wrong places at the right time. But she can do every style and do it a little better than the people who can't do any other. Maybe a generation from now those old discs and tapes of Eydie will be the collectors' joy, because she does it all true, does it all with pride, does it all with heart.

So I settled back and listened to her open her throat and let go, backed by the Trio Los Panchos, Mexican love songs in flawless Mexican Spanish. She eased the little itch of remembering just how good my Irish lady had smelled, tasted, and felt.

A lot of the good ones get away. They want to impose structure upon my unstructured habits. It doesn't work. If I wanted structure, I'd live in a house with a Florida room, have 2.7 kids, a dog, a cat, a smiling wife, two cars, a viable retirement and profit-sharing plan, a seven handicap, and shortness of breath.

God only knows how many obligations there would have been once we were living in the British Virgins. Sing to me, Eydie. I just lost a pretty lady.

Through the music I heard the bong of my warning bell. I put on the aft floods and trapped Meyer in the white glare, blinking. I turned them off and let him in. I could not use Eydie for background music, so I ejected the tape and put a nothing tape on and dropped the sound down to the threshold of audibility.

Meyer said, "I was here an hour ago, and there was a beautiful, angry lady here, all dressed up, with someplace to go but nobody to go with."

"Fix yourself a knock. She decided to go alone."

"I bet."

"I am a crude, selfish bastard, and she is through with me."

He came back with a drink. He sat and said, "They tell me that a ring in the nose bothers you for the first week or so and then you never notice it again."

"Until somebody yanks on the rope."

"Oh, she wouldn't do that without good cause."

"Who the hell's side are you on?"

"She'll be back."

"Don't put any money on it."

"Speaking of money . . ."

"Harry Broll?"

"Yes, indeed. I had a long, tiring day. I talked to twenty people. I lied a lot. This is what I put together. It is all a fabric of assumption and supposition. Harry Broll is a small- to medium-sized cog in the machine called Sea-Gate, Inc. It is Canadian money, mostly from a Quebec financier named Dennis Waterbury, and New York money from a syndicate there which has been involved in other land deals. They needed Broll because of his knowledge of the local scene, the local contacts, legal shortcuts, and so on. It is a privately held corporation. They are going public. The offering price has not been set yet, but it will be about twenty-six or twenty-seven dollars a share. Most of the shares will be offered by the corporation, but about a third of the public offering will be by the present shareholders. Harry will be marketing a hundred thousand shares."

Cause for a long, low whistle. Old Harry with two and a half mil before taxes was a boggling picture for the mind to behold.

"How soon does he get rich?"

"Their fiscal year ends the last day of this month. The national accounting firm doing the audit is Jensen, Baker and Company. They will apparently get a guaranteed underwriting through Fairmont, Noyes. I hear that it is a pretty clean deal and that SEC approval should be pretty much cut and dried after they get the complete audit report, the draft of the red herring."

I stared at him. "Red herring?"

"Do you know what a prospectus is?"

"That thing that tells you more than you care to know about a new issue of stocks or bonds?"

"Yes. The red herring is the prospectus without the per share price of the stock on it or the date of issue. And it is a complete disclosure of *everything* to do with the company, background of executives and directors, how they got their stock, what stock options they may hold, what financial hanky panky, if any, they've ever been involved in. Very interesting reading sometimes."

"Nice to see an old acquaintance get rich enough to afford a hell of a lot of alimony."

"When a company is in registration, they get very secretive, Travis. Loose lips can sink financial ships."

"What would he want Mary to sign? He said it was to protect his interest in SeaGate."

"I wouldn't have any idea."

"Can you find out?"

"I can try to find out. I suppose the place to go would be West Palm. That's where the administrative offices of SeaGate are. That's where they are doing the audit, starting early so that they can close the books as of April thirtieth. It would be futile to try to pry anything out of the Jensen, Baker people. But maybe somebody in the Sea-Gate organization might talk. What did you do today?"

I told him. It was complicated and a lot of it was wasted time and effort, so I kept to the things that had worked.

Then I got to my big question. I had been bouncing it off the back of my mind for an hour, and it was going to be a pleasure to share the trauma with someone else.

"Here is this distrait husband, Meyer. He says he doesn't chase women. The Canadian girl was an exception, a big mistake. He wants me to tell Mary he wants her back. They'll go on a nice trip together. He is so rattled and upset he takes out his little gun and tries to kill me. Suppose he had. His two and a half mil would do him no good at all. And Mary could do him no good by coming back. Okay. He stashed his Canadian tail in apartment 61 at his Casa de Playa, and it was right there that Mary caught him. Harry got rid of the girlfriend. Mary gloomed around for a time, and then she left him. He wants her back. He's sending messages through me, he thinks, to get her to come back to him. Let's say she decides to go back. She goes to their house and finds it closed up. She knows he has the apartment. So she'd go there next, and she'd find him all cozied up there with a blonde named Betsy Booker. Draw me some inferences, please."

"Hmmm. We'll assume that the Booker woman is living in Broll's apartment with him, and the signs of her presence are too numerous to eliminate with short warning. Thus, when Broll came to see you, he either was very sure that Mary *would* not come back to him or that Mary *could* not come back to him. Or, possibly, if Mary could come back to him and decided to come back to him, he would have an early warning system to give him ample time to get the Booker woman out of the apartment and maybe even move back to Blue Heron Lane. This would imply that he knows where she is and has some pipe line to her. In either case, there would be considerable insincerity in his visit to you. Yet a man playing games does not pause in the middle of the game to murder someone out of jealousy. So we come to a final postulate which is not particularly satisfying. We assume that he is and was sincere but is too comfortable with his current living arrangement to want to think it through and see how easily it could spoil his second chance with Mary."

"He's not that dumb. Dumb, but not *that* dumb."

"Logic has to take into account all alternatives."

"Would you consider eating Hungarian tonight?" I asked him.

"Considered and approved."

"Poker dollar for the tab?"

"Food and drink, all on one."

six

The way you find Mary is the same way you find anybody.
Through friends and neighbors. And patience. Through
shopping habits, money habits, doctor, dentist, bureau-
cratic forms and reports. And more patience.

You reconstruct the events of three and a half and four
years ago and try to remember the names and places, the
people who could be leads. You find out who Mary used
to be, and from that maybe you find out where she is.

To start with, she was Tina Potter's friend. Came down
to see Tina and Freddie. Came down from Rochester,
New York. It was just a visit, and then she got her own
place. Had some money, some kind of income. Didn't
have to work. Came down because she had just been
through a jolting and ugly divorce action. She'd gotten her
maiden name back by court order. Mary Dillon. Dillon
and Dolan. I seemed to be working my way through the
Ds. D for divorce.

A quiet young woman. We all got to like her. She had
been putting the pieces of herself back together very very
nicely. Then something happened. What the hell was it?

At last I remembered. Tina Potter had come over to the
Flush late one afternoon and asked me if I could sort of
keep an eye on Mary. Freddie had a special assignment in
Bogota, and Tina would go with him only if she was sure
somebody would watch over Mary. The incident which
had racked her up had been the accidental death of her divorced husband a few days before. A one-car accident on
a rainy night somewhere near Rochester. Left the road
and hit a tree.

I remembered Tina's earnest face as she said, "Two-bit psychology for whatever it's worth, McGee. I think Mary had the idea, hidden so deep she didn't even realize it, that one day her Wally would grow up and come back to her and then they'd have the kind of marriage she thought they were going to have the first time around. So with him dead, it can't ever be. She's trying to hang on, but it's very white-knuckle stuff. Would you mind too much? She trusts you. She can talk to you."

So I had spent a lot of time with Mary. Beach walking, driving around, listening to music. But if she laughed, she couldn't be sure it wouldn't turn into tears. She had no appetite. The weight loss was apparent. A drink would hit her too hard.

I suggested the aimless cruise. Get away. No destination. Mary knew by then it wasn't a shrewd way of hurrying her into the sack, because had that been the target, it would have happened one of the times when her guard was way down. She agreed without much enthusiasm, provided she could pay her share of the expenses and do her share of the chores aboard.

After two weeks she had really begun to come out of it. At first she had slept twelve and fourteen hours a night, as if her exhaustion was of the same kind that happens after an almost mortal wound. Then she had begun to eat. The listlessness had turned to a new energy. She could laugh without it turning to tears.

One day when we were anchored a dozen miles north of Marathon, among some unnamed islands, I took the little *Sea Gull* outboard apart, cleaned it, lubricated it, reassembled it, while she zipped around out there in the sailing dinghy, skidding and tacking in a brisk bright wind. When she came back aboard the *Flush* she was wind blown, sun glowing, salty, happy, and thirsty. Before she went off to take her very niggardly freshwater shower, she brought me a beer. She told me she hadn't felt so good in a long long time. We clinked bottles in a toast to a happy day. She looked, smiling, into my eyes, and then her eyes changed. Something went click. They widened in small shock and surprise, then looked soft and heavy. Her head was too

heavy for her slender neck. Her mouth was softer. Her
mouth said my name without making a sound. She got up
and left me, her walk slow and swaying, and went below.
It had been awareness, invitation, and acceptance all in a
few moments, all without warning. I remember hastily fastening the last piece of the housing back onto the small
motor and deciding that I could test it and stow it later.
The lady was below, and there was a day to celebrate, a
cruise to celebrate, a recovery to celebrate.

So try Tina and Freddie Potter. Long gone, of course.
Scrabbled around in the locker where I throw cards and
letters. Found one a year old. Address in Atlanta. Direct-
dialed Atlanta information, then direct-dialed the Potter
house. Squeals of delight, then desolation that I wasn't in
Atlanta. Freddie had just gone off to work. She had to
quiet the kids down, then she came back on the line.

"Mary? Gee, I guess the last I heard was Christmas
time, Trav. She wrote kind of a short dreary note on the
back of a New Year's card. She sounded pretty depressed,
so I wrote her, but I didn't hear from her. What's the matter? Why are you looking for her?"

"She left Harry Broll early in January."

"That doesn't surprise me much. I never could understand why she married him. Or the first one, Wally, either.
Some women seem to have to pick losers every time. Like
some women pick alcoholics every time. But . . . I'd think
she'd get in touch with you or with us. But you know
Mary. Doesn't want to be a burden to anyone."

"How about family?"

"Well, there was just her mother up in Rochester, and
she died two years ago. That was all she had, Trav. Gee, I
can't think of who you could ask. But I'd think she'd have
some friend she'd talk to. A neighbor or something."

She couldn't contribute anything more. She wanted me
to let her know when I found out where Mary was, and
she wanted me to come to Atlanta and stay with them and
tell them all the news about everybody around the marina.

I couldn't use the Rolls pickup to visit the neighbors

along Blue Heron Lane. There aren't any cover stories to fit that set of wheels. And housewives are very edgy these days. They have little peep holes set into the doors and outdoor intercom speakers and little panic buttons to push if they get too nervous. Respectability is essential. Nothing eccentric please.

So I borrowed Johnny Dow's Plymouth sedan, and I wore pressed slacks, a sincere jacket, an earnest shirt, and a trustworthy necktie. I carried a black zipper portfolio and a dozen of my business cards. I am Travis McGee, Vice President of CDTA, Inc. It is no lie. Meyer incorporated the company a few years ago, and he keeps it active by paying the tiny annual tax. CDTA means nothing at all. Meyer picked the letters because they sound as if they have to mean something. Commercial Data Transmission Authority. Consolidated Division of Taxes and Audits. Contractors' Departmental Transit Acceptance.

In my sincere, earnest, trustworthy way I was going to hit the neighborhood on this hot Friday morning with a nice check which I had to deliver to Mrs. Harry Broll in settlement of her claim and get her to sign a release. I used one of the checks Meyer had ordered. It was on an actual account. Of course, the account was inactive and had about twelve dollars in it, but the blue checks were impressively imprinted with spaces for his signature and mine. He borrowed a checkwriter from a friend in one of the shops, and we debated the amount for some time before settling on a figure of $1,093.88.

"Good morning, ma'am. I hate to bother you like this, but I wonder if you can help me. My name is McGee. Here is my card. I've got out a check payable to Mrs. Harry Broll in full payment of her claim of last year, and I have a release here for her to sign, but the house looks as if they're off on a long trip or moved or something. Could you tell me how I could find Mrs. Broll?"

It was not a long street. Three short, curving blocks. Large lots, some of them vacant, so that the total was not over twenty-five homes right on Blue Heron Lane. The Broll house was in the middle of the middle block on the left. The canal ran behind the houses on the left hand side, following the curves. Dig a canal and you have instant waterfront.

I made the logical moves. I parked the Plymouth in the Broll driveway, tried the doorbell, then tried the neighbors, the nearest ones first.

"I can't help you at all. We moved in here three weeks ago, all the way from Omaha, and that house has been empty since we moved in, and from any sign of neighborliness from anybody else around here, all the houses might as well be empty, if you ask me."

"Go away. I don't open the door to anyone. Go away."

"Mrs. Broll? Someone said they split up. No, we weren't friendly. I wouldn't have any idea where you could find her."

At the fourth front door—the fifth if you count the place where nobody answered—there was a slight tweak at the baited end of my line.

"I guess the one to ask would be Mrs. Dressner. Holly Dressner. She and Mrs. Broll were all the time visiting back and forth, morning coffee and so forth. That's the next house there, number 29, if she's home. She probably is. I didn't hear her backing out."

After the second try on the doorbell I was about to give up. I could hear the chimes inside. No answer. Then the intercom speaker fastened to the rough-cut cypress board beside the front door clicked and said, "Who is it? And, for God's sake, just stand there and talk in a normal tone of voice. If you get close to the speaker and yell, I won't understand word one."

I gave my spiel, adding that the lady next door told me she would be the one to ask. She asked me if I had a card, and she had me poke it through the mail slot. I wondered why she sounded so out of breath.

I heard chains and locks, and she pulled the door open and said, "So come in." She wore a floor-length terry robe in wide yellow and white stripes, tightly belted. Her short, blond, water-dark hair was soaked. "I was in the pool. Daily discipline. Come on out onto the terrace. I'm too wet to sit in the living room."

She was a stocky woman with good shoulders and a slender waist. She had a tan, freckled face, broad and good humored, pale lashes and brows, pretty eyes. The terrace was screened, and the big pool took up most of the space. Sliding glass doors opened the terrace up into the living room. The yard beyond the screening and beyond the flowerbeds sloped down to a small concrete dock where a canopied Whaler was moored.

She invited me to sit across from her at a wrought iron table with a glass top.

"Try that on me again, Mr. McGee. Slowly. Is this the check?"

She picked it up and put it down and listened as I went through it again. "A claim for what?" she asked.

"Mrs. Dressner, it's company policy not to discuss casualty claims and settlements. I'm sure you can understand why."

"Mr. McGee, may I ask you a personal question?"

"Of course."

"How come you are so full of bullshit?"

I stared at her merry face and merry smile. But above the smile the hazel eyes were expressionless as poker chips.

"I . . . I don't quite understand."

"Go back to Harry and tell him that this didn't work, either. What does he think I am? Some kind of idiot, maybe? Goodby, Mr. McGee."

"This isn't for Harry. This is for me."

"So who the hell are you?"

"How friendly are you with Mary anyway?"

"Very very very. Okay?"

"What happened to her when Wally got killed?"

She frowned at me. "She came apart. She flipped."

"And a man took her on a boat ride?"

"Right. And the way she talked about him, that's the one she should have played house with instead of Harry Broll."

"I almost thought about it seriously."

"You?"

"Travis McGee. *The Busted Flush.* Cruised the Keys

and up the west coast to Tampa Bay. Taught her to sail. Taught her to read a chart. Taught her to navigate."

She put her determined chin on her fist and stared at me. "That *was* the name. You, huh? So what's with the funny games, coming here with your funny card and your funny check? If you knew we're close friends, why not start honest?"

"I have not seen her or talked to her in over three years, Holly. And don't jump on my knowing your first name and try to make anything out of it. The woman next door clued me."

"Hitting the whole neighborhood?"

"One at a time. Mary is . . . low-key intense. She hides a lot of herself. She doesn't make friends easily. But she needs people, so I thought she'd have to have a friend in the neighborhood. A friend, not an acquaintance. Right?"

"So right, McGee. Coffee and tears. Most women bug me. Mary doesn't. I . . . still don't feel right about you. About taking you for granted. It *could* be some kind of a trick. I want to ask you things, but I can't think of anything to ask that you couldn't have gotten from Harry."

"He's trying to find her."

"You know it! I thought the silly son of a bitch was going to try to shake it out of me."

"When was this?"

"A couple of weeks ago. He'd had a couple. He got all weepy. He insisted I had to know where Mary is."

"Do you know where she is?"

"McGee, I know why Harry wants to find her. He wants her to come back to him and sign something and live happily ever after."

"It might be an ugly shock if she did come back."

"How?"

"She'd find the house empty, and she'd go look for Harry at the Casa de Playa, where he just so happens to be shacked with a divorcing blonde named Betsy Booker. In apartment 61."

I couldn't read her expression. "So?"

"So isn't that where Mary found him with the Canadian?"

"Only two people could have told you that. Or three. Harry, Mary, or Lisa—the Canadian quiff."

"Wrong."

"The hell you say."

"I got it out of Betsy Booker's best friend, Jeannie Dolan, also from Columbus, who got part of it from Betsy and part of it from the housekeeper. Jeannie and Betsy take turns manning the sales desk at the Casa de Playa."

I saw her buy it and give a small nod. "So help me. That rotten Harry. Jesus! The way I read it, Lisa was not the first. Just the first she caught him with. He really is one sorry bastard."

"How did she find out?"

"She thinks it was one of the girls in his office or a girl he'd fired, trying to make things rough for him. She got a phone call. The person on the other end whispered. Mary said it was spooky. Something very much to the point. 'Mrs. Broll, your husband has loaned apartment 61 in his new building to Lisa Dissat, and he'll be taking another long lunch hour today so he can drive out there and screw her.' So she drove out and hid somewhere until he arrived and went upstairs. Then she went up to the sixth floor and waited around until the door opened and he started to come out. She took a quick run at the door and knocked it open and charged past him and found the bareass Canadian getting ready to take a nice nap. I take it there was a certain amount of screaming going on for a while."

"Then Harry got rid of the girl friend?"

"She was packed and out of there the next day. Back to Canada, Harry told Mary. He confessed his sad story. He had gone to Quebec for business conferences with his Canadian partners. He had to dictate new agreements. They sent the secretary to the hotel. They worked very late. He was too tired to think clearly. She was pretty and available. It went on for the three days he was up there. He came back. Two days after he was back, she phoned him at his office from Miami. She had quit her job and followed him back to Florida. So he told Mary that while he was trying to talk Lisa into going back, he put her up at the apartment. I guess he was having a hard time convincing her. He talked from the end of November till two days before Christmas. That's a lot of long lunches and a lot of evening conferences."

"But Mary didn't leave him until January fifth."

"Harry told you that?"

I laughed. "I thought the silly son of a bitch was going to try to shake it out of me, too. This was just the other day. And he got weepy."

"So you're finding her for him?"

"May I ask you the same personal question you asked me?"

"Okay. Okay. I'm sorry. Why then?"

"For myself. Pride, I guess. Harry thought if she was really in trouble, she would come running to me. And the more I think about it, the more logical it seems. That she would. Besides—" I stopped suddenly.

"What's the matter?"

"When was Harry here, did you say?"

"Oh, two weeks ago."

"Can you pin it down to a day?"

"Let me go take a look at my kitchen calendar and see."

She came back and said, "Less than two weeks ago. It was a Monday morning. April fifth."

"He told me someone had seen Mary with me on April second. He was wrong, of course. Why would he come after you instead of me if she was seen with me?"

"Maybe he hadn't been told about it before he came to see me," she said.

"And maybe he was trying to get you to admit she'd moved in with me or some damn thing. What difference does it make anyway? He didn't act as if he was thinking very clearly."

"Mary was thinking about getting in touch with you. She was sitting in my kitchen wondering out loud if she should. That was after she'd decided to take off. Then she decided it would be better to have some breathing space in between, some time to herself first. I thought she would have written you long before now. It's over three months."

"She writes you?"

"Don't get too cute, McGee."

"Okay. Do you know where she is?"

"Yes."

"And she is okay?"

"I have no reason to think she isn't. If I was Mary, I would be relishing every damn moment. The farther from Harry, the better."

"That's all I wanted to know, Mrs. Dressner. That she is okay. I had to hear it from somebody I could believe."

"Hey! You're spoiling the fun. You're supposed to worm the whole story out of me. Or try to."

"It's Harry who has to know where she is. Not me."

"Friend McGee, I am not about to get you two men confused, one with the other."

"So she is a long distance from here. And should be relishing every moment. Right?"

"I've gotten some comedy post cards."

"I believe you. There are people you believe and people you don't. I don't need to know any more than I know right now."

She looked rueful. "Everybody believes me. Everything I'm thinking shows. I've got one of those faces. I'd make a rotten spy. Hey, sit down again. I haven't offered you anything. Coffee, tea, beer, booze? Even some lunch?"

"No thanks."

"Believe me, I'm glad to have anybody show up here. This is one of the days when the house gets empty somehow. David—my husband—has been gone all week. He'll be home tomorrow, probably about noon. He's gone a week or more out of every month. Our two little gals are tennis freaks, so who sees them at all when the weather is like this? I miss hell out of Mary, I really do. You could choke down some terrible coffee at least. Pretend it's delicious, and I'll tell you where Mary is. Even if you don't have to know."

She brought coffee from the kitchen to the glass-top

table on the screened terrace. Moving around had loosened the hitch in the terry belt, and when she bent to pour my coffee, the robe suddenly spilled open. She spilled coffee, clutched frantically, put the pot down, and gathered herself together and tied the robe firmly, her face dark red under the freckles. It was obvious she had not contrived it.

"Some people are solitary drinkers. I'm a solitary skinny dipper."

"It's habit forming," I said.

She got paper towels and mopped up the spilled coffee and filled my cup the rest of the way. She sat and stared at me, lips pursed. Finally she said, "Thank you."

"For?"

"For not jumping to any conclusions, for which I could not exactly blame you. Good God, I tell you my husband is away, my kids are playing tennis, I'm lonesome. I beg you to stay for coffee and then damn near drop my robe on the floor."

"Some days are like that."

"I like the way you can smile without hardly changing your mouth at all. It's kind of all in the eyes. Mary said you're a doll. She said big and brown and sort of beat-up looking. But you're bigger and browner than the idea I had of you. About Mary. That was a sordid scene at the Casa de Playa. It shook her. Friendship is friendship, but you don't tell your friends what to do when it comes to big emotional decisions. Through Christmas and the rest of December she spent a lot of time over here. I let her bounce it all off me. She was thinking aloud, arguing it out. Taking one side and then the other, while all I did was say 'um.' But I could tell which side was winning. Finally she said that if she hadn't already had one divorce, she would definitely decide to leave Harry. It was a lousy reason to stick around, just to avoid being divorced twice, which has a kind of ring of failure to it, failure as a person or as a woman. So she was going to leave him and go away and, to be real fair, think it all through. But the way she felt, she'd probably sue for divorce after the waiting period. I waited for her to really make her mind up, and then I questioned her to make certain she was sure, and finally I told her about a little problem I had once with her husband. There'd been a party down the street and the four of us, the Brolls and the Dressners, had walked back together, a little tight. They came over here for a nightcap. There were supposed to be falling stars. It was in the paper. I wanted to see them. We put out the lights on the terrace, and I stretched out on a sun mattress beside the pool, right over there, to watch up through the screening overhead. David went to the kitchen to fix drinks, and Mary changed her mind about what she wanted and went in the kitchen to tell him. Harry was on a sun mattress near mine. All of a sudden he rolled over and put his big old cigar mouth on mine and pressed me down with his big belly and ran his big paw up under my skirt and started groping me. I froze with shock for about one second, and then I gave a big snap of my back like a huge fishing shrimp and bucked him into the pool in all his clothes. It turned into a big joke. He said he'd gotten up and tripped and fallen in.

"When I told Mary about it, she was furious with me for not telling her sooner. I told her I hadn't told David, because he would have tried to beat Harry to death. I said that now she'd made her mind up, I could tell her about what Harry pulled that time. Frankly, what I was doing was trying to lock her into her decision to drop that jerk forever. Having her own money made it easy for her to get away. She got it from her trust officer at the Southern National Bank and Trust in Miami. Cash. A lot, I think. She didn't want Harry tracing her through credit cards or personal checks. She told me she didn't want to hear his voice or see his face once she left. Not for a long time anyway. We sat right out here one afternoon, a warm day for early January, and we looked at the travel folders she'd picked up from some little travel agency where she wasn't known. She wanted to go to the islands. Between the two of us we decided that Grenada looked the best, and it was certainly far enough, way down there at the bottom of the West Indies, almost as far as Trinidad. So the travel agency sent wires and cables and got her set up at what looked like a very plush place, the Spice Island Inn. She's sent me those joke greetings. Four or five, I guess. Airmail takes eight days! That place is a real hideaway."

"Harry told me she left on January fifth. He said he came home from work and she was gone."

"I think it was an impulse. She wasn't going to leave until Thursday or Friday. I was out most of that afternoon. Maybe she tried to say goodby. I guess she probably drove down to Miami and stayed in a hotel or motel until her flight left."

"I wonder what she did with her car?"

"I think she was going to leave it at Miami International."

"Which is two fifty a day, no matter how many days, so she is up to a two-hundred-dollar parking charge."

"McGee, the lady had decided to go first class all the way. That is what ladies do when they get mad enough."

"What would Harry be wanting her to sign?"

"I haven't the faintest idea."

"Good coffee."

"Come *on!* It tastes like stewed tire patches."

She walked me to the door. She got ahead of me and leaned back against the door and looked up quizzically. She stood a little taller than my elbow. "McGee, I just wondered. It seems like a hell of a lot of trouble you went to. The business cards and the funny check and the sales talk."

"No big thing, Holly. The cards and the checks were in the cupboard. I have to hunt for people sometimes. You learn to use something that works."

"Why do you hunt for people?"

"I do favors for friends."

"Is that a line of work with you?"

"I really wouldn't know how to answer that question."

She sighed. "Heck, I thought I could solve a problem for Mary. She never *was* able to figure out what it is that you do for a living."

"Salvage consultant."

"Sure. Sure."

When I glanced back, she was standing on her shallow front steps, arms crossed. Her hair was beginning to dry and to curl a little. She smiled and waved. She was a sturdy, healthy woman with a very friendly smile.

seven

I was on the beach by three o'clock that Friday afternoon and that was where Meyer found me at a few minutes to four. He dropped his towel, sat upon it, and sighed more loudly than the surf in front of us or the traffic behind us.

There were nine lithe maidens, miraculously unaccompanied by a flock of boys, playing some game of their own devising on the hard sand in the foamy wash of the waves. It involved an improvised club of driftwood, a small, yellow, inflated beach ball, one team out in the water, and one on the beach. Either you had to whack the ball out over the heads of the swimmers before they . . . or you had to hit it past a beach player who then. . . . Anyway, it involved a lot of running, yelping, and team spirit.

"A gaggle of giggles?" Meyer said, trying that one on me.

My turn. "How about a prance of pussycats?"

"Not bad at all. Hmmm. A scramble of scrumptious?"

"Okay. You win. You always win."

He slowly scratched his pelted chest and smiled his brown bear smile. "We both win. By being right here at this time. All the strain of a long, difficult, and futile day is evaporating quickly. Meyer is at peace. Play on, young ladies, because from here on out life will be a lot less fun for most of you."

"Grow up and be earnest and troubled?" I asked. "Why does it have to be that way?"

"It doesn't. It shouldn't be. Funny, though. They take all those high spirits, all that sense of fun and play into

74

one of the new communes, and within a year they are doleful wenches indeed. Somber young versions of American Gothic, like young wagon train mothers waiting for the Indians to ride over the ridge. And their men look like the pictures of the young ones slain at Shiloh. Idealism in our society is pretty damned funereal."

One of the players looked up the beach and gave a quick wave and then went churning into the water to capture the yellow ball.

"One of my constituents," Meyer said comfortably.

"You are a dirty old man."

"You have a dirty mind, McGee. I could not bring myself to ever touch the child. But in all fairness it does enter my mind. Lovely, isn't she?"

"Exquisite."

"Her last name is Kincaid, and I do not know her first name. She is known to everyone as Breadbox. She has an incredible appetite. She's an economics' major at Yale. Quite a good mind. Her father grows tobacco in Connecticut. She drove down in a five-year-old Porsche with two other girls. This summer she is going to work in a boutique aboard a cruise ship. She has a dog at home named Rover, which seems to have come full circle and is now an 'in' name for a dog. She is getting over a romance which ended abruptly and does not want to become interested in another man for years and years, she says. Tennis used to be her sport, but now she prefers—"

"So all right already, Meyer. Damn it."

"I think she was waving at someone behind us."

"What?"

"I never saw the child before in my life. I was just putting together into one package some of the things some of the other young ladies have told me."

"Have you been drinking?"

"No. But if you'd like to . . ."

With as little warning as a flock of water birds, the nine maidens dropped the club and went jogging north along the beach, one of them clutching the yellow ball.

Meyer said, "I did not do well today, Travis. Just a few

small items. Dennis Waterbury is in his mid-thirties, bland, shrewd, tough, quick, merciless—and completely honest. He gives his word and keeps it."

"Listen. I was able—"

"Let me deliver my few crumbs first. Harry Broll's cost on his one hundred thousand shares was ten dollars a share, and his money and the money the others put in was used to acquire the land, prepare sites, build roads, start the utility construction, water, waste processing, and so forth. A very golden opportunity for a man like Broll to get his foot in the door with people like Waterbury and friends. But in order to make it big, he had to pluck himself pretty clean, I imagine, and borrow to the hilt. Put up one million and drag down two million and a half. The odds are splendid, the risk low enough."

"About Mary, I—"

"I can't seem to find out what she would have to sign. She wouldn't have to sign anything in connection with the stock. It's in his name. She isn't on his business paper."

"Mary is alive and well and living in Grenada."

"In Spain?"

"No. The island."

"Dear chap, the one in Spain is Gran-AH-duh. The island is Gre-NAY-duh. The British corrupted it with their usual mispronunciation of all place names."

"You've been there?"

"No."

"But you know a lot about it?"

"No. I happen to know how to pronounce it. One has to start somewhere."

"Let's swim."

After about ten minutes Meyer intercepted me fifty yards from the beach, to ask, "How come you could find that out and Harry can't?"

"I found the only person who might really know for sure, aside from the travel agent. A neighbor lady, who shows her good taste by disliking the hell out of Harry Broll. She thought for a while Harry sent me. I softened her up. She makes terrible coffee."

"Did Harry try to pry it out of her, too?"

"Yes. Nearly two weeks ago. With tears. Without the gun. But rough. She said she thought he was going to try to shake it out of her."

Meyer nodded and went gliding away, head up, in that powerful, slow, and tireless breast stroke that somehow makes me think of a seal when I see his head moving by.

When I came out of the water, he was sitting on his towel again, looking petulant, a rare mood for Meyer.

"Something bothering you?"

"Illogical actions and illogical emotions bother hell out of me, Travis. His wife has been gone over three months. How about checking accounts, credit cards?"

I explained about the trust account and her taking cash so that she couldn't be easily traced by her husband. He said he knew one friendly face in the trust department of Southern National, but of course it would be Monday before he could learn anything there.

"Why bother?" I asked him. "I'm satisfied. We know where she is. I don't give a damn how jittery Harry Broll gets."

We walked back across the bridge together, squinting toward the western sun setting into its usual broad band of whisky soup. "I guess it doesn't matter in any case," Meyer said.

"What doesn't matter?"

"What happens to anybody. Look at the cars, McGee. Look at the people in the cars, on the boats, on the beach, in the water. Everybody is heading toward their own obituary notice at precisely the same speed. Fat babies, and old women like lizards, and the beautiful young with long golden hair. And me and thee, McGee. At tick-tock speed moving straight toward the grave, until all now living are as dead as if they had died in Ancient Rome. The only unknown, and that is a minor one, is how long will each individual travel at this unchanging, unchangeable pace?"

"Good God, Meyer! I was going to buy you dinner."

"Not today. This is not one of my good days. I think I'll open a can of something, go walking alone, fold up early. No need to poison somebody else's evening."

Away he trudged, not looking back. It happens sometimes. Not often. A curious gaiety, followed by bleak, black depression. It was a Meyer I seldom see and do not know at all.

Friday night. I took my time building a drink, showering, dressing, building a refill. Dark night by then, and a wind building up, so that the *Flush* moved uneasily, creaking and sighing against her lines, nudging at her fenders. I felt restless. I was wondering where to go, who to call, when Jillian came aboard.

She clung tightly and said she had been utterly miserable. She looked up at me with two perfect and effective tears caught in her lower lashes, her mouth quivering. The Townsend party had been desperately dull, really. She shouldn't have tried to force me to go. She shouldn't try to force me to do anything. She realized that now. She would not do it again, ever. Forgive me, Travis darling, please. I've been so lonely and so ashamed of myself etc., etc., etc.

Once forgiven, all the lights came on behind her eyes, and the tears were flicked away. Mood of holiday. She had been confident of reconciliation, she had brought hairbrush and toothbrush. And all the urgencies a girl could muster.

In the morning a rare April rain was coming down hard, thrashing at the ports beside the half acre of the captain's wrinkled and rumpled bed, bathing us in gray ten o'clock light.

"Is your friend in trouble?" she asked.

"Who?"

"That respectable married lady friend, of course."

"Oh. No, she's fine. It turns out she's hiding from her husband. She went down to Grenada."

She lifted her head. "Really? Henry and I went down there on the first really long cruise we took in the Jilly III. The Grenadines are one of the great sailing areas of the world. And the yacht basin at St. George's is really marvelous. You see people from everywhere, really. Yacht Services is very helpful."

"She's staying at the Spice Island Inn."

"Quite expensive. Is she alone down there?"

"Apparently."

"She can get into all kinds of delicious mischief if she wants. If she's even half attractive, she won't be lonely. The air is full of spice and perfume down there, dear. It's a fabulously erotic island. Always so warm and lazy, with the hot hot sun and the hills and jungles and the beaches. Quite near the equator, you know."

"I didn't know."

"Well, it is. Don't you think we should go there one day?"

"I guess so."

"You don't seem exactly overwhelmed with enthusiasm."

"Sorry."

"Are you going back to sleep, you wretch?"

"Not with you doing what you're doing."

"This? Oh, it's just a sort of reflex thing, I guess. Darling, if you're no longer worried about your friend, could we be ready to aim the *Jilly* toward home on Tuesday? I can get her provisioned on Monday."

"What? Oh, Tuesday. I guess so."

"You don't seem to keep track of what I'm saying."

"I guess I'm easily distracted."

"You're easily something else, too."

"What did you expect?"

"I expect, my dear, if we put our minds to it, we might make the Guinness Book of Records. Cozy? A nice rain always makes me very randy." After a moment she giggled.

"What's funny?"

"Oh, I was thinking I might decide we should go to Grenada during the rainy season, dear."

"Ho ho ho."

"Well . . . it amused *me*. When I feel this delicious, I laugh at practically anything. Sometimes at nothing at all."

The unusual cold front which had brought the rain ahead of it moved through late on Saturday afternoon. She went back to the *Jilly III*. She said she had a thousand things to do before we sailed on Tuesday. She said to come over on Sunday, sometime in the afternoon. She said

I could bring along some of my clothes and toys then, if I wanted.

She left and I locked up again, hot showered, and fell into a deep sleep. I woke at ten on Saturday night, drank a gallon of water, ate half a pound of rat cheese, and dropped right back down into the pit.

I woke with a hell of a start at four on Sunday morning, and thought there was somebody coming aboard. Realized it had been something happening in a dream. Made a grab for what was left of the dream, but it was all gone too quickly. Almost a nightmare. It had pumped me so full of adrenalin there was no hope of going back to sleep. Heart bumped and banged. Legs felt shaky. I scrubbed a bad taste off my teeth, put on jeans and boat shoes and an old gray sweatshirt, and went out onto the deck.

A very silent night. No breeze. A fog so thick the nearer dock lights were haloed and the farther ones were a faint and milky pallor, beyond tangible gray. I could hear slow waves curl and thud against the sand. The craft on either side of the *Flush* were shrouded in the fog, half visible.

Meyer's gloomy message had been delivered none too soon. Everybody else had been tick-tocked to the grave, leaving one more trip to complete—mine. Then, far away, I heard a long screeeeee of tormented rubber and a deep and ugly thud with a small accompanying orchestration of jangles and tinkles. The thud had been mortal, tick-tocking some racing jackass into his satin-lined box, possibly along with the girl beside him or the surprised folk in the other car.

A few minutes later I heard the sirens, heard them stop at what seemed a plausible distance.

So stop thinking about this and that, McGee, and think about what you don't want to think about, namely the lush future with the rich widow.

I climbed to the sun deck and went forward and slouched behind the wheel and propped my heels atop the instrument panel, ankles crossed.

That old honorary Cuban had simplified the question all to hell when he'd said that a moral act is something you feel good after. Conversely, you feel bad after an immoral act. But what about the act that is neither moral nor immoral, Papa? How are you supposed to feel then?

Look, we are very suited to each other. There is a lot of control either way on both sides, so timing is no problem at all. She pleases me. She knows how to intensify it. I like the textures and juices, spices and rhythms of her, all her tastes and tastings. We truly climb one hell of a hill, Papa, and when we fall off the far side together, it is truly one hell of a long fall, Papa, and we land truly and well and as zonked out as lovers can get. We laugh a lot. We like to hold each other afterward. We make bawdy jokes. She has a lot of body greed and finds me a satisfying stud. In her gratitude she takes a lot of extra effort to keep things varied and interesting. So?

There's this little problem. I go into the head, Papa, and look at this battered and skewed beach-bum countenance of mine, reflected in the mirror, and my eyes look dull, and my mouth looks slack, and I am wearing the remnants of a doggy little smirk. I know she is in there, a-sprawl on the bed, drifting in and out of her little love doze, and I look truly and well at myself in the mirror, and I do not feel good about anything or bad about anything. I just feel as if I had made one of those little diagonal lines you use to keep track. You know—four little vertical lines side by side and then the diagonal that crosses them out and ends the group.

In the mirror my nose looks too big, and my skin looks grainy. I wear the doggy little grin. The smells of her cling to my body. There is the feeling of marking something off on a long score sheet. Something well and truly done that will have to be well and truly done for whatever years we both have left, because that is the bargain. Chop that cotton, tote that bale, plow that little acre of God.

What about it when you don't feel good and you don't feel bad? When you just feel that it's done for this time and done reasonably well, and later on the slack dangle of flesh will turn tumescent, and it will and can be done again, just as well as the last time? With proficiency, determination, patience, understanding, power and skill. Isn't lovemaking as good a way as any to pass the time for the rest of your life? It tones the body, and it's acceptable exercise, and it makes two people feel good.

If I don't grasp the opportunity, somebody will find some quick and dirty way to let the sea air through my skull.

I'm overdue. That's what Meyer says, and that's what my gut says in a slow cold coil of tingling viscera. Overdue, and scared, and not ready for the end of it yet. The old bullfighters who have known the famous rings and famous breeds despise the little country corridas, because they know that if they do not quit, that is where they will die—and the bull that hooks their steaming guts out onto the sand will be a poor animal without class or distinction or style.

An animal as ordinary as Harry Broll.

I shifted position, dug the keys out of the pocket, and found the keyholes in the instrument panel. It is one of the tics of the boatman, turning on the juice without starting up, just to check fuel levels, battery charge. By leaning close, I could read the gauges in the pallid light.

Maybe it isn't just the woman. This woman. Or a passing of time. It is the awareness, perhaps, of the grasshopper years, of always pushing all the pleasure buttons. The justification was a spavined sense of mission, galumphing out to face the dragon's fiery breath. It had been a focus upon the torment of individuals to my own profit. Along with a disinterest in doing anything at all about all those greater inequities which affect most of us. Oh, I could note them and bitch about them and say somebody ought to do something. I could say it on my way to the beach or to the bed.

Who will know you were ever around, McGee? Or care?

Wait a minute! What am I supposed to be doing? Making up the slogan I shall paint on my placard and tote in the big parade? A parade is a group, and I'm not a group animal. I think a mob, no matter what it happens to be doing, is the lowest form of living thing, always steaming with potential murder. Several things I could write on my placard and then carry it all by myself down empty streets.

Up with life. Stamp out all small and large
indignities. Leave everyone alone to make it
without pressure. Down with hurting. Lower
the standard of living. Do without plastics.
Smash the servomechanisms. Stop grabbing.
Snuff the breeze and hug the kids. Love all
love. Hate all hate.

Carry my placard and whistle between my teeth and
wink and smirk at the girls on the sidewalk watching the
nut with his sign.

Am I supposed to go out with my brush and yellow
soap and scrub clean the wide grimy world?

If you can't change everything, why try to change any
part of it, McGee?

The answer lit up in the foggy predawn morning, right
over my head. A great big light bulb with glowing fila-
ments, just like those old timey ones over in Boca Grande
in the Edison place.

Because, you dumbass, when you stop scrubbing away
at that tiny area you can reach, when you give up the illusion you are doing any good at all, then you start feeling
like this. Jillian Brent-Archer is another name for giving
up your fatuous, self-serving morality, and when you give
it up, you feel grainy, studlike, secure, and that doggy little
smirk becomes ineradicable.

You are never going to like yourself a hell of a lot, T.
McGee, so what little liking you have must be conserved.
To become Jilly's amiable useful houseguest and bedguest
would turn you into something which you are not—yet
have an uncomfortable tendency to become.

You retain the fragile self-respect by giving Them the
increasingly good chance of ventilating your skull or
scragging you through the heart. There have been some
rotten little scenes with Jilly, but the next one will be the
most memorable of all.

So Mary Broll is okay. And there is a good lump of
cash money stashed behind the fake hull in the forward
bilge of the *Flush*. But it would be a good time, a very
good time, to go steaming out and find the plucked pigeon

and clean up its little corner of the world by getting its feathers back—half of them, anyway. Get out there on the range and go down to the pits and stand up for a moment and see if they can pot you between the eyes. If they miss, maybe you'll get your nerve back, you tin-horn Gawain.

eight

Sunday I did not feel up to facing the predictable fury of Lady Jillian. She wanted me aboard for drinks Monday evening. Time enough, I told myself.

Meyer came over to the *Flush* on Monday morning at about ten thirty. I was punishing myself for recent sensual excess by polishing some neglected brightwork on the instrument panel, using some new miracle goop that was no more miraculous than the old miracle goop.

Without preamble he said, "I phoned the trust department of the Southern National Bank and Trust Company and told the girl to put me through to somebody who could give me a trust account number. When another girl answered, I said that my name was Forrester, and I was with Merrill Lynch. I said we had received a dividend which apparently should have been sent to Mrs. Harry Broll's trust account. I wanted to advise New York and mail the check along, and to prevent further confusion, I wanted the trust account number and the name of the trust officer handling that account. Mary Dillon Broll or Mrs. Harry Broll, 21 Blue Heron Lane, and so forth. She told me to hold, and in a minute or two she came back and said the number was TA 5391, and the trust officer was Mr. Woodrow Willow."

"Interesting, but—"

"I asked her to put me through to Mr. Willow. When he came on the line I introduced myself correctly and told him that I was a personal friend of Mrs. Broll, and she had told me before going away on a trip that he handled her

85

account TA 5391. He said that was correct. He sounded guarded. Properly so. I told him that Mrs. Broll had asked me to give her some advice regarding rephasing her accounts to provide a maximum income, as she anticipated some possible change in her personal status."

"You are getting very crafty lately, Meyer."

"Please stop rubbing those damned dials and look at me. Thank you. He sounded huffy then and said they were perfectly competent to give all necessary investment advice. I told him I knew that and that was why I had called him. I certainly didn't want to usurp their authority and responsibility. I said I seldom make portfolio recommendations any more, only for old friends and at no fee, of course. I said that women often become confused about the way a trust account is set up. I said I understood she had discretion over it, that she could determine what she wanted bought and sold and so direct them. He said that was indeed the case. He sounded wistful, as if he wished it weren't true. I said that I had been trying to get in touch with her in order to clear my ideas with her before coming in to discuss them with him. I said her husband had been unable to help me. I said her house was closed, and her neighbors did not know where she had gone. I asked if he could help me. He said she had phoned him early in January and had come in and drawn out all the accumulated interest and dividends, a sizable amount, and told him she was going away for a month or six weeks. She did not know where. He said he wished he could help me."

"A month or six weeks?"

"Yes. Over three months ago."

"She could have decided to stay longer, you know."

"That's what Woodrow Willow said. He said she was quite upset when she came to see him. He said he could guess why she might be thinking in terms of independent income. So I said that, of course, maximizing income would enable her to live comfortably, but with a woman that young, inflation protection was important."

"Did it work?"

Meyer displayed an uncommonly wolflike smile. "He

hesitated and I heard a desk calculator rattling and humming, and then he said that with her equities reinvested in income holdings, she'd have a pretax income of from twenty-five to twenty-seven thousand. So I told him that we should probably think in terms of eighteen to twenty or, in case of substantial alimony, consider tax exempts. He said he'd be delighted to talk to me about it, but of course he would have to have clearance from her to discuss her affairs. I said I realized that. He said he expected to hear from her very shortly, before the end of the month. Travis, I couldn't push him any further."

"I can see that. He was all set to snap shut at any moment. You got a hell of a lot out of him. Congratulations."

"I braced myself and took a risk. I said, 'Oh, yes, of course. To sign those things for Mr. Broll.' He hesitated and then said, 'It's inconvenient for her to come here in person. So she told me when she came in what Mr. Broll was asking of her. It's something that they did once before, and it was paid off. I had her sign the note. The loan was later approved by the loan committee and the board. A sizable loan, secured by the assets in her trust, with her signed authorization to me to deposit the loan proceeds in Mr. Broll's personal checking account. The effective date of the loan was to be April fifteenth, last Thursday. He requires the funds before the end of the month. She requested me to get it all set up but not to go ahead with it until she gets in touch with me and tells me to proceed or to destroy the signed documents and forget it. That's why I expect her to be in touch with me soon.' Travis, I remember you telling me to always press the luck when it is running your way. So I told him that I had heard that Broll was getting very agitated about getting the note and the authorization signed, so I imagined that Mr. Broll had been in touch with him. Mr. Willow has a very weary laugh. He said he hears from Mr. Broll almost constantly. He said he saw no reason to tell Mr. Broll everything was signed and ready to go, awaiting only authorization from her. I got the impression Harry tried to bulldoze him, and Mr. Willow got his back up. Then he began to realize he had told me more than he should. I could *feel* him pulling back. So I jumped in and said that actually the documents aren't signed until she says they are signed. Until then it is an approved line of credit, and if she doesn't care to use it, she doesn't have to. I told him he was quite correct, and I could feel him trying to persuade himself I was not working for Harry Broll. I hope he did."

I put the cap on the miracle goop and swabbed up the few white places where it had dribbled on the varnish, miraculously removing the gloss. I spun the helmsman's seat around and looked at Meyer.

I said to him, "You are pretty damned intense about something I don't understand. We don't know whether Mary wants him to have that money or not. We know she's in Grenada, knowing he's sweating it out, and she's probably enjoying it every time she thinks about it. We know that Harry is getting so frantic he's losing control. He isn't thinking clearly. Are you?"

"She's been gone over three months now. Harry is living in a way that means he doesn't expect her to come back. You thought she'd get in touch with you if she was in trouble. She didn't. Who saw her leave? What travel agency did she use?"

I reached into the back of my mind and swatted something down. It had been buzzing in circles back there. I picked it up off the floor and looked at it. "Meyer, once on that cruise years ago we bought provisions and got a lot of green stamps. I think it was in Boca Grande. They got wet and got stuck together. Mary soaked them apart. It soaked all the glue off. She dried them between paper towels. Then she got a green stamp book and some Elmer's, and she glued them into the book. Meyer, she didn't even *save* green stamps. Another thing. We spent a lot of time anchored out, as far from marinas and boat traffic and shore sounds as we could get. So she kept turning off the generator, the airconditioning, even the little battery transistor radio. She made great things out of the leftovers from yesterday's leftovers. She's not stingy. If you asked for her last dime, she'd borrow two bits somewhere and give you thirty-five cents. But she has a waste-not, want-not twitch. I kidded her about it. She didn't mind. But it didn't change a thing. Holly Dressner told me Mary planned to leave her car at the Miami airport. Okay. Would Mary pay two and a half a day indefinitely? Ninety days is two hundred and twenty-five dollars. Not Mary. No matter how upset. She'd find out the rates and turn around, drive a few miles, make a deal with a gas station or parking lot, and take a cab back and catch her flight."

"If she had time."

"Unless she changed a lot, she'd get there two hours ahead when the ticket desk says one hour. She'd have time."

"So we should go look for her car?"

"Holly should be able to tell me what to look for."

"Travis, I don't want to seem efficient, but why don't we phone Mary in Grenada? I would rather go below and drink one of your Tuborgs and listen to you fight with the island operators than drive to Miami."

I struck myself a heavy blow in the forehead with the heel of my hand, said a few one-, seven- and ten-syllable words, and we went below.

I started at eleven thirty, and by the time I got the desk at the Spice Island Inn, I was in a cold rage. It was a radio link, and nobody seemed to give a damn about completing it. I had mentally hung Alex Bell and Don Ameche in effigy several times.

At last I got the faint voice of a girl, saying, "Spice Island Inn. May I help you?" It was the singsong lilt of the West Indies, where the accented syllables seem to fall at random in strange places.

"Do you have a Mrs. Broll registered? A Mrs. Harry Broll?"

"Who? I am sorry. What last name, sir?"

"Broll. Bee-are-oh-el-el. Broll."

"Ah. Broll. There is no Mrs. Harry Broll."

"Was she there? Did she leave?"

"There is a Mrs. Mary Broll. She is here since many weeks."

"From Florida?"

"Yes. She is here from Florida."

"Can you put me through to her, please."

"I am sorry."

"Do you mean you can't?"

"There is the instruction, sir. Mrs. Broll does not take overseas calls. Not from anyone, sir."

"This is an emergency."

"I am sorry. I can write down for her your name and the number of your telephone. I cannot say if she returns the call. She does not wish to be disturbed by telephone calls from overseas. If you can give me your name?"

"Never mind. Thank you for your help."

"I am sorry." She said something else but it faded away into an odd, humming silence. There were loud clicks. Somebody else said, "Code eighteen, route through Barbados, over."

I said, "Hey! Somebody."

The humming stopped and the line went dead as marble. I hung up. I stood up and stretched. "Mrs. Mary Broll has been there for a long time, but she doesn't take overseas calls."

"In case one might be from Harry, I suppose."

"That takes care of it. Right, Meyer?"

"I suppose so."

"It was your idea. I phoned. She's there."

"I know. But . . ."

"But?"

"The known facts now seem contradictory."

"Meyer, for God's sake!"

"Now listen to me. She wants to hide from her husband and think things out. She does not want to take any overseas calls. What would it cost her to get the operator and the desk clerk to deny that she's even registered? Ten Biwi dollars each, ten U.S. dollars total? No more, certainly. If she was sure her husband couldn't trace her, then the only call she *could* get would be from her friend Holly Dressner, and she would want to take a call from her I'd think. If she set it up so that he *can* find out where she is, then the refusal to take calls would mean she wants him to fly down, and the bait would be the loan he needs."

"First you simplify things, Meyer, and then you complicate the hell out of them. I don't know what to think now."

"Neither do I. That's my problem."

"So we drive to Miami anyway?"

Holly was home, and she was very helpful about the car. "It's one of those Volks with the fancy body. Oh, dear. What in the world are they called?"

"Karmann Ghia."

"Right! Two years old. Dark red. Hard top. Believe it or not, I can give you the license plate number even. We were shopping, and we went to the place you get the plates together, and mine is about the same weight, so we were in the same series. Hers was one digit more than mine, so hers is 1 D 3108."

We drove down to Miami in Miss Agnes, and I jammed her through the confusions of the cloverleaves and put her in one of the new airport parking buildings, halfway up the long wide ramp leading to the third level, nosing her against the wall between two squatty Detroit products which made her look like a dowager queen at a rock fest. A mediocre hamburger, gobbled too hastily on the way down, lay like a stone on the floor of my stomach.

I pointed out to Meyer how our task was simplified. Apparently there was some kind of stone-crushing plant in operation not too far from the open parking garages. The longer any car had been parked there, sheltered from the rain, the more white powdered stone dust it had all over it. And Mary's would be one of the whitest of all.

There were more than enough ramps and levels and separate structures. Finally, on a top level on the side furthest from the entrance and exit ramp, I saw Karmann Ghia lines, powdery white as a sugar doughnut. Even the

plate was powder white, but the bas relief of the digits
made it readable as I neared it: 3108. Three months of
sitting and accumulating stone dust and parking charges.

Meyer drew in the dust atop the trunk. It would have
been a childish trick except for what he drew. A single
large question mark. I wiped the windshield with the edge
of my hand and bent and peered in. Nothing to see except
a very empty automobile.

A police sedan drifted up and stopped close behind the
Ghia. "Got a problem?" the driver asked. His partner got
out.

"No problem, officer."

"Your car?"

"No. It belongs to a friend."

The driver got out. "And you can't quite remember the
name of your friend, I suppose?"

I gave him my earnest, affable smile. "Now why'd you
think that, officer? This belongs to Mrs. Mary Broll, 21
Blue Heron Lane, Lauderdale, for sure."

"Girl friend?"

"Just a friend, officer."

"Doesn't your friend have anything to say?"

Meyer said, "I was not aware that you were addressing
me with any of the prior questions, officer. I happen to
have here—"

"Easy. Bring it out real real slow."

"I happen to have here a page from a scratch pad
which, if you will examine it, gives the name of the owner
and the license number and description of the vehicle."

The nearest officer took the note and looked at it and
handed it back. "Repo?"

"What?" Meyer asked. "Oh. Repossession. No. We
happened to be parked here, and we knew Mrs. Broll has
been gone for three months, and we wondered if she'd left
her car here."

The other officer had gotten into their car. I heard his
low voice as he used the hand mike. He waited, then got
out again. "Isn't on the list, Al," he said.

"Parked here, you say. Now both of you, let me see

some ID. Slow and easy. Take it out of the wallet. Keep the wallet. Hand me the ID. Okay. Now you. Okay. Now show me your parking ticket. What kind of a car?"

"Officer, it is a very old Rolls Royce pickup truck. Bright blue. It's over there in that other—"

"I saw that, Al. Remember? That's the one I had you back up and see if it had the inspection sticker."

It stopped being confrontation and began to be conversation. "Nobody," said Al, "but nobody at all is going to arrive here in that freak truck to pull anything cute. Okay. For the hell of it, why were you wondering if this woman left her car here?"

"Not so much if she left it here, but to see if she was back yet. We were just wondering. If we didn't find it, maybe she left it someplace else, or she came back from her trip. But we found it, so that means she's still on her trip."

"She stays away too much longer, she can save money by forgetting the car." They got in and glided away without saying goodby or looking back. I guessed they cruised the garages from time to time, checking their hot car lists. It would make a good drop after a stolen car had been used for a felony. Leave it, walk across to the upper or lower level, leave the airport by cab or limousine. Or airplane. Or by private car previously stashed in the parking garage.

Meyer was very quiet, and he did not speak until we were approaching Miss Agnes. He stopped and I turned and looked back at him and strolled back to where he was standing.

"Are you going to break into tears?"

"Maybe. If you were as anxious to find your wife as Harry is, if it's financially important as well as emotionally important, wouldn't you report her missing and give her description and the description of her car with the tag number to the police?"

"I would think so."

"Then the number would be on their list, wouldn't it?"

"Yes. I mean, yes, damn it."

"And because you are thinking what I am thinking and because we happen to be right here, wouldn't it be a good time to find out about airline connections, McGee?"

"For two?"

"I have to finish my paper on the Eurocurrency which replaced the dollar. I promised the conference program chairman."

nine

I should have boarded my early afternoon BWIA flight to Barbados with stops at Kingston and San Juan, thoroughly, if not visibly, bloodied by Jillian. This was Tuesday, and I should have been sailing the sea not the air.

Cowardice is a very curious ailment. The attacks occur when you do not expect them. Instead of saying the rehearsed words, I heard myself say, "Jilly dear, the matter of the old friend has come up again. I wouldn't want to go cruising down to St. Kitts with that hanging over me. I wouldn't be able to stop thinking about it and wondering. It will take a few days . . ."

"Darling, I want you to be able to keep your mind on your work. Exclusively. Besides, the five-day forecast is foul. It might work out very nicely."

"No tantrum?"

"What sort of woman do you think I am, dear? That's hardly flattering, you know. All evidence to the contrary, I am not a spoiled little bitch who goes about whining and screaming and drumming her heels. I'm grown up, you know. And more patient than you imagine. I have waited quite a while to have you all to myself."

"This shouldn't take very long."

"I'll be here when you return, dear Travis. Grenada?"

The habit of caution took over. It is an automatic reflex. Never tell anybody anything which they might in turn tell the wrong person. "No. That information is obsolete. San Juan."

"Of course. By this time, Grenada must be well emptied

out. She could have more fun in Puerto Rico. Are you and she going to have a lot of fun, Travis? Just like old times?"

"I'm not planning to. But you never can tell."

"Really! You are the most—"

"You keep asking the wrong questions. It's a bad habit."

"As bad as giving the wrong answers."

For a moment the tantrum was on the edge of happening, but she forced it back, visibly, forgave me, kissed me a lingering farewell.

Now five miles over Cuba, I wondered if it would have been better for both of us if I had made it clear I was never going to become her tame houseguest. I wondered if it had been cowardice or if I was really, underneath, the kind of miserable son of a bitch who likes to keep something in reserve in case he happens to change his mind.

Our captain, being a pleasantly enthusiastic host, invited us to look down at Cuba. I was following the McGee rule of international travel and was in first class, alone in the window seat, the bulkhead seat on the starboard side. It was British West Indian Airways, BWIA, and the leg room in the bulkhead seats on the 727 is good.

A clear and beautiful day. The tilled-field geometry of Cuba looked like the geometry of any other of the islands, from five miles up. We moved across the southern coastline, and the shallow sea was a hundred shades, from the pale pale tan of shallow sand through lime and lavender to cobalt.

"Sir?" the clear, young voice said. She was a small, dusky stewardess with a high forehead, a blue-eyed stare of calculated innocence, a dark spill of glossy black hair. Her skin was a matte texture, and it was one half-shade lighter than milk chocolate. She was the one with the absolutely great legs I had noticed when I had clambered onto their airplane. "You are going to . . ."

"Barbados."

"Ah, yes. Thank you, sir. Can I get you something to drink?"

"The last time I was on BWIA there was fresh orange juice. Do you still—"

"Oh, yes."

"With vodka then, please?"

"Oh yes, right away, thank you." She twinkled at me and spun away, the short skirt flirting and snapping. It is changing in the islands, same as everywhere. The conservative island politicians and the white businessmen try to tell you there is no racism, that black and white are treated alike and live amiably together in happy understanding and compassion.

But if you are observant, you notice that the more desirable the job, particularly the jobs women hold—stewardesses, cashiers in banks, clerks in specialty shops, hostesses in restaurants—the more likely they are to be bleached by past miscegenation. There are some true blacks in those positions, of course, but in a far lower ratio than exists in the general population. Look at the cleaning women, the canefield workers, the laundry workers, to find the purest blacks in the islands. And the blackest blacks are, of course, probably seventy-five to eighty percent of the population of the West Indies, the Bahamas, the Windward and Leeward islands. The other twenty percent is a perceptible lightening of color, shade by shade, all the way to unleavened white. Regardless of all protestations, the whiter you are, the better you live. Blondes have the most fun. One of the most thoroughly ignored aspects of the Cuban Revolution is how happily the black Cubans embraced the new order. Though the percentage is smaller in Cuba than elsewhere through the Caribbean, the pattern of discrimination was the same. Black Cuba was entirely ready for anything at all which promised equality in education, jobs, and health care. It didn't have to be Khrush or Mao. They would have built statues to a big green Martian if it could have delivered on the promises.

The curious and immediate and personal result of the color prejudice in the islands was that my pale chocolate stewardess with the great legs identified with me. We were both part of the ruling cabal. There could be an earnest friendliness in her unlikely blue eyes, an uninhibited flirtatiousness.

Another little girl of exactly the same color, but a citizen of the US of A and working, say, for Eastern on a domestic run, would have been working hard on an Afro hairdo, would have given me the precise number of millimeters of smile as prescribed by Eastern, would have been entirely correct, but her eyes would have been as empty as the ice of a long winter, concealing nothing more personal than a propagandized hostility, a prepackaged contempt, an ability to see me only as a symbol of oppression, not as a living creature walking two-legged on the same untidy world, trying to live through the weird years with a little bit of grace and care.

Too bad, somehow. The real guilt is in being a human being. That is the horrible reality which bugs us all. Wolves, as a class, are cleaner, more industrious, far less savage, and kinder to each other and their young.

When she came back with the screwdriver, she leaned one round delicious knee on the empty seat beside me and reached and put the glass and napkin on the small, built-in service area between the seats. I could read her name tag. Mia Cruikshank.

"Mia?" I said.

"Yes, sir?"

"I just meant . . . it's a pretty name."

She made a droll mouth. "Better than what it was, I think. Miriam. Mia is smashing compàred to that."

"Smashing indeed."

So we went humming down across the blue séas under the blue skies of vacationland at approximately nine hundred feet per second, which is the muzzle velocity of the .45 caliber Colt automatic pistol, an ugly and cumbersome weapon. Our happy captain pointed out this and that. We stopped at Kingston and San Juan and points south. We lost more passengers than we took on. Each island had its quota of red tape, so that the stops were long.

Mia kept me happily supplied with drinks and food, and we found it easy to smile at each other. We stood together when the sun was low, on the little platform at the top of the rolling stairs at the little airport on St. Lucia.

"You are remaining at Barbados, sir, or continuing?"

"To Grenada tomorrow morning."

"Oh, yes. That is so lovely an island. Of course, Barbados is very nice, too. Just one night is a short time to stay."

"I didn't want to stay there at all."

"I know. There is no way. You fly with us or Pan Am to Barbados or Trinidad, from Miami everyone arrives too late for the last flight to Grenada. It has to be by daylight, of course, in the small aircraft. Where will you stay in Barbados?"

"I thought I would check it out after I get there."

"Oh, yes. The season is over. There is room everywhere. But really, there was room in most of the places during the season too this year. We did not carry so many people to Barbados this year."

"Why not?"

She glanced back over her shoulder and moved closer to me, lowered her voice. "I am not a rich, important person who owns a hotel, so perhaps they know what they are doing. But, sir, suppose this was in the season and you are traveling with a lady and you try to make a reservation for the two of you in Barbados, just to stay in a hotel room overnight to continue on in the morning. In your money, in US dollars, to stay at the Barbados Hilton, it will be seventy dollars for one night, and there will be ten percent service charge added to that, so that it will be seventy seven dollars. Even were you to stay at the Holiday Inn, sir, it will be fifty-five plus ten percent, or sixty dollars and fifty cents."

"Without meals? You have to be kidding."

"Oh, no. You see, sir, they will only make reservations for you on the Modified American Plan, which includes breakfast and dinner, even when it is clear you will have dinner aboard this flight and leave so early the next morning there is perhaps time for coffee and rolls. This is happening in all the islands, sir. It is perhaps the worst in Barbados, the worst of all. It is a fantastic greed. It is like some terrible animal out of control, so hungry it feeds upon itself and is killing itself. I should not say so much."

"I won't turn you over to the tourist board, Mia."

"Oh, thank you." She hesitated and scowled. "There is something I am trying to think how to say. It is really what is wrong now with the islands. It is why each year there will be fewer people coming to these lovely places."

"It's a shame."

She turned to face me directly and looked up at me. "Seventy-seven dollars is over a hundred and fifty dollars in our currency. In Biwi dollars. A house servant in Barbados *might* make fifty dollars, Biwi, a month. A waiter or waitress *might* make seventy-five dollars, Biwi, a month. So how does a human person feel serving or cleaning up after another human person who pays two or three months wages for one single night in a room? Sir, it is like such a terrible arrogance and thoughtlessness. It makes hate, sir. It makes contempt. So the cleaning is done badly, and the serving is done very slowly and badly, and there are no smiles. Then, sir, the person who is paying too much because the hotel owners are so greedy, he becomes very angry because, if he pays so much, the service should be of the very best, and everything should be very clean. When he is angry, then he seems to be more arrogant and rich and thoughtless, sir. Hate and anger back and forth, it is a terrible thing. There is no pleasure in work and no pleasure in vacationing here, and that is why each year, like this year, there will be fewer and fewer tourists, jobs, money. It is wicked. I keep thinking to myself, what can be done —what can be done? It is like the goose, sir."

"The goose?"

"The goose they killed to get at the golden eggs." She looked at her watch. An official was trotting up the stairs. "Now we will be going, sir."

After liftoff she gave me a final drink, and she and the other girls did their desk work and policed their area and changed to their ground uniforms. She had time to give me some advice. She told me that the nearest hotel to the airport was a five-dollar taxi ride, Biwi. The Crane Beach. She said the rooms were very small and primitive, but the beach was beautiful, and the food was excellent. She said the management was surly, and the waiters insolent, but it was only for overnight, and it would be almost empty. Besides, the Barbados Hilton and the other hotels were a lot closer to Bridgetown, and so were ten to fifteen Biwi dollars one way from the airport. In most of the islands it appears that committees of taxi drivers determine airport locations.

"Just laugh at whatever they want to charge you at the Crane Beach, sir. The season is over. Put down ten dollars, Yankee, and tell them the service charge percent is included, not extra. They will show you a rate schedule and tell you it is official and they cannot change it. Just laugh. They will take the money and give you a room. It is not so easy to get a taxi in the morning early from there. Just tear a Yankee dollar in two pieces and give half to the taxi driver and tell him when to come in the morning. He will be certain to return. Do not tip anyone at that hotel. They are shameless, and it is all included in the price of everything anyway."

I was genuinely grateful to Mia. I thanked her and said, "I hope I will get a chance to tell you how I made out."

"Perhaps, if you fly BWIA back to Miami, I will serve you again. How long shall you be in Grenada, sir?"

"A few days. Any idea where I should stay?"

"Oh, no. I do not know that island so well. This is not a vacation for you. Business, yes?"

"How do you know?"

"I think I can tell if a man is not one who would take a vacation alone, sir. Good luck, sir."

My taxi man arrived the next day three minutes before the stipulated hour. He smiled broadly when he saw me standing in the early morning light outside the hotel gates with my single piece of carry-on-luggage. He decided that it was a splendid idea, the half of the paper dollar. It left each of us with an investment to protect. He had brought some tape, and he put his dollar back together before we started off. His name was Oswald, and he was a thin old man with several gold teeth. He drove his elderly white Plymouth with that kind of care which is more involved with not breaking anything than not hitting anybody.

I took LIAT, a BWIA subsidiary, to Grenada, a direct flight of about forty minutes. It was an old Avro with the rows shoved closer together to increase capacity, so that the little oval windows did not match the seat positions. Two big propjet Rolls Royce brutes powered the small aircraft. The stewardess was about the same size and shape as Hubert Humphrey. The pilot had Walter Mitty dreams of being a fighter pilot. It was an interesting takeoff and an even more interesting landing.

At Grenada's grubby little airport I once again had to show my driver's license and turn over that card form which serves as embarkation and debarkation permit, depending on how you fill out the blanks.

And then came a fascinating ride in a taxi. The island is only twenty-one miles long and twelve miles wide. The airport is about as far as it could possibly be from the principal town, St. George's. The morning ride took one full hour, and I would not have wanted my man to have tried to shave five minutes off the elapsed time. I helped with the brakes so continuously that my right leg was nearly paralyzed when we finally came down out of the mountains to sea level. The driver—he gave me his card —was Albert Owen, and he had a Chevrolet assembled in Australia with a suspension system designed for the Outback of Australia. He had put fifty-three thousand incredible miles on it on that improbable road system, using up God only knows how many sets of brake linings. Drive on the left. Average width of road—one and a quarter lanes. No shoulders. Blind corners. Big lumps, deep potholes, children, dogs, pigs, donkeys, bicycles, trucks, buses, motorcycles. So honk the horn almost continuously, shift up and shift down, swerve, leap, squeal, slide, accelerate—and all the time Albert Owen was hollering back over his shoulder at me, pointing out bah-nah-nah tree, almond tree, sugar cane, sar. Over there mammy apple, coconut plahntation sar, cocoa, also you are seeing nutmeg, sar. Many spices.

Once when a small insane truck came leaping at us on the wrong side around a bend, Albert swerved smartly. It missed us by the thickness of a coat of paint. Albert laughed and laughed. He said, "That is one foolish driver, sar. He nearly mosh us."

But nobody actually did mosh us. It was hard to believe they were not trying. Were the fates to put Albert down on any weekday morning on the Palmetto Turnpike heading into Miami with the inbound torrent, the terror of it might put him into a dead faint. A Miami cabdriver suddenly transported into Albert's mountains might conceivably run weeping into the jungle.

People certainly did go about moshing people. The dead cars amid the lush vines and wild shrubs were proof enough of that.

Albert asked me where my reservation was as we plummeted down toward the town and blue late-morning sea beyond. I said I had none but would look about a little. He said there were no problems this time of year. There had been trouble with the government water supply. When the hotel cisterns had run out, many people had left. Now the water was on again, but there were not so many tourists as on other Aprils. I found out that the Grenada Beach Hotel was the place most centrally located on Grande Anse, the two miles of crescent beach just south of the town, looking westward. I asked him if he would wait there for me. We made certain financial negotiations.

I left my single piece of luggage with him. He parked in the vehicle circle outside the main doors. I walked in and through an open lobby area and found a thatched bar off to the left, open to the outdoors, looking out across a long expanse of green lawn and tall, graceful coconut palms toward the garden of beach umbrellas, toward the bright colors of beach chairs and towels on the distant sand.

A bored bartender in a red coat appeared from some unknown hiding place, yawning. He made me a delicious rum punch with grated nutmeg afloat on it. He asked for my room number, and I paid cash for my drink, then gifted him with some of the Biwi I had picked up at the moneychanger's booth in the temple of Miami International. He brightened visibly, and I asked him if he had a phone back there, and he said he did, and he said he would be glad to phone the Spice Island Inn for me. He did so and handed me the phone.

"What number is Mrs. Broll in, please? Mrs. Mary Broll?"

"Ah . . . yes, she is in cottage 50, sir. Shall I ring her for you?"

"No thank you," I said and hung up.

I finished my drink very very slowly. It is a very strange reluctance, a curious hesitation that can immobilize you at such a time. You are eager to prove to yourself that you've been quite wrong, that you've taken too many small things and built them up into a fantasy structure that cannot be true.

Yet, if by some chance the fantasy proves to be reality, most of the game is still left to play, and an ugly game it can be.

It could be a delicious surprise. I could see the shape of Mary's familiar mouth, the wide and startled eyes, and then the rush of pleasure, the embrace.

"The Spice Island Inn is close by?"

"That direction. Very close. A small walk, sir. Two minutes."

But in the hot tropical blaze of April a man in slacks and sport shirt, socks and shoes would be as conspicuous on that beach, I found, as in a Mother Hubbard at a nudist camp. I went back through the hotel and found Albert dozing in the shade. I woke him, and we got into the broiling taxi and rode south to the entrance to the Spice Island Inn.

Meyer and I had tried to cover all eventualities in the long planning session we'd had before I left. In the islands there appeared to be so little interest in any verification of identity that the risk factor seemed very minor indeed. If we were wrong, I was going to feel a little foolish. But if we were right, there was a chance I could feel something beyond mere foolishness.

And so, in Albert Owen's back seat I switched the cash money, all of it, from one wallet to another and became

Gavin Lee. Known as Gav. Known as Mr. Lee. This follows Meyer's theory that when you pick a new name, pick
one that has the same basic vowel sounds. Then you will
react if you hear somebody behind you say your assumed
name.

I was going to carry my own suitcase in. Albert did not
think that was appropriate. The desk was very cordial.
Nothing creates such a flavor of genuine, heart-felt welcome as a nearly empty hotel. They showed me the rates.
They told me I had a choice of plans. They showed me a
map of the place with all manner of accommodations.
What would please Mr. Lee, the ostensibly vacationing
land developer from Miami, Scottsdale, Acapulco, Hawaii, Palm Springs, and Las Vegas? Well, I'm kind of
curious about those with the private pool. These here on
your map. Just this row of them, eh? How about this one
right here on the end? Number . . . I can't read it upside
down. Thank you, 50. Full. Are all these full then? Just
50, 57, and 58. Well, in the middle then, as far from the
occupied ones as . . . 54? I can see there are two bedrooms, but I don't see any one bedroom ones with the
walled garden and the pool, so. . . . Now what will it be on
. . . a European Plan? After a few days I may change, depending on how the dining room is here. Of course. I'm
sure it's marvelous. All right. Quote me on a per day. . . .
That's $28, single? That's US? Hmmm. Plus ten percent
service charge and five percent tax, which is . . . $32.34
per day. Look, I'm carrying a bit more cash than I intended. Would you mind taking this hundred-dollar bill for
three days in advance? And I'll bring you an envelope to
put in the safe.

I paid Albert off and told him I would keep his card and
I would certainly get him to drive me back to the airport
some day. A bellhop led me down a long long path to the
newest line of attached bungalows, the ones with the pool
in the garden. The row was a good two hundred and fifty
yards from the hotel proper. He demonstrated the airconditioning, the button to push for food service, the button
to push for drink service.

Then he went away. I was left in silence, in the shadowed coolness of the tourist life.

Drive the clenched fist into palm. Pock!

"Be here, baby. Just *be* here!"

ten

The row of tall attached cottages with a double peak on the roof of each one was set at a slight angle to the beach, so that architecturally they could be set back, one from the next, to provide total privacy for the individual walled gardens where the small swimming pools were.

The row of cottages was back a hundred feet and more from the beach. Between the front gates of the cottages and the beach itself was a private expanse of sand, landscaped palms, sea grapes, almond trees with sun chaises spotted about at intervals far enough apart for privacy.

I put on swim trunks and took up a position on a chaise fifty feet from my front gate, turning it in such a way I could watch the gate of number 50. By then it was past noon. The tropic sun had such a hefty sting I knew that even my deep and permanent tan would not be immune, not without a little oil and a little limitation on the exposure time.

At twenty minutes to one the gate opened, and a young woman came out. She was of medium height, delicately and gracefully built. Her dark hair was quite long, and she had a white band above her forehead clipping it in place. She seemed to be somewhere in her twenties. I could not make a closer guess at that distance. She wore eccentric sunglasses with huge round lenses in dark amber. She wore a don't-swim-in-it bikini fashioned of white elasticized cord and swatches of watermelon-colored terrycloth. She was two shades darker than Mia Cruikshank, a perfect and even tan which could only have come from untold hours of total discipline and constant care.

A man came out with her. Youngish, lithe, laughing and
saying something which made her laugh. Awesomely mus-
cled, moving well so that muscles bulged and slid under
the red-bronze tan. A Riviera swimming outfit, little more
than a white satin jockstrap. She walked a few steps and
then turned in a proprietary way and went back and tested
to see if the gate was locked. She looked in her small white
Ratsey bag, apparently to make sure that her key was
there. Then they walked toward the hotel.

My heart had turned heavy, and there was a taste of
sickness in my throat. But you have to be certain, terribly
certain. Like a biopsy. Make absolutely sure of the malig-
nancy. Because the surgery is radical.

I gave them five minutes and then followed the same
route. I found them in another of the ubiquitous thatched
bars, having a drink at a shady table and still laughing. A
cheerful pair. I went to the bar and ordered a drink. When
I had a chance, I asked the bartender if the woman at the
table was a certain Lois Jefferson. He looked troubled. He
said he knew them by the numbers. Just a moment, please.
He went to the other end of the bar and came back with a
signed drink tab. Mary D. Broll. Number 50. He showed
it to me. I thanked him, said I was wrong. I winked at him
and said, "But that is not Mr. Broll?"

He had a knowing smile. "It is just a friend. He has
been a friend for a week, I think. He works, I think, on a
private boat. That is what I hear. It is easy to make friends
here."

I picked my drink up and moved along the bar to a
stool that was about a dozen feet from their table. I turned
around on the stool, my back to the bar, and looked at her
with obvious and amiable and very thorough appreciation.
She was worth appreciating, right from her brown,
slender, tidy little ankles right on up—not too quickly—to
a ripely cushioned little mouth, dark eyes set at an interesting tilt, a broad, immature, and vulgar little nose.

She put her glasses back on and leaned over and said
something to her nautical friend. He put his drink down
and turned around and stared back over his shoulder at
me. I smiled and nodded at him. He had a Prince Valiant

haircut, and his hair was the dark molten shade of some golden retrievers. His face had a tough, pinched, disadvantaged look which did not go with the Valiant hair or the beachboy body. I do not make any judgments about hair length, mine or anyone's. I own some Sears electric clippers with plastic gadgets of various shapes which fit on the clippers to keep you from accidentally peeling your hair off down to the skull. I find that long hair is a damned nuisance on boats, on the beach, and in the water. So when it gets long enough to start to make me aware of it, I clipper it off, doing the sides in the mirror and the back by feel. The sun bleaches my hair and burns it and dries it out. And the salt water makes it feel stiff and look like some kind of Dynel. Were I going to keep it long, I would have to take care of it. That would mean tonics and lotions and special shampoos. That would mean brushing it and combing it a lot more than I do and somehow fastening it out of the way in a stiff breeze. Life is so full of all those damned minor things you have to do anyway, it seems nonproductive to go looking for more. So I go hoe the hair down when it attracts my attention. The length is not an expression of any social, economic, emotional, political, or chronographic opinion. It is on account of being lazy and impatient. No reason why the male can't have long, lovely, dark-golden hair if he wants it. But it is a personal decision now, just as it was during the Crusades and the Civil War.

He kept staring right at me, and I kept smiling at him. So he got up fast and rolled his shoulders as he covered the twelve feet to stand in front of me, bare feet spread and braced.

"Chief, stop the birddog routine. You're annoying the lady."

"Me? Come *on* now! Don't let her kid you. Lois and I have known each other for a long time. She knows I like to look at her. Always have. And I know she likes being looked at. Right, dear?"

"You're out of your tree, chief. Knock it off. She isn't Lois."

I stood up. "She's Lois Jefferson. Believe me!" I edged

by him as he tried to block me away from the table. "Lois,
honey. It's Gav Lee, for God's sake. It was a good joke,
but let's not run it into the ground."

She took the glasses off and looked up at me. "Really,
I'm not Lois. I'm Mary Broll. Really."

I boggled at her. "Not Lois Jefferson from Scarsdale?
Not Tom's wife?"

It sucked in the fellow nicely. He was all alerted for
games. When you roam in public with an item like that
woman, you keep the guard way up. "Honey," he said,
"how about this clown? You get it? Tom Jefferson. Thomas Jefferson. Stop annoying us, chief, or I'll call the—"

I turned on him. "Really. Would it put too much of a
strain on you to have a little common courtesy? Her husband has always had the nickname Tom, for quite obvious
reasons. His real name is . . ." I turned back to her. "What
is Tom's real first name, dear?"

She laughed. "But I am really not your friend!"

I stared at her. "That can't be possible. It's the most
fantastic look-alike. . . . You wouldn't believe. . . . Miss
Broll, would you—"

"Mrs. Broll."

"I'm sorry. Mrs. Broll, would it be rude of me to ask
you to stand up for just a moment?"

"I guess not."

"Now just one goddamn—"

I turned on him again. "What harm can it do, Mr.
Broll?"

She stood up beside her chair. I moved closer to her,
and I stared into her eyes from close range. "By God, I am
wrong. I would never have believed it. You are a little bit
taller than Lois, and I think your eyes are a darker shade,
Mrs. Broll."

"Now go away," the man said.

As she sat down she said, "Oh, shut up, Carl. You get
so boring sometimes. The man made a mistake. All right?
All right. Please forgive Carl, Mr. . . ."

"Lee. Gavin Lee. Gav to my friends."

"I don't see any friends of yours around here," the man
said.

She gave me a very pretty and well-practiced smile. "Gav, this rude animal is Carl Brego. Carl, shake hands nicely with Gav, or you can damned well take off."

I saw the little tightening around his eyes and knew the childish bit he was going to try. So when he put his hand out, I put my hand into his much too quickly for him to close his hand to get my knuckles. I got my hand all the way back, deep into the web between thumb and finger. Then I could just maintain a mild, firm clasp and smile at him as he nearly ruptured his shoulder muscles trying to squeeze my hand to broken pulp.

"Sorry about the little misunderstanding, Carl," I said. "I'd like to buy you two nice people a drink."

He let go of my hand and sat down. "Nobody invited you to join the party, chief."

He had fallen into that one, too. He was scoring very badly. I said, "I don't expect to sit down with you, Carl. Why should I? I was going to go to that table way over there and have my own drink over there and send two to this table. You act as if I'm trying to move in on you. How far would I get, Carl? As you are not Mr. Broll, then this lovely lady is a friend of yours. You are having lunch together. Just the two of you. If I were having lunch with her, I would be very ugly about anybody trying to move in. I just think you overreact, Carl. I made a little mistake. You keep getting rude for no reason. But I'll still buy those drinks. I was thinking of it as an apology, not a ticket to the party."

So saying, I gave the lady a little bow and marched on over to my distant table and told the waiter to give them anything they might want. I sat with my back toward them.

It did not take her long. Four minutes, I think it was, before he appeared beside my chair, standing almost at attention.

"Excuse me. Mrs. Broll would be very happy if you would join us for lunch."

I smiled up at him. "Only if you are absolutely certain you don't mind, Brego."

It hurt his mouth to say it. It hurt his whole face. "Please join us, Mr. Lee."

All through lunch I knew Brego was waiting and planning. When I saw that he wasn't at all upset that I was living just a few doors—or a few gardens—away from his pretty friend, I could almost guess the kind of routine he had figured out.

And during lunch I had managed to steer the conversation in a direction that gave me a chance to awaken more than a flicker of interest in her eyes and at the same time gave her a chance to shove a little blade into Carl Brego and give it a twist.

I said, "I take little flyers in island property sometimes. Actually, that's why I'm here. Some associates said I ought to take a look at this one. Anyway, usually I like to pyramid, but quite a while ago I got into Freeport up in the Bahamas at the right time and got out at exactly the right time with much more than I'd expected, so I thought I'd give myself a little present. So I bought this great big, ridiculous brute of a schooner in Nassau and had the yard that sold it to me hire aboard a crew, and I actually set out for *this* island. But the guest I invited aboard for the trip became terribly seasick. We made it as far as Great Inagua and got off, both of us, at Matthew Town and arranged passage from there back to civilization. I had the crew take the boat back to Nassau. As I remember, my acountants told me the net loss was something like thirteen thousand dollars after I'd had the yard resell the schooner. But it would have been cruel and unusual punishment to have made the young lady sail one more mile."

Something behind her dark eyes went ding, and a cash drawer slid open in her skull. She counted the big bills and shut it again and smiled and said, "Carl knows all about yachts. He sails one around for a very fat rich lady, don't you, darling?"

"That must be very interesting," I said.

"He's waiting on Grenada until she arrives with friends," the woman said. "You know. Like a chauffeur, parked somewhere."

"Knock it off," Carl said in a small humble voice.

"Please?" she said.

"Please."

And that made it even more imperative. I decided I was reading her well enough to see that she knew the direction the tensions would take and would give the ceremony a chance to get under way at the first opportunity. And would want to watch.

When we got to her gate, there was no one in sight. The breeze had stopped. Sweat popped out immediately on all three of us. I felt it run down my back.

"Do come in, Gav," she said. "Do join us."

She was starting to unlock the gate. Carl said, "So it's enough already."

"Enough?" she said blankly. "Enough?"

"Honey, the guy is taking a cheap shot, and I'm going to run him off."

She licked her mouth. "Carl, sweetie, why do you have to be—"

"You can go in out of the heat, or you can stay and watch how it's done, Mary. Either way I run this smartass off."

"Any special direction?" I asked.

"Pick the one you like best, chief," he said with a jolly grin of anticipation. "Start now and save yourself grief."

"Take your best shot, Brego." He took it. I was worried that he might know too much about what he wanted to do. If he did, it was going to take a long time in the hot sun, and if he didn't, it could be reasonably quick.

He did a little bounce, a little prance. He pawed with the clumsy, measuring left and then came leaping in, following up on the right hook that he had brought up from about five feet behind him, practically at ground level. He did not know what he was doing. People who know do not go around taking the chance of hitting the solid bone of skull or jaw with the bare fist. A broken hand is incapacitating. It takes a long, tiresome time to heal. He wanted to pop me one and let the momentum carry him into me so he could get his hands and arms on me and put those muscles to work. He gave me lots of time for a decision. If I fell back away from it, he was going to tumble onto me. That way I might get a thumb in my eye before I could unwind and unravel him. The footing in the soft sand was a little uncertain for savate. So I moved forward, a little to my right, to take me inside that long, sweeping hook.

I felt it go around me, and I let his momentum then drive me back. I drove both hands, fingers spread, into his long hair, I clenched hard and went down pulling him on top of me but getting my knees up against my chest in time. One shoe slipped off his sweaty body, but the sole of the other stayed in place against his belly, and momentum gave me enough leverage to push him up and over. It was a good, high kick, and he spun well. By then I was on my back with my hands straight up over my head.

He hit the soft sand flat on his back with one hell of a whump. It exploded the air out of his lungs. I was up first, and I moved into position, waiting for him. He got up slowly, gagging for air. As he pushed up, I cranked his arm around behind him and put my other hand on the nape of his neck and ran him into the weathered boards of the garden fence, quite close to the woman. He splintered a board with the top of his head. She squeaked and chewed her fist. I dragged him back by the ankles, face down. I picked him up and stood him on his noodle legs and slapped him until he started to come around. Then I bent him over and ran him into the fence again. I dragged him back again, and I turned his feet until he rolled over onto his back. I slapped him where he lay, and when he stirred and his eyes came into focus, I levered his mouth open by bracing the heel of my hand against his chin. I packed his mouth full of soft hot sand, from the back of his throat to his pretty, white teeth. He came sputtering and gagging onto his hands and knees and coughed himself sick. I grabbed the hair and pulled his head up and back.

"Nod if you can understand me, Brego." He nodded. "Do you want me to break any bones? Do I have to do that?" He shook his head. "She isn't your woman any more. Understand?" He nodded. "Now I am going to start kicking your ass. You better head for the beach. If I ever see you back here, I'll break some bones."

I went around behind him and got a pretty good soccer kick into it, using the side of my foot. On the upswing. It slid him onto his face. He came scrambling up with more energy than I expected, but I got him again just as he got his feet under him and his hands free of the sand. Three running steps and he landed on his face again but didn't spend any time resting. He got up and went into a wobbly scuffling run, fists against his chest, not daring or wanting to look back.

I watched him and then turned and looked at the woman. She gave me a very uncertain smile. There was an unhealthy skin tone under that deep lovely tan. "I . . . I thought you were going to kill him."

"Kill him? What in God's name for?"

"Well . . . it was so quick and so terrible."

"He won't be back, Mary. Are you going to miss him, particularly? You going to be lonesome?"

"That would depend, wouldn't it?"

"Is there any of his stuff in there?"

"Not much. A few things."

"Anything worth his coming back after?"

"I wouldn't think so. No."

"Now you can invite me in again."

Her color was back. "You take a hell of a lot for granted."

I put a knuckle under her chin and tilted her face up and looked at it inch by inch, a long and interested search. "If you want, girl, I can throw you back, like an undersized mackerel. The world is full of Carl Bregos. It's up to you."

She twisted her chin free. "I guess I wouldn't want to be thrown back, Gav. I guess it wouldn't fit my image. Was there really a Lois Jefferson?"

"If you think there was."

"I don't think so."

"Then there never was such a girl."

"Poor Carl. Do you always get what you want?"

"I usually get what I *think* I want."

She tilted her shoulders one way, her hips the other. Her look was challenge. "And sometimes you find out you didn't really want it after all. Me, too. Win a little, lose a little, huh?"

"If you wanted Brego, you'd still have him. I wouldn't have gotten to say more than two words to you."

"Like I was saying when we were so rudely interrupted, you want to come into my house? It's hot out here when the wind quits."

So we went in, and I wondered why I could find no trace of a Canadian accent. She had to be Lisa Dissat.

eleven

Though the plantings were different, the patio furniture of a different style and arrangement, the pool and the cold water shower head were placed just as in my rented garden. I went to the shower and turned it on and sluiced off the sand that had caked thickly on my sweaty back and on my left side where I had rolled to get up quickly. The woman stood and watched me and then took a big, striped beach towel from a stone bench and brought it to me as I stepped out of the spray and turned the shower off.

As I dried myself, I realized how sexually aware of her I had become. Physical readiness. All her honey-brown curves and cushions were there, appropriate, ready for use.

It is such an old old thing, the pattern of male conflict that wins the female. It is deep in the blood and the secretions, a gut knowledge. We are mammals still caught up in all the midbrain mechanisms of survival. The bison female stood long ago and watched the males thud their brute heads together, tear up the sod with their hooves, watched the loser lope heavily away, and then she waited patiently to be mounted by the victor. The stronger the male, the stronger the calves, and the better protected the calves would be during the long months of helplessness. The victorious male, turning from battle to the prize of battle, would be physiologically ready to mate her and have no question about her readiness.

I knew the musky readiness of the woman. She told me in the way she stood, in the way she looked at me, in the shape of her placid mouth. Maybe ten percent of what we

117

can say to each other is with words, and words can conceal as easily as they can reveal. The rest of it is body language, our cants, tilts, postures, textures.

And who can prove there is not an actual telepathic signal being transmitted? Tiny electrical discharges occur in the living mind in great and complex profusion. Strong emotion, tautly focused, may send out an impulse so strong it can be read. Hate, fear, anger, joy, lust . . . these all seem contagious beyond all objective reason. I knew she was so swollen, so moist, so ready, that if I trotted her into the shadowy coolness of the apartment and into her bed, there would be no time or need for foreplay, that she would cling and grind and gasp and within a minute begin to go into a climax.

The violence had caught us up in the first act of the fleshy ceremony, and I wanted to take that quick, primitive jump so badly I felt hollowed out by the ache of it. Bed was her country. That was where, after the first great surge, she would take command. I would become what she was accustomed to and lose any chance of keeping her off balance. I shook myself like a big tired Labrador after a long swim, balled the damp towel, and flipped it at her face. She moved in her slow sensuous dream, getting her hand partway up before it hit her squarely in the face. It fluttered to the floor.

"Hey!" she said, frowning. "What's that for?"

"Pick it up!"

"Sure," she said. She picked the towel up. "What are you sore about? Why are you getting ugly and spoiling the fun?"

"He was supposed to hammer me to bloody ruin out there. That was supposed to be the fun. Thanks a lot."

She came toward me. "Darling, you've got it all wrong. I was getting *bored* with him! I was *so* glad you came along."

"Sure, Mary. Only I know the Bregos of this world. They don't start anything they don't think they can win. Their cheap women chouse them into it because they like the blood. You set me up by reacting to me. If you'd

cooled it, there'd have been no fight. He was going to
smash me around and that was going to turn you on for
him, so you'd hustle him into your sack for a quick hump.
A little midday entertainment. No thanks."

She leaned forward from the waist, face contorting,
voice turning to a squalling fishwife. *"Goddamn* you! *You*
moved in on us with all that crap about me looking like
somebody else. *You* thought I was worth the chance of
getting your ass whipped. Don't slam the gate on the way
out, you son of a—"

Her lips started to say the obvious word, but I had fitted my big right hand to her slender throat, just firmly
enough to cut off her wind, not firmly enough to crush any
of the tender bones and cartilage. The ball of my thumb
reached to the big artery in the side of her throat under the
jaw hinge, and my first and middle finger reached to the
artery on the left side of her throat.

Her eyes went wide, and she dropped the towel and put
her nails into the back of my hand and my wrist. I pinched
the arteries gently, drastically reducing the flow of blood
to the brain. It gave her a gray-out to the edge of fainting.
Her eyes went out of focus, and her mouth sagged. When I
let up, she tried to kick me, so I pinched again. Her arms
fell slack to her sides. When I released the pressure, adjusting my hand enough so that she could breathe, she
raised her hands and then hung them upon my wrist.

I smiled at her, pulling her a half-step closer and said,
"If you get loud and say nasty things, dear, if you get on
my nerves, I can hold you like this, and I can take this free
hand and make a big fist like this, and I can give you one
little pop right here that will give you a nose three inches
wide and a quarter inch high."

"Please," she said in a rusty little voice.

"You can get a job as a clown. Or you can see if you
can find a surgeon willing to try to rebuild it."

"Please," she said again.

I let go of her and said, "Pick up the towel, love."

She coughed and bent and picked it up and backed
away. I turned away from her and went to the cottage

apartment and pulled the door open and went in. I went to the kitchen alcove and checked the bottle supply. I heard her slide the glass door shut again.

I fixed some Booth's with Rose's lime juice and a dash of bitters, humming softly but audibly. I took my glass over to the couch and sat and smiled at her and said, "Did I ever tell you I read minds?"

"You must be some kind of a crazy person." It was not said as an insult. It was said softly, wonderingly.

I pinched the bridge of my nose and closed my eyes. "Many messages are coming through. Ah, yes. You are wondering if you can get the hotel management to throw a net over me and get me out of here. No, dear. I think they would believe me instead of you. If they make life difficult, I could go down to the harbor and find your friend Brego and bounce him up and down until he agrees to write out a personal history of your touching romance and sign it. Then I could go find your husband and peddle it to him. It would cut the heart out of any alimony payments."

"I just want you to—"

"Where and when did you meet Brego?"

"On the beach. Over a week ago. My neck hurts."

"Of *course* it hurts a little! How could I do that without giving you a sore neck? Let me see. What else is in your mind? You're wondering if I'm going to lay you and if I'll be nicer to you afterward. The answer to both questions, dear, is: time will tell."

She went over to the kitchen bar. Ice clinked into a glass. She came back with a drink and sat on a hassock five feet away from me. Her eyes looked better. Her confidence was coming back. She squared her shoulders, tugged the bikini top and bottom into better adjustment, tilted her head, and risked a meager smile. "I guess all that lunch talk about land investments was a lot of crap, huh?"

"What makes you think so? It's what I do."

"You don't act like it's what you do. Like the way you were with Carl and with me, Gavin. I mean . . . well, it's like you enjoyed hurting."

"Well . . . let's suppose there's a man with a good idea where a new interstate is going or a new jetport, and suppose we teamed up, and you had some nice long weekends with him, and he clued you about where to buy the raw land. Mary, I just couldn't stand having you get tricky with me about something like that. I wouldn't want to worry about you selling that information to somebody else. I'd have to have you so trained for the work that if I just stare at you for ten seconds, you start to have the cold sweats and the gags. Hurting is purely business. I guess I enjoy anything that helps make money."

She thought that over, sipping, frowning. "But it's not as if I was going to work with you, Mr. Lee."

"Time will tell."

"You keep saying that. Well, I'm not going to work with you or for you. For that kind of work you're talking about, what you want is some kind of a hooker, it seems to me."

"Does it seem like that to you? Really? I wouldn't say that. You're built for the work. You have just enough cheap invitation in the way you look and the way you handle yourself to keep a man from wasting a lot of time on unnecessary preliminaries."

"Now wait one goddamn minute—"

"Are you still with Brego? No. Then shut up."

"I'm sorry. Don't get sore."

"Fifty bucks makes you a hooker. For five hundred you're a call girl. Five thousand makes you a courtesan."

"What's that?"

"Never mind. But when we move the decimal point one more place, your end of the arrangement is fifty thousand. That makes you a career woman."

The pointed tongue moved slowly across the underlip. She swallowed and said, "I've got my own thing going, thanks."

"Alimony is a cheap hustle."

"It all depends."

"On how much he's got? On the evidence? On the law?

It has to be a cheap hustle, because when there's enough money involved, there's more profit from going in some other direction."

I had wanted to test just how deep the hardness went. Her eyes changed. She slopped some of her drink onto her bare knees, wiped it off with her hand. "That's crazy talk."

"Not for careful people who've got the right contacts."

"For me, no thanks. I just wouldn't have the nerve, Gav."

I got up and moved around, carrying my drink. I did not know where to take it from there. I could guess that she had been ordered to keep to herself in Grenada but had finally gotten so bored she had become reckless and picked up Brego. Now the Brego game had mushroomed into something a lot less comfortable for her. If she could live quietly at the inn for the length of time she was supposed to, she could get away with it. She wasn't too much shorter than Mary or too much younger. Dark hair. All American women look alike to the help.

I hadn't wanted to let myself think about Mary. From the physical description the housekeeper had given Jeannie Dolan, this woman was the Canadian, Lisa Dissat. If she was here, Mary was dead. I had the beginnings of an idea. I went back to the conversations at lunch. Neither the first name of her supposed husband nor her Stateside residence had come up.

After mental rehearsal and rewrite I sat once again and looked placidly at her and said, "The way you spell that last name is bee-are-oh-el-el?"

"Yes."

"Kind of unusual. It rings a bell someplace. Mary Broll. Mary Broll. It's been bothering me ever since I met you in the bar."

"Why bother with it? Want me to fresh up your drink?"

"Got it!"

"Got what?"

"Where'd you register from? One buck will get you five it's the Fort Lauderdale area. Sure! We had a syndicate

set up a couple of years back and we wanted a builder in
the Lauderdale area who could put up a hotel and marina
complex in a hurry. Heavy-set fellow name of Broll. Big.
Not old. Frank? Wally? Jerry? . . . Harry! Damn right.
Harry Broll."

"Maybe there's more Brolls than you know, Gav."

"Bring me your purse, honey."

"What?"

"Go get your purse. Your pocketbook. Your handbag.
Bring it to dear old Gavin Lee so he can look at your ID,
dear."

She gave me a broad, bright smile, and her teeth chattered for a moment before she got herself under control.
"Okay. My secret is out. You are speaking of the man I
used to love."

"How long have you been married to him?"

". . . Nearly four years."

"Any kids? No? Lucky. Kids seem to get the rough end
of the stick. Bring me the purse, honey."

"Why should I? I told you, didn't I?"

"Honey, if we stop getting along, we're going to have to
hurt your neck a little until we get squared away."

"Please. It makes me sick to my stom—"

"Get the purse!"

She brought it to me. I found the billfold. I examined
the identification. I looked at the signature on the driver's
license. I knew my Mary had signed it, and I knew, looking at it, that she was dead.

"Honey, go over to that desk and take a piece of paper
and sign your name on it. Mary D. Broll. And bring it
back here to me."

"Who *are* you? What do you want?"

"I am the fellow who sat across the table from Mary D.
Broll at Le Dome of the Four Seasons in Lauderdale two
years ago last month. There were about ten of us at that
dinner. Harry was making the big gesture, trying to sucker
us into letting him build for us. I spent the evening trying
to make his wife. She wouldn't give me a clue. I always

have a better memory for the ones who get away. Here's her signature right here. Go over there and forge it for me, honey."

"Who *are* you?" she demanded, close to tears.

I gave her a broad, egg-sucking smile. "Me? I am the fellow who all of a sudden owns himself a whole woman, right from dandruff to bunions and everything in between. Broads like you don't play games like this unless there's money in it. And now it's *our* money, dear. I am the fellow who is going to get it all out of you, and I am going to beat on you until you convince me there's nothing left to tell. Me? Hell, baby, I am your new partner."

"Please. Please. I can't tell you—"

"The little lady in this corner is getting one chance and one chance only, to go over to the desk and sign her real, true, legal name to a piece of paper and bring it back to the gentleman. And if it turns out that it is not her real true name, it is going to be one of those long afternoons. We're going to have to stuff a towel in the little lady's mouth so the screaming won't spoil anybody's vacation."

She walked to the desk, her back very straight. She wrote on a piece of paper and brought it back and handed it to me and began to weep. She covered her face and ran for the bedroom. Damned few women look well from a rear elevation, running away from you in a bikini. She was not one of them. She had written her name neatly. It was a schoolgirl neatness. Lisa Dissat.

I slowly crumpled the sheet of hotel paper. I felt tired. I got up and walked back to the bedroom where she lay upon the unchanged sheets she and Brego had stained, sweated, and rumpled. She was on her side, knees hiked up, clenched fists tucked under her chin. She made sucking sounds, whining sounds. Fetal agony.

In the better interrogations there is always a good guy and a bad guy. I had been the bad guy. Time to change roles. I went into the bathroom and took a hand towel and soaked it in cold water. I wrung it out, took it to the bed, sat on the side of the bed, and cupped my hand on her shoulder and pulled her toward me. She resisted and made protest sounds, then let herself roll onto her back.

I hitched closer and gently swabbed her face and fore-head. Her eyes went wide with astonishment. The last thing she had expected was gentleness. She snuffled. Her face looked touchingly young. Tears had washed away the challenge and the hardness.

"Have you got anything with you to prove your name is Lisa Dissat?"

"N-no."

"And you're pretending to be Mary Broll?"

"Yes. But I—"

"Does Broll know you're impersonating his wife?"

"Yes."

"Were you having an affair with him?"

"Yes."

"Where's the real Mary Broll?"

". . . I don't know."

"Lisa?"

"I didn't know what he was going to do! I *didn't!*"

"Lisa!"

"I couldn't have changed anything."

"Just say she's dead, Lisa. Go ahead."

"I didn't know he—"

"Lisa! Say it!"

"She's dead. Okay. She's dead."

"Harry killed her?"

She looked startled. "Oh, no!"

"Who killed her?"

"Please, Gavin. If he ever knew I told anybody—"

"You're in a real box, dear. You can worry about what's going to happen in the future, or you can worry about what's going to happen in the next ten minutes."

"I don't even know if he really meant to."

"What's his name?"

". . . Paul. Paul Dissat. He is . . . my first cousin. We worked for the same man. In Quebec. Mr. Dennis Water-bury. Paul got me the job there. I'm a secretary. I was a secretary. Paul is an accountant. He is . . . very trusted. I think he might be crazy. Really crazy. Maybe he really planned to kill Harry's wife. I don't know. I don't even know if he knows."

"How much money is involved?"

"An awful lot. Really, an awful lot of money."

"Stop crying."

"I want to talk about it, and I don't want to talk about it. I've been scared for so long! I *want* you to make me tell you all of it, but I'm afraid to tell you."

twelve

It was a very long afternoon for both of us. But longer for Lisa Dissat, because from time to time she tried to get cute. But the more she tried it, the more conditioned she became, and the more quickly she would correct herself.

At last I was able to bring the complex, wandering, fragments of the story into reasonably sharp focus.

Paul Dissat had hungered for a long time to share in some of the large profits Dennis Waterbury made on his varied operations and investments in resort lands, oil and gas drilling programs, new urban office structures, tanker leasing, and so on. Paul Dissat was well paid. There were staff bonuses when things went well. Paul Dissat was shrewd enough to realize that without investment capital he had no chance of participating in the profits and that if he used his skills to tinker with the records of the various corporations and their shifting, changing bank balances, sooner or later an audit would catch him.

He was single, she said, and did not look like anybody's idea of an accountant. Bachelor apartment, sports car. She said he was a superb skier, proficient at downhill racing and slalom. She said that three years ago, when she was twenty-three, she had run up bills she was unable to pay. She was afraid of losing her job. She had phoned Paul. She had not seen him in several years. He had taken her to dinner and back to his apartment and made love to her. He had paid her overdue accounts and arranged for her to be employed by Waterbury. After they had been intimate many times, he had told her of his plan to share in some of the fat profits from Waterbury's operations. He would arrange the necessary leverage through her. He said he would let her know when the right opportunity came along.

He arranged for her to seduce the particularly unattractive minor partner in one of the Waterbury developments and to pretend infatuation. Paul prompted her during the affair, telling her what her lines should be. Eventually, in order to safely end the affair without Lisa going to his wife, the man deposited a substantial amount of cash in her savings account. Paul told her that the cash was the proceeds from the stock in a Waterbury enterprise that the man had sold to get the money to buy her off. Paul had taken all of the cash except a thousand dollars.

They had done it once again prior to her affair with Harry Broll and made a little more than the first time. Paul explained to her that a man who has suddenly made a substantial profit tends to be generous with a mistress who is becoming too demanding and possessive.

I wanted to know why she kept so little of the take and let her first cousin have all the rest. She said it was because she was in love with him. At first.

"The third one was Harry," she said. "I went to the hotel and took dictation. Just like the first two men. Ten minutes after I looked at him in a certain way and told him how real brilliant he was, I was helping him take off my bra, because his hands were shaking so bad. Then after Harry went back to the States, Paul made me quit my job and follow him. I didn't want to. He said this could be the big one, worth a big risk. So . . . I did what he said. Harry got jumpy when I phoned him last November from Miami. He was glad, but he was nervous, too. I told him I had followed him because I was so in love with him I couldn't live without him, and I was putting my future in his hands."

Harry had set her up in the apartment in the Casa de Playa. At about that time Paul Dissat had been transferred to the administrative offices of SeaGate, Inc. in West Palm Beach, just as he had planned and expected. SeaGate was a large, complex situation with very complicated financing and special tax problems. Paul had been involved in it from the beginning.

"I called Paul once, but he got very angry. He told me to keep on following orders. The orders were to make myself just as agreeable as I possibly could, to make Harry as happy as possible, to really work on the sex part of it and do anything and everything to give him so much pleasure he'd never be able to get along without me. That wasn't easy, because Harry worked hard and he didn't keep in shape and didn't have much energy left for bed. But after I learned what turned him on the most, it got better for both of us. I had to pretend to be passionately in love with him. You know, it wasn't such a bad life. Go shopping, go out on the beach, get your hair done, watch your weight, do your nails, take naps. Not a bad life. Then a few days before Christmas, Paul wanted to know when Harry would be with me, definitely. I said I could make sure he'd come in the middle of the day on the twenty-third and spend an hour and a half with me. He told me not to be surprised if Mrs. Broll showed up. I couldn't understand what Paul was trying to do. He told me to shut up and do what I was told. She came barging in as Harry was leaving. Better looking than I'd thought from what Harry had told me about her. She called me some things, and I called her some things, and she went away crying."

Harry Broll had then become very upset. He had told Lisa Dissat that he needed her, that he wanted to get a divorce from Mary and marry her, but he couldn't do that yet. He had to make up with Mary, humble himself, promise never to see Lisa again. He said he had to do that because without her financial backing he was going to miss out on his great opportunity at SeaGate. He said he had to move her out of the apartment and be very careful about seeing her. He said it might last until May, but then he could leave Mary and marry her.

On the night of January fourth, shortly before midnight, Harry came to Lisa's motel, where he had moved her after taking her out of the apartment. He was drunk. He said that he and Mary had a terrible fight, and she was leaving him. As soon as Harry had passed out, Lisa phoned Paul to report, as required, any new development. Paul drove over to the motel, left his rented car there, borrowed Harry's car and house keys, and told Lisa to undress the unconscious Harry and keep him quiet for as long as she could manage.

"He wouldn't tell me what he was going to do. He acted all . . . keyed up, excited, on top of the world. He came back at daylight. He seemed very tired and very relaxed. He helped me get Harry up. Harry was confused. He knew Paul, of course, because of SeaGate and knew he was my cousin. But that was the first he realized that Paul knew about Harry and me. Paul pretended to be very upset about the affair, I guess to keep Harry off-balance. The three of us went back in Harry's car to Harry's house on Blue Heron Lane. Paul kept telling Harry he was in trouble. Paul made me wait in the living room. He took Harry into the bedroom. Harry made a terrible sound. A kind of bellowing groan. I heard heavy footsteps running, and then I heard Harry throwing up. When Paul brought him back into the living room, all cleaned up, Harry was like a sleepwalker. Paul kept saying it was an accident, and Harry kept saying anything like that just couldn't be an accident, and Paul kept telling him that everything could be worked out for the best if Harry would just pull himself together. Paul had me make coffee, a lot of it."

Mary had, of course, been interrogated by Paul Dissat and murdered by Paul Dissat when he finally had everything he needed—the air reservations and tickets from the travel agency, the hotel reservation, the complete details of her arrangement with her trust officer, the fact that only one friend knew where she was going and why: Holly Dressner at 27 Blue Heron Lane, a few doors away. And he had the ninety-two hundred dollars in cash she had drawn from the income account of TA 5391. Mary was half packed for the trip. She had bought resort clothes. At Paul's order Lisa finished the packing, hunting through Mary's belongings for what she thought she would need.

"It was weird with her on the bed all covered up. I tried some of the stuff on in her dressing room. She was a little hippier than I am. I mean some of the things were a size ten when I'd be better off in an eight. Harry was like a very sick person. He couldn't seem to get himself out of it. Tears kept rolling down his face. Once he just sort of hung on me. He grabbed me and put so much weight on me he nearly rode me right down on to the floor. He was asking me something, mumbling about how could Paul do that, how could he. They had a terrible argument later on. I couldn't hear most of it. It was about what to do with her body. Harry said he couldn't stand having her buried on the place. There was something about the seawall and a transit mix truck. Paul told Harry she was going to be buried right on the property, then Harry would not go back on any promises, ever."

She was given her orders, and Paul made her repeat them until there was no chance of her forgetting them. Drive to Miami International. Find accommodations for the night of the fifth and sixth. Stay in the room. Use Mary's ticket on the seventh. Use Mary's driver's license as proof of birthplace when needed. Use her immunization certificate if needed. Use her hairstyle. Wear big dark sunglasses. Travel in her new clothes. Go to Grenada. Register as Mary Broll. Live quietly. Keep to yourself. Send some post cards to Holly Dressner. Pick the kind which do not require a message. Sign with a little drawing of a smiling face.

"I *did* try to keep to myself. But, God, I've been here a long long time, Gav. I really have."

"What do you do next? What are Paul's orders?"

"On Monday, next Monday, I'm supposed to send a cable. Paul dictated it to me." I made her get it. It was to Woodrow Willow at Southern National in Miami. PROCEED WITH LOAN AS ARRANGED EARLY JANUARY. HAVE ADVISED HARRY BY PHONE. HOME SOON. MARY BROLL.

Harry's part in it would be to phone Woodrow Willow that same day, Monday, April twenty-sixth, and tell him that Mary had reached him by overseas phone call from Grenada to tell him she had cabled Willow to go ahead, tell him not to worry, tell him she would be home soon.

He would inform Willow that Mary had given him the name of the travel agency she had used and had told him that her neighbor, Mrs. Dressner, had known all along where she was.

Very nice. If Willow felt like double-checking after he got the cable, he could call the travel agency and call Mrs. Dressner.

"Can't they check back on an overseas call?" I asked.

"Sure. That's why I call him at his office next Sunday afternoon. I've got the number. He'll have a secretary there. It will be person-to-person. Mrs. Broll calling Mr. Broll. That's for afterward, in case they do a lot of checking."

"Checking what?"

"I'm reserved to leave here on Monday, the third of May. Paul just didn't have time to work everything out before I left. But the way he wants it to happen, Mary Broll will have some kind of accident. He's going to get a message to me telling me what to do. I just . . . leave everything of hers and arrive back home as myself somehow. Maybe a towel and a beach bag left on the beach, and nothing missing but a swim suit and a cap."

"Where does the money come from?"

"The way I understand it, Gav, Harry invested seven hundred thousand in SeaGate. The letter of agreement said that on or before April thirtieth, he has to pay in another three hundred thousand to make one million dollars. There is a block of stock escrowed for him and a note escrowed, saying SeaGate owes him seven hundred thousand plus interest. It is an . . . indivisible block. He takes it all and wipes out the money SeaGate owes him and pays three hundred more. If he doesn't, he just gets his seven hundred back with interest, and the hundred thousand shares go to increase the number of shares the corporation is selling to the public and to reduce the number the stockholders will offer. There is no way in the world Harry can get that money except from the bank on a loan on Mary's trust. He can't get an extension, and he can't cut down the number of shares he'll take. And he is borrowed to the hilt everywhere else."

"So he had to keep Mary alive for about four months after she died?"

She shivered. "Or lose a big profit, a million and a half."

"How much to your cousin?"

"He said a million. He didn't say that in front of Harry. I think he could get it all out of Harry." She frowned. "The thing about Paul, he stopped giving a damn *what* he does. It doesn't matter to him any more. It scares me. Once when I was little, a deaf boy took me to the movies, and he laughed when nobody else was laughing. Paul is like that now, sort of."

"And I suppose Harry has been making a big fuss, storming around, shaking up Mary's friends, demanding they tell him where they're hiding her."

"Maybe. I don't know. I guess it would make him look better later on, if people could testify to that. I don't know how he is. I keep wondering how he'll sound on the phone."

Her voice dragged. Her face looked puffy with fatigue. Her eyes were irritated because of the many times the tears had come. There wasn't much left of the day. She said, "Can we go for a walk on the beach? Would that be okay, Gavin?"

She got up and got a gaudy print dashaki and pulled it over her head, pushed her hair back into semiorder, put her big glasses on. "Gee, I feel emptied out, as if it's out of my hands somehow. I should be scared, but I'm too beaten down to be scared. You're in charge, Gav. You've taken over. I don't know where we're going, but you're running the ship."

It was so nicely done I had my mouth all set for the bait and the hook. Poor little victim of a sordid conspiracy, clinging to the first man who'd give her the benefit of the doubt.

Sweet little immature face and a busy, nimble little butt and all the conscience and mercy of a leopard shark. Let me be your little pal, mister. Nobody else has ever understood me but you. She had slipped up on one little detail, but it was a bad slip. She let me see how she must have

looked trying on Mary's new resort clothes while Mary lay
dead. Probably Lisa turned this way and that, looking in
the mirror, smoothing her rear with the backs of her
hands, wishing the damned dead woman had bought the
cute clothes one size smaller. She tried on clothes while
the men argued in the next room. "Look at it this way,
Broll. You had a look at her an hour and a half ago.
They'll want to know why you waited so long before reporting it. What do you tell them?" While Lisa hummed
and bit her lip and frowned at herself and wondered if the
colors were right for her.

thirteen

We walked up the beach in the orange and gold light of tropic sunset. The tide was moving out and the packed sand was damp and firm under our tread, a coarse, yellow-brown sand. The sun was behind us setting into the sea just out beyond Long Point. Far ahead, beyond the rocks that marked the end of Grand Anse beach and beyond St. George's harbor, was the toy-town look of the town at evening, spilled up the green slopes, small formal shapes with windows looking toward the sea.

We walked past the Grand Anse Hotel, the Grenada Beach Hotel, the Holiday Inn. Cars had come down to the public areas to park under the sea grapes and the almond trees. People swam in the relative cool of twilight, and people walked the long broad promenade of packed sand. Sloops and ketches and multihull sailboats were anchored off the two-mile crescent of beach. A fast boat was pulling a limber black girl on water skis between the anchored sailboats. Behind us was the blinding dazzle of the sun's path on the quiet sea, and our shadows ahead of us were long in a slanting pattern against the damp sand.

"You were going to talk, I thought?"

"I am. I am." She moved closer, linked her arm through mine, hugged it against her body, and looked up at me. "I have to, I guess. Do you know how things can happen to your life that . . . don't fit it somehow? Then everything else isn't real. When you forget, then everything around you is real again, but what happened doesn't seem as if it could have ever happened. Do you know what I'm talking about?"

"Not yet, girl. Not yet."

"I guess in my own way I was as numb as Harry was. It seems like ten years ago, practically."

"Didn't you think it was pretty damned stupid for Paul to kill Mary Broll? Didn't you tell him it was stupid?"

She had to wait until we had passed a group of people strolling at a slower pace than ours. She indicated a stubby cement pier at the far border of the Holiday Inn property. It projected only to the surf line and seemed to have no purpose other than as some sort of groyne to retain the sand. We went up the slope of beach, stepped up onto it, and walked out to sit near the end, our backs to the sunset.

She laced her fingers in mine, tugged at my hand, and rested it palm upward against the smooth, round brown of mid-thigh. She frowned toward the town.

"I've thought about it and thought about it, Gavin. I guess it got to be pretty obvious to Paul that an affair with me wasn't going to be enough leverage on Harry. Harry and his wife weren't getting along so great anyway. There wasn't anything real important to expose, you might say. So why did he tip off Mary Broll so she'd catch me and Harry together? Why did he make sure she *would* catch us? Why did he tell me to yell at Mrs. Broll and make a big scene out of it? Motive, right?"

The point was well taken. Mary would certainly confide her problem to someone. The scene at the apartment had attracted so much attention that even Jeannie Dolan heard about it later. Of late, Harry had been blustering around, threatening people, trying to locate his dead wife.

If the police were tipped, dug for Mary, and found her, even the most inept state's attorney could put together a case F. Lee Bailey couldn't successfully defend.

"So, Lisa, you think Paul had decided to kill her when he made the phone call to her. Does that make sense? He didn't know then she'd decided to go away. He didn't know then what she'd arrange about the loan. She could have left without any warning at all. He'd have to be some kind of warlock, reading the future."

"I know. I think about it until my head starts to hurt, and then I give up."

"Did you think he'd ever kill anybody?"

"You don't go around wondering whether people you know can kill other people, do you? I knew he was mean. I knew how nasty he could get. I knew there was something kinky about him, the way he got something special out of sleeping with me and then making me sleep with those older guys. It was something to do with him never getting married, I think. We look alike, like brother and sister. His eyes are the same as mine, the same dark dark brown and long black lashes and—see?—the left one set straight, and the right one slanty. His mouth is like mine, a lot of natural red to the lips, and the mouth small, and the lower lip heavy and curling out from the upper lip. We both look younger than we are, but that's always been true of the whole family. Aside from that there isn't the least thing feminine about him. Even my eyes and mouth don't look girlish on Paul, somehow. Except when he's asleep. That's strange, isn't it? I'd watch him sleeping, and then his eyes and lips would look the most like mine and make me feel strange. He is big! He's almost as tall as you are and as big through the chest. But he moves a lot quicker. I guess I mean his normal way of moving is quicker. Nobody is quicker than you were with Carl. Jesus! You looked kind of dumb and sleepy, as if you couldn't believe he was really going to beat on you. Then you were something else."

"I want to know more about Paul. How old is he?"

"He'll be coming up onto thirty-seven, I think in July. Yes. Other companies have tried to hire him away from Mr. Waterbury. So I guess he's a good accountant. He stays in great shape all year. He does competition slalom in the winter and tennis in the summer. His legs are tremendously powerful, like fantastic springs."

"An exercise nut?"

"With weights and springs and pulleys and things. And a sun lamp that travels by itself from one end of you to the other and turns itself off. He's real happy about those legs.

One funny thing, he's as dark as I am, and he has to shave
twice a day when he goes out in the evening, but on his
body, except for those places where everybody has hair,
he hasn't any. His legs have a really great shape, and there
isn't any hair on them or his chest or his arms. The muscles are long and smooth, not bunchy. When he tenses
them, his legs are like marble."

"You called him kinky."

She frowned and thought for a little while. I saw the
point of her tongue slowly moisten the curve of underlip.
"No. That isn't the right word. The whole sex scene isn't a
big thing with him. I mean it's there, all right. It was
something we would do. You know, when he couldn't unwind and get to sleep, he'd phone me to come over to his
place down in the city. We were five blocks apart. He
makes me feel . . . I don't know . . . like one of his damn
exercise machines, something with a motor and weights
and springs, so that afterward he could put it in his exercise log. Ten minutes on the rowing machine. Eight minutes on the Lisa machine."

"I can't really get the picture of you two."

"What's so difficult, honey?"

"You move to Quebec and change jobs because he tells
you to. You come over whenever he phones you. He tells
you to seduce Mr. X and then Mr. Y and tells you how to
extort money from them, and he takes most of it. He tells
you to seduce Harry, quit your job, and follow Harry to
Florida, and he tells you to come here and pretend to be
Mary. You are awfully goddamn docile, Lisa."

"I know. I know. Yes. It's funny about him. He's just so
absolutely positive you're going to do what he tells you to
do, it's a lot easier to do it than try to say you won't."

"Did you ever try to say you wouldn't do something he
asked you to do?"

"God, yes! In the very beginning, before he even got the
job for me. I was at his place, and he asked me to get him
something from across the room. I was sitting at the table,
and I said something like 'You're not a cripple, are you?'
He got up and went behind me and hit me on top of the
head with his fist. I blacked out and fell off the chair and

cut my chin. It did something funny to my neck, pinched a nerve or something, and I was in bed for three days with it, practically in agony. He was a darling. He waited on me hand and foot. He was so sweet and considerate. I guess . . . it's easier to do what he says, because you have the feeling that neither of you knows what he'll do if you say no. At work he's another person."

"How do you feel about the way you're crossing him?"

"It keeps making me feel as if I'm going to throw up."

She looked up at me with a piquant tilt of her dark head. It's funny," she said. "I never saw you before today. Then you scared me so. You really did. Now you're so nice and understanding. I can really talk to you. About everything."

Her fingers were laced in mine, and she pressed down on my hand, holding the back of my hand against the round, tan thigh, slowly swinging her dangling leg as she did so. I felt the smooth working of the thigh muscles against the back of my hand. It was a sensuous and persuasive feeling. She was a pretty piece, making her constant offer of herself in any way that she could.

"Why trust me?" I asked her.

She shrugged. "I don't know. I guess I'm trying to. I guess I can't go it alone, no matter what it is. I appreciate you didn't mark me up any. I mean I hate to get belted in the face where it shows. It cuts a person's mouth inside, and there's a big puffy bruise and maybe a mouse comes under a person's eye. It's a bad thing to do to a girl. She goes around ashamed."

"Paul belted you?"

"Sometimes."

"But you trust him?"

"He's a blood relative. Maybe I shouldn't trust him at all. He's strange. He really is. It doesn't show. You have to know him."

"I keep thinking of how boxed in you are."

"How do you mean?"

"Suppose after you go back, Harry is picked up for killing his wife. They have her body. It's certainly no big problem finding the girlfriend and proving you were there.

With that starting point, Lisa, how long before the state attorney's investigators learn about the impersonation? Would you want to explain on the stand why you took her money, her tickets, her reservations, her clothes, and her car?"

There was a sudden sallowness. "Come *on* now. Don't, honey! Jesus! I don't like jokes like that. We're in this together, aren't we?"

"Are we?"

"What do you *want* of me? What more do you want that I'm not ready and eager and willing to give, dear?"

"Do you think Cousin Paul is going to give you a short count on the money again?"

"If he gets the chance."

I pulled my hand away from her. "Now what would keep him from having the chance? Me?"

"Darling, please don't try to confuse me."

"How am I confusing you?"

"Well . . . you said you own me now, and you said there had to be money in it. So I guess you'll go after the money. I guess you'd have to have my help."

"Doing what?"

"That would be up to you, dear."

"To figure out how you can help me get rich?"

"That's the name of your game, I thought."

"Maybe Paul's game is over."

"How do you mean?"

"Harry Broll is not a complete idiot. Why couldn't he have gone quietly to the police and managed to sell them the truth? So they lay back and wait for you to return and for Paul to make his move, and scoop you both up."

"Damn! I forgot to tell you about the letter I wrote Paul. He was right there when I wrote it. He found Mary Broll's personal stationery for me to use. He told me what to write. I had to do it over because he said it was too neat the first time. I dated it January fifth. It said that Paul had been right and I never should have gotten involved with Harry. It said Harry had done something terrible while drunk and had gotten me to his house afterward to help him but I couldn't. I said I was frightened and I was going away and to wait until I got in touch with him. He held it in front of Harry and made him read it. Then he had me seal it in an envelope and put a stamp on it and address it to Paul's place in West Palm Beach. Paul put it in his pocket to mail as soon as he could."

The sun was gone. The world was darkening. The sky was a dying furnace, and the sea was slate. We walked back the way we had come but more slowly.

"Gavin?"

"Shut up, Lisa. Please."

The beach was almost empty. The outdoor torches had been lighted at the Spice Island Inn. Birds were settling noisily to bed, arguing about the best places. Canned music was coming over all-weather speakers, a steel band playing carnival calypso.

When we reached her gate, she said, "Now can I say something? Like, please come in?"

"I want to sit out in the breeze, thanks. Over there."

"Join you?"

"Sure."

"Bring you a drink, maybe?"

"Thanks. Same as before."

I sat deep in a chaise, legs up, trying to work it out in every possible combination and permutation. With Mary Broll dead, Woodrow Willow was supposed to slam the lid on that trust account. Harry was probably the beneficiary under her will, possibly a coexecutor along with the bank. But had she died in early January, even in a traffic accident, the chances of processing the estate quickly enough for Harry to get his three hundred thousand before April thirtieth were very damned remote. She had to die later on.

So what if Meyer and I had not had all those vague feelings of uneasiness? What if we had accepted my phone call as being proof enough that she was alive and well and living in Grenada?

Then it would have worked like a railroad watch. The timely loan. The news of pending reconciliation. Enough supporting information for Willow to consider the cable legitimate authorization. Then the ironic tragedy. Estranged wife on the point of returning home to her contrite husband, missing in mysterious drowning incident. Search is on for body. However . . .

"Here you go," she said. I thanked her for the drink. She had brought one for herself. She sat on the side of the chaise, facing me. I moved my legs over to make room. The stars were beginning to come out. I could see that she had brushed her hair, freshened her mouth. The bright, block print dashaki had deep side slits, and she adjusted herself and it, either by accident or design, so that the side slit showed the outside of a bare thigh and hip as high as the waist, a smoothness of flesh in the dying day that was not interrupted by the narrow encirclement of bikini I had seen there before.

"You certainly do an awful lot of thinking," she said.

"And here I am, dear, alive and well."

"But you have been terribly terribly hurt a few times, Gav."

"The times when I wasn't thinking clearly."

"Do I keep you from thinking clearly? I'd sure like a chance to try. Would you mind if I ask you politely to please make love to me?"

"What are we celebrating?"

"You're *such* a bastard! Gavin darling, I feel very very insecure about a lot of things. I've been alone a long time. Now I want somebody to hold me tight and make love to me and tell me I'm delicious. For morale, I guess. Why do you even make me ask? It doesn't have to be any big thing, you know. It doesn't have to take up a hell of a lot of your time. Hitch over just a little bit, darling, and let me . . ."

The way she started to manage it—to lie down beside me and hike her dashaki up and tug my swim trunks down and simultaneously hook one brown leg over me—certainly wasn't going to take up a great deal of anybody's time, the way she was going at it.

I pushed her erect and pulled the trunks back up. "Very flattering. Very generous. But no thanks."

She laughed harshly and picked her drink up off the sand near her feet. "Well, comparing you to Carl, I can say this. You've got a different kind of attitude. If I hadn't uncovered proof, I'd be wondering about you."

"I'm busy pretending I'm Paul, wondering how he has it all worked out."

"Different strokes for different folks."

"I hang back and make sure Harry Broll follows orders. I check with him about the Sunday afternoon phone call from you. On Tuesday morning, the twenty-seventh, I will get in touch with Mr. Willow, in my capacity as an employee of SeaGate, to verify that Mr. Broll will indeed have the funds to pick up his escrowed block of SeaGate shares. I am assured. The money comes through. And I am very very busy right through the thirtieth and through the weekend, because that is the end of the fiscal year for SeaGate. Right?"

"I guess so, dear."

"Then I have to do something about Cousin Lisa. She's expecting a message from me. I'll have to deliver it in person."

"To tell me what to do next?"

"Old Harry is twitchy about his dead wife. And Lisa is twitchy about Harry's dead wife. Harry and Lisa could testify against me if they ever join forces. Lisa is wearing the dead woman's rings. I just have to arrange a nice quick safe way to meet her in the islands and blow her face off and blow her dental work to paste. Then there's no mystery about a body. I can settle down and separate good old Harry from every cent of his gain and every cent he has left over when that's gone. When Harry is empty, it will be time to lay him to rest, too. By accident. Just in case."

I reached an idle hand and patted her on the shoulder. She remained quiveringly still, then was suddenly up and away, to come to rest five feet from the chaise, staring at me.

"No! No, Gavin. He's my first cousin. No."

"He couldn't do that?"

"Absolutely not. Not ever. Not any way."

"Then why are you so upset?"

"Anybody would be upset, hearing something so horrible."

"You know you are supposed to fake Mary Broll's death. There's less chance of a hitch if somebody plays the part of the body. You've been Mary Broll since January. Why switch now?"

"Don't be such a bastard!"

"It's the way I have to read him from everything you've told me. A quirky guy but very logical. A good improviser. If one logical plan doesn't develop the way he wants it to, he thinks up an alternative just as good or better. And . . . Lisa dear, just what the hell good are you to him? The end of usefulness. He knows there's a chance you'll make new friends who'll hear about how you died and get very upset about it and might run into you in an air terminal somewhere a year from now. All you are is a big risk, and an unnecessary risk."

"Shut *up!*"

"Think about it."

"I *am* thinking about it."

"It wouldn't be *my* style, but I have to admire it in a way. It ties up the loose ends. No way out for Harry. Or you."

She found her drink had been kicked over. "Ready for another?"

"Not yet, thanks."

"Want to come in?"

"I'll stay here awhile."

"Be back soon, dear."

fourteen

Though Lisa Dissat was not gone for more than ten minutes, it was full night when she came back, a velvet beach under a brilliance of stars. There were lights behind us from the Spice Island Inn cottages. The lights made a slanting yellow glow against the sand.

She sat beside me again. She had changed to tailored white shorts, a dark blouse with a Chinese collar and long sleeves. She smelled of perfume . . . and Off. The white fabric was snug on the round hip that pressed warm against the side of my knee.

"Took off your instant rape suit, eh?"

She pulled her shoulders up slightly, and her drink made the sounds of ice as she sipped. "I guess you made me lose interest."

"Are you a believer now?"

"Up to a point. I can't see any percentage in taking dumb risks. You are the loose end Paul doesn't know about. I guess I can be the bait in the trap. But we have to be awfully awfully careful. He's very sensitive to . . . what people are thinking. We can't give him any chance at all."

"How do you mean that?"

"If it's like you say, if that's what he's going to try to do, then he'll have it all worked out so there won't be any risk in it, hardly any at all. So if he really wants to kill me, we have to kill him instead, darling."

"Your very own first cousin?"

"Don't be a stinker, please. What other choice is there?"

"Then what?"

"Then we have to get me back into the States in some safe way. I guess there's no reason why I couldn't go back in as Mary Broll, come to think of it. What harm would it do?"

"None, if you don't try to keep on being Mrs. Broll."

"If he isn't thinking about killing me like you say, then we'll have to play it by ear."

"All goes well, and you and I are back in the States. Then?"

"We just go and see Harry. That's all. I'll tell him that unless he gives us lots and lots of money, he's going to have lots and lots of trouble. And you can beat him up if he tries to bluff us."

"How much money?"

"I don't think we should make him really desperate or anything. I think we should leave him with enough so he'll think he came out of it pretty well. I think we could ask for half a million dollars."

"Each?"

"No, dear. He has to pay taxes on the whole thing, you know. I think with the holding period before the sale to the public, it will be long term. Yes, I know it will. He should get his money next December. Hmmm. His taxes will be a half million. That leaves him two million, and I know he owes four hundred thousand and he will have to pay back the three hundred thousand. So out of his million and three, we'll take five hundred thousand, darling, and he'll have eight hundred thousand left. It would be neater if we took six hundred and fifty and left him six hundred and fifty, don't you think?"

"A lot neater. And you want half?"

"What I want and what you'll let me have aren't the same, are they?"

"They could be with cooperation all the way."

"Moving money like that around without leaving traces that people can find later is very hard. Do you know anything about that kind of problem? I'd think you would."

"If Harry Broll will hold still for the bite, yes."

"There's no problem, Gav honey. None."

"Leaving only Paul."

She finished her drink, bunted me with her hip.
"Scrooch over some, honey. Make room. No funny stuff
this time, I promise."

She turned, lay back, and fitted her head to my
shoulder, swinging her legs aboard.

After a while she said, "Want to order dinner in my
place or yours, dear?"

"I don't know yet."

"I'm not hungry, either. Gee, look at all the damned
stars. Like when I was a little kid, the night sky looked
glittery like this."

"Where was that?"

"Way up in French Canada on the St. Lawrence, north
of Riviere du Loup. A little town called Trois Pistoles.
Ten thousand saints, ten thousand churches all over that
country. Convent school, uniforms, vespers, acts of contri-
tion, the whole scene. I ran away when I was fifteen. With
my best friend, Diane Barbet. We got across the border
and into the States. Things got kind of messy for us. You
survive or you don't, I guess. I don't know what happened
to Diane. I think about her sometimes. A guy in Detroit
helped me really go to work on my hick Canuck accent.
Movies, television, radio, and using a tape recorder. I
think in English now, except if something startles the hell
out of me or scares me. I get scared in French. Another
man sent me to business school. To learn to be an executive secretary. That was in Cincinnati. He was a real old
guy. He picked me up. I was hitchhiking. He took me
home. He lived alone—his wife had been dead two years.
He wanted me to stay there with him and pretend I was
his grand-niece so the neighbors wouldn't turn him in. I
wanted somebody to send me to school so I could be a
secretary, so it worked out okay. He bought me pretty
clothes. I was eighteen by then. He bought me a little car,
even. He was retired. He cooked and kept the house clean
and did the laundry and made the bed. He even ironed my
things that needed it, and he rinsed out stuff. I was really
pretty rotten to old Harv. He was forty years older than
me. That is a lot of years. When he got on my nerves, I
wouldn't let him touch me. I cut off the supply. He didn't

really want me too often or give me much trouble. I finished school and got my certificate and got a job. The way I was living, I could put it all in the bank, and I did. I came home one evening, and he was on the floor in the utility room. His whole left side had gone dead. His eye drooped and spit ran out of the left side of his mouth, and he couldn't speak. He just made terrible noises when he tried. I packed all my things into the trunk of my car, and then I called the hospital. I parked in the next block and walked back to make sure they found him and put him in the ambulance. I went to a motel. I finished out the week after I gave notice. I got my money out of the bank. I left and went down to Mobile and sold the car there. You can sell cars easy in Alabama. Then I flew home to Canada and got a good job in Montreal. I kept missing old Harv. I still miss him, I guess. It was a pretty good way to live, you know? I wasn't very nice to him. If I had it to do over, I'd be a lot nicer. I'd never hold out on him the way I did. It never cost me a thing to make him feel good.

"Anyway, I had a wonderful life in Montreal. There was a great bunch of kids there. And then I fell really *really* in love. When my guy took off with a girlfriend of mine, I did what I always do when I hurt. Buy, buy, buy. Shoes, clothes, wigs. I like money. I guess I spend it to hurt myself. You know? I knew I was in real trouble unless somebody bailed me out. So I went up to Quebec and saw Cousin Paul. I think I could have gone the rest of my life without the kind of help *he* gave me. Hey, look!"

"Shooting star."

"I know. But such a big, bright, slow one, huh? It lasted forever."

"Did you make a wish?"

"Was I supposed to? Would it work?"

"The way to make a wish come true is to wish for something you're going to get anyway."

"Is it okay to wish a little late?"

"Go ahead. It wasn't my shooting star."

"Okay. I wished." My arm was around her. She turned in a twisting motion that slipped her breast into my hand.

Under the thin fabric of the blouse she wore no bra, and in seconds I felt the nipple growing and hardening. "Does that give you a clue, friend? Something I'm going to get anyway?"

I sat up, raising her with me, slid my hands onto her waist, picked her up, and dropped her onto the sand beside the chaise.

"Ow! That made me bite my tongue, you son of a bitch!"

"Just be a good girl and stop trying to hook me on the product. It's there anytime I want it. Stop pushing it."

She stood up. "Don't be too damned sure it's going to be served up on a damn tray when you decide to ask for it, Gav. And I wasn't trying to hook you on anything. I just think it's friendly and nice to get laid. It isn't a big thing, is it? And it got me going, what I was talking about."

"Old Harv, for God's sake?"

"No, you dummy! The money. Big gobs of money, just thinking about it makes me feel all hollow and crawly inside, and I guess it's so much like the feeling you get when you know you're going to get laid, it works the same way."

"Go take a cold shower."

"You're terribly nice to me. You're oceans of fun. I'm going to walk up and down the beach and think about blizzards and icicles and catheters and having my teeth drilled. That takes me off the edge fast."

"I should think it would."

So she went walking out there, clearly visible, scuffing barefoot through the foamy water that came running up the wet slope after the thud of each slow, small wave. A girl walking slowly, slow tilting swing of hips, legs shapely and dark below the white glow of the shorts.

She had deftly pushed a lot of my buttons. She had worked on proximity, touch, forthright invitation. She had talked in areas that accentuated sexual awareness. She smelled good, felt good, kept her voice furry and intimate. I knew she wasn't being made wanton and reckless by my fabulous magnetism. We were moving toward an association, possibly profitable. For maximum leverage within that association of two, she wanted to put that weapon to work which had profited her in the past, probably in every relationship except the one with her cousin.

I was another version of good old Harv, whom we last saw on the floor with spit running out of his mouth. She'd pushed Harv's buttons and got her secretarial training and a car and a lot of clothes. Her libido certainly wasn't out of control. It was just a useful thing for her to do, a nice little inexpensive favor for her to grant, and if it clouded the recipient's judgment, eventual profit from the relationship might improve.

Were I a great ape, a giant anthropoid, munching stalks torn from the jungle, and able to lead her to forgotten treasure, Lisa would take her best shot at making everything friendlier and nicer. As she said about Harv, it wouldn't cost a thing to make that big monkey feel good.

But knowing how and why the buttons are pushed doesn't diminish the physiological aftereffects of the button pushing. The tumescence is noticeable. The palm of the hand retains the shape of the breast—the precise size, warmth, and rate of erection. The eyes watch the slow walk, creating an increase in the heart beat and rate of respiration and blood pressure and surface body temperature, as the conditioned mind anticipates the simple progression of events of calling to her, bringing her close, shucking her out of the shorts, pulling her astride, and settling her properly for that sweet, grinding task that would end so quickly the first time.

The buttons tripped certain relays. I had to go back into the mind, into central control, and reset those relays, compensate for the overload, switch the current back to those channels designed for it.

I went searching through the past for the right memory, the one which would most easily turn growing desire to indifference.

I thought a memory of Miss Mary Dillon long ago aboard *The Busted Flush* would do it. There were more than a few, but they would not come through vividly enough to achieve turnoff.

Lisa made it so damned easy, so completely available,

there was no importance to it. And with no importance to
an act, why did it matter whether or not it happened? Why
did McGee need some cachet of importance in this world
of wall-to-wall flesh in the weekend livingroom where the
swingers courteously, diligently, skillfully, considerately
hump one another to the big acid beat of the hifi installation, good from 20 to 20,000 cycles per second?

Is McGee still impaled upon some kind of weird Puritan dilemma, writhing and thrashing around, wrestling
with an outdated, old-time, inhibiting and artificial sense
of sin, guilt, and damnation? Is that why he couldn't accept the lifetime gift Lady Jillian offers? Is that why he has
this sickly, sentimental idea that there has to be a productive and meaningful relationship first, or sex degrades? So
bang the doxy, because easing the ball-pressure is reason
enough.

Who needs magic and mystery? Well, maybe it is magic
and mystery that an Antarctic penguin will hunt all over
hell and gone to find the right pebble to carry in his beak
and lay between the funny feet of his intended, hoping for
her favor. Maybe sex is a simple bodily function, akin to
chewing, sneezing and defecation. But bald eagles fly as
high as they possibly can, up into the thinnest air, making
the elegant flight patterns of intended mating all the way up,
then cleave to each other and fall, fall, fall, mating as they
fall fluttering, plummeting down toward the great rock
mountains.

The way it is supposed to work nowadays, if you want
to copulate with the lady, you politely suggest it to her,
and you are not offended if she says no, and you are man-
nerly, considerate, and satisfying if she says yes.

But the Tibetan bar-headed goose and her gander have
a very strange ceremony they perform *after* they have
mated. They rise high in the water, wings spread wide,
beaks aimed straight up at the sky, time and time again,
making great bugle sounds of honking. The behaviorists
think it is unprofessional to use subjective terms about animal patterns. So they don't call this ceremony joy. They
don't know what to call it. These geese live for up to fifty
years, and they mate for life. They celebrate the mating

152 JOHN D. MACDONALD

this same way year after year. If one dies, the other never mates again.

So penguins, eagles, geese, wolves, and many other creatures of land and sea and air are stuck with all this obsolete magic and mystery because they can't read and they can't listen to lectures. All they have is instinct. Man feels alienated from all feeling, so he sets up encounter groups to sensitize each member to human interrelationships. But the basic group of two, of male and female, is being desensitized as fast as we can manage it . . .

"What the hell is there about me that turns you off?" Lisa demanded. She had walked up the slope to stand by the chaise, blotting out a Lisa-shaped abundance of stars as she looked down at me with a faint angle of pale yellow light laying across her cheekbone and lips.

"I was wondering what you'd do if I picked up a pebble in my beak and put it between your feet."

"I've heard of a lot of ways guys get kinky, but that is—"

"Why do you want reassurance from me? Take my word for it. You are a fantastic piece of ass. Ask practically anybody."

"I don't know. I haven't checked it."

She stood there for a few seconds in silence. Then she said, "If you ever do want some, friend, you're going to have to take it away from me, because that's the only damned way in this world you're ever going to get any."

"Goodnight, Lisa."

She walked away from the shoreline, a silhouette moving toward the yellow lights.

fifteen

Thursday I was up early. Awakening in a new place makes the day of arrival seem unreal. There had been no Carl Brego, no Lisa Dissat trying to be Mary Broll, no Lisa Dissat striding angrily away from me in the hot, buggy night. I went to my cottage after she left, swam in my minipool, two strokes per lap, changed, and went to the open dining room. The food was good, the service indifferent. There were some beautiful people there. A fashion photography team. Some yacht people. Some twosome guests had tried to get as far as possible from wherever they didn't care to be seen together. Some guests were ritualistic sun worshipers who had been there for many many weeks, using the intense tropic sun to add each day's tiny increment of pigmentation at the cost of blinding, suffocating, dazed hours and quarts of whatever oil they happened to believe in. Johnson's or coconut or olive. They were working toward that heady goal of becoming a living legend in Bronxville or Scranton or Des Moines.

"Tan? You think that's a tan? So you didn't see Barbie and Ken when they got back from Grenada that time. Dark? I swear to Christ, in a dark room all you could see were white teeth. And Barbie's diamonds."

I took a cab into town, memorizing landmarks all the way. I negotiated the rental of an Austin Moke. A Moke is a shrunken jeep with a very attractive expression, if you look at the front of it and think of the headlights as eyes. It looks staunch, jaunty, and friendly. It is a simplified piece of machinery. Stick shift which, like the wheel on the right, you work with the left hand. The horn, a single-

153

note, piercing beeeeep, is operated by pressing in on the
turn indicator with the right hand. A quick whack with the
heel of the hand is the approved method. Four speeds forward, small, aircooled engine, pedals so tiny that if you try
to operate one with your bare feet, it hurts like hell. Canvas top nobody ever folds down in the hot season, and all
they have in Grenada are two hot seasons, one wet and
one dry.

With the tourist season almost over, there were a lot of
them in stock. I picked one with a lot of tread, and the
rental man and I walked around it and tested lights, horn,
directional signals, windshield wiper (singular). He wanted his total rental in advance, which is standard for the
area. While we dickered, I practiced getting in and out of
the damned thing. I'd learned in Grand Cayman and Jamaica that with the length of my legs there is only one
possible way. Stand beside vehicle on right side. Bend over
at waist. Reach across body and grasp steering wheel with
right hand, while simultaneously lifting left leg, inserting it
into vehicle so that foot comes to rest on floor well beyond
pedal area. Swoop your behind onto the seat and pick up
right leg and lift over high broad sill (which contains gas
tank). In driving position both knees are bent sharply,
spread wide apart. Steering wheel fits between knees, and
lower part of legs must angle in to assure foot contact with
pedals. Adjust to inevitability of frequently giving oneself
a painful rap on the left leg while shifting.

We arrived at a mutually agreeable fee of five Yankee
—ten Biwi-dollars a day for a one week rental or any
period of less than a week. I buy the gas. I will phone him
when I leave and tell him to pick it up at the Spice Island
Inn. I promise not to leave it at the airport. I tell him I
would not drive it over that road to the airport for a
hundred dollars a mile. Can I drive safely on the left side
of the road? I suggest that perhaps no one in Grenada can
drive safely on any side of the road. But yes, I have so
driven on other islands of this British persuasion.

We accomplish the red tape, he gives me a free map of
St. George and environs. I note that, as expected, there is
at least one half-pint of gas in the five-gallon gas tank. I

edge carefully into the tourney and immediately am nearly
bowled over and over by a small pale bus with a name
across the front of it. The name is: I AM NOTHING.

After I have bought petrol and felt my way back into
the center of town, avoiding too intimate a contact with a
large gaudy city bus called LET IT BE ME, I park my Moke
and wait until I am certain my legs will work. ("You will
enjoy browsing in St. George's along the narrow, quaint
streets.")

I changed another wad of Yankee dollars into Biwi at
the Bank of Canada, picking that one from among all the
shiny banks downtown, from Chase to Barclay's to the
Bank of Nova Scotia, because there was a faint aroma of
irony in the choice. The girl standing behind the money-
changing counter was very dark, very thin, and totally antagonistic—so much so, there was no chance of ever making any kind of human contact with her unless you were
her identical anthracite color.

I asked some questions and was directed to a big busy
supermarket called EVERYBODY'S FOR EVERYTHING. As long
as I had kitchen facilities and I could make my own ice
cubes, it seemed useful to set up shop. Gin, rum, fruit
juices from Trinidad, mixes, and a couple of large substantial drink glasses. I am a fussy old party about glass-
ware. Nothing takes the pleasure out of drinking like the
tiny dim glasses supplied by hotels and motels. I always
buy heavy glasses, always leave them behind. Tiny glasses
turn drinking from a pleasure rite to a quasialcoholic
twitch.

The final purchase was on impulse at a shop I saw on
the Carenage on the way home. A great big planter's hat
of straw with a batik band. Put a man in a rental Moke
with advertising painted on the side of it and put a funny
hat on him, and he is a tourist. All tourists look alike. Regardless of age, sex, or the number of extra lenses for their
cameras, they all look alike.

I found my way back out to Grand Anse to hotel row,
and I found an overland way to get the Moke close to my
cottage. I carried my box of stuff in. From the moment I

had awakened until the moment I finished putting the stuff away and sat down, I had not let myself think about Mary, Lisa or the mechanics of impersonation.

It is a useful device. If you keep things in the front of your mind, you worry at them like a hound chomping a dead rabbit. Throw problems in the back cupboard and keep them there as long as you can. The act of stirring around seems to shuffle the elements of a problem into a new order, and when you take it out again, there are new ways to handle it.

I tossed my sweat-soaked shirt aside. The airconditioning felt good on my back and shoulders. Okay. Mary is dead. I want Paul Dissat. I want him very badly. The money is the bait, and Lisa is the bait in another sense. I want very badly to convince Paul and Lisa and Harry Broll that, if given a choice, they would elect retroactive birth control. I want them so eager to be out of it they'd dig their own graves with a bent spoon and their fingernails.

Secondly, as a professional, as a salvage consultant in areas of considerable difficulty, I want to come out of this with a little salvage for myself. If I walk away without a dime, with only expenses I can't reasonably afford, then I lose all respect for myself as a con artist. I would have kicked the hell out of their little wagon just to avenge one hell of a woman, Mary Dillon. Pure emotionalism is bush league.

So? So I do not advise Mr. Willow not to make the loan on Mary's securities. They go to Harry eventually anyway. That is, if Harry happens to be still around. The money has to be loaned to Harry, and Harry has to pick up his block of stock in time and get himself in position to make a great deal of money when the public issue comes out. But that is a long long time for me to wait for my money. I shall use the leverage to extract a reasonable chunk from Paul, maybe from Harry, maybe from both, before I set them to work with those bent spoons.

It may be enough to have Harry and Lisa dig their graves deep with the sides and ends properly squared off and stand in them without the slightest morsel of hope left.

Then I walk away and leave them standing there. But Paul is something else.

Program: Lisa must perform exactly as instructed, make her phone call to Harry, and send the cable to Mr. Willow at the bank. I want her to be desperately anxious to tell me all the details of any contact by Paul Dissat. Then I will prepare to greet him. Here. There. Somewhere.

I pulled on my salty swim trunks and put on my big tourist hat and went looking for the lady. She was not in cottage 50. I trudged around, squinting into the hot glare, and found her on a sun cot at the top of the slope that led down to the beach proper. She was face down. The bikini was yellow today. The top was undone, and she had rolled the fabric of the bottom so that it was about as big around as a yellow lead pencil where it cut across the tanned cheeks of her behind. She was glossy with oil. Her towel was on the sand. I sat on it. Her face was turned away.

"You wanna buy nice coconut, Miss lady? Peanuts? Nice spices?"

She slowly turned her heat-stricken, slack-mouthed face toward me. "I don't want any—" She shaded her eyes, squinted. "Oh. It's you."

"Me. Absolutely correct. Me, himself."

"Who needs you?"

She lay with her face turned toward me, eyes closed. "You need me," I told her.

"Not any more. Thanks a lot. But not any more."

"I don't mean that kind of need, honey. I'm talking about financial need. Commercial necessities."

"Thanks loads. I think I'd better take my chances with Paul."

"That should be a lot of laughs for both of you. I wrote an interesting letter last night."

She forgot her top wasn't latched. She sat up fast. "What kind of a letter? Who to?"

"What's the local policy about the tits on tourists?"

She picked up the top and put it on. "I know what *your* policy is, friend. You ignore them. What kind of a letter?"

"Double envelope. A sealed letter along inside the

sealed letter. If he doesn't hear from me on or before May tenth, he opens the second letter."

"Then what?"

"He takes action."

"*What* action?"

"Oh, he just gets in touch with the right people at the SEC and says that it looks as if one Mr. Harry Broll bought himself into SeaGate, Inc. with a final three hundred thou fraudulently obtained and that this fact might not be uncovered by the accounting firm preparing the material for the red herring and they should check with a Mr. Willow regarding evidence as to whether or not Mrs. Broll was alive at the time he released funds at her earlier request. My friend is an attorney. He knows all the steps in the new registration folk dance. Delicate, these new issues. They can die of a head cold."

"Oh God! Why'd you think you couldn't trust me?"

"Who said anything about that?"

"Isn't that why you did it?"

"Lisa, Lisa, Lisa. What if we miss? Suppose your dear cousin nails us both, lays us to rest in a ceremonial boat, lights the pyre and sends us out to sea. The last few moments would be a lot more enjoyable knowing Cousin Paul would never make a profit on the deal."

She swallowed hard and looked unhappy. "Don't talk about things like that." I knew that behind her sun squint her brain was ticking away, weighing and measuring advantages. I reached under the sun cot and retrieved her big sun glasses from the magazine on which they lay and handed them to her.

"Thanks, dear," she said, putting them on. "Sure. I see what you mean. And if he catches us sort of off base, it could maybe be handy to tell him about your lawyer friend."

"Yes. I think so. If he gives me a chance."

"Can't you see why I thought you did it on account of me?"

I thought it over. "Well, I suppose I can in a way. If you *did* decide he represents a better chance, you could tip him off about me and he could . . . tidy up the situation."

She turned over and put her feet down on the sand near my legs. Her hairline was sweaty. Trickles of sweat ran down her throat, and a little rivulet ran between her breasts and down across her belly to soak into the narrow yellow bikini. Her knees were apart, and the cot was so short-legged that her knees were on the same level as her breasts. Her eyes were even with the top of my head.

She leaned toward me, forearms on her knees, and said in a cooing voice, "You know, you act so weird about me, about us, that I'm afraid I'm going to keep on misinterpreting the things you say. We're going to keep on having misunderstandings. I waited a long time last night for you to come over to my place to say you were sorry."

I looked at her. Bright sunshine is as cruelly specific as lab lights and microscopes. There was a small double chin, caused by the angle of her head. There was a scar on her upper lip near the nostril. Her hands and feet were small, square and sturdy, nails carefully tended. Her posture made a narrow tan roll of fat across her trim belly. Her slender waist made a rich line that flowed in a double curve, concave, convex, into the ripe tan hip and thigh. She sat with her plump parts pouched into the yellow fabric, heavy and vital. Stray pubic hairs, longer than the others, curled over the top of the bikini and escaped at the sides of the crotch, hairs the color of dull copper.

Sweat, muscles, flesh, hair, closeness. So close the tightness of the yellow pouch revealed the cleavage of labia. This was the magic and mystery of a locker room, steam room, massage table, or of a coeducational volleyball game in a nudist colony. This was jockstrap sex, unadorned.

"Lisa, I guess we have to say things so carefully we won't have misunderstandings."

"Maybe I got the wrong impression yesterday. You wouldn't be queer, darling?"

"No more than any other true-blue American lad."

"Some kind of trouble? You can tell Lisa. Prostate, maybe? Or some kind of irritation?"

"I'm in glowing health."

"Honey, are you so strung out on some great broad that

you just don't want to make it with another girl? I could understand that. I've been through that."

"Nobody I've met lately has gotten to me."

Her mouth firmed, and her throat turned darker. "Am I some kind of pig woman it would turn your stomach to—"

"Whoa! It's just a little rule of mine. Save the dessert until last."

Her mouth softened into a sudden smile. "Dessert? Darling, I am also homemade soup, meat and potatoes, hot rolls and butter, and your choice of beverages. I am mostly meat and potatoes."

"There's another reason for waiting, Lisa."

"Like?"

She was ready again, I decided. Like training a mule. A good, solid blow between the eyes, and I should have her total attention.

"It's kind of a sad story, dear."

"I love sad stories. I love to cry and cry."

"Well, once upon a time there was this lovely, delicate little blond lady, and she and I were partners in a complicated little business deal. We took our plans and problems to bed, and talked them over during rest periods. I freaked over that little lady. She loved to make love. Then our business deal went sour. It fell apart. That was too damned bad because it was a nice piece of money for both of us. Well, one day a month later we romped all day together, happy as children, and that night I took her out in a boat, a nice runabout, out into the Atlantic. It was calm and beautiful, and I made her sit on the side rail, and I aimed a Colt .45 with the muzzle an inch from her pretty brow and blew the top of her head off. I wired the spare anchor to her waist and let her go in a half-mile of water, and the moon was so bright that night I could see her for a long way as she went down. Now you can cry."

Her mouth sagged open. She put a hand to her throat and in a husky whisper said, "Jesus H. Christ!"

"That idiot girl thought that by sleeping with me she was buying insurance, in case I ever found out she had gone behind my back and made her own deal for half again as much as she would have made as my partner. She was so convinced of it, she was starting to smile when I pulled the trigger. You're not crying."

"Jesus H. Christ!"

"You said that before, Lisa. After that I decided it's bad policy. I made the punishment fit the crime, but I hated myself. You know? I used to think of that little blonde a lot. It used to depress me. It seemed like a waste, all those goodies sinking to the bottom of the sea."

"What *are* you?"

"Me? I'm your partner, Lisa. And we trust each other, don't we? Nobody is going to try to be cute. But . . . just in case . . . let's save all the goodies until after we've made the money score?"

"T-that suits me, Gavin," she said. She clapped her thighs together so smartly they made a damp slapping sound. "L-later. I . . . I got to go for a minute. I'll be back."

"I'll probably be swimming."

She went off toward her place, walking slightly knock-kneed, head bowed and shoulders hunched.

An imaginary letter and an imaginary blond partner. I could imagine that dear imaginary girl sinking down down through the black water, hair outspread, getting smaller and smaller and more and more indistinct until she was gone out of my imaginary life forever. Poor kid. Gavin Lee was a mean son of a bitch. It made me almost want to cry. Now the Lisa-McGee contest could be declared no contest. The lady wasn't going to come out for the third round. She was cowed. She was going to do as she was told. She was going to have as much sex drive from here on as a harem guard. And at the first word from her cousin she was going to come on the run to tell me all about it.

That evening she was so prim it was as if she had never left the convent school. We walked on the beach and got back to the cottages just after dark. We went to her place. She unlocked the gate. We went in, and she screamed as the two dark shapes jumped me. It got very interesting. They both knew a lot more about it than Carl Brego had.

If they had been ready and willing to kill, they had me. But they weren't. And that gave me a better chance than I thought I was going to get.

I took punishment and gave it back. Whistling grunts of effort. Slap and thud of blows. Scuff of feet. I took one on the shoulder, off balance, and fell and rolled hard and came up near a yellow light bulb. A half-familiar voice said, "Hold it! I said *hold* it, Artie! I *know* this joker."

The voice was suddenly very familiar. "Rupe, you dreary bastard, what are you trying to do?"

"A favor for a friend. Lady, if you can get some Kleenex and some rubbing alcohol or some gin, I'd be obliged. And turn on some lights around here."

I told Lisa it was all right. She turned on the garden lights and the inside lights. She had some alcohol and a big roll of paper towels. All three of us were breathing hard. We were all marked, one way and another.

I said, "Mary, this is an old friend of mine. Rupert Darby, a sailing man. Rupe, Mary Broll."

"Pleased to meet you, Mary. And this here, Mary, is Artie Calivan. Artie is mate on the *Dulcinea,* and I'm hired captain. And this big rawboned bastard it's so hard to get a clean shot at, Artie, is an old friend of mine from way back. Trav McGee."

"McGee?" Lisa said blankly.

"It's a kind of joke name, honey," I said. "It comes from an old limerick. Trav rhymes with Gav for Gavin. And McGee rhymes with Lee."

If it had just hung there, I couldn't have brought it off. But Rupe came in very smoothly. "I'd like to recite you the limerick, Miz Mary, but it's just too dirty to repeat in front of a lady. I use that old name on Gav when I'm trying to get his goat. I think I've got one tooth here that isn't going to grow back tight again, dammit."

I looked at his mate. "You brought along a big one."

"Seems he was needed. I needed two like him."

"You were doing fine with just one of him. But *why?*"

"Oh, that damn Brego. What did you think? He whined all day about how us hired captains ought to help each other out, and he said this big fellow, quick and mean as a sneak, had filched his piec—excuse me, Miz Broll, his lady friend. So finally I said to Artie here, let's take the dinghy and run over there to the inn and bounce this tourist around some. Had no idea it was you, Tr—Gav. None at all. Sorry. But not too sorry. First time I haven't been half asleep in two weeks."

I dabbed at a long scratch on my jaw and moved over to Lisa and put my arm around her waist. "Honey, have you got any message you want these fine men to deliver to Mr. Brego?"

"Rupe? Artie? Would you tell him that Mrs. Broll suggests he stop by again and try his luck with Mr. Lee?"

Rupe laughed. "Sure."

"Would you mind taking some of his things back to him?"

"Not at all."

"Let me go gather them up. It won't take a second."

Rupe sent the young man down to keep an eye on the dinghy. Rupe and I sat in a shadowy corner of the garden.

"What happened to the *Marianne?*" I asked him.

"Two bad seasons, and the bank finally grabbed her. I don't really mind a hell of a lot. I work for good people. Good wages."

"Thanks for the nice job of covering."

"That? Hell, that's what a good hired captain starts with or learns real fast. When somebody clues you, don't stand around saying 'Huh?' Run with the ball. No point in asking you what's going on. I certainly know something is going on, and that broad in there must be part of it. She looks good enough, but there's better on the island. Any time you have to scruff up a clown like Brego to grab yourself that kind of ass—"

"Like you said. There's more than meets the eye."

"By God, Trav, you know something? That was fun off and on."

"Glad you enjoyed it. How's Sally?"

"Fine, last I heard. She went back to her folks. She married a widower fellow with four kids. Our three plus his four makes a lot of family."

"Sorry to hear about that, Rupe. I really am."

"It hurt some. But I hate the land and everything on it. I hate a tree, and I hate a mountain. The only death worth dying is by drowning. With the licenses I've got I'll stay on the water all the rest of my time. When our oldest girl drowned, that did it for Sally. That finished her, up, down, and sideways. No more oceans. Next time I write the kids I'll put in a note to her saying I saw you. She always liked you, Trav."

Lisa came out with a brown paper bag and gave it to Rupe. "This won't be too much trouble?"

"Not one bit, Miz Mary."

"Thank you so much. Excuse me, but is that mate of yours a mute?"

"Artie just doesn't have very much to say."

We both walked Rupert down to the dinghy. He stowed the bag aboard, and they picked the little boat up and walked it out past the gentle surf, scrambled in, and started the little outboard and headed back toward the yacht basin.

"*Imagine* that Carl sending them to beat you up!"

"They gave it a good try."

"Did they hurt you, darling?"

"Hardly at all. A month in bed and I'll feel like new."

"I mean really."

"Honey, the adrenalin is still flowing. So the pain is suppressed. Tomorrow morning when I try to get out of bed I'll know how much damage they did."

"Rupe has really enormous hands, doesn't he?"

"And very hard, too."

"And that gigantic boy is *really* handsome. Did you notice?"

"I wasn't thinking in those terms. Want to eat in the dining room?"

"Let's order it sent to my place. It's so much nicer, really. We can fix our own drinks and be comfortable. I won't make any passes, Gavin. None at all."

She kept her word. Long after we had dined, when the nightcap was down to the dregs, she came over to me and bent and peered at my face, teeth set into the softness of her under lip.

"You are going to have one great big mouse right on that cheekbone, friend."

"I can feel it."

She straightened up. "I can't read you, McGee."

"McGee? Who he?"

"Like the limerick. Tell me the limerick, huh?"

"Tell the truth, I can't remember it."

"Was it real dirty?"

"Not very, as I remember. But insulting."

"Funny, you knowing him. I would have thought he would have told Carl you were an old friend. Carl would have told him your name, Gavin Lee, and described you and all."

"Lee is a common name."

"Gavin Lee sure the hell isn't. And how many people are your size anyway?"

"Lisa honey, what are you trying to develop here?"

"I don't know. Is there anything you ought to tell me that you haven't?"

"Can't think of a thing."

"What are we going to do after we get rich, dear?"

"Live rich."

"Like this place?"

"And Las Brisas at Acapulco. And Cala de Volpe on Sardinia. The Reina Cristina in Algeciras."

"In where?"

"Spain, near Gibraltar."

She sat on the couch a couple of feet from me, eyes hooded, mouth pursed. "Will we travel well together when we're rich?"

"Get along?"

"Do you think we will?"

"We'll have to try it."

"Are you terribly dog-in-the-manger about things?"

"Like what?"

"If we had something going for us and I happened to

see somebody like Artie Calivan. As long as I didn't over-do."

"Get the guests?"

She shrugged. "When they come in pairs, dear. And both exciting."

"I don't like to set policy. Take each situation on its merits. Okay?" I put my glass down and stood up. Winced. Flexed my leg. It was going to stiffen up very nicely during the night. She walked me out to the garden gate. I kissed her on the forehead and told her to dream about being rich. She said she had dreamed about that ever since she could remember.

sixteen

I came bounding awake in the middle of the night from a dream so horrible I couldn't remember any part of it. I was drenched with icy sweat and trembling badly.

The dream made me recall lying to Lisa about sending a letter. A letter would be a comfort. I couldn't wait until morning. Leonard Sibelius, Esq., attorney at law.

The sealed letter inside was about the same, but the cover letter for the sealed letter varied. I asked him to read the sealed letter if he did not hear from me by the last day of May and then give it to some colleague wise in the ways of the SEC and the NASD.

After the lights were out again and the letter tucked away, I thought of how ironic it would be if Harry Broll ended up being defended by Lennie Sibelius on a charge of murder, first. Lennie would get him off. He would extract every dime Harry had ever made and put a lock on every dime Harry might make in the future, but he would get him off.

I felt myself drifting off and wondered what the hell there had been in that nightmare that had so thoroughly chilled my blood.

I was up early again on Friday and made another exciting run into town. I stopped at the main post office and sent the letter to Lennie by air, special delivery, registered mail. I drove through the one-way tunnel that leads from the Carenage area under Hospital Hill to the Esplanade and the main part of downtown. The *Queen Elizabeth II* was in, and it was her last visit of the season. She had spewed about two thousand passengers into the town and

onto the beaches. The ones in town were milling around,
arguing with each other about the currency and looking
for the nonexistent duty-free shops and being constantly
importuned to hire a nice taxi and see the sights. The big
single-stack ship was anchored out with fast launches running back and forth like big white water beetles.

I ambled around and admired one out of every forty-
three tourist ladies as being worth looking at and did some
minor shopping of my own, then tested my skill and reflexes by driving back to the Spice Island Inn.

It was on that twenty-second day of April that I risked
two lives instead of merely my own and drove Lisa out toward the Lance aux Epines area and had lunch at the Red
Crab—burly sandwiches on long rolls, icy Tuborg beer,
green salad—eaten outdoors at a white metal table by a
green lawn in the shade of a graceful and gracious tree.
After lunch we went exploring. We stopped and looked at
the sailboats moored in Prickly Bay. I drove past large,
lovely houses, and we got out of the Moke at Prickly Point
and walked down the rocky slope and looked over the
edge at the blue sea lifting and smashing at the rocks,
working away on caves and stone sculpture, biting stub-
bornly and forever at the land. A curiously ugly species of
black crab, big as teacups, foraged the dry sheer stone just
above the reach of wave and tide, scrabbling in swift
hundreds when we moved too near.

I studied my map and found, on the way back, a turn
that led to a stretch of divided highway, probably the only
bit of it on the little island. Weeds grew up through cracks.
It was the grand entrance to the site of what had been the
Grenada Expo of several years ago. I had heard that few
visitors came. Many of the Expo buildings were never
completed. The ones which had been finished lay under
the midafternoon hum of sun's heat, warping plywood
shedding thin scabs of bright holiday paint. Some faded,
unraveling remnants of festive banners moved in a small
sea breeze. We saw a VIP lounge where the doorsill brush
grew as high as the unused and corroded doorknobs. Steel
rods sprouted from cement foundation slabs where build-

ings had never stood. We found a huge and elegant motel, totally empty, completely closed, yet with the lawns and gardens still maintained by the owners or the government.

I drove down crooked little dirt roads, creaking and swaying at two miles an hour over log-sized bumps and down into old rain gullies you could hide bodies in. She clung and laughed, and we made it down an angled slope to a pretty and private little stretch of beach where the almond trees and the coconuts and the sea grapes grew closer than usual to the high tide mark because of the offshore protection of some small islands.

I parked in the shade. We walked on the beach and found one of the heavy local skiffs pulled well up between the trees, with red and blue and green paint peeling off the old weathered wood. She hiked a haunch onto the gunwale, near the hand-whittled tholepin, braced herself there with one knee locked, the other leg a-swing. The breeze moved the leaves overhead, changing the patterns of sun and shade on her face and hair, on her yellow-and-white-checkered sun top, her skimpy little yellow skirt. The big lenses of her sunglasses reflected the seascape behind me. She sucked at her cigarette, looked solemn, then tilted her head, and smiled at me.

"I'm trying to figure out why it should be so much fun, just sort of churning around in the heat of the day," she said.

"Glad you're enjoying it."

"I guess it's because it's like a date. Like being a kid again in Trois Pistoles and going out on a date. It's a feeling I haven't had in a long long time. It's sort of sweet, somehow. Do you know what I mean, Gav?"

"Not exactly."

"Ever since I left when I was fifteen, I've been with guys I've either just been in bed with or am just about to get into bed with or both. And if it was a guy I'd already had or one I was going to have, if we were alone in a funny, private place like this, we'd be knocking off a stand-up piece right here. I was thinking I don't want you to try anything, because it would take away that feeling of being on a date. There's something funny and scary about it, like being a virgin again. Or maybe it's you that's scary to me, about that girl sinking in the ocean. I dreamed about her. Jesus! You really did that? Really?"

"It seemed like a good idea at the time."

She slid off the gunwale and snapped her cigarette into the surf line. She bent and picked up a coconut in the husk and threw it with a shotput motion. She was wiry, and she got surprising distance with it.

"So this is just a little bit of time when nothing happens and we just wait, Gavin."

"For your cousin. After you make the phone call and send the cable."

I leaned on the boat. Some palm fronds had been tossed into it. I lifted them and saw the battered metal fuel tank for the missing outboard motor, and I saw a spade with a short handle, sawed off where it had broken and decided it was a clumsy, improvised paddle. Clumsy but better than none at all. With all that weight and freeboard she would be a bitch to try to paddle against wind or tide.

"Head back?" I asked.

"Can we keep on being tourists, dear? Let's look at that map again."

We went back to the Moke, studied the map and decided to try the road out to Point Saline and look at the lighthouse. It was a road so wretched that by the time we were halfway I had decided only a jeeplike vehicle such as a Moke could make it. Then around the next hairpin corner I was shouldered into the shrubbery by three taxis coming back from the lighthouse, whamming and leaping over the ruts and broken paving, chock-full of tourists off the *QE2*.

My gratis map had little paragraphs on the back of it about local wonders, so just short of the lighthouse hill we stopped and dutifully got out to walk for a moment on the white sand beach of the Caribbean, then crossed the road and went down a path for about fifty yards to walk on the black sand beach of the Atlantic. Then I roared the Moke up the twenty-degree slope to the lighthouse.

The attendant was there, obviously eager to be a guide, obviously eager for bread. We climbed the several flights to the glass enclosed top. The treads were very narrow, the steps very steep. Lisa was directly ahead of me, and I was staring at the backs of her knees as we climbed.

It was a view so breathtakingly, impossibly fabulous that it became meaningless. It was like being inserted into a living postcard. It does no good to stand and gawk at something like that. The mind goes blank as soon as you see it. Tourists take pictures and take them home and find out they have postcards. If they put Helen in front of the view, they have a postcard with Helen in it. The only way a person could accommodate himself to a place like that would be to live there until he ceased to see it and then slowly and at his own pace rediscover it for himself. When I found out what the attendant had to do to keep that fifty-mile light operating, I was happy to place some Biwi in his hand.

Lisa was quiet on the way back. When we were nearly back to the deserted Expo site, I glanced over at her and saw the tear running down her quiet cheek, coming out from under the sunglasses. I pulled over in a shady spot and said, "Hey!"

"Oh God, I don't know, I don't know. Leave me alone."

"Sure."

Glasses off. Dab eyes, snuffle, sigh, blow nose. Fix mouth. Put glasses back on. Light cigarette. Sigh again, huffing smoke plume at windshield.

"Everything is supposed to be so great," she said. "Everything is some kind of a trick. Every time. Some kind of flaky trick, no matter what it is. Fifty-mile lighthouse! Good God! What the hell is a Fresnel lens?"

"A Frenchman invented it long ago. It focuses light into a beam."

"Nothing is ever what you expect. That's what got to me, Gav. A fifty-mile lighthouse and all there is up there is a mantle like off a Coleman lantern and not a hell of a lot

bigger, and that poor scrawny black son of a bitch that has
to get up every two hours all night long and run up there
and pull on some goddamn weights like a big grandfather
clock so his fucking light keeps turning around for another
two hours. Fresnel! They fake everything in the world."

"What kind of a big deal did They promise you, Lisa?"

She pulled the glasses off and looked at me with reptil-
ian venom and coldness. "They told me, friend, to sing in
the choir, love Jesus, do unto others, pray to God, live a
Christian life, and then live in heaven in eternal bliss forevermore. They forgot to explain that the choirmaster
would give me free private voice lessons when I was fourteen and by the third lesson he'd have his finger up me.
They didn't tell me that if I didn't report him, I'd lose out
on all that eternal bliss. They didn't tell me that I wouldn't
want to report him, because then he wouldn't have a
chance to do it again. They didn't explain about it being
the temptation of the flesh and how finally you get to the
place where you either make a true confession or you run
away. They were running their big lighthouse and making
it look wonderful, shining its light all over the world to
save souls. But it was just a gas mantle and weights and
chains and a weird lens. The real thing they teach you
without even knowing it is: do unto others before they do
it unto you."

"My my my," I said in a gentle wonder, and the tears
came again. She got them under control at last.

"Will you laugh at me if I tell you what I *really* want to
do with the money, Gav?"

"I don't think I will."

"I want to join an order. I want to give the money to
the order. I want to take a vow of silence. I want to kneel
on stone floors and pray until my knees bleed and I faint. I
don't ever want to be screwed again the rest of my life or
be even touched by any man. I want to be a bride of
Christ. Now laugh yourself sick."

"I don't hear anybody laughing."

"You think I'd go over the wall in a week, don't you?"

"Do you?"

"If I can find the guts to start, I'll never leave. Never.

You're doing all this to me by making me feel the way I did a long long time ago. A lot of men ago. A lot of beds ago."

"I don't think people stick with projects they start because they think they should start them. That's image making. People stick to their truest, deepest gratifications, whether it's running banks, building temples out of beercans, stuffing dead birds, or telling dirty jokes. Somewhere early you get marked."

"I got it early. Stations of the Cross. Easter. Christ is risen. At about twelve I felt so marvelously pure. Jesus loved me, that I know."

"So you fight it all your life or go back to it. Either way, it is a deep involvement."

She found her glasses on the floor, picked them up and said wearily, "You know so goddamn much, don't you? You know something? You've got a big mouth. A great big mouth. Let's get back on the beach where I belong."

seventeen

That random afternoon had turned Lisa Dissat off in a way she either couldn't explain or didn't care to explain. It amounted to the same thing. We became like neighbors in a new suburb, nodded and smiling when we met walking to or from the main hotel building or up and down the two-mile beach or back and forth from sun cot to cottage.

I saw some of the cruise ship men, crew and passengers, take their try at her now and then when she walked the long wide beach alone. I saw male guests at our hotel and the other beach hotels make their approach, each one no doubt selecting the overworked line he thought might be most productive. They would fall in step with her, last about a half dozen steps before turning away. I followed her a couple of times and kept count. Prettier young women in bikinis just as revealing walked the beach unaccosted. It was difficult to identify those characteristics which made her such a frequent target. It was something about the tilt and position of her head, in relation to the shape in which she held her mouth while walking. It was challenge, somehow. A contempt and an arrogance. Try me, you bastard. Try your luck and see how good you are. Do you think you're man enough to cope, you bastard? There was both invitation and rejection in the roll of her hip. To describe everything that happened to tilt, curve, and musculature in one complete stride from start to finish and into the next stride would have taken a seventeen syllable word. Provocative, daring, and ineradicably cheap. That was what Rupe had seen so quickly, wondering why I risked even a bruised knuckle to take ass like that away

174

from Carl Brego. It was what I had seen when she sat with Brego for a drink and lunch.

It was a compulsive cheapness. I could not believe that it was deliberate in the sense of being something she had thought out. It had to be something she could not help doing, yet did not do out of some physical warp or out of any flaw in intelligence or awareness.

She had been uncommonly determined to give herself to me. It had been too early an effort. She wanted to be used, not loved. She wanted to be quickly tumbled and plundered. It was what she expected and what she wanted, and it was that need which exuded the musky, murky challenge.

I have a need to try to put people together out of the pieces they show me. The McGee Construct-A-Lady Kit. For those on a budget we suggest our cheaper, simpler Build-A-Broad Kit.

Once you Build-A-Broad, it pleases you more than it did before you took it apart and examined the components.

She had ripened young. They had drilled virtue into her so mercilessly that when she was seduced she believed herself corrupt and evil. Purity could not be regained. So she ran away and had spent a dozen years corrupting because she believed herself corrupt, debauching because she had been debauched, defiling because she was the virgin defiled.

When you cannot like yourself or any part of yourself in mind or body, then you cannot love anyone else at all. If you spend the rest of your life on bleeding knees, maybe Jesus will have the compassion to love you a little bit. She had been destroyed twelve years ago. It was taking her a little while to stop breathing.

I kept in close touch with her. She heard nothing. I killed time restlessly. So Saturday I got a clear connection and talked to Meyer. I told him to check out Paul Dissat in the SeaGate offices in West Palm. I had to spell the name in my own special kind of alphabet before he was sure of it. Detroit Indiana sugar sugar Alabama teacup.

"Dissat? Paul Dissat?"

"Yes. And be damned careful of him. Please. He bites."

"Is Mary there? Is she all right?"

"She's fine."

After all, what else could I say? Time to talk later.

Later on Saturday I drove until I finally found the way to Yacht Services. I parked the Moke and went out on the long dock and found the *Dulcinea*. She was a custom motor sailer, broad of beam with sturdy, graceless lines. Rupe Darby and Artie kept her sparkling, and she looked competent.

Artie had gone over to the Carenage in the dinghy to do some shopping. Rupe asked me aboard and showed me the below decks spaces, the brute diesels, all the electronics. He was fretting about the delivery of some highly necessary engine item. It was supposed to come in by air. They couldn't leave without it, and he didn't want to be late meeting his owners at Dominica. He hoped to be out by Wednesday.

I asked about Carl Brego, and he told me that Brego's rich lady had arrived with friends, and they had left early that morning for two weeks sailing the Grenadines.

A sunbrown and brawny woman in blue denim shorts and a dirty white T-shirt came along the dock and waved and smiled. She had a collie ruff of coppery gold hair, a handsome weathered face. Rupe invited her to come aboard and have some coffee with us. She did, and we sat in the shade of the tarp rigged forward. She was Captain Mickey Laneer, owner and operator of the *Hell's Belle,* a big businesslike charter schooner I could see from where we sat. Mickey had a man's handshake and a state of Maine accent.

"Trav, Mickey here has the best damned charter business in the islands, bar none."

"Sure do," she said, and they both chuckled and chuckled.

"Could be out on charter all the time," Rupe said.

"But that would take all the fun out of it, too much of the same thing," Mickey said.

"She charges high, and she picks and chooses and doesn't have to advertise. Word of mouth," Rupe said, and they kept chuckling.

"Five hundred bucks a day, US, and I don't take the *Belle* out for less than five days, and I won't carry less than three or more than five passengers. Price stays the same."

"That's pretty high," I said.

"I keep telling her she ought to raise the rate again."

"Would you two mind telling me why you keep laughing?"

Mickey shoved her hair back, grinning. "Rupe and I just enjoy life, Mr. McGee."

"She does a good trade with business meetings. Three or four or five busy, successful executives, usually fellows in their thirties or early forties, they come down to relax, get some fishing in, get a tan, do a little dickering and planning. You know."

"Why is everybody laughing but me?" I asked.

"She takes male passengers only, Trav."

I finally caught up. "I get it. Your crew is all female, Captain?"

"And," said Rupe, "all nimble and quick and beautiful and strong as little bulls. They range from golden blond— a gal who has a masters in languages from the University of Dublin—to the color of coffee with hardly a dab of cream. Eight of them."

"Seven, Rupe. Darn it. I had to dump Barbie. She was hustling a guest for extra the last time out. I've warned them and warned them. After I provision the *Belle*—the best booze and best food in the Windwards—I cut it down the middle, half for me and the boat, half for the gals. So on a five day run, they make better than three hundred, Biwi. Everyone from golden Louise all the way to Hester, whose father is a bank official in Jamaica."

"You need eight crew to work that thing, Mick?"

"I know. I know. We're going out Monday for ten days. Four fellows from a television network. Nice guys. It'll be their third cruise. Old friends. That means my gals will be topless before we clear Grand Mal Bay."

"And bottomless before you get opposite Dragon Bay and Happy Hill."

"Could be, dear. Louise flew up to Barbados today. She says she has a cute chum who loves sailing. It's a way for a certain kind of girl to combine her favorite hobbies and make a nice living. I don't take hard-case types. I like polite, happy girls from nice backgrounds. Then we have a happy ship."

She got up and said, "A pleasure to meet any of Rupe's old friends, Travis. Hope you'll sail with us sometime. Rupe has."

"Mickey invited four of us captains to a free five-day cruise last year."

"I had a cancellation," Mickey said, "and we were all wondering what to give the other captains for a Christmas present. Well, nice to meet you."

After she was on the dock, she turned and waved and said, "Tell him our motto, Rupe."

He chuckled. She walked lithely away. He said, "Mickey likes you. In her line of work she gets to tell the men from the boys in a hurry."

"What's the motto?"

"Oh. It's on her letterhead. 'Make a lot of lovely new chums every voyage.' "

"Enjoy the cruise?"

"Oh, hell yes. By God, it is different. There's rules, and Mickey enforces them. None of her gals get slopped. Any and all balling is done in the privacy of your own bunk in your own stateroom, curtains drawn. No pairing off with any special gal, even for a whole day. If a gal is wearing pants, long or short, it means hands off. Otherwise, grab whatever is passing by whenever you feel like it. The gals don't make the approach. The things you remember are like standing aft with a big rum punch in a fresh wind with Micky at the wheel really *sailing* that thing, putting on all the sail it'll take, and those eight great bareass gals scampering around, hauling on those lines, trimming sail. And like being anchored in a cove in the moonlight, the evening meal done, and those gals singing harmony so sweet it would break your heart right in two. Great food and

great drinks and good fishing. Everybody laughs a lot
aboard the *Belle*. Between all they got to do, those gals
put in a day full of work for a day's pay. I can't understand that damned stupid Barbie. Why'd she want to try
some private hustling? Her old man must own half the
state of South Carolina. Barbie's been a sailboat bum all
her life. And she gets this chance to make a good living
doing the two things in this world she does best and enjoys
most, sailing and screwing, and she blows the whole deal.
It's hard to understand. Anyway, we were out five days,
and it was like being gone a month, I swear. It's . . . it's
something different. If you ever see the *Belle* coming in
here or leaving, you wouldn't figure it out. Those gals look
like some kind of Olympic people training for a race. Nimble and slender and tough and . . . fresh faced. Scrubbed.
You know?"

On Sunday Lisa agreed without much argument to arrange her call so that I could hear both ends of the conversation. She placed it from the cottage. We had to wait a
long time before the desk called back and said they had
her party on the line. I sat close beside her, and she turned
the phone slightly so we could both hear, my right ear and
her left.

It was Harry's nervous, lying voice. "Mary, honey? Is
that you, Mary darling?"

"Yes, dear. Can you hear me?"

"Talk loud. You sound a million miles away, honey.
Where are you? I've about gone out of my head with
worry."

I hoped he sounded more convincing to his secretary
than he did to me. Lisa followed her prepared script, telling Harry to let Holly Dressner know she was all right and
that she had phoned. She said she was afraid he'd find the
travel agency she'd used. The Seven Seas. Down in Hal-
landale. Mrs. DeAngela had been very nice and helpful.

"Are you going to come home? To stay?"

"I think so, Harry. I think that's best, really."

"So do I. When, honey? When will you be home?"

"I've got reservations out of here May third. But don't

try to meet me. I don't know when I'll get in. And I'll have my car. By the way, you don't have to worry about the money. Not any more. I'm going to cable Mr. Willow tomorrow to activate the loan and put the money in your account, dear."

"I've been getting pretty nervous."

"I can imagine. I guess I wanted you to sweat a little."

And on and on and finally it was over, and she hung up. She gave me a strange look and then wiped beads of sweat from her upper lip and throat.

"It spooked me."

"I know."

"If I'd been Mary, I certainly wouldn't arrange a loan for that son of a bitch. I don't see much point in that phone call, really. There's enough without that."

"His secretary will make a good witness. Mary Broll is alive and well and in Grenada. She'll be home May third. She can say she was there when Mrs. Broll called her husband. Probably Harry will have his secretary get Mrs. Dressner on the phone and make sure his secretary hears him give her Mary's message."

"I don't have to send her any more cards. If I was supposed to, Paul would have told me. He thinks everything out."

"It's a good way to be, if you like to kill people."

"It's weird. You know? I've thought and thought about what you said, Gav. The smart thing for him to do would be kill me. Get word for me to meet him on the way back. Some other island. Arrange something. But I just can't believe he would. We're from the same town. We're family. I keep having this dream about him. He's standing watching me sleep, and I sneak my eyes open and find out he isn't really looking at me. He's looking the other way, and he has a mask just like his face that he wears on the back of his head. He's pretending to watch me, but he's looking at something else I can't see. When the dream wakes me up, I'm cold all over."

"We won't have long to wait, Lisa. After you send the cable to Willow tomorrow, you're no use to him."

"Stay close to me, huh?"

I reassured her. I wouldn't let the bad man get her. She'd be safe.

Sure.

eighteen

I was up very early on Monday morning when the sun was still behind the green mountains. I swam. The tide was low and getting lower, still running out. I went back to take my shower before dressing for breakfast.

By then, of course, he had talked with Lisa long enough to discover I was one of his priorities. He had immobilized her and come after me. Usually I am pretty good at surprises. Some sense I cannot describe gives me a few microseconds of lead time, and when I get that kind of warning, the reaction time seems to be at its best. Perhaps it is hearing or the sense of smell at subliminal levels.

I don't know where he hid. There were good places in the garden. He could have crouched behind the bar in the service area or behind some of the bigger pieces of furniture in the living room. He worked it out well. He saw me go swimming, and he nipped over the wall unobserved. I'd locked the gate but not the sliding door. He could assume I would come inside to take my shower, and I would have no reason to close the bathroom door. Standard procedure is to reach in and turn the handles until you get the roaring water to the right temperature, and then you step in. It is a moment of helplessness, and there is a useful curtain of sound.

I remember that when I got the water temperature the way I wanted it, I straightened to strip the swim trunks off. The whole back of my head blew up, and I went spinning and fluttering down through torrents of white, blinding light.

182

I know what he probably used. I made things easy for him. I had picked up the piece of driftwood in the surf a few days before. It was iron hard, less than a yard long, a stick an inch and a half in diameter with a sea-polished clump of root structure at the end of it the size of a large clenched fist.

Because he did not give a particular damn whether he killed me or not, he waited for the water roar, then came prowling into the bathroom with the club cocked, poising like a laborer to sledge a stake into hard ground.

The brain is a tender, gray jelly wrapped in membrane, threaded and fed with miles of blood tubes down to the diameter of thread. The gray jelly is a few billion cells which build up and discharge very small amounts of electric impulses. The whole wet, complex ball is encased in this bone, covered with a rubbery layer of scalp and a hair thatch which performs some small shock-absorbing service. Like the rest of the body, the brain is designed to include its own spare parts system. Brain cells are always dying at a rate dependent on how you live but are never replaced. There are supposed to be enough to last you. If a stroke should kill all the cells in the right hemisphere involved with communication—hearing and speaking, reading and writing—there is a fair chance of dormant cells in the left hemisphere being awakened and trained and plugged into the other parts of the system. Researchers can run a very thin electrode into an animal brain and hit a pleasure center and offer a chimp two levers—push one, and he gets a little electrical charge that makes him feel intense pleasure; push the other, and he gets a banana. The chimp will happily starve to death, pushing the pleasure lever. They can make a rabbit dangerously savage, a cat afraid of mice. They can put electrodes against your skull and trace pictures of your brain waves. If you have nice big steep alpha waves, you learn quickly and well. People who smoke a lot have stunted alpha waves. People who live in an area with a high index of air pollution—New York, Los Angeles, Birmingham—have rotten little alpha waves that are so tiny they are hard to find. No one knows yet why this is so. It may be a big fat waste of everybody's money, time, and energy sending kids to school in Los Angeles, Chicago, and lately, Phoenix.

Anyway, if you take a club to all this miraculous gray tapioca with a good full swing and bash the back of the skull a little to the right of center where a right-hander is likely to hit it, it is not going to function at all for a while, and then it is going to function in some partial manner for a varying period of time, which could be for as long as it lives. If you have any blood leaking in there and building pressure between the bone and the jelly, then it is not going to live very long at all.

Even if there is a perfect, unlikely, one-hundred-percent recovery, it is going to take a long time to gather up the scattered pieces of memory of the time just prior to the blow and the time just subsequent to the recovery of partial consciousness. The memories will never be complete and perfect. Drop one of those big Seeburg jukes off the back of a pickup truck, and you are not going to get any music at all, and even if it can be fixed, the stereo might not ever work too well.

Forget the crap about the television series hard guy who gets slugged and shoved out of a fast moving car, wakes up in the ambulance, and immediately deduces that the kidnapper was a left-handed albino because Little Milly left her pill bottle on the second piling from the end of the pier. If hard case happens to wake up in the ambulance, he is going to be busy trying to remember his own name and wondering why he has double vision and what that loud noise is and why he keeps throwing up.

Assembling the bits of memory into some kind of proper order is a good trick, too.

Here's one fragment. On my left side, curled up in a cramped, tilting, bouncing place where things dug into me. Very hot. Some fabric pasted to me with sweat. Head in a small place full of blue light. Something abrasive under my left cheek. Arms immovable, hands dead. Motor grinding. A woman making a keening sound somewhere near, a thin long gassy cry, over and over, not in fear, in pain, in sorrow—but as if she were practicing, trying to imitate something, like a broken valve in a steam plant. Blackout.

Another: being jounced and joggled, hanging head down, bent over something hard digging into my belly. Thighs clasped. By an arm? One brute son of a bitch to carry me that way in a walk, but this one was jogging! Begin shallow coughing that announces imminent vomit. Immediately dropped heavily into sand. Gag, choke, and drift back into the gray void.

There were others, more vague. Some were real, and some were dreams. The brain was trying to sort out the world and it took bits of input and built dreams. On patrol, clenching myself motionless against stony ground while the flare floated down, swinging a little, moving over to burn out against the shoulder of the hill that closed off the end of the valley they were using. A brilliantly vivid fragment of old nightmare of Junior Allen surfacing behind the cruiser, tough jowls wedged into the gap of the Danforth anchor.

Then along came a more detailed one that continued so long the brain was able to go to work on it, sorting out evidences of reality, comparing them to evidences of fantasy. I awoke slowly. I was sitting on sand, leaning back against something that felt like the trunk of a tree. My arms were fastened around behind me, painfully cramped. I tried to move them and could not. I tried to move my hands, wiggle my fingers, and I could feel nothing.

I stared down at familiar swim trunks and down the brown length of my very own legs with the curled hair sun-bleached to pure white against the brown hide. A quarter-inch-in-diameter nylon cord had been tied to both ankles. It had been pulled so tight it bit into the skin. My feet were puffed. There was a two-foot length of cord from ankle to ankle. My legs spraddled. A sea grape tree grew up out of the sand in the middle of the triangle formed by my spread legs and the ankle-to-ankle cord.

It took time to work it out. It was unlikely I had been there so long the tree had happened to grow there. Do trees grow slowly? Yes. Very slowly. Okay, could I have been fitted over the tree somehow? Long, careful thought. No. Too big. The ankles had been tied after they had been placed on either side of the tree. By me? No, the cord was too tight. My feet were swollen and blood dark. By somebody else then. Untie the cord? Not with arms I couldn't move and hands I couldn't feel. Remove tree? No way. I was supposed to stay there. No choice about it. I turned my head to the left, slowly, slowly. I was in shade. Out there the sand blazed under a high sun. Blue waves, small ones, moved in toward the sand and lifted, crested white, slapped and ran up the sandslant and back into the next wave. I turned my head the other way as slowly and looked to my right.

A man was sitting there. He was sitting on a small, inflatable blue raft I had seen afloat in Lisa's pool. He had a weathered brown basket made of strips of woven palm frond, and he was pressing it back into shape and working new green strips of frond into it. He sat crosslegged, intent on his task. He had a trim cap of dark curls. He had dark eyes and long lashes. He had a plump red mouth. He wore white boxer shorts. He wore a gold cross on a chain around his neck. He wore a wristwatch with a stainless steel band and a complicated dial. That was all.

As he tugged and pulled at the stubborn fronds, a lot of useful-looking muscles bulged and writhed and slid around under the smooth skin of arms and shoulders. He rose effortlessly to a standing position and turned the basket this way and that. It was crude. Conical. Half-bushel size. His legs were slender, but the long muscles looked springy and powerful.

A name tugged at the edge of my mind until finally I could fit my sour mouth around it. An articulated croak. "Paul."

He looked at me. There is a way you look at people, and there is a way you look at objects. There is a difference in the way you look at objects. You do not look at your morning coffee cup, at a runover toad in your driveway, or at a flat tire the same way you look at people. This was the way a man might look at a flat tire that he was going to have to attend to in a little while. Not like the owner of the car but like a service station attendant. Damage appraisal, estimate of time required.

I managed another word. "Untie." I was becoming a chatterbox. He looked back down at his basket repair job. I couldn't understand why he wouldn't talk to me. Then gray mists came rolling in from some swamp in the back of my head, and the world faded away ...

I was being shaken awake. I was going to be late for school. I was picked up and placed on my feet. I squinted into a dazzling world and saw Paul looking at me. I was leaning back against a palm bole, weak and dizzy. I looked down and saw the familiar length of cord from ankle to ankle. Where could my sea grape tree have gone? I could not imagine.

Paul pulled me away from the tree and turned me to face the sea. He walked me carefully, holding onto my upper arm with both hands, helping me with my balance. I had to take short steps. There was very little feeling in my feet. He guided me at an angle down the beach, the trees at my left, the sea at my right. We were out in the hot glare, away from the shade of the trees. He stopped me and said, "Sit." He helped me ease down onto the sea-damp brown sand, facing the basket I had seen him repairing. It was upside down on the sand, like a crude clown's hat. A wave slid up the sand and took a light lick at the edge of the basket and at my right foot.

With the slow grace that accompanies ceremony, Paul reached and plucked the basket away. It was a magic trick. Lisa's severed head was balanced upright on the sand, facing the sea. Magicians can fool you with things like that. He stood easily in front of her and extended his right foot and put his bare sandy toes against her left temple and slowly and gently turned the head so that it faced me. As he did so he spoke a rapid, guttural, unmusical French.

Lisa rolled mad and empty eyes toward me, eyes that looked through me at something on the other edge of the world beyond me and creaked her jaw wide and made a thin, gassy, aspirated scream, gagged for air, and screamed again.

He squatted, turned her head back, slid his palm under the chin to uptilt her face, spoke down at her, the French rapid but gentler, almost tender, chiding her.

A wave slid up and under him, and the edge of foam slapped the lower half of her face. She gagged and coughed. He stroked her dark, soaked hair back from her forehead with a tender and affectionate gesture, patted her cheek, said something else to her which ended with one word I understood. *Adieu.*

He moved toward me, and as he did so, I saw a bigger wave coming. She seemed to see it, too. She squeezed her eyes shut and clamped her mouth shut. It slapped against my hip. It washed completely over her head and reached six feet behind her and paused, then came sluicing back, leaving two small divergent ridges in the sand from the nape of her neck toward the sea, shaped like the wake of a boat. The sea had combed her hair forward, left it pasted down over her face.

He lifted me easily onto my feet, turned me to face up the slope of sand, urging me on. By dint of great mental effort I put three words together. "She can't see." Meaning, if she can't see, she can't see the wave coming the next time.

"Never mind," he said. His English was good, but there was a trace of the French-Canadian accent which Lisa had eliminated entirely. As we walked up the beach, I saw the old boat and remembered the day with Lisa. So she had guided Paul to this secluded spot. I saw the spade with the short handle stuck into the dry sand near the trees. Easy to dig a hole big enough for Lisa. With her knees against her chest, her ankles tied to her wrists, it wouldn't take much of a hole at all. I saw the Moke beyond the trees, on that rough little sand road, parked almost where I had parked it on that day of the lighthouse.

He helped me through the thick, dry sand and eased me down in the shade with my back against a rough tree trunk. "Dig her out?" I said. I was getting pretty good with three-word sentences.

He sat on his heels, began picking up handfuls of dry sand and letting it trickle out of the bottom of his fist. "It's too late. Not that it would make any difference. I shouldn't have used the basket. She hated the basket. She begged me not to use the basket. But I had to be sure she told every last thing. But something broke in her head. After she lost all her English. Something gave way. I thought seeing you might put her back together. I guess it was the basket. I'll be more careful with you."

I looked out at Lisa. I saw the biggest wave yet of the incoming tide. It did not curl and smash down at the packed sand until it reached her; then it bounced high off that dark roundness sparkling in the sun, the way a wave will bounce off a small boulder along the shore.

It was hard to believe it was Lisa. From the back only the dark hair showed. Her head looked like some large nut covered with a dark growth that had fallen from a tropical tree and rolled down, coming to rest in the incoming tide.

"If she holds her breath at the right time, she could last a long time, perhaps," he said. "But she is dead. Just as you are dead."

"And . . . Mary?"

There was a slight Gallic shrug. "That was bad luck. I went to her to try to convince her to leave Harry for good. Why should a woman like that have been loyal to a man like that? I wanted her to run, because without her, Harry would have to find three hundred thousand somewhere else. I have that much. I was going to squeeze Harry for half his stock. Waterbury should have let me buy in. Then nothing would have ever happened."

"Bad luck?"

"She tried to run. The house was dark. I caught her, and we fell badly. Very badly. It was an ugly situation. She knew who I was. I couldn't call an ambulance, could I? She knew how bad it was. I had to find out a lot from her while she could still talk. She was stubborn. I had to . . . amplify the pain to make her speak." He frowned. "I

thought it would sicken me to do that. But it was a strange
pleasure in a little while. As if we were lovers. So that is
bad luck too, I suppose, to learn that about oneself. Grati-
fication is expensive and very dangerous, eh?"

He stood up, clapped his hands to remove the loose
sand. "And it was the same pleasure with Lisa, and we
will discover if it is the same with a man, too. I should not
care to dig a hole big enough for you, Mr. McGee."

"McGee?"

"I am very good about details. Harry described you well
enough. Mary is dead. Lisa is dead. McGee is dead. But
we must find out who you sent the letter to and what it
said. We shall improvise, eh? There is a tire pump and a
jack in the tool compartment of that ugly little vehicle.
Something will come to mind. There will be enough time
to proceed slowly and carefully."

He walked up toward the car, a hundred feet away. The
equation was very simple. No unknowns. I could spend
the afternoon on this hideaway beach as Paul Dissat
whiled away the lazy hours with a question-and-answer
game with the penalty for wrong answers and right answers precisely the same. Improvised agony.

Or I could try to stand up. That was the first step. If I
couldn't, there wasn't any point in wondering about step
two. If I could stand up, then I had to see if I could walk
down the beach and into the sea. I had to hurry, but with
short steps well within the range of my constraining nylon
cord, and I had to keep my balance. The third part of it
was getting into the water at just the right place. I had
seen the place when I had been out there near Lisa's head
in the hot sun.

There is no such thing as an undertow. Not anywhere in
the world. All you ever find is a rip. To have a rip, you
have to have a partial barrier parallel to the beach. It can
be a sandbar or a reef. The barrier has to be underwater.
There has to be a hole or channel through it. A great volume of water comes in on wind and waves and tide over
the barrier, rushing toward the beach with waves marching
right along behind each other, hurrying in. Then that big
volume of water has to get out to make room for the water

coming in. So it goes flowing out through the hole or channel. A big volume and a narrow deep hole makes one hell of an outgoing current. It is sort of fan-shaped, wide at the beach end, narrowing toward the gap in the barrier, and going faster and stronger as it gets narrower.

You can read a rip on a sandy beach from the way it boils up the sand in a limited area and makes a foam line out toward the gap. If you get caught in one, you swim parallel to the beach until you are out of it, then turn toward the beach. Fight it and you can panic and drown, because they usually go faster than any man can swim.

I got up, scraping some hide off my back on the palm trunk. I went down the beach slope, stamping my feet wide for balance. The beach and the sea kept tilting, misting, merging, flowing. In nightmare slowness I passed the round, black, hairy thing, saw it vividly for just a moment. A wave had come in and covered it entirely. The top of it was a few inches under momentarily motionless water, at rest when a wave had come all the way in and gathered itself to run back out. Her black hair was fanned out, and in that instant of sharpened, memorable vision I saw the spume of sand drifting out of her open mouth, like a strange cartoon balloon, a message without sound. A sandy, tan farewell.

Paul was shouting above the wave noises. I was off balance, leaning forward. A wave slapped my chest and straightened me up. I took a deep breath and lunged forward. I counted on the exceptional buoyancy of the water, the high salinity of the dry season. I had to know if I was in the rip. I managed to roll and float and look back at the beach and saw him and the trees and the raft and the Moke moving into the distance at six or eight miles an hour. It was a good rip, and I hoped it was a long gap in a barrier reef, that the reef was well offshore, and that it would move me out into a current that would take me away from there. Any direction at all. Out to sea and drown while laughing at how Lennie Sibelius was going to nail Paul Dissat, nail him and sweat him and find out how it happened. All of it.

The swell had built nicely, and it was going to play hell

on him, trying to find me bobbing around in all that blue and white sparkle. If the hands are dead, it is less burdensome to drown, but you try not to drown if you can help it. I could arch my back and float high, my ears full of the drum sounds of the sea, a wave slapping me in the face now and then. Lift my head, pick a direction, and go kicking along. When all the luck has gone bad, do what you can.

nineteen

It was a good rip that carried me way out and put me into a sea current that seemed to be taking me due north at a hell of a pace, increasing speed the further out I got. The water was warm, and the sky was squinty bright, and I was gently lifted and dropped in the swell. It had been a good way to live, and given a choice of dying, it was as good as any that came to mind. I wanted to stay aware of the act of dying as long as I could. I wanted to touch it and taste it and feel it. When it is the last sensation left, there is a hunger to use all of it up, just to see what it is like at the very end, if it is peace or panic.

I kicked my bound legs slowly and easily. When I lifted up, I could no longer pick out the beach area where Lisa had died. I looked to the southwest and saw the checkerboard pattern of the town of St. George's to the northeast growing more easterly as I floated farther. Finally, I began to see more and more of Grand Anse beach as I drifted further out from shore, and it came into view beyond Long Point. When all of the beach was visible, I estimated that I was two miles from land. I saw the bright sails moving back and forth in the bay when a wave lifted me high. I could not guess how long I had been floating because I kept fading into a semidazed condition very much like sleep. The sun was so high I guess it was past noon.

There was a change in the direction of the current. I believed it had begun to carry me northwesterly, but I was too far from any reference points to be sure. I was opposite the town by then, and as near as I could estimate, I was just as far from the town as I was from Point Saline.

When I could no longer see much of the town, see only the green mounded hills, I knew I was at least three miles off-shore, possibly four.

I came out of a daze and saw a tall ship bearing down on me about a mile away. There was just enough angle so I could make her out as a three-masted schooner, and she had all the canvas on her, all the fore and aft sails flying, tilting her on a long reach.

I knew it could be reality or fantasy, and the smart money would bet on fantasy. I guessed she had come out of St. George's, and from my estimate of the wind, if she was headed north to the Grenadines, she would stay on that course until she was far enough out to come about and put her on the opposite tack for a single long run that would clear all of Grenada and head her for Carriacou.

I felt remote, as if working out a problem that had nothing to do with me. My arms had no feeling. I moved up and down on big, slow, blue swells. The crests were not breaking. I kept kicking myself back to an angle where I could watch her, see the boil of white water at her bows. My chance of being seen was one in ten thousand, even if she passed by me fifty yards away.

But then I had an idea. I suppressed it because it was going to involve a lot of effort and any effort did not really seem worthwhile. There would be fishermen aboard, people who always scanned the sea even when there is no hope of stopping for a chance at whatever quarry they see. The big fish smash the water, whack it to foam, send the spray flying. Go to work. Make a fuss. Give them something to spot. Hard to do. Double up and snap. Get the bound legs up and whack them down. Get into a spin, writhing and turning the body, kicking. Duck under and come out and kick as high as you can. Dizziness then. Sickness. Vision going. A sound of sails slatting, lines creaking, a thin cry. Sound of an outboard nearby. Hands grasping, lifting me. Fall onto hardness, onto oil stink, fish smell, and vomit up quarts and quarts of sea water . . .

Then came that burlesque of fantasy, an ironic parody of the seafarer's paradise. I was on a low, broad hatch cover, and I could feel the motion of a ship under me. I squinted up into brightness to see, clustered close around me—all their lovely faces somber, all their girl voices murmuring of concern—the sirens of all the legends, seawind stirring their tresses, their lovely skin in shades from antique ivory to oiled walnut. They were close around me, a multitude of them, prodding and massaging calves, ankles, and puffy feet—forearms, wrists, and swollen hands.

One lifted my dead left hand, and I stared at it with remote interest. It was a dark purple rubber glove, over-inflated, with deep dimples where the knuckles had been.

Suddenly I screamed. It astonished me. I am not the screaming type. There was a pain in my right hand equivalent to having all the fingernails yanked off simultaneously. Pain shoved me far enough into sudden darkness so that the raw scream seemed far away and I could think of it as an angry white bird, clawing and flapping its way out of my open throat.

I came out of blackness in time to get myself braced for the next pain. It was again in the right hand, and as it faded, I got a big one in the left hand, which caught me off-balance and so I roared. The enchantresses moved back a little, looking down at me in worried speculation. They were all in little sleeveless blouses in bright colors, no two alike, all in little white shorts.

Captain Mickey Laneer came into view and perched a haunch on the hatch cover beside my hip. She wore a khaki shirt and a baseball cap. "What the hell have you been trying to do to yourself, McGee?"

"Hello, Mick. Lost an argument."

"Somebody throw you overboard?"

"Ran away, got into a rip, floated out from shore."

She stared at me. "From shore? Jesus! You could be a little bit hard to kill. Gals, this is an old and good friend of our old and dear friend, Rupert Darby, captain of the *Dulcinea*. Say hello to Travis McGee." They said hello in smiling musical chorus.

"McGee, clockwise around you, starting with Julia in the yellow shirt, meet Teddie, Louise, Hester, Janey, Joyce, Margot, and Valerie. Teddie, get to the helm on the double and tell Mr. Woodleigh he's falling off to port, for chrissake, and bring him back on. Janey, Mr. McGee needs a big mug of black coffee with four ounces of Fernandez rum in it. Margot, you help me get Mr. McGee onto his feet, and we'll put him in my cabin while we run back in."

I started to say something to her, then had to clamp down on the pains. Very savage pain but not as bad as the first ones.

"Speak to you privately, Mickey?"

"Move back, gals."

"Somebody is going to make very damned sure I drowned. It could revise their plans if I didn't. They'll keep a watch on the hospital. They could get to me there, I think. It's a bad risk."

"McGee, I like you. But I can't get involved in anything. The government pretends I don't exist. They like the money I bring in. The black power types talk about me forcing blacks into prostitution. Bullshit! Hester is the only almost pure black, and there are three less than half. Every girl has freedom of choice, believe me. Any publicity of any kind, any infraction, they hit me with a heavy fine. Enough to hurt without driving me out of business. Don't kill the goose. But don't let her get fat. You need hospital attention for the head and the hands. So I'm going to come about and have a nice run back and turn you over to Rupe to put you in the hospital. I've got four good, regular customers aboard who've paid their money for a ten-day cruise. Sorry."

I started to fade out and couldn't have pulled myself back in time if a sudden pain hadn't hit my right foot, as if an electric icicle were being shoved through it.

"Mick. I'm . . . sorry, too. Rupe heading up to Dominica Wednesday. Take me up to Grenadines, set up a meet, transfer me. Reach him on radio?"

"Yes but, dammit—"

"Take me back, and I blow your tired businessman cruises right out of the water, captain. Sorry as hell. You probably fulfill a pressing need. No pun. Official complaint to your lady governor, if I have to. And the premier. And the *Miami Herald*."

"McGee, I like you less and less. You are a bastard!"

"Only when I have to be."

"But, damn you, you could *die* on me!"

"Sort of a risk for both of us."

"Valerie? VAL! Get it on over here, girl. This big ugly son of a bitch going to die on me? She was a nurse, McGee."

Valerie was of that distinctive and very special mix you see in Honduras. Mayan, Chinese, and Spanish. She looked at my hands and she had me roll onto my belly while she checked the back of my head. Her touch was firm enough to hurt but gentle enough to let you know the hurt was necessary.

They helped me onto my back again, and she bent close and thumbed my eyelids up and looked gravely into one eye and then the other, back and forth, several times.

"Well?" Mickey said impatiently.

"Eet wass a terrible blow on the head. I don't know. The pupils are just the same size. Probably no fracture because the skull is solid and thick right there. Concussion. Could be bleeding in the brain, captain."

"How do we tell? What do we do?"

"One girl has to be with him every minute, and what she has to do all the time she is with him is count his pulse for one full minute and write it down. Count his respiration for one full minute. Write it down. Over and over. One hour is the most a girl can do that and be accurate. Half-hour is better."

"So we set up half-hour shifts."

"Then she must write down a column of figures. Suppose it is like . . . 71, 70, 72, 69, 71, 70, 69. Fine. Then it is 70, 69, 67, 68, 66, 67, 65 . . . right then the girl on duty finds me and finds you, and we get a seaplane alongside to take him to a hospital. They'll have to open his skull and see if the clot is shallow enough so they can take it out and keep him alive."

"My hands?" I asked.

"They'll hurt like hell," Valerie said. "Like living hell. But you'll be fine. No nerve damage. No dead tissue. Good circulation, so that even something that tight couldn't cut it all off."

The pain hit again as I was fading, but it just held me on the edge, and when it stopped, I went the rest of the way on down. Blurred memories of being carried, of choking on hot, pungent coffee, of hearing the hiss of water along the side of the hull. Then memories of it being night time, feeling that slow swing and turn of an anchored vessel, hearing faint music from topside, of moving in and out of sleep and seeing girls, sometimes the same one, sometimes a different one, solemnly and intently taking my pulse, lips moving, writing on a pad, then staring back and forth from my chest to a watch, counting respirations, writing it down. A Coleman lantern was hung from the overhead with an improvised shade which left the bunk in relative shadow and filled the rest of the small cabin in harsh brightness.

I awoke to a gray morning light in the cabin. The lantern was out. A slender, dark-haired girl sat taking my pulse. She had a narrow, pretty face, sallow skin. Her forehead and the end of her nose were sunburned.

"Where are we?"

"I'm counting."

"Sorry. Tell me when you're through."

"You made me get mixed up."

I let her count, write it down. "We're at anchor in a cove by some pretty little islands north of Grenada. They're called the Sisters. Now I have to count your breathing."

"Who are you?"

"Joyce. I'm new. Hush, please."

"From Barbados, eh?"

It startled her. "How'd you know that?"

"I can even remember the words. You are Louise's 'cute little chum.' She flew up and talked to you about the job."

She blushed. "Yes. Let me count, please."

"Dear girl, do your counting, and then I have to get up and use the head."

She wouldn't let me without going and bringing Valerie back to check me over and give permission. I felt shaky and frail. When I came back from the nearby head, clutching at everything handy, Valerie was sitting on the bunk looking at the notebook tabulations, and Joyce was standing near her. They got out of my way, and I sighed as I got in and lay back.

"Now we can take you off the continuous count, I think," Valerie said. "Do you feel dizzy? Do your ears hum?"

"No."

"I think we'll take a count every fifteen minutes. Joyce, your hour will be up in . . . ten minutes. Stay another hour, okay? I'll have Margot take over from you at seven thirty, and you can go help with breakfast then."

"You're a good nurse," I told Valerie. "Isn't there a shortage of nurses around the islands?"

She was so still for a moment her pretty face looked like a temple carving. Her Indian blood was more apparent. "Oh, yes. A shortage of nurses. And damn lots of patients. And not so many reasons for keeping them living, I think. The children die. The old ones come back, over and over, trying to die."

She spun and left quickly. I tried to smile at Joyce. Maybe I managed it convincingly enough. I think she smiled back as her face tilted and blurred and faded into gray-black. I had to say something to assure Joyce and myself I was not going sour on them.

"What did you do in Barbados, dear?" My voice seemed to come from the bottom of a brass barrel.

"Does it matter?" she said from the far end of a hundred-yard corridor.

"I'm interested. I'm curious. That's all."

She began to emerge out of the humming mists and the metallic distances. I saw her face again, shifting as if underwater, then firming up. "Are you all right?" she asked, frowning. I felt her fingertips moving on my wrists, seeking the pulse.

"I'm fine."

"You looked different. Your eyes were funny. I work in a boutique in Bridgetown. My husband worked at the desk in a couple of the good hotels. We could live on what we made if we were careful. Maybe he got tired of being careful. He left over a year ago, and I have no idea where he is. What else do you want to know? I'm English and Portuguese mostly with a bit of colored. I make about two hundred and seventy-five to three hundred, Biwi, a month in the season and a lot less when the tourists are gone. I can't quite live on it. I've sold the things Charles and I owned, like the music system we got on hire-purchase and was all paid for, and I let them come and take the things which weren't paid for. The last thing I let go, the last thing worth selling, was my little sailboat my father built for me before he died when I was twelve." Her words were coming faster and faster, and she had stopped searching for the pulse. Her thin fingers were wrapped around my lacerated wrist. "It was the only thing I could use to get away, to be someone else, and I took it out in a gale before I let it go, telling it to drown me, but it would not . . ."

"Hey, now," I said.

Her eyes had filled. "I mean there is no end to it, Mr. McGee. I've been a decent woman. I have no family at all. A fat political gentleman wants to give me a cottage in a development he owns. There has been one girl every two years, I understand. He is quite old. They each end up with a cottage and some sort of small pension. I imagine a long street of them with the years marked on little signs in the little yards, with all of us sitting on our little porches . . ."

"Joyce, honey. There, honey."

Kind words started the flood. She put her forehead down into the bend of my elbow, and the stifled sobs wracked her thin body. I stroked her hair and made soothing sounds. I identified my own feeling of guilt. I had not really wanted to know about her life and her problems. I had been talking in an effort to keep the brassy mists from sucking me under. But the words had opened her up, and it had come spilling out.

She pushed herself away, stood with her back to me, blew her nose. "Why should you give a damn?" she said in a choked voice. "Why should anybody?"

"Is this cruise what your friend Louise described?"

She turned, snuffled, sat wearily in the chair. "Oh, yes.

Louise didn't lie. She called a spade a spade. It's a ten-day trial, you might say. I will do deck duty, scut work, help with the food, drinks, laundry, scrubbing, and all that. But I don't have to be . . . available unless I decide to be and tell Captain Laneer first. The men really seem quite nice. I can keep my clothes on, thank God. Louise said it took her three days to get used to pottering about the decks and below decks entirely starko. I think it would take me forever, and even then I couldn't adjust. The girls are so much nicer than I imagined. But an entirely naked woman is not really erotic, do you think? Of course, in a cold wind or offshore insects or one's time of the month or coming into port, clothes are definitely required." She had a brooding look, frowning down at her knuckles. "It's rather difficult for one to imagine being quite ready for it. I mean if one has taken a bucket of scraps aft after cleaning fish, it is so abrupt to be suddenly tweaked, then taken by the hand, and led below." She roused herself and looked slightly startled. She had been voicing her internal monologue. "I go on, no?" She forced a wan smile. "At any rate, once the ten days are ended, I shall either go back to the boutique to stay or go back to quit my job and pack. I shall fret about it later, not now. Valerie told me that it would be good for you to get as much sleep as you can now. Can you sleep, dear?"

I could. I slept and slept and slept. The dull ache in hands and feet and head did not inhibit it. In too many of the sleep periods Lisa was way down below the velvet black, waiting for me on the bright beach, the severed head propped on the delicate bones of the jaw, smiling at me.

It was another morning, and Mickey Laneer brought me a stone mug of coffee, nudged me awake, and put the coffee in my hand after I had hitched up, knuckled grainy eyes.

"You are some kind of a sleeper," she said.

"A long swim with your hands and feet tied will do it every time. We moved again, didn't we? Where are we, and what day is it?"

"Anchored in the lee of Frigate Island at eight o'clock on the morning of Thursday, April twenty-ninth."

"Thursday! But couldn't you get in touch with—"

"He'll be off to the west of here about opposite us at fourteen hundred. We'll make a radio check on him an hour beforehand. No sweat. We'll run out and intercept and put you aboard *Dulcinea*."

"I've been a lot of trouble to you and your crew, Mick."

Her smile was sour. "Better this kind than the kind you were going to lay on me if I ran you back in."

"Hard feelings, captain?"

She grinned, punched me on the side of the thigh. "My four passengers haven't made any complaints. Maybe because I run the only game in town. The gals have loved playing nurse. By doing it your way—with you having the grace not to die on me—I've kept my friendship with Rupe. And I put a high value on it. No, McGee. Except for having to give up my own cabin, no hard feelings. How do you feel anyway? Strong?"

I checked and tested. "Better than I should."

"You look good. If you feel strong enough, I can send you down a little sample of our recreation program here aboard the *Hell's Belle*. Courtesy of the management. Name your favorite nurse, man."

"Joyce?"

The taut smile was gone. "Now you really are a smart-ass, you know that? I know damned well you know that girl's arrangement aboard, because she told me about talking to you."

"I thought maybe she'd made her decision."

"And you were curious? I wouldn't want you aboard long. You'd make too much mischief. Nobody puts any kind of pressure on that kid. She works it out for herself. She makes her own decisions."

"What will she decide?"

Mickey Laneer stood up, looking weary and cynical. "She'll decide that every other choice she has is worse. I'll send your breakfast."

Teddie brought my breakfast. She was the big, creamy, Minnesota Swede who had learned her sailing on Lake Superior. She was the one who giggled. Her hair was sea-weathered to a harsh spill of pure white hemp. From the bulge of bland forehead down to the clench of prehensile toes, she was tanned to the shade of macaroons. She giggled as she presented the tray with the menu she had devised. Two giant rum sours. A stack of toast. A platter of flying fish, perfectly sautéed and browned, crisp and sweet. A big enameled coffee pot and two of the stone mugs. She latched the door, giggling, and we had breakfast. She took the tray over to the table and came back, giggling. In the moist hollow of her throat, from earlobe to collarbone and across the socket in front, around to the other earlobe, she smelled exactly like fresh cinnamon and Pears' Soap.

The rendezvous was made about fifteen minutes past two, an estimated seven miles due west of Frigate Island. I convinced Mickey that there was no need to use the tender to transfer me. It was a freshening breeze, the sea running sparkling high. I said that though I didn't want to test my skull by diving, I could certainly swim a little. Rupe put the *Dulcinea* dead in the water, rocking in the trough, and hung the boarding ladder over. Mickey at the helm took the *Belle* across the *Dulcinea's* stern, laying her over so that as I sat on the lee rail and swung my legs around to the outboard side, my feet were but inches from the water.

I dropped and swam the fifty or sixty feet to the *Dulcinea,* bringing from the *Belle* no more than I had brought aboard—the swim trunks, leaving behind somewhere in the sea the scraps of nylon cord they had cut out of my flesh.

There was no hand extended to help me when I clambered aboard the *Dulcinea.* Rupe and Artie stood staring at the *Belle,* jaws slack, leathery paws dangling. Mickey saw no need to change the uniform regulations for an old friend like Rupe. Mickey showed off by taking the *Belle* fifty yards past us, coming about smartly, working hell out of her girls, and then coming back aslant, waving as she angled across our bows on a northeast course not over forty feet away. The girls shouted, grinned, laughed, and waved.

"Fool woman," Rupe said. "All sailor, that fool woman. Artie. Artie? ARTIE!"

"Huh? Me?"

"Bring in that boarding ladder and stow it right this time."

"Boarding ladder?"

"ARTIE!"

"Oh. Sure. Yessir, Rupe. Right away."

Rupe put the diesels back in gear, opened them up to full cruise, checked the chart and gave Artie the compass course, and left him at the wheel. We went below.

"Now what the *hell* is this all about, Trav?"

"It'll take some time."

"Time is what we've got the most of."

twenty

Rupe loaned me the money to get home, and Artie loaned me the clothes, a set of fresh khakis that fit better than I would have guessed from looking at him. I had to buy straw sandals at Kingstown on St. Vincent. Customs and immigration clearance was at San Juan, and I had an interesting time there. People are supposed to have papers and luggage, a wallet and a toothbrush.

They wanted to take my citizenship away from me. I told them it was a little misfortune at sea. I told them we could make some collect phone calls. When I said a magic name they could call collect, they came to attention. They almost smiled. That was on Sunday, the second day of May. I pulled the home number, unlisted, out of the damaged recesses of memory and got his wife, then got him. He talked to the boss immigration fellow, and when they were through, the boss immigration type felt a compulsion to pump my hand and call me sir and ask me if there was any little thing he could do, anything at all.

Before my flight left, I tried Meyer again, and this time he was aboard his boat, and when he heard and recognized my voice, he said in a shaky voice, "Thank God. Thank God." I told him what I needed and what to do and not to be so sentimental, anyway.

It was a bright, clear day to fly across the Bahamas and the incredible tones and shades of the Bahama flats. I wanted to think but not very much. I wasn't very sure about being able to think things through. I wanted to depend on Meyer. The weather across my internal landscape wasn't very good. Patches of gray, like drifting clouds, obscured things I wanted to see. And sometimes in a waking state I would have the same feeling, the same jolt as when you awaken from sleep. For a little while I would not know where I was or where the plane would land.

I got off that flight and walked through the lower level and out to vehicle pickup, and there was Meyer, bless him, standing beside a dark blue rental Ford as ordered. A very anonymous car. I told him he had better do the driving, as I was not entirely sure of the circuitry in my head. He drove. I talked. We selected a ma-and-pa motel on the way into Lauderdale on Route 1, and he got me a room in the back with an airconditioner that sounded like an air hammer breaking up paving. I finished the story in the room.

I unpacked the stuff Meyer had brought from the *Flush,* using that spare key I gave him, which he keeps hidden aboard the *Keynes.* He had packed some Plymouth, which seemed a kindly gesture. He went and got ice from the machine, and we drank from sleazy disposable glasses that looked as though they were about five-room-guests overdue for disposal.

I sat on the bed, sipping the clean, cool taste of juniper. Meyer paced and paced. He would stop in front of me to ask questions. "I'm not clear on one point. You *did* write the whole thing to Lennie Sibelius, telling him to get moving, open the inner envelope if you hadn't checked in by the end of May?"

"I did. But I told Lisa the tenth of May. I wrote to Lennie later. And I did not tell her who I wrote to, of course."

"She believed you?"

"She very definitely bought it. And she told Cousin Paul everything he wanted to know. Assumption: he believed her the way she believed me. But by the time he found out about the letter, he'd gone too far with both of us to start making deals. His next step was to make me talk to him. And he could have. I'm stubborn, Meyer. Need I mention it? The pain threshold is high, as measured on the dolorimeter. But I could have gotten so anxious to talk I would have fallen all over myself. He scares me. What was your reading on him?"

"Humble beginnings. Very bright, very reliable. Full scholarship to McGill. Went back to his village to work for the man who helped him. Worked for that man about three years, and then one of Waterbury's companies acquired the benefactor's business in a merger situation. Waterbury was impressed by Paul Dissat and took him into the Quebec headquarters. Dissat is thirty-six, single, conservative, devout Catholic. He doesn't drink or smoke. He's apparently managed his own savings very shrewdly. Handsome. Very fit. Superb skier and superior tennis player."

He paced and I sipped, and the airconditioner kept up its whangbangroaring, leaking condensation down the blue concrete-block wall.

He stopped in front of me, using his lectern mannerisms. "He functions very well in a highly pragmatic profession. He is perfectly aware of cause and effect. He can weigh the degree of risk he is willing to take. He will assume that the man who gets your letter will be competent. Can his whole plan stand determined investigation? No. Even without a link as weak as Harry Broll enough could be learned to bring it before a grand jury. What would this sort of scandal do to the SeaGate stock offering? It would come out that a fraud had been committed to get funds from a bank to pay for a preoffering block of stock. Waterbury could not afford to proceed. Both Jensen, Baker, and Fairmont, Noyes would recommend the applications be withdrawn. This would all happen, if your letter exists, with or without Paul Dissat on stage. See where I'm going?"

"I think so."

"With no public issue to raise money through the sale of stock, SeaGate comes to a shuddering halt. Harry's indivisible block becomes worthless. I can think of a Dissatlike solution."

"Grab the three hundred thousand from Harry?"

"Yes. But don't burn the bridges. Not all the way. Kill Harry because he is the last useful witness left alive. Then take a leave of absence on an emergency basis, somewhere out of touch. Lay back and listen. If there is no letter at all, if it was a bluff, then come back after the deadline and pick up the project again."

I toasted him. "To you, Meyer. If he has left already, I get the letter back from Sibelius, and we wait for him to reappear. If he's still here and working closer to the deadline of the tenth and if he hasn't gotten around to Harry, we pluck Harry away from him and take Harry to a private place and have a long chat about Mary and Lisa."

"If he has left, or is preparing to leave, and wants a door ajar so that he can get back just in case, then he'll have given Waterbury some sort of cover story, I imagine."

"Can we arrange a secret meeting with Waterbury?"

"Travis?"

"Why are you looking at me like that?"

"If we can't find Harry Broll anywhere and if Paul Dissat is still around and if Harry never did buy that block in SeaGate, even if Mary's body is dug up and identified, there's no way you can get Paul indicted. You probably can't even get him fired."

"He's got pretty legs."

"I don't want you to do some damned idiot thing."

"Long black eyelashes, Meyer. Red lips."

"Travis!"

"Maybe I want to dance with him. Maybe I want to whisper in his ear. But I don't want to have him come to me. You see, he's a careful man. He knows I'll come back if I didn't drown. That's why I told you to be careful about being seen going aboard the *Flush*. Am I overreacting?"

"No. You are not overreacting."

"Don't let him get to you, Meyer, when he starts looking for that letter."

"I've never seen you like this."

"He scrambled my brains. We should get away. I know a great cruise we could take."

"A cruise! A cruise?"

"It's different. I'll tell you about it later."

"Do that. There's been no report of Mary Broll's death from Grenada. It's taking a long time."

"A guest is charged for the cottage whether she uses it or not and charged for the food whether she uses it or not. And in the absence of a body it is the kind of island where, if a lady gets invited aboard a yacht for cocktails or up into the hills to an estate for cocktails, a lady could decide to spend a week being entertained. It is, shall we say, an impulsive place. A carefree isle."

"I phoned Mr. Willow last Wednesday. He got the cable from Mrs. Broll on Monday, and he talked with Harry Broll on Monday. On Tuesday morning he activated the loan papers and deposited the funds in Broll's personal account. I thought you'd like to know. That's when I started trying to get you on the phone. Wednesday, Thursday, Friday, Saturday. It was . . . pleasant to hear your voice."

"Paul sent the cable in her name. No problem. I should have realized how easily he could do that." I looked at Meyer's watch after first staring at my empty wrist for the thousandth time. "Five o'clock on Sunday afternoon. About the only thing we can do is try to find Harry."

"How?"

"There is a name in the back of this scrambled skull. All the file cards are spilled on the floor. Let me crawl around back there for a minute."

I retrieved the red-brown hair, pale green eyes, the vital and expressive face, the lean, quick-moving body. I let her walk around and smile, and then I knew her. "Jeannie Dolan of 8553 Ocean Boulevard." I hitched along the bed and got her number from information and called her.

"Who?" she asked in a sleepy voice.

"McGee. The guy with the blue Rolls pickup."

"Hey! It's you! I'd about decided I hadn't made any kind of dent on you at all. And that doesn't help a girl's pride. Where are you? Ask me out and then sweat out about three minutes of girlish reluctance and then come and get me, huh?"

"I am going to do exactly that later on, but right now I can't do any stirring around."

"Oh! Are you sick?"

"Not too sick to take you out, Jeannie. But I am trying to give the impression of being out of town. For good reasons."

"Okay. I'm not even talking to you. I will go around saying, 'Whatever happened to good old whosis?' "

"You are one nice lady."

"Rrrr*right!*"

"For reasons I may tell you some day, right now I want to know how goes the course of true love and romance and convenience. Betsy and Harry."

"It isn't exactly a script Ali McGraw is going to want to star in. Right now Betsy is teed pretty good. He was real jumpy and mean last week, and Wednesday morning early, like five, he got a phone call. It woke her up, but she fell asleep, and then he's shaking her awake. It's just getting to be daylight, and he's dressed, and he's packed a suitcase. He tells her he's going away on business. By the time the front door slams, she has asked him where he's going and when he'll be back about three times—no answer. I told her I think she has been handed the personally engraved, natural-bristle brush and maybe she should move back down here onto four with me. She's been calling his office and getting brushed off there, too. She drove out there a couple of times, but there was no sign of his car. Maybe he is away on business. But it showed no consideration, the way he left."

"Sold any condominiums?"

"Not to that friend of yours. She never showed up. If she really exists."

"You are very suspicious of people."

"If you'd ever met my husband, you'd know why. He could walk into a phone booth and leave by a side door."

"I'm a sneaky type too, Jeanne."

"That's nice. It's what I'm used to."

"I'll be calling you soon."

"You do that, hon. Bye."

Meyer and I talked, establishing the new parameters. But it was like the game of guessing which fist contains the chess pawn. Harry had enough animal caution to know that if things went wrong for Paul Dissat, it was runaway time for Harry. So if it was Paul who phoned him, maybe Harry had started to run. Conversely, Paul would know Harry was shrewd enough to know when to run, and so if Paul gave Harry cause to run, he would make certain Harry wouldn't be able to.

"The money will be the clue," Meyer said. "The first thing in the morning, as soon as the bank is open. I don't think it was paid over to SeaGate. And I don't think it's still in the bank."

"How do you manage that?"

Meyer smiled an unexpectedly unkindly smile. "By almost giving Woodrow Willow a coronary. He deserves a jolt. One should not be able to con a trust officer out of any assets held in trust."

"I'm coming along."

"Do you think you—"

"In the disguise you're going to go out and buy me at Happy Sam's Giant Superstore Open Always Practically."

"And on the way back here I buy pizza and beer to go?"

The lobby of the Southern National Bank and Trust Company takes up half of the ground floor of their new building on Biscayne. It is like three football fields. People at the far end are midgets, scurrying around in the cathedral lighting. The carpeting is soft and thick, dividing the lobby into function areas through the use of colors. Coral, lime, turquoise. The bank colors are pale blue and gold. The girls wear little blue and gold bank jackets with the initials *SNB* on the pocket, curled into a fanciful logo, the same logo that's stitched into the carpet, mosaiced into the walls, embossed on the stationery, and watermarked into the checks. The male employees and officers up to ambassadorial rank wear pale blue and gold blazers. Everybody has been trained to smile at all times. The whole place looks like a huge, walk-in dental advertisment. There is probably also a bank song.

Meyer dropped me a block away, and while he found a parking space, I strolled back to the bank and went in. I wore a Hawaiian shirt, a straw ranch hat with a red band, a drugstore camera around my neck, sunglasses with big pale orange lenses.

A guard moved in from the side and asked if he could help me. I said I was meeting the little woman here because she had to cash a travelers check, probably to buy some more of those damn silly hotpants, and where would she go to cash travelers checks. He aimed me across a hundred yards of carpeting, under a forty-foot ceiling. Nobody else looked at me. Tourists are invisible, except to the man trying to sell them something. Otherwise, they are as alike as all the trees in the park. Only a botanist knows there is any difference between trees. Or an applegrower.

I kept moving, because if I stood still, one of the guards would come over and ask me if he could help me. I did not know how long it would take. Meyer said he would come in from the north side corridor after going up to the trust department and coming back down with Mr. Willow. Also, I kept moving because I wanted to make certain that by no ten-thousand-to-one chance was Cousin Paul doing a little banking business this hot, windy Monday morning. Sometimes his face would be completely gone from memory, and that would frighten me. Then it would pop back like a slide coming into automatic focus.

At long last I saw Meyer coming toward me, striding right along, and I guessed that was Mr. Woodrow Willow a half step to the rear. I watched Meyer. He was going to rub his nose if he wanted me to join the act. He looked through me and did not see me at all. Woodrow Willow was not what I expected. This was a young man, tall, fresh-faced, snub-nosed, round-headed with the same mouth old Walt used to draw on his chipmunks. I sauntered after them, and caught up when they talked to a man who had his own big blond desk in a solitary, private thirty-by-thirty area of coral carpet right out in the midst of everything. The man used a phone. Soon a rangy woman came over walking like one of those heel-and-toe competitors, elbows pointed outward. She listened. She picked up the phone. A far younger girl came, carrying a ledger card. She jogged. Every part of her jogged.

After she left, Meyer shook hands with the man at the desk, and Meyer, Willow, and the rangy woman walked all the way across to a line of teller's stations on the far side of the bank. The rangy woman spoke to a slender girl with brown hair. Then she spoke to a man patrolling behind the cages. The slender girl closed her window and came around and out onto the bank floor. Meyer turned toward me and rubbed his nose. The rangy woman was leaving.

I walked up, and Meyer said, "Mr. Willow, this is my associate, Mr. McGee. McGee, may I present Miss Kathy Marcus."

"Who *is* this person?" Willow said in a voice of despair. "Good God, I had no idea you were going to bring in—"

"A place where we can talk?" Meyer said. "Just to have Kathy tell us in her own words before we get into anything else. Then we won't be taking up so much of her time."

"Take a lot," she said. "I've got a three-dollar short that's driving me up the wall."

"We'd better use one of the small conference rooms upstairs," Willow said.

Upstairs was 1910 banking, as opposed to the 1984 version in the lobby. Oak paneling, green rugs, leather libraries. The computers were hidden off-stage. Park your Mercer under the elm trees and come in and talk about buying a block of Postal Telegraph.

There were six chairs around the table in the small conference room. There were two framed prints of clipper ships and a seventeen-pound glass ashtray on the polished walnut. As soon as the door was shut, I shed the ranch hat, shades, and camera.

"Enjoying your stay?" Kathy asked me with a quick wink.

"Little gal, when I come across those Everglades in that big old airconditioned Greyhound bus, I said to the little woman, I said, Mother, we shoulda—"

Kathy guffawed, stopping me. Willow rang the big glass ashtray with his pipe in authoritarian tempo, silencing everybody. "Please! This is a very serious matter. If I have your attention, Miss Marcus, we would like to find out to what extent you are involved—"

"Whoa, friend," she said sharply, no laughter in her voice or her level stare.

"Now you will *listen* to me, Miss Marcus! I was saying—"

She got up and went to the door and smiled and said, "When you go home to the wife and kiddies tonight, Woodie, tell her that nice Miss Marcus quit the bank and went right down the street to another bank. Some loyalty, huh?"

"Come back and—"

"Woodie dear, the banks are so hard up for anybody who is worth a damn, it's pathetic. They've been hiring people here if they're ambulatory and feel warm to the touch. And I am one very damned good teller, and I have been here four years, and I am not now, nor have I ever been, *involved* in anything hanky or panky."

"Please, come back and—"

"Woodie dear, you just can't have it both ways. You can't call me Kathy and fun around with me when we're alone in an elevator and give me a friendly little grab in the ass and a chummy little arm pressure on the tit and then expect me to sit meek and mild in front of these gentlemen and take some kind of accusatory shit from you. No thanks. I'll tell them downstairs who ran me out of this bank."

"Kathy," he said.

With her hand on the knob she looked at him with narrowed eyes and said, "That's a start at least. Say the rest of it."

"I'm sorry. I didn't mean to imply—"

"Do you want me to come back and sit down, Woodie?"

"Please. I would appreciate it very much."

She came slowly back to the chair, sat, and smiled and said, "If these men had been strangers, Woodie, I would have let you go on being a jackass, and I would have cooked you later. But I'm among friends. Friends who rescued an eerie blonde from the oldest floating houseparty in the world."

"I remember already," Meyer said.

I looked at her more closely. "Delmonica Pennypacker?"

"Just a little name I made up for my vacation. Anyway, as I understand it, Woodie, you want a play-by-play account of cashing the check for Mr. Harry Broll."

Woodrow Willow was coming out of shock. He cleared his throat and told how a Mr. Winkler, a vice president of the bank, had received a telephone request last Wednesday at closing time from Harry Broll, stating that he would be in at about eleven on Thursday to cash a check for three hundred thousand on his personal account. He wanted to make certain the bank would have cash available in hundred-dollar bills. This is not an unusual request in an area where large real estate deals are made.

Kathy took over and said, "The way our system works, everything has to go through teller records, or we're out of balance. The cashier is Herman Falck, and I suppose Mr. Winkler told Herm to have the cash on hand. Herm told me he would run it through my balance, and he said Mr. Broll would probably bring in a dispatch case for the money. That amount would fit with no trouble. We run a minimum cash balance in the drawer at all times to make the place less appealing to the knockover boys. We signal the vault for more cash or to come make a pickup when we get too fat. They come zipping in a little electric money cart.

"So at ten after eleven Herm brings these two men over to me. I put out my closed sign so that a line won't build behind them. He takes the dispatch case from the man with Mr. Broll and hands it around to me. Mr. Broll gives me the check, and Herm initials it. Then Herm goes back and brings the cash cart behind the cage. It's just a matter of packing the sixty wrapped stacks of hundreds into the case. A black plastic case, imitation lizard. I counted them out as I packed them. Five, ten, fifteen, on up to three hundred. The case was below eye-level looking from the floor of the bank. I snapped the snaps and slid it up onto the counter, and the other man took it, and they walked away."

"Had you ever seen Mr. Broll before?" I asked.

"I think so. He looked sort of familiar. Maybe I waited on him. The name seems familiar."

"How did he act?"

"Well, I guess he's really a pretty sick man. I don't think he could have managed without the other man helping him."

"In what way did he seem to you to be sick?"

"Well, he was very sweaty. His complexion was gray, and his face was wet. He kind of wheezed. Like asthma sometimes. He didn't have much to say. Usually, men joke about lots of money when they put it in or take it out. They joke with me because I'm all girl, I guess. His friend had to kind of support him walking to my window, I noticed. Mr. Broll walked slowly, a little bent over and taking small steps. His friend was very nice to him. Considerate."

"What did his friend look like?"

"Younger. Dark curly hair. Tall. Middle thirties, I'd guess. A very nice voice. Some kind of accent. Marvelous clothes. Conservative mod. But he was too pretty for my taste. Husky pretty. Great eyelashes. He called Mr. Broll 'Harry,' but Mr. Broll didn't call him anything. Let me help you, Harry. Here, let me take that, Harry. Come on, there's no hurry, Harry. Take your time, old man. It took them a long time to walk to the main doors. The fellow helped Mr. Broll and carried the dispatch case. I watched them. They didn't go right out. I guess Mr. Broll felt faint, because they stopped and sat down in that lounge area left of the main doors. It made me uneasy. You like to see three hundred thousand get to where it has to go and get locked up again. They sat side by side on the couch. I could see the fellow leaning toward Mr. Broll and talking quietly and confidentially. I saw Mr. Broll put his hand over his eyes. The other man pulled it away and took his handkerchief and wiped Mr. Broll's face, wiping the sweat away, I guess." She frowned. "Maybe I shouldn't say this, but the whole scene had a funny flavor. It seemed faggoty to me, like a wife with a sick husband. . . . No. The other way around. A youngish husband with kind of a fat, sick old wife he doesn't really love but feels sort of affection and gratitude and . . . a sense of duty to, if I don't sound flippy."

"Not flippy at all."

"I was busy, and when I looked again, they were gone. I would guess it was about twenty minutes before noon when they left the bank together."

Willow said, "Would you say Mr. Broll was drunk or drugged?"

She thought it over. "No. He kept his eyes sort of squinted up. He knew what he was doing. He just seemed . . . fragile. As if he was in terrible pain. As if he had the world's worst bellyache and was wondering if he was going to pass out with it. And . . . he smelled sort of sour. He was wrinkled, and he had beard stubble. I wondered if he'd been traveling all night or he'd slept in his clothes. I suppose it *could* have been the world's worst hangover."

"Thank you, Miss Marcus," Willow said. "Uh . . . Kathy."

"That means take off, huh?"

"With our thanks, Kathy," Meyer said. "You are a bright girl and a good observer. And if it ever becomes possible to tell you anything about this whole matter, we will."

"Thank *you*," Kathy said. She paused at the door and said, "McGee, do you still have that wild floating pad?"

"The Busted Flush. Slip F-18."

"I'll come visit. If you haven't gotten married up."

"Come visit, Kathy. Bring your swim pants."

"I'll bring a bowl of Greek salad. I make one hell of a Greek salad."

When the door shut, Willow said, "Good help is so terribly hard to find and hard to keep that one has to . . . uh . . . put up with a degree of impertinence that . . . uh . . . ."

"Like she said, Woodie," I told him, "it's a lot easier to get respect from the pretty ones if you don't keep grabbing them by the ass in the elevator. Right, Meyer?"

"Absolutely right. An executive can't have it both ways."

"Keep the pretty ones at a distance," I said. "Grab the dog-faced ones by the ass. Then you have a happy bank."

"A contented bank," Meyer said.

"Goddammit," Willow yelled. "Tell me what this is all about!"

Meyer said, "I'll ask you the same question I asked you before, Woodrow. Could you swear that you were absolutely, positively certain that Mary Broll was alive when you processed that loan?"

"The answer is still the same. But why are you asking the question?"

"I'll ask you another. What was Harry Broll going to use the money for?"

"To buy the SeaGate stock, to pay the balance due of three hundred thousand. Don't look at me like that. It's legal, you know. It is illegal to borrow money to buy *listed* securities."

"He'd lose a great opportunity if he didn't buy the block of stock?"

"Oh, yes! Really great."

"Would he have to have cash to buy that stock, Woodrow?"

"Of course not! A certified check would—"

"Do you think he bought it?"

"I don't know."

"Can you think of any way of finding out?"

"Don't go away."

We were left alone. Meyer sighed. I told him he was pushing Woodie around beautifully. All he did was sigh again. When Meyer gets the silents, he isn't very good company.

twenty-one

As Meyer drove conservatively back toward Lauderdale in fast traffic, he said, "We can summarize what we know, if you think it will help."

"You do it, and I'll tell you if it helps."

"We do not care whether Harry Broll was running from Dissat or hurrying to meet him. Immaterial. Dissat had him from some unknown hour early Wednesday morning until they walked into the bank Thursday at ten after eleven. By three o'clock Wednesday afternoon Harry Broll was forced to make the phone call to Mr. Winkler about the large cash withdrawal. Dissat had to then sustain Broll on that depressed level where he could make his appearance at the bank without creating suspicion, yet would have no interest in appealing for help. Total emotional and physical defeat. A person reduced to Harry Broll's condition is beyond feeling terror. Only despair. The only part left would be the details of disposal, or if he'd already planned how to do it, to go ahead with it. If it required darkness, he would have to have a place to take Broll to wait for night, or better yet, a place to immobilize him safely so Dissat could put in an appearance elsewhere. If we are building the structure of limitation, the parameters of time and space, we need to know if Dissat appeared at the West Palm office on Wednesday, and if he did, the time spent there."

"And where he is right now," I said. "When I wonder where he is right now, I wonder if he's crouched on the floor behind us. That's what he does to me, Meyer. Sorry. He was so *pleased* with himself, so damned *delighted*

219

when he reached out with his bare toes and turned her head so she looked at me with those empty, crazy eyes. It was a funny kind of innocent pleasure, as if he had no idea there was anything really wrong about it. He was like a little kid who'd built a kite that would fly, and he wanted me to tell him how great it was. He tried to talk tough. Movie tough. But it was like something that had to be said. An obligatory part of the ceremony. After that we were going to share something, he and I. Some special personal important relationship. Dammit, I can't say it so that you can understand how it was."

"He fits the pattern of a certain kind of damaged personality I have read about, Travis. He could be called the activated sociopath sadist. Bright, healthy, energetic, competent. Excellent in areas requiring ritual. Mathematics, accounting, engineering. Quite cold inside. Tricky. Unable to concede the humanity of people around them because, having no basis of comparison, they think all of us have their same dry and barren soul. They are loners. They can charm when they choose. Sexually stunted, inhibited, often impotent. When Mary tried to escape from him and he caught her and they fell badly and injured her seriously, that activated him. Now he knows what he wants. He wants inventive episodes like the one with Lisa. The money will be meaningful only in how many such episodes it will buy. He isn't aware of evil. Only of being caught. You have to think of him as a bored child who suddenly discovers that it is wonderful fun to go to the pet store and buy a mouse and bring it home and do things to it until it is dead. Life is no longer boring. It is full of rich and wonderful excitement. The mouse shares the experience, so he feels fond of the mouse for as long as it lasts. You could say that the child loves the mouse to the extent he can feel love."

"Jesus!"

"I know. Stroking Lisa's forehead, drying Harry's sweaty face, are imitations of emotion. We can imagine he spoke tender words to Mary because she was pleasing him, giving him release. He's not a madman in any traditional sense. He cannot feel guilt or shame. If caught, he would feel fury and indignation at the game ending too soon. He'll go to great lengths to stay free, unsuspected. His career is a lot less important to him than it used to be. My guess is he'll be gone by the deadline, the tenth, a week from today."

We rode in silence for a time. "Meyer? How did you get that Woodie Woodchuck to snap to attention?

"By reminding him that he had informed me of the approximate value of the assets in one of his trust accounts without any authorization from the trust customer or the senior trust officer. Banks take all confidential relationships very seriously. He soon said he would be very happy to help me find out all about the three hundred thousand."

"How did he find out Harry had forfeited his option?"

"I don't know. Probably phoned a contact at SeaGate and asked what value, as collateral, Harry's hundred-thousand-share block would have. The stuff is too closely held to have an OTC quote."

"Couldn't he have borrowed against the stock he was going to get?"

"Not if he had already done so."

"Sick condominiums and a sick construction business. How about the seven hundred thousand he's supposed to get back from SeaGate?"

"If it went into land improvements at the site, then I guess he'd have to wait until the public issue money comes back to SeaGate."

"So that goes to pay off other debts, and then Harry's business quietly fades away and dies?"

"Reasonable guess."

"He had to take Harry somewhere and keep him there. Harry and Harry's car. Transportation problems, Meyer. Logistics and tactics. If he took him to wherever he lives—"

"A cluster apartment complex at West Palm on the bay shore. Rental apartments. Not likely."

"I suppose you have his phone number?"

"You asked me to check him out. Remember?"

"And your overall impression?"

"A very dull fellow, competent and humorless."

"You know the name of the cluster apartments?"

"I'd rather not say it. Palm Vista Gardens. D-2."

"The first phone booth after we get off the pike, please."

He parked at a gas station by a shiny row of vending machines under a roof made of plastic thatch, incredibly green. I phoned from the hotbox provided by Gen Tel out on the cement wasteland. I hoped Palm Vista Gardens was big enough to have a rental and administration office on the premises. It was. The lady's voice came right from the resonant bridge of her Indiana nose.

"Yes, maybe you *can* help me. Have you got any furnished one-bedroom vacancies?"

She was not a well-organized lady. She tended to ramble. She gave information and then with cries of dismay retracted it and called herself names, mostly "old fool."

She finally discovered that one of their renters, "a nice young man" who had been on the special month-to-month basis with one month in advance (an arrangement they made with the "nice young people" from that new Sea-Gate company) had come in on the last day of April, just last Friday, and given his notice. He said he was vacating in a week. And that would make it . . . the eighth? No. The seventh. Yes. Next Friday. They could start showing it again the following Monday if there wasn't too much to be done. That was number D-2, which meant apartment 2 in cluster D. Just stop at the office. But don't wait too long. They go very quickly to nice young people, providing they don't have any pets. Or any babies, of course. I wondered how they felt about noisy goldfish, the kind that do a lot of leaping and splashing and churning around.

I tried to blot out all rational thought with a lot of peripheral items. Goldfish. Lead-free gasoline. Diminishing aquifer. I walked to the car, realizing I had left the cheap camera on the back seat. An essential part of my tourist costume. Meyer stood beside the rental car, drinking a can of orange pop, and it suddenly seemed insane that Meyer wore no tourist disguise. Paul Dissat knew exactly who I was and where I lived. And if he had gone to Bahia Mar and poked around as such a thorough chap would, he would have learned that Meyer was associated with me in certain obscure but apparently profitable ventures. Though believing me safely drowned off Grenada's lovely beaches, he might conclude that it was a very good chance my letter of self-insurance had been sent to Meyer to stow in a safe place. And so, as a percentage play . . .

It worked on me to the point that Meyer stared at me and said, "What the hell is wrong, Trav?"

My mouth wasn't going to work. Alarm is contagious. He trotted around and got behind the wheel, whipped us out into the traffic flow with a good imitation of teenage technique. At last I managed two words. "No hurry."

I saved the rest of it for my rackety motel unit. I tried to smile at Meyer. "Pure chicken. Sorry. I just don't know what the hell is . . ." Then I felt the sudden and humiliating sting of tears in my eyes and turned quickly to blink them away before Meyer could see them.

I stood with my back to him, staring out between the slats of the battered tin blinds at the side wall of a restaurant and a row of trashcans haloed with bluebottled buzzing. I spoke too fast and chuckled where there was no need, saying, "It's the old bit of the brave and noble hunter, gliding silently through the jungle, following the track of the big black panther, and slowly beginning to realize that the panther is also a-hunting and maybe he's flattened out on top of that thick limb up ahead or behind that bush over there or in the shadow of that fallen tree, with just the tip of his thick glossy black tail moving and the shoulder muscles rippling and tightening under that black hide. I'm spooked because I kept telling myself the son of a bitch would be gone by now, but he isn't going until Friday, and—"

"Travis. Come on. Slow down."

Can't ever really fool ol' Meyer. I sat on the bed. We're all children. We invent the adult facade and don it and try to keep the buttons and the medals polished. We're all trying to give such a good imitation of being an adult that the real adults in the world won't catch on. Each of us takes up those shticks that compose the adult image we seek. I'd gone the route of lazy, ironic bravado, of amiable, unaffiliated insouciance. Tinhorn knights of a stumbling Rosinante from Rent-A-Steed, maybe with one little area of the heart so pinched, so parched, I never dared let anything really lasting happen to me. Or dared admit the flaw. Maybe in some crazy way Paul Dissat was a fun-house mirror image of me, a warped McGee with backspin, reverse English.

The adult you pretend to be convinces himself that the risk is worth the game, the game worth the risk. Tells himself the choice of life style could get him killed—on the Daytona track, in the bull ring, falling from the raw steel framework forty stories up, catching a rodeo hoof in the side of the head.

Adult pretenses are never a perfect fit for the child underneath, and when there is the presentiment of death, like a hard black light making panther eyes glow in the back of the cave, the cry is, "Mommy, mommy, mommy, it's so dark out there, so dark and so forever."

Cojones are such a cultural imperative, the man who feels suddenly deballed feels shame at reentering the childhood condition. Papa Hemingway will never take him fishing. George Patton will slap his face.

In all my approximately seventy-six inches of torn and mended flesh and hide, in all approximately fifteen-stone weight of meat, bone, and dismay, I sat on that damned bed and felt degraded. I was unmasked as a grotesque imitation of what I had believed myself to be.

Frowning, I tried to explain it in halting fashion to Meyer. "You talked about . . . the reflexes slowing, the warning system not working; the instincts inaccurate when . . . the only reason Harry Broll didn't kill me was because he lacked one more round in the clip. Then in Grenada I didn't even think of being careful . . . didn't sense his presence, got such a shot in the skull bone my head is still blurred. Meyer, people have been a few steps ahead of me other times. I've played pretty good catchup. This time I have this feeling that there's no way. He's going to stay out in front, and if I get too close, he'll turn around and take care of the problem. Maybe I've gotten too close already, and I have ten more minutes or ten more hours."

"Travis."

"I know. I'm scared. It's like being very very cold. I can't move well, and I can't think at all."

"So I do the thinking?"

"I wish you would. Don't go back to your boat. I have a very ugly hunch about your boat."

"We have to talk to Dennis Waterbury in absolute privacy, and I have to make contact in such a way that he will trust us to the limited extent that rich and powerful people can trust anyone."

"Can you do it?"

"I don't know. I have to try to reach some people by phone. In Montreal and Toronto and Quebec."

"Start trying."

"If I can get through to someone he knows and trusts, who can tell him I am reputable, not a shakedown artist, then we are going to give him whatever lead time we can spare before I go to the law."

"With what?"

"With enough. Woodrow Willow's contact said Broll didn't buy the stock. So there's a missing three hundred thousand and a missing Harry Broll. If they dig around the seawall at Blue Heron Lane, they'll find Mary's body. Kathy Marcus and the other bank people could pick Paul Dissat out of a lineup. Maybe it will sink the SeaGate public issue without a trace. Even if Dissat never took a penny from the Waterbury enterprises, a breath of scandal can make the accounting firm and the underwriters back off."

"So why don't we go to the law? Why do we screw around with Waterbury if we've got all this?"

"Think about it, Travis. Think about it."

I instinctively fingered the place on the back of my skull where I had been so soundly thumped. Meyer was right. SeaGate was a very large thing, and Dissat was an operating officer in the SeaGate power structure. The lower echelons of the law would never go cantering into battle on the say-so of an apparently unemployed beach bum and a semiretired and eccentric economist. It was a two-county operation with both state and federal implications. Lower echelons would take the eccentric pair into skeptical custody and sweat them both.

Suppose you go to the top level, such as approaching the United States attorney in the area and suggesting he refer the problem to the FBI for investigation because of possible violations of the criminal code insofar as banking regulations are concerned. Then the approach would be made so tentatively—due to the SeaGate clout and the dubious source of the tip—that Dissat would be alerted, and he would disappear into his large countryside or ours.

First, you sell Dennis Waterbury on the idea that his boy, Paul Dissat, has been a very very bad boy lately and any publicity given his activities can founder the SeaGate plans. You convince him and give him some facts he can quietly check. You speak to him in absolute privacy and secrecy. Then, when *he* picks up the phone and relays his unhappy suspicions to the highest level, Dissat will be pounced upon first and investigated later, giving Waterbury additional time to plug up the holes and protect the upcoming public issue from scandal.

I said, "Okay. Do you think I'll ever be able to think things out for myself any more? Or will you have to be on permanent standby?"

"I think they start you on baskets and work up to needlepoint."

"I am supposed to laugh. All right, Meyer. Ha ha ha. Make your phone calls. What if the bastard won't listen even if we can get him alone?"

"Men who are rich have times when they don't listen. Men who are quite bright have times when they don't listen. Men who are both bright and rich *always* listen. That is how they got the money, and that is how they keep it."

"Then do we go to Canada, or does he come here?"

"He's here now. I found that out when I was learning all I could about Paul Dissat. Waterbury is in a guest cottage on a Palm Beach estate. The owners are in Maine now, but they left enough staff to take care of Waterbury. Pool, tennis courts, security system, private beach."

He started making calls. He had to push the thermostat high enough to kill the compressor before he could hear. I lay a-doze, hearing his voice come from metallic distances, sounding like the voices of grownups when I had been a child half-asleep in a moving car or train.

twenty-two

He found an old friend at last, a Professor Danielson in Toronto, who knew Waterbury well and was willing to try to set it up. Meyer gave Danielson the motel number and unit number and asked to have Waterbury phone him as soon as convenient. If Danielson found that Waterbury was unable or unwilling to phone Meyer for a secret meeting, Danielson would phone back.

Nothing to do but wait and try to digest a roast beef sandwich which lay in my stomach like a dead armadillo. The motel television was on the cable. We turned the sound off and watched the news on the electronic printer, going by at a pace for a retarded fifth grader, white on black printing with so many typos the spelling was more like third grade than fifth.

The woes of the world inched up the screen. Droughts and murders. Inflation and balance of payments. Drugs and demonstrations. Body counts and new juntas.

Spiro was dead wrong. The trouble with the news is that everybody knows everything too fast and too often and too many times. News has always been bad. The tiger that lives in the forest just ate your wife and kids, Joe. There are no fat grub worms under the rotten logs this year, Al. Those sickies in the village on the other side of the mountain are training hairy mammoths to stomp us flat, Pete. They nailed up two thieves and one crackpot, Mary. So devote wire service people and network people and syndication people to gathering up all the bad news they can possibly dredge and comb and scrape out of a news-tired world and have them spray it back at everybody in con-

228

stant streams of electrons, and two things happen. First, we all stop listening, so they have to make it ever more horrendous to capture our attention. Secondly, we all become even more convinced that everything has gone rotten, and there is no hope at all, no hope at all. In a world of no hope the motto is *semper fidelis,* which means in translation, "Every week is screw-your-buddy week and his wife too, if he's out of town."

The phone rang, and Meyer sprang up and cut off the compressor and took the call. He made a circle of thumb and finger to tell me we had gotten through the corporate curtain. He listened for several minutes, nodded, and said, "Yes, thank you, we'll be there." Hung up.

"A Miss Caroline Stoddard, Mr. Waterbury's private secretary. We're to meet with him out at the site at Sea-Gate. We go through the main entrance and follow little orange arrows on sticks that will lead us to the storage and warehouse area. There are two small contracts going on now out there. Earth moving and paving. They stop work at four, and the crews leave. The area is patrolled at night, and the guard shift starts at eight at this time of year. Mr. Waterbury will meet with us at an office out there in the end of one of the warehouses behind the hurricane fencing near the vehicle park and the asphalt plant. We can find the place by looking for his car. If we meet him out there at five, we should have plenty of time for uninterrupted talk."

We got to the area a little early, so we drove down A-1-A for a little way, and when we found a gap in the sour commercial honky-tonk, Meyer pulled over. Down the beach there was a cluster of fat-tire beach buggies, some people swimming. Meyer and I were walking and talking over our plans when a chunky trail bike came growling up behind us, passed us, and cut in and stopped, and a fellow with enough black beard to stuff a small pillow glowered at us and gunned the bike engine. He looked very fit and unfriendly.

"You've got a problem?" I asked.

"You are the guys with problems. How come there are

so many of you characters so cramped up you got to come
creeping around to stare at naked people?"

"Where, where, where!" Meyer said, smiling. "If it's required, I'll stare. But as a rule, it's dull. If you have some
graceful young girls cavorting, that is an aesthetic pleasure
for a certain amount of time. Doesn't sand get into the
working parts of that thing?"

Meyer is disarming. Maybe a completely frantic flip,
stoned blind, could run a knife into him. Otherwise, the
belligerent simmer down quickly.

"It's sealed so it doesn't happen too bad. But you can
mess it up if you try. I thought you were more guys with
binoculars, like the last pair. See, if you walk down this
way far enough, then you can see around the end of the
buggy and see the girls."

Meyer said, "Excuse me, but I was of the impression
that the current belief is that the flaunting of the natural body cures the woes of society by blowing the minds of
the repressed."

"A lot of people think that way. But we're opposed to
the brazen display of the body and public sexuality. We're
here on a pilgrimage mission for the Church of Christ in
the Highest. And we have permission to camp on this part
of the beach while we're bringing the word of God to the
young people in this area."

"Wouldn't it be a lot easier to cover those girls up?" I
asked him.

"Four of our sisters have got the crabs, sir, and they are
using the salt water and the sunshine to cure them. The
drugstore stuff didn't work at all, hardly."

Meyer said, "I have worked and studied in primitive
countries, and I have caught about every kind of body
louse a bountiful nature provides. And I have yet to contract a case that did not respond immediately to plain old
vinegar. Have your girls soak their heads, armpits, and
their private parts in vinegar. It kills the crabs and kills the
eggs, and the itching stops almost immediately."

"You wouldn't kid me?" the beard asked.

"It is the most useful and generally unknown information in the modern world."

"They've been going up the walls. Hey. Thanks. And God bless you guys."

He roared away. I told Meyer he was fantastic. Meyer said that my continual adulation made him uncomfortable, and it was time to see The Man.

We turned around, and where A-1-A curved west, away from the Atlantic beach, Meyer drove straight, down a road that was all crushed shell, ruts, and potholes, and marked private. Soon we came to the entrance pillars, a huge billboard telling of the fantastic city of the future that would rise upon the eleven square miles of sandy waste, where no child need cross a highway to get to school, where everything would be recycled (presumably vitiating any need for cemetery zoning), where clean industry would employ clean, smiling people, where nothing would rust, rot, or decay, where age would not wither nor custom stale the fixed, maniacal smiles on the plastic faces of the future multitude who here would dwell.

Once past the entrance pillars we were on a black velvet vehicle strip (trucks stay to right, off blacktop) which restored to the rental Ford the youth and ease it had lost during a few months, a few thousand miles of being warped, rocked, and crowded by the dozens of temporary owners.

We followed the small, plastic orange arrows and saw some yellow and green and blue arrows on yard-tall sticks marching in other directions, forming a routing code for workmen, planners, delivery people. A small sign in front of a wilderness of dwarf palmetto said starkly: SHOPPING PLAZA E   400,000 SQ. FT. ENCL. Yes, indeed. A multilevel, automated, air-controlled, musicated selling machine, where—to the violins of Mantovani and the chain gang shuffle of the housewife sandals—only those processed foods would be offered which the computer approved of as being saleable in billion-unit production runs.

We turned away from the sea and against the glare of the high western sun saw the construction headquarters, the belly and stack and hoppers of a portable asphalt plant, saw the trucks and spreaders, piles of aggregate, loader, and loading ramp. That area outside the warehouse and office compound enclosed by hurricane fencing was deserted, as if a flock of Seabees had slapped blacktop on it and been airlifted out. There was a big, vehicle gate in the hurricane fencing, and it stood wide open. In the fenced area were some above-ground fuel tanks and pumps for the vehicles, outdoor storage of some unidentifiable crated items, a generator building, and six small prefab steel warehouses backed up against a truck loading dock. A dark green Lincoln Continental limousine was parked by the next to the last warehouse.

Meyer parked nearby, and we got out. Meyer said in a low voice, "He'll be tempted to think it's some kind of a shakedown. Give us money, and we'll keep quiet about Dissat and let the public issue go through. But Danielson says Waterbury is honest by choice, not as a matter of necessity or operating policy."

There were three crude steps up to the crossbraced plywood door. It stood a few inches ajar, the hasp folded back, a thick padlock opened, hanging from the U-bolt in the door frame.

I gave the door a couple of thumps with the underside of my fist. It made a nice booming sound in the metal structure.

"Hello?" said a pleasantly feminine contralto voice, elusively familiar. "Are you the gentlemen who phoned? Come in, please."

It was dim inside. There were no windows at the end where we entered, only at the far end. We were on an elevated area with a floor made of decking with steps leading down to the slab floor of the warehouse proper. The office was at the far end. The air was very thick and still and hot in the warehouse portion, but I could hear the whine of airconditioning in the enclosed office at the far end.

"I'm Caroline Stoddard," she said. "So nice to see you again, Mr. McGee."

I located her off to the left, standing down on the lower level. At first I thought she was one very big secretary in some kind of slacks outfit, and I blinked again, and my eyes adjusted, and it was Paul Dissat. That odd feeling of having heard the voice before was because of the slight residual accent.

"Be very nice," he said in his normal voice, "and be *very* careful. This is a new automatic nailer. They use it to knock the forms together for footings and pilings and so on. That hose goes over there to that pressure tank, and the compressor is automatic, and the generator is on."

It seemed heavy, the way he held it. He turned it to the side and triggered it. It made a hard, explosive, phutting sound, and nails zinged off the concrete and whanged the metal wall twenty feet away. He turned it toward us again.

"I'm a bad shot," he said. "But these things spray. At more than six inches they begin to turn. They'd make a ghastly hamburger of your legs, I think. I don't know why I've always been a poor shot. I'm well coordinated otherwise. Harry was a fantastic marksman. I guess it must be a natural gift."

"Fantastic marksman?" I asked numbly.

"Didn't you know? You could throw three cans in the air, and with that silly little popgun of his he could hit each one of them twice before they hit the ground without even seeming to aim, just pointing at them by some kind of instinct."

"When he came to see me—"

"He was coming apart. I was having trouble keeping him quiet. He had to make some mock show of being terribly concerned about Mary so that later people could testify he was almost out of his mind with worry. He said you moved so quickly and startled him so badly, he nearly hit you in the foot."

"Where is Mr. Waterbury?" Meyer asked in a tired and wistful tone.

"Playing tennis, I should imagine. This is his time of day for it. Cool of the evening. When word came this morning of the request for information from Mr. Willow, I called him back and after a little hesitation he told me one McGee and one Meyer had initiated the request. Don't keep edging sideways, McGee! It was really a shock. I thought you dead. From drowning or brain damage. You

pranced like a sick, ugly stork, and you went floating out
at a incredible speed. You are very lucky and very hard to
kill."

"Where is Mr. Waterbury?" Meyer asked.

"You are a bore," Dissat told him. "I went to his emi-
nence and told him I had confidential information that two
sharpshooters were going to try to get a private audience
with him and try to frighten him into parting with money.
I gave him the names. He told me to handle the problem. I
handle a lot of problems for the man. When the information came in from Toronto, he had me take the call. Don't
you think limousines allay all suspicions? They're so symbolic. Sit on the floor slowly and carefully, Travis. That's
very good. Now, Meyer, make a wide circle around behind him and come down the steps. Fine. Walk over to
that coil of wire on the floor next to the pliers and stretch
out on your face with your head toward me. *Very* good.
Now, Travis, you can come down and go around Meyer
and kneel on the other side of him. Hold it. Now I want
you to wire your friend's wrists together and then his ankles. The better job you do, the better all three of us will
get along."

It was a heavy-gauge iron wire, quite soft and mallea-
ble. It was such dim light I felt I could do a fairly sloppy
job. Dissat moved back to the wall, and an overhead bank
of daylight fluorescent tubes winked on.

"You're doing a lot more talking, Paul," I said. "All
keyed up, aren't you? All nerves?"

"Pull that strand tight. There. That's fine. Let's say I'm
more talkative because you're more receptive. Would you
like to know how the wave action affected Lisa's body?"

"I bet it was fascinating."

"It was. I sat and watched the whole thing. After the
waves were breaking way in beyond where she was, the
outgoing wash started to scoop the sand out from around
her until she was almost uncovered. Finally she toppled
over onto her left side. Then the waves began digging the
sand out from under her, settling her lower and lower and
flowing and forming around her as it began covering her.
The very last thing I saw of her was her right shoulder,

and it looked like a little, shiny brown bowl upside down on the smooth sand. And then that disappeared, too. I imagine that on all beaches the sea is a scavenger, burying the sad, dead things and the ugly litter every time the tide comes and goes. Now one more turn *under* the other wrist and then twist it and cut it. Good!"

I wished the pliers were heavier. I rehearsed the motions in my mind. Whip the arm up and hurl the pliers at his face, falling forward at the same time to give the throw more velocity and also shield Meyer from the expected hail of nails. I could scramble forward and take the nails in the back and get to his ankles and yank his feet out from under him, provided no nail went head-deep into the spine. And provided he didn't swing the muzzle down fast enough to drive a close pattern into my skull.

I hesitated, thinking how badly I had missed Harry with the ashtray, and while I hesitated, Dissat moved, making plier-throwing a much worse risk.

He shifted the heavy nailer, swinging the pneumatic hose out of the way, much as a singer manipulates the mike cable. In the bright fluorescence he looked almost theatrically handsome. He was like a color still shot for those strange ads Canadian Club used to use. (I never knew how challenging it would be to hold two men captive with an automatic nailing device until I tried it.)

"Talkative?" he said. "Perhaps. Relief, I suppose. I've made a decision and simplified the future. Harry's money and mine make enough, you know. I've sent it to safe places. You two are the last loose ends. I'm taking sick leave. Actually, I'm retiring. Maintaining two identities compounds the risk factor. I told you in Grenada what I learned about myself from Mary Broll and poor Lisa. Now I shall have a chance to devote all my time to exploring it further. Very thoroughly. Very carefully. Mostly it's a matter of selecting people who might logically disappear of their own accord. I suppose the challenge excites me. So I talk a great deal, don't I? There's nothing I can reveal you can't guess, so it's not a help to you, is it? We shall explore the matter of the letter you sent from Grenada. As a matter of form. It isn't really important whether I learn about it or not, so I don't have to be awfully careful, do I? To keep everything tidy, I might leave with a traveling companion. A certain Mrs. Booker. Betsy. Would you know about her? Never mind. His ankles are finished? Walk backward on your knees. Further. Further. Right there. Sit down there, please, and wire your own ankles together, leaving a length of wire between them, the same length as the nylon cord that day on the little beach."

One uses any small frail idea. From handling the thick, soft wire I guessed that if one bent it back and forth enough times, it would snap. So I took a couple of turns around my ankles, tight enough to keep the wire from turning on my ankle. I made the binding turns, squeezed the wire knots with the plier jaws, nipped away what was left. With luck, management, and timing the wire might part at the squeezed place after enough steps.

He moved to stand over Meyer. He bent over and held the business end of the nailer almost touching the base of Meyer's spine. "I have this on single fire, McGee. Or single nail. If you can wire your own wrists nicely, I'll be so pleased with you, I'll give up the pleasure of finding out just how he'd react to one nail right here. Use ingenuity, McGee. Do a nice job. After Grenada, I take no chances with you."

I did a nice job. I was even able to nip off the extra wire by wedging the pliers between my forearm and the flooring. By holding my wrists together, exerting pressure, I could make it look as if there was no slack at all. Cheap little tricks never do any good at all, except to give the trickster false hope when he needs it.

Dissat came lithely over, bent, and inspected, kicked the pliers away with the edge of his foot. He grunted with satisfaction and walked over and put the nailer down beside the pressure tank, then swung and flexed his arms. "It got much too heavy," he said. He picked up a short, thick piece of metal. I thought it was steel pipe with a dull, gleaming finish, but as he walked toward Meyer, flipping it and catching it, I guessed from the way he handled it that it had to be very light metal, probably aluminum bar stock. It spun and smacked neatly into the palm of his hand each time.

"I don't even know what we use this for," he said. "There's a lot of it in the last warehouse. I've been taking an inventory personally, to check on pilferage of materials, small tools, and so on. That's where I kept Harry, in that warehouse. This piece just happens to have perfect weight and balance. I picked it up by accident the first time. After that, every time I picked it up, old Harry would start rolling his eyes like a horse in the bull ring."

He bent suddenly and took a quick swing, very wristy, and hit Meyer on the back of the right leg, just above the knee. It made an impact sound halfway between smack and thud. Meyer bucked his heavy frame completely off the floor and roared.

"See?" Paul said. "Heavier stock would crush bone and tissue, and lighter stuff would merely sting. I experimented with Harry and went a little too far. I whacked him across his big belly once too often and possibly ruptured something in there, God knows what. For a time neither of us thought he could walk into the bank for the money."

"I'll trade Meyer for all you want to know about the letter."

He looked at me owlishly. "*All* of Meyer? Alive and free? That's naive, you know. Meyer is dead, and you are dead. There's no choice now. I *could* trade you, say, the last fifteen minutes of Meyer's life for information about the letter. He would approve a deal like that when the time comes. But what would be the point? I'm not that interested in your letter, really. I learned a little bit from Mary and more from Lisa and a little more from Harry. Now I can check what I learned and learn a little more. Why should I deprive myself?"

"Why indeed?" Meyer said in a husky voice.

"I like you both," Paul said. "I really do. That's part of it, of course. Remember, Travis, how Lisa became . . . just a thing, an object? It moved and made sounds, but Lisa was gone. I made the same mistake with Harry but not until the very end. The problem is to keep the person's ac-

tual identity and awareness functioning right to the end.
Now we have to get Meyer out of here. Get up and go
bring that hand truck, Travis, please."

I got the truck, and at Paul's request I bent and clumsily wedged and tugged and lifted my old friend onto the
bed of the truck. Meyer ended up on his right side. He
squinted up and me and said, "I have this terrible pun I
can't seem to get out of my head, like one of those songs
you can't get rid of. Let's hope his craft is ebbing."

"How is your leg?" I asked him.

"Relatively shapely, I think, but considered too hairy
by some."

"Are you trying to be amusing?" Paul asked.

Meyer said in his public speaking voice, "We often notice in clinical studies that sado-sociopathic faggots have a
very limited sense of humor."

Dissat moved to the side of the truck, took aim, and
clubbed Meyer right on the point of the shoulder, and
said, "Make more jokes, please."

Meyer, having exhaled explosively through clenched
teeth, said, "I hope I didn't give the wrong impression,
Dissat."

"Are you frightened, Meyer?" Paul asked politely.

"I have a lump of ice in my belly you wouldn't believe,"
Meyer said.

Instructed by Paul, I rolled the hand truck along the
warehouse flooring, turned it, and backed laboriously up a
ramp, pulling it up. He unlatched a big metal door with
overhead wheels and rolled it aside. The white sunlight
had turned yellowish outside as the world moved toward
evening, but it was still bright enough to sting the eyes. I
wheeled the truck along the loading dock and down a
steeper ramp where it almost got away from me.

I pushed the truck along the concrete roadway, the steel
wheels grating and clinking. I became aware that with
each stride I could feel less resistance to bending in the
wire joining my ankles, and I was afraid it would snap before I wanted it to. I took shorter steps and changed my
stride, feet wider apart to put less strain on the wire. We
went through the big gates in the fence and over toward

the asphalt plant. Dissat told me to stop. He put a foot against Meyer's back and rolled him off the hand truck. We were in a truck loading area with a big overhead hopper. The concrete was scabbed thick, black, and uneven with dried spills of asphalt tar. Paul motioned me away from the hand truck and pushed it back out of the way. Above us was the hopper and a square, bulky tank that stood high on girder legs.

"Do you see that great big wad of wasted asphalt over there, Travis? Meyer is facing the wrong way to see it. Vandalism is always a problem. Last Thursday night some hippies apparently came over from the beach, and for no reason at all they dropped at least two tons out of the holding tank. That's the big, square tank overhead. It's insulated. Just before the shift ends, they run what's left in the plant into the holding tank. It's hot enough to stay liquid all night in this climate, and in the morning while the plant is being fired up and loaded, the trucks draw from the holding tank. But last Friday morning they couldn't drive the trucks under the hopper until they got a small bulldozer over here to blade that solidified hunk of warm asphalt away from where I'm standing. It's all cooled now, of course. And our old friend, Harry Broll, is curled right in the middle of that black wad, snug as nutmeat in the shell."

I remembered being taken on a hunt when I was a child and how my uncle had packed partridge in clay and put the crude balls into the hot coals until they baked hard. When he had cracked them open, the feathers and skin had stuck to the clay, leaving the steaming meat. Acid came up into my throat and stayed, then went slowly back down.

I swallowed and said, "And the patrol checks here tonight and finds more vandalism?"

"You belabor the obvious, McGee. They'll have to blade your hydrocarbon tomb, big enough for two, over next to Harry's. It's hotter now, of course, in the holding tank than it will be by morning." He moved over to the side. "This is the lever the foreman uses. It's a manual system. If I move it to the side . . ."

He swung the lever over and pulled it back at once. A black glob about the size of your average Thanksgiving turkey came down the chute, banged the hanging baffle plate open, and fell—swopp—onto the stained concrete, making an ugly black pancake about four feet across, very thin at the perimeter, humped thick in the middle. A couple of dangling black strings fell into the pancake from overhead. A tendril of blue smoke arose from the pancake. Meyer made a very weary sound. Pain, anger, resignation. The pancake had formed too close to him, splattering a hot black thread across his chin, cheek, and ear. In the silence I heard the faraway flute call of a meadowlark and then the thunder rumble of a jet. I smelled that sweet, thick, childhood scent of hot tar.

When Meyer spoke, his voice was so controlled it revealed how close he was to breaking. "I can certify. It comes out hot."

"Hardly any aggregate in it," Paul said. "It cools and hardens quickly. Travis, please turn Meyer around and put his feet in the middle of that circular spill, will you?"

I do not know what started the changes that were going on inside me. They had started before the meadowlark, but they seemed related somehow to the meadowlark. You used to be able to drive through Texas, and there would be meadowlarks so thick along the way, perched singing on so many fenceposts, that at times you could drive through the constant sound of them like sweet and molten silver. Now the land has been silenced. The larks eat bugs, feed bugs to nestlings. The bugs are gone, and the meadowlarks are gone, and the world is strange, becoming more strange, a world spawning Paul Dissats instead of larks.

So somehow there is less risk, because losing such a world means losing less. I knew my head was still bad. It was like a car engine that badly needs tuning. Tromp the gas and it chokes, falters, and dies. It has to be babied up to speed. I had a remote curiosity about how my head would work with enough stress going on. Curiosity was changing to an odd prickling pleasure that seemed to grow high and hot, building and bulging itself up out of the belly into the shoulders and neck and chest.

I knew that feeling. I had almost forgotten it. It had happened before, but only when I had turned the last card and knew the hand was lost, the game was lost, the lights were fading. I had been working my wrists steadily within the small slack I had given myself, bending a tiny piece of connecting wire back and forth, and the bending was suddenly easier as the wire began to part.

The hard, anticipatory joy comes not from thinking there is any real chance but from knowing you can use it all without really giving that final damn about winning or losing. By happenstance, he'd made a bad choice of wire. And maybe the twisted child was so eager to squash his mice, he might give one of them a chance to bite him.

The wrist wire broke as I put my hands on Meyer to move him. "Can you roll?" I asked in a voice too low for Paul to hear. Meyer nodded. "Roll on signal, to your left, fast and far."

"What are you saying!" Paul Dissat demanded. "Don't you *dare* say things I can't hear!"

"Careful, darling," I told him. "You're going into a towering snit. Let's not have any girlish tantrums."

He quieted immediately. He picked up his chunk of aluminum. "That won't do you any good, and it isn't very bright of you to even try it. You disappoint me when you misjudge me. You take some of the pleasure out of being with you again." I looked beyond him and then looked back at him very quickly. I couldn't be obvious about it.

The instant he turned I broke the ankle wire with the first swinging stride. He heard me and spun back, but by the time he raised the aluminum club, I was inside the arc of it. I yelled to Meyer to roll clear.

My head went partly bad. I knew I had turned him back into a kind of corner where the girder legs of the holding tank were crossbraced. I was in gray murk, expending huge efforts. It was a stage. Somebody was working the strings of the big doll, making it bounce and flap. At times its doll chin bounced on my shoulder. It flailed and flapped its sawdust arms. I stood flatfooted, knees slightly bent, swaying from left to right and back with the cadence of effort, getting calves, thighs, rump, back, and shoulder into each hook, trying to power the fist through the sawdust and into the gristle and membrane beyond.

Pretty doll with the graceful, powerful, hairless legs, with the long lashes, red mouth, and hero profile. Sawdust creaked out of its throat, and Raggedy Andy shoebutton eyes swung loose on the slackening threads.

Soon a blow would burst it, and it would die as only a doll can die, in torn fabric and disrepair. I had never killed a doll-thing with my hands before.

Somebody was shouting my name. There was urgency in the voice. I slowed and stopped, and the gray lifted the way a steamed windshield clears when the defroster is turned on. I backed away and saw Paul Dissat slumped against a crossbrace, one arm hooked over it. There was not a mark on his face.

I backed away. I imagine that what happened next happened because he did not realize what punishment to the body will do to the legs. He was conscious. I imagine that from belly to heart he felt as if he had been twisted in half.

The shapely, powerful legs with their long muscle structure had carried him through the slalom gates down the long tricky slopes. They had kept their spring and bounce through the long sets of tennis. So perhaps he believed that all he had to do was force himself up onto those legs and run away on them.

He tried.

When his weight came onto them, they went slack and rubbery. He fought for balance. He was like a drunk in a comedy routine. He flailed with both arms, and his left arm hit the load lever, and he staggered helplessly toward the thick, gouting torrent of asphalt from the overhead hopper. He tried to claw and fight back away from it, screaming as I once heard a horse scream, yet with an upward sliding note that went out of audible range, like a dog whistle. But it entrapped, ensnared those superb and nearly useless legs and brought him down in sticky agony. I ran to try to grab him, yank him out of that black, smoking jelly but got a steaming smear of it across the back of my hand and forearm. I turned then and did what I should have done in the first place, went for the lever and swung it back to the closed position. The last sight I had before I turned, was of Dissat buried halfway up his rib cage, hands braced against the concrete slab, elbows locked, head up, eyes half out of the sockets, mouth agape, cords standing out in his throat, as the black stuff piled higher behind him, higher than his head.

I yanked the lever back and spun, and he was gone. A part of the blackness seemed to bulge slightly and sag back. The last strings of it solidified and fell. It was heaped as high as my waist and as big as a grand piano.

I remembered Meyer and looked over and saw him. He had wiggled into a sitting position, his back against a girder. I took a staggering step and caught myself.

"Pliers," Meyer said. "Hang on, Travis. For God's sake, hang on."

Pliers. I knew there wasn't time for pliers. The gray was coming in from every side, misting the windshield as before. I found my way toward him, fell, then crawled, and reached his wrists. I bent the wire, turning it, freeing it. I saw a sharp end bite into the ball of my thumb, saw blood run, felt nothing. Just one more turn and then he could . . .

twenty-three

I was not entirely asleep and not yet awake, and I could not remember ever having been so completely, perfectly, deliciously relaxed. The girl voices brought me further across the line into being awake.

Rupe had said how very sweet their voices were, how touching, how heartbreaking, aboard the *Belle*. Their harmony was simple, their voices true and small.

"What a friend we have in Jeeeeee-zusss. All our sins and griefs to baaaaaaaare."

I wondered why the extraordinary crew of the *Hell's Belle* should select a number like that. Yet there was the tidy warmth of Teddie's thigh under the nape of my neck, a sweet, firm fit. Fabric over the thigh. I opened my eyes, and it was night. Light came slanting and touched the girl faces, touching their long, hanging hair. I realized I was on a blanket, and there was the unmistakable feel and consistency of dry sand under the blanket. Teddie's face was in shadow. I lifted a lazy, contented arm and put my hand over the young breast under thin fabric so close above my face. It had a sweet, rubbery firmness.

She took my wrist and pushed my hand down and said, "No, brother." They had stopped singing the words of the song. They were humming the melody. "He has awakened," the girl said. It was not Teddie's voice. They stopped singing.

A man's voice said, "How do you feel, brother?"

I raised my head. There were five or six of them in a

244

glow of firelight. Bearded, biblical men wrapped in coarse cloth. I had been hurled out of my historical time and my place.

I sat up too quickly. I felt faint and bent forward to lower my head down between my knees.

A hand touched my shoulder. Meyer said, "I was trying to get you to a doctor and ran off into the sand. This one here is their healer, and he—"

"I was a third year medical student when I heard the call. I'm the healer for the tribe on this pilgrimage mission."

I straightened and looked into a young bearded face. He nodded and took my pulse and nodded again. "We got that tar off your arm and hand with a solvent, brother, and treated your burn and dressed it."

My arm was wrapped with gauze. There was a bandage on my thumb. I turned my head and saw the beach buggies and several campers. A baby was crying in one of the campers.

I lay back very carefully. The thigh was there, cozy as before. The face leaned over me and looked down. "I will comfort you, brother, but no more grabbing me, huh?"

"No more, sister. I thought I was somewhere else with someone else. A . . . different group of girls."

"On a pilgrimage, too?"

"In a certain sense of the word, yes."

"There is only one sense, brother, when you give your heart and your soul and your worldly goods and all the days of your years to the service of almighty God."

"Did your . . . healer put vinegar on my burns?"

She giggled. "That's me you smell, brother. Blessed providence sent you and your friend to us this afternoon before I flipped right out of my tree. If it isn't sacrilege, my sisters and I are enjoying a peace that passeth understanding ever since."

I tried sitting up again, and there was no dizziness. One of the sisters brought me a cup of hot clam broth. She wore a garment like an aba, made out of some kind of

homespun. She too smelled of vinegar. There was a crude
cross around her neck with green stones worked into it.
The automatic slide projector in my head showed me a
slide entitled "The Last Known Sight of Paul Dissat in
This World." A small gold cross hung free around his
straining throat.

After I drank the broth, I tried standing, and it worked
reasonably well. They were not paying any special attention to me or to Meyer. We were welcome to be with
them. Feel free to ignore and be ignored. Listen to the
sweet singing, taste the broth, and praise the Lord.

I found the vinegar girl and gave her back her cup with
thanks. Meyer and I moved away from the fire and from
the lights in the campers.

"I panicked," Meyer said. "I got the rest of the wire off
me and threw you in the damned car and drove like a
maniac."

"Where is the car?"

"Up there on the shoulder. It was in deep. They pulled
it out with a beach buggy."

"What about that limousine?"

"Good question. Joshua and I went back in there on his
trail bike. The keys to it were on the desk in the office. We
put the trail bike into the trunk. I locked everything in
sight, and we were out of there before seven thirty. I took
the long way around, and we left it at the West Palm airport, keys in the ash tray. Call it a Dissat solution. By the
way, I made a contribution to the pilgrimage mission collection plate in both our names."

"That's nice."

"One of the wrapped stacks of hundreds from the
Southern National. Initialed. Unbroken. There were four
stacks in a brown paper bag on the desk in the warehouse
office."

"What did Joshua say?"

"Thanks."

"No questions about the kind of help you asked of
him?"

"Just one. He said that before he took the name of

Joshua, he had clouted cars to feed his habit. He said all he wanted to know was whether, if we had committed a sin, we repented of it. I said that even though I didn't think of it as a sin, I was going to pray for forgiveness. That's when he nodded and said thanks and riffled the stack with his thumb and shoved it into the saddlebag on the trail bike. I walked out of the airport parking lot, and he drove the bike out and waited for me down the road from the airport. Long way around coming back here, too. I had the idea you'd be dead when I got here."

"Meyer?"

"Yes?"

"Get me home. Get me back to the *Flush*. Please."

"Let's say goodnight to the tribe."

I did a lot of sleeping. I was getting to be very good at it. I could get up at noon, shower, work up a big breakfast, and be ready for my nap at three. The gray fog rolled way back into the furthest corners of my mind. People left me alone. Meyer made certain of that. He passed the word. McGee has pulled the hole in after him. And he bites.

Meyer would come over during that part of each day when I was likely to be up and about.

We'd walk over and swim. We would come back and play chess. I did not want to be among people. Not yet. So he would cook, or I would cook, or he would go out and bring something back.

The longer we delayed the decision, the easier it was to make. The random parts fell together in a pattern we could find no reason to contradict. Harry Broll had grabbed his three-hundred-thousand loan in cash and fled with Lisa, the girlfriend he had promised to give up. Except for some irate creditors nobody was looking for him diligently. Harry's wife had been reported missing in the Windward Islands, presumed drowned while swimming alone. Paul Dissat was missing too, possibly by drowning, but in his case it would more likely be suicide, emotional depression, and anxiety over some kind of disease of the blood. He had requested sick leave.

Jillian had been astoundingly sweet and helpful and had even lived up to her promise to ask no questions. She had flown down to Grenada and stayed a few days and with the knowing assistance of an attorney friend had obtained my packet from the hotel safe and my other possessions from their storage room.

The favor was, of course, Jilly's concession to apology, to regret. When she and her new friend got back from Grenada, she came over with him to give me back my belongings. They had a drink with us, and they did not stay long. Meyer arrived before they left.

"I keep forgetting his name," Meyer said later.

"Foster Cramond. Still a close personal friend of both his ex-wives."

"Rich ex-wives."

"Of course."

"Likable," Meyer said judiciously. "Good manners. No harm in him. Good at games, what? Court tennis, polo, sailing. Splendid reflexes. Did you notice the fast draw with that solid gold lighter? Twelfth of a second. Interesting phenomenon when they looked at each other."

"What? Oh, you mean the visible steam that came out of her ears? And the way he went from a sixteen collar to an eighteen? Yes. I noticed."

"Travis, what was your reaction when you met her new friend?"

"Relief at not running into some big fuss about breaking my word to visit her for a week. And . . . some indignation, I guess. In all honesty, some indignation."

"And you wished you could change your mind again?"

I let his question hang in the air for a long time, for three moves, one involving tightening my defense against his queen's bishop. I found a response that created a new problem for him. While he was studying it, I leaned back.

"About changing my mind. No. My instincts hadn't turned bad when Harry came here. He had no intention of shooting me. So let's suppose I'm slower by a half a step or a full step. Maybe I'm old enough and wise enough to move into positions where I don't need the speed. The only thing I know is that I am going to run out of luck in the future, just as I have in the past. And when I run out, I am going to have to make myself some luck. I know that what counts is the feeling I get when I make my own luck. The way I feel then is totally alive. In every dimension. In every possible way. It wouldn't have to be Jillian. I could lay back, watch the traffic, select a rich lady, and retire myself to stud. But that would be half-life. I have an addiction. I'm hooked on the smell, taste, and feel of the nearness of death and on the way I feel when I make my move to keep it from happening. If I *knew* I could keep it from happening, there'd be no taste to it at all."

Meyer gave that a lot of thought, and then he gave the game a lot of thought. Finally he said, "When in doubt, castle." He moved his king into the short corner, the rook standing guard. "Travis, I am very very glad that you were able to make us some luck. I am glad to be here. But . . ."

"But?"

"Something else is wrong with you."

"I dream some rotten things. I've got my memory almost all straightened out. Picked up nearly all the cards off the floor and put them back in the right order. But I have real rotten dreams. Last night I was buying a shirt. The girl said it was made in the islands, and they weren't sized correctly and I should try it on. When I put it on and came out, I realized that it was exactly the same print that Lisa had worn that first night I knew her. A dashiki. As I started to tell the girl that I didn't want it, she came up to me quickly, and she reached out, and she snapped something onto the front of the shirt. It made a clack. It was a big, round, white thing, too heavy for the front of a shirt. I turned it around, and I saw that the sound had been the lower jaw of a skull being closed with the fabric caught between the teeth. It was a very white, polished, delicate skull, and at first it looked feral, some predator's skull. Then I knew it was Lisa's skull. I tried to get the girl to take it off, but she said it went with that particular shirt. No other shirt. Just that one. And I woke up."

"Good Christ," Meyer whispered softly.

"But usually I don't dream at all."

"Be thankful. Travis. Is something else wrong?"

"Yes."

"Do you have the words for it yet?"

"I think it's getting to the point where there will be words for it. When there are words, I'll try them on you."

"Are you going to check me with that knight? Go ahead. See what happens if you do."

On the following Sunday afternoon, a Sunday late in May, Meyer and I were over on the beach. When the wind died, it got uncomfortably hot in the sun, so we moved to a bench in the shade. I watched two lovely ladies approaching along the beach, consciously keeping shoulders back and tummies in as they strode along, laughing and talking. Elegant lassies. Total strangers. They were walking across the edge of my life and right back out of it, and I would never know them or touch them nor two million nor ten million of their graceful sisters.

"Maybe I can put that problem into words now. But it's just a try. Maybe you can be patient?"

"How often do you see me impatient?"

"This starts with a word Rupe Darby used down in Grenada. A phrase, not a word. It designates a condition. Womaned out. He meant it in the physical sense. Total sexual depletion to the point where you think you never want to see another woman. I think I'm womaned out in a different way. All my love life is pre-Grenada, and that was a lifetime ago."

"So. Womaned out but not in a physical sense."

"God, no. Those two who just went by created the intended reaction. And I keep remembering how neat and warm the thigh of the little Jesus singer felt under the nape of my neck. Physical capacity is just dandy. No, Meyer. I feel foundered and wind broke in some other dimension of myself. I feel sick of myself, as if the prospect of me in action would turn me off, way off."

"How?"

"Everything I thought I believed about making love to a

woman sounds very stale. I hear myself talking to too
many of them. There has to be affection, dear. Respect for
each other. We must not hurt each other or anyone else,
darling. There has to be giving on both sides and taking on
both sides, honeybunch. Oh Meyer, God help me, it all
sounds like a glossy sales talk. I was kidding them, and I
was kidding myself. Look. I was holding out a package
deal. And on the bottom of the package in small print was
the guaran-goddamn-tee. Mary Dillon picked up the package. I didn't force it on her. I just left it around where
she'd see it. She picked it up, enjoyed the product, and
then married Harry Broll, and now she's buried in a wash-
out behind a seawall under transitmix concrete. So something is wrong with the small print or the service contract
or the damned sales force, Meyer. I just can't . . . I can't
stand the thought of ever again hearing my own sincere,
manly, loving, crap-eating voice saying those stale words
about how I won't ever hurt you, baby, I just want to
screw you and make you a more sincere and emotionally
healthy woman."

"Travis, Travis, Travis."

"I know. But that's what's wrong."

"Maybe there is some new kind of industrial waste in
the air we breathe."

"Fractionated honesty?"

"Don't suffer all over me, McGee. You are a good man.
There is no man alive who is not partially jackass. When
we detect some area of jackassery within ourselves, we feel
discontent. Our image suffers."

"What should I do?"

"How do I know what you should do? Don't make me
an uncle. Go get lost in the Out Islands and fish for a couple months. Go hire onto a tug and work yourself into a
stupor. Take five thousand of what was in that brown bag
and lease the *Hell's Belle* all by yourself for ten days. Take
cold showers. Study Hindustani."

"Why are you getting sore?"

He bounded off the bench, whirled, bent over, yelled
into my face, "Who's getting sore? I'm not getting sore!"

And he ran down to the water, bouncing hairily along, and plopped in and swam out.

Everyone was not acting like himself. Maybe there *was* some new kind of guck in the air lately.

By the time we had finished our swim, Meyer had gotten over his unusual tizzy. We walked slowly back across the bridge, and as we neared the *Flush,* I could see a figure aboard her in the shade of the sundeck overhang, sitting on the shallow little afterdeck.

I did not recognize her until we were within thirty feet. She lay asleep in the deck chair with a tidy, boneless look of a resting cat. There was a big red suitcase beside the chair and a matching red train case, both well scuffed by travel. She wore a little denim dress with white stitching. Her white sandals were on the deck under the chair. Her sleeping arm clamped her white purse against her.

Suddenly her eyes opened wide. There was no sleep-stunned transition. She lept back into life and up onto her feet in the same instant, all smiling vitality. "Hey! McGee! It's me. Jeannie. Jeannie Dolan. I should have looked over on the beach, huh?"

I introduced them. Meyer said he had heard nice things about her. He seemed to approve of the lively mop of red-brown hair and the quick glinting of the gray-green eyes.

I unlocked the *Flush,* and we went in. She said, "Leave my stuff right there, unless you've got thieves. Hey, can I look around? Say, this is a great kind of boat, Trav! Look, is the timing bad? Am I in the way or anything? If you guys have something all lined up . . ."

"Nothing," Meyer said. "Nothing at all."

"Wow, what a great kitchen."

"Galley," I said.

She looked at me blankly. "Galley? They row those with big oars. And a man walking around with a whip. Do you row this thing, for God's sake?"

"Okay, Jeannie. It's a kitchen," I said.

"Does it have engines in it? I mean, it will cruise around and so forth?"

"And so forth," Meyer said, looking happier.

"Wow, would I ever like to go someplace on a boat like this."

"Where's your friend?" I asked her.

"Betsy? We got tossed out of that Casa de Playa by the bank that took over. Not we, just me. Because she was gone by then. She went back to cleaning teeth. For a widower dentist in North Miami."

"Vodka tonic for you?" I asked her.

"Exactly right! It's wonderful when people remember things, isn't it? What I'm going to do, I'm on my way back to Columbus. No, not back to Charlie, that creep. But I called my old job, and I can make enough money so I can save enough to fly to the Dominican Republic and get a quickie divorce, instead of beating my brains out down here."

"Won't you sit down, Jeannie?" I asked her.

"I'm too nervous and jumpy, dear. Whenever I impose on people, I get like this. I've got the bus schedule and all, and then I thought, oh, what the hell, I wanted to see that McGee guy again and never did. A girl sometimes has to brassy or settle for nothing, right?"

I looked at Meyer. He was wearing a very strange expression. I handed Jeannie her drink and said, "Sometimes a girl gets brassy at just exactly the right time, and she gets invited on a private cruise. What would you say to that?"

"Aboard this wonderful ship! Wow! I'd say yes so fast—"

"HOLD IT!" Meyer roared, startling her. He trotted over to her and with raised finger backed her over to a chair. She sat down on command, staring up at him with her mouth open.

"I am going to ask you some very personal questions. Mrs. Dolan."

"What's the *matter* with you, huh?"

"Have you been in a lot of emotional turmoil lately?'

"Me? Turmoil? Like what?"

"Are you at a crisis point in your life?"

"Crisis? I'm just trying to get myself a plain, ordinary divorce-type divorce."

"Mrs. Dolan, do you feel like a pathetic little bird with a busted wing who has fluttered aboard, looking for patience, understanding, and gentleness and love which will make you well and whole again?"

She looked at me with wide, round eyes. "Does he get like this a lot, Travis?"

"Pay attention!" Meyer ordered. "How do you relate to your analyst?"

"Analyst? Shrink? What do I need one for? Chee! You need one, maybe."

"Are you in love?" he asked.

"This minute? Hmmm. I guess not. But I sort of usually am. And pretty often, I guess. I'm not a real serious kind of person. I'm just sort of dumb and happy."

"One more question, and I must ask you both this one."

"You answer him, honey," Jeannie said to me.

"Would either of you two happy people mind too much if I spend the next few weeks in Seneca Falls, New York?"

"Speaking for the two of us, Meyer, I can't think of a serious objection, really."

He trotted to the doorway to the rear deck and opened it. He picked up the two pieces of red luggage and set them inside the door, gave us a maniacal smile, and slammed the door and was gone.

Jeannie stood up and sipped frowningly at her drink. Then she looked at me. "McGee?"

"Yes, dear."

"Everybody I know is acting weirder all the time. Have you noticed that too?"

"Yes, I have. Meyer isn't often like that."

"It's pretty weird and pushy for me to barge in on you like this. I'm not like this, really."

"It does have engines."

"That's nice. But do you feel like you've been maneuvered into something you'd just as soon not do, huh?"

"The more I think about it, the better I like it."

She put her drink down and came over and gave me one quick, thorough, and enthusiastic kiss. "There! Now it's just a case of getting acquainted, huh? Want to start by helping me unpack?"

We carried the luggage back to the master stateroom. She asked me what Meyer had meant about her having a broken wing. I said he was one of the last of the great romantics. I said there used to be two. But now there was just the one left. The hairy one.